Richard saw the point of a sword blade sticking out from between the man's shoulder blades. He spun back toward Richard after throwing the woman out of the opening, ready to attack. It seemed impossible, but the man looked unaffected by the blade that had impaled him through the chest.

It was then, in the weak light from the fire pit off to the side, that Richard got his first good look at the killer.

Three knives were buried up to their brass cross guards in the man's chest. Only the handles were showing. Richard saw, too, the broken end of a sword blade jutting out from the center of the man's chest. The point of that same blade stuck out from the man's back.

Richard recognized the knife handles. All three were the style carried by the men of the First File.

He looked from those blades that should have killed the big man, up into his face.

That was when he realized the true horror of the situation, and the reason for the unbearable stench of death.

THE THIRD KINGDOM

TERRY GOODKIND

TOR®

A TOM DOHERTY ASSOCIATES BOOK
NEW YORK

This is a work of fiction. All of the characters, organizations, and events portrayed in this novel are either products of the author's imagination or are used fictitiously.

THE THIRD KINGDOM

A Tor Book
Published by Tom Doherty Associates, LLC
175 Fifth Avenue
New York, NY 10010

www.tor-forge.com

Tor® is a registered trademark of Tom Doherty Associates, LLC.

ISBN 978-0-7653-7067-9

Tor books may be purchased for educational, business, or promotional use. For information on bulk purchases, please contact Macmillan Corporate and Premium Sales Department at 1-800-221-7945, extension 5442, or write specialmarkets@macmillan.com.

First Edition: August 2013
First International Mass Market Edition: April 2014

Printed in the United States of America

0 9 8 7 6 5 4 3 2 1

THE
THIRD
KINGDOM

Wе should eat them now, before they die and go bad," a gruff voice said.

Richard was only distantly aware of the low buzz of voices. Still only half conscious, he wasn't able to figure out who was talking, much less make sense of what they were talking about, but he was aware enough to be disturbed by their predatory tone.

"I think we should trade them," a second man said as he tightened the knot in the rope he had looped around Richard's ankles.

"Trade them?" the first asked in a heated voice. "Look at the bloody blankets they were wrapped in and the blood all over the floor of the wagon. They'd likely die before we could ever trade them, and then they'd go to waste. Besides, how could we carry them both? The horses for their soldiers and the wagon are all gone, along with anything else of value."

The second man let out an unhappy sigh. "Then we should eat the big one before anyone else shows up. We could carry the smaller one easier and then trade her."

"Or save her and eat her later."

"We'd be better off trading her. When else would we ever get a chance like this to get as much as she would fetch?"

As the two men argued, Richard tried to reach out to the side to touch Kahlan lying close up against him, but he couldn't. He realized that his wrists were bound tightly together with a coarse rope. He instead pushed at her with his elbow. She didn't respond.

Richard knew that he needed to do something, but he also knew that he would first need to summon not just his senses, but his strength, or he would have no chance. He felt worse than weak. He felt feverish with an inner sickness that had not only drained his strength but left his mind in a numb fog.

He lifted his head a little and squinted in the dim light, trying to see, trying to get his bearings, but he couldn't really make out much of anything. When his head pushed up against something, he realized that he and Kahlan were covered with a stiff tarp. Out under the bottom edge he could see a pair of vague, dark silhouettes at the end of the wagon beyond his feet. One man stepped closer and lifted the bottom of the tarp while the other looped a rope around Kahlan's ankles and tied it tight, the way they had done with Richard.

Through that opening Richard could see that it was night. The full moon was up, but its light had a muted quality to it that told him the sky was overcast. A slow drizzle drifted through the still air. Beyond the two figures a murky wall of spruce trees rose up out of sight.

Kahlan didn't move when Richard pushed his elbow a little more forcefully against her ribs. Her hands, like his, lay nested at her belt line. His worry about what might be wrong with her had him struggling to gather his senses. He could see that she was at least breathing, although each slow breath was shallow.

As he gradually regained consciousness, Richard realized that besides feeling weak with fever of some sort, he hurt all over from hundreds of small wounds. Some of them still oozed blood. He could see that Kahlan was covered with the same kinds of cuts and puncture wounds. Her clothes were soaked in blood.

But it was not only the blood on the two of them that worried him. Damp air rolling in under the tarp carried an even heavier smell of blood from out beyond the men. There had been people with them, people who had come to help them. His level of alarm rose past his ability to gather his strength.

Richard could feel the lingering effects of being healed, and he recognized the shadowy touch of the woman who had been healing him, but since he still ached from cuts and bruises, he knew that while the healing had been started, it hadn't gone beyond that start, much less been completed.

He wondered why.

On his other side, the side away from Kahlan, he heard something dragged across the floor of the wagon.

"Look at this," the man with the gruff voice said as he pulled it out. For the first time, Richard could see the size of the man's muscled arms as he reached in and lifted the object he had dragged closer.

The other man let out a low whistle. "How could they have missed that? For that matter, how could they have missed these two?"

The bigger man glanced around. "Messy as everything looks, it must have been the Shun-tuk."

The other's voice lowered with sudden concern. "Shun-tuk? You really think so?"

"From what I know of their ways, I'd say it was them."

"What would the Shun-tuk be doing out here?"

The big man leaned toward his companion. "Same as us. Hunting for those with souls."

"This far from their homeland? That seems unlikely."

"With the barrier wall now breached, what better place to hunt for people with souls? The Shun-tuk would go anywhere, do anything, to find such people. Same as us." He lifted an arm around in a quick gesture. "We came out to hunt these new lands, didn't we? So would the Shun-tuk."

"But they have a vast domain. Are you sure they would venture out?"

"Their domain may be vast and they may be powerful, but the thing they want most they don't have. With the barrier wall breached they can hunt for it, now, the same as us, the same as others."

The other man's gaze darted about. "Even so, their domain is distant. Do you really think it could be them? This far out from their homeland?"

"I've never encountered the Shun-tuk myself, and I hope not to." The big man raked his thick fingers back through his wet, stringy hair as he scanned the dark line of trees. "But I've heard that they hunt other half people just for the practice until they can find those with souls.

"This looks like their way. They usually hunt at night. With prey out in the open like this, they strike fast and hard with overwhelming numbers. Before anyone has time to see them coming, or to react, it's over. They usually eat some of those they fall upon, but they take most for later."

"Then what about these two? Why would they leave them?"

"They wouldn't. In their rush to eat some of those they captured and to take the rest back with them, they must have missed these two hidden under the tarp."

The smaller man picked at a splinter at the end of the wagon bed for a moment as he carefully scanned the countryside. "I hear it told that Shun-tuk often come back to check for returning stragglers."

"You heard true."

"Then we should be away from here in case they come back. Once they are overcome with the blood lust, they would devour us without hesitation."

Richard felt powerful fingers grip his ankle. "I thought you wanted to eat this one before he dies and his soul can leave him."

The other man took hold of Richard's other ankle. "Maybe we should take him to a safe place, first, where the Shun-tuk wouldn't be so likely to come across us and interfere. I would hate to be surprised once we get started. We can get a good price for the other. There be those who would pay anything for one with a soul. Even the Shun-tuk would bargain for such a person."

"That's a dangerous idea." He thought it over briefly. "But you're right, the Shun-tuk would pay a fortune." The wolfish hunger was back in the bigger man's voice. "This one, though, is mine."

"There's plenty for both of us."

The other grunted. He seemed already lost in private cravings. "But only one soul."

"It belongs to the one who devours it."

"Enough talk," the big man growled. "I want at him."

As Richard was dragged out of the wagon, he was still struggling to gather his wits in order to make some kind of sense of the strange things he was hearing. He remembered well the warnings about the dangers of the Dark Lands. He was aware enough to realize that for the moment his life depended on not letting the two men know that he was beginning to come around.

As he was swiftly dragged by his ankles clear of the wagon bed, his upper body dropped to the ground. Even though he tried to round his shoulders, with his hands tied he couldn't use them or his arms effectively to keep his head from whacking the rocky ground. The pain was shockingly sharp, followed by an enveloping, inviting blackness that he knew would be fatal if he couldn't fight it off.

He focused on the surroundings, looking for an escape route, to try to keep his mind engaged. From what he was able to see in the murky moonlight, the wagon sat alone and desolate in the wilderness. The horses were gone.

While he didn't see anyone else about, he did spot bones nearby. The bones were not bleached by weather, but stained dark with dried blood and bits of flesh. He could see gouges where teeth tried to scrape every bit of tissue from the bones.

The bones were human.

He recognized, too, shreds of uniforms. They were the uniforms of the First File, his personal bodyguards. Some of them, at least, had apparently given their lives defending Richard and Kahlan.

The smaller man still had hold of Richard's ankle, apparently unwilling to let go of his prize. The other man stood to the side, looking at the thing he had pulled across the floor and out of the wagon.

Richard realized that it was his sword.

The man holding the sword pulled Kahlan partway out from under the tarp. Her lower legs bent at the knees and swung lifelessly from the end of the wagon bed.

While the man was distracted looking at her, Richard used the opportunity to sit up and lunge, trying to snatch his sword. The man yanked it back out of the way before Richard could get his fingers around the hilt. With his hands and feet tied, he hadn't been free enough to grab it in time.

Both men stepped back. They hadn't thought he was conscious. Richard had lost the advantage of surprise and gained nothing in return.

In reaction to seeing him awake, both men decided not to waste any more time. Snarling like hungry wolves, they descended on him, attacking him like animals in a feeding frenzy. The situation was so bizarre that it was difficult to believe.

The smaller of the two pulled Richard's shirt open. Richard could see a glaze of ferocious savagery in the man's eyes. The bigger one, teeth bared with a feral fury, dove straight for the side of Richard's neck. Richard reflexively drew his shoulder up, deflecting the lunge at the last instant. In protecting his exposed neck, the move instead presented his shoulder to the attack.

Richard screamed out in pain as teeth sank into his upper arm. He knew that he had to do something, and do it quick.

He could think of only one thing: his gift. He mentally reached down deep within, desperately summoning deadly forces, urgently calling on the power that was his birthright.

Nothing happened.

With his level of anger and desperation, along with his fear for Kahlan, the essentials were there for his gift to respond. In the past it had answered such critical need. The power of it should have come roaring forth.

It was as if there was no gift there to summon.

Unable to call it forth, with his wrists and ankles bound, he had no effective way to fight off the two men.

2

Frustrated and angry that he couldn't get the mysteries of his gift to respond in order to help himself and Kahlan, Richard knew that he didn't have the time to try to figure it out. Instead, he resorted to using what he could depend on—his instincts and experience.

As the men lunged for him, Richard thrashed wildly, trying to prevent them from being able to hold on to him and muscle him under control. Being on the ground with the weight of his attackers above him left him at a decided disadvantage, but he knew that he couldn't let that stop him from doing everything he could to fight them off.

Their eyes wild, both men threw themselves over the top of him to hold him down. At the same time they tried to rip into him with their teeth. Richard had heard stories of people being attacked and eaten by bears. The two men piling onto him reminded him of the helplessness that came across in those stories, but with the frightening new dimension of human malevolence behind it.

Several times their teeth began to sink into his flesh,

but each time Richard managed to jerk, twist, or elbow them away before they were able to get a good enough bite to rip off pieces of him. He couldn't understand why they didn't simply stab him to death. They were both carrying knives, and they had his sword.

It was almost as if they knew what they wanted to do, but their inexperience was making them less effective than they might have otherwise been. Still, the partially successful attempts left gaping, horrifically painful wounds that gushed blood. With Richard quickly tiring from fighting under the weight of the two men, to say nothing of losing blood, he knew it was inevitable that they were going to succeed in what they intended.

Incomprehensibly, between trying to bite off pieces of him, the men paused to lap at the blood as if they were dying of thirst and didn't want to let a drop of it get away and run into the ground. The interruption from biting to go after all the blood at least gave Richard time to get a breath.

Frustrated by not being able to get him under their control, the bigger man pressed a muscular forearm against Richard's throat and leaned his weight on it. Richard fought to breathe as he tried to squirm out from under the pressure of the arm compressing his throat. It was terrifying to have both men on top of him, trying to tear him apart with their teeth, and not be able to move, much less get them off.

Pressed down with all his weight, the man's arm abruptly slipped on all the blood. As he fell forward he had to throw a hand out onto the ground for balance. In a flash, with strength powered by fear and desperation, Richard pulled his own blood-slicked arms up from under the man stretched out over him and looped one arm over the man's head.

Richard elbowed the man's arm, knocking it aside. Without a hand on the ground, he lost his balance and fell farther forward. Richard arched his back, at the same time blocking with his knees, forcing the man around onto his back. Finally in a position to apply leverage, Richard pulled the rope binding his wrists together tight across the man's throat.

Straining with every ounce of strength, Richard hauled back on the coarse rope binding his wrists, using it as a garrote to choke the big man.

Surprised, the man hadn't had time to draw a breath before Richard had control of him. He gasped, straining for urgently needed air as he desperately clawed at Richard's forearms. His fingernails ripped gashes across Richard's flesh, but all the blood made for a greasy grip on Richard's arms and the man couldn't get himself free. Not able to escape the hold, he reached back, trying to claw Richard's face or gouge out his eyes, but Richard's face was out of reach and the man's fingers caught only empty air.

The second man rushed in to help. He, too, tried to lever Richard's arms away from his companion, but could find no spot to get his fingers under for a solid hold. Richard, fighting for his life, kept the first man locked in a death grip.

Not able to break Richard's hold, the second man hammered his fists against Richard arms, trying to make him let go of his companion. Lost in rage, Richard hardly felt the blows.

Seeing that his efforts were doing no good, the man quickly realized that he had to try something else. Yelling for his companion not to give up, he struck out with a fist at Richard's face, trying to get him to let go. With the way Richard had the big man pulled in tight against himself, the blows weren't direct enough. Several times the man's fist glanced off Richard's jaw as he screamed for Richard to let go.

Richard had no intention of letting go. To let go would mean certain death.

The big man Richard was choking squirmed frantically, his arms flailing as he desperately reached for something, anything, that would help him escape or at least get a breath. He kicked with his heels, aiming for Richard's shins. Richard pulled his knees up to keep his lower legs out of range. Most of the blind kicks landed on the ground and the ones that did connect weren't direct enough. Gritting his teeth with the effort, Richard tipped the man back even farther just to make sure that he couldn't do any damage with his heels.

Richard saw a knife blade rising in a bloody fist of the second man. He pulled the man he was strangling over on top of himself as best he could to shield himself against a knife attack. He didn't know how effective it would be, but it was the only thing he could do.

Suddenly, there was a loud, bone-cracking thump. The man faltered as he tried to turn. Another, sharper thump swiftly followed. With the third blow, blood rained down.

The man dropped the knife as he collapsed in a limp heap across the top of the man Richard was choking.

Richard wasn't sure what had happened, but he was not about to let go to find out. Without the second man fighting him, he was able to focus all his strength on the task at hand. The big man's movements had already become slow and weak as not only his wind was being cut off, but also the blood to his brain.

Richard screamed with rage to power his own aching muscles. As the man's struggling became sluggish, Richard swiftly changed his hold, throwing an arm around the man's neck, getting him in a headlock. Hard as he could, he twisted the man's head. In the quiet drizzle, when he reached the point of resistance, he pulled back a bit to gather more force, then slammed the man's head over even harder. When he did, he finally felt the neck snap. The man's whole body immediately went slack.

Powered by fury, Richard continued strangling the man even though he was no longer fighting.

A hand gently reached down with a reassuring touch to Richard's bulging biceps.

"It's all right. He's dead. They're both dead." It was a woman's voice he didn't recognize. "You're safe," she said. "You can let go now."

Still panting from the effort and the rage, Richard blinked as he looked up into several shadowed faces crowded in over him.

They were not soldiers. From their simple clothes, they appeared to be country folk. Two women and two men leaned in, looking down at him. Back beyond those four, a handful of other men crowded in closer. They, too, looked like country folk.

3

Richard gradually released the pressure on the dead man's neck. As the remaining air hissed from his lifeless lungs, his head flopped crookedly to one side.

One of the men standing above him lifted the limp arm of the other, smaller of the two dead men atop Richard and pulled him off to the side. Even in death, there was still a bloody snarl frozen on the face.

A mask of blood had run down to cover the side of the man's face. Fragments of bone stuck up from his matted hair. Richard saw that the back of his head had been bashed in with a large rock that one of the other men crowded in close still held in a tight grip.

As the man with the broken neck began to slowly slip off to the side, one of the women, the one who had touched Richard's arm, used a foot to shove the bigger of the two dead men aside. It was a relief to have the suffocating weight finally off.

The woman picked up the bloody knife that the second attacker had dropped when his skull had been crushed in. Leaning close, she sliced at the rope binding

Richard's hands and they at last parted. She moved down and cut the rope tying his ankles together.

"Thank you," Richard said. He was more than relieved to at last be free. "You saved my life."

"For the moment," a man in the shadows said.

"We hope you will return the favor," another added.

Richard didn't know what he meant, but he had bigger worries at the moment.

With an angry gesture, the woman with the knife hushed the men before turning her attention back to Richard.

He saw in the weak light of the full moon that illuminated the cloud cover that she was middle-aged. Fine lines creased her face in an agreeable way. It was too dark to tell the color of her eyes, but not the determination in them. Her expression, too, was one of grim resolve.

The woman leaned closer to press a hand to the bite wound on the side of his upper arm to try to stop the bleeding. Her gaze turned up to his as she held pressure in the wound.

"Are you the one who killed Jit, the Hedge Maid?" she asked.

Surprised by the question, Richard nodded as he looked around at all the stony faces watching him. "How do you know that?"

With her free hand, the woman pulled stray strands of her straight, shoulder-length hair back from her face. "A boy, Henrik, came to us a little while ago. He told us that he had been her captive, and that she intended to kill him like all the others she had killed. He said that two people rescued him and killed the Hedge Maid, but now they were in trouble and needed help."

Richard leaned forward. "Was there anyone else with him?"

"I'm afraid not. Just the boy."

Even though Richard had killed the Hedge Maid, he and Kahlan had both been grievously hurt. Their friends had brought a small army to get the two of them out of the Hedge Maid's lair and take them home. Now, those friends were all missing. He knew that none of them would have willingly left Kahlan and him alone like this.

"Henrik was the one who told my friends what had happened and where they could find us," Richard said. "They should have been with him."

The woman shook her head. "I'm sorry, but he was alone. Terrified, and alone."

"Did he tell you what happened, here?" Richard asked. "Did he tell you where those who were with us are now?"

"He was winded and in a panic to find help. He said there was no time to explain. He said we had to hurry and help you. We came right away."

Now that Richard was free and the rush of the fight was over, the shock of pain had begun to bear down on him in earnest. He touched his forehead with trembling fingers.

"But did he say anything else at all?" Richard asked. "It's important."

The woman glanced around in the darkness as she shook her head. "He said that you had been attacked and needed help. We knew that we had to hurry. Henrik is back at our village. When we get back you can question him yourself. For now, we must get in out of the night." She gestured urgently to the woman behind her. "Give me your scarf."

The woman immediately pulled it off her head and handed it over. The woman kneeling beside Richard used the scarf as a bandage, wrapping it high around his upper arm several times. She swiftly knotted it, then stuck the knife handle under the knot and twisted it around to tighten the tourniquet. Richard gritted his teeth against the pain.

He couldn't seem to slow his racing heart. He was worried about all those who had been with him, worried as to what could have happened to them. He needed to get to Henrik and find out what was going on. More than that, though, he was worried about getting help for Kahlan.

"We shouldn't be out here any longer," one of the men in back quietly cautioned, trying to hurry the woman.

"Almost done," she said as she quickly appraised some of his more obvious injuries. "You need these wounds sewn closed and treated with poultice or they will be infected by morning," she told Richard. "Bites like this are not to be ignored."

"Please," Richard said as he gestured with his other arm toward the wagon. "Help my wife? I fear that she is hurt worse."

With a quick gesture from the woman, two of the men hurried to the wagon.

"Is she the Mother Confessor?" one of the men called back as he checked on her.

Richard's sense of caution rose. "Yes."

"I don't think that we can do anything for her here," he said.

The other man spotted the sword and picked it up from the ground. His gaze glided over the ornately wrought gold and silver scabbard before taking in the word TRUTH made of gold wire woven through the silver wire wrapping the hilt.

"Then you would be the Lord Rahl?"

"That's right," Richard said.

"Then there is no doubt. You are the ones we came looking for," the man said. "The boy, Henrik, told us who you were. We came to find you."

Richard's concern eased at hearing that it was Henrik who had told them exactly who he and Kahlan were.

"Enough," the woman said. She quickly turned back to Richard. "Glad we were in time, Lord Rahl. I'm Ester. Now we have to get you both back to safety."

"Richard will do."

"Yes, Lord Rahl," she said absently, as if no longer listening as she pressed at wounds, checking their depth.

Ester motioned to some of the other men behind her. "You will need to help him. He's badly hurt. We have to get out of here before those who did this come back."

Several men, relieved to hear that she was finally ready to leave, rushed in to help Richard to his feet. Once up, Richard insisted on going to Kahlan. The men steadied him when he staggered to the wagon.

Richard saw that Kahlan was still unconscious, but breathing. He laid a hand on her, aching with fear over her condition. Her clothes were soaked in blood from the ordeal with the Hedge Maid. The thought of that vile creature and what she had been doing to Kahlan again awakened Richard's anger.

The Hedge Maid had been drinking Kahlan's blood.

He slid his hand through the long slit in her shirt, feeling where Jit's familiars had slashed open Kahlan's abdomen to bleed her and collect her blood for the Hedge Maid to drink. He was worried not only about the severity of the terrible wound, but how much blood she had lost. To his astonishment, he found only a few swollen ripples in her skin where the long wound had been nearly healed.

Richard recalled, then, the touch he had felt—the

touch of a healing begun, but not finished. Zedd or Nicci must have healed the deep wound on Kahlan, but from the rest of the wounds still evident on her, Richard could see that, as with him, they hadn't finished what they had started. Because he remembered that it had been Nicci's healing touch on him, he suspected that it would have been Zedd who had started healing Kahlan.

Richard was thankful that Zedd had managed to heal the terrible gash in Kahlan's abdomen, but he hadn't had time to heal everything. She had a number of wounds that still bled. He knew, too, that she must have other serious injuries or she would not be unconscious.

"Do you have someone who can help her?" Richard asked. "A gifted person?"

Ester hesitated. "We have someone gifted who may be able to help," she finally said.

One of the men behind leaned close, taking hold of Ester's dress at her shoulder to pull her back a bit as he whispered in her ear. "Do you think that wise?"

The woman turned an angry look on the man. "What choice is there? Should we instead let them die?"

He straightened, his only answer a sigh.

"But we must hurry," Ester said. "She can't heal them if they're dead."

"Besides that," another man reminded her, "we need to get all of us in out of the night."

At his words, others glanced around in the darkness. Richard noted that they all seemed terrified of being out after dark. Having once been a woods guide, he had often visited country folk. It was a relatively common attitude among them to want to shut themselves in when the sun went down. People in more remote places tended to be more superstitious than most, and the one common thing they all feared was darkness.

Although, he had to admit that these people certainly had real things to fear.

Richard watched as several men gently lifted Kahlan and then placed her over the shoulder of the biggest man. Richard wanted to carry her himself, but he knew that he couldn't even walk by himself. He reluctantly let two of the men put their shoulders under his arms to help him stay upright.

In the faint moonlight and soft golden glow of lanterns that several of the people carried, Richard looked back beyond the wagon. For the first time, he saw countless bodies. They weren't the men of the First File. Strange, pale, half-naked people lay sprawled across the ground everywhere. Given their gaping wounds, it looked like the First File had fought a fierce battle. Given the numbers of the dead, it was no wonder that the damp air smelled of blood and gore.

Nearby, just beyond the corner of the wagon, one of the dead men lay sprawled on his back, mouth agape. His dead eyes stared up at the dark sky.

The man's teeth had been filed to points.

Richard's grandfather Zedd and the sorceress Nicci had brought elite soldiers with them to see Richard and Kahlan safely back to the People's Palace. None of them would have abandoned the two of them. Richard scanned the scattered bones among pieces of uniforms, insignias, and the weapons of the First File lying scattered across the ground. It was a horrifying sight. But he didn't see anything that looked like it belonged to Zedd or Nicci or Cara.

Cara, his and Kahlan's personal bodyguard, was Mord-Sith. She would not have left him for any reason short of death, and he'd always suspected that even then Cara would come back from the world of the dead to protect him.

He feared that out there in the darkness where he couldn't see them, the bones of all those he cared so much about were among the dead. Panic at the thought of losing those so close to him tightened his chest.

"Hurry now," Ester said, pushing at the men helping to hold Richard up. "He's bleeding badly. We have to get back."

The others were more than happy to start away from the sight of so much death and head back to safety.

Richard let the men half carry him onto a narrow path through the wall of trees and into the night.

4

O n their swift journey through a forest so dense that the floor of the trail remained nearly untouched by moonlight, all of the people around him kept a wary watch of the surrounding darkness. Richard, too, scanned the woods, but he could see little beyond the weak lantern light. There was no way of telling what might be back in the black depths of the woods, no way of telling if the mysterious, half-naked people who had slaughtered his friends might be following him.

Every sound caught his attention and drew his eye. Every branch that brushed against him or snagged on his pant leg elevated his heart rate.

From what he could see, the people he was with carried nothing more than utilitarian knives. They had used a rock to dispatch the man attacking Richard. He would hate to encounter the hordes of killers on the dark trail and have to fight them off with little more than rocks.

He was glad to have the tooled leather baldric back over his right shoulder and his sword again at his left hip. From time to time he absently touched the familiar hilt of his sword for reassurance. He knew, though, that he was in little condition to fight.

Still, just touching the ancient weapon stirred its latent power and the silent storm of rage it held within it, stirring its twin within him and enticing him to call it forth. It was reassuring to have that faithful weapon and its attendant power at his beck and call.

Because some of the people had lanterns, Richard scanned the blackness for eye shine that would reveal the presence and position of animals beyond the limited range of the lantern light. While he did see some small creatures like frogs, a raccoon, and some night birds, he didn't see any eyes of larger animals watching them.

Of course, it was always possible that something larger could have been hidden among the dense clusters of ferns and shrubs or back among the tree trunks so that Richard wouldn't have seen them.

And, of course, there would have been no eye shine if the eyes watching them were human.

Since he couldn't really see anything in the black depths of the woods, he depended instead on sounds and smells that might tip him off to a threat. The only thing he smelled, though, was the familiar scent of balsam, ferns, and the mat of pine needles, dried leaves, and forest litter covering the ground. The only sounds he heard were the buzz of insects and sometimes the sharp call of night birds. Distant, faint cries of coyotes occasionally echoed through the mountains.

All of the people taking Richard and Kahlan to the safety of their village refrained from talking on the journey. The wary group walked swiftly but nearly silently, the way only those who had spent a lifetime in the woods were able to do. Even the man ahead who was carrying Kahlan made little noise as he moved along the trail. Richard, unable to walk very well and sometimes dragging his feet as the men on either side helped him, was making more noise than any of the rest of them, but there was little he could do about it.

With all the bodies of strange people he had seen back near the wagon, to say nothing of the two men who had attacked him and the things he had overheard, as well as all the warnings he'd previously gotten about venturing into the Dark Lands, Richard could easily see why these people were nervous and being so careful. The two men who had attacked him had looked nothing like the bodies he had seen. If those two men had been right, then the dead were the mysterious people they had mentioned, the Shun-tuk.

It seemed that unlike other country folk Richard knew back home, the people with him had more reason for their fears than simple superstition.

He appreciated it when people took real dangers seriously. The people who most often invited trouble were the willfully ignorant who didn't want to believe trouble was possible, so they dismissed the potential for it. You couldn't be ready for what you never considered or were unwilling to consider. Worry was sometimes a valuable survival tool, so Richard thought it foolish to ignore it. But still, since they were so lightly armed, he didn't think these people took the threats seriously enough.

Either that, or perhaps the threats they faced were something new to them.

It wasn't long before they abruptly emerged from the confining, oppressive darkness of the forest into the open. A light mist borne on cooler air dampened Richard's face.

In the distance across the slightly rolling ground out

ahead of them, lit by the muted moonlight, Richard saw a sheer rock wall rising up. Partway up the cliff face he could see faint, flickering light, probably from candles and lanterns, in passageways that looked to go back into the rock.

Making its way ever onward toward the cliff, the trail passed between large fields, some planted with grain, others with vegetables. Once among the fields spreading out from the foot of the soaring cliff, the people with him finally felt safe enough to start whispering among themselves.

As they got closer to the rock wall, they came upon pens made of split rails. Some of the pens held sheep, others rather skinny hogs. A few milk cows stood together in a tight cluster in the corner of one pen. Long coops set among boulders fallen from the mountain towering over them looked like they were for chickens that were no doubt roosting for the night. Richard saw a few men tending to the animals.

One of the men was checking on the sheep, patting their backs to make them move aside as he wove his way back through the small but dense flock crowded together in a large pen.

"What is it, Henry?" Ester asked as she got closer. "What are you men doing down here at this time of night?"

The man couldn't help staring for a brief moment at the strangers being carried in, one being helped on foot and a woman with a long fall of hair draped over a man's shoulders. He lifted a hand out, gesturing to the neat grid of pens.

"The animals are restless."

Richard looked back over a shoulder. The palm of his left hand rested on the familiar hilt of his sword as his gaze swept the fields between them and the dark mass of woods. He didn't see anything out of the ordinary.

"I think you had better leave the animals and get inside," Richard said as he scanned the dark tree line.

The man frowned as he lifted his knit cap to scratch his thinning white hair. "And who might you be to tell me what to do with our animals?"

Richard looked back at the man and shrugged, but then, feeling his legs about to give out, he put his left arm back around the shoulder of one of the two men standing beside him. "I'm just someone who doesn't like it when animals are restless, and I've seen a lot of frightening things this night not all that far behind us."

"He's right," Ester said as she started out again toward the rock wall. "You'd best get up inside with the rest of us."

Henry replaced his cap on his head as he cast a worried frown toward the silent wall of the woods hard against the far edge of the fields. The tall spruce looked like sentinels keeping the moonlight from entering.

Henry conceded with a nod. "I'll bring the others up right behind you."

With the help of the men to either side, Richard followed behind Ester, who in turn followed behind the man carrying Kahlan. Out at the head of the small group making their way toward the cliff, a man with a lantern looked back from time to time, making sure everyone was still accounted for.

Kahlan, her long hair matted with blood, her arms dangling, hung limp and unconscious over the shoulder of the man carrying her. In the moonlight Richard could see the wounds from the thorny vines the Hedge Maid had used to bind and imprison her. From time to time blood from those and other wounds dripped from her fingertips.

Richard had the same kinds of cuts, but not as many as Kahlan. The thorn vines must have had a substance on them that kept wounds from closing up properly because his, too, still oozed blood. At least he had managed to kill the Hedge Maid before she could completely drain Kahlan of all her blood. Although seriously hurt, at least she was still alive.

As they had made their way through the forest on

their way toward the village, he had ached to stop and heal her himself, but he knew that he was in no condition to be able to accomplish such a task. It took a variety of strengths on the part of the one doing the healing to be effective, strengths he didn't have right then. It made more sense to get help for her.

Once he knew that Kahlan was safe, he needed to find out what had happened to the soldiers of the First File and the friends who had been with them. He refused to believe that those he cared so much about were already dead. He remembered all too vividly, though, the human bones he had seen. He was distressed that any of his people had died, but especially in such a horrific fashion.

As they approached the base of the cliff, the small group made their way through a sprawling boulder field of broken rock built up over time as rock cleaved from the cliff face to accumulate below. In some places those with Richard, making their way single-file among the boulders, had to duck under massive slabs of stone that had fallen from the face of the mountain and now rested atop the jumble of rock slabs.

Richard was surprised to see the people ahead of him start up a narrow path right up against the face of the rock wall. Set back in a tangle of scrub, it would have been easy to miss, had he not seen people ahead beginning to climb upward.

He had thought that maybe they had ladders going up to the inhabited caves, or even an interior passage, but it appeared that the only way up was along the path made up of natural crags and ledges of the rock face. Where there were no natural footholds, the rock looked to have been laboriously cut away to create a trail. In the weak yellow light of the lanterns carried by some of those ahead, he could see that the rock underfoot had been smoothed by people treading across it to ascend the cliff wall for what had to be thousands of years.

"What is this place?" Richard asked in a whisper.

Ester looked back over her shoulder. "Our village, Stroyza."

Richard missed a step. He wondered if she knew what the name meant. Few people still alive understood High D'Haran. Richard was one of those who did.

"Why do you live up there? Why not build down among the fields and then you wouldn't have to climb up and down this treacherous trail all the time?"

"It is where our people have always lived." When that seemed not to be reason enough for him, she showed him a patient smile. "Don't you think that it would also be treacherous for anyone who would come to attack us in the night?"

Richard glanced to the bobbing dots of lantern light out ahead as people carefully made their way ever upward. "I suppose you're right. A single person up top could easily hold off an army trying to make their way up this trail." His brow twitched. "Do you have a lot of trouble with people attacking your village?"

"This is the Dark Lands," she said, as if that was explanation enough.

With the drizzle making the rock slick, Richard stepped carefully as they made their way up the narrow ledge of a path. The path wasn't anywhere near wide enough for a man to walk on either side of him to help him walk, so one of the men instead followed close behind, ready to steady him if he faltered. Fortunately, there were iron handholds pinned into the face of the rock in particularly narrow spots.

Unfortunately, the handholds were on the left side, and his bandaged left arm was the one most severely injured. He was in so much pain that his fingers could barely grip the iron holds, so he sometimes had to cross his right hand over to grip the bars. It made it more difficult to climb, but kept him from falling. The man following close behind held on to the iron bars with one hand and from time to time used his other to help prop Richard up and to keep him from falling. Glancing downward in the faint moonlight revealed a dizzying drop.

When they finally reached the top, a small cluster of people waited to greet them. As Richard stepped onto the open area the crowd moved back to give the arriving party room. He could see that the naturally formed, broad cavity narrowed down in places into several cavelike, wide passageways going deeper back into the mountain. Concern masked the faces of the people watching the injured strangers being brought in.

Several cats emerged from the darkness to greet the returning people from the village. Richard spotted several more of the cautious creatures back in the passageways. Most of them were black.

"We're thankful to see you all safely back," one of the waiting men said. "With you out after dark for so long, we were worried."

Ester was nodding. "I know. It couldn't be helped. Fortunately, we found them."

Before Ester could introduce him, Henrik spotted them from the shelter of the shadows and ran out to greet them.

"Lord Rahl! Lord Rahl! You're alive!"

Whispered astonishment swept back through the small assemblage of villagers. Apparently, not everyone in the village had been informed who the party had gone out to rescue.

"Lord Rahl . . . leader of the D'Haran Empire?" one man asked as whispers continued to spread among those gathered.

Through his pain, Richard nodded. "That's right."

They all started going to a knee. Richard hurriedly waved away the show of deference. "None of that, please."

As they all hesitantly returned to their feet, Richard managed a smile for the boy. "Henrik, I'm relieved to see that you are all right."

The man holding Kahlan eased her limp form down off his shoulder. Several people rushed in to help.

Ester quickly introduced a few of the people gathered around, but then cut it short. "We need to get them inside. They are both badly hurt. We need to see to their injuries."

The small crowd, shadowed by several cats, followed behind as Ester hurriedly led them back into one of the broader tunnels. There were a number of rooms built into natural clefts and crags along the way back into the cavern. Many of the rooms and network of tunnels had been excavated from the semisoft rock. The faces of some of the rooms had mortared stone walls filling in the gaps. Some places had wooden doors while others were covered with animal skins to create what looked to be a community of small homes.

The honeycomb of dwellings throughout the warren of burrows looked like a grim existence, but Richard supposed that the safety of the place high up within the mountain was comfort enough. The clothes worn by the people around him also spoke to the austere nature of existence in their small village. They all wore similar types of crudely made fabric that blended in with the color of the stone.

Ester snatched the sleeve of a woman ahead of her and leaned closer. "Get Sammie."

The woman frowned back over her shoulder. "Sammie?"

Ester confirmed it with a firm nod. "These two need to be healed."

"Sammie?" the woman repeated.

"Yes, hurry. There is no time to waste."

"But—"

"Go," Ester commanded with a flick of her hand. "Hurry. I will take them to my place."

As the woman rushed off to get the help Ester had called for, the crowd all funneled into a smaller passageway. Finally arriving at a doorway covered over with a heavy hanging made of sheepskin, Ester and several of the people with them ducked inside. Once inside the small room one of the men hurried to light dozens of candles. In contrast to the simple wooden table, three chairs, and chest to the side, crude but colorful carpets covered the floor. Pillows made of unadorned material similar to the material their clothes were made from provided the only other seating.

Ester directed the men carrying Kahlan to the side of the room, where they gently laid her down on a lambskin backed with a row of plain, well-used pillows. The men with Richard helped ease him down to sit on the floor against several pillows.

"We need to tend to your wounds right away," Ester told Richard. She turned to some of the women who had followed them in. "Get some warm water and rags. We will need a poultice made up. Bring bandages as well as needle and thread."

As the small cluster of the women hurried back out of the modest quarters to do her bidding, Ester knelt beside Richard. With a gentle hand she carefully lifted his arm and loosened the tourniquet so she could look under the blood-soaked bandage.

"I don't like the color of your arm," she said. "These bite wounds must be washed out. Some of them need to be stitched up." She glanced up at his eyes. "You also need more talented help."

Richard knew that she meant he needed a gifted person to heal him. He nodded as he leaned to the side, carefully pulling strands of hair back from Kahlan's face so that he could press the inside of his wrist against her forehead. She felt feverish.

"I can wait," he said. "I want you to take care of the Mother Confessor first."

When he looked back at Ester, apprehension tightened her features. She was clearly worried that he was the one who needed the immediate help.

Richard softened his tone. "I'm grateful for all you and your people have done, but please, I want you to help my wife first. You're right that my bite wounds need to be tended to, but she's unconscious and obviously in worse trouble. Maybe my wounds could be sewn and bandaged while your gifted person sees to helping the Mother Confessor first. Please, I'm worried about her condition. I need to know that she will be all right."

Ester studied his eyes briefly and then smiled a bit. "I understand." She turned and flicked a hand. "Peter, please go make sure that Sammie is on her way."

Richard turned from Kahlan when he heard people approaching out in the corridors. The first woman who ducked in under the sheepskin covering the doorway was carrying a bucket of water. A few of the other women brought in another bucket of water along with bandages and other supplies.

He was surprised to see some older women enter next, ushering in a wisp of a girl only beginning to blossom into womanhood. A long mass of black hair framed her small face. Her dark eyes were wide with wonder as she stood stiffly among the sheltering cluster of women. The smooth skin of her narrow face set back in among the dark mass of curly locks looked pale in the candlelight.

Ester rose up and held a hand back down toward Richard. "Sammie, this is Lord Rahl. The woman lying there is his wife, the Mother Confessor. They've both been badly hurt and need your help."

The girl's dark eyes briefly turned down to take a look at Kahlan before they turned back up at Ester. At Ester's urging, the girl hesitantly stepped forward. She lifted out the sides of her long skirt and performed an awkward curtsy before Richard.

Richard could easily see that she was not simply shy; she was terrified of him. Being from such a small, isolated place, she probably rarely saw strangers, much less strangers such as this. Despite the pain he was in and his worry for Kahlan, he made himself smile warmly to reassure her.

"Thank you for coming, Sammie."

She nodded as she hugged her slender arms to herself. Without answering, she moved back against the shelter of the older women.

"Sammie, would you excuse us for just a moment, please?" He looked up at Ester. "May I speak with you privately?"

Ester apparently knew why he wanted to talk to her alone. She forced a quick smile in answer before shepherding the small group to the doorway. They paused, looking confused, but finally obliged as Ester gently shooed them out. Once they were gone, Ester pulled the sheepskin down across the doorway.

"Lord Rahl, I know that—"

"She's a child."

The woman straightened her back and clasped her hands as she took a deep breath. She stepped closer and chose her words carefully.

"Yes, Lord Rahl, and though she is only just fifteen years, she's a gifted child. Right now that's what you both need. I can tend to cuts and scrapes, treat fevers with herbs, sometimes I can even set a broken bone"— she gestured to Kahlan—"but I don't know how to help her. I don't even have any idea what's wrong with her. Yes, Sammie is young, but she is not without knowledge and abilities."

Richard remembered when he had been as young as

Sammie. He had thought that he was all grown up and had the world mostly figured out. While he had known more than most adults gave him credit for, as he had grown older he had come to realize that despite how much he did know, he knew less than he thought he did, mostly because he never appreciated how much more there was to learn. Now, as an adult looking back on someone that age, despite how much they might know, he understood how limited a young person's scope of the world really was.

That age of early confidence was something like a false dawn. The real thing was coming, yet despite being close at hand it was still not quite there. And even when it did begin to arrive, there was always more to learn. He remembered Zedd telling him that old age meant that the only thing he really knew was that he would never know it all, much less know enough.

Putting Kahlan's life into the hands of someone with such limited experience was more than a little disconcerting to him.

"But she's a child," Richard said softly so that those outside wouldn't hear. "This is a difficult and complex task even for someone experienced in such things."

Ester bowed her head respectfully. "Lord Rahl, if you don't want Sammie to try, that is of course your decision and I will abide by it. I will do my best to sew up the worst of your wounds and tend to other injuries as I know how. I can try to guess at what the Mother Confessor might need and prepare some herbs and such that might help her."

The woman lifted her head to look him in the eye. "But I think you know as well as I do that it isn't going to be enough. You both need gifted healing.

"If you don't want Sammie to try to do that bigger

task of what is needed, then all I can suggest is that you will have to travel elsewhere in the hope of finding someone more to your liking. It would be a difficult journey. In the Dark Lands there is no telling how far you will have to go to find such a person. I can tell you that there are not many with such abilities as you need. Not many I would trust, anyway.

"Because of that, Jit was able to prey on those desperate to find help. Occasionally she would help someone in need so as to create hope among other desperate people and in that way draw in more victims.

"Do you think you have the ability to undertake a journey to find someone trustworthy who could help you? Do you think the Mother Confessor can make such a journey? Are you willing to risk her life on waiting until you can find someone else? If you become desperate will you risk her life on someone with veiled motives and perhaps end up in the hands of someone like Jit?

"You have already seen that we are willing to help you, even at the risk of danger to ourselves."

"And why would you do that?" Richard asked.

Ester shrugged. "We help because we would want someone to help us if we were in danger. It is our way. It has always been our way, handed down from generations long forgotten. We teach our children to help those in need because one day we might be the ones in need, and we can only hope to earn such help if we are worthy, if we are the kind who would give it and not just receive it. We believe in treating others as we would want to be treated."

"I guess that's the way I've always tried to live my life as well," Richard said.

"Lord Rahl, I am telling you that Sammie may be only fifteen, but she is gifted and has a good heart. That is all we are able to offer. That is the best we can offer. Are you so sure that you want to turn down our help, such as it is?"

Richard knew that he was in no condition to heal Kahlan himself. Worse, though, he didn't think that he could. Back at the wagon he had tried to summon his gift to save her life, and his gift had not responded. It was evident that there was something seriously wrong with his gift. If it wouldn't save her from being murdered, it would not respond to heal her, either.

He didn't know what could be wrong with his gifted ability. He knew only that it wasn't working. They both needed help.

He also knew that in his present condition he couldn't make it far. He remembered that Zedd and Nicci had started healing them even as they lay in the back of the moving wagon. They wouldn't have been doing that if it wasn't urgent.

Still, he didn't entirely trust the motives of these people.

If he wasn't willing to accept the girl's gifted help, then having Ester tend to their wounds with needle and thread, herbs, and poultices was the only other choice. He knew that Ester was right that such help wasn't enough, especially for Kahlan.

Richard had been wounded in the past. This time, though, he felt something different, something more than simple injuries. He wanted to ignore the way he felt, but he knew he couldn't, at least not for long. He knew, too, that whatever the grim shadow of affliction he felt within himself was, Kahlan was suffering from it far worse than he was.

Zedd and Nicci had been trying to heal him and Kahlan, but they hadn't been able to finish that work. Now they were missing. Richard knew that the lives of not only Kahlan but also his friends depended on him making the right decision. He didn't think that there was any time to waste.

But gift or no gift, he didn't know if he dared to trust Kahlan's life to such a young and inexperienced girl. Where the gift was concerned, a mistake could be fatal.

"Do you trust her abilities?"

Ester hiked up her gray dress and again knelt beside him. "Sammie is an earnest girl. Her mother was a sorceress. That may account for Sammie seeming to be grown beyond what her years would otherwise suggest. Being ungifted myself, I don't know much about such abilities, but I do know that her mother passed the gift on to Sammie. There is no doubt about that much of it."

"Where is her mother?"

Ester's gaze fell away. "Not long ago we found the remains of Sammie's father, but not her mother. We think that her mother was captured and taken. Though Sammie holds out hope, I don't think she is still alive."

"Taken?"

Ester's gaze rose to meet his. "As your people were. As nearly happened to the Mother Confessor.

"The Dark Lands have always been a dangerous place. We have long lived with those dangers and know how to remain fairly safe. But now, terrible things are happening that we don't understand and can't fight. We need help."

Richard wiped a hand across his mouth. As he had thought, this was what the men who had helped save him back at the wagon had meant. Although they might have always lived their lives by the code of helping others as they would want to be helped, in this case they needed help that they thought only one such as the Lord Rahl could provide. Considering the frightful things he had seen, it wasn't hard to see why they were desperate for help. He couldn't blame them for their motives.

His gaze turned to Kahlan. He briefly watched her shallow breathing. Did he dare to risk her life on such an inexperienced girl?

What choice did he have?

"All right," he finally said with a sigh of resignation.

As soon as she had Richard's agreement to let Sammie help, Ester sprang up. She pulled back the thick covering over the doorway and ducked under it to rush out into the hall. Richard could hear her asking the others to please give the Lord Rahl and the Mother Confessor privacy. The people murmured their understanding.

In short order Ester ushered the girl back in, leaving all the others to wait down the corridor. With a reassuring hand on the girl's shoulder, Ester steered her into the room as she once again let the heavy sheepskin fall across the doorway.

A black cat ducked in under the sheepskin and casually followed the girl into the room. The cat sat off to the side, lifting a hind leg as it licked the glossy fur on its tummy.

Sammie stood stiffly just inside the room, looking too fearful to approach. Her flawless skin laid over her immature features not yet fully emerged made her almost look like a statue carved of the smoothest marble.

Richard held out his good hand and waggled his fingers in invitation. "Please, Sammie, come sit here beside me."

When Sammie shuffled closer, he gently took her hand and urged her to kneel down beside him. She sat back on her heels, wary to get too close. Her big eyes sparkled in the candlelight as they remained fixed on him. If she only knew that he probably had more to fear than she did.

Once Ester saw that the girl was in his hands, she used her foot to slide the bucket of water across the floor with her as she carried the bandages and other supplies over to Kahlan, where she squatted down and hurriedly began cleaning the worst of Kahlan's wounds.

"I'm very sorry to hear about your father and that your mother is missing," Richard said.

Sammie's eyes welled up with tears at the mention of her parents. "Thank you, Lord Rahl." Her voice was as thin and timid as the rest of her, and it carried the lonely, painful tone of inconsolable grief.

"Maybe if you can help us, then when I'm able to, I can help find your mother."

Sammie's brow twitched. She looked confused. "You are the ruler of the D'Haran Empire." She wiped the tears from under her eyes. "Why would you be concerned with helping someone from the little village of Stroyza?"

Richard shrugged. "I didn't become a leader because I wanted to rule people. I became a leader because I wanted to help protect our people from harm. If one of the people I'm sworn to protect is hurt or in danger, no matter who they are, then that is my concern."

She looked perplexed. "Hannis Arc rules all the Dark Lands, including our village. I've never met him, but I've never heard anyone say that he is concerned about protecting us. Far from it; I've heard that he only cares about prophecy."

"I've heard the same thing," Richard said. "I don't share his concern for prophecy. I believe we make our own future. In part that's what brought me here. The Mother Confessor and I were both hurt while making sure that a terrible prophecy did not come true and harm our people. Our free will, not prophecy, made the ultimate difference in what happened."

The girl glanced at Kahlan out of the corner of her eye. "I'm sorry about your wife being hurt." Her big eyes turned back to Richard. "My mother often said that I was gifted, but it was up to me, not fate, to make something of it."

"Wise advice. And did she teach you about using your gift?"

A bit of the tension went out of the girl's bony shoulders. "All my life she taught me things about my gift, but mostly in little ways."

"Little things are a good place to start. Larger understanding is built on little things. We put those little things we learn together into larger concepts."

With a thumb, Sammie smoothed a fold in her dress along the length of her thigh. "She was just starting to teach me more, to teach me about using our calling to heal. She said that I was old enough to start learning more. But I'm still only a young sorceress. My ability is nothing compared to my mother's gift, and especially nothing compared to one such as yours must be, Lord Rahl."

Richard couldn't help but to smile. "I didn't even find out that I had the gift until I was a lot older than you are now. No one taught me about it as I was growing up. I imagine that with all your mother taught you, you must know more about the gift than even I do."

Her smooth brow bunched skeptically. "Really?"

"Really. I've since used my ability, but in a different way than most gifted people. I've both destroyed and healed with my ability, but I've done it through instinct and desperate need, through letting my gift guide me, rather than from anything I was taught."

Sammie sat over on her hip as she thought it over. The black cat strolled over to rub against the girl before padding on silent paws toward Kahlan.

"That must be frightening to have the gift and not know how to use it, not know how to control it."

Despite the pain he was in and his worry for Kahlan, he couldn't help letting out a small ripple of laughter. "You don't know the half of it."

She regarded him with an unreadable look. "But still, you must be able to use your power well enough. After all, you are the Lord Rahl. I've heard it said that the people of D'Hara are the steel against steel so that you might be the magic against magic."

Richard didn't tell her that at the moment his power didn't work.

Out of the corner of his eye, he saw the cat cautiously stretched forward to smell Kahlan's boot. The little black nose glided along, hovering just above her leg and then up along her arm, not quite touching her skin. The cat abruptly drew back. Its lips curled with a hiss that bared sharp little teeth. Richard thought that it must not like a stranger who smelled of blood being among them.

"Are all the cats that live here black?" Richard asked Sammie.

She looked up at him from under her brow. "They are when they need to be."

Richard frowned. "What does that mean?"

"In the dark they are all black," she said, cryptically.

Ester, kneeling beside Kahlan, flapped her rag at the cat, chasing it away. Ears laid back, the cat scurried out of the room.

Richard looked back at Sammie. He wasn't sure what she meant, but he had more important things on his mind. He turned the conversation to the matter at hand. "So what do you know about healing?"

Sammie's brow twitched as she considered her answer. "My mother was just starting to teach me how to heal people. She talked to me about the fundamentals and then had me help with small things. I've only done simple healing—cuts and scrapes, a sick stomach, headaches, rashes. Things like that. She guided me in how to let my ability go down into a person to feel the trouble within them."

Richard nodded. "I've experienced that when I've healed people." He stared off into grim memories. "On occasion, because the need was so great, I've had to let myself go so far down into a person that it felt as if I lost who I was as I sank into their soul to lift their pain away and take it into myself."

"I've never gone that deep." Sammie looked uneasy. "I don't know that I'd ever be able to go down into a person's soul."

"If you've healed people then I suspect you have, even if you didn't realize it," Richard said. "That's how it works. While healing, you are venturing down into the essence, in other words the soul, of who they are. At least, that's how it works for me."

"That sounds . . . frightening."

"Not if you really care about helping them."

She watched his eyes for a moment as if they held some deep secret. "If you say so, Lord Rahl."

Richard looked over at Kahlan lying not far away. Ester, her face set in a frown of focused concentration, carefully cleaned and inspected cuts along Kahlan's arms.

"I've healed Kahlan before," Richard said, "but I'm not strong enough to do it now and I'm terribly worried for her."

Sammie's gaze left Kahlan to wander over some of his more serious bite wounds. Her worry about the task he was asking of her was clearly evident in her tense expression.

"I don't know how deeply I may have gone into a person's essence, but I do know that I've never healed such terrible injuries. I've only healed small things. I've never tried to heal anything so grievous."

"Well, from my experiences I can tell you that, to a certain extent, anyway, the severity of the injuries is irrelevant. Of course, in some cases it isn't, such as when the person is near the veil and in the process of crossing over from the world of life into the world of the dead. That's different."

Sammie's eyes widened. "You mean as the person is crossing the boundaries of the Grace?"

Richard regarded her more seriously. "Your mother taught you about the Grace?"

Sammie nodded. "The symbol that represents the spark of creation, the world of life, the world of the dead, and the way the gift crosses those boundaries to link everything. Those with the gift, she told me, must know about the Grace so as not to violate it. It defines how the gift flows and how it works—its capability and its limits—as well as the order of creation, life, and death. All our work, my mother said, is represented by the Grace, guided by it, and ultimately must be governed by it."

"That's what I learned as well," Richard said. "By allowing myself to flow along those lines of the gift as represented by the Grace, I've found that healing most injuries is basically the same process. If you let the person's need guide you, then through your gift you can feel what is necessary. Through your empathy you lift away the hurt and hold it within yourself so that the healing power of your gift can then flow into the person you're helping. I have always found that the person's need actually guides me, draws me onward toward it."

Except that for some reason his gift had stopped working.

The girl frowned. "I think I know what you mean. My mother had me feel deep down into people, feel the trouble within them."

"And did she teach you to lift that pain out of them and take it into yourself?"

Sammie hesitated. "Yes. But I was afraid. It's hard when you can feel the pain they feel. I've done that. I've felt what they felt, though it was for smaller injuries. Then I try to lift it away from them and, like you say, let the warmth of the gift flow from me and into them to heal them."

Richard was nodding as she spoke. "That's been my experience as well."

"But you said that you have healed people when they have been at the boundaries of the Grace, when they have been crossing over into the world of the dead. You have flowed along those lines of the Grace that flow into the world of the dead."

It didn't sound at all like a question so much as a lecture for doing things she had been taught were forbidden.

"You would be surprised, Sammie, what you would do for ones you love." He again looked over at Kahlan. "I love her very much and I'm afraid for her, but this time I don't have the strength for the sustained effort needed to heal her. Can you do that for her?"

Sammie's gaze glided over to watch Ester gently cleaning blood from Kahlan's face. "What's wrong with her?"

"I don't know for sure. A Hedge Maid had captured her and was starting to drink her blood and—"

"Jit?" Sammie abruptly leaned toward him, her eyes intent. "Are you talking about Jit?" When Richard nodded she asked, "How did you ever manage to get away from the Hedge Maid?"

"I killed her."

"Indeed he did," Ester said back over her shoulder. She dipped the cloth in the bucket and then wrung red water out of it. "That's how they were both hurt," she said with a last look before going back to her work cleaning Kahlan's wounds.

Sammie seemed not to notice Ester. She instead stared in wonder at Richard.

"Then you really are a protector of your people." She caught herself, glanced at Ester busy with her work, then leaned closer to Richard and spoke confidentially. "You are the one."

Richard didn't know what she meant about him being the one. He was having enough trouble remaining upright and besides, he had far greater concerns at the moment.

"Will you help Kahlan, then? I need you to help us both, but I want you to help Kahlan first. I need to know that she's out of danger."

Anxiety tightened the gentle features of Sammie's face. "She's the Mother Confessor."

Richard wasn't sure exactly what she was getting at. "That's right."

Sammie winced a little with a sideways look, apparently fearful of posing the question. "Won't I, well, you know, won't I be harmed by her power? When I go down into the essence of who she is, won't I be taken by her Confessor power?"

Richard was shaking his head even before she had finished the question.

"No, it doesn't work that way."

"How can you be sure? You said that you don't know a lot about magic."

"Because besides me, both a wizard and a sorceress have healed her before. None of us were harmed. In fact, a sorceress was in the process of healing her earlier today, but we were attacked before she was able to finish.

"Kahlan's power won't harm you. It's not a danger for you to heal her. So, will you do it?"

Sammie pressed her lips tight. Her mouth contorted as she weighed her inner doubts. She finally nodded.

"I'll try, Lord Rahl. I'll do my best."

"That's all I can ask."

Sammie squatted down beside Ester and leaned in over Kahlan. She turned her head to get a better view as she looked down at Kahlan's still face.

"She's very beautiful," Sammie said back over her shoulder.

Richard nodded, trying to be understanding of Sammie's young age and not show his tense impatience. He was afraid that if he wasn't careful he might frighten her and then she wouldn't be able to concentrate properly on the job ahead of her. With his stomach in knots and Kahlan's life hanging in the balance, it wasn't easy to show the girl a calm expression.

"She is beautiful on the inside, too," he said. "Right now she needs help. It's up to us to give her that help.

"Maybe you should start out with the small things, first. Maybe concentrate on healing some of the cuts on her arms. That way you will be doing what you know. After you get comfortable with what it feels like to be healing her, then you can move on and deal with her bigger problem."

Sammie nodded, liking the suggestion. "That sounds like the guidance my mother would give."

She gently took hold of the older woman's elbow and urged her back. Ester moved out of the way, pulling the bucket of bloody water with her.

"Take your time and think it through, child," Ester told her. "Your mother taught you well. I know that you can do it."

"I'll do the best I can," Sammie said as she rested a hand on Kahlan's abdomen, feeling her slow breathing. "I hope it's enough," she whispered to herself.

Ester stood off to the side, watching nervously. "Your mother would be proud of you, Sammie. She would say that you can do it, and that it's in your hands now."

Sammie, already concentrating on what she needed to do, answered with an absent nod. She momentarily touched various wounds along Kahlan's arms, evaluating them with her gift. Her fingers tested the place on Kahlan's stomach that had already been mostly healed by Zedd. Her hand lingered there, as if inspecting the work, perhaps hoping to learn from it.

Finally, Sammie scooted around so that she was kneeling above Kahlan's head. Leaning in, Sammie pulled wet strands of Kahlan's hair aside and then pressed her hands to Kahlan's temples. Her splayed fingers lying along Kahlan's cheeks were so small and frail-looking that Richard feared she didn't have the strength needed for such a difficult task, to say nothing of the experience to accomplish it.

He reminded himself that he had healed people without any experience or training. He supposed that in that respect Sammie was more knowledgeable than he was. Still, it was Kahlan, and he couldn't seem to quiet his worry, or his racing heart.

The girl's eyes rolled back in her head as her eyelids slid closed. Still holding Kahlan between her hands, Sammie stretched her arms out straight as her head tilted back in the effort of calling for the needed strength.

Richard had learned some time back that he had the

unique ability to see the gift radiating power around sorceresses. He could see that aura of power around Sammie as she opened herself up to her gift. The aura looked like shimmering, colored distortions to the air around her, something like the heat waves above a campfire.

Richard had seen the auras of gifted people before. It was reassuring to see such a marker of gifted power glimmering in the air around Sammie. While Sammie's aura wasn't nearly as strong as many he had seen, and especially not as powerful as that of a sorceress such as Nicci, it was definitely the gift he was seeing warming the glow around the girl.

He hoped that power would be enough.

Richard listened to the soft hiss of the candles as Sammie leaned forward again and bowed her head in concentration. He knew what she was experiencing, what it felt like to let yourself dissolve down into the person you were trying to help, to immerse yourself in their being, to be intimately close to their innermost self. He watched as the flames of the candles slowly wavered and the wax dripped down from time to time as they burned. He wondered all the while what Sammie was experiencing, what she was feeling within Kahlan.

Several of the candles in the room abruptly extinguished at the exact same instant. Richard's gaze darted around the small room, searching shadows.

Sammie shrieked and leaped to her feet.

Richard sprang up in surprise. Ester shrank back.

Before he could ask her what was wrong, Sammie began screaming in a high-pitched shriek born of what looked to be unbridled panic. Arms flailing, she retreated blindly until her back smacked into the stone wall. In the grip of terror, still screaming, unable to back away any farther, she clawed at the air while shrieking in fright. Her head twisted from side to side as if she did not want to look at what she was seeing.

The shrill screech was painful. Ester fearfully backed away as far as she could. As Sammie turned to run for the doorway, Richard caught her, closing his arms tightly around her slender body to keep her from getting away. Her spindly arms thrashed frantically, as if she was trying to escape something only she could see. She screamed in unbridled terror the whole time, twisting madly in Richard's arms as she fought to escape.

Richard cocooned the squirming girl until he finally gathered her wildly flailing arms and pinned them to her sides.

"Sammie, what is it? What's wrong?"

Tears streamed down her cheeks. "I saw it in her . . ."

"It's all right. You're safe, now. What did you see?"

When she turned in his arms and pushed at him, crying hysterically as she again tried to get away, Richard grabbed her firmly by the sides of her shoulders to keep her right where she was. Despite his injuries, she was no match for his muscle.

"Sammie, tell me what you saw!"

"I saw . . ." was all she could get out between sobs.

Richard shook her. "Sammie, stop it. You're safe. Nothing is going to hurt you." He shook her again. "Stop it now. Lives are at stake—your mother's life could very well be at stake. You need to get control of yourself and tell me what's going on. I can't help fix it if I don't know what's wrong. Now tell me what you saw in Kahlan."

Sammie, tears coursing down her face, shook from head to toe.

"I saw what is in her," she sobbed.

"What do you mean? What did you see in her?"

Sammie's face contorted in horror. "I saw death."

Again Sammie tried to turn away. Again Richard turned her back.

"What do you mean, you saw death? You need to get yourself under control and talk to me. What do you mean?"

Panting in fear, Sammie swiped at the tears running down her cheeks. She gulped a few quick breaths and pointed, as if it was plain as day, as if he should be able to see it, too.

"She has death in her."

As she again tried to twist away, Richard tightened his grip on her shoulders. "Calm down. Take a deep breath. Kahlan is unconscious. She can't hurt you. I'm here with you. I need you to explain what you're talking about so that we can figure out what you saw. Kahlan is alive. She's not dead."

Sammie's face wrinkled up as tears sprang anew. "But I saw—"

"You're a sorceress," he said in a firm voice. "Act like one. Your mother is gone. She may need help, too. This is important. She would want you to stand in her place and do what is needed. You can do that, I know you can."

Sammie sniffled, trying her best to hold back her tears. She finally nodded.

Ester laid a hand on the girl's back. "You're safe, Sammie. Do as Lord Rahl says, now."

Sammie's lower lip trembled. She looked from Ester back to Richard.

"Is that what my father saw when he died? Is that what it's like? Did he have to face that? Did my mother see that too? Is that what we all face when we die?"

Richard squeezed her shoulders in sympathy and spoke softly. "I'm sorry, Sammie, but I can't answer that. I don't know what we see when we die. I don't know what you saw in Kahlan. Now, take a deep breath."

She took two.

"Better?"

She nodded as she pushed her thatch of dark hair back from the sides of her face.

"All right," Richard said, "now explain to me what happened."

Sammie took another steadying breath and then flicked a hand toward Kahlan. "I was connected to her, feeling her pain—you know, the pain of her smaller injuries, like you suggested. I was, well, I was trying to gather up a lot of that pain, collect it, and take it into myself."

"I understand," Richard said as he cautiously released her shoulders. "Then what?"

Sammie put one hand on a hip as she pressed the trembling fingers of her other hand to her forehead, trying to remember what had happened. "Well, I don't know exactly. I don't know how to explain it."

"Do your best, child," Ester urged.

Sammie glanced at her and then looked up at Richard's eyes. "Do you know the way the sensation of beginning to do a healing is like being caught up in a flow that draws you in, draws you deeper, seeking more of the trouble within the person?"

"Yes, I know what you mean," Richard said. "It's like you lose your sense of who you are as you become more and more focused on them and their pain. It feels like you are dissolving into the other person, losing yourself as you slip down into who they are. It seems to gather power from you and in that way pulls you onward."

Sammie was nodding as he spoke. "That's what it felt like. When I've healed other people, though, I wasn't pulled in like that. This was stronger than I've ever felt before."

"That's most likely because they weren't as badly hurt. It's the need that draws you toward it. The more serious the trouble, the stronger the need, so the more powerfully it pulls you in. You don't need to be afraid of that sensation. From what I know, that's not unusual."

"That wasn't the frightening part," Sammie said as she cast a worried look at Kahlan. Her lower lip started quivering again. She seemed transfixed, unable to look away from Kahlan lying so still on the lambskin.

Richard put a finger under Sammie's chin and turned her face back toward his. "Go on. Tell me what you saw."

Sammie knitted her fingers together as she frowned while recalling the experience. "When I started slipping down into her, I began to be drawn in faster and faster. It took me deeper than I had expected. I realized that I wasn't trying to go down into her, it was just that something kept pulling me down. It was like losing my footing as I slid down a steep, slippery slope."

"I told you, that's pretty normal."

"That's what I thought at first. But I soon realized that I wasn't simply going down into her need the way

I have with others I've healed. I wasn't just being pulled in. I was being drawn toward something."

"Toward something? Toward what?" Richard asked.

"Something dark. Something dark and sinister. As I got closer, I heard voices."

That was something Richard had not expected. "Voices? What kind of voices?"

"At first I didn't know what the sound was. At first it was a distant buzzing. As I sank ever faster toward the darkness within her, I realized that what I was hearing were screams."

Richard frowned. "Screams? I don't understand. What do you mean, you were hearing screams? How could you hear screams?"

Sammie stared off, as if experiencing it again. "It was like a thousand screams all melted together." She shook her head at her own description, or maybe in an effort to escape the memory. She looked back up at him. "No, not like a thousand. Like a million. Like a million million. It was like an infinite number of screams welling up from a dark place. They were the most horrific, terrifying, anguished screams you can imagine. The kind of screams that seemed as if they might sear the flesh from your bones."

Richard couldn't help glancing back down at Kahlan. "Did you see anything?" he asked. "Did you see where these screams were coming from?"

Sammie twisted her hands, bending her fingers as she tried to find words. "I, I was being pulled toward darkness. But then I saw that it wasn't darkness, exactly."

"What do you mean?"

"It was more like a writhing mass of forms. That was where the screams were coming from. A turning, churning, tumbling mass of spirits that were all wriggling, struggling, squirming, and screaming at once."

Richard stood stunned, unable to imagine what was going on.

Sammie looked frustrated trying to come up with the right words for what she had seen. "I'm sorry that I can't explain it very well, but when I saw it, felt it, I knew that it was death I was seeing. It was death itself. I knew it, that's all."

Richard made himself take a breath. "That certainly sounds frightening, and while I can't explain it, that doesn't mean that it was death you were seeing."

Sammie tilted her head to the side as she frowned up at him. "But it was, Lord Rahl. I know it was."

Richard was impatient to get the young sorceress back to the task of healing Kahlan, but he reminded himself that he had to be understanding of not only her age and inexperience, but her fears. This was all new to her, and her mother was not there to help her. He suspected that she was simply misinterpreting the pain resulting from the seriousness of Kahlan's injuries.

"Sammie, it was probably the terrible pain, the profound hurt within Kahlan, that you were encountering. I've healed grievously injured people before, so I know how frightening it can be. Being immersed in their suffering is a dark and daunting experience. Time seems to stop. The world of life can seem distant. Lost in that strange place with their pain, you know that what is hurting them could kill them, and only you can stop it. You know that they're facing death if you can't help them."

"No," Sammie insisted as she shook her head. "When I looked through that shimmering green curtain, I knew I was looking beyond the veil into the world of the dead."

Richard froze still as stone. The room seemed too quiet, too small, too hot.

"What did you say?"

Her tongue darted out to wet her lips. "When I looked beyond that curtain, I knew that I was looking beyond the veil into—"

"You said it was green."

Sammie's brow bunched as she fought back new tears. "That's right."

"Why would you say it's green?"

Perplexed, she frowned up at him. "Because it was. It was like a shimmering green curtain of fog. It rippled, brighter and darker, something like a wispy, sheer, transparent green curtain moving in a breath of breeze. It's kind of hard to describe.

"Beyond that awful veil of green I saw what looked to me like a churning mass of spirits. They were all screaming as if in terrible agony. That was the sound I heard. Some of the forms ripped apart as they screamed, while yet more of them constantly boiled up from the blackness below to take the place of those that disintegrated, in turn adding their ghastly screams to the sea of souls, all fusing into one, long, hopeless cry.

"Some of them saw me and tried to grab for me, but they couldn't reach through that green veil. Others beckoned me to come to them instead. It was death calling to me, trying to pull me in."

Richard turned and stared down at Kahlan. He had encountered the underworld a number of times. The veil before the world of the dead was always an eerie green color.

He slowly sank to his knees beside the unconscious form of the woman he loved more than life itself. "Dear spirits, what is going on?"

10

W hat is it?" Ester looked back and forth between Sammie and Kahlan. "Lord Rahl, what is it? Do you know what it means? Do you know what's wrong with her?"

Instead of answering, Richard laid a hand on Kahlan's shoulder, feeling her warmth, her breathing, the life in her. Despite how sick he felt, he ignored his own pain. She was in grave trouble and needed help. She needed gifted help.

She needed more help than Sammie was able to give.

He shut himself off from everything around him as he retreated into the calm center within himself. The people outside in the corridors and rooms of the cliff dwelling no longer seemed at all close. The faint undertone of their voices gradually faded away. Ester's and Sammie's voices became distant murmurs as he focused on what needed to be done, on what Kahlan needed done.

In that inner silence, he sought to release himself into Kahlan to heal her, or at least to try to sense what the problem was. He wanted to see it for himself. He wanted to deal with it himself. He wanted to extinguish that hidden terror. Most of all, he wanted to take away her pain. He ached to see her open her eyes and smile up at him.

Even though he had healed Kahlan before when she had been grievously hurt, this time as he tried desperately to call forth that healing ability within himself, he couldn't seem to find the way to do it. It didn't exactly feel as if he was having difficulty recalling how to heal—it felt more like he had never known how to do it. It was maddening to feel like he knew where he wanted to go, to know that he had been there before, but not to be able to find the path back.

Whatever he had done in the past to heal people seemed simply to no longer be there. If he didn't know better, he would think that he had never healed anyone before. He couldn't imagine what component was missing, or how to find it.

Where he should have felt his inner empathy coming to the surface to take him into Kahlan's suffering, he felt nothing.

As desperate as he was to help her, he realized that wasn't the only trouble on his hands.

He knew without a doubt that he should have at least felt something, but he didn't. He remembered all too well that it had been much the same back at the wagon when he had reached down inside himself to call on his gift to help him protect Kahlan from those men. Nothing had happened then, either. If there was ever a case where his gift should have worked, it would be to protect her and to heal her.

It wasn't that he was simply too injured himself or too weak to heal her. He knew now that something more was going on. Whatever the problem, he didn't know how to compensate for it.

His level of fear and alarm rose as he wondered if his gift was gone.

In place of the healing power of his gift that he should have felt, he realized that he could hear the slightest of sounds. As he concentrated on listening, trying to hear what it was, his blood ran cold as he realized that it sounded like distant screams.

He didn't know if those screams were coming from something he felt in Kahlan . . . or in himself. He wondered if he might be imagining it. He couldn't help feeling haunted by the things Sammie had told him she had experienced.

He fought back a rising sense of panic. He had told Sammie to calm down, that panic wouldn't help. He knew that he had to take his own advice. He had to think if he was to act effectively.

For whatever reason, what he was doing to try to heal Kahlan was not working. He opened his eyes, rose up, and took a long stride back to the girl.

"Did you sense it in her, too?" Sammie asked.

Richard shook his head. "What else did you sense in her?"

Sammie looked confused by the question and intimidated by him towering over her. "Nothing. I was afraid. I drew back out of her."

Richard turned to look down at Kahlan, pinching his lower lip as he thought it through.

Whatever was wrong with Kahlan, it had to have happened in the Hedge Maid's lair. Whatever was wrong with him had started there as well. He and Kahlan had both been unconscious when Zedd, Nicci, and Cara found them.

Richard remembered killing the Hedge Maid. He had been warned that his sword, and his gift, would not work against her. The Omen machine, though, had given him a prophecy: *Your only chance is to let the truth escape.*

With that clue, he had realized that the way to stop that vile creature was to cut the leather strips sewing her mouth closed. Doing so had caused her to release an inner scream held back for most of her life by those leather strips. It had brought about the release of the corruption and death that had been contained and festering within her.

First, though, knowing what he had been about to do, Richard had wadded up small pieces of cloth and stuffed them in Kahlan's and his own ears to keep both of them from hearing that malevolent cry born in the world of the dead—to prevent them from hearing the call of death itself.

At least, he thought it had kept them from hearing it.

He turned back to Sammie. "I need you to use your gift on me, the way you did when you tried to heal Kahlan. I need to know if you can sense that same thing in me that you sensed in her."

Sammie shook her head as she shrank back.

"Listen to me!" he yelled, freezing her in her tracks. "Lives are at stake. I'm not asking you to go beyond that green veil and cross over into what you sensed as death, but I need to know if the same thing you sensed in Kahlan is within me as well."

When she again started backing away he grabbed her slender wrist. "Listen to me, Sammie. You were able to back out of Kahlan, weren't you?"

Her eyes turned fearfully toward Kahlan. "Yes."

"So then it can't pull you in. Whatever you sensed in her doesn't have the power to do that. You are in control. Even though you went down deep into her you pulled yourself back out, didn't you?"

She didn't answer.

"Didn't you?" he repeated.

He knew that he was frightening her, but it couldn't be helped.

"I suppose so," she finally said.

"Then you are the one in control, not what you saw in her. That evil may try to pull you toward it, but you have free will and are able to resist that dark call. You make the choice not to be pulled in by evil."

Sammie let her arm drop when he released her wrist. "I guess you're right."

"I know I am," Richard said. "I know because you came back of your own free will. But I also know because others were healing Kahlan and me when we were attacked. They both have vast experience and know a great deal more about healing than either you or I will likely ever know. They would have sensed what was in her and they wouldn't have been trying to heal her if it was a lethal trap."

"But how can you be sure that they were healing her?"

"They healed the wound on her stomach."

Sammie thought it over for a moment. "You're right," she finally admitted. "I felt that healing. I could tell that it was fresh, that not long before me someone else had been there healing her."

"And they came back. You were able to come back, too. That means you are in control. You aren't helpless to that call of death."

She looked considerably more calm, even if she didn't look at ease. "That makes sense."

Richard took a step closer to her. "I need you to check me. I need to know if that same sickness is in me."

She appraised his eyes for a moment with a look that was well beyond her years.

"You suspect that you have the same thing in you

that she has in her, and you think that may be what's keeping your gift from working," she said.

It wasn't a question.

Richard arched an eyebrow, then sat on the floor and crossed his legs. "Come on. Do it now. I need to know."

Sammie let out a frustrated sigh, then gave in and sat before him. She followed Richard's gaze to see a cat that had just sauntered into the room, peeking in the dark places behind the pillows against the far wall the way cats liked to do.

"I think that the cat sensed what I saw in the Mother Confessor," Sammie said.

"The cat?"

She nodded as she crossed her legs, the way he had done. "My mother says that cats are sensitive to spirits, to things from the world of the dead."

Richard looked at the girl for a moment without saying anything, then held his hands out. "Take my hands. Try to heal a few of my wounds. Do what you did with Kahlan."

Sammie gave in with a sigh and finally took his hands. Richard, having trouble holding his left arm up, rested his forearms across his knees. His bite wound had started bleeding again.

Her hands looked tiny holding his. It occurred to him that right then, despite her young age and her inexperience, she wielded more power than he did. Not a comforting thought.

The girl closed her eyes and slowed her breathing. Richard did the same, hoping to help her do her job. Ester stood off to the side wringing her hands as she watched.

Richard tried not to think about what Sammie was doing, about what she might find. Instead, he thought about Zedd, Nicci, Cara, and Cara's husband, Ben, the general who had led the troops to come find Richard and Kahlan. Richard needed to know what had happened to them. They would never have willingly left him and Kahlan to their fate.

He remembered the bones and remnants of uniforms. He remembered what the two men had said, that those with Richard and Kahlan had been attacked by people called the Shun-tuk. He remembered seeing masses of dead attackers. He remembered the vulgar visage of one of those dead whose bloodstained teeth had all been filed to points to better rip into flesh.

With the Hedge Maid dead, he had thought that the battle was over. It appeared that it had only just begun. Something more was going on. Something more than he understood.

He needed to find answers and he knew that time was working against everyone. If those people he cared so much about were in the hands of the Shun-tuk, then every day that went by made their survival less likely. The longer Kahlan went without gifted help, the worse he feared she was going to get. He was not much better off himself.

These people, too, the people of Stroyza, were in trouble, probably a great deal more trouble than they realized. They were used to the harsh conditions and dangers of the Dark Lands, but these savages who ate human flesh appeared to be something new.

Sammie gasped suddenly and yanked her hands back, releasing his as if they had burst into flames.

Richard leaned in. "What did you see?"

Sammie's eyes were wide with terror and brimming with tears. Her breathing was ragged and quick.

"I felt your pain," she whispered. "Dear spirits, how can you stand it?"

"I don't have a choice. The lives of those I love and

the people I am sworn to protect are at stake. That's what matters to me the most at the moment. Now, what else did you feel?"

Sammie swiped tears from under her eyes. "I felt the same thing, Lord Rahl. You have the same thing in you as the Mother Confessor. Death, behind the veil of green. You both have death in you."

Richard couldn't say that he was surprised. He hadn't really expected anything different. Both he and Kahlan had been exposed to the Hedge Maid's screams, screams that had been unleashed from the underworld itself.

He looked up at Ester's ashen face. "Bring Henrik to me."

"You want the boy?" she looked confused. "Now? Lord Rahl, your wounds must be tended to. Your arm is bleeding again and it must—"

"Now," Richard said.

Richard turned from Kahlan's unconscious form when he heard the sound of feet shuffling out in the passageway. Ester lifted the sheepskin out of the way for Henrik to duck in under it. When the boy saw Richard, he smiled, but the smile clearly betrayed his worry.

Richard returned the smile, trying to convey a sense of his own worry. "Thanks for coming, Henrik. Come, sit by me."

Henrik cautiously sat on the floor, close to Richard and Sammie. His eyes, reflecting points of candlelight, lingered on Kahlan. He would be dead if not for her coming into Jit's lair and freeing him.

"Is the Mother Confessor going to be all right, Lord Rahl?"

Richard shook his head. "I don't know yet. We don't know enough about exactly what's wrong with her. I'm hoping that you can fill in some of the blanks and tell me something that will help us to know how to heal her."

"I don't know much about sickness and such, but I don't think you can heal her."

Richard was taken by surprise. "Why do you say that?"

"Because of what I overheard Zedd and Nicci talking about. They said that they could only hope to help both of you temporarily, until they could get you back to the People's Palace."

Puzzled, Sammie scooted a little closer. "The People's Palace? Really? A palace? Did you hear why?"

Henrik nodded.

Seeing that they would be busy in conversation, Ester took the opportunity to pull the bucket of water and the bandages closer so that she could go back to her work on Kahlan's wounds.

Richard lifted a hand, stopping Henrik from answering Sammie's question. "I need you to start at the beginning. Tell me everything that happened. It's important that we know all the details. Don't leave anything out. Sometimes the little details have meaning that you may not realize are important, but I would."

Richard couldn't help thinking of all the times Zedd had told him the same thing. Zedd always wanted every little detail. Richard felt a little uncomfortable finding himself repeating those same things that he used to find so frustrating when Zedd had insisted on them.

Henrik pushed his disorderly fall of hair back from his eyes. "Well, the Mother Confessor came in and cut me out of the walls made of thorny vines that the Hedge Maid had used to imprison me, but then Jit showed up and captured her right as I was able to escape—but you already know that much of it because I ran into you as I was running out of Jit's lair.

"You told me that your friends were on their way from the People's Palace to help you, and you asked me to go and tell them where you and the Mother Confessor were. So I kept running and not too long after that I found the whole column of cavalry accompanying Zedd, Nicci, and Cara. They were pretty impatient to find you both. I told them where you were, and that Jit had the Mother Confessor. I told them that you were going to go in to save her.

"I went with them so I could show them the way. When we finally got to the Hedge Maid's place we found you and the Mother Confessor inside. Jit was dead. She looked like her whole body had been torn apart from the inside. There was blood everywhere. It was a frightful sight.

"You and the Mother Confessor were both unconscious and bleeding badly. After Cara and the soldiers cut you out of the thorny vines where the Hedge Maid had you both trapped, Zedd burned that awful place to the ground. It was strange seeing such a fire burning in the middle of a watery swamp. It was a fierce fire. It lit the bottoms of the clouds. There's not a scrap of Jit's place left."

"I'm glad to hear that much of it," Richard said half to himself. "Then what?"

Henrik's mouth twisted a little as he frowned in recollection. "The soldiers laid you both in the back of a wagon. Cara was so angry that you and the Mother Confessor were hurt that she looked ready to spit fire herself."

Richard couldn't help smiling. "I can only imagine." His smile faded when he thought about the danger Cara and the rest of them were in. He needed to find them, and soon.

"Go on."

"With the cavalry leading, we started back, headed for the People's Palace," Henrik said. "Zedd and Nicci were tending to the both of you. At first, Zedd was really upset about how badly you were both hurt.

"As they were walking along beside the wagon, Zedd found a little wad of rolled-up cloth in your ear. Nicci found the same thing in Kahlan's ears. She said 'No wonder they're alive.'

"Zedd didn't understand. Nicci told him that it was said that the scream of a Hedge Maid, if she were ever to open her mouth all the way and let it out, was the sound of the Keeper of the underworld himself. Nicci said that the sound of such a scream would pull the Hedge Maid and anyone who hears it into the underworld. She said that the unleashed scream of a Hedge Maid is death, even to herself, so at a young age, before they can fully develop a voice capable of calling death into the world of life, a Hedge Maid's mother sews her lips shut with leather strips imbued with occult powers that hold death back.

"Nicci said that she suspected that you both were alive because you stuffed those wads of cloth in your ears and that shielded you from the full power of that scream.

"Zedd wanted to know how she knew so much about such things. Nicci said that she knew because she had once been a Sister of the Dark serving the Keeper of the underworld. She said that Hedge Maids were vile creatures who use a kind of occult conjuring that is directly linked to the world of the dead.

"She said that such powers were a perversion of the Grace and as such not able to be touched by regular gifted ability. She said that was what made a Hedge Maid so dangerous, that Lord Rahl and the Mother Confessor would have no power against her.

"Nicci explained to them, then, how you both were touched not just by the Hedge Maid's occult conjuring and the things she was doing to you, but more importantly you were both touched by her scream. She said that through that scream you both were touched by death itself and therefore infected with it."

Sammie gave Richard a look, as if to say "I told you so."

Richard rolled his hand for Henrik to go on.

"Well, Zedd didn't exactly believe everything Nicci was telling him about the power of such a scream born in the underworld and death infecting you both."

"Sound familiar?" Sammie asked under her breath.

Richard gave her a sideways look but didn't say anything.

Henrik was involved in his story and didn't hear her. "So Nicci put two fingers on Kahlan's head. She told Zedd, 'Here, see for yourself.' He leaned in and put two fingers on Kahlan's head next to Nicci's fingers. She asked if he felt it.

"Zedd said that he felt some kind of frightening, deathly darkness. Nicci told him that what he was feeling was the touch of death from the Hedge Maid that you both carried in you."

"Just like I said," Sammie noted.

Richard nodded. "You were right."

She smiled at the triumph as Henrik continued his story.

"Zedd was really afraid because of what he'd felt in Kahlan. Cara got scared, too. She asked if you both were going to die because you had death hiding in you. Nicci said not if she had anything to do with it.

"Nicci said that you both were only alive because the wads of cloth you had stuffed in your ears blunted the full sounds of death's call, but it still had infected you both."

"Did they say how to heal them?" Sammie asked, suddenly excited about the possibility of having an answer to the riddle.

"Nicci said that she thought she could do it, but that it had to be done in something called a containment field."

Richard felt as if the floor fell out from under him. It was no longer a simple matter of being healed by a gifted person. This was no simple injury. It was going to take more than a simple healing if the real threat within them was to be addressed.

"A containment field?" Sammie's nose wrinkled up. "What's a containment field?"

Henrik shrugged with the discomfort of not having the answer for her.

"It's a place that keeps any foreign spells out while you work on or open up dangerous forms of magic," Richard told her. "More importantly, though, it also keeps contained those things you unleash—either intentionally or accidentally. Things you wouldn't want escaping."

Sammie looked stunned by the description. "Where can we get one of these containment fields? How do you make one?"

"They're ancient," Richard said. "As far as I know, they were made ages ago by powerful wizards. I only know of a few, and they're thousands of years old."

"There's one at the People's Palace," Henrik said.

"That's right," Richard said as he nodded. "The Garden of Life is a containment field."

Henrik squinted as he tried to recount it all accurately. "Nicci told Zedd that she needed a containment field to shield you and the Mother Confessor while she did what was needed. She said that she had to remove the touch of death lodged within you both.

"She said that because the Grace was corrupted and twisted within you both by that infection, if they tried to remove it outside a containment field, then the call of death would draw the Keeper of the dead to you and both of you would die. She said that they could heal your other injuries, though, and they should do that right away to keep you alive until they could get back to the containment field."

Sammie was astonished by such exotic tales. "I would love to see a palace. I bet it's magnificent. I never heard of a containment field before. What does it look like?"

Richard gestured overhead. "This particular one at the People's Palace is a beautiful garden with a glass roof and—"

"Glass roof!" Sammie's jaw fell open. "I've never even dreamed of such an incredible thing. I'd give anything to see such a grand palace."

"Maybe someday you can," Richard said. He was impatient for Henrik to go on with the story. "Then what?"

"Zedd said that they needed to hurry back to the palace, because you were both hurt so bad. He bent in over Kahlan, worried about the terrible wound on her stomach. Bouncing in the wagon made it open up and it was bleeding a lot. While he started to heal her, Nicci walked along on the other side of the wagon and reached down to start healing you, Lord Rahl.

"Cara was relieved to see that Zedd and Nicci were finally working on healing you both, so she got up into the wagon's seat and sat next to her husband, General Meiffert. She helped pull me up to sit next to her while Zedd and Nicci worked."

"So why didn't they finish healing us?" Richard asked. "What happened to everyone?"

Henrik looked like he wished he didn't have to tell that part of the story.

12

Henrik's face turned grim as he stared off into his memories.

"Well," he said at last as he went on with the account, "we were going as fast as General Meiffert said he dared push the horses. Everyone was worried about you and the Mother Confessor and they all wanted to get you out of the Dark Lands and back to the palace.

"Zedd and Nicci both had to climb up in the wagon so they could work on healing you. Zedd cursed, then, and told them that they were going to have to slow down because the Mother Confessor was hurt bad and he needed to close up the wound, but he couldn't do it when the wagon was bouncing around."

"Did they say anything at all about what they were going to do to heal them?" Sammie asked the boy as she eagerly leaned in. "Did they say how they were able to do it with that touch of death in them?"

Henrik shook his head. "I don't know anything about healing or how magic works. I only know that I heard Nicci say to Zedd that they could heal the injuries, but would have to leave the touch of death in them until they got to the palace and the containment field."

"That much of it is good news," Richard told Sammie. "It confirms what I thought, that you can do a healing of the other problems even with what you saw in us."

She nodded in thought as she listened to Henrik go on.

"It was getting dark. Zedd and Nicci bent over you both, using their gift to heal you." As he stared off into his memories again, his voice occasionally broke. "As they worked, everyone else was keeping a close watch on the surrounding countryside. The Dark Lands are a dangerous enough place in the daylight, but everyone knows that out here you don't want to be outside at night if you can help it."

Henrik idly fingered the edge of the coarse carpet they were sitting on. "I guess we couldn't help it."

"I guess not," Richard said, feeling guilty for being the one responsible for bringing his friends into the Dark Lands to help him.

"We were going along for a while without talking, going pretty slow as Zedd had instructed so he and Nicci could concentrate on trying to heal both of you. Then, all of a sudden, they both looked up."

"At the same time?" Sammie asked.

Henrik nodded.

"If they both looked up at the same time it must be because they sensed something through their gift," Sammie said to Richard.

Richard only nodded, not wanting to interrupt Henrik's story.

"Zedd whispered to the general, up on the wagon seat on the other side of Cara from me, that there were people out there in the darkness. The general asked how many people. Zedd paused a moment, and then said, 'A lot of people.' I looked around but I couldn't see anyone."

Henrik stared off into the distance, as if seeing it in his mind's eye again. "Even though I couldn't see them, it seemed as though I could feel their eyes watching us from back in the darkness of the trees. There was forest all around, and it gave whatever Zedd and Nicci sensed plenty of places to hide.

"With the clouds, the moon didn't provide much light. It was hard to see much of anything. Whoever was back in those dark woods, we couldn't see them."

Henrik swallowed. "I was afraid. Really afraid. I think everyone kind of knew that we might be in some kind of trouble, but no one knew what to expect. I saw some of the soldiers get a better grip on their lances while others touched their swords, all of them making sure that their weapons were ready.

"Then, all of a sudden, we saw movement off at the tree line to the right. Even as dark as it was, there was still enough light that we were able to see masses of people as they poured out of the woods. None of them made a sound as they came rushing out of the trees. They weren't yelling battle cries or anything. That silence from those people made it even more frightening to watch them coming. There were so many that it looked like the ground was moving. I was scared to death.

"Cara asked her husband if we shouldn't try running with the wagon. Before the general could answer, Zedd spoke up to say that we couldn't outrun them. He said that they were out ahead of us as well as behind. He said we were surrounded.

"The soldiers pulled their horses around to shield the wagon. All the lancers formed an outer ring and lowered their lances toward the advancing horde. It was hard to imagine anyone trying to run up on those lancers.

"At the same time, other men, in an inner ring behind the lancers, drew their swords. Yet others pulled battle-axes from hooks on their weapon belts. There weren't a lot of soldiers with us and seeing how many people were rushing in toward us I wished there were more, but they were D'Haran soldiers, after all. Seeing all those big men draw their weapons made me think that maybe we had a chance."

They would not have been regular D'Haran soldiers. Richard knew that the men who had come from the palace with Zedd, Nicci, and Cara would have been men of the First File. The First File, led by General Meiffert, were the Lord Rahl's personal guards at the People's Palace. They weren't simply the biggest and best of the D'Haran troops, they were the elite fighters. They were disciplined, skilled in combat, and prepared to fight. They lived for just this sort of duty. They had competed all their lives to earn their place at the point of the spear.

"Zedd stood up in the wagon trying to see better," Henrik said. "Nicci stood up too, growling in anger over having to stop working on healing you, Lord Rahl, saying that she needed more time. As people kept streaming out of the woods, all of them running toward us, Zedd told her that it looked to him like their time had run out.

"General Meiffert told his men that he didn't want to stand and fight, but it looked like they were going to have to. Cara suggested putting you and the Mother Confessor over the back of horses. She said she and a couple soldiers could run for safety while the rest of the soldiers held the horde at bay. Zedd said in a low voice that it was a bad idea. When she asked why, he said that the worst thing you could do was run from predators because it excited them to chase. He said that there were people coming in from all directions and they would run down anyone who tried to get away."

The room was dead silent except for the soft, sputtering hiss of the candle flames. Sammie sat frozen, wide-eyed as she waited to hear what had happened next. Even Ester had stopped working. Her hand, holding a poultice, floated frozen above Kahlan.

"Then Zedd threw his hands toward the sky, sending up a flare of light," Henrik said. "At first, as it rose high up into the air, it was only a spark, but then it exploded into a bright, sparkling fire that lit the countryside all around."

Henrik's eyes brimmed with tears. "In that flare of light, we could finally see the thousands and thousands coming for us. I saw not only men racing toward us, but women, too. Most of the men had no shirts and were bare-legged. I didn't see any of them with swords or spears or shields. A lot of them had knives, though. So did the women. Our men were on horseback and had much better weapons. I would have felt better about that were we not so overwhelmingly outnumbered.

"The fire that Zedd had sent up started to die out, and it was getting harder to see all the people racing toward us. As they got even closer, he tried to send up another flare of fire to replace the one that was fading, but nothing happened. Nicci asked what was wrong. Zedd looked confused. He stammered and said that he didn't know. So Nicci tried then, but it didn't work for her, either."

Henrik swallowed again and looked down for a moment. Richard put a hand on the boy's shoulder but didn't say anything, instead giving him the time to find his words.

Henrik cleared his throat. "When they were close enough that they would be able to hear him, the commander of the cavalry stood in his stirrups and yelled at the people running in toward us, warning them to stop, to stay back, or they would die. It didn't do any good.

"All the people had been silent up till then, but after the general told them to stay back or they would die, they started yelling battle cries, like they were eager for such a fight. It wasn't the battle cries of soldiers, but some kind of shrill shrieks. It sounded to me like they were evil spirits charging out from the world of the dead. Their yells all jumbled together into an eerie howl that made my hair stand on end.

"When General Meiffert saw that they weren't going to stop, and we could see the knives raised, there was no doubt that they intended to attack us, so he ordered the cavalry to cut them down before they could get too close. About half the men raced away across the open ground while the other half shielded the wagon.

"The cavalry sliced into the leading edge of the swarm, cutting them down like scything down a wheat field at harvest. Even though it was dark, there was enough light from the moon that I could see people falling in great numbers.

"I was relieved, thinking that such powerful cavalrymen would cause the attackers to break and flee in fright. But then I saw that the enemy didn't fear the men on horseback. Most didn't even cry out as they were cut down. Even though the cavalry was slicing down hundreds of enemy, it seemed that for every one that fell ten more appeared out of the trees.

"Then I saw the first man unhorsed. He was a big man, fighting fiercely, cutting down attackers by the dozens as he charged through the leading edge of the enemy. Unafraid, the people paid no attention to the danger and swarmed in around him as he was attacking. He hacked them to pieces as they came. His horse trampled a number of them. But he was overwhelmed by the incredible numbers pressing in on him.

"There were so many people piling in that there was no room for all those who were trying to get at him. They swarmed in, climbing over the backs of others both living and dead, trying to be the first to get at him. People were trampled and crushed by their own kind. None of them seemed to care about the dead and dying. They only cared about getting at the man on horseback.

"Despite how the soldier and his powerful horse struggled and fought, the weight of all the people finally dragged the big animal to a stop. Even as other soldiers raced to try to help him, hacking at the enemy to get through, I saw dozens and dozens of arms flailing, stabbing at the horse until it went down."

Henrik swallowed again, and again wiped at his eyes. "Then they all piled on the man like a pack of wolves. The thing was, they weren't stabbing at him, like they had been stabbing at the horse."

Sammie frowned when Henrik fell silent for a time. "What were they doing, then?"

Richard knew the answer. It had almost happened to him.

"The throng seized his arms, legs, even his hair, and from what I could see it looked like they were all ripping into him with their teeth. They were tearing into him like a pack of wolves on a lamb."

Sammie glanced at the bleeding bite wound on Richard's arm. "Just like the way they were starting to use their teeth when they attacked you, Lord Rahl."

"It would seem so," Richard said, waiting for Henrik to gather his thoughts and go on.

Richard knew that what he was hearing from Henrik about the bizarre attack fit with what he had overheard from the two men who had attacked him. As he had been waking up, he heard them talking about the Shuntuk eating people. He remembered all too well seeing human bones and parts of D'Haran uniforms not far from the wagon. He didn't know how many more such remains there might have been out in the darkness. He feared to imagine.

From what Richard knew, as crazy as it sounded, the two men had thought they could somehow capture his soul by eating him. Had it not been for the people of Stroyza, they surely would have killed him in the attempt.

"I saw more of our men going down," Henrik said,

his jaw trembling. "I heard some of those men scream in pain as they were pulled from their horses and torn apart while they were still alive and struggling."

"What about Zedd and Nicci?" Richard asked. "Weren't they using their gift to try to stop this horde of people? I've seen Zedd use wizard's fire on enemy troops. It's devastating, even when the enemy was coming in great numbers like you describe. The two of them should have been able to do something."

Henrik wiped his nose on his sleeve. "Zedd was trying, Lord Rahl. As the charge of all those people got closer, more of our men joined the battle to try to fight them back and keep them away from you and the Mother Confessor in the wagon. The soldiers fought fiercely but the swarm of people were all howling like demons that had escaped the underworld and they just kept coming.

"With all the yelling and screaming, it was hard to hear. But I did hear Zedd and Nicci talking. The two of them were pretty frantic to do something that would help keep the advancing people away. I don't know much about such things and I didn't hear all of what they were saying, but I could tell that they were both trying their best to conjure things and cast their power out to fight back the waves of people charging toward us. It seemed that nothing they were doing, though, was working the way they expected. I don't know what was wrong, but I can tell you that as hard as they were trying, if their gift would have been working right they might have been able to stop the enemy.

"Sometimes, though, something they did would work. At least, it worked to a degree. When nothing else seemed to work, I saw both Zedd and Nicci push their arms out together, with their palms raised, as if pushing against an invisible wall. When they did that, occasionally groups of people were thrown back and tumbled across the ground, knocking down others behind them. It blew them back like leaves in a gust of wind. While it did work, it only worked against small numbers at a time. It was taking them a lot of effort to do that much but it wasn't nearly enough to cope with the endless numbers that were racing toward us across the open ground.

"Zedd looked over at Cara, then, and told her what even I could see, that something was wrong with their abilities and it wasn't going to be enough. The general said that above all else they had to protect you, Lord Rahl, and the Mother Confessor. He told Zedd, then, that if they all took a stand to defend the wagon, the people coming for them would know that we were protecting something important.

"Nicci asked what he was proposing. The general said that they had to abandon the wagon.

"I thought Cara might break his neck for saying that. She yelled at him, saying that as long as she was alive and could fight, she wouldn't leave you for anything. He shouted her down, saying that if they left the wagon, like it didn't mean anything to them, and instead made it look like they were running to try to escape, then the enemy would come after them and leave the wagon, thinking it was unimportant. He said that they appeared to want to attack and kill them. He said that they weren't dying by the hundreds just to steal what looked to be nothing more than an empty wagon.

"Nicci said that he was right. Zedd said that he hated to admit it, but he agreed. He also said that they had better hurry and decide or it was going to be too late for the plan to do any good.

"Cara's jaw was clenched so tight she couldn't speak. Her face was as red as her leather outfit. Finally, she growled and leaped down into the bed of the wagon.

She hurried to unfurl an old tarp that was shoved in the corner and with Nicci's help pulled it out and along the wagon bed, covering up the both of you so that it looked like it was just a mostly empty supply wagon."

Richard finally understood the mystery of why he and Kahlan were all alone in the back of the wagon, unconscious, lying under a tarp.

"I don't know that I would have thought of doing that," Richard said. "Ben is a general for good reason. So what happened next?"

"Cara lifted me off the wagon seat and set me down in the bed of the wagon with her. While her husband, Zedd, and Nicci jumped to the ground, she bent close and pointed her Agiel at my face. She told me to listen, and listen close. She quickly glanced toward a spot in the woods to the other side from most of the attackers, to where I didn't see anyone.

"She leaned close again and asked if I saw the path into the woods. I didn't see it, but I was afraid to say so. She said that she wanted me to run for that path and get away."

"Run?" Sammie asked. "If there was a place where there were no people, then why didn't all of you go that way and try to escape?"

"I asked her that. I begged her to come with me. She said that carrying Lord Rahl and the Mother Confessor would slow them down and not only that, but they couldn't see to run fast enough in the woods. She said that with that many of them running to try to escape they would be spotted and chased. She said they would be caught in there, and then the enemy would have Lord Rahl and the Mother Confessor.

"She said that above all, saving you, Lord Rahl, and the Mother Confessor was what mattered to D'Hara and to the future of everyone.

"She told me that Benjamin was right, that this was the only chance they had to save you both, but they had to act fast. She said they would run in another direction making it look like they were trying to get away so that the people would chase after them and hopefully not even realize that the two of you had been left hidden in the abandoned wagon.

"I asked what was going to happen to her and the general, and Zedd and Nicci, and all the rest of the men." Henrik paused briefly to choke back a sob. "Cara gritted her teeth and said they were doing what they had to do to protect you."

Henrik dissolved into tears, choking back sobs. Sammie put a hand over his and softly told him that she understood. Her eyes, too, brimmed with tears. She told the boy that the same thing had happened to her father, and that her mother was missing. She told him that she knew what it felt like to hurt inside from losing people you loved.

Henrik was surprised to hear about her parents. He told her that he was sorry. Sammie squeezed his hand and told him that there was grave trouble at hand, and they all had to be brave.

When she asked, Henrik finally went on with the story. "Cara lifted me down over the side of the wagon and set me on the ground. The general yelled back to her from the other side of the wagon, telling her to hurry. She nodded then turned back to me.

"She pointed her Agiel at my face again and told me to run like the wind and get away. She told me that I had to get away so that I could find help for Lord Rahl and the Mother Confessor. She said that they were all counting on me. She said that they would try to lead the enemy in the other direction to buy me time so that I could slip away through the woods and find help.

"I was terrified. I didn't want to leave them. I asked what was going to happen to her and the others.

"She said not to worry about them. She said that my job was to run, to get away, and to find help. I stood there trembling, staring at her, unable to believe it was happening. Cara grabbed my jaw and said, 'Run. Don't look back. Don't stop for anything. Get help for them. Understand?' I nodded that I did. I couldn't answer because I was too afraid to talk.

"Cara pointed off into the darkness with her Agiel and said, 'Go!' I turned to go, but then she grabbed my arm.

"I turned back and she was real close, looking right into my eyes. She said, 'Don't let us die for nothing, Henrik. Find them help no matter what. Make our lives count for something. Get them help.' I said, 'I promise, Cara.'

"As I turned to run, I saw her race around the wagon to join the others. And then they all ran, the howling enemy right on their heels."

Henrik's words dissolved into sobs.

Richard was in so much pain that his hands shook. His breathing was ragged. But the pain seemed distant in the numb haze of his grief.

He rubbed the boy's shoulder, understanding his emotions, feeling great sorrow for his ordeal. His own heartache felt as if it would crush his chest.

"As I ran toward the woods, I finally spotted the trail," Henrik said, trying mightily to pull himself together enough to finish the story. "I heard the howls around me. I raced onto the trail without slowing to look back. Before I had taken ten strides down the dark trail, I saw someone moving back in the trees. I froze. They didn't spot me. I saw dark shapes moving through the brush. I realized that the enemy was in the woods and remembered that Zedd had said that they were all around us. They had been lying in wait in case anyone tried to escape in that direction."

"It was a trap," Richard said. "They made it look empty and inviting as an escape route to draw people in. They were waiting in ambush."

Henrik nodded. "I guess. Because I'm small, or maybe it was because I was alone there in the dark and there was so much noise going on back the way I'd come, they didn't spot me. Once they realized that the cavalry and the others were running to try to escape in the other direction they all went crazy, howling as they raced out of the cover of the woods to join the chase.

"When I saw them coming I knew that if I kept going down the trail they would soon have me. I was trapped and there was nowhere to run, so I dove behind a fallen tree. I clawed through the soft moss and decayed wood to squeeze in under the trunk.

"I lay as still as I could, holding my breath where I hid. I could just make out dark shapes moving through the trees. Closer in a lot of legs ran past me. More and more people kept running by all the time. Thousands, it seemed, ran past. I could hear the sound of all their feet rumbling through the forest.

"I was terrified that any moment one of them would spot me and then reach down and pull me out. I knew that if they did, they would tear me apart with their teeth the way they had the man I saw pulled off his horse and killed.

"I stayed hidden a long time, too afraid to move. I could hear them making that awful shrieking sound as they charged through the trees like a pack of wild animals on the scent of blood."

Henrik looked up at Richard. "The general and the others were right not to have tried to take you and the

Mother Confessor back through those woods. If they had, you would be dead now."

Richard knew that he owed his life, Kahlan's life, to his friends. It didn't seem fair that he should live at the cost of their lives. He desperately wanted to find a way to help them . . . if they were still alive.

"Finally," Henrik said, "after what seemed forever, I didn't hear any more people running past. I could hear all the howls and cries from them as they went after Cara and the others. That noise kept getting farther away.

"After it was quiet in the woods for a time, I finally dared to crawl out and take a careful look around. The woods were dead still and I didn't see anyone. I started running."

"So then, as you were running along the trail, you came to this place?" Richard asked.

Henrik nodded. "I found people here caring for their animals. I begged them to come help you. Thankfully, they did."

14

After Cara told me to run, I never saw what happened to all of them." Henrik's head hung as he cried quietly in sorrow for those he had left behind to their fate.

Sammie put a comforting arm around Henrik's shoulders. Her eyes glistened with tears as well. With her father murdered in the same way as Henrik described and her mother missing, very possibly a victim of the same grim end, she clearly empathized with Henrik's misery.

Ester turned to Richard as she spoke into the silence, taking up the rest of the story. "When the boy showed up here we couldn't understand what he was talking about. He wasn't making much sense. He was frantic to get help, that much was clear, but we were having a hard time of getting him to slow down enough so we could understand what kind of help he needed. He kept pointing and telling us to hurry.

"When we began to grasp that he had been with people who had been attacked, and that there were two injured people who needed help, we knew that we couldn't wait for him to tell the whole story. It's dangerous in the Dark Lands at night, and it was evident that your party had somehow fallen victim to something awful. We knew that we had to go right away to find you and get you both out of danger. We figured we could get all the details later.

"As reluctant as we were to venture out into the wilderness at night, we also feared what would happen if we didn't help. The Dark Lands are sparsely populated. There are dangers, to be sure, and it can be especially dangerous at night, but we had never heard of so many people as it seemed Henrik was describing attacking them.

"We thought that maybe he was imagining things because he was so afraid. It was not only difficult for us to believe what we thought he was telling us, he was having trouble telling us the whole story because he was frantically concerned with us hurrying to go help you. We had no trouble believing, though, because of his panicked state, that you had been attacked by someone and the situation was serious.

"Henrik didn't know where you were, exactly. We finally got it out of him that you had come from Kharga Trace, from the Hedge Maid. That was enough to tell us what we needed to know. There is only one, seldom-used road that goes in the direction of that swampy place, so we had a good idea where to look. We left the boy up here where it was safe while we went out to look for you."

"You did good, Henrik," Richard told the boy. "You saved our lives."

Henrik managed a small smile. "Just returning the favor, Lord Rahl. You and the Mother Confessor saved my life." He gestured toward Kahlan. "The Hedge Maid had me. Jit would have bled me dry like the other poor souls who were trapped like I was, but had no one come

in time to help save them. They died in her lair. The
Mother Confessor got me out."

Richard nodded. "That's the kind of person she is.
She has always fought for life." He rubbed his forehead as his gaze sank. "Now she's fighting for hers."

He was feeling dizzy, both from his injuries and from
fear for his friends and loved ones after what Henrik
had told him about the mysterious attack. The long war
had ended. He had thought they were finally at peace
and that life was returning to normal. He guessed that
there was no such thing as normal out in the Dark
Lands. He knew, though, that even for the Dark Lands
this was out of the ordinary.

Sick with worry for the fate of his friends, his bite
wound throbbing painfully, and his head pounding
with what might be a developing fever, he needed to lie
down.

After learning a little more about Zedd and Nicci
beginning to heal them despite the Hedge Maid's vile
touch of death, he needed to have Sammie see to helping
Kahlan. He needed help as well, but he knew that he
could wait a bit. He didn't know if she could.

Richard was about to ask Ester if she knew anything
at all about the people who had attacked his friends,
when he saw the cat across the room suddenly turn to
the doorway and arch its back.

Teeth bared, the cat hissed. Its dark gray fur lifted
until it was all standing on end.

Richard felt the hair on his own neck stiffen.

"Does it do that often?" he asked in a quiet voice.

Sammie pulled a long lock of curly black hair back
from her face as she frowned at the cat. "No. Just when
it's frightened for some reason."

The flames of several candles withered and died out,
leaving a wisp of smoke to curl up into the still air.

Richard heard other cats out in the corridors beyond the doorway let out feral yowls.

Ester started to get up. "What in the world . . ."

Richard caught her arm, pulling her back, keeping her from going to the door. Henrik's eyes widened at the chorus of feline screeches. Sammie's frown deepened.

And then, someone in the distance let out a blood-curdling scream.

Richard sprang up. Dizzy and light-headed, he struggled to keep from falling over as he focused his attention on the sounds outside in the corridors.

His hand instinctively found the hilt of his sword resting in its sheath at his hip. His fingers tightened around the wire-wound hilt as sudden cries of terror and pain rang out and echoed through the halls. At first there was only one scream, but others soon joined in a chorus of terror.

The sword's anger instantly inundated him. The suddenness of it felt like being abruptly dropped into an icy river. The shock of it made him draw a sharp breath.

His own anger rose up out of those dark waters to join with the rage spiraling up from the ancient weapon. The icy shock turned hot with rage as a storm of power from the sword called forth its twin from somewhere deep within him.

With his hand on the hilt of that ancient weapon, whatever sickness he felt, whatever pain, whatever exhaustion and weakness weighed on him, it melted before the heat of rage that had sparked to life. The sword's power, its anger, crackled within him, hungry for violence in reaction to the screams of terror and pain he was hearing from out in the passageways.

The unique sound of steel rang through the room as Richard drew his sword.

It felt exhilarating having it out, intoxicating to hold

it in his fist. With the blade free, with the sword's anger awakened, the Seeker and the Sword of Truth were now forged together in purpose and fierce intent.

They were now a singular weapon.

Ester shrank back at seeing him with his sword to hand. Distantly, Richard realized that his grim expression, and especially the look in his eyes, was probably frightening her.

Henrik scooted back toward the wall, wanting to be out of his way.

Sammie crouched protectively over Kahlan, ready to protect her from whatever might come through the door.

Richard didn't intend to let anything come through the door.

He pointed the sword back at Kahlan as he spoke with quiet fury to Sammie. "Stay here and protect her."

Looking determined, Sammie nodded.

Richard flipped the sheepskin covering up out of the way as he ducked under it and out into the hallway, headed toward the sound of the screams.

15

As Richard raced out into the hallway, he heard not only terrified screams, but a kind of animalistic growl that could not have sounded more out of place in the world of life. The malevolent roar, a manifest threat to the living, reverberated through the dark passageways.

Richard didn't know the layout of the labyrinth of corridors excavated through the soft rock of the mountain, or where all the passageways led and connected, but he knew the direction the screams were coming from, so he raced to follow the sound. He knew that the kind of cries he was hearing only came from people in mortal terror. Other screams he recognized as coming from those who were grievously injured or dying. He had heard those dreadful, primal shrieks before. With the war over, he had hoped never again to hear such gut-wrenching cries.

As he raced down the passageways, he began encountering clumps of people racing away from the screams of the injured and bone-chilling bellows of the attackers. Many of the people he ran past were screaming as well, but they were crying out in panic, not the kind of screams that people let out in the throes of death.

As he ran, Richard realized that he was getting lost in the confusing maze of passageways, but it wasn't hard to follow the agonized cries toward their source. It didn't really matter if he knew where he was, only that he knew where he was going, and the screams marked the route all too clearly. With his own pain and sickness forgotten for the moment—a distant concern banished by the rage of the sword—his only need was to get to those being hurt.

The part of the rage that came from his sword wanted to get at the ones doing the hurting. That part of the rage wanted the blood of the attacker.

Some of the people saw him coming with his sword to hand and flattened themselves against a wall to stay out of his way, but many others didn't see him coming and he had to shove them aside. Women hurriedly herded children past, paying attention only to their charges. A few men helped older people. At times, as people desperate to escape the threat came racing past Richard, he had to use an arm to shield them from running into his sword. Other people, men and women, old and young alike, stampeded through, too terrorized by what was behind them to care about what was in front of them.

Before he saw the threat, he encountered a smell that was alien to the cavelike village of Stroyza. It was the unmistakable stench of decomposing flesh, a smell so sickening, so repulsive, that it made his throat clench shut to lock his breath in his lungs. He had to force himself to breathe.

As he rounded a curve in the passageway, Richard saw a broad open area out ahead. It was the entrance cavern of the village, the place where he first came in after he had climbed the narrow trail up the side of the mountain. Out the opening a gentle rain fell through the dark night.

A few lamps hung on pegs in the walls to one side and a fire burning in a pit to the other side provided the only light. In that dim, flickering light he could see people trying to stay out of the clutches of two big men. Both of the dark shapes stormed clumsily around the room, charging first one way, then another, swiping at people trapped in the room. Both of the big attackers glistened in the lamplight, wet from the climb up in the rain.

Some of the people cornered in nooks and crannies around the broad cavern pressed themselves back against the walls, hoping not to be noticed. Others inched toward openings, hoping for a chance to escape. Men keeping what they hoped was a safe distance waved their arms and threw stones, trying to distract and confuse the attackers.

In the center of the chamber the two figures, like bears in a cage, raged at the people around them, their thunderous roars echoing off the domed ceiling of rock. The smell of death and decay was overpowering.

Men popped out of dark passageways from time to time to pelt the attackers with rocks, trying to keep them from attacking. Most of the rocks missed or glanced off, though sometimes it did distract one of the two into taking a swing at the stones. A man on the right side raced in closer to heave a good-sized rock at one of the intruders. The rock hit the big man in the back of the head and bounced off, but it sounded like it had succeeded in cracking the man's skull, yet the man wasn't slowed and didn't show any evidence of being harmed by the blow.

The other shadowy shape roared and rushed to intercept people trying to escape into a passageway. The two big men couldn't control everyone, though, and when they turned away a few people managed to slip away into the dark opening. A few others sprang suddenly, ducking under the outstretched arms as the big men tried to snatch them. The lucky ones managed to dash into a corridor or over the edge and down the treacherous trail that came up the side of the mountain.

Not everyone was lucky enough to escape, though. Richard saw several broken bodies sprawled in a way that suggested that they had been killed and then thrown to the side. The floor of the cave glistened not only with rainwater but with pools of blood.

Even as Richard was racing across the room toward the dark shapes, one of them lunged and took a sudden swipe, catching a woman pressed back against a wall. With that one powerful blow, his clawlike hand ripped open her soft middle, splattering blood across the wall. Frozen in panic, the woman seemed unable to believe what had just happened. Richard knew that she did not yet feel the full pain of it. Stunned, eyes wide, she let out only small, panting cries as the realization of what had just happened began to sink in.

In that moment of frozen shock, the big man who had done the damage leaned in and snatched the stunned woman's wrist. With frightening speed, the other dove in and grabbed the cornered woman's ankle, pulling her feet out from under her. She hit the floor hard, letting out a grunt on impact.

As Richard charged across the cavern toward the two attackers, several cats leaped out of the darkness and onto the man holding the woman's leg. He swiped one cat off his shoulder. The other clawed at his face. The man held on to the woman's ankle, not seeming to be hurt by the cat's claws. He swatted at the cat, trying to get it off his face, as if it were merely an annoyance.

At the same time, the other man twisted the woman's arm around, ripping it away from her shoulder. With her remaining arm, she struggled weakly, clawing at the ground, trying to escape a fate past changing. The other man still had a firm grip on her ankle, keeping her from squirming away. Her screams lost their power as she mercifully lost consciousness.

As Richard charged in, screaming in rage, his sword flashed through the dim night air, coming down with lightning speed to sever the arm of the big man holding the woman's disembodied arm. With a cracking sound, the bone splintered. Both disembodied arms, that of the woman and the other holding it in a death grip, tumbled to the floor.

Unconcerned with Richard, the man clutching the woman's ankle turned toward the cave opening, swinging the woman around and up into the air. She sailed in an arc out into the rainy night, streaming blood and viscera behind her as she silently sailed out over the side of the cliff and down toward the rocks below.

Richard saw the point of a sword blade sticking out from between the man's shoulder blades. He spun back toward Richard after throwing the woman out of the opening, ready to attack. It seemed impossible, but the man looked unaffected by the broken blade that had impaled him through the chest.

It was then, in the weak light from the fire pit off to the side, that Richard got his first good look at the killer. Three knives were buried up to their brass cross guards in the man's chest. Only the handles were showing. Richard saw, too, the broken end of a sword blade jutting out from the center of the man's chest. The point of that same blade stuck out from the man's back.

Richard recognized the knife handles. All three were the style carried by the men of the First File.

He looked from those blades that should have killed the big man, up into his face.

That was when he realized the true horror of the situation, and the reason for the unbearable stench of death.

16

Richard found himself staring into the face of a corpse.

But it wasn't the broken sword blade or the knives buried in his chest that had killed him.

It was all too obvious that the man had been dead long before he had ever been stabbed.

The man standing before him looked like a corpse that had been freshly dug up from a grave. The repulsive stink of death was as singular as it was overpowering. The smell alone was enough to drive Richard back a step.

The man's outfit was so moldered and filthy that it was unrecognizable as to what it might once have looked like. In places the dark tatters of cloth were stained and discolored by bodily fluids that had oozed out during decay. As it had eventually dried, the cloth had stuck to the rotting flesh so that it became almost one with the body.

The lips had shriveled back to reveal the skull's death grin of broken, blackened teeth. A thin veneer of dark, blotchy skin with a few sparse patches of pale hair covered the crown of the skull. The taut hide had rotted and parted in a few places—on one cheek, on the forehead, and in a long split over the top of the skull—allowing the stained bone beneath to show through.

Although he clearly looked cadaverous, the eyes were something altogether different. The man's eyes momentarily stopped Richard cold in his tracks.

Richard had seen the indistinct but unmistakable glow of inherent power in the eyes of gifted people before, a glow that he had learned most others didn't see. Such a light had always seemed to him to be too ethereal to be real, something he saw only through the eyes of his own gift. This man's eyes also clearly carried a glow fired by the gift, yet that inner light was unlike any light of the gift he had ever seen before, and he didn't need his own gift to see it. Rather than the transcendent light he had seen in the gifted, this was a fiery luminosity that everyone could see, an announcement to all of the evil lurking behind those eyes.

It was at once dead and empty, but at the same time alive with menace.

In the near darkness, the penetrating reddish glow of those eyes sent ripples of goose bumps up Richard's arms.

Although he wasn't an expert on the gift, he had read a great many historical documents on those ancient times when both sides of the gift were common. From what he had learned from the gifted he knew, and from those historical accounts, he had never heard of the gift being able to reanimate the dead.

He knew that those glowing eyes betrayed what animated this man—not life, not the gift, but some kind of occult sorcery.

Even though the dead condition of the man, the stench, and the glow in his eyes had stopped Richard in

Without waiting to see if it would stop or slow the man, in quick succession Richard rained more blows down on the invader, taking off his other arm, then swiftly hacking his body into several pieces, finally taking the legs that were still standing before him down at the knees.

The roars of both attackers were finally ended. Injured people around the cavernous room screamed or moaned in pain. Others wept in terror. Many of those not hurt rushed out of hiding places to help those who were.

Richard nodded his thanks to the man who had tried to help by stabbing the attacker through the neck. Now back on his feet, the man stood wide-eyed at all that had just happened.

Panting from the effort and repulsed by the nauseating smell, Richard covered his mouth as he turned to the group of men who had been throwing rocks to try to stop the attack.

He took his hand away from his mouth. "What happened? Why wasn't anyone watching? Didn't you see these men coming up to your home?"

The men blinked in surprise and confusion, still clearly startled from the unexpected attack and stupefied by the bloody consequences.

"I'm sorry, Lord Rahl," the man with the knife said. "We do keep a watch, but I guess not a very good one. With as dark as it is, and the rain, and with the dark clothing the men were wearing, we didn't see them coming or even realize they were here until we heard the screams. Some of us came out to see what the trouble was but by then they were among us and it was already too late. That's when we found ourselves in the middle of a fight for our lives."

Richard clenched his jaw with the anger of the sword raging through him. He supposed that with the darkness and rain it would have been difficult to have seen the men or hear them coming.

"If someone had done a better job of standing watch," he said, "all they would have had to do would have been to put a boot to these men as they tried to climb into here and that would have sent them crashing down the mountain."

With sheepish expressions their gazes sank to the ground.

"You're right, Lord Rahl," another man said. "But nothing like this has ever happened before. I'm afraid that we weren't expecting such an attack."

Richard pointed his sword out into the night. "With that attack earlier tonight that Henrik came here and told you about, you should have been alert for trouble. Nothing like that has happened, either. You should have known that something was going on and been prepared, or at least on alert."

The men hung their heads but said nothing.

"I'm sorry," Richard said as he took a deep breath and tried to cool his anger. "I shouldn't blame the victims."

Some of the men nodded before moving off to help those who were down.

"Nothing like this has ever happened before, Lord Rahl," the man with the knife said. He looked griefstricken. "We just weren't . . ." He swallowed back his heartache as his eyes wandered among the dead and injured.

With one hand, Richard gripped the man's shoulder in sympathy. "I know. I'm sorry to sound so angry. These dead men were obviously being driven by some sort of occult conjuring. It could even be that whatever magic was animating them hid them from you so they could get up here. But you need to be on the alert and ready next time."

The men brightened a bit at Richard's suggestion that the attackers might have been hidden at first by magic.

The man with the knife used it to gesture toward the cavern opening. "I'll make sure that there is a watch from now on, Lord Rahl. It won't happen again." His haunted gaze swept over the carnage. "I promise, we at least won't be caught unaware again."

Richard nodded as he turned back to the dead and injured, making sure that people who could be helped, were being helped.

He spotted an arm of one of the dead attackers nearby. The fingers were still moving, closing and opening, as if still trying to get hold of someone, still trying to attack.

Richard picked up the still-moving, desiccated arm and tossed it into the fire pit, where flames flared up as it caught fire.

As he looked around, it occurred to Richard that with so many people injured, Sammie was going to need to help them before tending to Richard and Kahlan. A number of people were dead. While a few weren't badly hurt, some of the others had been seriously injured. They needed to be healed by a gifted person, and Sammie was the only one around.

He hoped the girl was up to the challenge. He knew that it would be difficult work even for an experienced sorceress.

As he was about to sheath his sword, he heard screaming break out farther back in the passageways.

When he heard the roar, he realized that there had been more than two invaders come to attack the village of Stroyza.

17

Richard stood stock-still for an instant, appraising which direction the sounds were coming from. Once he had the direction and approximate distance fixed in his mind, he raced into a passageway, following the sound of the screams. At least a dozen men followed close on his heels.

This time the men all had their knives out instead of bringing rocks. This time they would have a better understanding of what they faced and what they would need to do. Nothing less than hacking the attacker to pieces was going to stop him.

Richard knew that he was going in the right direction because the screams were getting steadily louder. Yet as he ran through the hallways, he occasionally had to pause briefly at intersections to listen again. The tricky way that sound echoed through the passageways made it difficult to tell right away which he needed to take. He ran as fast as he could through the confining, honeycombed network of rooms and passageways, knowing that any delay meant that more people would be hurt or killed. It was frustrating to have to stop at intersections to check for the sound of cries for help so that he could be sure to go in the right direction.

As he got closer to the screams, he realized that they were coming from the direction of where he had left Kahlan.

That realization would have spurred him to run even faster, but he was already going as fast as possible, racing with wild abandon down halls and flashing through intersections without slowing.

Coming around a dark corner, he ran square into a big man. He was as hard as an oak tree and barely moved when Richard crashed into him. Richard hadn't seen him because he was dark and dried-out like the first of the two dead men he had fought. He stank of death like the others. The walking corpse was so blackened with decay that he blended right into the shadows.

As he staggered back, Richard saw that he had interrupted the invader as he was strangling a woman. As the lanterns from the men coming up from behind threw light on the attacker and his victim, Richard saw that the woman's face was blue and her wide eyes were fixed and still. She would do no more screaming.

The attacker had both hands around the woman's throat, holding her off the ground as he crushed her throat. Bone and dried tissue cracked and popped as his head turned. He glared at Richard with glowing red eyes as he bellowed in threat.

As Richard's sword came down, the powerful blow severed both of the man's arms at the crook in his elbows. The woman dropped to the ground like a sack of grain, slumping in a lifeless heap. The man roared again as he charged Richard, the stumps of arms held up, his jaws open wide, prepared to attack with his teeth since most of his arms were gone.

A swift blow cut the man's head in half right across

his open mouth. The skull shattered into fragments. Sinew and flesh crumbled under the powerful blow. Two more swings of the sword chopped the man apart. Richard saw the fingers of the disembodied arms on the floor grasping, trying to attack but unable to find or reach a victim.

Richard, still hot with rage from his sword, turned back to the men. "You need to burn all the pieces of these men to ashes. Collect it all and burn it."

The men looked down, watching the fingers of one of the hands trying to pull its way across the floor toward Richard.

Richard crushed the still-moving hand under a boot heel, grinding the fingers to dust.

"I have no idea what's going on," Richard said, "but it seems pretty obvious that some kind of occult conjuring is involved. I don't want any part of that conjuring left among you. Burn it all. Understand?"

The men all nodded earnestly, fearful of the heat in Richard's voice even if they knew it wasn't directed at them.

Hearing yet more screams, Richard turned to the sound. He realized that there were yet more than three of the dead men among them.

He again sprang into a dead run, headed toward the sound. He wondered how many attackers had made it up into the cave. If there were many more, they could wipe out half the village before Richard could find and destroy them all.

As he made his way down narrow passages, he had to squeeze past men, women, and children frantically trying to escape the threat. Some of them cried as they ran, some of them screamed, but they were all panic-stricken, not knowing what to do except run from the danger.

At an intersection of several halls, Richard followed the chilling roars into a broader corridor. He recognized it as the passageway to Ester's small home. The monster was near. He was getting close. As he panted from the run, he drew in the putrid stench of death. It was like a reminder of the touch of death from the Hedge Maid that lurked within him.

In the distance he saw a flash of movement as a dark shape disappeared around a corner. As Richard ran he stopped suddenly at a doorway with a sheepskin covering. He ducked inside and in the candlelight saw Kahlan on the lambskin rug where he had left her. Ester was there, a knife in her fist as she stood protectively over Kahlan. Richard knew that she had no chance of stopping one of the walking dead, yet she was prepared to try.

Sammie was gone.

Richard let the covering drop back over the doorway as he started out again in pursuit of the threat. He raced toward the screams of startled people apparently awakened in the middle of the night by the attack. He had to shove some of the sleepy people aside when they stood dumbly in the dark passageway.

Out ahead, he saw a blur of movement again as a small figure darted across an intersection only to vanish down a side hall. A dark shape roared as it chased after her. A second shape entered the tunnel, following behind the first and Sammie.

It paused momentarily and turned to look in Richard's direction. Back in that dark tunnel, Richard couldn't make out much of the walking corpse, but he could see the piercing reddish glow of its eyes. It was like it was glaring out from the darkness of not only the tunnel, but death itself. And then it was gone, vanishing into the shadows of a side passageway, chasing after Sammie.

Richard ran after them, racing as fast as he could. He ran so fast that the men following behind him couldn't keep up. As Richard chased after the threat, and put distance on the men behind, he was losing the help of the light from their lanterns. He kept running despite how hard it was to see. Occasionally a room to one side or the other was lit with candles so that their faint light spilled out into the hallway, giving him enough of a glimpse of the tunnel to keep from having to slow.

In the dark, he came upon the second of the two men running after his companion and Sammie. It was hard to see, but he could see well enough to tell that this man, too, was a walking dead man. Even without a good look, the smell alone was unmistakable.

As the man stopped and turned back to see who was behind him, Richard was already there, swinging his sword down with all his might. The ceiling wasn't very high, so he couldn't put as much power into a full swing as he would have liked. Still, it was a blade powered by more than mere muscle, the same as these men were powered by more than life.

As the man opened his mouth to bellow a threat at Richard, the sword came down with all Richard's force and strength behind it. The blade cleaved the man from the top of his head down to the center of his chest. Parts of the head and neck fragmented off the corpse.

Richard didn't wait to see if it was enough. He hacked furiously at the man, screaming in rage the entire time, cutting the threat to bits. As the men with the lanterns caught up from behind, Richard could finally see that the threat from this particular intruder was no more than rubble in the hallway.

With that one threat ended, Richard looked up. In the distance, faint candlelight came from a room to the right. Richard saw the silhouetted shape of the other man headed for that light. In that light, Richard could see that the hallway was a dead end beyond the room. Sammie was trapped down there. She had nowhere left to run, no way to escape.

Richard charged down the passageway, knowing that he was in a race to kill the man before he could kill Sammie. He yelled as he ran, trying to distract the killer. The man paid no attention to Richard. His attention was on his prey.

The hulking corpse stood just outside the doorway, looking in. Richard wasn't close enough. The dark shape glanced Richard's way with glowing eyes, then turned back to the room. He roared with menace as he stormed into the room.

Richard ran with all his strength. The dark shape disappeared into the room at the dead end of the hall. Richard wasn't close enough. He wasn't going to make it in time. He knew that Sammie didn't stand a chance.

Just as he was about to reach the doorway, the big, dark shadow of the man flew backward out of the room and crashed into the wall on the opposite side of the tunnel. Dust billowed up from the impact.

The man was clearly stunned but he recovered quickly. As he regained his footing, Sammie appeared in the doorway.

Richard was almost there, but he wasn't yet close enough. Sammie and her attacker were too far away for Richard to help her.

The man again let out a thunderous roar of rage as he rushed the girl. Sammie lifted both arms out straight, with her palms up, as if she actually thought she could stop the charge of the big man.

To Richard's surprise, the man flew backward again, again slamming into the wall.

This time, as he came off the wall, flying toward the

girl, she shrieked when she tried a third time to stop him and it didn't work.

But this time Richard was there. With one mighty blow, the sword cleaved away the monster's head and one shoulder. A second strike came like lightning, severing the other arm as it tried to strike at Richard. With quick swings, Richard hacked the body down to the waist, and then chopped the legs down at mid-thigh.

The head, with the neck, a shoulder, and one arm still attached, lay on the ground, looking up with menacing, glowing red eyes. The hand reached out and snatched Richard's ankle. Richard brought the sword down a half-dozen times in quick succession, hacking the arm and head apart. He crushed the hand with his boot after smashing the head to bits.

Richard stood panting, sword in his fist, feeling the rage of it storm through him, drawing yet more of his own rage forth. He cocked his head, listening, but he didn't hear any other screams or roars. It seemed that this was the last one.

Sammie stared up at him.

"Are you all right?" he asked her.

She nodded as she let out a deep sigh of relief.

He pulled her to him and with his sword arm, embraced her around her small shoulders, thankful that he had been in time. She had managed to buy a few precious seconds until he could get to her and end the threat for good.

"You're sure you are all right?" he asked again. "You're sure that he didn't hurt you?"

She held some of her dusty, frizzy black hair back out of the way as she looked down, taking a good look at the remains.

"No, I'm fine," she assured him. She sounded remarkably calm.

"Then do you mind telling me what you were doing?" Richard gritted his teeth as his fist tightened around the hilt of his sword. He leaned down toward her. "I told you to protect the Mother Confessor. When I left, I clearly told you to stay there and watch over her."

"I was watching over her."

"Until you ran. I trusted you to protect her, and instead you ran. I can't fault you for being afraid, but I was counting on you and you didn't stay there and protect her."

Sammie shook her head. "I was protecting her—"

"They came back in the caves after her. You ran."

Sammie folded her spindly arms and glared up at him. "They weren't after the Mother Confessor. They were after me."

"You don't know that."

"Yes I do." She was still glaring from under a lowered brow. "That's why I ran—to protect her by drawing the attackers away from her. That was the best way to keep her safe."

Richard straightened. "What are you talking about?"

"Is she hurt? No. Are there monsters back there ripping her to pieces? No. Why do you suppose that is?"

When Richard didn't answer, she leaned toward him. "They aren't back there killing her because they were after me. When they came into the room they didn't even look at her. They were both looking at me with those glowing red eyes. As they came toward me I moved to the side of the room to see what they would do. Their gazes stayed locked on me. Do you know what they did then?"

"They came after you instead of her," Richard guessed in a considerably quieter voice.

"That's right. They didn't even seem to see her. They

were focused only on me. They came after me. I tried every bit of magic I knew to stop them. I admit that I don't know a lot about such things or have much experience, but I tried everything I know. Nothing worked.

"Then I remembered what Henrik said about what your friends did, so I threw a fist of air like they had done. It didn't harm those two the way it should have, but it did knock them back just long enough for me to get to the door. When I did that, they left the Mother Confessor and came after me. Once I saw that they really were after me and not her, I ran to get them to chase after me so I could lead them away from her. They weren't interested in the Mother Confessor. They both came after me."

She tapped her chest. "Me, not her. Me. So yes, I ran, but I ran to protect her the only way I could—by getting those monsters to chase me so I could lead them away from her.

"I was afraid. Even though I was afraid, I knew that I had to think of something. I wondered if I could somehow trap them in a dead-end tunnel. Then, when I got down here, I had the idea to get them into that room and slip past them like I had before, and then I would collapse the hallway in to bury them down here in this room."

In the light from the lanterns carried by the men waiting back a ways up the passageway, Richard looked around. It was indeed a dead end, with only the one room at the end. If he hadn't gotten there in time her plan might have worked. Of course, it might not have. She very easily could have been slaughtered.

Yet, of all the people in the small village, she was the only one who had thought of something to stop the threat. She was the only one with a plan and she acted on it.

Richard ran his fingers back through his hair as he let out a sigh. "Sammie, I'm sorry. You're right. You did a very brave thing. Thank you for doing what you did to protect Kahlan."

"You don't need to apologize," she said as she showed him a small smile. "I can see in your eyes that you are in the grip of the magic of the sword. I can also see that its anger is all that's keeping you on your feet. I need to heal you. It can't wait any longer."

As he nodded, he realized that his wounds had opened back up in all the fighting. The blood running down his arms dripped off his fingers. Now that the urgent demand of fighting off the attack was over, he was feeling increasingly light-headed and the pain was again pressing in on him.

"Listen, Sammie, there are a lot of your people back there who are hurt. Some are hurt pretty badly. They need your help. Please, tend to them first."

He was frantic to have help for Kahlan, but he knew that helping some of the others was more urgent. Without help, many would die. He thought he could wait.

Sammie's gaze swept over the remains on the floor outside the room where she had intended to trap her pursuers. She didn't merely look worried for her people who were injured; Richard thought that she looked somehow older than she had earlier.

She started back out of the dead-end tunnel. "We'd better hurry, then," she said back over her shoulder.

"Right," Richard said as he sheathed his sword.

When the blade slid home, the anger from it extinguished. His own rage went out with it.

In that instant, the entire weight of the ordeal and the staggering pain of all his wounds set in with a vengeance. The sword had been all that had been holding it back.

He couldn't feel his fingers.

It felt like the tunnel was collapsing in on him and the suffocating weight of it was crushing him.

He managed to take one step, and as he did the world tilted as the floor began rushing toward him. Everything seemed strangely distant, as if he were looking through a long, dark tube at the world off in the distance. The concerned shouts he heard somewhere around him sounded eerily muffled.

Before the floor reached him, the blackness closed in and shut the world away.

When Richard woke, he didn't recognize his surroundings. He was lying on a woven straw mat in a windowless room softly lit by candles clustered along recessed shelves that had been meticulously carved into walls of the same stone as the rest of the cave village of Stroyza. The surface of the walls themselves had been flattened and finely smoothed, mimicking the look of plaster. From what he had seen of the rest of the excavated cave system, these were luxurious quarters.

Kahlan lay on another mat close beside him. She was still unconscious and didn't respond when he touched her shoulder. To his relief, he saw that she was breathing more evenly and easily than she had been before.

He was surprised to see that her clothes were no longer soaked with blood. Not only were her clothes clean, the rips, tears, and cuts in them had been carefully sewn up so that it almost looked like the shirt had an embroidered design on it. Most importantly, though, she was no longer covered with cuts and hundreds of puncture wounds. From what he could see, it appeared that they had all been healed.

He was relieved by that much of it, if not by the fact that she was still unconscious.

He looked down, then, and saw that his own clothes were just as clean as Kahlan's. Checking his arm confirmed his suspicion that the horrific bite wound had been healed. Running his fingers over the spot revealed only a slight swelling where the wound had been. A great deal of the pain, too, was gone, though he could still feel a lingering ache in the muscle. He was able to sense a hint of a tingling sensation that he recognized as the residual effect of having been healed.

Even though his outward wounds seemed to all have been healed, he could still feel the awful, dark weight of a grim, inner sickness that was the touch of death left there by the Hedge Maid. That merciless weight was always there, trying to pull him down into its darkness. He knew that the same call of death itself still lay within Kahlan as well.

Richard sat up, looking around. The place was bigger than Ester's place, where they had been at first. The carpets were thicker, better made, and the colors in them were a little brighter than others he had seen. There were a few chairs and a table that, while not fancy, were well made. The door was wooden rather than a simple hanging. By the way the walls looked square and true, as well as the way they had been smoothed, he suspected that it was the home of someone important.

When she saw him sit up, realizing that he was awake, Ester rose from a bench to the side. "Don't try to stand, yet, Lord Rahl. How are you feeling?"

"Better." Richard blinked up at her in confusion. "What's going on? Where are we?"

"We're in the home of our sorceress." She pressed

her lips tight with grief. "Well, it used to be her home, before . . ." She reconsidered and then swept a hand around. "Actually, I guess it still is the home of a sorceress. Sammie still lives here, and she is the only sorceress we have left. It was her parents' home, but now I suppose it's her home."

Richard looked around. "Where is she?"

Ester gestured to a door to the back of the room. A few simple designs carved around the outside of the door were a luxury in a village that existed in such a harsh place.

Carved in the center of the door, though, was a Grace, the design that represented Creation, life, and out beyond the bounds of the world of life the eternity of the underworld. Radiating out through the world of life and the underworld beyond were lines representing the gift.

Such a design would not be a luxury, especially not in the home of a sorceress. A Grace was often used as a serious tool of the gifted, and often served as a symbolic reminder to the gifted of their duty, their purpose, their calling. It was never drawn or used merely for the purpose of decoration.

"Sammie is resting. Poor girl, she was exhausted."

"Exhausted? Then she helped the injured people? She healed all the people who had been hurt?"

"Yes, yes, she worked hard healing people," Ester said as she waved off his concern, seeming eager to change the subject. "Then she said that she needed to heal you both, as best she could, anyway. I told her that she needed to rest before she took up such a demanding task, but she insisted that it couldn't wait any longer. She said that she had to do what she could for you and the Mother Confessor right away or you both would slip beyond what help she would be able to give."

Richard glanced over at Kahlan. He had known that she was in grave trouble. He also knew that Sammie couldn't heal everything that was wrong with her. That healing would take someone with more ability and experience than Sammie, and it would take a containment field. He was thankful, though, for what Sammie had been able to do to help Kahlan.

He knew that he needed to find Zedd and Nicci, and then they had to get back to the People's Palace before it was too late if death's touch was to be removed from both him and Kahlan.

What he didn't know was how much longer they could survive with that poison inside them. Kahlan, especially, was in urgent need of such help. She wouldn't be able to survive in this unconscious state for long. Without food and water her condition would only worsen.

Richard was about to ask Ester about the people who had been hurt, and if there had been any more trouble, when the door to the rear of the room swung open. Sammie stood in the doorway, rubbing sleep from her eyes, before peering out into the candlelit room.

"Lord Rahl—you're awake." Her initial surprise quickly turned to relief.

Richard nodded. "I am, but Kahlan still isn't."

Sammie briefly glanced Kahlan's way. "I know."

Before he could say anything else, Sammie bowed her head to Ester. "Thanks for watching over them for me, Ester. I'm awake now. You can go get some rest. You look like you need it."

Ester yawned. "You sure? You've only been asleep for a few hours. After all the long and difficult work you've done, don't you think you need to get some more rest?"

Sammie smoothed back her disheveled black hair. "You've been working hard to help people, too, and you, too, have been up for two nights, now. At least I got a little sleep. Lord Rahl is still going to need to rest so his body can finish healing. I can watch over them as they rest. Why don't you go get some sleep?"

Ester let out a heavy sigh. "All right. I admit that I could use it, but I want to go check on some of the others, first." Ester flashed a quick smile at Richard. "I'll be off, then." She lifted a cloth bag from beside the bench. "Come get me, Sammie, if you need my help for anything."

Sammie nodded as she saw the woman to the door.

Richard held his knot of questions for the time being as Ester bid him a quick farewell and left. Once the door closed, Sammie promptly returned to put two fingers on his forehead, testing with her gift.

"Well?" he asked after a moment of silence in which she showed no sign of what she might be detecting.

Sammie took her hand back, rubbing her fingers as if she had touched something wholly unpleasant. "Hard to tell for sure, Lord Rahl, but the healing that I was able to do, such as it was, seems to be holding."

Richard knew that she meant that it was hard to tell much of anything with death's touch still in him. "You were afraid to heal us before," he said. He thought it a little strange that she had gotten past her fear of healing them both without him having to do any more convincing.

"Henrik's story about how the wizard you know—"

"My grandfather, Zedd."

Sammie nodded. "Yes, him and the sorceress. Once I knew that they were healing you even though they saw the same thing in you both that I saw, I knew that I could at least try to do the same."

Richard was still suspicious. "You weren't afraid?"

Sammie's little nose scrunched up. "Yes, but I knew

that it had to be done, so I tried not to think about how afraid I was and just concentrate on what I needed to do."

"What about Kahlan. Why isn't she awake like I am, if her injuries are healed?"

Sammie cast a brief, worried glance at Kahlan. "I'm sorry, Lord Rahl, but I did everything I could. The presence of death seems to be stronger in her. That's something I can't heal and it was harder to get around it in her in order to work on what I could heal. Death is casting a darker shadow over her than you."

Richard nodded as he heaved a worried sigh. Even Zedd and Nicci had said that they couldn't remove that dark force within her without being back at the palace. Considering the difficulty, Sammie had done well to be able to do as much as she had done.

"Thank you for doing what you did for her." He hoped it would be enough to keep Kahlan alive until he could find Zedd and Nicci, and then get them all back to the palace.

"Keep in mind that I'm not an expert in such things, Lord Rahl, but I think that with her injuries healed as best as I could do, and her not losing any more blood, it may just take some more rest for the healing to complete enough for her to wake. You've been asleep a long time. I'm hoping that she, too, will wake up once she has had some more rest. She was hurt worse than you, so she may just need some more sleep before she wakes."

Richard wanted to believe that was true, but he didn't know if it was just wishful thinking. "What about the others? All the people who were hurt. Did you heal them first?"

Sammie was a long moment in answering. "Some of them."

Richard looked up. "Why didn't you heal them all, all the ones who could be healed, anyway?"

"Because had I not stopped so that I could heal you, you would have died. The Mother Confessor is in more serious trouble because that awful shadow of death is a lot stronger in her, but you were in more immediate danger from your injuries and loss of blood. You were in danger of dying from the things that I could heal. I had to make a choice."

Richard's heart sank. "You mean, you had to let some of your people die to instead save me?"

Sammie swallowed. "Yes."

Richard's brow drew tight with concern. "Those were your people, Sammie. Why would you abandon them to heal us? To heal strangers?"

Sammie sat on the chair close beside him. She put some of her weight on her hands beside her small hips and rocked a little at the thought of how to answer his question.

"I'm only one person," she said in a quiet tone. "I worked on those I could save, worked as fast as I could, did what I could. Some people were going to die no matter what. I knew that if I spent the night trying to save some of those, they would still die in the end and then others that I might have saved would also die.

"There were many people needing healing. There wasn't enough time to heal all of them, even if I would not have healed you. I was never going to be able to save them all.

"This is the second night since the attack. You slept that night of the attack, all day yesterday, and most of last night. It will be dawn soon. That first night, after you had ended the threat and the battle was over, you passed out.

"I had you brought here while I stayed out there and

healed a number of people. More needed healing. Some people died as they waited, died while I healed others that I thought had a better chance. Some had wounds that are beyond my skill. I knew I had to leave them. Ester and others comforted them as best they could.

"Throughout the night, between healing people, I checked on you and the Mother Confessor to make sure that you both hadn't gotten any worse and that you could wait a little longer for me. There were so many who were hurt. Some not badly, so I left them to people like Ester to help with what they could do. I worked on those in more need for as long as I could. But then it could wait no longer.

"I had to choose who I was going to help, you and the Mother Confessor, or some of the others still waiting. I knew that if I helped you, then some of those I couldn't get to would die. But I also knew that if I didn't do what I could for you and the Mother Confessor, you both would die that night.

"I had to decide. I decided to heal you while I still could."

Richard ran a hand back over his face, distressed to hear that she had been faced with such a choice, that saving his and Kahlan's life had cost others theirs.

"I never had to make a decision like that before," she said. "My mother never talked to me about how to make such a choice. Such a thing never came up. I don't know—maybe she wouldn't have known what to do, either. There was no one else who could tell me what to do. All I knew was that I had to figure it out on my own."

Richard had made such gut-wrenching decisions before. They left scars that never entirely healed.

"I decided that I had to heal you while I still could,"

she finally said. "You saved a lot of people that night. I know that, in reality, you saved us all. Most of the people here would have been killed that night—we all could have been killed—if not for you being here. You are the one. You need to live. By helping you, I am helping many more people here to live than just those I could have healed."

She had said that about him when she had first met him. Richard frowned. "What do you mean, I'm the one?"

Sammie shrugged uncomfortably as her gaze drifted away. "You are the one I chose."

He knew that wasn't what she had meant. She was evading the answer, but he didn't press her on it. She would tell him when she was ready.

"I understand, Samantha."

She frowned as her eyes turned up to him. "Why did you call me that?"

"Because," he said, "Sammie is what you were called when you were a child. You made a very difficult, adult choice. You are becoming a woman, now. You used your head and made choices like a woman, not like a girl. I think Samantha is a more fitting name for you, if you don't mind me being so forward."

Samantha began to beam with pride at the unexpected acknowledgment. "Thank you, Lord Rahl. I've always wanted to be called Samantha—it sounds so much more grown-up—but to everyone else I have always been seen as Sammie. It's hard when you're still a girl trying to find out how to be a woman. You're the first one to see me as Samantha. Thank you."

Richard bowed his head in a single nod.

"Now, Samantha, please tell me the real reason you let others die and chose instead to heal Kahlan and me."

She looked very much the woman she was growing into as she gazed into his eyes. "Because you are the only one who can save us all."

"I think you had better explain what that means."

Samantha nodded. "I think I had better. We are running out of time. We are all running out of time."

19

W hat do you mean, we're all running out of time?" Richard asked.

She took a deep breath as she gathered her thoughts. "Well, there were other gifted people here, but they're all gone, now, so I guess that no matter how ill prepared I am for the task, it's up to me to explain it all to you."

"There were other gifted here? You mean besides your mother?" When she nodded, he asked, "So what happened to them?"

"I had three aunts, all gifted. Two were my mother's sisters, the other was my father's sister. They were all sorceresses serving our people.

"My father's sister, Clarice, was much older. She had never married. While among the gifted here in Stroyza there is no official leader, as such, it always seemed that she was our matriarch. She was the elder gifted and everyone deferred to her judgment. It had been that way my whole life. It seemed the natural order of things.

"Some time back, a little over a year and a half ago,

she was found dead in the woods not far from here. People assumed that she must have died because she was old. Everyone in Stroyza was shaken by her passing."

"Did she really die of natural causes?"

"I don't know. At the time we all thought so—we didn't have reason to suspect anything else. Now, I'm not so sure.

"After she died, people turned to my mother to fill Clarice's place." Samantha gestured around at the room. "That was when we moved in here. These quarters are where the foremost of the gifted of our village lives. It's an ancient tradition that is part of our ways.

"Not long after Clarice's death, when my parents and I moved in here, we first started hearing rumors of people encountering a strange woman with her lips sewn shut. It was only later that we found out that she was called Jit the Hedge Maid and that she had a strange lair in Kharga Trace. We didn't know where she'd come from or even how long she had been back in the Trace. We weren't even sure of exactly what she was.

"From traders passing through here who visited many of the people of the Dark Lands, we heard all kinds of rumors about Jit. Some thought she was death come among us, marking the end of time. Some thought she had remarkable, even miraculous abilities to heal those who could not otherwise be healed.

"My mother was able to learn that Jit used some kind of magic that was unlike ours, some kind of occult power that we had never encountered before." Samantha looked up at his eyes to make sure he was paying attention. "Some kind of magic that could maybe do things we never knew could be done, like maybe make the dead walk again."

"You mean like those walking corpses who attacked the other night?"

Samantha nodded. "There were rumors of such things, of bodies stolen from graves. Rumors of the dead walking the Dark Lands."

Richard wondered if Jit was the one who had reanimated and sent the dead men to attack the village. He wondered, even though he had killed the Hedge Maid, if there were more of her dead minions wandering the countryside.

"My two aunts Martha and Millicent were convinced that Jit could be nothing less than some kind of evil creature that had escaped from beyond the north wall."

Richard leaned forward. "The north wall?"

Samantha briefly gestured in that direction. "I'll get to that. Anyway, after they'd heard enough worrisome stories, my parents, two aunts, and their husbands all decided that since we were the closest village to Kharga Trace and were the ones potentially most at risk, we needed to investigate and find out the truth.

"Aunt Martha's husband was gifted. Not a wizard, as was explained to me—I've never met a real wizard, neither has anyone I know. Aunt Millicent's husband Gyles was supposedly gifted as well, but in a different way. He was mostly given to small prophecies, or at least so he said. No one much believed him, though. My mother humored his claims.

"But Uncle Gyles was one of those who had long been warning of a dark force he said would one day come into the Dark Lands. Then we heard about Jit having built a lair in the Trace. Gyles thought it was proof of his prophetic abilities.

"My mother always said that if you predicted rain long enough, sooner or later you would get wet and be proven right. She said that there were good times in life and bad, and if you predicted bad, you would eventually be proven right, but if you predicted it loud enough, you would be proven a prophet."

Richard smiled at that. He had always thought much the same thing.

"What kind of stories were your people hearing about Jit?" he asked before he became lost in the family tree.

Samantha shrugged. "The stories were mostly whispered to my parents and aunts and uncles behind closed doors. My mother never told me what was said, but I knew that she was concerned."

"You didn't ask?"

"No. I knew better. When my parents wanted me to know something, they told me. If they didn't tell me, I knew that meant I wasn't to ask, that it was an adult matter. The six of them—my parents, both aunts, and both uncles—discussed such matters privately, between themselves. Especially if it was a decision about the safety of our people."

"The gifted rule here, then? Even if informally?"

"Not exactly." Samantha squinted in thought, looking for the words. "The gifted have always been the ones people of Stroyza turned to. I don't know that you would say they rule, exactly. We're a small place, not an empire, and it never much seemed that we needed someone to rule. Maybe to settle arguments, occasionally, but not really to rule.

"It's always been more like the people here respect the gifted and seek their advice, much like people respect elders and seek advice from them, but don't necessarily want to be ruled by them. When something needed deciding, people would often come to one of the gifted—my parents or aunts and uncles—seeking advice, and on occasion, a decision."

"You mean like when we were first brought here,

they sent for you because they respect your ability, but they wouldn't expect you to think you could rule them."

Samantha smiled at the analogy. "I guess that's a good way to put it. So in this matter that seemed to somehow involve magic, the gifted decided among themselves that Aunt Martha and her husband, since he was gifted too, would go look into what was happening in Kharga Trace, what this Hedge Maid really was, and what she might be up to back in that swamp.

"Last fall, when the water level was at its lowest, Aunt Martha and her husband set out for the Trace to look into it."

"And they never came back," Richard guessed when she brooded silence for a moment.

Samantha confirmed his suspicion with a shake of her head. "Our people searched, but my aunt and uncle were never found. The wilderness of the Dark Lands is vast so they couldn't search everywhere, of course. More than that, though, people were afraid to go too far into the uncharted depths of the dark swamp of Kharga Trace.

"Then, this past spring, someone found their remains when the overflow of spring waters washed them out of the swamp."

Richard knew that there couldn't have been much left of the bodies. He tried to ask a gruesome question as gently as possible.

"After all that time, being out in the swamp and all, how could you be sure it was them?"

Samantha lifted a hand in a forlorn gesture. "My mother identified their bones. She said that the bones carried the telltale trace of the Grace—of the gift—and she recognized it as that of her sister."

Samantha stared at her hands nested in her lap. "She also said that she could read in the bones that they had died a violent death. She said they had been murdered."

Richard wondered if it was true that a gifted person could actually tell such things from bones, or if it had been grief speaking, trying to find blame. He didn't know enough about the gift to know the answer to that question.

He did know, though, that the Dark Lands were a dangerous place, and Kharga Trace certainly more so. He had been warned about going into the Dark Lands by soldiers who grew up in that mysterious part of D'Hara. Given everything he knew, not only of the warnings he had heard, but his own experience, it was not at all unreasonable to believe that Samantha's aunt and uncle had been murdered.

"Not long after," Samantha said, "my other gifted aunt, Aunt Millicent, and her husband Gyles, were taken away by soldiers from the abbey."

Richard frowned in surprise. "The abbey?"

"Yes, it's a distant place off somewhere near the city of Saavedra. It's run by Abbot Dreier. It's a place that has something to do with collecting prophecy for Hannis Arc, who rules Fajin Province from his citadel in Saavedra."

"What do you know about this place, this abbey?"

"Not much at all, really, other than that they collect prophecy, like I told you. I'm not sure anyone knows much about it. No one likes to talk about the abbey, or the citadel."

Richard knew Abbot Ludwig Dreier, but he didn't say so. Ludwig Dreier had stirred up trouble about prophecy at the People's Palace. He had, in fact, turned a number of lands away from their alliance with the D'Haran Empire in favor of throwing their lot in with Hannis Arc, who promised to share prophecy with them, and reveal its secrets.

"Any idea why they would pick out your aunt and uncle to go to the abbey?" he asked.

Samantha idly rubbed the edge of the chair. "I don't know, for sure. But Uncle Gyles was the one I told you about who claimed to have a bit of the gift for prophecy. Maybe that had something to do with it. Maybe they wanted him to speak of what prophecy says about our future.

"All I know for sure is that soldiers showed up and said that Aunt Millicent and Uncle Gyles had to go with them. The soldiers said that because they were gifted, they had been chosen to go to the abbey to help with prophecy. They said that it was for the good of the people of Fajin Province, that prophecy belonged to all the people."

"And they never returned after helping with prophecy?"

By the way Samantha looked down as she shook her head, Richard got the point that no one ever returned from the abbey. He wondered why.

"That left my mother as the only gifted person left in Stroyza."

"There's you," Richard said. "You're gifted."

Samantha shrugged one shoulder. "I guess. I guess I should say it left my mother as the only adult gifted person in Stroyza. Now, she is gone. That means the ancient duty we were given has fallen to me."

Richard didn't think he liked the sound of that. He flicked a piece of straw off his pant leg.

"Do you know what the name of your village, your people, means? What 'Stroyza' means?"

Samantha pushed back some of her black hair as she frowned up at him. "No. I thought it was just a name. I never heard anyone say that it meant anything."

"It's a High D'Haran word."

"High D'Haran is an ancient, dead language. No one today understands High D'Haran."

"I do."

"Really?" Intrigued, she leaned in. "So what does it mean, then?"

"It means 'sentinel.'"

Samantha's smile ghosted away as her face lost its color.

"Dear spirits," she whispered.

"Does that word in an ancient language have something to do with your ancient duty?" Richard asked.

Her eyes beginning to brim with tears, Samantha nodded.

"That's what my mother had been doing. She had been keeping watch. My parents left Stroyza to report what she had seen, but she was never able to complete that duty. They didn't make it far when my father was killed. My mother is missing and I fear that she has also been murdered."

"We don't know that, yet," Richard said. "What was she watching?"

Samantha gestured toward the door with the Grace carved into it. "I need to show you."

20

S amantha touched her slender fingers lightly to the design of the Grace carved into the door.

"This is our duty," she said. "Our duty to the world of life."

"You mean, to be guardians of what the Grace represents?"

"That's right," she said as she pushed open the door.

Richard couldn't imagine how these people in this remote place could be guardians of the Grace. That symbol embraced all that existed. He looked back at Kahlan, making sure she was still breathing peacefully, before following Samantha through the doorway emblazoned with a Grace, as if it was meant to serve as a reminder of that duty.

The room inside, as well made as the outer room, was dimly lit with a few candles. A rumpled blanket lay pushed to the side of a mat where she must have been sleeping as she waited for him to wake. A simple but well-made tall cabinet stood to the side of a curved bench with a small pack and waterskin under it.

Samantha led him into a dark hallway at the back of

the room. She took a lantern from a shelf, lighting it with a gesture, a flick of her hand, that sent a flame sparked by her gift into the wick. The lamplight sent a mellow glow down a hallway that was longer than he expected it would be.

The hallway led them past a few rooms that he thought were likely to have been more bedrooms. There was a small recess cut into the wall. Three plank shelves in the niche held a few small, simple clay statues. One of the figures was a shepherd standing beside several sheep. Another was of a man, hand shielding his eyes, apparently gazing into the distance. On the lower shelves were a few books, and some folded linens. After passing several more darkened rooms to the sides, the hallway continued on without interruption, going deeper yet into the mountain, finally ending at a rather strange dead end.

The single opening at the end of the passageway was closed off on the far side by what looked to be a slab of stone. Carved in the center of the stone blocking the passageway was another Grace. To the side of the doorway Richard spotted a metal plate set into the wall. The plate was so corroded and pitted with age that it looked like part of the stone of the wall and he almost missed it.

Richard had seen similar metal plates before, though they had been in better condition. They had also been located in important restricted areas. Such plates were a kind of lock requiring the key of the gift.

Richard's gift had in the past allowed him access to many such shielded passageways and restricted areas. It had even allowed him access to areas with the kind of deadly protective shields that required both Additive and Subtractive Magic in order to pass, places no one had been able to enter for hundreds of years.

"No one else in your village, none of your ungifted people, can get through here, can they?"

Samantha shook her head. "No. This is a place meant only for those who are gifted. Others are never allowed in here. Most people are at least a little fearful of the gifted and none of them ever enter the gifted's quarters unless invited, and I've never known of anyone invited back this far into this place. I've never heard anyone but the gifted even mention this place. I'm not sure, but I don't think that anyone but the gifted among us even know that this place exists."

Richard pressed his hand to the plate to open the door. Nothing happened.

"My gift doesn't open it," he said, a bit surprised.

He recalled that his gift hadn't worked to protect Kahlan, or to heal her. It was further confirmation, as if he needed any, that for some reason his gift was not working.

In a fluid gesture, Samantha's fingers traced the lines of the Grace carved into the stone blocking the opening, doing it in the proper sequence in which a Grace was to be drawn. First the outer circle representing the limits of life, then the square inside that circle that represented the world of life, then another circle inside the square that represented the beginning of life, then the eight-pointed star, representing Creation, within the inner circle. Lastly she traced the lines coming from each point of the star, crossing the inner circle that marked the beginning of the world of life, and then the outer circle that represented the end of life and the beginning of the world of the dead.

"The gift," Samantha said as she traced the last of the eight lines going outward, "as it is meant to be."

Richard frowned, wondering what she was getting

at. "The world of life and the spirit world, with the spark of the gift connecting it all."

"As it is meant to be," she again prompted. "In the proper order," she stressed. "The world of life, and then after life ends, the spirit world—the underworld, the world of the dead."

"I know," he said, still frowning, still not understanding what she was getting at, but a bit unsettled by how easily she slipped into the enigmatic temperament of a sorceress.

"You said that your gift does not work."

"That's right."

"From the things my mother taught me about the gift and its connection to everything as shown in the Grace, I think your gift isn't working because it is corrupted."

"Go on. I'm listening."

"You have death in you, do you not?"

"I'm afraid so."

"Death in the world of life," she said as she arched an eyebrow. "That can't be. That is not the order of things, not as the Grace shows it should be.

"There is supposed to be the world of life, and the world of the dead. They each exist in their own place, as shown by the Grace. You have both at the same time, in the same place. That violates the Grace."

Richard felt goose bumps on his arms. He had not thought of it in that way before.

"That is how I know you are the one," she said in a confidential tone as she leaned in.

Richard's brow drew even tighter. "What do you mean?"

"Right now, you are neither of the kingdom of life, nor the kingdom of death."

"How does that make me the one you think you're looking for?"

"I have to show you," she said as she straightened.

She placed the flat of her hand against the metal plate. At her touch, the stone blocking the doorway began to roll to the right, revealing a passageway beyond. Richard stood in silence, staring into the darkness, as the heavy stone rumbled to a stop at the side.

"What is this place?"

"A place for the gifted of Stroyza. For those who keep watch."

Richard wondered what they were keeping watch for. He stepped through the opening, to a bracket holding a glass sphere just on the other side. He knew what that was as well. He had often used the light spheres left from ancient times.

But this time, as he approached, the glass sphere remained dark. He brushed his fingertips along the smooth surface, but it remained dead and dark.

As Samantha came closer and reached for the glass sphere, it began to glow, lighting the hall. She picked up the glowing sphere and then set her lantern down back in the hall before touching another metal shield placed on the inside to shut them in. The massive stone began to roll back into place across the opening.

"My gift doesn't work for that either, I guess," Richard said in frustration as he gestured to the light sphere.

"What I don't understand," she said with a twitch of a frown, "is why, if your gift doesn't work, the magic of your sword did. It seems a contradiction."

"If your theory is correct, and I think it is, then it isn't a contradiction at all. My gift is something within me." Richard lifted the sword a few inches and then let it drop back into its scabbard. "The sword, on the other hand, is external magic, something constructed. It doesn't need the gift to work. Anyone, including those who are not gifted, could use the sword and its magic would work for them. Its magic is independent of any person. It only requires the intent of the person wielding it."

Samantha nodded thoughtfully at the explanation. "That makes sense."

Richard looked back the way they had come. "But that means that Kahlan's Confessor power likely won't work. She was born a Confessor. It's innate in her, just as I was born with my gift."

It was a troubling realization that Kahlan very well might be without the protection of her Confessor power.

Samantha nodded. "She has that same touch of death in her as you do, so you must be right. It's corrupting the order of her existence the same as it's corrupting yours. Like you, even though she is alive, she, too, carries death within her. Except that with her that presence of death is stronger than it is within you.

"In that way, you both exist in two worlds—the kingdom of life, and the kingdom of death." Samantha leaned a little closer in the sphere's light, lifting an eyebrow to be sure he was paying attention. "Those two worlds don't belong together."

"Great," Richard muttered, now concerned that on top of everything else, Kahlan didn't have the protection of her power.

"Come on," Samantha said as she started down the stone corridor.

CHAPTER

21

Richard followed behind the wisp of a girl, engulfed in the glowing cocoon of light from the glass sphere she was holding. The stone of the passageway walls had been laboriously smoothed and precisely squared with the floor and ceiling, much like the rest of the quarters where Samantha now lived. There were no decorations of any kind on the smooth walls, other than the very faint natural variations in the consistency of the rock.

The corridor, devoid as it was of furnishings or so much as a shelf or niche or bench, had an odd feel to him, a deliberately sterile sense, as if it had been built with the intention that there be no distractions of any kind, no reason to linger, for those meant to use this hallway. The skill and time invested in creating the flat precision was in and of itself the decoration.

In an odd way, it put him in mind of some of the private corridors in the People's Palace, the ancestral home of the Lord Rahl. They were lined with beautiful paintings and statues that were meant to be a subtle reminder to the Lord Rahl, as he passed through those halls, of his duty to protect the sanctity of life. This corridor, devoid of anything that might be a distraction, in a contrary and subtle way seemed meant to remind those whose business it was to pass this way of the deadly seriousness of their purpose.

He wondered what that purpose could be.

In places the corridor curved gently. By the way it bent its way through the mountain, Richard had the impression that the meandering route was not for aesthetic reasons. The curves, being shallow turns rather than straight sections connected by corners, seemed yet another aspect of the guiding principle of minimizing distractions.

After a time, they arrived at another door similar to the first one. It, too, had a capstone covering the far side of the square passageway, to stop anyone who might have made it past the first from getting any farther. Without delay, Samantha pressed the flat of her small hand against the metal plate on the wall to the side.

Richard noticed that when she did, the light sphere glowed brighter as the magic recognized her as someone permitted to pass the shielded doorway. That told him that this shield was stronger than the first. In addition, this stone looked bigger and considerably heavier than the previous one, apparently another means to keep what was beyond more secure.

The mountain itself rumbled as the great, round stone disc began rolling to the right, its tremendous weight grinding small bits of dirt and popping flakes of rock, crushing them under the weight. The stone rolled back into a slot cut into the mountain. Once through, since the first had been closed, she left the second stone open.

Beyond the doorway, Richard noticed that the corridor was half again wider than the one they had just come from. The walls of this place were also smoothed, but to a far greater degree, so that they had a sheen to them. He ran his fingers along the cold, creamy surface of the stone, marveling at what it would have taken to accomplish such an effect. The light from the sphere Samantha held reflected off the wall in a way that revealed that the stone had been smoothed and then polished in much the same way marble statues were polished to create flesh in stone.

When they rounded a curve and abruptly encountered symbols on the walls to the left, Richard stopped in his tracks.

The designs had been incised into the featureless rock walls, making those symbols more enduring than paint would ever have been. Whoever had done this wanted those symbols to remain as long as the mountain stood. He could see that farther on into the passageway the symbols and designs proliferated to cover most of the wall.

Richard recognized the symbols.

Samantha turned back. "Come on. This way."

Richard had a hard time pulling his gaze from the flowing designs, the circles within circles, the unique devices, and varied emblematic shapes. He started out again, hurrying to follow Samantha.

As he rushed along the hallway to catch up with her, scanning the patterns carved into the wall, Richard saw that the designs grew not only more numerous the farther he went, but more complex. Soon they covered much of the wall to their left from floor to ceiling. Their very number conveyed a sense of urgency to the messages contained in the symbols.

Coming around another curve in the passageway, he was surprised to see a soft blush of light up ahead. He realized that it wasn't more of the light from the spheres. This was daylight. It seemed to be coming from some kind of window or opening on the wall to the left. The muted light coming in that opening fell on the wall on the opposite side of the corridor, brightening the whole hallway, making all the designs on the wall to the left stand out all the more plainly.

"Here," Samantha said, placing her glowing sphere in an iron bracket among the symbols before going on ahead to stand in the radiance of natural light. She gestured to the round opening in the wall that was letting that light in.

Richard rushed up and looked in. He saw that an opening had been bored through the rock to the outside of the mountain. He stuck his head into the circular portal to take a look out. The opening had been cut precisely and was perfectly round. It started out about four feet across but tapered slightly as it went through the stone toward the outside of the mountain. It looked to be eight or ten feet long, with smooth sides similar to the hallway, but not polished. By the time the hole reached the far end where it emerged out on the side of the mountain, letting in the daylight and fresh air, it had narrowed down to less than three feet in diameter.

The strange hole allowed him to look out in a different direction than the cliff opening where he had come up into the cave village.

This hole faced north.

Richard frowned at Samantha. "What is this?"

She pointed through the opening. "Look."

He put his hands on the edge and leaned in a little, looking out through the cylindrical opening into a murky dawn. He saw in the gloomy light a valley spread out before them. Not much of the dense forest of the valley far below was visible. The length and shape of the cylindrical opening restricted the view to a specific place off in the distance.

The opening framed a gap in soaring mountains many miles away. He bent down, trying to look up, trying to see how high the mountains were, but they were so immense and because of the way the opening was made it wouldn't allow him to see the mountaintops. All he could see were impassable walls of stone rising up from a valley below.

A deep canyon between the rock walls appeared to be the only way through the barrier of the mountains. Having been a woods guide, Richard understood the difficulties of finding passable routes through rugged wilderness. There was often only one passage through such mountainous country. It appeared to him that the valley was the only way back into and beyond those mountains.

He backed away. "What is it I'm supposed to see?"

"Well," she said, gesturing to two small metal plates in the wall around the opening, "you need to use these."

Framing the opening was a design with several distinct motifs. Like the others, Richard recognized the symbols that made up the designs. To each side, where Samantha pointed, within elements of the design where he hadn't noticed them at first, there were small metal plates, each about half the size of his palms. The metal was in better condition than the first shield plates he'd seen. It looked to be worn smooth by the touch of countless hands.

"Here, let me show you." Since his gift didn't work, she ducked under his arm and popped up in front of him so that she could put her hands on both plates for him. She was tiny enough that she could easily slip into the space between him and the wall. The top of her mass of black hair came up only to the middle of his chest.

"Lean around me and look in," she said.

As Samantha bent to the side, keeping a hand on

each plate, Richard leaned past her to put his head inside the circular opening.

To his surprise, the air wavered, similar to the way the air above a fire wavered, except that it did it in a circular pattern, more like ripples in a pond radiating outward. It was a dizzying sight that made his stomach feel a bit queasy.

But then the ripples in the air cleared, so that the distant view out the hole through the rock suddenly appeared much closer. It was as if he were abruptly shifted much closer to the mountains than he had been only a moment before.

As his eyes adjusted to the light and the resolving clarity of the scene, he realized that there was something built across the valley. Framed in the center between the two mountains, at the base of the canyon, a wall that was obviously man-made stretched between the cliff walls to either side.

Richard squinted as he studied the detail of the wall. It was enormous. It was as colossal as any man-made structure he'd seen. The lofty wall towered over the forest at its base.

In the center of the wall, also made of stone and rising up higher yet, was what appeared to be a monster of some sort, jaws gaping open, with fangs hanging down over a massive portal, as if walking through it would be like walking into the waiting maw of some grotesque stone beast. In that opening, great doors stood taller than the tallest trees. The doors were nearly as colossal as the wall holding them.

The doors stood open.

Richard backed away from the round portal. Samantha removed her hands from the metal plates to each side and the view through the portal wavered, re-

22

But when my mother and father left, they were going there to warn the wizards' council. That's what they said." Samantha's gaze looked lost as it darted about. "They said that the wizards' council at the Keep would be the authority on the matter of the north wall. That's what my mother told me—that she had to go to the Keep to warn those who would know what to do about it."

Richard was only now starting to realize just how isolated the village of Stroyza was from the rest of D'Hara, not just in distance, but in knowledge of the outside world. He felt sorry for these people, thinking they were serving a vital mission for wizards who no longer existed.

He spread his hands in regret. "I'm sorry, Samantha, but there is no such council there at the Keep. There used to be, but that was long ago. There is no longer a wizards' council at the Keep, or anywhere, for that matter.

"It's not like it used to be. Those gifted born as wizards have become extremely rare. There aren't many left today. I'm one of those who was born with that gift, but I grew up without knowing anything about it, so I'm afraid that I'm no expert on the subject.

"My grandfather is First Wizard and knows a great deal about such things as the history of the wizards at the Keep, but he's missing. If I can find him and the others with him, maybe he would be able to tell you more."

While Zedd probably knew a great deal about the history of the wizards' council, Richard didn't think that he knew anything about a north wall in such a forgotten place.

On the verge of panic, Samantha grabbed a mass of black hair in each fist. She looked out the opening through the rock wall as if looking for an answer. She looked like she wanted to pull her hair out. He could see that her world, her duty in life, was coming apart at the seams.

Richard laid a hand on her shoulder. "Slow down, Samantha. Take a deep breath and then why don't you tell me what happened next."

She nodded and then swallowed to help slow her breathing. "Some of our people found my father's remains not far from here. My mother's things—her pack and traveling supplies—were found scattered about on the ground nearby. There were drag marks, they said, that looked like she had fought them. Our people couldn't find her anywhere. The ground was rocky and they couldn't follow the trail.

"After that, with the north wall breached, and me being the only gifted person left, I knew that it was up to me, now." She flung her arms up. "But I didn't know how to get to a distant Wizard's Keep. I don't even know where it is, except I think it's far to the west somewhere. I hadn't yet learned the things I still need to learn. I didn't know what to do."

She looked up at him. "Fortunately, you showed up.

I don't know if it was coincidence, or fate, or if it was the good spirits themselves intervening to send you here when I needed you most."

Richard cast her a sideways look. "I don't believe much in coincidence."

"Well, all I know is that you're the one meant to hear about this—especially since you tell me there is no longer a wizards' council. After all, you said yourself that you're one of those who is gifted in that way."

Richard let out a deep breath of his own. "I'm not so sure."

"I think that it all happened this way because you're the one."

"The one." Richard cast her a skeptical look. "I'm glad you think so. I'm not so sure."

Some of the tension eased out of her shoulders as she let out a deep sigh. "I am."

He arched an eyebrow. "Wouldn't you think that if I was 'the one' I would know something about all this? I've never heard of any of it. I only recently heard of the Dark Lands for the first time."

"You killed Jit. Only you could have done that. Only the person we needed could have done that."

In frustration, he gestured out the round opening. "Yes, but I don't know anything at all about this north wall. This is the first I've ever heard of it. I killed Jit because she had captured Kahlan, then me, and she was going to kill us both if I didn't stop her. I was just trying to survive, to live. That's all there was to it. Kill or be killed."

Richard paused as a thought occurred to him. He wondered why Jit had gone to so much trouble in the first place to draw them both in.

She had first gotten her hands on Henrik, then cast some kind of spell over the boy. Making him helpless to do otherwise, she had sent him on a mission to deliver her occult conjuring to Richard and Kahlan in order to get both to come to her in Kharga Trace. Because of the calculated intent of that spell, the Hedge Maid had been able to draw Kahlan to her lair and imprison her there. That, in turn, had drawn Richard to her.

Now that he thought about it, he couldn't really imagine, living as she did way back in the depths of that forlorn swamp, that she would have had any way to know anything about Richard and Kahlan off in the distant People's Palace. It didn't make any sense, unless she had merely been looking to take down anyone who was a leader and that just happened to be Richard and Kahlan.

Unless someone else had a motive and they had directed her to do it in the first place.

"That's what we're all doing," Samantha said. "We're all just trying to survive."

He put the distracting thoughts of Jit's intentions out of his mind and returned to the matter at hand. Samantha was still looking up at him, waiting.

"I understand," he said, "but that doesn't mean that I'm the one you need to tell about all this north wall business. Like I told you, I never heard of it before."

"Well, you are the Lord Rahl," she said with simple logic. "To my mind, that makes you even more important than a wizards' council. You rule all of the D'Haran Empire, don't you? This is part of your empire."

Richard grudgingly had to concede her point. "I guess you're right about that much of it, but that's not enough to make me the one you need to tell about the north wall."

"But that's only a small part of it. The main reason is that you are of that place beyond the north wall."

Richard put his hands on his hips as he looked down at the wisp of a girl. He tried to keep the frown off his face. He couldn't imagine that it was comforting to have a big man, and the Lord Rahl besides, towering over her.

"I'm from Hartland." He aimed a thumb back behind him toward the west. "That's a small place in Westland, on the far side of the Midlands. That's a very long way from here. I'm not from beyond that north wall."

"I don't mean it in that way," she said in a calm voice as if he were dense and she was trying to be patient.

She was showing that exasperating side of sorceresses that made them all tend to talk in circles and riddles in a way that never failed to make him feel ignorant. He had once surmised that such a demeanor was a product of age and wisdom. But he could see now that it wasn't. That inborn nature of a sorceress was showing in Samantha even at a young age, much like the color of her hair or her small frame. He found it annoying the way it made him feel a bit dim-witted.

"When I say that you are of that place, I don't mean that you grew up there," she said, patiently, when she saw that he wasn't following her meaning. "What I meant is that you are from there . . . well, inwardly. You are of the place." She tilted her head as if to ask if he finally understood.

He didn't. "Of the place? What place?"

"The third kingdom," she said in simple explanation.

"The third kingdom?"

"Yes," she said as she dipped her head in a single nod, seeming to think that it was now as plain as could be. "The Grace explains the way it is all supposed to be."

"Samantha," he said, trying to be calm, "I don't know what you're getting at."

"There are two kingdoms represented in the Grace, right? The kingdom of life starting with the inner circle, and the kingdom of the dead beginning at the outer circle."

"So then what's this third kingdom?"

She stretched up on her tiptoes and pointed out the opening. "That is the third kingdom, beyond the north wall that has kept it locked away for all this time, since the time of the ancient war."

Richard had been dealt years of grief, misery, and trouble because of that ancient war. It was a war that had never been fully resolved back when it had raged. That ancient conflict had reawakened to spawn a new war that had caused untold suffering and had taken hundreds of thousands of lives. But that war, both the ancient one and the new one it had given rise to, was at last over. He had ended it for good.

Richard glanced out the opening and then back at Samantha. "What does a place have to do with the Grace."

"No, you don't understand. Not a place, as such. Although, it is a place—"

"It is, but it isn't." He made an effort to control his voice and keep it composed. "Samantha, if I'm going to help, you need to be more clear."

"Sorry." She pushed some of her hair back, took a breath, and lifted both hands as she started over. "The third kingdom is neither the kingdom of life, nor the kingdom of death." She lifted each hand alternately as if to illustrate both of those kingdoms in balance. She brought her hands together. "The third kingdom is both, together, in the same place, at the same time."

Richard felt goose bumps tingle up his arms to the nape of his neck. "That's not possible."

An uncomfortable thought immediately came to

him. He had once ventured to the underworld to go to the Temple of the Winds, which had been banished there for safekeeping during that ancient great war. He was life, and he had been in the world of the dead. So, in a way, both life and death had been in the same place at the same time.

When he first met Kahlan she had come looking for help from beyond the barrier that separated Westland from the Midlands. That barrier, slicing through their world, like a crack in their world, was an opening into the underworld. He had gone through that barrier with her.

So, in a way, he realized that such things were in some ways possible. Great trouble, certainly, but possible.

He turned back to the opening, this time looking at the symbols circling it, rather than looking out the opening itself to the distant valley. He surveyed the symbols, deciphering them in his mind as he studied the entire band of elements. It was then, for the first time, that he saw that the symbols translated to "the third kingdom."

It was naming what the opening showed.

When he had first seen that encircling emblem, and had recognized the device within the design that meant "kingdom," he had assumed that the circle of symbols would merely be the name of an ancient kingdom. After all, what was now D'Hara had once been made up of many kingdoms.

Samantha reached up and tapped her finger on his chest. "You have both life and death in you at the same time. Right now, you are neither of the world of life, nor of the world of the dead. Right now, you belong in both places. You have both life and death in you at the same time, as does the Mother Confessor. If that touch of death is not removed from you, it will claim you both and you both will die. But for now, you carry both life and death within you."

Richard stared at her.

"That is why I say that you are of that place." Without taking her eyes from him, she flicked a finger toward the opening looking out into the distance. "You are of the third kingdom beyond the north wall."

The north wall? Why do you keep calling it that?" She frowned at him, puzzled by the question. "Because that's what it's called."

"No it's not," Richard said.

Her smooth brow creased. "What are you talking about?"

Richard gestured back at the symbols stretching back along the wall. "It's called the barrier wall. There is no mention of a north wall anywhere in these writings. It only speaks of the barrier wall. So why do your people call it the north wall?"

Samantha's dark eyes grew large and round. Her face looked pale against the dark frame of her hair.

"Do you mean to say that you can read those strange markings on the walls?"

"Yes." He pointed to the circle of symbols around the opening. "This one here says 'the third kingdom.' It's naming what it shows: 'the third kingdom.'"

Richard ran the flat of a hand along the wall to the side, where ancient symbols had been carefully cut into the smooth, polished surface. "This here speaks of the barrier wall. See, right here? This symbol combined with this one under it means 'barrier wall.' Nowhere does it call it the north wall."

Samantha followed behind him, ignoring where he pointed, instead gaping up at him. "You can read these markings? Are you saying that you really know what they all mean? You really understand them? For real?"

He nodded as he swept his hand past another grouping of symbols. "These markings, here, all deal with the barrier. There's a tremendous amount of information written here. I'd have to study it awhile to be able to translate it all, but I understand enough of what I see to know that it all pertains to the barrier and the third kingdom that lies beyond." He glanced back over his shoulder. "So why do you call it the north wall?"

She looked at a loss. "I don't know. It has always been called the north wall. We've never had any reason to think it might be called something different."

It was Richard's turn to be taken aback. He stopped and stared at her.

"Do you mean to say that it has been the duty of the gifted people here in Stroyza to watch the barrier so they could warn others if the gates ever opened, and none of you could read the information about it all, the instructions and warnings that have been left right here on the walls?"

She looked bewildered, confused, and somewhat embarrassed. "I'm sorry, Lord Rahl, but from what I've been taught, the markings are an ancient, dead language. I never heard my mother, aunts, or uncles say that the things on the walls here were important. Aunt Martha always smiled when she saw them and called them the pretty decorations our ancestors left for us.

"My mother mentioned that others used to think it might be some kind of message, but I was always told that if it was, their ancient meaning had long ago been lost."

"But your people have been here all this time, apparently since the time that this was all built and this information was placed here. How could you not know what it says? Why wasn't the understanding of these writings passed down? Why weren't young people taught how to read this?"

She gazed at the wall a moment before looking back at him. "I'm sorry, Lord Rahl, but I don't have an answer."

"It doesn't make any sense." Richard lifted a hand and then let it drop. "Why wouldn't the gifted here teach their descendants, teach their children, to read this? After all, this was apparently their purpose, their duty—to be sentinels. This wall tells them about their purpose."

Samantha scratched her brow as she considered the problem. "Well, sometimes a skip is born—you know, a person who doesn't inherit the gift."

Richard nodded as he rested the palm of his left hand on the hilt of his sword. "The gift skipped my mother."

"I guess that there must have been gaps like that in the lines of gifted who serve Stroyza," she said. "It must be that there weren't enough sorceresses with gifted children, so their knowledge wasn't able to be passed on. When those ungifted children eventually had gifted children, maybe the only sorceresses still alive were old and the grandchildren weren't yet old enough to learn it all. It could even be that older sorceresses had passed away by then and the young gifted had no one to teach them.

"After all, you say that you're gifted but no one taught you about using your gift. That knowledge that could have been passed on was lost to you. Who knows what you failed to learn as a result."

Richard's mouth twisted with an exasperated expression. "I guess you have a point."

"Our understanding of these markings must have been lost during the times of those skips, so that the gifted who were eventually born were only able to learn sketchy pieces. It could even be that young people weren't taught for some reason. You weren't.

"Like me with my mother gone, those young people during times of skips likely were never even aware of what areas of knowledge had been lost. After all, once I have children I can't ever teach them the things my mother knew because she never had the time to teach me all she knew. I don't even know what I'm missing from her, or how much she might have known that I will never know. I guess that must be why the meaning of these markings were never passed down to her."

Richard let out a weary sigh. "I guess that makes sense. I didn't mean to make it sound like your people were negligent. It must have been hard for them. All this time they've lived way out here in this desolate place, all the time losing the knowledge of their reason for being here."

That was one of the reasons Richard had always considered books to be so important, why he sought them out, and why he put so much effort into gleaning information from them. Books were links that spanned such missing human bonds or even times of savagery and its resulting ages of ignorance.

It was helpful if you had an elder who could pass on their knowledge, but if there were no elders to teach you for whatever reason, books filled the void, not merely in generations, but often in centuries and sometimes even millennia. Books served to keep hard-won knowledge safe. They endured. Books could almost be immortal.

He glided the flat of his hand over the symbols carved into the stone wall. But you had to know how to read to extract that information. All the invaluable information written here on the walls was useless if young people weren't taught how to read it.

Samantha frowned suspiciously as she scrutinized the wall of symbols she couldn't understand. "If you had no one to teach you about your gift, then how can you understand a dead language?"

"In the course of some of the things I've been through, on my way to becoming the Lord Rahl, I've had to learn a lot of different things, such as High D'Haran"—he gestured at the wall—"and this."

His gaze drifted back to the round opening. "But in all I've learned, I've never learned anything about a third kingdom. I've never heard this place mentioned anywhere."

"I guess your elders failed to teach you many things, too."

He succumbed to a crooked smile. "I guess so."

"But what about this dead language?" she asked, still looking perplexed. "You really do understand these strange markings and know what they all mean?"

"Yes." He again ran the flat of his hand over one of the designs. "This one here, for instance, involves what it calls barrier spells. It says that the barrier spells, not the stone walls, or iron gates, or even the mountains are the true strength that keeps such a great evil contained."

"Great evil . . ." she said with a worried look.

He nodded as he gestured with a finger. "This composition here, beside it, mentions gravity spells being part of the barrier spells. I'd have to read more to try to find out what that means." He looked down at her. "Do you happen to know what gravity spells are?"

She shook her head, still staring at him in wonder, as if he could be nothing less than a good spirit with mystical knowledge come into the world of life to stand before her and explain the unexplainable. It made him feel a bit uncomfortable.

He went to another series of designs, studying the different elements for a moment. He tapped the wall. "This, here, talks about the gifted who settled here in this place called 'Stroyza' to watch over the barrier. It says they must stay in this place and watch for a deterioration of the gravity spells, which would in turn degrade the effectiveness of the barrier."

"I feel terrible that we lost all this knowledge. They went to so much trouble to pass on their knowledge, and we lost its meaning."

Richard nodded absently as he pinched his lower lip in concentration, studying the symbols, unable to resist translating them in his head as he scanned the elements. He wagged a finger at the wall.

"This is interesting. It seems that the people who did this were aware that the barrier couldn't last forever. That's why they left people here to watch over it in the first place. It says that the spells, though powerful and long-lived, would eventually decay over time. It says that when that starts to happen some of those on the other side will begin to escape out into the world of life."

"Jit," Samantha whispered in realization. She looked up at him. "She was one of those things that we should have known to watch for. My mother was worried about the Hedge Maid, and where she might have come from, but she didn't know anything about these barrier spells as you called them."

Samantha walked along the wall, gazing at all the markings in a new light. "To think, I never even knew that this was a language. I can't believe that none of us ever knew that these odd markings were important instructions on our duty."

"It's called the language of Creation."

Samantha turned back to him, her brow drawing together. "Do they teach you this language of Creation in Hartland, where you are from?"

Richard smiled at the notion. "No. I learned it not long ago, as a matter of fact."

The language of Creation was what the ancient machine Regula, or the omen machine as some called it, used to communicate or to set down prophecy. Regula issued prophecy by using focused beams of light to burn the symbols composing the language of Creation onto metal strips. There was part of a book, also called *Regula,* back at the People's Palace. Not all of it was there. Part of it, the part explaining the purpose of the machine, had long ago been removed and sent to the Temple of the Winds for safekeeping.

Regula seemed to be an instruction book of some sort for the device. With the help of the book Richard had learned to translate the symbols and in the process learned the language of Creation.

The language of Creation was a condensed, efficient form of writing. It used symbols representing concepts, rather than words. Once Richard caught on, he had come to realize that for years he had used parts of the language of Creation without realizing it. Many symbols in the Keep as well as spells drawn by the gifted used elements of the language of Creation. In many small ways, the language of Creation influenced all that came after it.

"I don't see how such a thing is possible," Samantha said with a frustrated sigh. "I don't see how something can be communicated merely with symbols and designs." She swept a hand past the wall. "How do circles, triangles, and all these different kinds of squiggly emblems and elements and such really tell us anything? At least anything complex?"

"The Grace is a symbol, isn't it?" he asked as he scanned the writing on the wall.

"Well, yes."

"It's a symbol from the language of Creation."

Her eyes grew big again. "It is?"

"Sure. And it's a pretty complex concept, don't you think? Look here." With a finger he revealed a circular element nested in one of the symbols on the wall. "Here is a symbol that talks about life, and the dangers to it from what lies beyond the barrier. See how it contains some elements of the Grace?"

Samantha's jaw dropped as she came closer and touched the motif of life. "I've never noticed that before. I always came here with my mother to look out through the opening into the distance to check the wall. Since I never knew what any of the things carved on the wall meant, or that they meant anything, I've never really paid much attention to any of it. I walked past it all the time without ever really looking at it."

"It's all the language of Creation," Richard said.

"You are the one," she said, staring up at him again with awed conviction. "Only the right one, the one who can help us all, would understand this writing and be able to tell what we must do about the third kingdom breaking through its barrier."

"Just because I understand the language of Creation,

that doesn't mean I understand the problem or I know what to do about it. I have my own problems to . . ."

Richard turned back suddenly to the opening that looked out at the wall between the mountains in the distance.

"Dear spirits," he whispered aloud, "I think I might know where they are."

Samantha looked puzzled. "You know where who is?"

"My friends who came to the Dark Lands to rescue me and Kahlan," Richard said, distracted as his mind raced, trying to fit together the pieces of the puzzle. "My friends were attacked much like your parents were attacked."

"What are you talking about? How do they connect to this?" she asked as she swept a hand out toward the expanse of symbols.

"Barrier spells," Richard said, turning back to the description on the wall. "When I first woke, there were a couple of men there standing over us. I was only just regaining consciousness, but I remember some of what they were saying. They were speculating about who might have attacked the soldiers and my friends who had been taking Kahlan and me back to the People's Palace.

"One of the men said that he thought our group had been attacked by people called the Shun-tuk—"

"Shun-tuk? I've never heard any such people in the Dark Lands."

Richard looked toward the opening out through the wall. "I don't think the Shun-tuk are from the Dark Lands. The other man was skeptical about it being the Shun-tuk. The first said 'With the barrier wall now breached, what better place to hunt for people with souls? The Shun-tuk would go anywhere, do anything, to find such people.' "

Samantha looked horrified. "So, then, you think these Shun-tuk came from beyond this barrier?"

"Sounds like it. The second man said that they had a vast homeland of their own. He wanted to know why they would come this far. The first man said, 'Same as us. Hunting for those with souls.' "

Samantha's nose wrinkled as she made a face. "Hunting for souls?"

"That's what he said. I don't think their homeland is on this side of the barrier. I think it's out beyond."

Richard returned to the wall, scanning the progression of symbols and designs, looking for something about souls. As he read in silence, Samantha walked on ahead, her footsteps echoing through the hall as she dragged a hand along the stone, gazing at the symbols she couldn't understand, but was now starting to see in a new light.

"Lord Rahl," she called back.

Richard, concentrating on the symbols, glanced back to where she had a finger pressed to the wall. "What is it?"

"I think there's a name here."

"A name? Are you sure?"

"Well, I don't know," she said as she leaned closer to the wall, "but it's not a symbol. I think it must be a name carved into the stone. It says 'Naja.' "

"Naja?" Richard was surprised that she could read something on the wall.

"Yes, right here. I can't believe I've never seen it before. I guess I never noticed it because it's so small, and it's almost lost in the crazy swirl of designs."

Richard scanned the wall off to the right of where Samantha stood holding a finger under the name. The area was slightly different than the rest of the carving on the corridor walls. The lines etched into the smooth stone of the wall stood out in stark relief in the glow of the glass sphere. They were packed tighter, into their own section, creating what was a block of symbols unto themselves. The section created a core among the expanse of symbols flowing out around it.

Richard looked above Samantha's slender finger resting on the wall. There was indeed what looked to be the name Naja carved into the wall. After the name he saw a crescent with three rays below it cut into the stone—the symbol for the word "moon."

"What do you suppose it means?"

Richard quickly translated some of the other symbols. "You're right. It is a name. The first part can't be written in the language of Creation, only the second part can."

"So what's the name, then?"

"Naja Moon."

"That's a beautiful name," Samantha said as she considered the sound of it, "but what do you suppose it's doing here?"

Richard was only half listening. He was already looking for the answer to that very question. He scanned the symbols to confirm his initial impression.

"This is a personal account," he said half to himself, half to Samantha.

"A personal account?"

Richard straightened. "That's right."

Gazing at all the symbols, Samantha slowly shook her head in wonder. She pointed, then, a little farther into the maze of symbols.

"Look over here—there's another name. Magda Searus."

Richard's knees grew weak under the weight of meaning behind that name. Goose bumps rippled up his arms at seeing it written there in the stone, written in such a far-off, lonely, forgotten land.

Samantha frowned with concern when she saw the look on his face. "Lord Rahl, what's wrong? Does that name mean something to you?"

"Magda Searus was the first Confessor."

"The first Confessor. You mean Magda Searus was a Confessor like your wife?"

Richard touched his fingertips to his temples as he stared at the name from legend.

"That's right," he said at last. "Magda Searus was the very first of her kind, the first woman to become a Confessor. It all began with her." Richard pointed after her name at another: Merritt. "Merritt was her wizard, her protector, much like I am Kahlan's protector."

Samantha looked back at the names and shook her head in wonder. "The first . . ." She looked back at him. "What does it say about them?"

Richard's fingers reverently brushed the names and then the following emblems incised into the stone. "It says that this is Naja Moon's firsthand account, set down here at the behest of Magda Searus and Wizard Merritt so that all those who come after would never forget."

Samantha swallowed. "I'm shamed to say that our

people have forgotten." She looked up at him hopefully. "So, can you read it then? Can you read the account so that it might once again be known?"

Richard cleared his throat as he found the beginning and started working out the translation. Right there at the beginning of the account, he found another name—Sulachan—tangled in among the symbols.

"It says that Emperor Sulachan's makers—"

"Emperor Sulachan? Who is that, and what is a maker?"

Richard shook his head. "It doesn't say, exactly, but by what comes next it appears that makers were wizards of some sort." He tapped a finger against the next complex of designs. "It says here that Sulachan, emperor of the Old World, commanded his makers to develop new and powerful weapons for use in their war against the New World. It says that in doing his bidding they created terrible new spells for him."

Richard felt an icy chill at realizing that the war he had fought against Emperor Jagang and the Old World had first been ignited here, in Naja Moon's time, in Magda and Merritt's time. It was a time of the creation of some of most terrifying spells ever conceived. That same, distant age was also the time when the spells creating the first Confessor had been constructed.

That was the balance that magic needed for the terror conceived and loosed on the world.

Richard was seeing an account of the birth of a war that had caused unimaginable suffering and death. It was the beginning of a struggle for domination that had raged across the millennia. The flames of that war had never entirely died out but instead smoldered for thousands of years only to reignite in Richard's time.

It had begun in the time of the first Confessor and her wizard, Merritt, and reignited into full fury again in the time of the last living Confessor, Kahlan, and her wizard, Richard.

This account was from that time when Kahlan's Confessor power was born.

These makers mentioned here must be wizards who made things with magic," Samantha was saying, bringing him out of his thoughts. "I've heard my aunts talking about how wizards make constructed spells. It must be that Naja is talking about constructed spells."

Richard cast Samantha a look. "No, not constructed spells, at least not at first, not at this stage. First, they made new forms of magic itself. Later they then used those new forms in constructed spells. They also used new forms of magic to create weapons out of people."

Her mouth dropped open. "They changed people into weapons?"

Richard nodded. "Terrible weapons, like Emperor Jagang from the Old World. His ancestors were weapons first created back in Naja's time. They were called dream walkers."

"Really?" she whispered in wonder. "My mother never taught me of such things."

"Not a lot of people in our time knew of such things from that ancient war. Some of us learned about them after that war started up again. We were all pretty horrified to learn about such weapons."

"But how are new forms of magic possible in the first place? I thought that magic was magic, that it was always the same, and that we must learn how it works. I never heard anyone say that it's possible to make new kinds of magic."

Despite appreciating her endearing curiosity, Richard was too distracted by the appalling nature of what he was learning to want to get into it right then, so he simply said, "Yes, it's possible."

"Does it say what kinds of new magic they created?"

Richard's brow lowered as he looked down at her. "Samantha, let me decipher more of it and I'll tell you."

Her head sank between her shoulders a bit. "Sorry."

Richard went back to translating the story. "It says the makers developed spells to use the dead—"

"Use the dead! Are you serious? Use them for what?"

"It says they were used as warriors, of sorts. Through these new spells, corpses were awakened from what was called their death sleep and made to serve the emperor's cause."

Samantha clutched his forearm. "You mean like those monsters that attacked us the other night? Those creatures that looked like corpses pulled from graves and brought back to life?"

"Apparently." Richard shook his head at the ghastly account he was seeing written in the stone. "It says that by altering elements within the Grace, the emperor's makers learned how to manipulate the spirits of the dead in the underworld—"

"Why would they do that?" Samantha interrupted yet again, impatient for him to translate faster.

He waved a hand to silence her so he could finish

studying a grouping of symbols before continuing. She sighed and waited quietly.

Richard wiped a hand across his brow. "It says that they invested powerful magic into dead bodies while at the same time using Subtractive Magic on their spirits in the underworld, in that way linking those spirits back to their worldly remains."

Samantha hugged her arms to herself as if feeling a sudden chill. "I never imagined that such things were even possible."

Richard hadn't either. He translated another line before continuing to explain. "This says they were able to do it by manipulating that connection in the Grace— the spark of the gift—that runs from creation, through life, and into death, connecting it all. In this way they were able to create walking dead that had no will of their own. These reanimated corpses were given a purpose by those who had awakened them.

"It says that in this way Sulachan's makers were able to create an army of bloodless, relentless, remorseless killers. It says that when awakened from their death sleep in this way, they don't know hunger, pain, fear, or pity. They never get weary. They don't ever retreat. They have no ambition but the one given them, and they can't be killed because they are already dead.

"It says here that the dead could be animated as needed. When awakened they are tirelessly committed to their purpose. The magic that drives them also gives them terrible strength. They are so strong they can tear people limb from limb."

"That certainly sounds like what we saw the other night," Samantha said.

"I'd have to agree with that." Richard tapped the tightly packed line of symbols. "It also goes along with what it says next. It says that they are so single-minded that if they lose their legs they will not feel it and will instead use their arms to pull themselves after the ones they were sent to kill. I wish I could say that it sounds too preposterous to believe, but I saw that very thing with my own eyes.

"It says they must be hacked to pieces, but warns that magic hardens them so doing so is difficult. That same magic that animates them also protects them, acting as a kind of shield, and makes using most forms of the gift against them virtually useless. It says you can burn them, though, either with normal fire or wizard's fire."

"Wizard's fire. I've never seen wizard's fire. Have you?"

Richard grunted that he had as he concentrated on working out more of the translation. "This says that shields don't protect against them because shields key off life."

He gestured back up the corridor. "I was wondering why the shields protecting this area move those large stones out of the way. It struck me as out of the ordinary for shields."

"Really? In what way?"

"With all the shields I've seen before, touching the metal plate allows those with the right gifted ability to pass through the shield without being harmed. Those shields never used anything but magic to block a passageway. Some of them would repel those who don't belong by using uncomfortable sound, heat, or even tingling pain to keep people from passing, but there are dangerous shields that are strong enough to kill intruders if they continue to try to get through. There were shields that would strip the flesh from your bones if you continued to try to pass after they gave you a warning.

"All those shields used magic. These shields here must use those big stones instead because the dead they are intended to shield against are protected by the same magic that animates them, so they aren't affected by a regular shield's power. They could pass right through a conventional shield, but the simple physical barrier of those round stones is too massive for them to move aside."

As she thought it over, Richard worked out the next section of symbols. "Well, this is frightening," he said. "It says that these reanimated dead are often sent against specific targets, such as the gifted." He glanced down at her. "Looks like you were right about them being after you."

She looked aggrieved. "I told you so."

"And do you know why they would have been after you?"

She seemed surprised by the question. "To eliminate the gifted so they can't use magic to stop them?"

Richard tapped the wall of symbols. "Magic doesn't work against them—except maybe wizard's fire, and you certainly can't wield that. Besides, I don't think they killed my grandfather, Zedd, or Nicci. Zedd is a wizard and Nicci a sorceress. I suspect someone wanted them taken captive for some reason. I wonder if they took your mother as well. After all, your father's remains were found, but hers weren't."

"All right, then, why do you think these monsters would come after me?"

"The gifted here watch the barrier in order to warn others if those in the third kingdom ever start to escape. I suspect their intent was to prevent an alarm. They may have killed your other relatives to keep them from warning anyone until they could completely breach the barrier spells. It's possible they murdered your mother as well as your father, but capturing her would also have prevented her from warning anyone and maybe they have some purpose in mind for the gifted. That only left you, here in Stroyza. I think they wanted to kill you, or maybe even capture you as well, to keep you from sending out an alarm."

Samantha looked shaken. "I don't even know how to send out an alarm."

"They don't know that."

"I suppose not." She looked up hopefully. "Do you really think my mother is alive?"

Richard was a long moment in answering. "I hope so, Samantha. I hope my friends are still alive as well. If they are, I have to try to rescue them. As easily as these monsters could have killed them, I wonder if whoever brought them back to life wanted gifted people captured alive for some reason. If they really do have your mother along with my friends, maybe I can get her out as well."

Samantha glanced to the opening overlooking the third kingdom. "You mean go there? Surely, you don't mean that you're thinking of going to that terrible place that is in part the world of the dead? A place where the dead walk the world of life? That sounds like suicide."

He regarded her with a resolute look. "Besides wanting to free them from harm, if I don't rescue my friends and get them back to the containment field where they can remove death's touch from us, then Kahlan and I are going to die."

Samantha swallowed before she answered. "I know."

Richard asked the question to which he already knew the answer, but couldn't help asking. "Do you see any hope for us, any way to get this sickness out of us and save our lives, other than what Henrik overheard must be done?"

Samantha glanced back over her shoulder, as if she could see Kahlan lying back there. When she looked back at him her eyes looked considerably older than her years. There was no doubt or uncertainty in her young features, or her sorceress eyes.

She shook her head. "I'm afraid not, Lord Rahl. The Mother Confessor is very sick. I'm hoping that with what I was able to do for her she will soon recover enough strength to wake and be able to eat and drink, but she is deathly sick. So are you, even if you don't yet feel its full effect. You soon will. She will die if that death within her is not removed. She does not have a lot of time left. You will last a little longer, but not much. The path for both of you is set, unless something is done to change it."

Richard nodded, unable to say anything, unable to stop himself from imagining Kahlan lying dead.

"I'm sorry, Lord Rahl, but I don't think you are the kind of man who would want me to tell you anything other than the truth."

Richard stared into Samantha's dark eyes. "No, I wouldn't. Only the truth can help us. That's why I need to translate this message. I need to see if there is any information here that can help us."

He couldn't say out loud that if Kahlan died, he would not want to live. Life held nothing for him without Kahlan. Life held nothing but imminent death for both of them if he couldn't find Zedd and Nicci. To do that, he needed to go to the third kingdom, but first he had to learn what he faced.

He looked briefly at the account on the wall highlighted in the eerie light of the sphere. "Maybe I can find something here that will help us, give us some answers we can use."

She nodded solemnly. "I hope so."

He turned back to the language of Creation and read to himself for a moment. It was grim reading.

"Naja's account says that the dead are always plentiful and more corpses were animated as needed, often in vast numbers. Oftentimes they used their own soldiers who had been killed. She says that as part of its function the magic that possesses them forestalls the decay process, but because such dark forces are used in the world of life, the magic invested in the dead has limits. For one, because everything in the world of life breaks down over time, so does this magic. As it does, its effectiveness degrades and the dead it possesses will begin to resume natural decomposition. She advises that while they know that the magic animating the dead eventually fails, she doesn't know how long that process takes."

"Great. So these killers, these walking dead who don't rot for ages, are plentiful and now they're escaping the third kingdom to walk among us."

"It would seem so," Richard said in desolate agreement.

Samantha shook her head in dismay. "Even Jit stayed in her lair. As dangerous as the rest of the Dark Lands can be, we've never before had to face anything as terrifying as these walking dead. I can't imagine anything worse."

Richard, still reading ahead in Naja's account, lightly skimmed his fingers over the next line written in the language of Creation inscribed in the wall.

"It says here that the half people are far worse."

L ord Rahl, your face just turned white. What's wrong? What in the world are half people? Does it say what they are?" Samantha leaned in. "Lord Rahl, answer me. What's wrong?"

Richard pressed his fingertips to his forehead a moment as he double-checked the translation. He ran it through his head again while trying to grapple with such an alien concept.

"It says that the half people are living people who have been stripped of their souls."

"Stripped of their souls?" She cocked her head toward him. "Are you serious?"

Richard couldn't help scanning it yet again before going on to read the following section of the sobering account. He finally backed away, staring at the writing on the wall.

"I'm afraid so." He pointed out a complex symbol. "This is the part here where it warns that those beyond the barrier have no souls."

"That doesn't make any sense. How can people not have a soul? Our souls are part of us all. They are 'us.'

It's like saying . . ." She cast about, trying to find the words. ". . . that, that living people aren't alive."

"I'm afraid that in a way that's exactly what it's saying. Naja says that the half people aren't exactly human, but they almost are. She says they are somewhere in between human and not human."

Samantha's nose wrinkled as she made a face. "How can that be?"

"Apparently, the dead and the half people share certain things in common and that's what keeps the half people from being fully human. At least not in the accepted sense."

Samantha leaned in with a look of dismay. "Accepted sense? What does that mean?"

Richard took a deep breath. "Well, the accepted sense is that living people have souls. But what does that mean? How does it make us human? In some part, having a soul means having the full intellectual ability to reason. Do you understand?"

"I don't think so. What does reasoning have to do with it?"

"The ability to reason is what gives us our capacity to have empathy for others, to value life itself. Our ability to judge right from wrong, to value all life, is only possible through our ability to reason. Reason is what powers morality.

"Naja says that these half people have no empathy and she also makes the specific point that they don't have the ability to reason fully. I think that she wanted us to see that the two are connected. That part of them that enabled them to reason out their larger self-interest has been destroyed through Subtractive Magic. That ability to reason was the source of their empathy, their humanity.

"She says that because of the way their minds have

been reduced, with what is left of them they can only reason in part, the way a predator reasons in order to hunt.

"Without the ability to reason in that broader sense, they are not the same as us. They are not human. They have no context for their lives, no transcending aspirations, no understanding or feelings for others. They make weapons, they hunt, they kill, they eat, they reproduce. They have human form, but that's all."

Samantha gave him a crooked look. "I can understand Sulachan wishing to have this mindless army, but do you think that it's really even possible to do such a thing?"

"Apparently," Richard said as he scanned the symbols, translating the gist of it for her. "In this line here, Naja says that the Grace and so their very being was ripped asunder. After that, they invested them with magic that is similar to that used to reanimate the dead. In this way the emperor's makers were able to create a race of half people to serve him.

"What's more, because of what was done with Subtractive Magic to the husk of their living bodies, half people age very slowly, almost imperceptibly."

Samantha, looking more than a little skeptical, folded her arms. "Magic can do a lot of things, but it can't slow people from aging. If it could, the gifted would all do that to keep themselves from getting old."

"It can be done," Richard said. "I've seen it myself at the Palace of the Prophets. Ancient spells altered time there. The people living inside that spell seemed to age slowly compared to the rest of us. It was originally done when the palace was built in order to give the sorceresses there enough time to complete the task of training young wizards.

"I know people who once lived there who are hundreds of years old—at least by our measurement of time outside that spell, if not theirs from within it. I even know an ancestor of mine, Nathan Rahl, who lived there most of his life and is close to a thousand years old."

"A thousand years. . . ." Samantha stared for a long moment, finally shaking her head. "I wish I could see such wonders that must exist out beyond the Dark Lands. I've always known that I'm doomed to stay here in this little isolated place, like all my ancestors, never to see the world beyond. But I've dreamed of seeing such wonders."

"I don't know if I would call them 'wonders.' Oftentimes, like with what we're facing here, it's nothing more than a whole lot of trouble."

After considering his words a moment she finally returned to the issue at hand. "But, how was it possible to keep these half people from aging? They're not living inside a spell like you described."

"It necessarily involves Subtractive Magic—"

"But only those ancient wizards back when they created these half people could wield Subtractive Magic, right? No one now has the ability to use Subtractive Magic."

"Even today there are a very few who can still call upon that side of the gift." He didn't go into the fact that he was one of those—at least when his gift was working. Her eyes were wide again, so he simply continued with what he had been explaining.

"So, in this case, since Subtractive Magic had been used to bring about such changes in the Grace, that would inescapably involve the underworld and in that way their aging was slowed."

"The underworld? Why would involving the underworld slow their aging?"

"Because our lives have limits—we are born, we live, and then we die—but we're dead forever, right?"

"Right," she conceded with a confused nod. "So?"

"So, we live for a finite time, but since death is forever there is no way to measure it. Life gives dimension to time."

"But our spirits begin their time in the underworld when we die, much the same as we begin our lives when we are born into the world of life."

"Except that our lives have an end, so we can say how long a person's life was. In the underworld there is only that beginning when we die. Since there is no end to being dead, there is no way to measure time in the underworld. That's why the Grace shows life with a beginning at Creation and an end at death, but once our spirits go beyond into the underworld, it goes on forever."

She still looked confused. "But that is when the length of time there starts. You start measuring time from that point."

"Yes but there is only that beginning point. It's like trying to determine how long a rope is when there is only one end. If you can't ever reach the other end because the rope goes on forever, then how could you measure how long it is? Life, from beginning to end, is a known quantity. Death has no end."

Samantha squinted as she tried to imagine such a thing.

"Each day lived," Richard said, "is one less of our limited number of days gone forever. Time therefore has relevance and meaning to us. Life is precious, so time is precious. Time is how we put value on things such as love. We give our most precious commodity, our time—a part of our lives—over to those we love."

"I never thought of it in that way. I know how much I treasure the time I spent with my parents, and how much I miss my time with them. What about time in the underworld?"

"We're dead forever. So a spirit in the underworld has no sense of getting old because spirits don't get old. They have no sense of their time running out because it doesn't run out. They remain dead forever, so in the underworld a day or a thousand days or even a million doesn't measure anything meaningful out of an infinite amount of time. You are still dead and you always will be.

"As a consequence, because death is inalterable and the length of time you will be dead is limitless, there can be no value in being dead, and thus no value to time."

"But what does that have to do with these half people living a long time?"

Richard arched an eyebrow. "The half people have no soul. That part of them is already dead. Time for the dead is limitless. The half people exist in a third kingdom in violation of the principles of the Grace, in a kingdom with its own set of principles where life and death exist together without clear separation, where they can intermingle in unexpected ways.

"Each of those half people carries that third kingdom, thus death, within them, so time moves differently for them. Emperor Sulachan's makers apparently used that link to the timeless world of the dead to make these people they turned into weapons long-lived so they could better serve his cause. Time was important to Sulachan because he was alive, so he used the opposites of both life and death to manipulate time for his purpose."

She stared at him. "That's all pretty hard to take in."

Richard nodded, aware that he had seen things she couldn't yet imagine and were hard for her to grasp.

He was also all too aware that because of the Hedge Maid, death now held a claim on both him and Kahlan, and in that way made the two of them a part of that third kingdom. The difference was that they were not going to be able to live a long time. Their contact with that kingdom, through the touch of the Hedge Maid, was deadly, and the world of the dead would soon call that debt due.

"I know," he said in a measured voice. "I have to admit, it's pretty hard for me to take in, too."

Richard turned his attention back to the symbols carved into the wall and read ahead for a few minutes as Samantha waited patiently. Her eyes tracked his finger from time to time as he traced a particularly difficult emblematic design while working out the translation in his head.

"So what else does it say?" she asked, her patience finally growing thin.

Richard swiped a hand back across his face. "Well, there's a lot about how Emperor Sulachan wanted to convert as many people as possible into this new race of subhumans, these half people living without a soul in this altered timeline so that they could continue to serve his cause. He also planned on eliminating any opposition to his grand scheme by first eliminating any of the gifted who would oppose him."

Samantha frowned up at him. "What grand plan is she talking about?"

Richard went to the next line, taking it all in for a moment. He read it twice, making sure it actually said what he thought it said.

"Well?" Samantha asked. "Can you read it or not?"

Richard let out a troubled sigh. "I can read it. I'm having trouble believing it, but I can read it. It's no wonder that the people of the New World were willing to go to war to stop him."

"Why, what does it say?"

"It says that Emperor Sulachan wanted to unite the world in what he called the People's Alliance, with him ruling over it all."

Richard had fought the Old World over many of these same kinds of tyrannical ideas of a greater good that some people believed transcended the lives of individuals. What that greater good always came down to was submitting to the rule of a tyrant and sacrificing to their cause, or dying. Enforcing the belief in a greater good required the massacre of anyone who disagreed, since such beliefs could not endure the light of differing beliefs.

Richard had thought that with the latest emperor from the Old World dead, the struggle was at last over. Now, he wasn't so sure. Evil always seemed to emerge to try to destroy any good that came about, any peace that had settled in, or any prosperity that had emerged. As long as mankind existed, he supposed that there would always be those who thought that their vision of a better world required murdering anyone in the way.

It was now evident that the ancient struggle, started so long ago by Emperor Sulachan, and the frightening weapons he had developed, hadn't been entirely eradicated. Some of those weapons loosed on the world of life had long ago been sealed away behind barriers and walls where they waited to fight another day. Where other barriers had come down, so, too, had this one finally given way.

"Seems to me like someone always wants to rule,"

Samantha said as she scanned the writing she couldn't understand.

"That's certainly true enough," Richard said as he tapped the wall of engraved symbols, "but the dangerous difference is that Sulachan believed that his cause transcended life as a larger cause for the good of all existence."

Samantha's mouth twisted a bit. "I don't understand."

"Sulachan envisioned the world of life and the world of the dead as one grand, interconnected entity, one whole, just as the Grace is one whole, interconnected concept. He wanted to unite the world of life and the world of the dead under his rule."

Samantha shook her head as she watched him reading the language of Creation. "That's madness."

He looked over at her. "I don't disagree with you, but sometimes lunatics are so driven they can take the whole world into madness with them."

"I don't see how normal people could go along with such beliefs."

Richard straightened with a sigh. "Oftentimes it's easier for lunatics to attract impassioned followers than it is for sensible people to get people to listen to reason. People are often more willing to believe lies than the truth. Lies can be made to sound pleasant. The truth, by its very nature, isn't always so attractive.

"That leaves peaceful people no choice but to fight for their lives or fall to the blades of madmen. In such a situation, there is no middle ground. There is no such thing as compromise between civilization and savagery. Civilization must always defend itself against savagery or else fall to it."

"I guess that's our part in this?"

Richard nodded. "I've never wanted to fight, to be in a war, to see good people die, to have to kill. I just wanted to live my life in peace. But others wouldn't allow me that life of peace. The battles I fight have always been a fight to survive and live in peace, not to conquer. That's how I came to be here instead of back in Hartland where I grew up."

He swept his hand past the writing on the wall. "In this case, here, with the people of the New World, it looks as if they had no stomach for fighting and kept out of the conflict as long as possible, but those of the Old World didn't care that these people wanted to live in peace. In such a case, the aggressor prevails unless those wanting peace are willing to fight back.

"According to Naja, Emperor Sulachan and his followers were determined to create whatever weapons they needed, no matter how terrifying or deadly, in order to conquer all those who opposed their plans. The reanimated dead and the half people were two such weapons. She says here that Sulachan's plan was to eventually rule both the living and the dead, from the world of the dead."

Samantha paced off a few strides in agitation, then returned. Her mood was as black as her hair. "I can understand a madman starting a fight, I've seen such things happen on a very small scale among pigheaded people here in our village, but what you're describing sounds just plain crazy." She jabbed a finger at the side of her head. "Crazy, crazy."

"Naja says the same thing, but she also warns that even if his ideas were as deluded, impractical, or preposterous as many knowledgeable people believed them to be, and even if in the end they did indeed prove to be impossible to carry out, he was willing to slaughter untold numbers of innocent people in the attempt, and that was what mattered to those in his way. The people of the New World were in his way.

"She says that he had no intention of stopping the killing as long as life existed. He believed that in the end, there would be only the reanimated dead and the legions of half people here in the world of life, and he would control their souls forever from the underworld."

"Are you sure that he wasn't the Keeper himself brought to life?" Samantha asked, sarcastically, as she folded her arms.

"He was just a man," Richard said. "A man like so many others who in one way or another, whether they have been aware of it or not, have been devoted to death.

"I guess he was simply more shameless about it than most madmen. Naja says, in fact, that he believed the act of bringing death to so many and on such a grand scale was a transcendent experience."

Samantha threw up her hands. "This sounds so deluded that I can't even fathom it. But the thing that really confuses me is why people would believe in such a madman and fight for his crazy cause. I mean, I'm not even grown up yet, and I can see that this is lunacy."

Richard turned from the account on the wall. "There are plenty of people drawn to such a way of life. Following such a leader gives them license to be savages themselves, to be an anonymous thug and take what they have been told they are entitled to. Some people find it intoxicating to have the power and permission to destroy others.

"But that's really beside the point. The point is that Sulachan was powerful enough to bring about immense destruction and loss of life. Even if he was deluded and his ideas were crazy, he, his gifted, and his vast, rampaging armies had the might to bring the world under the darkness of a great war.

"Fortunately, Naja and the people back then seem

to have been able to at least create this barrier and contain some of the most menacing creations of his makers. It has protected the world for a very long time.

"But those half people in the third kingdom, locked away for so long behind the barrier, have over the centuries likely continued growing in numbers. Now they are loose in the world of life. They are now again a problem."

Samantha, looking more than a little bitter, folded her arms. "You mean they're our problem."

"Our problem," Richard agreed with a nod. "All that really matters now is that the creations of Sulachan's wizards in those ancient times have now once again been unleashed against the world. If we don't figure out how to stop them, then we will be the ones who are wiped out."

28

Samantha paced in nervous agitation while Richard read ahead in Naja's account on the wall. He could sense the anguish in that account by the way the mysterious woman from so long ago went to great pains to ensure that future generations would understand the reasons behind the fears of the people back in her time and their horror at what had descended on them at the hands of so evil a man.

They knew that life for the people of the New World would become one long dark night of terror if the half people were not stopped or somehow contained. It was obvious that she wanted to make sure that all those who came after her would also appreciate the danger that was locked away behind the barrier.

"Dear spirits," he murmured to himself.

"What?" she asked, having heard the comment he hadn't realized he'd said aloud.

Richard took a deep breath at the description of the grim specifics. "Well, Naja says here that the half people began hunting for souls to replace the one they no longer had."

Samantha paused in her pacing and turned back to him. "Hunting for souls? What is she talking about?"

Richard squinted in concentration, making sure of the translation before he went on with the account. "According to this, not having a soul drove the half people into a form of insanity that compelled them to hunt those who did have a soul in the hopes of taking that soul for themselves."

Richard abruptly paused in surprise.

"And . . . ?" Samantha asked when he fell silent.

"And . . . they ate any living people they could catch in an attempt to take possession of their soul. Such an effort was futile, according to Naja, but that didn't stop the half people from continuing to try."

Samantha rushed closer. "They eat living people? Are you sure that's what it says?"

Richard nodded. "It was an unintended consequence of the process used in creating the half people. The unanticipated behavior developed suddenly, Naja says, not long after they were stripped of their souls to make them into these living weapons for Sulachan. They unexpectedly became so compelled by a deranged need for a soul to replace the one they had lost that it overrode everything else. Although they had been created as weapons, they became uncontrollable. Despite all the efforts by the wizards who had been in charge, the half people were driven by a frenzied need for a soul.

"Driven by this mad, single-minded lust to consume the living, they can't comprehend that this thirst for a soul is impossible to quench. She says they would hunt alone but often they would congregate in order to coordinate a more effective attack on the living."

"You mean they started hunting in numbers? Like packs of wolves?"

"So it would appear," Richard told her. "Naja says

that at first they rampaged out of control, in the beginning attacking those who had created them and then the troops they had been assigned to serve with before escaping out into the population at large. The half people tore through the ranks of makers who had created them. The wizard makers who hadn't been eaten were terrified of their own creation. Many fled.

"For a time, they had no way of stopping them. For a time, the half people owned the night. People quickly learned to lock themselves inside once the sun went down and hope those without souls didn't come for them in large numbers.

"Fearful whispers called these demonic hunters of souls the unholy half dead."

"Unholy half dead. That sounds like a pretty good description of them to me," Samantha said.

Richard agreed. "Naja says that Sulachan's makers were eventually able to come up with a solution. They modified the magic they had used to create them and directed this need to kill against their enemies—the people here in the New World."

"Against us?" Samantha asked in alarm.

Richard nodded. "I'm afraid so. She says that the half people, although no stronger than a normal person and nowhere near as strong as the awakened dead, are more dangerous because they are quicker, but more importantly because they still have the ability to think like a predator and hunt those with souls.

"Although stripped of their higher reasoning functions, they learned to amass and attack in overpowering numbers. After the makers gained control and were able to modify the magic used create them, their savage nature and their ability to think was finally turned against Sulachan's enemies."

Richard was weary from the effort of translating

such complex symbols, but he couldn't afford to miss anything or to stop. He rubbed his eyes and went on reading.

When he was silent for a time, Samantha shook his sleeve. "What does it say? What are you reading? Speak it out loud."

Richard let out a deep sigh as he straightened. He gestured vaguely, dismissively, at the wall.

"There's no new information in this part. It's just some material describing how the half people kill their victims."

"I need to know," Samantha said when he fell silent. "They will come after our people, after me. Don't try to protect me by keeping me in the dark. It's no help to be ignorant of the truth. I need to know."

Richard glanced briefly to the determination in her eyes. He supposed that she was right. He gestured at the description.

"They tear people open, believing the soul they crave is inside. The half people often eat the victim's insides first because they think the soul resides in them. They drink the blood, fearing that the soul might escape by leaking away. When they aren't satisfied because they still haven't been able to get what they crave, they strip all the meat from the bones, devouring every bit of it in an attempt to find and consume the soul they think is hiding somewhere in the still-warm flesh.

"Groups of them will compete for scraps, each hoping to get the soul for themselves. They eat everything— muscle, blood, organs, even the face. They suck the brain out of the skull, or crush it with a rock to get at it. They leave only some of the bowels and the bones, but often crack open larger bones and devour the marrow, still trying to find the elusive soul."

Samantha looked dumbfounded. "How do they possibly think they can get a soul by eating people?"

"It's a madness that drives them. It doesn't make sense to us, but it does to them. They think that souls reside within a person or hide in bodily tissues. They're looking for that moment when the spirit departs the dying body. They think that at that moment they can devour it, pulling it into themselves for their own. So, they eat everything, hoping to get it while it is hiding in the body, before it can escape the warm flesh."

Samantha's eyes grew more liquid. "They are unholy demons."

"Soulless demons," Richard agreed. He gestured to the symbols as he went on. "Failure to gain the soul they seek only makes them more frantic, more enraged. The more they kill, the more they fail to be sated, the more obsessed they become to possess a soul.

"Naja says that the half people can sense the presence of a soul, the way a predator can smell blood."

Samantha grabbed his sleeve again and leaned in. "You mean they can use that ability to track and hunt people?"

Richard nodded. "Naja says that the half people are death itself, with teeth, coming for the living."

He had to pause to take a breath. The account was graphic and making him sick. He had only given her the highlights so that she would understand what they faced. He judged it enough.

Samantha, looking on the verge of tears, shook her head in horror. "Death with teeth, coming for the living," she said to herself. "That's what happened to my father, then. And maybe my mother. If they hadn't already eaten her alive when they caught her, they would have by now."

"We don't know that." Richard put a hand around the girl's small shoulders and hugged her against his side. "I'm sorry, Samantha, to have to read this to you."

She wiped her tears on her sleeve. "A kind lie would hardly serve me well. I'm the only gifted person left here. I need to know the truth of what my people face. I may be too young to really defend them, but I'm all they have." `

Richard understood how she felt. He was terrified for Zedd, Nicci, Cara, and the rest of them. He redoubled his focus on translating the account. Any time he might have left was quickly running out. But he needed to understand what they faced and then go find them.

Richard knew that with his gift corrupted and not working because of the touch of death in him, that meant that his bond to the people of D'Hara would not work. And if that bond didn't work, then Cara's Agiel, like Zedd's and Nicci's gift, would not work. Like the rest of them, she was virtually defenseless.

"This is disturbing," Richard told Samantha. "Naja says that when the emperor's makers created the half people, their spirits, once pulled from the victim, were not allowed to go to the spirit world. Because of how the spells to reanimate the dead worked, the spirits of those dead are pulled from their place in the underworld. Those spirits, both of the dead and of the half people, are thus kept trapped between realms.

"Unable to get to either the person they were pulled from or go through the veil into the underworld, these lost spirits sometimes drift back in this direction and end up haunting this plane of existence." Richard looked over at Samantha. "Naja says that not all of them who drift back into the world of life are friendly."

She made a sour face. "Great."

Richard could only imagine the vengeful anger of such lost spirits.

The account became more complex with some terms involving magic, both Subtractive and Additive, that Richard didn't understand. While there were elements describing conjuring that he had never seen before, he was able to grasp the general meaning of what Naja was explaining. And what she was explaining was frightening.

He scanned the next line of complex symbols twice before he was sure of what it said. He wished he weren't, but he was sure.

S o," Samantha prompted, "is that all of it?"

He thought she sounded like she was trying to be hopeful even though she knew better.

He wiped a hand across his eyes and read the last of Naja Moon's account, hoping to at last come to some word of the solutions to the problems of the half people and the reawakened dead. He was disheartened by what he found.

"She says that the best minds and most talented wizards of the New World were unable to come up with a way to eliminate the threat. She said that they fought the half people and the walking dead, often to victory, but even in victory they steadily lost valuable people. The Old World's losses were meaningless to them because there are vastly more people there. Besides that, they could reanimate as many dead as they needed— often the very enemy we had been able to kill—while the losses on our side were costly and continually drained strength and resources from the New World.

"She says they all knew that if something wasn't

soon done to end the threat, or to at least somehow contain it, the New World, and life itself, was going to lose the war to Sulachan's forces.

"Unable to come up with an effective counter or a way to destroy such a threat, she says they were desperate for a solution that could save them from annihilation as well as preserve the world of life. Eventually they came up with an answer that was not as much as they had hoped, but it was the best that they could do.

"She says that what the people here ended up doing was to use gravity spells that inexorably drew both the dead and the half people to this place beyond the mountains that we see out the portal. Once they had all been drawn in, the wizards in the New World were then able to seal these demons without souls behind a barrier of keeper spells."

"Gravity spells, keeper spells—I've never heard of any such magic."

"Me neither," Richard said. "Naja doesn't go into detail about the nature of those spells, but they seem pretty self-explanatory. She does say that in this way they were finally able to protect everyone from these demons without souls loose among the living.

"She then goes to great lengths to apologize on behalf of her people that they were forced to pass this terrible danger on to some unknown future generation, but there was nothing else they could do because otherwise Sulachan would have won the war and then there would be no future generations.

"She says that the best they could do was place the barrier and create a sentry village to watch over it and warn the wizards' council of the mortal danger if and when the barrier failed."

Richard tapped the next symbols. "This is alarming.

She says that hopefully by then, the wizards' council will have come up with a way to eliminate the threat once and for all."

"Well, we pretty much know that never happened," Samantha said. "And now there is no longer even a wizards' council."

"I'm afraid you're right. She implores people here to keep watch, for when that barrier finally fails those without souls will come for the living and the world of life itself will again be at risk."

Richard leaned in a bit, studying the next symbol. "She says that it's important to know that the half people will seek those with the gift."

"The gifted?" Samantha asked with a frown. "She said before that the gift doesn't work against these walking dead and the unholy half dead, so why would they bother to come after the gifted?"

Richard shook his head. "I don't know. She doesn't explain."

His anger boiled just beneath the surface thinking about what had happened to the First File troops and to his friends. He couldn't afford to wait any longer. He needed to know what he could learn from Naja's account, but time was running out.

Samantha was still frowning in thought. "Why would the half people want the gifted? I can see that in their madness they would want to steal a soul, crazy as that notion is, but why would they seek out the gifted?"

Richard sighed in frustration as he scanned the rows of symbols. "It doesn't say. Maybe they think the gifted have some way to give them souls." He glanced over at Samantha out of the corner of his eye. "Or maybe these half people, in their deranged obsession to possess a soul, think that there is something special about a gifted soul. Maybe they think it's easier to get, or maybe they even think that if they got a gifted soul, then besides having their soul they would also possess the gift."

Unable to fathom why the half people would seek out the gifted, Samantha leaned in closer, examining the symbols carved in the wall as if maybe by studying them more carefully she might somehow suddenly be able to read them. Unable to learn anything, she finally turned to Richard.

"Lord Rahl, are you sure of everything that you told me it says, here? That the half people really would eat people? That their souls and the souls of the awakened dead are really lost and left to wander between worlds? I mean, it's all pretty hard to believe."

"I know what it says, Samantha."

"But these"—she waved a hand at the wall—"these symbols all over the wall are pretty complicated. I don't doubt your knowledge of such things, Lord Rahl, but are you sure that you got the whole translation right?"

He scanned the symbols he had just finished translating for any little thing, any clue, he might have missed. While there were a few elements he wasn't completely positive about, they were minor points that didn't alter the meaning or essence of Naja's frightening story.

"I translated it accurately."

Samantha's nose wrinkled with a look of skepticism. "Isn't it possible, though, that you could have gotten some of it wrong? Or that maybe you misunderstood the intent of some of the things it says? Don't you think that with a language this old and strange and complicated that you might have interpreted at least some of it wrong?"

He looked down at her, wishing there were some legitimacy to her doubts. "What about the barrier being breached for the first time since it was put in place? And what about those wounds on me that you healed? They were bite wounds. Those two men, come from beyond that barrier, were trying to eat me alive, just as it is described here."

Her mouth twisted a little as she struggled with the idea of it. "But do you really think their intent was to steal your soul? Maybe they were cannibals from beyond the barrier. Maybe they have a famine there and they have to eat people to survive."

"They were both healthy, strong, and looked well fed. They weren't suffering from starvation. Just ask Ester if you doubt my memory. She was there, she saw them. The only thing they were hungry for was my soul.

"What I heard them talking about when I was waking up is still a bit fuzzy, but as I read what's written here about the barrier, some of the strange things I heard the two men saying started to make sense. They talked about eating me and taking my soul for themselves. Ester and the others arrived just in time to stop them and save my life."

Samantha pressed her lips tight in resignation. "Well, I'm glad they got there in time." She tipped her head toward the wall. "After all, you're the only one who knows how to read this. I guess you must have the translation right. I don't really doubt you, Lord Rahl, it's just that . . ."

"I know, I wish I was wrong about it, too," he said before going back to working the translation to the next part of Naja's account.

"It says here," he said after a moment's study, "that in the end, not knowing how to stop the single-minded attacks by Sulachan's unholy half dead, the only hope for survival had been to lock all of them behind the barrier spells."

Looking forlorn, Samantha hugged her arms to herself. "Lord Rahl, I'm not saying that you aren't translating it right, but could this all be a myth? Some kind of ancient legend they were passing down? A parable or lesson? Might that be all this is?"

Richard wished she was right, but knew she wasn't. He shook his head.

"When I started to wake up, I remember hearing those two men saying that they were going to take Kahlan with them because they were afraid that the Shun-tuk would return, looking for survivors. The men were going to eat me then and there, then eat Kahlan later, or trade her. They said that the Shun-tuk would do anything to get people with souls. Those men and the Shun-tuk came from beyond the barrier, not from legends recorded here."

He tapped a finger to a sequence of several symbols. "There can be no doubt that this has to be true. I wish it was otherwise, Samantha, but it's not."

She looked miserable, like she couldn't take any more such talk. "That's what they did to my father. They must have taken my mother to do that to her later, at their leisure, or else to trade her. I can't imagine her misery at what they did to my father, and her terror at what they were going to do to her."

Richard realized, then, why she had been so persistent about his translation being wrong. She had been hoping it was wrong for a very personal reason. He pulled her close in a gentle hug.

He had become so lost in trying to understand what was going on that he had started thinking of her as a sorceress, rather than a girl who had lost both her parents to this madness, a girl who was only now blossoming into a young woman and who until recently had not seen such terrible things.

"I'm sorry, Samantha. I understand. I saw bones of some of my friends as well. They took the others the way they took your mother. I know how you feel."

She wiped at her eyes. "No, I'm sorry. I can't let my weakness interfere with trying to find a way to stop those demons from coming for us all."

Richard cast a sideways look at the symbols on the wall, at the end of the account he had been reading on that very subject.

"I don't know if that's possible."

She looked up, tears still brimming in her eyes. "What do you mean?"

Richard turned back to the language of Creation on the wall, putting aside his feelings before going on with the account. He knew that time was working against him.

"It says that they, too, were seeking a way to protect people of the New World and end the threat. Despite the best efforts of their wizards and hard work of other gifted people, they were never able to find a way to end the threat. Part of the reason was because Emperor Sulachan's minions had been given otherworldly powers against which we had no defense."

"What kind of otherworldly powers? Does she say?"

Richard nodded. "She says that the unholy half dead

are able to use some kind of occult magic which was very ancient, very rare, and very powerful. It was widely feared because it was so little understood. She says that not only are the unholy half dead protected by these dark forces, some of them were even able to use this ability to awaken the dead.

"Naja says that in the end all those on our side were able to do for the time being was to seal the threat away behind the barrier. Short of doing that, she says that the people of the New World would have been slaughtered.

"She warns that one day the barrier would weaken and fail. She says that once the threat eventually breaks through that barrier, there is only one way to stop it from ravaging the world of life."

Samantha stepped closer. "There's a way?"

Richard nodded, still staring at what it said on the wall. He worked the symbols again, hoping he was wrong. He wasn't.

"Well, what is it, then?" Samantha tugged on his shirt. "Lord Rahl, what does it say? How do we stop them?"

Richard cleared his throat.

"It says 'The threat from the third kingdom can be ended only by ending prophecy.'"

31

Samantha's eyes darted around in confusion. "Stop the threat by ending prophecy? What are they talking about? How can prophecy be ended?"

Richard, more troubled than ever by what he was reading, traced a circular symbol containing a complex maze of twisting, supporting elements radiating out from the center.

"This circular symbol here, where she says that ending the third kingdom can only be done by ending prophecy, is some kind of time element, but I can't quite figure out its context."

"Time element? I don't understand. What do you mean, time element?"

Richard looked back through all the supporting designs and then the devices coming from the center of the primary symbol as he tried to think of how to put the concepts he was seeing into words. There were parts that made no sense to him, and other parts that had no direct translation.

"I'm not exactly sure what Naja is saying here in this part. It's not that I can't translate it accurately, it's that she is obviously familiar with the concept and I'm not. Because of that, it isn't clear enough for me to fully understand the precise meaning of the things she's talking about."

"What kind of thing is she talking about? Do you understand that much of it?"

"To an extent. I understand the words, but not what they mean. It's some kind of representation having to do with time that I'm not familiar with. She calls it the Twilight Count."

"The Twilight Count?" Samantha considered for a moment. "Like counting days? Keeping track? Is that what she means?"

"I think so," he said. "But it seems to be more than that. It seems to be some kind of formal calculation I don't recognize."

"Do you think it could be a calendar or something? Calendars have to do with counting time. All the things on calendar calculations—like the moons phases, star positions in different seasons, things like that—can get complicated to calculate into the future."

Richard pressed his lips tight for a moment as he tried to make sense of it.

"That's true enough, but I'm not sure if that's what she is referring to in this case. Since it's some kind of computation involving counting, you might be right, but it's hard for me to say for sure because she doesn't explain it. People back then must have been familiar with the term, so she didn't feel the need to explain it. She merely calls it the Twilight Count.

"It's also possible that it has to do with the chronology of prophecy."

Samantha frowned as she considered. "Chronology of prophecy? What do you mean? Prophecy is prophecy, isn't it?"

"Well yes, sort of." Richard looked up from studying the symbols. "Most people don't realize that chronology is always one of the great difficulties of understanding prophecy. It's hard to tell if a particular prophecy is about an event that will happen tomorrow, or a thousand years from tomorrow, or even if it may have already happened two hundred years in the past."

Samantha was hanging on his every word. "That complicates matters."

Richard nodded and gestured to the wall. "Since these symbols in Naja's account have to do with time, or more accurately with counting time, and it mentions it in conjunction with prophecy, it could be that the Twilight Count is a forgotten way of determining prophetic events in the flow of time."

Samantha looked at the wall with newfound interest. "So what does it say about this Twilight Count?"

"Naja says that they were able to determine by the Twilight Count that prophecy holds the key to stopping the threat."

"I thought you said that prophecy had to be ended."

Richard raked his fingers back through his hair as he tried to make sense of what came next, and even more than that, how to explain it to her. It was a difficult combination of symbology to decipher. Some of the elements seemed strangely familiar, but he couldn't place them.

"I did, but then it goes on to explain, here, that ending prophecy can only be accomplished by bringing death."

Richard frowned as he stared at the unusual network of symbols with a strangely shaped figure nine at the center. It was similar to a hooked nine he had seen before.

It suddenly came to him.

"No, wait, that's not exactly what it says."

"So what, exactly, does it say, then?" Samantha asked with exaggerated patience after he had fallen silent for a time.

Richard touched his fingers to his forehead. He suddenly felt hot and a little dizzy.

"It doesn't say that ending prophecy can only be accomplished by bringing death."

He stepped back from the wall and stared.

"It says that ending prophecy can only be accomplished by *the bringer of death*."

Samantha's brow lifted. "The bringer of death? What does that mean?"

"*Fuer grissa ost drauka*," Richard whispered.

Samantha's nose wrinkled. "What?"

Richard was still staring at the grim symbol, lost in a rush of tumbling thoughts. Now that he remembered some of the elements and had fit the pieces together, there could be no doubt about how it translated.

"It's High D'Haran. *Fuer grissa ost drauka* means 'the bringer of death.' That's who Naja is talking about."

"You mean that this bringer of death has to end prophecy if we are to have any hope of survival?"

"Yes."

Samantha watched him for a time as he scanned the symbols carved into the wall. "Do you know who that is? Do you know where we can find this bringer of death?"

Richard nodded slowly, transfixed by the symbolic, hooked, serpent figure nine. He tapped his chest.

"It's me. Ancient prophecies have named me *fuer grissa ost drauka*. I am the bringer of death."

Richard could not help thinking that he now carried death in him. In more ways than he could have ever envisioned, he was *fuer grissa ost drauka*.

32

"You're the bringer of death?" Samantha looked up at him from under her brow. "You're the one who is supposed to end prophecy? Are they serious?"

Richard was still staring at the symbols, certain at last that he understood their meaning. There could be no doubt as to the translation.

"That's what it says."

There had been a time when he would have been rattled to read what others thought he was or what they thought he needed to do, was destined to do, or must accomplish. But such things had often turned out to be quite different than they sounded at first, so his response to such news was more tempered than it once might have been.

But still, what he saw written on the wall in the language of Creation, the same language used by the ancient omen machine he had discovered buried deep within the People's Palace, was more than a little troubling.

Samantha paced off a short distance, considering.

She returned to stand close beside him. The contentious sorceress in her, young as it was, was coming to the surface.

"How in the world can prophecy be ended?—And how are you supposed to do such a thing? Did Naja say?"

Richard shook his head. "Naja says only that they had a great many remarkably talented wizards working feverishly on a way to eliminate the threat of the half people and the walking dead. But the magic the enemy used was too strong and they didn't understand it well enough to know how to counter it. There was, however, no doubt as to how dangerous it was.

"She says that if they knew how to bring an end to the menace, they would have done so. Since they didn't have a solution or access to the one named in prophecy as the bringer of death—or even know how to find him—in the end all they could do was build a barrier to contain these conjured weapons until such time as the wizards' council was able to come up with a solution or the bringer of death arrived to do what was necessary.

"She goes on to say that the terrible task of actually eliminating the threat presented by such conjured weapons would unfortunately have to be left to those who will one day again face them when the barrier eventually fails. It will be up to them when the time comes, she says, up to the bringer of death, to find a way to finally eliminate this evil."

"How could they know that such a thing was possible—you know, that prophecy really could be ended? Where would they come up with such a notion? What makes them believe this is the answer? What makes them so sure of it?"

Richard put a finger to the smooth wall, following

along as he translated the complex symbols and designs cut into the stone so that he could relate the gist of it to Samantha.

"Explaining that part of it wasn't her purpose in writing this account. However she does mention in passing that they know it's possible from information that predates the star shift."

Samantha was staring at him again. "What's a star shift?"

"I haven't the slightest idea."

"But you have to know."

Richard glanced back down at her. "Why do I have to know?"

"You're Lord Rahl. You are the magic against magic." She wagged a finger at the symbols he had just translated. "You said yourself that it names you as the one, just as I have known all along that you are the one. So you must know."

Richard sighed. "I wish it were so, Samantha, but I'm afraid it isn't."

"Lord Rahl," she said, again with the sort of serious intensity that could only be summoned by a sorceress, "do you think that what Naja really means, that what she is really saying here, is that he—you—can only destroy the half people and the awakened dead by destroying the world of life itself? You know, by bringing death to everyone and everything? Do you think she is saying that you are the one, the bringer of death, who is meant to end the world of life?"

Richard scratched his temple as he glanced over at her out of the corner of his eye. "She said end prophecy, not life itself."

"Maybe she was afraid to say it out loud." Samantha gestured at the wall. "You know what I mean, say it in writing.

"After all, prophecy is about the future, right? So saying that prophecy must be ended is like saying that the future has to be ended, don't you suppose? How can there be life if there is no future? If there is no future—if the bringer of death cuts off the future—then life ends.

"As you explained before, the world of life is about time. If there is no future, then time stops, doesn't it? And if time stops, then the world of life stops."

Richard stared at her for a long moment. "What you say makes a certain amount of sense, I'll give you that."

"So then, we're all dead? Sulachan's mad scheme is finally coming to fruition to end the world of life. And it is to be by your hand?"

Richard squatted down and gently grasped her delicate shoulders as he smiled a bit of reassurance.

"While what you say makes some sense, there's more to it."

"More to it? From what Naja is saying, one way or another, the future, time, and therefore life itself are soon going to end. It seems to me pretty clear that we've all run out of time. What more can there be to it?"

"Well, for one thing, this is tied into prophecy and prophecy rarely turns out to be anything at all like it seems when you read it. I've seen the most dire predictions turn out to be insignificant events that only sounded important. On the other hand, I've seen harmless-sounding prophecy take us all to the brink of destruction.

"Some of the most troubling prophecy of all time have turned out to exist on false forks, with the critical event creating the fork safely passed centuries before without anyone knowing it. It turned out in those cases that a great many people, many of them gifted, had worried their entire lives over something that was actually a long-dead fork in prophecy. This could be one of those. In the past, while people worried about such dire-sounding warnings, prophecy that didn't sound like any cause for concern in fact turned out to be the real trouble."

"How does that help us, here, now?"

"What I'm trying to explain is that it's a mistake to base your fears and decisions on prophecy. Naja is talking about a prophecy. Prophecy almost never turns out to be anything at all like it sounds."

"How can that be? It sounds so clear."

"Well, for example, what if a prophecy said that if you go out tomorrow you will get wet. Does that sound profoundly dangerous. Would you worry about it?"

Samantha shrugged. "No, not really."

"What if it turns out that the true meaning is if you go out, someone will cut your throat and your clothes will get wet because they will get soaked with your own blood?"

Her hands reflexively went to her throat. "Oh. I see what you mean."

"People commonly believe that written prophecy is the prophecy, but it's not."

"It's not? I thought prophecy was prophecy."

"Prophecy is intended for future prophets to grasp through visions triggered by the words. The written words are not the actual prophecy. They are a kind of catalyst intended for other prophets. Frequently, the words deliberately veil the truth behind a prophecy. Because prophets aren't common anymore, a true understanding of prophecy has for the most part been lost."

Samantha let out a deep sigh. "I never knew it was so complicated. I guess I kind of see what you mean, but I don't see how we're not supposed to worry about the bringer of death ending prophecy. That sounds pretty clear to me."

"Just because it sounds clear, doesn't mean it really is. I've learned not to be guided by prophecy or the fear of it. It's better to make rational choices and prophecy is just one of many things that has to be taken into consideration. People not schooled in prophecy often fall into the trap of thinking it's perfectly clear so they let it guide them. Your mother was right to teach you not to pay a great deal of attention to it."

"But it must be important sometimes." She gestured to the wall. "After all, Naja went to all the trouble to warn us about the barrier and what was beyond it. They apparently placed Stroyza here for us to be sentinels to watch the barrier. Her warnings all come down to this prophecy—and they had plenty of prophets back in her time. The prophets back then must have known it was important or they wouldn't stake so much on putting this message here about ending prophecy."

Richard glanced over at the expanse of writing again. "You may have a point, but it could also mean something entirely different that we don't yet understand. After all, the prophecy itself is not here, only a fragment of it."

Samantha's mouth twisted. "I don't know, Lord Rahl. This sounds like it means for us—for you—to do something about what is beyond the barrier that is now breached."

Richard stood, facing the wall as he rested the palm of his left hand on the pommel of his sword. His gaze swept over the ancient symbols carefully incised in the stone of the wall.

"That's true enough. That much of it doesn't necessarily have anything to do with prophecy, but with the threat."

"But you said yourself that prophecy named you the bringer of death." Samantha flung her arms up in frustration. "I'm sorry, Lord Rahl, but I don't understand. The whole thing doesn't make a lot of sense to me."

Richard nodded. "I know. But often the truth is complicated. That's why so many people get in trouble with both the truth and with prophecy."

"Then what are we to think of Naja's account? I mean, parts of it, like the part about ending prophecy, are pretty confusing to me. But those corpses who came in here and killed so many people are all too real." She pointed toward light coming from the opening. "That's what matters most. I'm not sure about all the things that happened back in Naja's time, but I know what's happening now. Does all this help us or not? What are we to do about it? What are you going to do about the barrier being breached and about ending prophecy?"

Richard's gaze scanned across Naja Moon's account of that ancient war before he went to the opening overlooking the barrier standing before the third kingdom, a barrier that had stood for near to three thousand years, holding back an unspeakable evil. A barrier that had now been breached.

"I'm going to do what I thought I would never have to do again."

"What would that be?" she asked as she watched him glaring silently out into the murky morning light.

Richard lifted his sword a few inches to make sure it was clear and then let it drop back into its scabbard.

"I'm going to war."

"Going to war?"

"Yes, with a madman who has been dead for three thousand years," Richard said as he marched away.

33

Samantha hurried to catch up with him. "What do you mean you're going to war?"

Richard, his mind lost in a jumble of thoughts, started back through the corridor the way they had come in. Samantha was right on his heels by the time he reached the opening with the round stone that had been blocking the passage on the way in, but now stood open.

"Shut this," he said as he marched through without pause.

Samantha growled, slapped the metal plate, and then rushed to catch back up with him. Richard could hear the stone grinding across the floor as it slowly rolled back in front of the opening to block off the corridor to the portal for viewing the ancient barrier to the third kingdom.

Samantha grabbed his wrist and dragged him to a halt. "Lord Rahl, what do you mean you're going to war?"

"I've read everything Naja wanted us to know. There is still a lot I don't understand, but the one thing that's clear is that if we have any time left, it's rapidly running out—for everyone. I have to do something to stop what is happening, and I have to do it now or it will soon be too late."

"Like what?" Samantha sounded as exasperated as she looked. "What are you going to do? What can you hope to do?"

Her voice echoed back from the distance through the simple stone corridor. What she meant, but didn't say, was what could he possibly hope to do without the help of his gift. He didn't have an answer to that unspoken question. He only knew that he had to stop what was coming after them all.

He had not told Samantha all the gruesome details written on the wall. He had wanted to spare her the anguish of some of Naja's words. But those words echoed in his own mind and he knew the ghastly extent of what the people back in the time of the first Confessor had faced and what the world of life now faced again.

Samantha's black hair looked even darker in the spectral glow of the light sphere she was holding. "Lord Rahl, answer me. What are you going to do?"

Richard clenched his jaw a moment before answering.

"I have to go in there."

"Go in there?" She leaned toward him with urgency. "Go in where?"

Richard flicked a hand back in the direction of the portal looking out over a barrier that had for thousands of years held back an unspeakable evil.

"I have to go in there, to the third kingdom. Knowing, now, what's beyond that barrier, I fully expect that I will have to fight a war to do it."

She snatched a quick look back the way they had come. "Go into the third kingdom? Are you crazy?"

"It's the only thing I can do, the only answer I can come up with."

"Answer? Answer to what? How to get yourself killed?"

Richard ignored the sarcasm as he started out again. "No, the answer to how to stay alive, how to keep us all alive."

"Lord Rahl," she said, her mass of black hair bouncing softly as she jogged along beside him, "you can't go in there."

He tapped his chest. "What do I have in me?" he asked without slowing.

Samantha pushed some of her hair back out of her face. "In you? You mean that touch of death?"

"That's right."

"What of it?"

"You can't remove that touch of death from me or Kahlan." Richard glanced down at the concern on her face. "If we don't rid ourselves of this link to the world of the dead, then it will claim us both. You said yourself that Kahlan didn't have much time, and I have precious little more than she does."

"I still don't think—"

Not in the mood to argue, he jabbed a finger toward her. "You're the one who told me that I would soon start getting as sick as she is. You know very well that once I get to that point, I won't be able to do anything to help myself, much less anyone else. Would you have me lie down and wait for death?"

She rushed along beside him in silence as they made their way back through the hauntingly empty tunnel.

Richard came to a halt in front of the doorway closed off by the first shielded stone they had passed on their way in.

"Open this, will you?" he said as he flicked a hand

toward the metal plate on the wall. "My gift doesn't work, remember?"

"I remember." Samantha grumbled as she moved close to slap the flat of her hand to the metal plate. "Which is why it's crazy for you to go in there."

Richard snatched her wrist, stopping her before she could touch the metal plate. He thought he saw some hint, some glimmer, of something in the center of the stone.

"Wait," he said.

She frowned up at the stone and then him. "Wait for what?"

Instead of answering, Richard reached out and pressed the flat of his hand to the metal plate. The massive stone shielding the doorway did not move, but in the center of the round stone, where he thought he'd seen something glimmer, stone dust started to crumble away. Powdery silt poured out of incised lines in the center of the stone. It was as if from centuries of rolling back and forth into the slot in the side wall, the engraved lines had become packed with dirt and dusty, crushed stone. Only now, as it spilled out, did the engraved symbols reappear.

"Would you look at that," Samantha whispered in amazement.

There, linked in a circle in the center of the stone blocking their way out, was a small triangular assemblage of symbols in the language of Creation. The three emblems formed a complex message. Richard squinted at the small designs as he worked the translation.

The first of the three emblems said, *If you are reading this it is because you are the bringer of death and the barrier has been breached. What we could not stop you now face. War is upon you.*

The second of the three emblems said, *Know that*

you are the only chance life has, now. Know, too, that you are balanced between life and death. You have the potential to be the one to save the world of life or end it. You are not destined for anything. You make your own destiny.

The third of the three emblems said, *Know that you have within you what you need to survive. Use it. Seek the truth. Know that our hearts are with you. Make your own destiny and make it true, for life hangs in the balance. We leave you a reminder to keep with you, of all that is important.*

Richard felt an icy chill run across his skin when he saw that it was signed Magda Searus, Mother Confessor, and Wizard Merritt.

They had been speaking to him personally. He half expected to see his own name engraved in the stone.

He stared for a long moment at the symbols, at the names. He had read a number of ancient texts and accounts. This was the only thing he had ever seen from the very first Confessor.

He touched the name, imagining the time so long ago when she must have stood in this very spot as they engraved the words meant for him. His fingers on that name felt like a connection from Magda, across the ages.

Perhaps more than anyone alive, Richard understood what it meant for a woman to be a Confessor. His life was devoted to a Confessor, as had been Merritt's. Richard knew precious little about the legendary figure of Magda Searus, but he knew Kahlan, and so in that way he knew Magda. In a way, by loving Kahlan he knew Merritt. In that way, he felt a personal connection to Magda, and to Merritt.

As his fingers brushed the names in stone, he looked again at the words saying they left him a reminder.

His fingers drifted to the center between the three

symbols, where there was a slight depression. He rubbed with his fingers and the stone dust there began to fall away until it revealed that underneath there was a piece of ancient leather tightly stuffed into a hole in the stone.

He pulled the leather out and opened it in his palm. There, in the center, rested a ring. He and Samantha stared at the silver ring. On the top face of the ring was a Grace. It looked like a ring used for sealing wax on messages.

The message they had sent him was the ring itself. It was a Grace he was to wear to always remind him of what was at stake. He slipped it onto the ring finger of his right hand, the hand he used with the sword. It fit perfectly.

Samantha gave him a look that said more than words could. She was as amazed as he. She knew well the importance of the Grace.

When Richard gestured at last, Samantha pressed her palm to the metal plate and the rock rumbled aside to allow them to pass. Once through, she touched the plate on the other side to shield the doorway.

Samantha didn't ask to have the message translated. She must have sensed by the look on his face and his silence that the words were for him and no one else.

When he hadn't said anything for a time as they swiftly made their way through the passageway, she couldn't remain silent any longer. "So, have you finally come to your senses and realized that you can't really go in there?"

"Look, Samantha," he said, "you know as well as I do that you can't get that deadly touch of the Hedge Maid out of me—only my friends can do that. The only way to save myself and Kahlan, and in turn hope to help everyone else, is to get my friends out of the hands of the Shun-tuk and then get us back to the containment field at the People's Palace. After they do cure us, then I can work to figure out how to put an end to the threat from the third kingdom before it's too late. Simple as that."

"Simple as that? And what if Zedd and Nicci and all the others are dead?"

"Then I'll soon be dead, too, and soon after that so will everyone else. I need Zedd and Nicci. If there is a chance they're alive, then I have to try to find them."

"But, but it's a land filled with half people and walking dead. And who knows what other unholy monsters might be in the third kingdom. It's too dangerous."

"I'm the one, remember?"

"Yes, which is exactly why you can't go there. We all need you!"

"What's your plan, then?" He looked down at her. "Hm? How are we going to stop the half people and the dead armies that have come back to life? Without a cure I'll soon be dead so you'll have to fight them alone. So, what's your plan?"

She pressed her lips tight for a moment. "Well," she finally said, "I guess, there's good reason you're the Lord Rahl. But I still don't like your plan to go in there."

"I don't much like it myself, but I can't help anyone if I'm dead, now can I? Basically, that is what the message back there on the stone door said. It was a message to me, saying that I'm the bringer of death and war is now up to me. I'm a war wizard. This is what I have to do, what only I can do."

"A war wizard without his gift," she reminded him.

When he didn't answer, Samantha sighed in frustration as she replaced the glowing light sphere in the iron bracket on the wall and followed him out of the hallway into the room where Kahlan lay on the mat. There was no one else in the quiet room.

Richard knelt down beside Kahlan, watching her slow but steady breathing. Every time he looked at her he was struck by how beautiful she was. Since the first time he had seen her, he had known that she was the one. Seeing her face always lifted his heart.

She was the one. The only one for him. The last one of her kind. He was going to find a way to help save her life.

Samantha had told him that with some of her injuries healed, and her resting and recovering after the healing, she should soon wake up. The main problem would remain, but she would regain consciousness and at least no longer suffer from all the injuries and blood loss at the hands of the Hedge Maid.

Richard pressed his hand to Kahlan's forehead. He was relieved to feel that while she was warm, she was not burning up with fever. That was a good sign, he told himself, a sign that she would hopefully wake soon. But he didn't know how long that would take and time was working against him.

If Zedd and Nicci had been killed by the half people who had captured them, then there could be no hope for Kahlan, for him, or for anyone else. Magda Searus had said that he could save the world of life. Or end it.

"I don't have any time to waste," he said in a voice now calmer in the presence of the person he loved more than life itself. "I have to go."

Samantha sighed unhappily. She considered quietly for a moment before speaking.

"I wish I had some other answer, Lord Rahl. I hate to say it, but I think you may be right."

"I know I'm right."

His decision final that he had to go into the third kingdom to look for Zedd, Nicci, and the others, Richard turned his attention to Kahlan, checking to make sure that all of her wounds looked properly healed. Samantha lit a few more of the candles so he could see better and then watched him in silence as he touched her cheek, silently asking the good spirits to watch over her.

"I'll need some traveling supplies," he told her as he smoothed back Kahlan's hair. "Maybe you could get some things together for me?"

Samantha nodded. "All right. I can get us some supplies. I'll put together some of the things we'll need for such a journey."

Richard looked up. "Just supplies for me, Samantha. You're not going."

"Yes, I am," she said in a calm voice laced with iron determination.

"It's too dangerous. You said so yourself."

"I know it's dangerous. That's why I have to go with you."

"If it's too dangerous for me, then it is definitely too dangerous for you. You don't know anything about dealing with such dangers."

"I was dealing just fine with those walking corpses that were after me," she said under her breath as she went to a chest across the room and opened the lid.

Richard didn't want to argue the point. He turned his attention once more to Kahlan, wishing she would wake before he left. He had so much to tell her. She had no idea of all the things that had happened. The last thing she probably remembered was being Jit's captive, being bound into those thorn walls, and being bled to death. She wouldn't know about Zedd, Nicci, and Cara coming to help get them out. She wouldn't have any idea about the mysterious people who had attacked them and been intent on eating her alive.

He didn't want to leave her when she was in the dark about everything that had happened. He especially didn't want to leave her in the dark about where he was going and why. She was also defenseless against such an enemy. But waiting for her to wake up would in reality only further endanger her life. His first duty was to find a way to get the vile contamination of death out of her. To do that, he had to find Zedd and Nicci.

"Your gift doesn't work," Samantha said as she rummaged through the contents of the chest. "My gift works. You'll need me to go with you."

"I have my sword."

"Good for you. You still don't have the use of your gift." She pulled out a small backpack, then gestured to the hallway at the back of the room. "You couldn't even get past a shield without me. What are you going to do if you need some kind of simple magic like that? I may be young and inexperienced, and I admit that I have a lot yet to learn, but at least my gift works."

Richard knew that she had no real concept of the danger she would be facing and he didn't have time to explain it to her.

"I appreciate the concern, but it would only make it more difficult if I were to take you with me. I've fought a lot of battles before without my gift helping me. I'll be fine."

She flipped open the flap on the pack, checking the contents still inside. "There are things I can do with my ability, things my mother taught me that I know how to do, that you can't do and may need done. After all, I healed you of those terrible bite wounds, didn't I?"

"Indeed you did," Richard admitted. He was grateful that Samantha had been brave enough to do what she had been so fearful of in order to save Kahlan's life—his, too. "And I deeply appreciate it. But this is different."

Bending over the chest, digging something out, she looked back over her shoulder at him. "I thought your plan was crazy, but you convinced me that it's vital that you go in there to try to rescue your friends." She pulled a knife in a sheath out of the chest, looked it over a moment, and then put it into the pack. "You convinced me that all our lives may depend on this. You were right.

"So if it's really that vital, which it is, then I have to go along so that I can help make sure you succeed." She glanced down into the chest. "Do you think we need to take soap?" She snatched it up and stuffed it into the pack. "Never mind, I had better take it."

"Samantha, it's simply too dangerous for you to come with me," he said with calm finality. He was worried about Kahlan and wanted to be on his way to get help for her. Samantha would only slow him down.

He was not in the mood to argue, but he hoped to make Samantha at least understand that he had good reason not to let her come along on such a journey. "You could easily be killed. I could never forgive myself if I let you go with me and something terrible happened to you."

She shot him an impatient look. "If you don't accomplish what you are going in there to do, Lord Rahl, then you will die, and if you die, then the Mother Confessor dies, I die, we all die. You said so yourself. You're putting my safety ahead of saving the Mother Confessor, ahead of saving everyone.

"I can help you and you may need my help. I may be able to use my gift to get you out of trouble. That may be the edge you need in order to rescue your friends and succeed.

"Even if it costs me my life, anything I do that helps you might very well be the very help needed to save all the people of my village, along with everyone else. Stop worrying about one young woman and start worrying about how important it is for you to succeed. Think of all those words you read back there, and how important this is.

"You're a pretty smart man. You should be able to see the sense in what I'm saying."

Richard started to object. Samantha held up a finger to silence him before he could answer.

"Are you really going to turn down gifted help? That's your plan? Do without what could make the difference?"

"My plan is to move swiftly, strike fast, and get out. You would slow me down."

She arched an admonishing eyebrow. "And if you break a leg in a badger hole while moving swiftly, who is going to help you? I'm going with you, Lord Rahl, and that's all there is to it."

Richard let out a long sigh. "You make a lot of sense,

Samantha, you really do, but I know a lot more about these kinds of things than you. I've fought for years in the war with the Old World. You've never had to face anything remotely like the dangers out there."

"Those dangers came here, into my home, looking for me, remember?" She shrugged with one shoulder as she looked away from his eyes. "Not only that, but my mother may be held captive with your friends. You said so yourself. If there is any way for me to help rescue her, too, then I want to go to make sure we get her away from those unholy cannibals."

Richard had thought that might have had something to do with it. "I know how you feel. I really do. I promise you that if she is being held captive, I will fight to get her safely out the same as I will fight to get my people out. But I'll handle it. I can't allow you to come along."

She stood and faced him.

"All right. You are the Lord Rahl. You do what you think best." She planted her small hands on her narrow hips and cocked her head with a serious look. "But you know, of course, that if you don't let me go with you, I will simply follow you. You can't stop me from following you. Being separated like that, each of us alone rather than traveling together, will only be more dangerous for both of us. It would be better if we were to travel together. You could do what you can to protect me that way, and in turn I could do what I can to protect you.

"But one way or another, with you, or following in your footsteps, I'm going. That's all there is to it."

Richard pressed his lips tight as he appraised the determination in her dark eyes.

"You are one stubborn little girl."

"Not a girl," she said with conviction. "Samantha, sorceress serving the Lord Rahl."

Richard couldn't help but to smile. "So you are.

Well, I guess you give me no choice in the matter, and what you say does have some good points." He shook his head to himself. "All right, I'll take you with me."

Samantha smiled. "You won't be sorry, Lord Rahl."

"I hope not, and I hope you won't be sorry. Let's hurry and get supplies together for the two of us, then. And I want someone to watch over Kahlan while we're gone."

"Ester will watch her."

Richard nodded. "Why don't you go get her. Before we leave, we need to tell Ester a little bit of what we learned so that she can warn the others and then tell Kahlan when she wakes."

I'll get Ester," Samantha said on the way across the room. She turned back from the doorway, looking a bit suspicious. "Don't forget, if you leave without me, I will simply follow you. I hope you know better than to try to trick me."

"I told you that you could come with me," Richard said in an earnest tone. "I keep my word."

"All right, then." She looked just a bit sheepish for floating the accusation.

He didn't want to put her young, inexperienced life in such terrible jeopardy, but he knew that she was right about her potential value to him. With the touch of death lurking within him, he didn't know how long it would be before it might start to become a real problem that could slow him down. If he didn't succeed, then everyone was going to be at the mercy of whatever could now escape from the third kingdom.

He could already feel the drag of that sickness making him feel unusually drained and weary. He could feel himself being inexorably drawn toward the darkness of death within. The inevitability of dying had always existed in the background of his mind, but it was a distant reality that most of the time went unnoticed. Now, death felt close, and coldly real.

In a way, that darkness trying to draw him in was beginning to feel appealing, inviting him to cross the veil of life into the unfeeling eternity of nothingness. It offered the comforting release of all effort, all cares, all fears.

Richard might very well need Samantha's help before their journey was over. Even if she was a small help, it might be enough to make a difference.

Richard remembered his grandfather once telling him that wizards had to use people. He didn't like the feeling that he was using Samantha, even though he knew she was willing, and even if she was not really giving him a choice. He knew in his own mind that it was really by his choice, not hers, and that she very well might lose her life on such a dangerous journey. They both might.

"I'll need a pack as well," he told her. "I don't have any supplies with me. Most everything I had, except my sword, was in the wagon." He checked in his pocket. "Wait, I've got a flint and steel for starting a fire, at least."

Samantha nodded. "I'll tell the men that we need just about everything else, then."

"We need traveling food so that we don't have to spend a lot of time hunting for something to eat, but we should have some small items in case we do need to hunt. Some line and fishhooks, things like that. If someone has a bow, that would be a big help as well."

"I'm sure that one of the men would be honored to provide a bow and arrows to help in the effort of stopping the threat. We have supplies of food that keeps well for traveling. It doesn't taste very good, though."

Richard smiled a little. "It never does."

"The gifted kept journey supplies—dried meat, fish, hard biscuits and such—in case they ever had to go to warn . . . well, I was going to say to warn the wizards' council, but I guess they're long gone." She gestured to the hall. "The travel supplies are kept in the second room to the right, in a cabinet. Take what you think we'll need. I'll be back as soon as I get Ester and gather up some of the other things we'll need."

When Richard nodded, Samantha dashed out the doorway. After she was gone, he knelt back down beside Kahlan, lifting her limp hand to hold it in his for a moment. He wished she would wake so that he could tell her where he was going and about the threat from the third kingdom. The last thing she knew about had been the threat from Jit.

He watched her steady breathing, watched her peaceful expression. He wished she would wake, but wishing couldn't make it happen. She was going to need help if she was to live. They both were. He had to try to get that help.

In the quiet stillness before the storm that he knew was about to break, he leaned down and gently kissed her soft lips, hoping it would last him, and that it would not be the last time he ever kissed her. He knew that if she were awake, she would tell him not to worry about her, but to go do what he needed to do.

Knowing that time was short, he rushed to the second room and found the journey supplies. He collected what he thought they could carry without slowing them down, piling it neatly in the front room. In short order, Samantha, carrying a second pack for him and two hooded traveling cloaks over her arm, hurriedly ushered Ester into the outer room.

"Some of the others are getting some supplies together for us," Samantha told him as she closed the door.

"Lord Rahl, what is it?" Ester asked, looking back and forth between the two of them as she squeezed one hand with the other. "Sammie said it's important, but she wouldn't say what it was about. Is the Mother Confessor . . . ?"

"She's all right for the moment," Richard said. "But we need your help. Samantha and I have to go—"

"Samantha?" the woman asked with a puzzled look.

"Sammie. You called her Sammie," Richard said. "I call her Samantha because I think she is growing into a woman, and she now has to face some very grown-up challenges. Samantha seems a more appropriate name. Like I was saying, I have to go and Samantha is going with me."

"Going with you? Where?" The woman looked more bewildered than ever. Richard didn't want to add to her sense of confusion, but he needed her to be aware of what was going on. She needed to be able to let everyone else know of the threat and she needed to tell Kahlan about it when she woke up.

"There is trouble," Richard told Ester. "You know those two men who were attacking me? The ones you helped save me from?"

Ester nodded. "Of course."

"Well, those men were cannibals."

"Cannibals!"

"Yes. Don't you remember how they were attacking me with their teeth? Biting me?"

"But, but, I don't—"

"I don't have time to explain everything. The important part that you need to understand is that this village was put here long ago, in ancient times, to watch over the barrier—"

"The north wall," Samantha told Ester. She looked over at Richard. "Everyone in the Dark Lands knows it as the north wall."

Richard nodded. "The north wall. The problem we're all facing now is that the north wall was keeping some very dangerous threats locked away to prevent them from harming the people of the New World. It has kept everyone safe since the ancient war, the great war thousands of years ago."

Ester nodded with a troubled look. "I know some about that history. I've heard tales since childhood about otherworldly dangers lying in wait beyond the north wall. No one ever knew what was on the other side, but we all knew it was evil."

"Those tales probably fall well short of the reality. With the barrier breaking down, what was on the other side is now getting out. What no one knew was that Jit was only the beginning of that evil escaping from beyond that north wall."

Ester leaned forward a little. "What is it that's on the other side?"

"You remember those creatures that looked like walking corpses that came up here the other night and hurt so many people, killed so many?"

Her knuckles were white. "How could I forget such a thing?"

"They were corpses animated by occult magic from beyond the north wall. They were the walking dead."

Unable to speak, Ester stiffened with a look of horror.

"The people from beyond that wall aren't like us," Richard said. "They're a kind of cannibal."

She frowned in confusion. "A kind of cannibal? What do you mean? How can there be different kinds?"

"They eat living people, eat them while they are still alive, to try to steal their souls," Samantha said.

Ester gasped but said nothing. She looked at a complete loss for words.

"Those from beyond the wall," Richard told the woman, "attacked my friends who were taking us back to the People's Palace. They were also the ones who killed Samantha's father and likely took her mother. I think that my friends and Samantha's mother may still be alive. We're going in there, beyond the north wall, to try to get them back out."

Ester looked at Samantha before looking back at Richard. "Are you serious? Do you so soon forget Henrik's story? They attacked a whole column of your elite troops, your personal guard from the palace, and overpowered them, and you think that you two can go in there alone and not be slaughtered the moment you step through the north gate?"

That same thought had occurred to Richard.

"He won't be alone," Samantha said. "I'll be with him."

"Sometimes it's safer to be few in number," Richard said. "We won't be noticed the way a whole column of troops would be."

"Lord Rahl, far be it from me to tell you your business, but you were alone when those two men attacked you, and had we not come along when we did you would be dead now."

Richard sighed as he rose up from beside Kahlan. "I know. But there's no choice. It's something I have to do. This threat could kill people in numbers beyond your ability to imagine. I'm the Lord Rahl. I have to do what is necessary to protect all the people of the New World."

Ester dipped her head. "I can't argue with the word of the Lord Rahl." Ester gestured at Samantha. "But why is she going?"

"Because she is stubborn," Richard said.

For the first time, a small smile touched Ester's lips. "I see you have gotten to know her."

"I have the gift," Samantha said in her own defense. "Lord Rahl and the Mother Confessor are sick with Jit's touch of death in them and their magic doesn't work. I can at least help Lord Rahl with my gift. And if we can get my mother out, then she can help him, too."

Ester considered briefly. "I see. That's very brave of you . . . Samantha. Well, what can we do to help, Lord Rahl?"

"You can watch over Kahlan for me and when she wakes up tell her what's happening. I'll be back as soon as I can get my friends out. Then we must rush back to the People's Palace so that they can cure us of the Hedge Maid's deadly touch. After that, I will deal with the threat from beyond the north wall.

"When she wakes, tell Kahlan what I've told you, and that I said it's important for her to wait here for me. I will be back for her. I will be bringing help.

"I need to briefly explain some of what I've learned so that you can tell the others here about the threat that is now loose. The people of Stroyza need to stay up here as much as possible. They shouldn't go out alone, only in large groups. Keep a watch at all times. The unholy creatures from beyond the north wall may try to get up here to attack your people."

"You mean, to eat us alive?"

Richard took a breath. "I'm afraid so. From up here you have a better chance of holding them off. Hopefully I'll be back before you have any trouble.

"We need to leave right away," Richard added.

"There's still plenty of light left. We need to get as far as we can before dark."

"It's a pretty long way to the north wall," Ester said. "It will take you days to get there."

"I know. That's all the more reason I have to hurry."

CHAPTER

36

The climb down the side of the mountain in the damp drizzle was harder than the climb up had been. As he led the way, Richard idly wondered how many people from the village of Stroyza, over all the time the cave village had been up there, had slipped in the wet on the narrow trail and fallen to their death.

Looking up at one point, Richard saw crowds of people lining the rim of the cavern, gazing down at him and Samantha as they made the treacherous descent on the way to an even more treacherous unknown land beyond the mysterious barrier they knew as the north wall. They were probably wondering if the two would ever be seen again.

Richard dared not entertain such doubts. Kahlan was up there and he needed to bring help back for her. If he failed, he was failing her and she would die.

As Richard and Samantha had swiftly put together their supplies, he had briefly explained the dangers from the barrier failing to those gathered around helping. With no time to explain things to all the people of Stroyza, Richard told Ester and those gathered around that they would have to be the ones to let all the rest of the people know what had happened with what they called the north wall and fill them in with more of the details of the new dangers.

The Dark Lands were already a dangerous place. With the menace of the Hedge Maid recently appearing out of nowhere and mysterious hordes attacking, killing, or carrying off all the soldiers and gifted who had been with the Lord Rahl, to say nothing of the grotesque creatures that had attacked and killed so many people up in the caves, the people of Stroyza were already on high alert. He had no doubt that they would take the warnings seriously.

While he'd had the chance, Richard had impressed on those gathered around the previously unknown sort of threat that those from the third kingdom represented. Like him, none of them had ever imagined people, or half people, who thought they could steal another person's soul by eating them alive.

He had told the people listening to come down the mountain only for something essential, and then only in groups prepared to fight off an attack. He'd been glad to hear that they had already avoided coming down ever since the attack by the walking dead. They told him that groups of men had quickly rushed down to tend their animals as necessary, but they didn't linger. They feared that more of those corpselike monsters might be lurking down below. Richard had told them that they could very well be right. That was before they knew of the threat of the half people. Fortunately, as of yet, they had not encountered any more of the awakened dead.

He was glad that the trail up was so strenuous. The difficulty of coming up that mountainside trail to attack the cave village was probably the best defense these people had, now that they were properly on alert. They had been careless in keeping watch before, but he doubted that they would be that inattentive again.

As he paused to gaze out over the gloomy wilderness, the thought occurred to him that those back in Naja Moon's time probably planned the cave village high up in the mountain with defensive safety in mind. It was even possible, if not likely, that they were the ones who had constructed the cave homes in the first place for just this eventuality. The more he thought about it, the more likely it seemed.

Still, whether it was by initial intent or the village had come to be this way over time, these were not a people who were schooled in the art of fighting. They had, after all, fought off his attackers with a rock, even though they carried simple knives. He had to admit, though, that in that instance it had been pretty effective. He had told them that they shouldn't depend on such methods in the future, and told them that when they went down to tend the animals to always have knives on them. A rock was all well and good, but a blade would serve them better in a fight for their lives.

These people, though, were meant to wait and watch. They were sentinels, watchers, the ones who were supposed to raise an alarm. It was clear to Richard that it was never intended that they would be the ones to be the first line of defense and fight the war they were here to warn about. Now that the ancient war had flared anew, they were going to have to defend themselves as best they could until Richard could do something to stop the threat.

Henrik had seen all the rushed preparations and had wanted to come with Richard and Samantha. Richard asked the boy to instead stay and help watch over Kahlan. When she woke, Henrik would then be able to fill in a lot of the blanks for her about what had happened after Richard had killed Jit. Ester could fill Kahlan in on what Richard had since learned about the barrier failing, and what he and Samantha had gone to do.

Kahlan had rescued Henrik from the Hedge Maid's clutches. Because of that, he had a special kind of loyalty and attachment to her so it hadn't taken a lot of convincing for Richard to get the boy to stay behind and help Kahlan.

Richard hiked the bow up onto his shoulder before negotiating a particularly treacherous turn on the steep trail. Between frequently looking down to watch his footing and looking ahead for handholds, he scanned the forest spread out in the distance below, looking for any sign of half people lying in wait. He didn't see anyone or anything out of the ordinary, but that didn't allay his concern. The unseen threats were what worried him the most.

Samantha seemed completely comfortable on the trail. She danced down behind him like a mountain goat, pausing to wait for him to make it past difficult spots where he was more careful. It wasn't that he was going slow—he wasn't—it was simply that she had grown up ascending and descending the trail and she was intimately familiar with it. Either that, or she was not properly cautious.

When they finally reached the boulder field at the bottom of the mountain, he again scanned the gloomy countryside out beyond the small sheds, buildings, and shelters housing the village's animals and tools. The open fields out beyond allowed him to see a goodly distance, all the way to the dark swath of sodden forest in the distance. What he could see looked deserted.

The chickens and geese were making a racket. They

had been quiet until Richard and Samantha had made it down near their coops and that was probably what disturbed them, so he wasn't alarmed.

Moving out of the boulders, he noticed that the rest of the animals seemed strangely quiet. The sheep huddled together under a roof of a small pole building. They were either staying out of the drizzle, or they were afraid of something. The hogs were likewise quiet and crowded together in corners of their pens.

Richard checked the damp ground, looking for fresh tracks that would indicate someone was about. There were tracks everywhere from people going about the work of looking after the animals. In fact, there were so many tracks through the mud that it made it difficult to make out anything suspicious.

But then he spotted a track that bought him to a halt. The people of Stroyza all wore shoes or boots. The print from this particular left foot was bare. What was so disturbing, though, was that the right footprint wasn't bare, but it wasn't a bootprint, either. It was a soft, irregular impression. It looked like the person's foot might have been wrapped in cloth.

At the same time as he saw tracks that concerned him, Richard looked up just as a man with dark, sunken eyes stepped out from behind the chicken coop.

CHAPTER

37

The man wasn't one of the villagers. His clothes were little more than tattered rags draped over his bony frame, exposing oozing lesions. In places, corners of different kinds of cloth hung like rotted flags.

His left foot was bare. His right foot was wrapped in muddy rags.

Considering his clothes alone, as filthy and frayed as they were, Richard's first thought was that this was another of the walking dead dug up out of a grave somewhere and sent on a mission to attack the people of Stroyza.

But this was no walking corpse. This man was alive, although by the looks of him he was well on the way to being dead. He stared with sunken eyes rimmed with dark, reddish circles. The skin of his exposed arms was riddled with open sores and scabs. Except for not looking to have any other deformities, he looked to be a leper.

There was no time to feel sorry for the man.

Almost as soon as he spotted Richard, the man rushed at him, his lips curling back. As he came, he let out a bellowing roar, an otherworldly, feral, fierce sound, a sound born of savage hunger. His jaws were open wide, and his teeth were bared for the attack.

Richard pivoted to his left as he threw his leg out, planting his boot squarely in the center of the man's chest as he charged in. The swift, powerful blow drove a grunt from the man and also drove him back, gaining Richard precious fighting room.

The man stumbled backward several steps as he struggled to catch his balance. As soon as he regained his footing, he immediately lunged toward Richard again.

Twisting to the left, coiled like a spring, Richard now had not only the time he needed, but also the fighting room.

The clear ring of steel in the still midday air announced the Sword of Truth clearing the scabbard.

The sword's rage came out with the blade. Richard's own anger was already there, waiting. Together, those twin storms fired the fury powering the blade's magic.

Samantha let out a squeak as she dove behind Richard both for cover and to get out of the way of his deadly blade.

Richard's gaze was fixed on the threat again rushing toward him. As his sword cleared the sheath, Richard uncoiled and whipped the blade around in a backhanded arc, following the path needed to take it where he was looking.

Before the man could take another step, the blade was already there to meet him. The silence was broken by the crack of bone. A red mist filled the damp morning air.

Before Samantha had finished diving behind Richard, the man's head was off and tumbling up through the air. It bounced down on the top rail of a hog pen, leaving a splash of blood, and then came down with a thud in the mud among the pigs. The pigs snorted, pushing back against one another, at first trying to get away from the threat, and then, as the head rolled to rest, the smell of fresh blood swiftly overcame their fear and they were on it, jostling one another to get at the gory prize.

The headless man toppled forward, hitting the ground hard at Richard's feet, splashing blood and mud across his boots.

Already, Richard was scanning the trees, fields, and nearby buildings for any other sign of threat. He expected a horde of half people to emerge suddenly and attack all at once, hoping to overpower and rip into him with their teeth before he could fight them all off, but he didn't see anyone else. Stillness settled once more over the countryside out beyond the animal pens. The pigs snorted and squealed as they fought to get at the head. The chickens, rattled by the man's roar, were in a frenzied, flapping panic.

Samantha, clutching his cloak, peeked out from behind Richard. Her face was white.

"Are you all right?" he asked, his voice still alive with the twin rage within him.

Samantha's mass of black hair jiggled up and down as she nodded, her eyes wide.

Richard, still holding the sword, looked back up the mountain to the cave opening. All the people up top gaped down in horror. He didn't think it was necessary to yell up to them to ask. They got the point.

"He was right here, among us," Samantha said, clearly surprised that one of the half people had been hiding this close. "They've found where we live."

"They will find where everyone lives," Richard said. "They're on the hunt for souls."

Richard laid a hand on Samantha's shoulder, holding her back, and told her to wait where she was while he checked the area. She looked forlorn as she waited, standing all alone with her elbows pulled in tight to her sides and her hands clenched in a tight knot under her chin as she watched him searching the area around the small buildings.

More than anything, seeing that thin, frail young woman standing there all alone made him realize how alone she really must feel with her father murdered and her mother missing. She was only now stepping away from being a girl into a world that demanded she grow up or die. Richard reminded himself again that if there was anything he could do to rescue her mother, he was going to do it.

Samantha watched as Richard looked inside the buildings and coops and all around the firewood piles for anyone who might be hiding. As he went around each structure, making sure there was no one hidden behind them, she snatched glances to the sides for any sign of trouble.

After Richard had satisfied himself that the area was clear and that there was no one lying in wait, he signaled for Samantha to come on ahead. She raced to catch up with him as he started down the lane between the pens.

"Are you starting to see why coming along with me is going to be so dangerous?" he asked as he slid his sword back in its sheath. As he released the hilt, he let the anger go as well.

"I'd rather be with you than back there with my people," she said. "They have numbers. You have a sword. After seeing them attacked the other night, and after seeing you use that sword just now, I'd rather be with one of you and your sword than with all of them."

Richard had to admit that she had a point.

"Did you sense that man at all with your gift?"

Samantha frowned. "Sense him? What do you mean?"

"Gifted people—wizards and sorceresses—can often sense when there is someone around. They can often sense someone in the darkness, or someone hiding like that man was hiding."

"Really?" Her mouth twisted with displeasure. "I wish my mother would have taught me that trick."

"Stroyza doesn't have any horses, do they?" he asked, even though he thought he knew the answer.

Samantha shook her head. "Just oxen to help in the fields."

It struck him that they lived here; they had nowhere to go. Unless, of course, in their duty as sentinels they had need to put out a warning about the gates to the third kingdom being open, but that had not been necessary for thousands of years.

Since they didn't have horses, there was no choice but to walk. From some of the terrain he had seen through the viewing port, horses could not make it all the way to where they needed to go, so it wasn't as big a hindrance as it might seem. They would have to make do and cover the most ground they could on foot.

As they took the turn, making their way down the path leading north through the fields, Samantha pulled the hood of her cloak up over her hair. The drizzle was getting thicker. By the look of the overcast, Richard thought that it might soon be raining. It was going to be miserable traveling weather.

At least the forest, still some distance off, would offer them some protection. He hurried his pace to make it to the trees quicker.

Samantha didn't look to be bothered by the gloom.

"Does it get gloomy like this often, here?" he asked her.

She nodded. "It's dark and dreary here a lot. I've often

wished that I could live someplace sunny, rather than in the Dark Lands."

Before they reached the edge of the fields, off ahead among the towering trees, Richard thought that for just a brief moment he spotted eyes back in the darkness of the thick forest.

38

Richard put his right arm out when he stopped, bringing Samantha to a halt as well. She looked up at him with a puzzled expression.

"Do you notice anything up ahead?" Richard asked in a hushed tone, gesturing with a slight nod of his head.

Samantha looked toward the trees and then frowned back up at him. "I see trees. What do you mean? Like what?"

"I mean, do you see eyes watching us?"

She turned her frown toward the dark forest rising up before them.

"Eyes?" she asked in a voice drawn thin and high with alarm. She leaned a little bit to each side, then forward a little, peering into the dark places among the trees.

Richard carefully, methodically, studied the dark shadows back in behind the trees. The woods weren't too far off. In fact, at the moment, they were feeling uncomfortably close. He saw a few sparrows darting among the pine boughs, and a squirrel or maybe a mouse rummaging among the leaf litter, nothing larger.

"No, I don't see anything," she finally said. "You saw eyes watching us? Where?"

"I think I saw them up ahead, back in the trees, just off to the right of the trail."

Samantha's gaze darted back to the forest, checking where he said he saw something. "Are you sure?"

"No. I only saw it for a moment. I've spent most of my life in the woods and I know that sometimes light reflecting off wet leaves, or a few light patches of moss— things like that—can sometimes look like eyes. Sometimes it can really fool you."

"Maybe that's what you saw this time." She sounded more hopeful than confident.

"It's possible. But now I don't see it." Richard took two steps back to replicate where he had been, trying to see if it was a reflection off wet leaves when seen from just a certain angle. He didn't see it again, so he doubted it was a reflection he'd seen. As he came forward to step up beside her, he still didn't see it again.

"That's good, if you don't see it, right? That means it was nothing, right?"

Richard stared into the dark recesses of the forest, back among the bases of the towering trunks and the smaller shrubs. "Maybe. It might have been a trick of the light, or some water dripping off leaves. But it could also mean that it was somebody, and when I spotted them they moved back and hid behind cover."

Samantha scanned the fields to their left. To the right the rocky ground rose up sharply into the mountain home where she lived. She looked back to the forest waiting for them at the end of the lightly traveled trail.

"What should we do?" she asked.

Richard surveyed the lay of the land. To the right the mountain made passage impossible. To the left, skirting the path, looked like an option but not a good one.

"Are there any other paths or roads going in this general direction?"

Samantha shook her head. "There are more populated areas to the south. Very few people live in this direction. This is the only path going north and it only goes north for a ways.

"If we go off the path it will be slow going through the forest. We will have to do that eventually because the path doesn't go all the way north to the wall. It turns off to the west less than halfway to where we're going. It eventually turns some more to go to the southwest as it makes its way around rugged, rocky ridges. But to the north, after the trail turns away, is uncharted wilderness.

"It only goes north as far as it does because of rugged mountains due west of here. The trail only goes north as far as it has to in order to get around impassable country, then it turns on its way to the few other villages to the west and south."

"Do many people travel through here?"

She tilted her head to the west. "Those villages are distant over those mountains. Most of the people there trade with places to the south of them, which are closer, so people rarely travel here because Stroyza is not only pretty isolated, it's not on the way to anywhere. This part of the Dark Lands is just too rugged and uninhabited to be worthwhile for most traders to have any reason to come this way, so we don't see many people other than a few trappers, merchants, and traders trying to scratch out a living."

Hands on his hips, Richard nodded as he studied the lay of the land. "I should have realized it."

She looked up at him. "What do you mean?"

"Well, in Naja Moon's time, they were trying to save everyone from the danger of the half people and the walking dead, right?"

"Right," Samantha said, not really following what he was getting at.

"Well if you wanted to stick something dangerous somewhere where it would have the least chance to harm anyone, where would you put it?"

Samantha's gaze shot back to the north. "Someplace deserted. Someplace people never went. Someplace where no one was likely to ever go near."

"Right."

She lifted her arms a little. "So what are we going to do? We have to head north if we're to get to the north wall. You saw it through the viewing port. The barrier that runs between a gap in the mountains is to the north. That gap in the mountains isn't very wide and there doesn't seem to be another way in. We have to go north if we are going to get into the third kingdom. This is the only path that heads in that direction, at least for part of the way, and then we'll have to go through uncharted woods."

"That's exactly why I don't like walking up this path into the trees. It makes a perfect place to ambush any unsuspecting traveler"—Richard looked down at the concern on her face—"in order to try to steal their soul."

Samantha rubbed her arms as if having a sudden chill in the damp but warm air as she contemplated people who would try to eat them alive to get at their soul.

"They have just as much chance of that as our pigs have of becoming human by eating that fellow's head."

Richard huffed a chuckle of agreement.

She peered up expectantly. "Then what are we to do? We haven't really even begun the journey. We've only been walking for a short time. We have a long way to travel."

Richard flicked a hand to the field off to the left of

the path. It was mostly dirt with a few clumps of weeds here and there. Whatever had been growing in it had been harvested and the ground plowed in preparation for planting another crop.

"Let's cut through this field. Maybe we can find a trail used by animals to go through the woods. Deer runs often make a usable path, then at least we wouldn't have to fight our way through dense brush."

"All the way?" she asked, incredulous. "You think we should follow deer trails all the way north? Lord Rahl, deer trails usually run hither and yon. Deer aren't looking to make time and get somewhere. They just wander around looking for forage."

Richard was nodding as she was talking. "I know, but what I'm thinking is that if someone is lying in wait, they would be right up there, waiting to catch anyone unsuspecting who follows the trail into the woods. I'm thinking that if we can make our way through the woods and around the path for a while, then we can finally catch back up with it farther north, in a few hours, maybe, and then make time on the regular trail."

"But if someone is waiting in ambush on the trail, they could be waiting in ambush all along the trail."

"Possibly, but if these half people are as desperate for souls as Naja says, then they wouldn't want others to get the first chance when people follow the trail north into the woods. They have probably already learned from the planted fields and animals that people live here, and they have probably been watching, so they know that very, very few people travel north like this."

"So? What good does that do for us?"

Richard rested the palm of his left hand on the hilt of his sword, still surveying the lay of the land, looking for an opening they could use.

"Well," he finally said, "if their pickings are slim, if

there are few souls for the taking, then they aren't going to want to leave those souls to other half people who are waiting right at the trailhead. If the first in line caught anyone happening by on the trail, then there wouldn't be anyone left for other half people lying in wait farther north. It seems to me that half people would be eager and want to be first to get any soul."

Samantha nodded as she thought it over. "That makes sense. They would be jealous of others getting first chance at any souls, so they would all want to be right here, like a pack of hungry wolves, where they can hide in the woods at the beginning of the trail north."

"That's what I'm thinking." Richard turned, looking back the way they had come. "I bet that fellow back there by your animals got the idea that he would wait even closer. He probably thought that he would get first pick of the souls living here. By the looks of him, he was desperate and not a very clear thinker. Being alone like that didn't give him as good a chance at success as some of them working together to overpower people."

"Well then, it seems that you're saying that you expect them all to be waiting just up ahead."

She started to lift her hand to point. Richard pushed her hand down.

"Don't point. If there are half people out there, they will be watching us."

Samantha was looking alarmed again. "So, what do we do?"

"I think we should try to go around them and pick up the trail farther north."

"Maybe we should wait until dark, so they wouldn't see us doing that. I mean, if you're worried about pointing where we are thinking of going because they might be watching us, they will certainly be able to see where we head off to skirt the trailhead unless it's dark out."

"That certainly makes the most sense, and I'd rather wait until dark, but there's two problems with that."

"Like what?"

"First, it's overcast. That means there won't be any moonlight or even stars to help us navigate through strange countryside in the pitch black. It's dangerous enough when you know where you are and you're following trails you know. In the dark, in unfamiliar country, trying to cross trackless woods, it's really dangerous.

"It only takes one mistake in the dark and your journey is done. You could hit dried branches that could blind an eye, or step in a split in the rock and snap the bone in your leg, or you could even fall over a cliff. Even a small cliff, not much higher than I am tall, is enough to kill you in the dark."

"I could heal you if you got hurt like some of those things."

"And what if it was you who fell and split your skull open on a rock?"

Samantha made a sour expression as she thought it over for a moment. "What's the second reason?"

Richard started off across the field to the left. "The second reason is that we can't afford to lose any time. Every moment we're delayed could mean the lives of the people we're on our way to help could be lost."

Samantha hurried to follow after him across the rough, plowed ground, stepping high over clods of dirt to keep from tripping.

"Well, I know that I would hate to arrive the day after my mother was killed and for the rest of my life wish I would have hurried just a little faster."

"Exactly," Richard said as he steered a course across the rough, open ground for a small opening into the woods that he had spotted off in that direction. It looked like a small deer trail, but it was their best option.

The only problem was that if there were half people back at the trail, they would be watching and know where the two of them were headed. It wouldn't give the two of them much of a head start.

It couldn't be helped. It was the best of a bad situation.

As they made their way as quietly and swiftly as possible across the field of broken ground, the half people began to emerge from the woods. At first there were only a dozen or so, but in short order they were emerging from the woods in droves. It was not only alarming to see them breaking cover and coming out onto the open ground, it was alarming to see their numbers growing so quickly. What was only a moment before a handful that Richard could have handled had become a crowd that could easily overwhelm him on open ground.

Richard could see that he and Samantha weren't going to make it to the woods in time. The people running across the plowed field were going to cut them off before they reached the tree line.

Richard didn't see any weapons being carried by the half people—they looked like a ragtag mob—but as they ran, rapidly closing the distance, they began to howl like demons hungry for blood. A chill ran through Richard knowing that was exactly what they were hungry for.

At that point, Richard wasn't exactly sure what to do. They would have a better chance in the woods because it was easier to fight large numbers in confined spaces. With limited room they couldn't all attack at once because it would be too hard to crowd in around their prey. Out in the open Richard and Samantha stood almost no chance. The howling masses could pile in from all sides at once. Richard's sword could only cut down so many, and could only cut them down so fast. It couldn't stop an avalanche of people descending on him and Samantha out in the open.

More than that, though, these were people in only a limited sense. He couldn't expect them to think like an ordinary enemy in a battle. From what Naja's account had warned and from what Richard had seen of the man back by the animal pens, these people, if they could be called that, didn't seem to fear for their own lives the way an ordinary enemy fighter would, or any ordinary human, for that matter. In the war, Richard had seen enemy troops making a mad charge without regard for their own lives, but this was different. These people were this way by their nature.

Since they weren't going to be able to make it to the woods, Richard slowed and finally came to a stop. He looked back the way they had come as well as off to each side. None of those other choices were a good option because on open ground these unholy half dead would likely be able to run them down in short order. Now that these beasts had two souls in sight, they were unlikely to stop for anything.

Richard felt, for the first time, what it must have felt like for Zedd, Nicci, Cara, and all the rest of his friends and soldiers as they had watched the howling menace coming for them.

It was as horrifying as anything Richard had ever faced.

Samantha, rather than panicking and asking him what they should do, started twirling her arms in a most peculiar manner. He couldn't imagine what she could be doing. She wasn't twirling them fast, but in a labored way, as if she were moving something invisible but heavy.

Richard saw, then, some of the dirt in the field out in front of them start to be lifted by gusts of wind building out of nowhere. He at last understood what she was trying to do.

She was gathering wind, calling it to do her bidding, gathering it into a focused windstorm.

"Can you do more?" he asked, checking the distance to the people running toward them, calculating how long they had before they would be overwhelmed.

"Trying" was all she could manage to say as her arms built speed, twirling faster and faster. Richard could see beads of sweat on her forehead.

As the gusts of wind she was calling forth built speed and power, they began picking up more dirt with every fitful gust. Pieces of straw and grass were lifted into the swirl of dirt and debris that was rapidly building into a whirlwind.

"It's too bad that the ground is wet!" he called out to her over the howl of the crazed attackers and the ever-increasing howl of the wind. "If it was dry, it would be dusty and the dust could hide us long enough for us to escape into the woods! That way, they wouldn't see where we went!"

Samantha briefly glanced up. He could see the spark of an idea in her eyes and the slight curl of her lips before she turned her attention back to the task at hand.

She added an alternating whipping motion to what she was doing with circling her arms, as if casting something out.

Richard understood as he began to feel the heat she was generating with what she was doing. The gifted could gather heat from the air and focus it, the same way they could gather the air itself.

Soon, it felt like standing near a bonfire. She was not only gathering the air into gusts to build those into a whirlwind, she was gathering heat out of the air and casting it against the ground. Richard had seen sorceresses, and even Zedd, gather heat from the air, or even pull heat out of the air to freeze water. Samantha was doing the same thing.

The heat was intense enough to confuse the onrushing horde, and in their confusion they slowed their mad rush. Some of them began to shield their eyes from the dirt and debris blowing at them while others rubbed at their eyes, trying to get the dirt out so they could see.

In what seemed a sudden turn, under the withering heat the wet ground flashed to dry as the moisture was driven out. In short order, great billowing clouds of dust rose up, lifting into the air in brown curtains.

As some of the half people started to run to the sides in an attempt to find a way around the wall of dirt, dust, and debris, Samantha recognized what they were doing and again started to whirl her arms around over her head. The hot winds along with all the dust she was stirring up started to rotate. A wall of the dirt and debris blew in around Richard and Samantha, rotating around them faster and faster, picking up both speed and dust as they stood at the center of the howling storm.

Before long, Richard couldn't see a thing. He knew

that if he couldn't see anything, including the half people, they couldn't see him.

He knew where the deer trail was in relation to where they stood out in the field. He kept the place fixed in his mind, even though he couldn't see it anymore. In mere moments, he had lost sight of the forest as well as the confused half people that had been darting around, trying to find a way to get at them through the blinding wall of dust.

The dust now rotated in towering walls around Richard and Samantha and had became so thick that it closed in completely, darkening the light that could get down inside. It felt like dusk inside the rotating storm of dirt and dust and getting darker by the moment. Meanwhile, Samantha's arms continued twirling around over her head, keeping up the momentum of the wind.

Once everything had grown dim and dark and Richard couldn't see a single one of the half people, and hardly more than the hand in front of his face, he leaned close to Samantha so she could hear him over the howl of the wind.

"Can you move while you're doing that?"

She glanced over at him, clearly in the throes of intense concentration. "I don't know," she yelled over the noise. The look on her face, though, told him that she didn't believe she could, even if she knew she had to try.

It was plainly evident that it was tremendously difficult for her to keep up such focused effort. He knew that they only needed to get to the trees without the half people seeing where they went and then they would have a chance.

Richard was struck with a sudden idea. He bent down and leaned in close. "You just keep doing what you're doing Samantha! Don't stop!" he yelled over the roar of the wind.

The howl of the wind had grown so loud that he could no longer hear the howls of the half people screaming for blood.

Samantha glanced over at him, clearly puzzled by what he intended. She couldn't spare the energy to answer. She simply nodded.

Richard slipped his arms around her waist and lifted her up. "Keep doing what you're doing! Don't stop! I'm going to get us to the woods!"

Samantha's arms kept twirling even as he lifted her. The wind kept blowing and gusting up a dust storm around them as Richard hoisted the slim young woman up, sitting her atop his shoulder. He held her tightly by the waist to steady her as he started running.

Richard knew that she had to be getting tired from the effort, but she didn't slow the pace or complain. She kept it up, and kept the curtain of dirt and debris rotating around them in a massive dust storm that blanketed the field all around. Richard had no idea how large the dust storm was, but he did know that it was hiding them and that was what mattered.

Before it had become opaque, though, he had seen that it was not some isolated little whirlwind. It was massive, covering a lot of ground and enveloping the entire swarm of half people charging out of the woods and coming after them.

It was sweltering hot inside the rotating dust cloud. Richard could hardly breathe from the heat. His nose was filling with dust, making it difficult to breathe. He didn't slow though. This was their only chance.

He ran until he heard the dirt and flying debris hitting the leaves and pine needles of trees. He could hear it pelting wet trees. He could hear the litter of the forest floor pulled up into the whirlwind and clattering against trunks. He could hear tree limbs whipping in the wind. Some of those limbs snapped in the gusts.

Richard suddenly spotted the deer trail and without pause plunged into it, into the woods, Samantha still up on his shoulder twirling her arms, still calling the wind around them.

CHAPTER

40

Richard had to swing Samantha down off his shoulder as he dove into the woods for fear that he would smack her face into a limb and break her delicate little neck. He held her against his right hip, slung on his arm. He had to duck forward himself as he ran into the deer run to keep from hitting low limbs and saplings that were bent in over the tunnel-like trail. Like others Richard had used before, the deer trail was not very tall but it was wide enough. As he ran, small saplings leaning in here and there slapped at his arms.

Samantha's arms finally stopped their frantic flailing and spinning. She slumped, panting with exhaustion from the effort. He could see that it had taken every ounce of strength that she had.

Now, it was up to him to get them away from the horde of half people who had been after them. He didn't think that they had seen which way Richard had run, but he imagined that they could probably guess that he would head for the woods. He expected them to show up at any moment.

Through the blur of branches, brush, and green flashing by, Richard spotted one of the half people. He was dressed better than the man Richard had beheaded, but not much better. As soon as he spotted Richard and Samantha he raced in from the left side. As he got close, he bared his teeth. Richard could see that he was missing a few. His jaws started snapping in anticipation of catching flesh and ripping it off.

Without pause, as soon as the man was within reach, Richard put his hand behind the man's head and used his momentum to propel him forward. Richard, bigger than the lone man and already running while he carried Samantha under his right arm, used his hand on the back of the man's head to steer him onward, moving him so fast that it not only took control of his direction but almost took him from his feet.

As they raced up on a tree, Richard ran the man's face hard into the thick trunk, right over the stump of a dried, broken-off limb, driving it straight through the man's face. The impact was so hard Richard could feel the man's head crack apart like a melon on a rock. With fluid movement, Richard released the man as he smacked into the tree and kept running. That was one attacker who wouldn't be following them.

After he had gone on a short distance more, Richard stopped to listen for signs that they were being closely pursued. He panted, catching his breath as he quickly appraised the situation. He tried to breathe as quietly as possible so he could listen. Samantha pushed at his arm, wanting down, so he eased her down to the ground.

She bent forward, her mass of black hair hanging down around her face, hands on her knees, as she panted, trying to catch her breath after the exertion of creating the windstorm.

"That was brilliant," Richard whispered to her.

She could only nod as she gasped for air. Richard let her recover as he listened for sounds of the half people in hot pursuit.

And then in the distance he heard them crashing through the woods, coming toward him and Samantha. It sounded like hundreds of people charging through the woods. Even though they were still a ways off, it wouldn't be long before they reached their prey.

"Can you run, or should I carry you?" he asked.

She answered by snatching up his hand and starting out at a trot. Richard started running, rapidly passing her and half pulling her along with him as he raced up the deer trail. As fear overcame her exhaustion, she had no trouble racing to keep up with him. The trail wound haphazardly through the woods as it made its way past trees, steep ledges, and drops, so they didn't encounter any obstacles in the path. As open as it was, Richard was able to keep moving along the winding deer trail at a rapid pace.

It seemed, though, that no matter how much ground Richard covered, the half people were still coming and getting closer all the time. He noticed that while they were mostly coming in from the direction of the trail off to Richard's right, some were coming up from behind, back in the direction of the field.

Richard knew that he had to do something to slow them down so that he and Samantha could vanish. He just couldn't imagine what would slow them. He was only one person, and it sounded like there were hundreds in pursuit. He knew that he could fight them off for a while in the woods, but if their numbers were great enough it would eventually be a losing war.

"How did you know to do that?" he asked Samantha.

"My mother taught me the wind trick," she said,

gulping for air as she was sometimes pulled up and over steeper places by his hand holding hers.

"And the heat to dry out the dirt?"

"I don't know. I guess it was just something I put together on my own out of desperation."

Richard smiled down at her. "Inventing magic?"

She smiled back with a breathless "I guess."

"Well, do you have any magic tricks to use to slow them down so we can escape and disappear into the forest?"

"Sorry, Lord Rahl, but I don't know what else to do."

Richard nodded as he pressed onward. The trees around them were becoming larger and farther apart, while at the same time the forest floor began to thin out of underbrush that couldn't grow in the deep shade. The Dark Lands seemed to have precious little sunlight in the first place, but on the hushed floor in under the massive pines it was darker yet.

Although that made it easier to run, the problem was that as the forest became more open, they could more easily be spotted.

Richard spotted them first, though. He saw ten or twelve of the half people in tattered clothes racing through the woods, dodging trees and jumping rocks and rotting logs as they steadily angled in to intercept Richard and Samantha. The deeper into the woods they went, the more open the forest down below became. The immense pines had no boughs down low. The huge trunks stood in sprawling beds of fern, beside streams, and among exposed rock ledges. The more ground that Richard and Samantha covered, the rockier the ground became and the broader the girth of the trees grew.

To make progress, Richard had to start climbing

over the occasional layer of rocks and lines of ridges thrusting up through the leaf litter of the forest floor. The problem was that while he was slowed by the lay of the land, the half people, still some distance off on flatter ground, were able to run faster and close some of the distance.

More than that, though, they ran headlong, utterly careless as they ran, driven by the mad need to devour a soul. Richard saw one man hit a tree square, rebound, and go down. Another tripped jumping over a log. He didn't rise out of the brush. Another caught a limb across the throat. His feet went flying out and he went down on his back onto rock with a heavy thud. The odd person running would occasionally catch a foot in a hole or under a downed limb and snap their leg.

But for every one who went down, it seemed like a dozen more showed up to join in the chase.

Richard frantically tried to think of a way to slow them, or to gain enough distance that he and Samantha could disappear into the trackless forest. He couldn't come up with a way to slow so many people. The trick with the wind that Samantha had used to such great effect in the open field would not work in the forest. It might be inconvenient and distracting, but it wouldn't stop their pursuers.

Richard had a sudden idea. He looked over at Samantha running beside him. Having to take two or three steps for every one of his strides, her feet seemed to fly over the ground, sometimes not even touching as he occasionally pulled her over an obstacle as they raced through the woods.

"That thing you did with heat, to dry the dirt and make dust, how did you do that?"

"Just gathered heat out of the air," she said, sounding a bit perplexed by the question. "It was pretty simple."

"Did your mother teach you to gather heat like that? Did she teach you how to make things hot?"

Samantha made a face. "I don't know. A little, I guess. She taught me a lot of things growing up. Not necessarily a lesson, just little things, like pulling heat out of the air and putting it someplace."

"Did she teach you how to heat rocks to keep you warm on cold nights?"

Samantha smiled even as she ran, still trying to catch her breath. "Yes. When I was little, she would do that and put the warm rocks in my bed. Then later she showed me how so that someday I could do the same thing for my little ones."

"So you know how to put that heat you gather from the air into things? You can focus it."

She nodded when he looked back at her, perplexed by what he was getting at.

Richard dove behind a long ledge, pulling her over it with him. He caught her around the waist and pulled her down behind the far side of the rock. He squatted down, turning her face toward him to make sure that he had her attention.

"Did she ever teach you how to make trees explode?"

Samantha's brow lifted in surprise. "Make trees explode? Are you serious?"

"Yes, I've seen it done. Especially in war. Wizards and even sorceresses would focus the heat they gather, kind of like you gathered it to dry the dirt. Only they would then focus that heat into a spot inside the trunks of trees, kind of like you do inside rocks to warm them. When they focused enough heat, and it was intense enough, it would make the sap in the tree trunk instantly boil and vaporize. They would do it so quickly, so suddenly, that as the sap vaporized it would make the tree trunk explode."

Her jaw was hanging open. "Really?"

"Really. The flying splinters and pieces of wood could cut down anyone nearby. It would shred them to pieces. It could stop a line of troops, bring a headlong assault to an abrupt halt."

"But, I don't know how to do such a thing."

Richard peered out over the rock ledge and then leaned back down close to her. "You need to learn fast. It may be the only thing that can save us." Richard carefully lifted his head and pointed off into the distance. "There, see that handful of men over there who stopped, trying to see where we went?"

She peeked over the edge of the rock. "Yes. I see them."

Richard put his hand on her head and pushed it back down so the men wouldn't spot her. "Try to gather heat and put it into that tree trunk beside them. See if you can focus the heat really fast. If you can, if you can do it fast enough and with enough intensity, you can make the trunk explode. I've seen it done, Samantha. I know it can be done. You've got to try."

She pressed her lips tight for a moment and then peeked over the rock again. She took a deep breath and then laid both arms on top of the rock, aiming her palms out at the tree.

She squinted with the effort, her fingers trembling as she tried.

Finally, the breath she had been holding left her lungs in a rush. "I'm sorry, Lord Rahl, but I can't do it. I just can't."

Richard let out a disappointed sigh of his own and finally nodded. "I know you did your—"

A man suddenly dove over the top of the rock behind them. Richard seized the man's ragged clothes in his fists as he came diving in and used the man's momentum to heave him out over the rim of ledge.

As the man tumbled away, three more men came over the top of the rock.

CHAPTER

41

Richard drew his sword as he sprang up. Powered by the anger of the blade's magic, as well as his own fury, he spun to the attack.

The first man to come in at him lost his head for it. The second figure to leap in at him was a woman, equally vicious in her frenzied attempt to rip into him with her teeth. As Richard kicked her legs out from under her, a powerful swing of his sword caught the back of her head, taking off the top half of her skull. The large disc of bone, with the scalp of ratty hair, cartwheeled down the rock ledge. Strands of hair flung outward as it tumbled away. Richard spun back to the side just in time to meet another woman's charge. With one powerful swing, the blade cut her ribs open to her spine. As she fell at his feet, her insides erupting from the massive wound, Richard drove the point of the steel pommel back into a man's face. On the rebound he thrust the sword forward through a man reaching for Samantha.

He used his foot to shove the man back off the blade while at the same time reaching back with his free hand to seize Samantha's arm. The mortally wounded man fell back across the rock, clutching the wound through his chest, choking on his own blood.

Richard yanked Samantha up and out of the way as two more men dove in at them, hands clawed as they snatched for her. Their fingers caught only empty air. When they missed as they grabbed for her, they sprawled forward. Richard stomped the back of one man's head, smashing his face into the rough granite, while he stabbed the other twice in quick succession. The man Richard had stomped clutched his hands over his ruined face as he writhed in agony.

"Let's go!" Richard yelled at Samantha.

Speed of movement was life. Richard wasted no time in continuing to engage the enemy unless he had to. Instead, when he could, he simply slipped through their ranks to escape their reaching hands as he pulled Samantha along with him through every sharp evasive turn he took. As he ran, he beheaded anyone that came in close enough, or took off the arms of those reaching in to keep them from getting hold of either Samantha or himself. He wasn't interested in fighting them if he didn't have to. There were too many to hope to eliminate them all. He was more interested in escaping, because fighting would risk being taken down and then having them get hold of Samantha.

It amazed him the way the half people charged in without any regard for their own safety. They showed little or no fear of his sword, only avoiding it sometimes as if it were nothing more than a mere nuisance on their way in to try to get to him. That made it all the easier for Richard to cut them down. They fell with terrible gaping wounds, or fell dead, in great numbers. The problem was that there were simply so many of them.

It was clear to Richard that their single-minded goal was to get at someone with a soul. That seemed to be all that mattered to them. Though they carried no weapons other than an occasional knife at their side, which he never saw one of them draw, their unwavering purpose in and of itself made them incredibly dangerous. In that purpose, their teeth were their weapons of choice.

As they attacked, they did little to protect themselves, and almost nothing to escape the certain death of his blade. They were determined to get what they were after. Nothing else mattered. Some were able to get in closer because he was so busy handling the great many presenting themselves for slaughter. But when he did get to them, they made easy targets of themselves.

Richard was only too happy to oblige them. The sword's fury demanded their blood, and Richard's anger was more than enough to provide the muscle the blade needed. He just wanted these monsters to stay away from him, and if killing them was the only way, then he killed them as fast as they came at him.

Holding Samantha's wrist in his left hand, he pulled her like a rag doll, this way and that, to keep her out of the reaching hands of the half people. He danced over the tops of rock as soon as a slight opening in the rush of half people presented itself. He dodged from side to side to avoid reaching fingers, occasionally kicking men and women out of the way if that was all it took. If they presented a more serious threat and it took more than a kick, he used his sword to cut them down. As he raced through the woods, using the tops of outcroppings of ledge as stepping stones, he swung the sword one way, cutting down those to one side, and then with a backhanded swing slashed those on the other side, leaving a trail of blood, the dying, and bodies in his wake.

Some of the attackers growled or roared in their mania to get at the souls they wanted, or cried out in anger as they missed snatching his and Samantha's legs. The ones he killed made very little noise as they were stabbed or slashed. Even the ones who lost a limb didn't let out the kind of screams that a normal person would have had they taken such grievous wounds.

When the opportunity presented itself, Richard leaped down from a rock onto the forest floor. Once back on more even ground and with a brief opening, he broke into a dead run. Seeing what he was doing and where he was heading, Samantha stayed a half a step ahead of him. Those chasing them on the more open ground, of course, could run faster as well, so Richard periodically had to turn to cut down any of the faster pursuers that got close. Sometimes, simply dodging to the side was enough to throw the horde of half people off stride long enough for Richard and Samantha to be able to put distance on them. Unfortunately, others came charging in from the sides and then they, too, had to be either dodged or dealt with.

Richard knew that he had to be effective with every single thing he did. If he missed once, darted the wrong direction, or made any mistake at all, they would be on him.

It felt like trying to outrun a cloud of angry gnats.

When he glanced back over his shoulder after he swung the blade, splitting the face of a woman who sprang up in front of him, he saw that most of those coming up from behind were trying to snatch Samantha rather than get to him.

Samantha was frantically using her hands to try to cast some kind of magic. Those coming for her showed no ill effect from her ability and it certainly wasn't slowing them. Whatever she was doing obviously wasn't working.

This was the same thing Henrik had reported about the attack on the column of troops. Henrik had told him that nothing Zedd or Nicci had done seemed to have had the desired effect. Samantha was now having that same difficulty with her gift. The whirlwind was the most effective thing Samantha had so far conjured, but in the forest, on the run, that kind of thing would do them little good.

He supposed that in a fight, those with the gift instinctively fell back on what they knew. But using her instincts was doing them no good. It was only using up her strength to no effect and slowing them down.

That was why Richard had wanted her to use her ability to make trees explode. Magic didn't work directly against these unholy half dead, but exterior things, such as his sword, or even a rock to their heads, did work. They could be hurt, but not with magic directly. He had wanted her to make trees explode in order to cut down their attackers. That was how he had figured out magic could be used against them.

But Samantha had tried and she couldn't do it.

Coming over the top of a rise, Richard lifted Samantha from the ground, spun her around, and set her down behind him out of the way. With both hands now on his sword, his swift blows cut into two men and a woman who rushed in at him. They all fell, clutching gaping wounds to try to hold their insides from spilling out. Richard knew that they would spend hours lying there on the ground, suffering a slow and agonizing death.

When he saw that the forest was getting ever more crowded with mobs of growling men and women closing in from all sides, he turned, looking for something they could use for a defensive position. Defense was not the way to win a battle, but at the moment he was rapidly running out of options.

He pointed with his bloody sword. "There!" he yelled at Samantha. "Get between those rocks! Get back in far enough that they can't reach you!"

Without question or hesitation, Samantha scrambled to dive into a narrow split in the jumble of ledge jutting up from the forest floor. She was small enough to squeeze way back into the narrow split in the rock. He hoped she could go back in far enough to be out of the reach of all the half people grabbing for her, at least for a brief time, time enough to give him the chance to fight off the closest attackers.

Richard knew, though, that it wouldn't protect her for long. Defensive action was not going to save them. There were simply too many half people swarming in from all around. It would only be a matter of time before some of the smaller among them squirmed far enough into the split in the rock to be able to reach in, get hold of her, and drag her out. If they did that, they would tear into her with their teeth and eat her alive on the spot.

Richard's heart pounded with the fear of such a thought. He forced aside the horrific notion, making himself think instead of how to prevent such a thing from happening. He had made a calculated decision to keep her safe, if only temporarily. Now he had to make use of the chance that gave him to turn from defense to offense. Having her crouched back in the protection of the rock gave Richard at least a brief opening to fight off the half people without having to try to keep them off Samantha at the same time.

He knew that fighting off the hordes coming in at them wouldn't be enough to save them, but it would stall the inevitable while he tried to come up with a better solution. It bought them both a bit of time, that was all. How much depended on him, on how hard he could fight, on how ferocious he could be.

It was already obvious that hacking them to pieces didn't instill a sense of fear in the half people. They showed virtually no fear of anything. They wanted one thing, and one thing only. There was no way to outrun the half people, so he stood his ground and hacked away at them without pause.

Despite how hard he tried to come up with a solution as he fought, he couldn't think of anything. He had no time to think, really. It took all his effort to continue to swing the sword, to continue to cut down the packs of people charging in all around him.

Richard stood on the high piece of ground he had staked out and unleashed the full fury of his anger at the throngs flocking in around him. He used the obstacles close in around him—tree trunks and a projection of rock—to keep his attackers from rushing straight in. He was merciless in the way he hacked apart clusters of people when they rushed in close enough. At the same time, he had to fight over and around growing piles of bloody corpses.

The tightly focused battle was an orgy of slaughter. Limbs, heads, and parts of bodies from men and women alike littered the ground. Some of the fallen, still alive, twitched in shock and agony. The rocky ledge was painted in a grotesque patchwork of viscera, vomit, urine, and blood.

As he fought, Richard had to be careful not to fall over the bodies or slip on the gore as he swung his sword and dodged fearless charges. The ground everywhere was spattered with a red rain. Blood dripped from the tips of leaves on the trees closest in all around and ran down the face of rocks. Severed fingers from people trying to grab the blade of his sword lay scattered over the rock, like fallen red leaves in autumn.

Richard's arms began to feel as heavy as lead. It was

tiring to swing the sword without pause. There was no time to catch his breath. Stopping for any reason would mean certain death.

He remembered the pain caused by the men who had attacked him, the pain of them biting him, trying to tear his flesh off with their teeth. That memory, that fear, that terror of such a gruesome end, not only for himself but for Samantha as well, drove him on with renewed fury.

Bodies and body parts lay in tangled heaps. The people running in to attack were tripping and falling over them before they could even get to Richard. Others were slipping on the blood and gore. Sprawled on the ground, they were all the easier to kill. As the ones still alive scrambled to their feet, they were covered in the blood of those they had fallen among, making it hard for Richard to know who he had cut and didn't need to cut again, and who might still represent a threat, so he simply cut any of them within range.

The most they ever did to defend themselves was to lift an arm before their faces. That cost them the arm and then their head. It was ridiculously easy to kill such single-minded half people, but their sheer numbers were going to win out in the end, and then he and Samantha would be the ones butchered.

Richard turned when he heard Samantha suddenly scream in terror. He saw a clot of people crowded in around the narrow opening in the rock, all of them leaning in the opening from every direction at the same time, dozens of arms reaching, hands grabbing at her, trying to get even a fingerhold on her to try to drag her out.

Richard swung the sword in a wild frenzy, severing half a dozen arms at a time as if he were hacking away a thicket of brush. When he had slaughtered all those around the opening to her hiding place, he could see her wide eyes back in the darkness, tears of terror streaming down her face.

She reached out to him, pleading with her open arms, wanting him to come to her.

It was a sight of such abject misery that it nearly broke his heart.

Richard looked out at all the masses of people flooding in toward him from every direction.

There was nothing he could do.

He dove into the split in the rock, over Samantha, covering her, protecting her, with his own body. He put his back to her. He felt her arms close around him, clutching him in tight against her.

Richard pointed his sword outward to try to stall the inevitable as he waited for the end.

Richard felt Samantha's arms tighten around him. "I'm sorry" was all he could whisper back over his shoulder. "I'm so sorry, Samantha."

He felt shame for letting himself so easily be talked into allowing her to come along, for how miserably he had failed to protect her, how he had failed Kahlan, failed Naja, Magda, and Merritt's efforts, failed everyone else who depended on him as the Lord Rahl to be their protector.

He should have never agreed to bring Samantha. She was one of the watchers. She was supposed to warn others. She had done that. She was not meant to fight the evil she was born there to warn others of.

He was supposed to be the one to end prophecy and end the threat. It was his responsibility, not hers.

Zedd had always told him to think of the solution, not the problem. He tried, but this time he had no solution. He had failed. He wanted to think that sometimes there simply wasn't a solution, but that would be absolving himself of responsibility, when it had been his responsibility. To think there was no solution was to surrender.

It was to come to nothing, though. Despite how hard he tried, he could think of no solution, and he couldn't fight any harder, couldn't fight off such an overpowering mass of half people all wanting to rip him and Samantha apart and steal their souls. Not even Zedd, Nicci, Cara, Cara's husband, Ben, the general of all those elite troops of the First File, had been able to hold off such overwhelming numbers.

Still, that was no excuse. He was the Lord Rahl. In the end it didn't really matter that they failed. It only mattered if he failed.

Richard watched out through the opening in the rock. He could see all the hands reaching back into the darkness for him. Fingers clawed the air, trying to catch hold of his clothes. Some of them grabbed the sword instead, and lost those fingers.

He could see the shapes of hungry mouths growling with sick need. They bared their teeth for the task for which they so desperately lusted, for the taste of human flesh.

It was all coming to an end before his journey of rescue had even begun. They hadn't even made it beyond the outskirts of Stroyza. They hadn't even made it safely across the fields and into the forest.

"Don't be sorry," Samantha whispered back from the darkness behind him. "Don't be sorry, Lord Rahl. You had the idea. It's not your fault. It's mine."

"What?"

Samantha put her hand on the top of his head and pushed it lower. "Keep your head down," she whispered as if from some distant, dreamlike place.

Richard frowned and was about to ask her what she

was talking about when her small fingers tightened on his head, keeping it down.

And then the ground suddenly shook with a thunderous explosion.

An instant later a deep shock wave hammered his chest. He couldn't make out its source.

Three more deafening explosions came in rapid succession, almost on top of one another. The earsplitting cracks of the detonations were like lightning hitting a tree right beside him. Each booming blast made him flinch. The explosions being so close left his ears ringing.

There was a brief moment of silence before another series of explosions, only there were more this time. All around the wallop of explosions shook the ground like a thunder and lightning storm gone crazy. The staggering concussions, one on top of another in rapid succession, sent shock waves ripping through the air. They shook the ground so powerfully that it made his head hurt. Dirt and small rocks rained down.

Again there was a preciously brief pause in the deafening thumps, and then the thunderous explosions erupted again, coming so close on top of one another that it reminded him of the sound of canvas ripping.

After the briefest of pauses, another series of explosions began, the echoing booms in a measured pace, one right after another, like some celestial blacksmith hammer raining down mighty blows on the anvil of the world. The very air shook with the power of those blows.

Then Richard heard clattering against the rock over his head as a rain of debris began falling. Some of it struck the rock with astounding violence. Other sharp impacts sounded like the crack of a whip. Some of it sounded like it might fracture the rock over his head.

And then pieces of wood began cascading down. Splinters of wood, some no bigger than sewing needles, pelted him while other pieces as big as oars crashed into the rock, bouncing back into the air to eventually come raining down all around. Richard saw that many of the pieces were covered in blood. Some even held skewered pieces of mangled flesh.

He could hear tree limbs under great weight snap in rapid succession, then the sound of massive trunks fracturing as trees crashed down through the forest canopy. The colossal trees shook the ground when they hit. The rumbling sound of trees toppling to the ground boomed all around them.

One of the enormous trunks smashed down with a jarring impact onto the rock they were cowering in. Richard thought that the rock might shatter from the blow. Instead, the impact of the great weight snapped the trunk in half above where Richard and Samantha crouched. Trees in the forest all around upended, ripping great limbs off as they fell. The ground shook with loud, booming blasts that reverberated through the woods.

As the tumultuous explosions continued at an unabated pace, the detonations moved ever outward, ever farther away, the ground shaking with each powerful blow until it all joined together to feel like an earthquake. It felt powerful enough to bring down mountains.

It seemed like it went on forever, but Richard knew that it had all happened in a mere moment in time, a thunderous, violent, murderous moment that had ripped through the forest with incredible brute force and merciless violence.

Almost as soon as they had started, the explosions came to an abrupt end.

Though the explosions stopped, trees continued to fall, each giant monarch snapping limbs of other trees on the way down, even splintering the trunks of neighbors that in turn were knocked over. Richard could hear the muffled sound of roots popping under the tremendous pressure as toppled trees fell against others. The ground shook with the impact when each one finally came to ground.

Giant splinters still rained down for another long moment. Tree trunks cracked in long ripping splits before they came crashing down. Gradually, the noises of all the destruction came to an end as one last tree smashed down not far away, making the ground rumble.

When the world finally went silent, Richard still didn't move. He wasn't sure he should, wasn't sure it was really over. Samantha still had her hand protectively over his head, holding it down.

Samantha slowly withdrew her hand. "Lord Rahl?" she asked in a soft voice choked with tears. "Are you still alive? Are you all right? Dear spirits, please be alive."

Richard blinked as he brought his head up. He had to push piles of bloody splintered wood off himself. There was so much debris piled into the narrow opening in the rock where he and Samantha hid that they were nearly buried.

"I'm alive." He rotated and bent his arms. "I think I'm all right. Are you?"

He rocked his shoulders back and forth in order to squeeze himself out of the opening enough to turn and look back. Tears streamed down Samantha's face. She looked more than miserable, more than merely exhausted.

She managed a nod. "I think so."

Richard flicked his sword, shedding all the debris covering it, and then uncurled himself enough to stand up and take a quick look around to check for any threat from the half people, even though he truly didn't expect to see anyone standing. He didn't.

It looked like the world of life had been blasted out of existence.

The dense forest that had closed them in from overhead with a thick canopy that shut out the sky and daylight had been completely ripped open. Overhead, there was a large, open patch of sky, thickly overcast with leaden clouds. He could smell fresh, wet wood, as if from sawing logs. The scent of fresh wood was mixed with the gagging stench of blood.

Off in every direction around them, not a single tree still stood. All around them the trees lay felled.

Here and there a few grotesquely splintered trunks jutted from stumps. In other places toppled trees had pulled up mats of forest floor along with their broken roots.

It was a scene of such mass destruction that it was hard for Richard to believe what he was seeing. Timber lay everywhere like hundreds of broken sticks cast to the ground by a giant. The patches of forest floor he could see between downed trees were covered with a deep layer of shattered, splintered wood, sticking up every which way in fragmented, spiked debris.

Everywhere under tree trunks, enormous limbs, branches, and man-sized splinters, lay a carpet of bloody, shredded bodies. No one could have lived through such a fierce storm of fragmented splinters driven by so many violent explosions.

Gazing out over the expanse of that destruction, Richard didn't see a single movement.

The half people caught in that violent rage of explosions had been torn to pieces. The pieces of bloody flesh he could see were unrecognizable. Most of what he saw looked like ground meat.

Richard turned back to Samantha. She watched him from the darkness of that split in the rock, as if not sure whether she wanted to come out or not.

Richard held his arms out to her in invitation. When he did, she sprang out of the narrow cleft in the rock and raced into his arms, finally giving in to sobs.

43

I t's all right, Samantha," he said softly as he smoothed her wild tangle of black hair, gently holding her head to his chest. "It's all right. We're safe."

She cried in racking sobs.

He gently shushed her, letting her know that it was all right, that it was over, that she was safe, now.

"I'm so sorry," she sobbed.

Richard frowned. "Sorry? Why would you be sorry?"

"Because I almost got us killed."

"What are you talking about?"

She looked up at him, her big dark eyes brimming with tears. "You brought me along because I said I could help you. I convinced you that you needed me, that it was important to take me because I'm gifted.

"Then, when you needed me most, when everything was at risk, you told me what I needed to do. You even explained how to make the trees explode. You brought me along to help you, and when you told me what I needed to do and how to do it, I failed you.

"You could have easily been killed any one of a hundred times fighting off those monsters while we tried to get away. I didn't do anything to help you.

"You are the one. I recognized that from the beginning, and I failed to do as I promised and as you asked of me. You were nearly killed. You are the one to save us all. It would have been my fault that the world of life ended. All because you told me what to do, and how to do it, and I didn't do it."

Richard shook his head reassuringly. "Samantha, that's not true. You were doing your best."

"No I wasn't."

"What do you mean?"

She hesitated, looking for the words. "I was afraid. I was afraid to do what you said. I was afraid that I'd mess it up, that I'd do it wrong, that I wouldn't be able to do it good enough, and that I'd fail you, fail everyone. So I couldn't do it. I tried, but I was afraid that I'd fail."

Richard smiled as he looked down at her, smoothing her hair. "You didn't fail, Samantha." He swept an arm out, gesturing around them. "You stopped the threat."

She wiped at her eyes and finally looked around, really looked around. She blinked, seeing the totality of it for the first time.

"I did this?"

"It wasn't me," Richard said.

"It's just as you said," she whispered, mostly to herself. "It would save us if I did what you told me."

"But you said you tried and couldn't." Richard was puzzled. She had tried—he'd seen her try—but she hadn't been able to do it. "So why did it finally work?"

Samantha stared off for a time, perhaps looking into her own visions as she seemed to search for the words to explain it.

"When I was back in that hole," she finally said,

"shaking and terrified that I was going to die, that those unholy half people were going to drag me out of there, rip me apart with their teeth, and eat me alive, I suddenly thought of my mother."

"Your mother? What do you mean?"

"She saw that happen to my father. That's what they did to him. She saw those monsters, like a pack of wild animals, using their teeth to rip into the man she loved, the man I loved, and devour his flesh and blood. I could finally, truly, understand how horrified and afraid she must have been.

"Then they took her. After murdering the man she loved, they took her. Can you imagine what she must have been thinking? How horrified, despairing, and afraid she must have been?

"If she really is still alive, then you are her only hope of rescue. I'm her daughter, the one who loves her more than anything, who insisted on coming along because I'm supposed to be helping you so that you can get her away from these savages. You're my mother's only hope, her last hope, and there I was cowering in a hole, shaking from head to foot."

"You shouldn't be ashamed of being afraid," Richard offered in solace. "I was afraid, too."

She looked up. "You were?"

"Of course. I can't imagine not being afraid in such a situation. It's a normal reaction of anyone with a soul. But I was also afraid because I was thinking that it was me who failed us, failed everyone depending on me."

She laid a hand, her tiny fingers, against his chest.

"But you brought me to help you. You gave me the chance. Then, when we were attacked, you had the idea of how to get us out of such a tough spot and you told me what to do. You knew what was needed because you are the one. You even explained how it worked. I'm the one who failed."

Richard looked around at the scene of destruction. "I don't think you failed at all, Samantha. In the end you didn't give up. You redoubled your effort and then you did it. You protected me. You stopped the threat. That's what matters."

She smiled with a bit of relief, if not pride, as she looked around with him. "When you told me about doing this, I didn't know that it would do this much damage. I never imagined."

Richard turned more serious as he glanced across the expanse of destruction. "Well, I have to tell you, I never saw a sorceress create quite so much havoc. But you did what was needed. Anything less, I think, would have not been enough to save us."

She looked out where his gaze went across the leveled forest. "I never imagined I could do such a thing. I didn't know the gift could be so destructive."

"Destruction in the cause of good is a glorious thing."

She smiled at such an odd sounding concept.

"So," he finally asked, "if you tried and couldn't do it, then what happened? How were you suddenly able to do it?"

"I got angry," she said rather quietly, almost as if she were ashamed of it.

"Angry?"

She nodded. "I was back in the hole, thinking about how I was about to die, and then I thought of my mother, like I told you, about what had happened to her. That made me angry, angry at myself for failing myself, for failing her, for failing you, for failing everyone. I was so angry.

"But mostly, more than being furious with myself, I was enraged at these half people, enraged that they would harm so good a man as my father, as so many others, as you. I was enraged at what they were doing, at what they want to do to everyone. Our souls are ours. What gives them the right to our souls?"

"I don't think they can really steal our souls, Samantha. Naja said as much."

"Yes but they want to. They intend to. They try to. That they can't doesn't really mean much if we're dead. They murder innocent people to try to get their souls, and that's what matters.

"What makes them think they have the right to someone else's soul, someone else's life?"

Richard could only shake his head.

"I was so angry," she said, "that it just sort of boiled over. I wanted more than anything to wipe them all out of the world of life. So, when I got that angry, trying to think of how to strike back at them for what they were doing, I latched on to what you told me to do with the trees.

"I let that anger build toward the ones who were causing so much suffering and death. When I did that, I realized that I was beginning to feel the trees all around us."

"Feeling the trees?" Richard asked.

"That's right. I reached out to them with my mind, feeling where they all were, and I focused all that anger boiling over inside me into putting intense heat in a spot inside the trunks of those trees I could feel, just like you told me to do. I guess I couldn't do it at first because I was only scared. I couldn't really do it until I was angry."

Richard studied her big eyes a moment.

"That's how my gift works—through anger."

"Really?"

He nodded. "I sometimes wish I was able to control my gift more so I could direct it to the tasks at hand, control it intentionally, but I'm afraid that as a war wizard my gift works differently than in others. It's anger or intense need that summons my gift, gives it its power. Yours seems to work both ways—by intent and then also through anger."

She looked around again. "But even so, I never could have imagined that I would be able to do this. I never imagined that I could muster this much force, create this much destruction. It's kind of, I don't know . . . frightening."

"I guess that you put the force into it that the task required, and the task was just. If you want to lift something light, it's easy. Lifting something heavier takes more muscle.

"I guess that in this case, anything less would have failed to do the job and evil would have won out. Your mind directed your gift to do what was needed, the same way you would use more muscle to lift something heavy. You don't have to think about it, your mind and body simply adjust to the weight of the task.

"I would guess that in this case, that's what happened when you used your gift." Richard gazed out across the open area. "And this is what was needed."

Still, the level of destruction was astounding and he could understand her apprehension at seeing what she had done. He had seen a number of things done by gifted people, but he didn't think he had ever seen anything quite like this.

He remembered the way Ester seemed to have a shadow of fear for Samantha. Samantha had even mentioned how people feared her and her relatives because they were gifted. That was certainly true enough with the gifted anywhere. Most people who couldn't wield magic feared those who could. They feared the unknown, feared what the gifted might be able to do.

Richard remembered when he first met Kahlan, how surprised he was when he learned how much people feared her. He had seen people, even queens, quake in her presence. A Confessor was in many ways much more frightening to people than an ordinary gifted person.

A gifted person could take your life. A Confessor could take your mind.

He guessed that, in essence, a Confessor could take your soul.

In much the same way, ordinary people feared prophets. They feared what a prophet might see of their future. They feared what secret knowledge they might have of coming events. Because of that, while they feared prophets, they also wanted to know what prophecy foretold about coming events for them.

Right before he had come to the Dark Lands to get Kahlan out of Jit's clutches, Richard had a great deal of trouble back at the palace because visiting rulers, there for Cara's wedding to Benjamin, wanted to know about prophecy. They thought Richard was hiding prophecy from them, that he didn't trust them to hear it. For that reason, some of those leaders had abandoned him and the unity of the D'Haran Empire to throw the lot of their lands and people in with Hannis Arc, the head of Fajin Province, all for the promise of leadership guided by prophecy.

While Hannis Arc was the ruler of the Dark Lands as part of Fajin Province, Richard ruled the D'Haran Empire, and the D'Haran Empire ruled Fajin Province. Hannis Arc and his followers appeared to want to break away from that alliance to instead follow prophecy.

He glanced over at Samantha, lit by the heavy overcast of the now open sky. He was beginning to see her in a new light.

He had thought she was an inexperienced sorceress

who was only now beginning to come into her own. As he looked around at the destruction, he wondered if she was something more.

He wondered about the role of Stroyza and the gifted living there. He wondered if Naja Moon's people back in ancient times had left gifted in Stroyza to be more than mere sentinels meant to watch for the barrier failing. He wondered if they had a larger purpose than to warn others, as he had thought at first.

As he scanned the massive destruction wrought by this small, frail-looking young woman, he began to wonder if those people in ancient times with such mysterious abilities had perhaps given the gifted here at Stroyza more than an explanation written in the language of Creation on their walls.

He wondered if they had given them some ability to fight. Naja said that they didn't have a way to end the threat, so they wouldn't have been able to give such an ability to any of the gifted of Stroyza, but they might have at least been able to give them the ability to fight.

Samantha had certainly demonstrated more resolve and strength than he would have expected.

He wondered if she was perhaps intended to be more than a mere sentinel.

He wondered if she was in fact a weapon left by the ancients.

This day she had certainly proven herself to be so.

After retrieving his bow from the split in the rock that had protected them and hooking it back over his shoulder, Richard stepped to the edge of the rock outcropping where he and Samantha had been protected from the lethal storm of splintered trees. He used his foot to clear the thick covering of sharp, bloody fragments off the top part of a torso. There wasn't a lot of it left, but there was enough to see that, like the others, it was clothed in little more than filthy rags.

"These half people are different," he said to himself.

Samantha regarded the remains with revulsion. "Different? What are you talking about? What do you mean they're different?"

Having been deep in thought, Richard hadn't realized that he'd said it out loud. He gestured out across the shattered landscape as he started out.

"Well, look at them all," he said, pointing here and there along the way toward the undamaged forest some distance off.

Samantha hurried to stay close as she followed behind, glancing at each place he pointed. Along the way, as he walked through the ruin, he paused to point out a headless corpse.

"See? They're all dressed basically the same, like that one, there. They're wearing little more than rags. It almost looks like they dug up corpses and stole their clothes."

"Disgusting," she muttered.

"The men who attacked me and Kahlan in the wagon were bigger than most of these people here."

"You mean those men who gave you those terrible bite wounds?"

"That's right. Those men were strong, well fed, and dressed in simple clothes that you and I would think of as normal. They were half people, intent on eating me to try to get my soul, but they didn't dress much differently than the men in your village.

"These people here are smaller, thinner, and a lot of them look sickly." He gestured to a disembodied arm sticking up out of the rubble. It was covered with open sores and scabs. "Most of them look to be diseased, like that. They all appear ill fed. They look like they live like animals.

"Besides the difference in size and apparent health, the men who attacked me talked. They sounded relatively intelligent. They thought through what had likely happened before they came across us and made plans for what they wanted to do."

"Plans? What do you mean? What kind of plans?"

"They wanted to eat me on the spot to try to get my soul, but they were going to take Kahlan for later, possibly for her trade value." He flicked a hand around, pointing out a head, a shoulder with an arm still attached, a few headless torsos, all of the torn remains peppered with everything from splinter-sized fragments to long, sharp spears of wood. "Did you ever hear any of these half people speak? Tell us to stop, anything like that?"

"I only heard them growling and howling," she said as she hugged her arms to herself.

Richard nodded. "So, even though the men who attacked me at the wagon and these here are both half people who want to steal our souls, they're considerably different."

Samantha pushed her tangle of black hair back out of her way as she looked around, stepping carefully among all the debris as she followed him.

She frowned as she thought it over. "It seems odd that these half people would be so different."

"And then there were the bodies I saw," Richard said as he sat sidesaddle on a fat, splintered fallen tree trunk and then swung his legs over.

It was too big for Samantha, so she went around. "What bodies?" she asked.

"Many of the half people who attacked us before I woke up were killed by the troops with us, and for all I know maybe by some kind of magic Zedd and Nicci managed to conjure. It was dark and I was only just waking up, but then, and later when Ester and the rest of them came to my rescue, I saw a number of bodies from what looked to me to have been a bloody battle. I only got a brief look, but from what I saw all of them looked the same, and they didn't look at all like any of these half people here, or anything like the men who attacked me. I overheard the men say that they thought they were Shun-tuk."

"Shun-tuk? What do they look like?" she asked.

"They wore little clothing. Some of them had trousers while others had only cloth wrapped around their waists. None of them had shirts, other than what I thought of as decorative vests covered with beads, charms, and talismans.

"All of them, though, were smeared with what looked like a whitish ash. Their eyes were darkened with dirt, or soot, or something. The rest of their faces were covered with a milky colored substance, probably wood ash. Their heads were shaved. A few of them had tufts sticking up on the tops of their skulls. Those with the tufts of hair had what looked like beads and teeth and bones wrapped around it to make the tufts of hair stand straight up."

Samantha hugged her spindly arms to herself again. "That sounds frightening."

Richard nodded. "Warriors of all sorts try to make themselves look intimidating, and these Shun-tuk certainly looked the part."

"So then, you're saying that all three of these different kinds of people, these sickly ones here in rags, the men dressed normal who attacked you, and the wild-looking, painted-up Shun-tuk are all half people."

"Right. All different, but all half people. The thing is, in Naja's account, when she talked about the danger from the half people, she didn't mention that they were different. She only said that Emperor Sulachan's makers down in the Old World had created the half people to be used as weapons. Later, Naja's people up here in the New World managed to collect them, along with the walking dead, and trap them all behind the barrier."

Samantha scrambled over a log to follow after him. "So then, what's your point?"

"My point is something has happened since they were locked behind the barrier and they are no longer the same."

Samantha looked puzzled. "Does it really make a difference for some reason?"

Richard looked back over his shoulder and arched an eyebrow. "According to Naja some of them had the ability to use occult magic."

Her alarm showed in her expression. "These didn't show any evidence of it."

Richard paused and looked back at her. "That's what has me so concerned. Maybe these here are just the outliers, the scavengers. We might be talking about half people who have developed since Naja's time, who are now more dangerous, who are even better at hunting those with souls than the half people were back in the great war, or than these dead ones here."

As they walked on through the rubble, Samantha's only answer was a worried look.

After a time, they made it to the edge of the site of the destruction and flattened trees. At the outer edge of the leveled forest a number of big trees leaned against others still standing in the forest beyond. From what Richard knew of wind-fallen trees, such tremendous weight leaning on other trees would cause some of them to eventually fall as well. The destruction in this part of the forest wasn't yet over. It would continue for some time until the weaker trees finally fell. Eventually, this place would grow back over, but it was going to be a long time before the clearing filled in among the fallen bones of the old-growth trees.

"Careful," Richard said as he stepped around several smaller trees leaning outward, all resting against a forest giant. "If the branches holding those trees here were to give way, they could fall at any moment. Stay in my tracks and follow me until we're safely back into the woods again."

Richard wove his way in among the destruction of damaged but standing trees, trying to avoid the ones that looked like they were in the most danger of falling, but he couldn't avoid them all, because there were hundreds of partially fallen trees hanging precariously in branches of others. All of them were riddled with splinters, some as small as a finger, and some bigger than his leg. Many of the leaning trees were buckling along splits and would never survive.

"So then it sounds like these Shun-tuk might be the ones who have our people," she said after some thought. "How will we find them?"

"From what the men were saying, the Shun-tuk live beyond the barrier in a distant land." Richard carefully ducked under a partially uprooted tree that was pulling up a section of the forest floor. "The men were surprised that the Shun-tuk had traveled so far. From what I overheard them say, the Shun-tuk nation is vast."

"Great," she muttered under her breath. "So, you're saying that the half people who are likely holding your friends and my mother captive are going to be deep into the third kingdom."

"It seems likely," Richard said as he entered the shadowy world of the forest. He gestured back toward the ruins of the woods. "I don't think that these half people here would be the kind to take captives. I think if they caught someone they would eat them on the spot. The Shun-tuk seem to be different. They act out of larger motives."

"That means we need to look for the Shun-tuk, and when we find them we'll face even bigger problems than we did here."

"I'm afraid so." Once farther back into the dark shadows of the still forest, Richard paused and turned back to Samantha. "The part that worries me the most is the occult magic Naja says they have. It may have been growing stronger as they were locked away behind the barrier."

Her nose wrinkled with her frown. "Why would it grow stronger?"

"Nature seeks balance."

"What do you mean?"

"Like all of nature, predators and prey seek balance. If there are too many rabbits, for example, more wolves will be born and they will have an ample food supply. Wolves will grow in number and cut down the overpopulation of rabbits. If there are too many wolves, then they overhunt the food source and they run out of prey. So, fewer wolves survive starvation. Then more rabbits are able to survive, and so on, as nature seeks balance."

"But that's just with animals."

"All of nature seeks balance. Even within the wolf population, such as the balance between male and female. Additive Magic is balanced with Subtractive Magic. Free will is the balance to prophecy."

Samantha pushed some of her hair back from her face as she walked close behind him. "Well, that much of it makes sense, but what does balance have to do with occult magic?"

"Occult powers may be the balance to the gift."

She stopped in her tracks and stared at him. "That's a frightening thought."

"I'd have to agree."

"But why would magic need balance?"

"Maybe it has multiplied too much and nature is seeking to balance it by letting occult power grow."

Samantha tilted her head toward him a little. "So are we the hunters or the prey? Who's hunting who?"

"Good question," Richard said before he turned back to the slightly open, low, mossy area that led back into the deeper woods. "The trail should be this way. It shouldn't be far, and then we can make better time."

CHAPTER

45

Richard was right. Before long they picked up the remote forest trail. It was a dark burrow of exposed rocks and roots tunneling through the thick vegetation. Over the centuries it had seen only random, occasional travelers, but lately it served hordes of half people coming down it to hunt souls. Now it was cloaked in a threatening silence.

Richard stood for a long moment, listening, watching, trying to pick up any sign that would indicate trouble. Samantha stood silently beside him, waiting for him to pass judgment.

"You said before that the gifted people can sense others," she whispered. When he nodded, she went on. "So, do you think you could explain it to me, like you explained how to make trees explode, so that I could help us by sensing if anyone is out there? I could at least try my best."

Richard pressed his lips tight in frustration. "I wish I could, but I'm afraid I don't have any idea how they do it. I just know that they can. No one has ever explained it to me, like with the trees, so I can't explain it to you."

She looked dejected at the news that she wouldn't be able to learn the trick so she could help them.

Richard laid his hand on her shoulder. "Come on. We'll just have to find your mother and get her away from whoever has her, and then she can teach you how to do it."

Samantha returned the smile. "You seem to have a way of making me feel better, even right in the middle of a terrible situation."

"As long as we have choices in life and use our heads, there is always the possibility of turning around the worst situation."

Her smile widened a little. While he returned the smile, he was concerned because he could see the exhaustion in her eyes. She obviously didn't want to admit how much it had taken out of her to do what she had done with the trees when back in that split in the rock.

"I'm dead tired from fighting off the half people with my sword. How about you? You must be worn out from the effort of using your magic back there. I know that, for me, using any kind of magic is tiring, even the magic of my sword."

"Well," she admitted, "I guess a little. But I won't slow you down. I promise."

Richard pulled his pack off his shoulder and flipped back the flap. He dug around a moment until he found some dried meat. He pulled out two pieces and handed one to Samantha.

"Here, chew on this as you walk. It will help build your strength back up."

Richard tore off a piece between his teeth. She took a bite of her own before following him as he started up the trail.

He hated to use the trail because it was such an obvious ambush point. When there was this kind of manifest danger, he would much rather make his own way through the woods than follow the choke point of a trail. The problem was, cutting their own way through the woods any more than they needed to would slow them down considerably. They had a long way to go to reach what Samantha's village knew as the north wall, and the trail went only part of the way. With every passing moment being a threat to the lives of those they were going to try to rescue, Richard knew they had no time to waste.

The choice was a hard one, though. They couldn't rescue anyone if they were killed on a trail by half people waiting in ambush. But on the other hand, Richard was terrified of being too late. Being a moment too late meant Kahlan would die, claimed by the touch of death lurking within her. He would soon follow her into the dark forever. It likely meant that untold numbers, if not the world of life itself, would die.

Magda Searus and Merritt had told him that he had the power to save the world of life, or destroy it. If he made the wrong choice, and was killed in an ambush on the trail, then that might be the cause of the end of life that the first Confessor was talking about. If he didn't take the trail, the delay might mean they lost their chance, and that could mean the end of all life as well.

In the end, he reasoned that the half people who had been chasing them would probably have all been together. It didn't seem likely that some of them would have hung back. They were driven by the lust for a soul, so it was reasonable to think that they were all dead back in the blasted forest.

In light of all that, Richard chose to use the trail in order to make the best time they could. His sense of urgency was too well founded to ignore. Of course, he was well aware that other half people, different kinds of half people from other parts of the third kingdom, could very well come down the trail or be waiting in ambush. All the more reason to stay alert.

Decision made, he forged ahead, determined to make the most of the time the trail saved them. The path through the woods was similar to secondary trails Richard knew back in Hartland. It wasn't a well-groomed trail that made for swift travel, but it was still much easier than pushing their own way through virgin forest. It also wasn't wide enough for them to walk side by side, so he led the way and Samantha followed, sometimes having to trot to keep up with his pace. Richard constantly scanned ahead and to the sides as he moved as quietly as possible.

There were occasional wind-fallen trees that lay across the path that they had to climb over. Saplings grew in close at the side of the trail in places, making it a narrow green tunnel with branches and boughs continually slapping at their arms and legs.

The leaden overcast, coupled with the thick forest canopy, conspired to make the tunneling pathway a dark and gloomy place. Off in the distance he occasionally heard the cries of birds or chatter from squirrels, but for the most part the woods were dead silent. Mist and drizzle combed out of the air by pine needles collected until the drops were heavy enough to drip down on them.

For their lunch, Richard stopped only briefly to get a bite to eat. Samantha was looking somewhat better after having eaten the dried meat earlier, so he didn't want to take any more time than necessary to catch their breath for a moment as they retrieved food and water from their packs.

After the brief stop, they were quickly back on their

way and walked the rest of the afternoon without seeing anyone or anything out of the ordinary. The journey through the forest was in a way comforting. It reminded him of his life growing up in the Hartland woods, and his time as a woods guide. It had been a time of peace and contentment, before he knew of any of the troubles of the wider world.

He caught himself looking at all the various mosses growing on rocks, making them look like green pillows, and the places where it crept across the ground and grew up the bases of tree trunks. In some places he saw beautiful, delicate little white flowers. In a way, the flowers seemed out of place because the journey was fraught with such danger and anxiety that it didn't seem like beauty belonged. He guessed that it was the balance to the lack of peace he was feeling.

Samantha kept her hood up to help keep her hair from getting wet in the drizzle and random drops falling from trees above. She kept her head down as she hurried to keep up with him. He could see in her posture how tired she was, but she didn't complain. He felt bad for setting such a swift pace, but it couldn't be helped. He suspected that she was thinking of her mother, and didn't mind the pace.

When it started getting dark, Richard led them off the trail to find a place to sleep. He didn't want to be anywhere that people—or half people—would likely come across them. He walked off the path for quite a ways, deliberately choosing the roughest terrain and the places with the thickest underbrush. People who went off trails to go through the woods almost always picked the easiest places to walk, so he wanted to go where it was least likely anyone might explore off the trail.

He eventually found a secluded spot he liked in the crook of a rock cleft that rose up for thirty or forty feet. He surveyed the area for any signs of dangerous animals, including humans. He saw no indication that anyone had ever been in the spot. Richard and Samantha were likely the first people who had ever seen this place. He saw no caves where bears or wolves might den, and no snakes.

With the light failing and the mist getting heavier, he swiftly cut some saplings and leaned them up against the rock. After having made a framework, he piled on pine and balsam boughs, and on top of that, brush to cover up the evidence of human construction. By that time it was nearly dark.

"I wouldn't know it was there even if I walked right by it," Samantha said.

"That's the whole point," Richard told her. "Ordinarily, in such a place I'd want to take turns standing watch, but I think this is hidden well enough. There is no evidence that anyone ever comes this way, so I think it's more important that we both get a good sleep. We're going to need it tomorrow."

She nodded. "I'm really tired. Sleep sounds good."

He gestured to the side of the lean-to structure. "Go on, then, go around there and get inside."

She looked puzzled. "Aren't we going to have a fire to keep warm?"

"Fires attract people. Even if you don't see it, you can smell the smoke from a fire from a long way off. By itself, someone would almost have to fall on top of this shelter to know it's here. But a fire would broadcast our position and let other people, especially half people, know that we're here."

She looked around at the surrounding woods. "Oh. I guess that makes sense." She glanced around again. "What about wild animals?"

"I'm not worried. I have a gifted sorceress with me."

She smiled. "I guess you're right."

"It won't be too bad, you'll see. Go on, get inside."

She had to crawl on her hands and knees to get in under the leaning roof of the shelter. Richard followed her in, pulling a thick mat of pine branches over the opening. Inside it was snug, relatively dry, and nearly pitch black. He fished around blindly in his pack until he found the tin travel housing for a candle.

He held it out and put her hand on it. "Here, can you use your gift to light this?"

He saw a small spark in the darkness and a flame sprang up onto the candlewick.

Richard hung the candle in front of them. "You can put your hands over it to warm them if you're cold. It's likely to get chilly tonight."

She frowned over at him. "Why don't I just put some heat in a couple of rocks? Then we could hold them in our laps to keep warm."

"Oh," Richard said. He hadn't thought of doing that. "Well, that works, too."

He used his fingers to pull a rock the size of a loaf of bread up from the ground to the side and handed it to her. Samantha put her hands to either side of it for a moment. He saw her briefly close her eyes in concentration; then she handed it to him. The rock was toasty warm.

"I guess you are coming in handy for something," he said as he pulled up another rock for her to heat for herself.

She let out a soft giggle.

They picked some travel biscuits and dried fish out of their packs, along with some fresh nuts, and had a simple meal that was better than he expected, probably because he was so hungry he would have eaten just about anything.

When they were done eating, Richard pulled off his

cloak and laid it over both of them like a blanket. "This will help keep us warm. Sorry, but the woods aren't the most comfortable place to sleep, especially in conditions such as this."

"I don't care," she said quietly. "I only care about getting there in time. I can sleep the rest of my life, after I get my mother out of the hands of those soulless, unholy half-dead monsters."

Richard agreed with her sentiment.

He pulled his cloak up to their chins. Samantha leaned against him for warmth, putting her small hands around his biceps and locking her slender fingers together. She laid her head against his shoulder.

Richard rested his right arm across his lap so that he could keep his hand on the hilt of his sword. That would make it a lot easier to respond in a hurry if he had to.

He could hear Samantha's soft, even breathing, along with the whisper of rain pattering against leaves. He was so exhausted that he started sinking into sleep almost immediately.

His last thoughts were of Kahlan.

46

By late the next day they reached the place where the trail began to bear left, toward the west. The trail had taken them as far as it could. It was frustrating, because they had been making good time, but the trail was no longer headed north, so they were going to have to start making their way through uncharted forest toward the third kingdom.

Richard scanned the edge of the forest along the side of the path, searching for the best area to take them through the woods, when he spotted a place that almost looked like a trail. A fresh trail.

"This looks like a good place," Samantha said as she pointed. "The way north looks more open through here."

"There's a good reason for that." He gestured to the trampled shrubs and broken twigs, the kicked up dirt, and the overturned moss. "Do you know what this is?"

Samantha looked puzzled. "No."

"It looks to me like the place used by all those half people traveling down here from the third kingdom. Look up in there at how someone dragged their feet along the ground." He pointed to another spot. "Looks like someone stumbled there and broke that branch. They walked without paying any attention to what they stepped on. There, they trampled those mushrooms. Back in there a lot of the ferns are broken.

"This is not the way a regular traveler walks. This is the way careless people who know little about traveling, or the woods, would walk. It looks to me the way those half people who tried to ambush us would walk. This is probably where they came down from the north."

"Really?" she asked. She looked up at him. "Then all we have to do is follow this and it will lead us right to where we're going. It will lead us right to the barrier, to those open gates in the north wall."

"No," he said, "if we follow this new trail we are liable to run into more half people coming down from the third kingdom to hunt for people with souls. Those dead half people back there aren't the only ones. The others are likely to be different, like the men who attacked me, or the Shun-tuk. They're smarter. We don't want to run into that sort if we don't have to."

She took a step back, as if the place was suddenly threatening. "I guess it isn't such a good idea, then."

With a hand on her shoulder, Richard turned her to the left. "We'll go on a little ways farther up the trail and then turn north through the woods to go parallel with this route taken by the half people. I want to stay far enough away from it that if there are more half people coming south by this same route, they won't hear us.

"At the same time, by staying close enough, then from time to time I can check on this trail they made so that I can make sure we're going to the place they came from. That way it will help lead us where we're heading, right to the third kingdom, but we won't be as likely to run into trouble.

"It shouldn't be too difficult to keep track of this route they've made trudging through the woods. From the looks of it they were simply taking the route that was the easiest because of the lay of the land. I can do the same thing, but stay off to the side so we don't accidentally run across their trail at the wrong time."

She made a face. "How do you know all this stuff?"

Richard shrugged. "I've been doing this all my life, since I was younger than you."

After following the established trail on for some distance, Richard finally judged it far enough away from the path made by the half people to be safe, so he turned north into the woods. He regretted having to leave the trail, even as rough as it had been, and make their own trail through uncharted forest, but it was something that he was experienced doing. Because of his experience, he knew how to select the best route to take through the dense woods.

For a time as they traveled north they were able to follow a deer trail, but it eventually veered off and they had to plunge back into the thick of the woods. In several places they had to climb rock ridges to avoid taking time and trouble to find a way around. Once, they had to backtrack when Richard abruptly found himself at the edge of a cliff that would be too dangerous to climb down.

When nightfall came, Richard again found a well-hidden spot, where he built them another small shelter for the night. The drizzle had picked up as darkness closed in. They had managed to complete the shelter in time to keep themselves mostly dry. He was sore from sleeping sitting up the night before, but he was tired and his hip sockets ached from the long day of hiking through dense woods, so he was happy for any rest he would be able to get. Like the previous night, he and Samantha huddled close for warmth and fell asleep quickly.

The next morning dawned cool and humid but at least the drizzle had stopped. That didn't mean a lot, though, because both the humidity and the previous night's drizzle and fog had left everything inside their shelter damp or dripping. Droplets of water dotted his cloak and ran off it in little rivulets when he took it off them and gave it a brief shake.

It was even more uncomfortable when they emerged from the warmth of the little shelter. It was a disagreeable feeling to see that it was another gloomy day. Richard was getting sick and tired of the endless dark days under a constant, heavy overcast. He wished for a sunny day that would dry everything out. He was beginning to see why it was called the Dark Lands. It was a dark and depressing wilderness.

They had a quick meal of sausages and travel biscuits along with a few slices of dried apples. After packing up, they were quickly on their way. Before long, they came upon a small brook that made travel through the dense undergrowth a great deal easier. As they walked, Richard checked the burbling, clear water for any sign of fish, but he didn't see any.

After an hour of walking along the rocky bank of the brook, he decided to scout to make sure that they weren't too close to the half people's haphazard trail. Richard had Samantha crouch down between a rock and several small spruce trees where she was well hidden and could wait while he went off to scout. The trail the half people had made meandered aimlessly at times, so he wanted to make certain that they were still distant enough from it that they would be safe.

The trail turned out to be a goodly distance. Richard

checked but didn't see any sign that there had been anyone on the trail overnight. Happy after he saw that they weren't too close to it, they were able to move on, using the brook as a path through the woods.

Mostly cedars grew along the sides of the brook, with a luscious carpet of moss covering the banks in places. The brook created a bit of an opening through the forest, so they were able to make better time. The moss growing in thick beds made for soft walking, but what Richard liked most about it was that it made their progress almost silent, while the running water of the brook also helped cover any sound they might make. Silence was safety because even if there were half people about, if they couldn't hear Richard and Samantha passing nearby then they wouldn't come after them.

Rounding a turn where the brook went around a rock outcropping, they came suddenly on a man kneeling beside the brook, scooping up water in his hands for a drink. He hadn't heard them walking upstream on the mossy banks. He looked up from his cupped hands, water leaking through his fingers, surprised to see Richard and Samantha as they came around the rock. He was dressed better than the half people that Samantha had killed, and had a huskier build, like the men who had attacked Richard at the wagon.

Richard wasn't as surprised as the man, because this possibility had always been in the back of his mind. Richard knew that with the new trail so well used by the half people, it was possible that some of them might wander off that trail, so he had been on the lookout. Still, it was an unpleasant jolt to suddenly come upon someone after having the woods all to themselves for so long.

The man, at first frozen in surprise, quickly recovered from his shock. His eyes immediately filled with the kind of savage hunger any predator had at seeing prey unexpectedly appear within reach.

The man sprang up in a full charge. He bared his teeth with a growl as he lunged at Richard. As he raced in, the man reached out to tackle his prey.

Richard had been ready and, rather than meeting the threat directly, dodged to the side at the last possible instant. Richard threw an arm around the man's neck as he fell past and put a choke hold on him to keep him from crying out for help.

The man struggled, reaching back to claw at Richard, trying to get to his face, to gouge out his eyes. The man's teeth were bared, but he couldn't get a bite of flesh. Richard lifted the brawny man while putting pressure on the sides of his neck to cut off the blood supply.

The man's struggles slackened as he quickly grew weak.

"Who are you?" Richard asked.

The man only growled, even as he did his best to keep his eyes open.

"How far to the north wall?" Richard asked.

Drool ran from the corners of the man's mouth as he gasped for breath, as he fought to remain conscious and at the same time fight back.

"How far," Richard asked again through gritted teeth.

"A day away, maybe."

"And the Shun-tuk? How far to their land once beyond the north wall?"

When the man didn't answer, Richard increased the pressure. The man's eyes bulged. His tongue bulged from his mouth as his face turned red.

"How far is the kingdom of the Shun-tuk?" Richard asked again in a dangerously calm voice.

"Don't know . . . never been that far. I'm not that stupid."

"How far?"

"Days. A few days more. But they will catch you, eat your flesh, and drink your blood. They will have your soul."

"You can't gain someone's soul by drinking their blood or by eating them. There is no way to get someone else's soul. It's not possible."

The man struggled even harder, trying with renewed fury to reach back and get hold of something. He couldn't. Richard wasn't taking any chances and twisted harder to make his point.

"Lie!" the man gasped, red-faced from lack of air. "You want to keep it for yourself. All of you with souls are greedy. You soil the world with your nature. We will have your souls. We deserve them. We will have all of your souls!"

Samantha stepped up before the man's face, regarding him calmly. "How do you figure you deserve our souls? What gives you the right?"

Richard had him tightly by the neck, but the man's glare turned up to Samantha. He gave her an evil, lustful grin.

"We will eat your warm flesh and drink your warm blood and have your souls. We will rule the world of life."

Richard twisted until the man cried out. "Are you with anyone else?"

"No!"

"Good," Richard said under his breath as he snapped the man's neck.

As Richard let the dead weight slip to the ground, he gestured to Samantha. "Let's get going. Better that we are away from here in case others of his kind find him."

47

Richard was exhausted after a day of difficult travel over rough terrain. The farther north they went, the more uneven the ground became, and the darker and gloomier. At times the clouds were so low that the tops of the trees vanished in the gray overcast.

It was tiring to climb up steep, rocky rises only to have to descend the far side, and then do it all over again when the next steep ascent appeared through the trees. It was made worse in places by stretches of brush so dense that it was tiring to get through it and it bogged down their progress. In other places they encountered underbrush with tangled layers of thorny vines that were impassable and had to be skirted.

Richard hadn't slept well the night before, after talking with the soulless man they found drinking at the brook who wanted to eat them alive. Richard wished he could have killed the man twice.

Samantha looked tired as well. She had been uncharacteristically quiet the night before and then all day as they trudged through the trackless forests of the

Dark Lands. When Richard had asked if she was all right, she'd said that it had unnerved her to hear such an evil man say such terrible things—to have him look her in the eye and tell her that he wanted to eat her warm flesh, drink her blood, and take her soul.

Richard knew that what probably unnerved her the most was knowing that others with the same sentiment had murdered her father and were likely holding her mother captive.

At least, he hoped they were still holding her mother captive, and that they hadn't harmed her. Richard hoped that Zedd and Nicci and Cara and Benjamin and the rest of the soldiers were all still alive as well, and that they hadn't been slaughtered. He knew what a dim hope that really was, though. It had to be terrifying to be in the hands of such merciless cannibals. He couldn't help being constantly haunted by fear for their safety. That fear kept him pushing forward as swiftly as he could.

Besides wanting to rescue his friends—to save the lives of those people he loved and cared about—he always had in the back of his mind that the only way to save Kahlan's life as well was to get her back to the containment field at the People's Palace along with Zedd and Nicci so that they could remove the Hedge Maid's touch of death.

Richard glanced around when he noticed that the woods were growing darker all the time. It was still only late in the afternoon, not yet late enough for it to be getting dark. He looked up from time to time but the dense forest canopy was closed in so tightly overhead that he couldn't see any sky, so he couldn't tell how cloudy it was. He felt warm even though there was still a cold mist.

Moving along a narrow, marshy low area, Richard

went to a knee. Overwhelmed with how weary he felt, how exhausted, he couldn't seem to take another step. He had to stop, had to pause to rest a moment.

"Lord Rahl, what is it?" Samantha asked as she rushed to his side. "What's wrong?"

Richard pulled a deep breath as his head hung. "I'm just so tired, that's all." He dismissed it with a gesture. "It's nothing. It's just that it's been hard traveling and I didn't sleep well. . . ."

Samantha laid her small hand against his forehead. "You have a fever."

He wasn't at all surprised. "Feels like it."

She pushed against the front of his shoulder with one hand while gesturing with the other. "Here, sit back on that rock for a minute."

Richard looked around behind and then sat back on the leaf-covered rock she was pointing to. Samantha stood in front of him, her face almost even with his. She pressed her fingertips to his temples. He could feel the slight but familiar tingle of magic.

She finally pulled her hands back. "It's the darkness in you," she told him in a quiet voice. "The touch of death. It's what the Mother Confessor has in her, too. It's the same dark evil that is trying to claim you both. It's getting worse, as I told you would happen."

"You did," Richard said as he nodded. "Is there anything you can do?"

She was a long moment in answering. "I'm sorry, Lord Rahl. I've already healed you all I can. I wish I knew more about healing. I wish I knew of some trick or something to help, but I don't. It will take your grandfather now if you and the Mother Confessor are to be truly helped."

"What if you try to use the gift to strengthen me, rather than healing me?"

She thought it over and then put her fingertips to his temples. He again felt the warm tingle of her gift. He could hear birds in the distance, and feel a soft breath of damp air on his face. Inside him, he could feel the warm glow of magic. He felt the familiar suspension of time in the grip of that magic.

She removed her hands. "Did it help?"

Richard stood and rolled his shoulders, trying to sense if he felt stronger. At least he was able to stand.

"I think it helped. I do feel a little stronger. Thank you."

"I wish it was more, Lord Rahl, but I'm afraid that it isn't the real solution you need, just a temporary boost. Rest would help more until you can be healed properly."

He nodded and managed a small smile to reassure her. "I think I can walk, now. Let's get going. Getting more rest will have to wait."

Richard forced himself to move despite how much he wanted to slow down or stop to rest. He knew, somewhere deep down inside, that if he gave up and lay down, he would die, much the way people caught in winter storms would get tired, lie down, and go to sleep, and never to rise again.

When he died, he told himself, he would have all eternity to rest. If he wanted to live, if he wanted others to live, it was going to take effort.

As they came to the top of each new rise he wished that he could see through the dense green leaves, pine boughs, and dark shadows among the endless tree trunks to what lay beyond. He wished he could get to a vantage point so he could see how much farther, but there was no such vantage point in the endless, dark, forbidding forest.

As he walked, he glanced up at a tree, thinking that

if he climbed up high, he might possibly get a view of what was ahead. But he didn't have the energy to spare, much less the time, to go climbing trees. He supposed that he knew where he was going, and he knew that they were going in the right direction, so he simply needed to put one foot in front of another and they would eventually get there. Looking out from a high vantage point wouldn't get them there any faster.

As the day wore on, he realized it was getting a little brighter. At first he thought the overcast might be breaking up, but then, coming over a rise, through an opening in the thick layers of limbs, he finally saw a patch of light.

He trotted toward a narrow opening in the trees and in the misty distance was rewarded with his first glimpse of the barrier. He had been impatient to get to it for days, and now, suddenly seeing it, he was stunned. He stopped dead in his tracks and stared. Samantha stood beside him, staring as well.

48

Richard and Samantha stood with their backs to the dark woods, staring out into the gray light of a heavily overcast day at the enormity of the structure standing before them.

There was no way to see the ancient power invested in this wall to make it a barrier keeping evil contained. But what he could see—the wall itself—was a physical barrier of staggering proportions. It had looked big when he had seen it through the viewing port back at Stroyza, but seeing it up closer, seeing the sheer size of it, was bone-chilling.

Despite the strength and size of the physical barrier itself, and the power of spells cast by wizards with abilities Richard couldn't entirely imagine, whatever was on the other side had still managed to escape.

From where they stood in a small clearing among a bed of cinnamon ferns and scraggly holly oak that gave them a broken view off through the pines standing guard at the edge of the forest, Richard could see that they were still some distance off to the side of where the opening would be, which was what he had wanted so as not to encounter any half people coming south through those gates from the third kingdom beyond. He wanted to remain hidden to give him an opportunity to survey the area.

"Come on," he said to Samantha as he started out again.

He moved more quickly now that he knew for sure that they had finally reached the wall. Samantha had to trot to keep up with his long strides. Even as he put more effort into moving quickly, he still kept a wary eye on the surrounding countryside for any sign of trouble. He didn't want to be surprised and find himself unexpectedly having to fight off a forest full of half people.

"What are we going to do when we get there?" Samantha asked, breathless from the effort of keeping up with him.

"I'm not exactly sure, yet. First, we have to get through the gates. After that we need to keep heading north until we find the land of the Shun-tuk."

"Then what?"

Richard frowned back over his shoulder. "Then we rescue our people being held captive there."

"How are we going to do that?"

Richard carefully danced across rocks to cross a small, slow-moving stream. "I wish I knew. We'll have to look over the situation once we get there, then we can start to figure out a plan."

"Maybe I can use magic to help somehow. You know, create a distraction, or something."

"Or something," Richard said.

At first animated now that they were close, Samantha fell to silent worry. She finally got around to the heart of her concern.

"Lord Rahl, you know the way Jit held you captive?"

Richard pushed a low pine bough aside, holding it

out of the way to let her pass. "You mean the way she had us bound up in all those thorny vines?"

Samantha nodded as she ducked under the bough he held out of her way. "Well, what if they're doing that to all the people we're going in there to save?"

Richard's brow drew together. "I don't know what you're getting at. Do you mean what will we do if they have all of them tangled up in thorn vines?"

"Not exactly." She peeked around her mat of black hair to look over at him. "You know what they were doing to the Mother Confessor? What they were going to do to you?"

It suddenly dawned on him what she was getting at. "Oh. You mean the way they cut Kahlan and were bleeding her."

"That's right. You said they were draining her blood and collecting it in bowls and then feeding it to Jit."

Richard half turned to her as he marched among the towering trees, his mood darkening. "Go on."

"They were bleeding her, Lord Rahl. They would have done that to you had you not managed to kill Jit and escape. Jit was collecting and drinking the Mother Confessor's blood, the same as she did with all her victims."

Richard came to a stop. "What's your point?"

"Remember what that man back at the brook said before you killed him? He said that he wanted to drink my warm blood. Naja spoke of them drinking every drop of blood, thinking that a soul might be in the blood and trying to escape. See what I mean? They think that the soul inhabits a living person and that it can escape. So, they drink people's blood, hoping that they will capture the soul as it tries to escape."

"So you're wondering if the Shun-tuk, unlike the other half people you killed back in the forest, have evolved even more to think of blood as the 'lifeblood' of a person, that it's the stuff of a person's soul, and maybe they want captives in order to bleed them in an attempt to drain out the soul and drink it in themselves."

Samantha shrugged her small shoulders. "I don't know. Maybe. After all, Jit was from the third kingdom, so maybe what she was doing to the Mother Confessor tells us something about what the people there are like and how they think. That man seemed to feel that same way, even if the ones I killed back in the woods were more wild about wanting to eat us."

Richard hadn't thought of it that way. "I suppose it's possible."

"My mother said that she should have realized that Jit being in the swamp was a sign that she was one of the first to have escaped from behind the north wall. She said that she should have recognized it as one of the first indications that the north wall was failing.

"What if Jit is also a good indication of the way these half people think and what they do? What if the Shuntuk wanted captives to keep for their blood, like we keep animals for their milk. What if they have those people imprisoned in order to drain them of their blood, thinking that fresh, warm blood is the way for them to gain their soul."

"That does make some sense," Richard said with a sigh, "but then why would they seem to be more interested in taking the gifted captive?"

Samantha didn't have a ready answer.

"Unless they think the blood of the gifted has some special quality," Richard said, following along with her line of reasoning. "Of course, they might have a more sinister reason for wanting to take the gifted captive."

"A more sinister reason? Like what?"

Richard considered it in brooding silence as he made his way past branches and boughs on his way toward the gray light out ahead. "I don't know. It could be something more complex. The main thing, though, is that the exact reason is really a secondary consideration. What really matters the most right now is the solution, not the problem. If the Shun-tuk do have them, and if our people are alive, we have to get them out of there. That's what matters."

Almost as soon as he said it, the forest began to grow lighter. In a few dozen more steps they emerged from the oppressive greenery on the edge of a small ridge that provided an opening in the forest, allowing them an expansive view.

They were face-to-face with an immense, towering wall.

Richard put his arm out, stopping Samantha from stepping too far out of the woods into the open, where he feared they might be spotted. She stood beside him, silently gazing at the sight.

From the edge of the slight ridge they had a good view through the opening in the trees. They were looking down somewhat on a wall that rose up from the forest floor, up well past the tallest trees, so that they had to turn their heads up to see the top. The wall made the towering old-growth trees look like they were nothing more than saplings.

"From seeing it through the portal, I always knew it was big," Samantha said, "but I still never realized that it was this big. Until you're standing here in front of it, you don't really know its true size."

Richard understood what she meant. Sometimes, when the scale of something was so far out of the ordinary, or so far outside your frame of reference, so much larger than anything you'd ever seen before, and viewed from so far away, it was hard to comprehend its true size. Up close, such monumental sights often seemed even more incomprehensible.

The stone wall seemed impossibly high, even to Richard, and he had seen a number of spectacular sights, both natural and man-made. It made him a bit dizzy just looking at the size of the soaring stone face of the wall.

The wall stretched left and right to where it ended in the distance against enormous cliffs soaring upward as high as any mountains he had ever seen. High up, past broken clouds, he could see patches of snow lying on the steep rises. Another layer of clouds higher up, above the ragged shreds of clouds drifting by lower down, obscured the tops of the mountains so that he wasn't even seeing the mountain peaks and thus their full height.

The wall standing before them was constructed of stones of different sizes and shapes, all fit precisely together like a complex puzzle. All the edges looked to be in solid contact with every part of each block locked in around them. He didn't see any spot where so much as a piece of paper could have been pushed between the tightly fit blocks of stone. The wall appeared to have been constructed without mortar, with the exacting fit and enormous weight locking it all tightly together. It was as perfectly built a wall as Richard had ever seen. He had seen a number of spectacular man-made structures, but this one was remarkable in its singular simplicity and sheer scale.

Down the slope, off to the right, Richard could see the opening in the wall where the gates stood. There was a structure over the opening for the gates that he remembered seeing from the viewing port.

He didn't see anyone anywhere. There were no people down in the area in front of the wall, no one watching from atop the wall, and no one coming and going through the open gates. It seemed odd to him that after thousands of years of the wall standing as an impenetrable barrier, now that the gates were open the area around them would be so deserted.

He wondered for a brief moment if all the half people from the third kingdom had already poured out of those gates to go south into the world of life, seeking souls they believed were there for the taking. He didn't know what their motives would be—to stay near their homes, or now that they were free to go on a rampage out into the world, to gorge themselves on flesh and blood.

For a time, Richard stood silently watching as he felt the cool speckles of mist on his face. He checked all along the top of the wall, trying to see if there was anyone watching them, if any guards looked out from time to time. It was impossible to tell for sure, of course, but he didn't see anyone. He didn't know if they might have some kind of small openings for looking out. Although, what would be the purpose? The wall was there to keep them in, not for defense.

He thought that it could be that all those who wanted to leave had already left, and those who didn't had stayed back to the north, where they had lived for millennia. It was also possible that they only left at certain times, hunted, and then returned to the safety of their kingdom, like bats that emerged at nightfall to feed on blood.

What he wondered most, though, was how he and Samantha were going to get in without being spotted out in the open. There was certainly no hope of scaling the wall. The outside of it looked to be too smooth for them to get a handhold or foothold anywhere. Of course, closer up he might find that there were small handholds in between the stones, but he doubted it. More importantly, even if they could scale the wall they would be exposed and out in the open for a long time and could easily be picked off with arrows. Possible or not, Richard discounted the practicality of climbing the wall.

The mountains to either side looked even more formidable. Mountains offered better opportunities for climbing than the smooth wall looked to provide, but still, the cliffs appeared incredibly difficult if not impossible for him and Samantha to scale, especially in the wet. Besides, the cliffs, too, would leave them out in the open and exposed for far too long.

Richard knew, too, that Naja's people would not have put the barrier here if there was an easy way over or around the mountains. Certainly the barrier spells would be the primary means to keep the threat contained, but like the wall, the mountains also presented a formidable barrier once the spells began to weaken. Climbing those mountains was no more a realistic option than climbing the wall.

Besides, the reason he was looking for a way in without having to go through the gates was to stay out of the open so they wouldn't be spotted. Scaling either the walls or the cliffs wouldn't get them in without being seen.

Surprise was their greatest weapon. He didn't want to give it up without a very good reason.

He wished he had a dragon handy to fly them in over the imposing wall filling the gap between the mountains, but it had been a very long time since he had seen a dragon.

That left the gates as the only realistic way into the third kingdom.

As Richard stood gazing at the enormity of the wall, he realized that what he was actually seeing was the physical manifestation of how much the people back in Naja's time feared what was beyond that wall. That was not a comforting thought. He knew that there was no choice, so he deliberately pushed the thought aside and went back to thinking of solutions.

"Let's make our way down closer to the gates," he said in a quiet voice so that his voice wouldn't carry. "We need to get a better look."

50

A nd what if there are people down there, near the gates? What if there are guards standing watch?"

"I can't imagine there would be guards," Richard said. "After all, the barrier was built to keep the half people in, not to keep us out. Why would anyone want to go in there? They'd be slaughtered.

"The half people obviously want out so they can hunt souls. So why would they have guards?"

Samantha shrugged. "I don't know. But what if there are homes or buildings right inside, a village or town of some kind, and the half people there would—"

"Samantha," he said in a quiet voice, cutting her off to get her to stop talking. "Let's not invent problems. We have enough real ones to solve. Let's first take a look and see what we're facing, then we can decide what we need to do. All right?

"Keep in mind, too, that this wall was not built to be a fortress wall. In many ways, as enormous as it is, it's only symbolic. The real barrier was the gravity spells and the barrier spells keeping evil on the other side.

Those spells are what kept the half people and the walking dead behind the wall for thousands of years.

"If that weren't so, then over all this great expanse of time they could have cut through the wall, or dismantled it, or tunneled under it, or something, wouldn't you think? If someone can put something together, then someone else can always find a way to take it apart. Especially given enough time and motivation. The half people had both.

"That means it's the spells that matter, not the stone or the gates. The spells are the barrier, not the wall. Those spells are what would be of concern to anyone inside, not the stone or the gates. That works in our favor."

"How?"

"Because it likely means they don't care about the gates. Why would they? The gates wouldn't hold any real significance to them except as a passage for them to get out into the world of life."

Richard started making his way down the slope, staying in among the denser growth of trees and using the shadows and foliage for cover as best he could. Since he now knew precisely where he was going, he could cut through the dense woods to remain hidden in case anyone was watching.

The forest was strangely quiet. He was used to being in the woods and, night or day, there being signs of life and activity, but these ancient stands of trees seemed forlorn and empty. He had no way of knowing if that was out of the ordinary. Animals could sense things that humans couldn't, so it was possible that such powerful magic had discouraged animals from living in the area near the wall.

Either that, or something else, some threat, had frightened them into silence. That was the possibility that worried him and kept him on high alert.

As he moved downhill, ever closer to the gates, he stopped periodically to peer out from behind the cover of the trees, checking for anyone. He still saw no one, no movement of any kind. The world felt so eerily empty outside the wall that in a way he wished he would see someone.

As they moved steadily down the slope, down lower toward the level of the ground outside the gates, the wall soaring up above them seemed even more impressive. To Richard, the enormity of the wall seemed a tangible representation of how much people in ancient times feared what was on the other side.

Richard paused. Something out of the corner of his eye caught his attention. He thought he saw lightning, or some kind of light, flicker from beyond the gates, but as soon as he focused his attention toward the gates, it was gone.

He carefully scanned the area around them before starting out again. He wished he could climb a tree to have a look over the wall to see what danger might lie beyond, but the trees, despite how huge they were, didn't begin to reach the top of the wall. The only thing he could do was to keep moving toward the gates so that he could look in.

Coming down the hill, he began to see that there was no road, clearing, or even a path outside the open gates. That made sense, of course. No one had gone in or out of it for thousands of years.

He could see, though, that the bushes, small trees, ferns, and grasses in that area had been trampled by heavy foot traffic, most likely from all the half people leaving. The ones who had attacked him and Samantha had probably come this way not long ago. There were also the men who had attacked him and Kahlan at the wagon. There might have been a lot of others like them who had come out through the gates.

And then there were the Shun-tuk who had attacked Zedd, Cara, and the others. Those Shun-tuk had obviously come out through the gates. From all indications, though, it looked like they probably took their captives back to their own land.

Richard wished he could remember better what he had heard as he woke up.

He had no way of knowing what other nations or groups of people might be living in the third kingdom beyond the wall, living in a land where life and death existed together. There could be vast numbers of half people of all sorts, just as in all the various lands of the world of life.

As they finally reached the ground down by the gates, Richard led them closer to the wall, but stayed in the shadow of the woods where possible as they worked their way closer. The gates opened out, so that also helped provide some cover.

"Stay there, behind the trees, while I get a closer look," he whispered to Samantha.

She nodded and quickly moved back into the shadows of young maples and spruce growing in an area of windfall pine that had opened the forest canopy.

The gates themselves were impossibly tall. They were considerably taller than the tallest pines in the surrounding forest. As he got closer, he thought that they looked more like movable walls than real gates. He supposed that made sense. They weren't designed, after all, to open and close regularly. It was most likely that the gates had been closed only after the wall had been completed. Once closed, they were meant to stay closed.

As he came up into the deep shadow behind the

nearest of the great gates, he saw that they were sheathed in squares of some kind of metal that had not rusted, although it did have the patina of great age. He reached out and put a hand against the metal. It was cool to the touch.

Signaling Samantha to stay where she was in behind the trees, Richard hiked his bow up on his shoulder, got down on the ground, and carefully crawled on his belly to the edge of the great door to have a look beyond. The edge of the door was several feet thick. It put him in mind of what an ant must feel like when around buildings.

As he peeked around the edge, he saw an open, rather barren landscape with broken, rocky terrain. The uneven ground was dotted here and there with a few scrub trees. There was no great forest like that outside the gates.

What alarmed him the most, though, was what he saw next.

In the distance, in various places, he saw flickering greenish light.

He had seen that specific kind of green light before. It was the same kind he had seen when he had first met Kahlan and they had crossed the boundary between Westland and the Midlands.

He had encountered the underworld a number of times since then. The veil before the world of the dead was always an eerie green color, an opaque green curtain of light.

That eerie green light was a boundary layer to the underworld itself.

When he inched out beyond the edge of the great gates to get a better view, he didn't see anyone inside the gates. It was a dark, barren landscape dominated by towering rock jutting up from the ground like spikes pounded up through the surface from below. But that was not the worst of it. It looked all the more forbidding because of the specter of greenish light flickering here and there among those rock towers.

Richard signaled for Samantha to come out of the trees. He aimed his thumb behind him, indicating that she should stay near the wall and to come up behind the door to join him.

She rushed out of the cover of the trees and quickly made her way through the smaller brush to crouch close behind him.

Not seeing anyone, Richard finally stood up and leaned out around the door for a better look into the third kingdom.

What he saw then both shocked and frightened him.

"What do you see?" she whispered. "What's wrong? Do you see half people?"

"I don't see anyone, but we have a problem and you need to know about it right now."

CHAPTER

51

"W hat?" Samantha asked. "What is it? What's the problem?"

Richard turned and squatted down in front of her. "Listen to me. This is important. The third kingdom is what?"

She frowned a little, not sure what he was getting at. "It's both the world of life and the world of the dead mixed together in the same place at the same time. It's neither the kingdom of life, or the kingdom of the dead. It's both, existing together."

Richard nodded. "That's right."

She put a finger on his chest. "But besides being a place, it is also what you are. Life and death together where they shouldn't be. You are of that place where life and death exist together at the same time."

"Good," he said with a single nod. "Beyond the gates is the third kingdom. The world of life and death together in the same place. There are places in there where there is greenish light—"

She frowned as she leaned toward him. "Greenish light?"

"Yes, kind of like . . . well, have you ever seen the sheets of light in the night in the northern sky?"

"Sure, of course."

"Like that. It looks something like that, only it's all a shimmering green light. That's the boundary layer to the underworld, the world of the dead."

She frowned suspiciously. Her head darted out to peek around the gate.

"Dear spirits . . ." She pulled back, her wide eyes staring into his. "Lord Rahl, that's the same eerie green glow I told you I saw when I tried to heal the Mother Confessor for the first time. Remember? I saw the same thing within you."

Richard wiped a hand across his mouth before letting out a deep sigh. "That green luminescence is death."

"I told you so. I saw it in her. That's when I first told you that she had death in her."

He nodded reluctantly. "So you did. I remember. But that was in her. This here is out in the open." Richard pointed a thumb behind him, beyond the gates. "If you walk into it, into that green veil of luminescence, you walk into the world of the dead. Understand?

"It's the boundary between life and death, just like you described seeing in Kahlan, the place that tried to tempt you in. If you had crossed over when you were in her mind, you would have entered the world of the dead. You would never have come back.

"This here is the same. Beyond that luminescent glow is the world of the dead. If you step over, even a little, you will never come back."

Her big dark eyes wide, she swallowed. "Then I guess it would be best not to walk through it."

"Exactly. When we go in there you can't ever let your guard down. You can't ever relax. I don't know the exact properties of how it works here, where the openings into the underworld will be, but in other places I've been you sometimes don't see it until you get really close. The greenish light is kind of like a warning that you are inches away from death, that you are about to cross over.

"Since you are so close to the underworld, the spirits of the dead beyond sometimes call to you, trying to entice you to cross over to them."

She nodded. "They did that to me, when I was trying to heal the Mother Confessor and saw that green veil of death. I heard the spirits beyond."

Richard nodded his understanding. "It seems that we can encounter death in a number of places, in a number of ways. You encountered that boundary to the eternal beyond in Kahlan, and in me. You saw and heard some of what was on the other side.

"In some places I've been that green wall will appear as a warning, much the way shields placed by wizards try to warn you with color and light if you start getting too close. In this case, it's a warning that you are getting close to the boundary.

"In other places I've seen, the walls to the world of the dead are static. They stay in the same place, shimmering, so that you can see them from some distance off and know where they are. But here, it seems like those green boundaries into the world of the dead are flickering in and out of existence. That means they aren't in one place. They move around."

"That makes sense," she said. "Life and death in the same place and at the same time, a kind of soup of ingredients mixing together."

"That's right, but it also means that this boundary between worlds may be different from what I've encountered before, where the lines between life and death were fixed and you could avoid them. Here, from what I saw beyond the gates, those boundaries appear to be fluid, moving like a gossamer carried on a breeze. That's what's different here. That's what makes it so much more dangerous here.

"It means that you may not necessarily need to walk into that boundary to be lost. In this place, they may drift in and come right over you."

"That would be bad," she said in a deadpan, stating the obvious.

Richard nodded. "You have to be extremely alert at all times and respect that danger. If you let your guard down for an instant, you could unintentionally find yourself pulled into the underworld. If that happens, you are never coming back."

Samantha nodded solemnly. "I understand. Keep my eyes open and be prepared to move out of the way."

"Right," he said with a firm nod. He took a quick look around. "We need to get going. But don't forget what I told you, not for a second. I don't know exactly what we will have to face in there, but this is already something I didn't expect. We can't ever let our guard down."

"I won't, Lord Rahl."

"One other thing."

"What's that?"

"If anything happens and we somehow get separated, then getting those people out, my friends and your mother, is the priority. Understand?"

"I understand, Lord Rahl. Find the wizard Zedd and the sorceress Nicci and get them out so that they can heal you of the death inside you so that you can end prophecy and end the threat to the world of life now that the barrier is down."

Richard would have smiled at how insane that sounded, and at her intensity, but the seriousness of the situation was nothing to smile about.

"Good. Now listen to me, Samantha. You may think I'm the one, but there are other people who are smarter about these kinds of things than me. Zedd knows more than I do about such things. Nicci perhaps more yet. They are both incredibly powerful people with vast experience and knowledge. Don't discount the importance of that—they may be able to stop the threat even without me."

"If they're so powerful, then how did they get overpowered and caught in the first place?"

Richard let out a sigh at her simple insight. "No matter how powerful you are, that doesn't mean you can always win. Sometimes, no matter how good you are, things just go wrong."

Samantha nodded. "What now?"

"Now we go in there and find them. Stay close and stay alert."

After she agreed, Richard peeked out around the gate. He saw no one out in the jumbled landscape of dark rock and flickers of the phantom luminescence here and there across the sprawling wasteland. In the distance a haze of smoke hung over the forbidding landscape.

As they made their way around the gate, stepping into the broad opening, Richard looked up and saw the great stone arch over the gateway. He remembered seeing it from the viewing port back in Stroyza. Up close, in all its detail, it was more imposing, more frightening, than he remembered.

The arch formed a head with glaring eyes made of some kind of red marble. Two enormous, sharp fangs hung down, as if ready to strike at anyone who tried to enter. It was meant as a warning that crossing through these gates would be like entering the jaws of some monstrous creature. It was a clear statement of the lethality of the place.

It was so obviously threatening that it was almost like a warning not to be stupid enough to enter the place.

Once through the open gates, Samantha pointed. "Lord Rahl, look," she whispered.

Richard turned and looked up. The insides of the gates had symbols embossed into the surface of the metal plates. When the gates were open, the enormous central emblem was broken in half, but when the gates were closed the symbol would have been whole and united. The element was in the language of Creation, like what Richard had seen on the omen machine, like Naja Moon's account back in the cave at Stroyza.

Richard didn't understand every component in the symbols, but he could clearly see that they were elements of a powerful spell. These symbols were meant to conjure powers Richard had never seen described before and didn't entirely understand.

What he did understand from the meaning in parts of the designs was that these were barrier spells. The writing, in the language of Creation, was not meant to convey information so much as to call forces together.

With the gates standing open, that enormous barrier spell, that lock in the center that had spanned both doors, was now broken.

With a chill, Richard realized that the seal was off the gates to the underworld itself.

He didn't want to take any more time to study all the symbols on the insides of the gates. Since the symbols and the spells they represented were now broken, what they had once meant was no longer important. Now, prepared or not, it was up to Richard to deal with the results.

He led them swiftly beyond the broad opening, toward rocky outcroppings off to the right that provided cover. They continued to move farther in beyond the gates and away from the wall, using the rocks as cover to stay out of sight as much as possible in case there were any half people traveling down to the gates out of the third kingdom.

In places, moving through the rocks, sheets of the greenish luminescence wavered off to the sides. He paused, watching veils of the eerie light drift lazily across the landscape, dragging a hem of light that flickered where it touched the ground. Richard kept an eye on the veils, making sure none were near, before starting to move again.

He had never seen the boundary to the underworld move like that. In the past it had always remained in place, an unmovable barrier to the world of the dead. The disconcerting sight of that boundary moving about the landscape sent a chill through him.

Coming around a column formation of stacked layers of slightly different colored rock, Richard abruptly spotted a man not far away, moving in their direction.

In that frozen moment, he realized that it was too late to hide. When the man looked up at the same instant and saw Richard and Samantha, the look in his eyes told Richard that this was a predator, one of the unholy half dead, that was always ready to exploit any opportunity it came across.

In a heartbeat, Richard had the bow off his shoulder. He whipped it around into position. He snatched an arrow from the quiver lashed to the side of the pack on his back. In another heartbeat he had the arrow nocked.

Time seemed to slow in Richard's vision as the man's lips curled back and he broke into a dead run toward them.

Richard was in that place where he controlled the world around the bladed point of his arrow. He settled the arrow and, in another heartbeat, it was away.

In his headlong rush to close the distance, the arrow entered through the man's left eye socket, right where Richard intended, where the bone wouldn't be as dense and possibly deflect the arrow's flight before it could do its work. It still had enough power behind it to erupt partway out the back of the man's skull.

Still flying at a dead run, the man crumpled and crashed facedown to the rocky ground, dead before he hit.

Richard looked both ways to check for any other sign of threat before he rushed out from the cover of the rocks. He grabbed the man's shirt at his shoulder and dragged him back in among the rocks.

"What are you doing?" Samantha asked, arms spread in alarm. "Why are you bringing him back with you?"

"We need to hide him. If someone else sees him it will alert them that there is someone with a soul in here, on this side of the gates, on their ground. I don't want to give them reason to suspect such a thing, or to start hunting for us."

"It's too open out here," Samantha said as she looked around. "How in the world do you think you're going to be able to hide him?"

"Easy," Richard said as he grabbed the man's simple shirt in his fists and lifted his dead weight.

Pulling him over onto his back, Richard was sorry to see that the arrow was broken when the man fell on his face, or he would have recovered it. He never liked to waste arrows.

Richard strained to hold the dead man up off the ground and get a better grip as he waited for the right moment.

And then, with a grunt of powerful effort, Richard heaved the man into a wall of shimmering green luminescence drifting toward them.

The light flickered at the contact. The greenish curtain wavered a little as the dead man tumbled through.

The man vanished.

"Well," Samantha said, "isn't that something. I guess it's pretty plain to see what you mean about not stepping through the green light."

"It would be the last step you took, that's for sure."

"I don't get it, though," Samantha said. "Dead I get, but where did his body go? When people die, their body doesn't vanish, just their consciousness, their spirit. Where did it go?"

"I don't know, Samantha," Richard said in a distracted tone. He had bigger things to worry about. "I don't know the answers for how everything works, especially not in the third kingdom."

Richard looked carefully around as he kept an eye on the curtain of greenish light, the wall before the underworld itself. The eerie, opaque glow of flickering light drifted past them before beginning to fade away as if it had never been there. Richard kept scanning the area for any other threat, but he didn't see anyone else. The man had apparently been alone.

"Let's go. Stay close."

"All right," Samantha said, scrambling to keep up with him. "But it just seemed strange the way his body vanished, that's all."

"The whole concept of this place is strange," Richard said as the two of them moved deeper into the third kingdom.

CHAPTER

53

Kahlan woke with a start.

She heard a confusing commotion. As she tried to focus her attention, she became dimly aware of the muffled sound of distant voices. She couldn't make out what they were saying, only the anxiety in their tone.

She blinked at the smear of blurry candlelight. Her mouth was so dry her tongue felt swollen and stuck to the roof of her mouth. She swallowed, trying to work up some saliva. She was too weak to lift much more than a finger.

Though the room was probably softly lit by candles, she still had to squint because the light from the flames seemed so bright to her. After what seemed like an eternity of bewildering darkness, the light hurt her eyes.

She realized that she was lying on a mat on the floor in a small, simple room. She didn't recognize the place. She had no idea at all where she might be. She couldn't even guess.

The fat candles were clustered together on shelves that looked to have been set back into simple plastered walls. The floor was spread with thick carpets with colorful designs. She saw a few chairs and a table that, while not fancy, were nicely made. A wooden door off across the room stood closed. As her vision began to clear, she saw that there were no windows, so she had no way of telling if it was day or night.

Out of the corner of her eye, Kahlan saw a middle-aged woman, with short, straight hair and wearing a simple gray dress, sitting on a low chest not far to the side. The woman's head was turned toward the muffled sound of voices in the distance. With her attention diverted, she didn't realize that Kahlan had opened her eyes.

She was glad to see the woman distracted by the same voices that Kahlan heard. Kahlan thought that most likely meant she wasn't imagining the voices and they weren't part of the dark world she seemed to have been trapped in for so long. She'd heard the frightening whisper of voices in that world, too. They had beckoned from somewhere beyond the darkness.

Kahlan wiggled her tingling fingers, working feeling back into them. She rolled a stiff wrist. On the second attempt she managed to sit up a little, enough, at least, to get up onto her elbows. She had to lean back on her hands for support as she rested a moment before she was able to finally sit up the rest of the way.

She leaned forward, bracing herself with one hand so she could use her other to feel her stomach where she had been cut by Jit. She expected it to hurt. She expected to find a horrible, bloody wound. Instead, she found a tidy seam sewing her shirt closed. She didn't find a wound. She looked around, but didn't see Richard.

As she turned her head, searching, she saw another door at the back of the room. While there were simple designs carved around the outside of the door, in the center a Grace had been carefully carved into the wood. It was somewhat comforting to see the Grace. Her anxiety lowered a notch at seeing the familiar symbol depicting the ordered nature of the universe.

Kahlan had a pounding headache. Worse, though, was that she was confused and couldn't make sense of anything. It was frustrating that she couldn't put the pieces she knew into proper order, frustrating that there was so much that seemed missing between the parts she did remember, frustrating that she didn't know why so much was missing. Fragments of things—voices, images—floated in complete disarray.

It felt as if she had been on some long and difficult journey, but she didn't properly remember any of it. It seemed like maybe she had been having terrible dreams for ages as she lay unable to wake from an endless ordeal. It was hard to tell what was real and what was still the strange, echoing, blurry dreamworld that wouldn't quite let her go.

"Please," she managed to say in a hoarse voice, "water . . ."

The woman sitting on the bench to the side jumped. She put a hand to her chest, panting in surprise.

"You gave me a start."

"Sorry" was all Kahlan could get out. Her tongue felt thick and wouldn't move the way she wanted it to.

"At last," the woman said as she rushed in close to kneel at Kahlan's side. "I was so worried waiting for you to wake. But Sammie—well, Samantha, I guess it is now—she said you would wake. And you did. She was right."

Kahlan weakly lifted a hand, laying it on the woman's arm. "Please . . . water . . . please."

The woman threw up her hands. "Oh! I'm sorry! Yes, water. Right here. I have some right here. Let me get it."

Kahlan saw her rush to the table and pour water from a pitcher into a mug. Carrying the mug of precious water in both hands, she hurried back to Kahlan.

She gently laid a hand on Kahlan's back to steady her as she put the mug to her lips. "Easy, now. Don't try to go too fast at first. You've been asleep for quite a while. Sammie—I mean Samantha—managed to make you drink when you were still asleep, but I fear it wasn't nearly enough for how long—"

"Who?" Kahlan asked, confused by the woman's babbling.

"Sorry. Not important at the moment. Take a sip. Go on, but go slow."

The water was more luxuriously delicious than anything she had ever tasted. Kahlan managed to gulp down a few swallows before the woman pulled the mug away to slow her down. "Easy. Go easy."

Kahlan nodded to earn the mug back. The second time she sipped slower, rolling the water around her mouth, relishing the wetness. She was able to swallow properly.

Kahlan noticed that the woman's eyes kept turning toward the door every time she heard the voices in the distance.

When she turned back, she saw Kahlan looking at her. "Oh, I'm sorry, Mother Confessor. I'm Ester. Richard asked me to watch over you until you woke up."

"Richard," Kahlan said with sudden relief and excitement. She glanced around, looking for his things. "He's here? Where is he?"

"No, I'm sorry. He and Sammie—"

"Samantha."

The woman let out a bit of a giggle. "Yes, Samantha."

"Who is Samantha?"

Kahlan was relieved that with the water her voice was finally starting to work. She thought that she almost sounded like herself.

"Samantha is our sorceress. We had more. But now she's the only one we have, since her father was murdered and her mother vanished."

Kahlan put a hand over her face in confusion as she closed her eyes for a moment to rest them from the light. She felt like she might still be in a dreamworld where nothing in the swirl of the things she was hearing made any sense.

"Forgive me, Mother Confessor, I'm talking too fast and only confusing you."

Kahlan nodded. "Richard?"

"He and Samantha had to go."

Kahlan's heart sank. "Go? Go where?"

Ester took a deep breath. "Well, it's a long story, Mother Confessor. You've only just now woken up. I don't want to throw it all at you at once. Sip the water. I should get you some soup. You look like skin and bones. You need to eat."

Kahlan looked down at herself. She did look to have lost some weight, but not a lot.

"The Hedge Maid had me . . ." she said, trying to orient herself in the world, trying to understand how she had come to be in this strange, stone room.

"Jit," Ester said.

Kahlan looked up. "Yes, that's right. Jit." She squinted, trying to remember. "Richard . . . I think Richard was there . . ."

Ester was nodding. "Yes, he told us that he went there to get you away from that awful woman. The Hedge Maid was an evil creature. Unfortunately, Jit captured Richard as well, but then he killed her—"

"Richard killed Jit?" Kahlan put a hand to her forehead, trying to remember such an important event, but she couldn't.

"Yes, but, but there was trouble in that."

Kahlan shook her head. "Trouble? I'm confused." It all felt like so long ago. "I'm sorry, Ester, but I don't understand what you're talking about. I don't understand what's going on. I don't know who you are or where I am or how I got here."

Ester looked toward the door. The voices were getting closer. Besides the tension in Ester's face, Kahlan, too, recognized that the voices did not sound friendly. She thought she heard a man demanding something.

Ester finally turned back. "Lord Rahl—and Henrik—"

"Henrik." She remembered Henrik. "Is he here? He's all right, then?"

"Yes, yes," Ester said as she nodded. "Lord Rahl and Henrik told us most of what has happened. Not all of it, I expect, but much of it. Lord Rahl had to go, though, so he wanted me to explain it to you—to let you know what had happened."

"Go? Where did he go?" That didn't sound like Richard, leaving her somewhere when she was unconscious. "Why would Richard leave me here?"

Ester put a hand on Kahlan's shoulder when she saw how frustrated she was getting with trying to understand.

"Mother Confessor, I will explain it all in more detail once you have had something to eat and you get your bearings. All right? For now, what you need to know is that Richard went to rescue you, and he killed Jit. But as she died, she touched you both with death."

Kahlan put her fingers to her forehead. She wasn't sure that she had heard correctly. She frowned as she leaned toward the woman.

"What?"

"You both have the touch of death in you from the Hedge Maid. Apparently, the Hedge Maid released death itself from within her as she screamed. That's what killed her, as I understand it. That sound would have killed anyone nearby. It would have killed you and Lord Rahl as well, but he was able to do something that protected you both from the worst of it. While it didn't kill you both, it did still leave death's touch in you both—you worse than he.

"You were both in a very grim way, not only from the wounds you received when being held captive by the Hedge Maid, but also from that touch of death in you. Your friends, a man named Zedd, and some others—a sorceress Nicci, and another woman . . ."

Ester put a finger to her lip and looked up, trying to remember the name.

"Cara?" Kahlan guessed.

Ester snapped her fingers. "That's the woman. Cara. Anyway, your friends and a lot of soldiers had come to help. They got you and Richard out of Jit's lair and were on the way to take you both back to the palace when they were all attacked by half people from the third kingdom."

Confused, Kahlan put her open fingers back over her face. She felt like she had just lost the thread of the story.

"The what people from where?"

"The half people from the third kingdom," Ester said, as she glanced toward the voices again, listening for a moment. The voices were still an indecipherable drone. As Kahlan again started to object, Ester waved a hand for patience so that she could explain.

"You, your friends, and the soldiers were attacked. Everyone but you and Lord Rahl were either killed or captured. The attackers didn't see you two because the woman—Cara—put a tarp over you both to hide you in the back of a wagon. It worked, but the rest of them were all killed or captured."

Kahlan covered her mouth in shock. Her heart pounded out of control at the news. She wasn't so sure she hadn't awakened to a world gone crazy.

"Do you know if any of them are safe? Do you know if any of them who were captured are still alive?"

"Sorry, we don't know. Apparently, after you and Richard were being taken from Jit's lair, the people with you were trying to heal your wounds, but they didn't have time before they were attacked. It appeared that at least some of them who weren't killed in the attack may have been carried off. Lord Rahl doesn't know who is dead, and who might be held captive.

"Henrik was with them when the attack began. When the woman, Cara, hid you and Lord Rahl under a tarp, she told Henrik to run and to try to find help for you both. Fortunately, he soon arrived here seeking help.

"We rushed to the scene, and when we got there a couple of men were dragging you and Lord Rahl out of the wagon where you had been hidden."

"Men from the attack?" Kahlan asked. "They were still there?"

"No, they were different men."

"Different men?"

"I know it all sounds confusing," Ester said, forestalling Kahlan's questions. "I guess you could say that the attackers were gone, and these men were scavengers who happened by."

"I see. I guess that makes sense. Then what?"

"These other men were trying to kill Lord Rahl and were going to carry you off. We got there just in time. We killed one of the men while Lord Rahl, even though he had horrible bite wounds from the men, was able to kill the other attacker."

"Dear spirits . . ." Kahlan whispered through her fingers.

"You were both in bad shape. Sammie—sorry, Samantha—was able to cure both of you from your normal wounds and injuries, but she couldn't cure the touch of death that was left in you both by the dying Hedge Maid. To do that, Lord Rahl says you both need the others—Zedd and the sorceress—and they have to get you both back to the palace in order to do that kind of special healing."

"All right," Kahlan said, trying not to lose track of the details as she followed along with the story, or get too impatient. "I guess that makes sense."

Ester put a hand compassionately on Kahlan's forearm. "I'm sorry to have to tell you this, Mother Confessor, but if this wizard, Zedd, and the sorceress Nicci, can't get you back to a special place in the People's Palace—"

"Special place? What do you mean, special place?"

The woman made a bit of a face as she shook her head. "I'm sorry, but I'm not familiar with such things. It was a field of some sort. I think that's it, a field."

"A field? Do you mean a containment field?" Kahlan suggested.

Ester smiled suddenly in recognition. "That's it. A containment field." Her smile faded. "If they can't get you back there to that field, then the dark sickness within you will kill you both. Jit will have claimed you at last. Your only hope to be saved from the touch of death is for your friends to do what only they can do in order to cure you both, and they must do it there, in that containment thing."

Kahlan had little trouble believing the seriousness of her sickness. She could feel the dark shadow of something evil within her, sapping her of life. She instinctively grasped the truth of what Ester was saying. Her level of alarm rose as she now understood why Richard would have left her.

She rolled a hand to get Ester's story back on track. "So then what?"

"So then Lord Rahl and Samantha went to try to rescue your friends who had been captured. They hope to find that Sammie's mother is with them and rescue her as well."

"I see," Kahlan said, trying to take it all in. She was still disoriented and having trouble reconciling it all in her head and fitting the different pieces together.

She had at first been confused, then relieved to be awake, then even more relieved to know that Richard was alive and that they had escaped the Hedge Maid's lair.

But now, she felt terror seeping back in.

Able to see that Kahlan was getting upset, Ester returned her hand to Kahlan's forearm.

"Mother Confessor, Lord Rahl wanted—"

The door burst open. Ester flinched, letting out a little squeak.

A tall man strolled into the room. He carried himself with an air of authority. A woman followed behind, but there were no candles on that side of the room and in the man's shadow Kahlan couldn't see much of her.

The severe-looking man wore a simple black coat with a turned-up straight collar that went all the way around his neck. The black coat was buttoned to his neck, keeping the collar closed at his throat. A rimless, four-sided hat that looked to be made from black material similar to his coat covered a head of blond hair cut short on the sides.

Kahlan blinked in surprise. "Abbot Dreier?"

He looked as surprised to see her as she was to see him. He recovered quickly.

"Mother Confessor." A sly smile that Kahlan didn't like one bit slowly spread across his face. "Well now, isn't this quite the pleasant surprise."

As Ester rose up from beside Kahlan, he removed the rimless hat in an act of formality. He turned the smile on Ester. The woman took a deferential step back.

"Abbot Ludwig Dreier," he said in a smiling introduction.

"Ester," she said as she bowed. "Welcome to Stroyza, Abbot Dreier. Our humble village is honored to have you here."

"Yes," he drawled, the smile remaining on his lips.

After making a show of looking around, he turned a cunning look back to Kahlan. "And is Lord Rahl with you, Mother Confessor? The both of you taking a tour of the Dark Lands and the remote little village of Stroyza, are you?"

Kahlan twitched a frown. "Where?"

He lifted a hand about. "Stroyza. Don't you know where you are?"

"May I be of service, Abbot Dreier?" Ester asked, drawing his attention, seemingly trying to rescue a confused Kahlan from the questioning.

He flashed her an empty smile. "We're just here to see if some volunteers would be willing to come with us to be of assistance at the abbey."

He looked back at Kahlan, clearly more interested in the unexpected guest of the village. As he did, the woman who had come in with him stepped out from behind him.

Kahlan was shocked to see that it was a Mord-Sith.

More surprising yet, Kahlan didn't recognize her.

Not only did Kahlan not recognize the Mord-Sith, but the woman was wearing black leather.

Kahlan had seen Mord-Sith in brown, white, and of course red leather. She had never seen a Mord-Sith in black.

It was a chilling sight.

For a moment Kahlan doubted her initial thought, questioning that the woman really was a Mord-Sith. The blond hair pulled neatly back into a single braid was the same style worn by all Mord-Sith, but that didn't prove anything—a hairstyle didn't make a Mord-Sith. Nor did wearing a leather outfit, even if it wouldn't have been such an odd color. Not even the tall woman's perfect shape or the dangerous demeanor meant that she was Mord-Sith.

Any number of women could wear their hair like that and have a leather outfit made to look like that of a Mord-Sith. Looking the part didn't make her a real Mord-Sith. It could even be that she was playing the part at the request of the pompous abbot. It would certainly fit Kahlan's impression of Ludwig Dreier to want to play the part of an important man by having such a woman with him.

What worried Kahlan, though, was the simple-looking red rod hanging on a fine gold chain from the woman's right wrist. That marked her as Mord-Sith. That was what told Kahlan that this had to be a Mord-Sith. Only Mord-Sith carried an Agiel. It was hard to imagine any woman carrying a fake Agiel just to play a part. If she was caught trying to pull off such an impersonation, a real Mord-Sith would skin her alive.

The woman's cold blue eyes were fixed on Kahlan.

"I'm afraid that we've had a great deal of trouble just recently," Ester said, trying to sound apologetic, "so I'm sorry, but no one here would be in a position to . . . volunteer to help with prophecy at the abbey."

"Trouble?" the abbot asked, sounding surprised to hear it. "What sort of trouble?"

Kahlan got the distinct impression that he knew exactly what sort of trouble, even if she didn't know what Ester was talking about.

Ester's gaze darted about. She dry-washed her hands as she tried to think of a way to explain it.

"Well, ah, well, we had an attack here. The village was attacked."

"Attacked!" the abbot sounded shocked and even concerned. Kahlan didn't think it was sincere. "Well, that does sound serious."

"It was, I'm afraid," Ester said, nodding furiously. "Very serious."

"In peacetime? In Fajin Province? The bishop will be quite disturbed to hear of any such trouble in his beloved land. Hannis Arc will not like to hear that his people have been attacked. He will not like it one bit, I can assure you of that."

"I'm sure he wouldn't," Ester said in a small voice.

Abbot Dreier leaned toward Ester. "An attack by whom?"

Ester cleared her throat. "Well, you see, it was these . . . well, I don't know how to adequately describe them."

"Simple is usually best," the abbot said, his tone turning cool as he straightened and clasped his hands before himself.

"Well," Ester stammered, "we were attacked by these, by these . . . dead men."

The abbot frowned as he again leaned toward her a bit. "Dead men?"

Ester shrank back at his tone.

Kahlan was getting confused again, wondering if she could possibly be back in the rolling, wavering, wandering dreamworld. She had felt like she had been trapped in it forever. She wondered if she really was, and this was part of it.

But the tension in the air was no dream. She had never liked Abbot Ludwig Dreier, but in the past, as the Mother Confessor, she had always had the upper hand and he had known it. Her last dealings with the man were at the People's Palace, at Cara and Benjamin's wedding and reception. The abbot had been particularly troublesome, insisting that she and Richard reveal prophecy to everyone, and that they should use prophecy to guide their rule of the D'Haran Empire.

At the time, Ludwig Dreier had stirred up a great deal of trouble among many of the leaders from various lands by suggesting that the people had a right to prophecy. Kahlan suspected he had stirred up murder as well.

While she had not been afraid of the man before, this was different. Now, she was feeling particularly vulnerable.

Of course, despite how weak and sick she felt, she

could always resort to her Confessor power, if need be. That thought gave her comfort. She was not defenseless. Far from it.

It would take but one touch and that would be the end of Abbot Ludwig Dreier. He would not stand a chance against such a touch. It would be wise for him to be more cautious.

"You said dead men," he repeated when Ester looked too intimidated to go on, too afraid to explain any further.

She fumbled with a button on a pocket as Dreier stared at her, waiting for her to speak.

The Mord-Sith glared unflinchingly at Kahlan.

"Well, yes. They looked like dead men, anyway," she explained in a rush. "I know it sounds crazy, and I can offer no explanation. I can only tell you what we saw. We were attacked by men that looked like corpses freshly dug up from a grave. They looked like the walking dead. They appeared suddenly in our midst and killed a number of people in the village. They injured many more."

Kahlan thought that it did indeed sound crazy, but Ester didn't strike her as the crazy type.

"Really," the abbot drawled. He turned to the Mord-Sith. "Dead men. Have you ever heard of such a thing?"

The blond woman's eyes turned to him as she shook her head. "Can't say that I have."

He turned his attention back to Ester. "And how were you able to stop this attack?"

"Lord Rahl killed them all."

He arched an eyebrow. "I thought you said that they were dead men. How could he kill men who were already dead?"

"Not killed them, exactly." She made little swishing motions with her hand. "Hacked them to pieces, actually. Hacked them to bits and had us burn the pieces."

He sighed audibly. "Ah, well, thank goodness Lord Rahl was handy, at least. It might have been a slaughter, otherwise."

"Yes," Ester said, "it would have been, but it was still a horrible ordeal for the people here. Many people lost their lives. Many more were seriously injured. We are all still trying to recover from it, trying to help those who were hurt and are still suffering."

"Well," the abbot said, "I can certainly understand that the people of Stroyza have a lot on their hands at the moment." He rubbed a finger back and forth on his chin, frowning in thought. "Maybe we can find someone else who would want to volunteer in place of someone from your village."

Ester quickly dipped her head. "The consideration would be very much appreciated, Abbot."

His deliberate gaze turned to Kahlan.

"What are you doing here, Dreier?" Kahlan asked in a cold tone to bring the phony chitchat to a halt.

He shrugged with a smile. "Why, seeking help with prophecy, Mother Confessor, that's all. I am but a humble servant of Bishop Hannis Arc. I provide him with prophecy so that it might help guide him in his rule of Fajin Province. And, I suppose, the rule of other lands that have so recently come to him for such guidance as he may be able to provide."

Ester inched forward, still fumbling with the button. She gestured toward Kahlan.

"Abbot Dreier, I'm afraid that the Mother Confessor is quite ill. She has been through a terrible ordeal herself. I was just tending to her. She is very weak and needs rest.

"I know that you would want her to get that crucial rest so that she might get well as soon as possible." She tilted her head forward just a bit. "I'm sure that Lord

Rahl would appreciate your understanding about his wife's recent ordeal, and be grateful to you for leaving her to her rest."

Dreier stared at the woman for a moment with that frozen smile of his and then made a show of glancing around. "Lord Rahl—is he about, then? He hacked those dead men to pieces, so he must be around. I would like to congratulate him, personally, on behalf of the people of not only Stroyza, but all of Fajin Province for his brave assistance in stopping such a dire threat. He has once again proven himself the protector of innocent people. I would personally like to thank him."

Ester cleared her throat. "I'm afraid that he had to leave—briefly. He should be back anytime, I'm sure. Anytime."

"I see." The abbot smoothed the front of his coat. "Well, in the meantime, I myself have a bit of talent with healing. I should lend a hand, as it were, to assist our Mother Confessor."

"But Samantha already . . ." Ester's voice trailed off when he turned an icy glare on her.

After the look had backed Ester a step, he turned back to Kahlan and went to one knee beside her. He reached out to touch her forehead. She pulled her head back, out of his reach as she put her arm up to block his hand.

"That won't be necessary. I only need rest, now."

Before she could stop him, he pushed her arm away. "Now, now, Mother Confessor, don't be shy about accepting my small offer of help. Won't take but a moment to see if there is anything more that I might be able to do."

His first two fingers touched her forehead. He bowed his head in concentration. "Let me just check to see . . ."

The oddest look came over his face. His eyes abruptly turned up to meet her gaze.

And then the slightest hint of a smile turned up the corners of his mouth as he leaned back.

"Well," he said, "it seems that you have had a healing recently. A fine one at that. I can feel it. I can sense the residual effects of the gift used to heal you."

Ester stole a quick glance at Kahlan. "As I said, Sammie worked some healing on her. She said that the Mother Confessor now only needs to rest."

The abbot stood, giving the Mord-Sith a meaningful look.

"I think she is well enough to travel. I can be of invaluable assistance with her recovery once we get her back to the abbey."

"No," Ester said, more firmly in spite of her fear of the man. "No, she needs to rest right now, right here. Lord Rahl will want her to rest. He won't want her moved."

The abbot casually lifted a finger toward Ester. The woman shuddered. Her fingers trembled as she blinked in confusion. Panting as if in pain, she backed away a few steps. Kahlan wasn't sure exactly what the man had done, but it was now clear that he was powerfully gifted and that he was hurting Ester.

In all his time at the palace, Abbot Dreier had kept that relevant fact hidden, never revealing that he was gifted.

"Now," he said down to Kahlan, "I think you should come along with us. We will be better able to see to your needs at the abbey."

"I'm afraid that I must decline your kind offer," Kahlan said in a chilling tone.

Abbot Dreier stared for a moment without showing any emotion and then turned to the Mord-Sith. "Please bring the Mother Confessor along. I will wait out front."

He seized Ester's arm and pushed her out of the

room ahead of him. He paused and from the doorway looked back at Kahlan.

"Mord-Sith can be quite persuasive. I advise you to cooperate as she helps escort you out to our waiting coach."

With that he left, pulling the door closed behind himself.

CHAPTER

56

After Dreier closed the door, the Mord-Sith smiled the way Mord-Sith smiled that could make you forget to breathe.

"We weren't introduced. I am Erika. Mistress Erika to you."

Kahlan glared.

Erika heaved an impatient sigh. "So, it's going to be like that, is it?"

"Get out," Kahlan said.

Erika spread her hands with mock decorum. "I'm afraid that the abbot has invited you to come along. He asked me to assist you. He would be very disappointed in me if I didn't do as he asked. Believe me, I have no wish to disappoint the abbot."

"We all are bound to disappoint someone now and again," Kahlan said.

The Mord-Sith dispensed with the smile. She rolled her fingers in a commanding gesture.

"Get up."

"I can't. I'm rather weak from my recent injuries that have only just been healed."

"Perhaps you misunderstood me. You must have thought that I was asking you." The smile reappeared. "I wasn't. I was telling you. Now, get up."

Kahlan thought the wordplay was childish. She was not about to be intimidated by a Mord-Sith, of all people. This one, by all rights, shouldn't even exist. If she even was a real Mord-Sith.

It occurred to Kahlan once again that the woman might simply be window dressing for an arrogant man, a woman who had convinced herself she could play the part of a real Mord-Sith. She appeared to be a woman who enjoyed pretending to be important and powerful so she could intimidate people and watch them cower.

Kahlan was not about to cower before this woman.

She rocked forward enough to get her feet under her. After being unconscious for so long, she found that the effort made her heart pound. She hadn't been on her feet for quite a while and she felt incredibly weak.

She crouched a moment, getting her balance, trying to summon enough strength to not show this haughty woman any weakness. Kahlan was, after all, the Mother Confessor.

With effort, she stood, if not to her full height, then at least most of the way. She couldn't stretch the last little bit at her waist. It felt like all of her abdominal muscles had shrunk, keeping her from straightening to her full height, which would have probably been an inch or two taller than the Mord-Sith if Kahlan could have stood fully upright.

"Now," Kahlan said through gritted teeth as she looked the woman in the eye, "get out. I will not ask you again."

An eyebrow lifted over one cold blue eye. "Or what?"

"I don't know where you came from, but you appear not to know much about anything."

Erika shrugged. "I know that Abbot Dreier asked me to bring you along. That is enough. What else is there to know, Mother Confessor?"

"'Confessor' is the operative word."

The Mord-Sith frowned a little. "Really? In what way?"

"You are apparently unaware of the danger a Confessor poses to a Mord-Sith—or a woman posing as a Mord-Sith."

"Danger? From you?" She smiled again, this time with what appeared to be genuine amusement. "I don't think so."

"Do you have any idea what a mistake it is for a Mord-Sith to attempt to use her Agiel on a Confessor? The results are beyond gruesome and all Mord-Sith know it. It is a death they all greatly fear."

"Really?" Erika cocked her head with an earnest frown. "How interesting. Well, I don't have to use an Agiel on you, you know. You look to be pretty weak." A dangerous look came into the woman's eyes. "Even if you were in the best of health, I don't think I would need to use my Agiel to handle you."

Kahlan didn't know what was going on, or how it had come to this, but she knew in that moment that she was going to need to unleash her power on this woman, and it was not going to be pretty.

"You are about to cross a line from which you will never, ever be able to step back," Kahlan warned in a deadly tone. "I suggest you call it quits now, Erika, while you have the chance."

"I don't think so, Mother Confessor. Like I said, I can handle you without my Agiel. More importantly, as I told you before, it is Mistress Erika to you."

The Mord-Sith spun the Agiel up into her fist.

It was an open threat, a hostile act that had now

gone too far. For whatever crazy reason, this woman was not going to stop until Kahlan stopped her.

In Kahlan's mind, the deed was already done. This woman had crossed a line from which there was no walking back. Kahlan was already letting the restraint on her power begin to slip its bounds in preparation for releasing her inherent ability.

The Mord-Sith gritted her teeth. "But in this case I prefer to use my Agiel."

With that, the woman slammed the weapon into Kahlan's middle.

Kahlan expected the ignition of power that would bring the attack to a halt before it could ever be completed. She expected to feel the hammering thump of silent thunder that would shake the walls and forever change who this woman was.

Instead, Kahlan's mouth opened in a shock of pain the likes of which she had only felt a few times in her life.

The nerve-shattering shock of it stunned her, took her breath. She doubled over around the Agiel. It felt like a bolt of lightning threatening to rip her in half. Her mind went blank of everything but the complete and total understanding of that terrible, all-consuming agony.

She heard herself screaming.

She felt herself hit the floor.

The pain of the Agiel, even though it was no longer touching her, had been so overwhelming that waves of jolting shocks still filled her mind, preventing her from forming a thought or even getting her breath.

Confused, disoriented, trembling from head to foot, Kahlan rolled over onto her back, her knees pulled up, her arms pressed across the pain knifing through her abdomen. Through tears of agony, she looked up at the woman in black leather standing tall and still over her, watching her.

An eyebrow lifted. "You were saying?"

"How . . . ?" was all Kahlan could manage to get out through the still-shuddering pain pulsing through every nerve in her body.

Erika shrugged a shoulder. "Well, Mother Confessor, as you have probably surmised by now, your power does not work. For you to be a threat to me—as you have so vividly described and as you so wholeheartedly intended—your power has to work." The cruel smile returned. "Don't you suppose?"

Kahlan couldn't understand what was happening. She was having trouble forming the simplest of thoughts. A cascade of questions and confusion overwhelmed her ability to think clearly.

"But even if it doesn't respond for you, that power is still resident within you and you fully intended to use that power on me, now didn't you? You tried to. You committed to it." She waggled a finger. "That was enough."

Kahlan didn't understand any of it. At that moment, she could only understand that she was in trouble and there was no one who could help her.

The Mord-Sith planted a boot in Kahlan's middle, over the spot where she had used her Agiel, and leaned over enough to rest an elbow on her knee. "And now you are mine."

Kahlan still couldn't talk and with the boot pressing down, couldn't draw a full breath. The Mord-Sith removed the boot from Kahlan's middle and straightened, rolling her Agiel in her fingers in a threatening manner.

"Now, I asked you a question, Mother Confessor. When I ask you a question, I expect an answer." She leaned down, gritted her teeth, and pointed her Agiel at Kahlan's face. "Is that clear?"

Kahlan couldn't make herself stop trembling from the still-lingering pain. She supposed that if she weren't in such a weakened condition, she might be able to better tolerate the touch of the Agiel. But, given what an Agiel was capable of, probably not a whole lot better. If a Mord-Sith wished it, the touch of an Agiel could be fatal.

What Kahlan couldn't reconcile in her own mind was how this woman could really be Mord-Sith.

For a moment Erika watched Kahlan's agony with

grim satisfaction. Finally, she reached down, seized Kahlan's hair in her fist, pulled her to her feet, and shoved Kahlan toward the door.

Kahlan finally drew a full breath. Her anger flared. She spun to the woman, determined to put a stop to the situation.

The Agiel again rammed into Kahlan's middle.

Kahlan didn't know how long she lay curled up on the floor the second time. She didn't think she lost consciousness, but the pain had been so overwhelming, so all-consuming, that it was hard to tell if she had remained fully awake or not. She couldn't reconcile how long it had been. The concept of time seemed to become meaningless and the world made no sense.

There was only the pain. She could think of little else but wanting the pain to stop. As angry as she was, as much as she wanted to strangle Erika, she wanted the pain to stop.

Erika leaned over, snatched Kahlan by the hair again, and yanked her to her feet. "Enough of this. The abbot is waiting."

This time, when the Mord-Sith pushed her toward the door, Kahlan didn't try to fight her.

"My, my, but you learn quick."

Kahlan paused at the door. "How?" That was the only word she could get out.

"How? How what?"

"How . . . You are not loyal to Richard."

The woman made a sour face. "Dear Creator no. What would give you such a grotesque idea? No, my dear Mother Confessor, I am not loyal to the Lord Rahl."

"But, that loyalty, that bond to the Lord Rahl, is what powers a Mord-Sith's Agiel."

Erica smiled at the chance to reveal the delicious truth. "Lord Arc powers my Agiel."

"Lord Arc . . . ?"

"That's right. Lord Arc is my master. Lord Arc will be everyone's master, just as soon as he finishes getting rid of your dear, dear husband."

The Mord-Sith opened the door and shoved Kahlan out into a hallway. Kahlan stumbled. She managed to get a hand up against the far wall to catch her balance and keep from smacking her face against the rock. The hall was dimly lit by a few candles and lamps. The hallway, like the room, looked to be carved entirely out of stone, but it was much less refined.

She walked hunched from the pain, clutching her middle, panting as she waited for the lingering sting of the pain to ease. It was not dying out the way regular pain would.

But more than the pain of the Agiel, far worse than the pain of the Agiel, was the agony of how much she missed Richard. It seemed like forever since she had seen him. The last time she remembered seeing him was back at the palace, not long after Cara and Ben's wedding. She wanted nothing more right than to be in his arms.

Kahlan thought that she remembered while in the dreams that he had kissed her. She didn't know if it had been part of one of the dreams or if it had been real. She only knew that she missed him more than anything.

Erika shoved Kahlan onward through the halls and corridors. Each time they reached an intersection, the Mord-Sith pushed her along, shoving her this way or that. Kahlan didn't know where she was, or where she was going. She had been unconscious when she had been brought in and it was all a confusing maze to her.

Kahlan thought she might throw up. She thought she might faint. She did neither. Still in lingering pain, she simply stumbled along ahead of the woman in black leather.

As she reached lighter areas with lamps hung on the stone walls at regular intervals, areas that widened with some kind of doorways off to either side that looked like a honeycomb of homes back in the rock, people lined the hallway. All of them stood grimly to the side, heads hanging, eyes watching her pass. Kahlan imagined that the Mord-Sith was enjoying the spectacle.

Around a corner, more people stood silently aside in the wide corridor. As she passed them, their eyes turned up to peek, unable to resist watching the dismal sight of Kahlan stumbling past, groaning in helpless agony from both times the Agiel had been used on her.

The cave broadened out, becoming bright with daylight streaming in through a wide opening that was the mouth of the cave. Erika snatched Kahlan's hair and jerked her to a halt. There were people all around the cavern, standing back out of the way to the sides of the cave.

Not one of them lifted a finger to try to stop the Mord-Sith or dared to voice a protest. Kahlan knew it would have done no good. Worse, it would likely only get them hurt.

She could see through the cave opening that it was heavily overcast outside. To her surprise, she saw treetops far below and realized that they were some distance up in the side of a mountain, with ground level far below.

Abbot Dreier stood near the edge of the precipice, watching with obvious satisfaction at the condition Kahlan was in as well as her humiliation.

Erika dragged Kahlan by her hair near to the edge of the cliff opening, beside the abbot.

"Well there you are, at last," he said, sounding in good spirits. "I see that you and Erika are getting along splendidly."

Kahlan glanced out the opening, down the side of the mountain. She saw a bit of a trail leading off down the cliff, but she couldn't imagine using such a narrow pathway down the side of the mountain, especially in the drizzle.

"Well, we really must be on our way," Dreier said.

Kahlan looked over at him. "You do know, of course, that I am going to kill you."

His hand instantly came up, halting the Mord-Sith from ramming her Agiel into the small of Kahlan's back.

"There will be time enough for that," he said to the Mord-Sith.

Erika bowed her head. "As you wish, Abbot."

"Now," he said to Kahlan as he gestured to the edge of the cliff at the mouth of the cave, "we really must be on our way. Get going." He gestured to the edge of the opening. "Down that way, there."

Kahlan took three steps back from the edge. She knew that in her shaky condition she would not be able to climb down such a treacherous trail without falling. It was all she could do to walk across a flat floor.

Dreier heaved an impatient sigh.

"Well, Erika, it seems the Mother Confessor prefers the quick way down."

Without question or delay, Erika took two quick, wide steps toward the edge, in the process yanking Kahlan right off her feet by her hair.

The powerfully strong Mord-Sith stopped abruptly at the edge and with a mighty effort swung herself around at the waist and flung Kahlan out the opening of the cave, out into the cold gray light.

She released her grip on Kahlan's hair as she flew out into thin air.

Kahlan gasped in shock as she sailed out from the cave opening.

Her fingers grasped, catching only air.

She saw nothing below but the ground—

As that ground raced toward her at an alarming rate and the rush of air sucked her breath away, her last thought was how much she loved Richard.

Richard carefully scanned the area ahead as he made his way down through the towering rock formations rising up all around them. Samantha peeked out from behind an irregular column of layered rock and looked both ways before tiptoeing after him, staying close so as not to get separated.

The spikes of rocks jutting from the rough ground sloped at an angle toward the lower valley floor below. The jumble of jagged, rocky spires above the low ground rose at a slant that made progress too difficult. They needed to get down to lower ground where they could make better time.

Richard had to always balance staying hidden with being able to make good progress. Both had their dangers. Too slow and they might be too late to save anyone. Trying to go too fast would allow them to be spotted and caught.

At the far side of the broad expanse of more open ground, dark, mountainous rock formations rose up, and beyond them the ground lifted into ever-higher mountains where tattered gray clouds drifted past imposing cliff faces.

All around them in every direction he could see the occasional flicker of the greenish veils of light. Some were far away, but others were uncomfortably nearby. Fortunately, in the gloomy daylight the flickering, eerie light stood out all the more and always caught their attention. Richard remained especially wary whenever the ominous curtains of shimmering luminescence came toward them. Whenever that happened, Richard was quick to move out of the area.

The third kingdom was an ever-changing landscape of rocky ground with the green walls of the underworld wandering and mixing with the world of life. It was not a place where he could ever feel safe.

Richard was exhausted from lack of sleep, the difficult journey, and the constant tension that kept them on high alert. Once through the gates, they had pressed on almost the entire night before, not wanting to stop, fearing to stop, fearing to fall asleep for long in such a place.

Besides that, they knew they were getting closer to the land of the Shun-tuk, where they expected that their friends and loved ones were being held, and both he and Samantha were eager to press on. They suspected that they were close to the strange half people's homeland, because they had spotted a number of them making their way south along the broad valley floor.

It confirmed that progress down lower would be quicker, but Richard also realized that down lower they were more likely to encounter half people.

The people Richard saw making their way along the valley floor all looked like the bodies he remembered seeing near the wagon, after he had woken up. Traveling in clusters of at least a few dozen, these people he was seeing now had the same ashen coloring wiped all over their bodies, with shaved heads and black around their eyes. Many had what looked to be dangling strings of teeth and bones. There was no doubt in Richard's mind that these were the Shun-tuk. The farther north they went, the more of them they saw, so he figured that he and Samantha had to be getting near their domain. At least he knew they were going in the right direction.

Getting closer to their objective, and in such dangerous country, neither Richard nor Samantha had wanted to stop for long the night before. They had found a small opening in the confusing jumble of the rock formations and wedged their way in, out of sight of anyone passing nearby. It reminded him of the place they had weathered the storm of wood fragments when Samantha had unleashed such devastation that wiped out the half people who wanted to eat them.

They had gotten precious few hours of fitful sleep, but it couldn't be helped, not when they were this close. Not when Richard could imagine the captives nearby, hoping for help, hoping for rescue. He didn't want to waste a moment for anything, even sleep. Samantha was of the same mind.

He knew that sooner or later they would need to rest, him even more so, but he knew he couldn't allow it to slow him down. He could feel the inner poison working on him. He knew that it was only going to get worse. Samantha had said as much, so to his way of thinking, the faster he could pull Zedd and Nicci out of captivity, the faster they could heal him. He knew the options and had made the choice he thought made most sense: press on.

Speed was life—his, and everyone else's.

He kept thinking that if they slowed, and if he then reached the captives and they had been killed only a few hours earlier, he would never forgive himself for not making the best speed he possibly could.

He supposed that he wouldn't live long enough to feel the pangs of regret if he didn't succeed, but the fear still kept him moving.

Crossing the open area, Richard didn't see any of the Shun-tuk, only flocks of black birds off in the distance against the slate gray sky. It was so heavily overcast that it nearly felt like dusk. He wondered if some of that dimness to the day was from his inner darkness.

The floor of the valley was strewn with broken shale, and in a swath along the valley floor stretched a broad expanse of standing water. It looked like it might be runoff from farther north that had settled in the low area in the center between the rising land to either side. The water was slightly chalky-looking, but clear enough to see that it was never more than ankle-deep. Because the shelves of rock jutting at an angle from the ground to the side had grown so tightly packed, they needed to cross the expanse of water to get to an area where they could make easier progress. Unfortunately, it was also the area that anyone else would have to use.

"Do you think it's awfully dark here?" Richard asked as they trudged into the shallow lake. "Or is it just me?"

"No," Samantha said in a quiet voice, trying to walk through the water without splashing too much of it up onto herself, "it's not you. It is darker here." She pointed. "Look over there. Looks like storm clouds gathering."

"It's a good thing we're crossing now, then. If there is a storm it could bring a flash flood down through here and wash us away."

Richard was relieved when they finally made it across the open, shallow water and were back on dry ground. Random fingers of rock jutting up from the uneven ground provided some cover. They wove their way through that rocky landscape, staying down closer to the valley floor and away from the taller spires that congregated in great enough numbers to hinder progress.

Spikes of rock thrust up all around, as if a porcupine were trying to emerge from beneath the ground. It made for an endless, confusing maze. Often the rock hid any point of reference. Richard tried to keep the taller mountains on their left in sight so he could know that he was going north, but in among the rocky spires it wasn't always possible.

At least the darkness was making it easier to see the flickering veils of green luminescence that came into the world of life from time to time. At times they watched as the curtains of eerie light dragged across the landscape and among the columns of rock like ghosts looking for a place to haunt. It occurred to Richard that that might not be too far from the truth. In a place where the world of life and the world of the dead existed in the same place, death probably looked to harvest any life it could catch.

After crossing another section of open ground, as they reached the concealing safety of columns and jumbles of rocks, Richard had to come to a stop. Blocking his intended course was an undulating green wall that abruptly rippled up into view before them between two towering fists of rock.

This time, through the greenish veil they could see dark figures on the other side—arms and legs writhing in continual turmoil. The shadowy shapes looked like the dead, lost beyond the veil, seeking a way out, or maybe seeking company in their misery.

It was a sight that brought both Richard and Samantha to an uneasy halt. At once frightened and at the same time beguiled, they had a hard time looking away.

It was a sight seen by few people on the living side of death.

Richard put a hand on Samantha's shoulder and nudged her off ahead of him, to his right, on a different route through the rocks. Even as she turned, her gaze stayed fixed on the moaning shapes beyond the billowing greenish veil.

"This way," Richard said. "Try not to look at them."

"It's hard not to," she said back over her shoulder.

"I know," Richard said in soft reassurance.

Almost before he had finished saying it, another wavering greenish veil abruptly loomed up before them, as if it had just risen from the underworld itself.

It came into view so swiftly that Richard almost stepped into it, almost touched it. It was so close that he could see forms moving beyond the opaque wall, pushing against it in places to make it stretch and bulge outward.

Richard took a quick step back.

"Lord Rahl?" Samantha called from the other side of the green veil.

He had pushed Samantha out ahead, directing her to a different route, and the veil had come up between the two of them as she had been out in front of him.

"It's all right, Samantha. I'm all right."

"Lord Rahl, I can hear you, but I can't see you."

There was no mistaking the alarm in her voice. "It's all right, Samantha. I'm right here. Stay back from it. Don't go near it. I'll come to you."

He turned a different way, going around it to get to Samantha. He made his way around a few of the imposing spires of rock to find a passage around the green veil.

Another curtain of the undulating green luminescence materialized, sliding in among the stone crags, as if carried in on an ill breeze. It stopped him in his tracks, preventing him from going the way he had intended in order to get around the first veil separating them.

"Lord Rahl, you're scaring me. Where are you?"

"Right here. I'm okay. I just have to go around another way, that's all. Hold on. I'll be right there."

The soaring rock spires all around created a maze that was made all the more difficult to navigate by routes being blocked by the flickering greenish veils of light.

As he turned to the left to go around a different way, another green veil appeared. This time, it felt deliberate, as if it somehow intended to block him from advancing and getting around. When he turned back, there was another already blocking his way.

"Lord Rahl?" came her voice in among the rock walls as another greenish curtain drifted in behind him, blocking any retreat.

There was only one way left open, and when he raced for it he had to skid to a stop as it, too, became blocked with the menacing green veil. He realized that he was surrounded. He would have to wait until the boundary walls to the underworld moved on.

"Samantha, listen to me. Do you have green walls blocking your way?"

"No. But I can't find you. I can't see you anymore. I can hear you, but not very well. I can't see you."

Richard was now completely surrounded by flickering, wavering, greenish light spanning every gap and escape route in the rock. He was trapped.

He knew that something was going on. This was not random.

This was deliberate.

Richard knew that he had only moments before the walls closed in and enveloped him.

"Samantha, can you hear me?"

"Barely."

"Are you all right?"

"Yes."

"Listen to me. Don't ask questions. Don't talk back and don't hesitate. Just do what I say. Understand?"

"Yes, Lord Rahl?"

"Run. Get away. Do it now."

Richard heard the crunch of small rocks from her footsteps. She was running. He sighed in relief at that much as the sound of her footsteps disappeared into the distance.

And then Richard was alone, surrounded by the world of the dead. He could see them—spirits of the dead—writhing beyond that eerie, opaque, greenish veil, hungry to get at him, to pull him in.

Richard began to see another shadowed form through the slowly swelling, flowing, rippling curtain of glimmering greenish luminescence.

This form, though, was different from all the others. This one was not moving.

The green veil on that one side in front of him began to fade, then to dissolve. It dissipated into the air before him until Richard was once again able to see the rocky world beyond. The green walls of the underworld to the sides and behind remained in place, blocking any retreat, but the way ahead was once more open.

Richard glanced to the sides, as much as he could, anyway, to look beyond the stone spires and the remaining prison of green, looking for any sign of Samantha. He didn't see her anywhere. He was relieved that she had done as he said.

Something was going on and he was thankful that she hadn't been trapped along with him. As long as she was still free, she might still be able to do something to help the others escape. Although she was still very young, Richard didn't discount her ability or her determination.

As long as one of them was still free and could act, there was still a chance to save the others.

In the deep shadows between the spires of stone not far in the distance a man in dark robes stood silently watching. It was the same form Richard had seen, unmoving, beyond the veil of the underworld. Now that the green shroud was gone, the shadowed form remained, confirming that this was not one of the dead from beyond the veil of life. Behind the man, off to his left side just a bit, was another form in the deeper shadows that he couldn't quite make out.

Once the green luminescence over the underworld had evaporated from the world of life, the man who had been waiting beyond that opening into the underworld began to step forward out of the shadows.

When he came into the muted light of the overcast afternoon, Richard stood in stunned silence.

The whites of the man's eyes were bloodred.

It looked as if his eyes had been deliberately tattooed a bright blood red, making the dark iris and pupil seem as if they were looking out from a fiery world—or perhaps from the underworld itself. It was as disconcerting as any gaze Richard had ever seen.

Even as otherworldly as his eyes looked, this man was clearly not an apparition from the world of the dead. Richard could tell that he was real enough, that he was flesh and blood.

Although it was that flesh that was the most disturbing aspect of the man. It was perhaps the most ghastly thing Richard had ever seen this side of death.

Every bit of the man not hidden by his dark robes was covered with tattooed symbols.

Symbols Richard recognized.

His flesh was not simply covered with the designs, but rather the tattoos were layered over the top of one another countless times so that the skin looked something other than human. As far as Richard could see, there was no spot that was not tattooed with some part or element of the circular designs, each one randomly laid over others that lay over yet others, all layer upon layer so that there was not one spot of untouched skin visible anywhere.

The top layers appeared to be the darkest, with designs underneath being lighter, and the ones under those lighter yet. It was as if they were continually being absorbed down into his flesh and new ones had to be constantly added over the top of those already vanishing down into his flesh. It gave them an endless, bottomless appearance, a tangled complexity that was dizzying, as if the symbols were continually seething up from underneath in a sea of something dark and dreadful.

The ever-deeper levels of the designs gave the man's skin a three-dimensional appearance. The endless layers made it hard to tell just where the surface of the skin actually was in all the floating elements, lending the flesh a shadowy, somewhat hazy, somewhat ghostly aspect.

The way the underlayers were lighter than the ones on top of them made each symbol distinct and recognizable, regardless of how many layers down in the design it lay, or how tightly packed they all were. All the different symbols, linked designs, and complex elements varied in size. There seemed to be an endless variety to the patterns within the designs, but each of those symbols contributed meaning to the larger, circular elements.

The man's hands and wrists, from what Richard could see of them where they emerged from his black coat, were completely covered with the same kinds of designs. Even his rather long fingernails appeared to be tattooed beneath, with the designs visible right through the nail itself.

His neck above his tight collar, like everywhere else, was covered with the designs ringing his throat. His face—every part of his face—was covered with the same sort of emblems. There were hundreds, if not thousands, on his face alone. When he blinked those terrible red eyes, Richard saw that his eyelids were tattooed as well. Even his ears, every fold and as far down inside as Richard was able to see, were completely covered with the symbols on top of circular symbols on top of yet more of the symbols. There were so many circular symbols that, in a way, it almost looked less like simple tattoos and more like they were a manifestation of black thoughts boiling to the surface from within.

While the man's bald head was covered over with the same kinds of designs, one of them, larger than all the rest, dominated them all. The bottom edge of that large circle crossed over the bridge of his nose, going out over his cheeks to each side beneath his eyes, and then up and around just above his ears to cover the rest of the crown of the skull. Inside the circle was another, and between them a ring of runes.

A triangle sitting within the inner circle crossed horizontally just above the man's brow. Smaller, secondary circular symbols floating outside the points of the triangle that broke the circles covered each temple with the third at the point of the triangle on the back of his head. The way it was laid out made it appear as if the man was glaring out with those haunting red eyes from within the circular symbol itself, as if he were glaring out from the underworld.

In the center of the triangle, toward the front of the man's skull, was a backward figure nine.

Richard recognized not only all the designs, but that one in particular.

That familiar tattoo covering the top of the man's bald head was darker than all the others, not just because it looked to be the most recently added, but because the lines composing it were heavier. Even so, lying as it was over layers of hundreds of other random emblems, it was evident that it was merely a part of a much larger purpose.

All the tattoos, in all their many different designs, were still variations of the same basic themes, much as letters in an alphabet were all of a set. There were symbols laid out in circles of every size, even circles within circles within circles, with some of the symbols contained within those circles made up of other, smaller designs and elements that Richard recognized as well. It was a disturbing sight to see a man so given over to such an occult purpose.

It all made him a dark, living, moving, fluid illustration, with every design down through the countless layers clearly discernible, and clearly with a purpose.

Richard was especially disturbed by the central design covering the top part of the man's face and skull, the one with the backward figure nine. Like the rest of the symbols all over the man, it, too, was in the language of Creation.

Richard also recognized all too well that looking out from the symbol as the man was, the figure nine at the heart of it would not be backward to him.

That particular symbol was the same one as on the omen machine, and on the cover of the book, *Regula,* that went with the machine. It was a symbol that linked it all to Richard.

The man's red eyes went to Richard's hand gripping the hilt of his sword still sitting in its scabbard, before returning to look into Richard's eyes, as if he were looking into his soul.

"Lord Rahl," the man said in a voice that was as unsettling as his flesh, "how kind of you to visit my land of Fajin Province."

Richard's brow twitched. "Bishop Hannis Arc?"

Hannis Arc was the leader of Fajin Province.

The man bowed his head. "Actually, it's Lord Arc."

L ord Arc," Richard said in a flat tone. "I was told
that it was Bishop Hannis Arc."

The man smiled insincerely. "My previous title."
He dismissed it with an annoyed flourish of a tattooed
hand. "I am now Lord Arc, soon to be . . . well, it's of
no concern at the moment. We have more important
business that awaits us."

The shadow behind the man finally stepped forward
to stand beside him.

Richard was stunned to see that it was a Mord-Sith
in red leather—a tall, very attractive, and a very
dangerous-looking Mord-Sith.

He was more stunned to see that the blond-haired
woman was not a Mord-Sith that he recognized—and
he knew them all. At least, he thought he did. This one,
he thought, must have been hiding under a rock. A
rock in the dark lands.

Hannis Arc held out an introductory hand as he
smiled in satisfaction at Richard's surprise. "This is
Mistress Vika."

Not only did he not recognize her, Richard had never heard any Mord-Sith mention the name Vika.

Hannis Arc turned to the woman. "You see, Vika? You worry for nothing. It is as I said. I leave the bread crumbs, and Lord Rahl follows them."

She smiled in response but held Richard's gaze with her steely blue eyes. "Yes, Lord Arc."

Hannis Arc turned back, also looking Richard in the eye as he spoke. "He is but a little pet, thinking he is going when he chooses, when he wants, and where he wants, when someone else is actually holding his leash."

"What's this about?" Richard asked as calmly as he could, reminding himself not to lose his temper.

He needed to think, to figure out what was going on. He knew that he couldn't do that if he gave himself over to a fit of rage, as satisfying as that might be. Better to stall for time and find out all he could. Better to find out exactly what kind of danger he was really up against. He knew that the more questions he could ask, and the more he let these two talk, the more time he would gain himself to try to think of a way out of the trap he found himself in.

"Well, you see, Lord Rahl, everything was going along as I wanted, but then the Hedge Maid nearly spoiled my plans. Seems as though she had an obsession with that blood lust that so overpowers her kind. But I guess that you have already learned all too much about that.

"Because of her failure to carry out my perfectly reasonable and carefully thought out requests, it became necessary to change my plans. In the end, however, I saw to it that it worked to my advantage, as all things eventually do.

"You see, I always take into account the alternate paths that others might choose to take because of their more limited nature so that if need be I am able to alter my own plans. Because of that, I was prepared and able to take advantage of the situation as it presented itself. You were only too accommodating and as a result it worked to my advantage even better than I could have dreamed up in the beginning.

"You see, in the beginning, I was wondering how I would deal with your well-known and quite dangerous abilities, but now, thanks to the obstinate nature of that filthy little Hedge Maid, that hazard has been taken care of as well."

Richard wasn't sure exactly what the man was talking about. When he didn't respond, Hannis Arc, as Richard expected, leaned forward a little to elaborate.

"I am referring to the touch of death she planted within you that prevents your gift from functioning. Its presence within you interferes with the function of the Grace." The sly smile reappeared. "Yes, I know about that. Seems she did me a favor by defanging you for me. Knowing her nature I allowed her to play out her own needs in order to serve mine. I knew what she would try to do, and I knew you would have to stop her."

Richard wondered what part prophecy had played in that.

Hannis Arc straightened, pleased with himself. "You see? My patience serves me well and it all works to my advantage in the end."

Richard saw that back in the shadows figures were beginning to appear as if materializing out of the rock itself. At first he saw only a few, but within moments there were hundreds emerging from behind the rock. They all looked the same.

Shun-tuk.

"So what is this grand plan of yours, anyway?"

Richard asked as offhandedly as he could, still stalling for time. "What's your little scheme all about?"

"All in good time." He couldn't seem to keep himself from adding "And not so little."

"Really? You expect me to believe that from the dark recesses of Fajin Province in your dark little domain, you have cooked up some elaborate grand plan that the world is going to care about?"

Fajin Province had contributed soldiers to the effort of stopping the Imperial Order. Some of those men even served in the First File back at the palace. It was disheartening to realize that this place that had fought with them was never really on their side. Or, at least, their leader wasn't. He had only pretended loyalty.

Richard wondered how many other leaders of other lands who smiled so pleasantly to his face really wanted to stab him in the back.

They had won the war, won the peace. Richard found such treachery not only infuriating, but disheartening. He had thought that there was going to be peace. Zedd had warned him that there was nothing so dangerous as peace. Richard should have taken his grandfather's words more seriously.

Hannis Arc smiled, as if trying to decide whether he wanted to kill Richard on the spot for disparaging his revelation of a carefully planned grand scheme, or continue to torment him to some purpose. In the end, he turned and bowed a little as he held an arm out in feigned, polite invitation.

"Come with us, if you please, Lord Rahl, and we will show you a bit of my grand plans. Then you can decide for yourself if you think the world will care."

The green walls of death still stood to the sides and behind, preventing any escape.

"Do I have a choice?" Richard asked.

Hannis Arc smiled in a way that made Richard's blood run cold.

"Not really."

"Well, even so, I'm sorry," Richard said. "I'm afraid that I have other plans, and they don't include you."

The shadow of a dark look came across Hannis Arc's tattooed face. The man lifted a finger in Richard's direction.

Sudden pain knifing through Richard's skull took him to his knees in a heartbeat. His eyes bulged as his hands went to the sides of his head. It felt like bolts of lightning were crackling in through his ears. The sound of it inside his head was deafening, the pain withering.

Hannis Arc withdrew the pointed finger, and the pain lifted with it. Richard fell forward onto his hands as he gasped a breath.

"I can do this all day," the man said. "Can you?"

Richard struggled to return to his feet, still panting to catch his breath.

"I think I can, Bishop," Richard said, deliberately using the man's lower title. "Please continue."

"Let me have a few minutes with him, Lord Arc," Vika said with menacing impatience. "I will teach him to be more respectful."

He dismissed her suggestion with a wave. "Later."

She bowed her head. "As you wish, Lord Arc."

Richard wished he knew where in the world she had come from, and why he didn't know anything about her.

"Enough of this," Hannis Arc said, dispensing with the polite tone, falling back on his true nature. "If you want to see your friends again," he said to Richard, "you will come with me."

He started away, but then turned back. "By the way, I believe you understand how the power of a Mord-Sith works. Draw your weapon, and Vika will own you."

"Vika," Richard said, addressing her directly and ignoring her master. "What are you doing here, with him? Mord-Sith serve the Lord Rahl."

"Not all of us," she said with that unique, chilling smile of a Mord-Sith. "Not anymore."

"What do you mean, not anymore?"

"We used to serve the House of Rahl, as had always been our tradition, but when Darken Rahl sent us on missions to Fajin Province in his name, some of us accepted Lord Arc's invitation to join with him, instead. We chose to serve him, and remain under his protection from the Lord Rahl."

Richard nodded. "I understand, Vika. Darken Rahl was an evil man. I know how he treated the Mord-Sith. Believe me, he harmed me as well. In the end, I killed him."

She smiled again. "Good for you." The smile vanished. She spun her Agiel up into her fist. "Now do as you were told and come along, or I will make you wish that you had not hesitated."

Richard knew that there was a time and place for everything, including a time and place to stand and fight. There was even a time and place to try to explain things. This was not either. Especially not in front of Hannis Arc.

He also knew what Mord-Sith were made of. They were universally feared for good reason. It was not a fight he really wanted to have. He looked at the determination in her steely blue eyes, and beyond to the hundreds of Shun-tuk that had appeared from nowhere.

This was not the time and place to stand and fight.

More than that, though, he knew these people were likely responsible for capturing his friends. Going with them was bound to be the quickest and easiest way to find out where Zedd, Nicci, Cara, Ben, and all the rest of them were being held.

Once he knew that, then maybe it would be the time to stand and fight.

Richard bowed his head. "Please, Bishop, Mistress Vika, lead the way."

61

In a grim mood, Richard followed behind Hannis Arc as he marched off in the direction of the rock towers in the distance. As he passed the mass of rugged stone spires, yet more of the chalky-looking Shuntuk emerged from the shadows to close in on both sides of him and from behind.

They were as forbidding a people as he had ever seen. All of them, even the women, were bare-chested. The most they wore above their waists were strings of beads, bones, and teeth, much of those worn around their upper arms.

All of them were smeared with a chalky white substance over every bit of skin not covered with their simple, sparse clothing. In a way, the white pigment was their dress. Most of them, including a number of the women, had shaved their heads. A few of them, including a few of the women, had topknots of hair wound with strings of bones and teeth to make the hair stand up in a plume. He didn't know if it was a mark of rank, another method of adornment, or meant to make them look more intimidating.

Smeared in the chalky white coloring, they were an unpleasant, savage-looking lot. They looked human, but in a way they looked less than that.

They all peered at him with hungry, grim expressions. The eyes of all the Shun-tuk looked haunted, surrounded as they were with rough circles of dark, greasy soot. Some of their faces had a skull's death grin painted over their lips and cheeks with the same dark grease, so that they looked like skulls rather than living people with flesh on their bones. It was as if they wanted to celebrate the part of them that was dead.

That made sense in view of the fact that these weren't really living people. They were half people, part of the third kingdom that existed somewhere between life and death. These people had no souls, no connection to the Grace, no spark from Creation that would follow them through their lives and into the underworld.

For now, they existed in neither the world of life nor the world of death. They were of a third kingdom.

Richard was unhappy to know that he, too, was of that kingdom and he had the shadow of that netherworld haunting him.

It was more than unsettling to be among such a gathering of half people. These were beings who, given the chance, would fall on him, rip him apart, and devour him to try to steal his soul.

As they went deeper into the endless expanse of spiked rock sticking up from the ground everywhere, the air grew darker overhead with a hazy layer of smoke. It smelled like sulfur. It was so thick in places that Richard couldn't see the tops of the taller rock projections.

The endless march felt like walking through a stone forest, with drifting smoke for a forest canopy. He began to spot places where that smoke was rising from cracks in the ground. The farther they went, the more prevalent the fissures became until he sometimes had to step over them and through the choking gray smoke. Green light shone up through many of those cracks, as if they were walking on rock that floated on the surface of the underworld itself.

To the sides, Richard saw openings in the craggy stone walls. Some looked shallow, but others went back into blackness. Acrid smoke rose from the cracked ground around them to add to the hazy layer overhead.

Deeper into the canyons among the stone columns, the spires began to take on the look of massive bundles of reeds that had turned to stone. Many of the individual stone rods that were bundled into the rock spires were broken off at different lengths, giving each column a jagged top. The ground was littered with those broken rodlike pieces of stone. In some places towers had fallen apart and had collapsed across the ground to leave a deep detritus that was difficult to walk through. In the distance off to the sides the columns merged together to become immense stone buttes.

As they made their way along a winding course among the network of deep, dark canyons created by the spires, Richard saw more of the Shun-tuk back in the dark recesses, peering out with those haunting, hungry, painted-on black eye sockets.

Farther into the confusing landscape, the rock changed and in among the spires was rock that looked to have once been liquid that flooded the place and then froze to stone. It was darker and full of holes. Richard saw more frequent openings in the rock. The larger masses of rock were riddled with every size of jagged hole. In places the flow of stone closed in overhead to make bridges and arches. Those, too, grew in number, creating a network of covered chasms. In places, the rock covering them thickened so that for brief spans it was like going through caves.

It felt as if the rugged landscape was bit by bit swallowing them up.

The Shun-tuk seemed to grow in number by the moment, coming out of openings in the rock to either watch, or join the procession. As they moved deeper into the snarled mass of rock, it seemed as if they began making their way through a cave system that over time had become partially exposed to the world above. The farther they went, the more the stone closed in overhead, until after a while, they were in a network of passages that were almost entirely underground. From time to time he saw gray overcast, but then they would again move into dark underground passageways.

As those passages, those holes riddling the rock, grew dark enough, torches were finally used to light the way. Eventually, as they moved deeper, the rock completely closed in overhead so that they were totally underground. Many of the grim, chalky half people brought torches with them as they emerged from holes, tunnels, and gaps everywhere in the rock.

In some of the passageways off to the sides, Richard saw silent figures standing, as if guarding the passage. They were not Shun-tuk. They were the awakened dead. The corpses, one with a shoulder bone sticking out from dried, crumbling, leathery skin, all watched with glowing red eyes.

Richard gave up trying to keep track of how he would ever find his way back out of the place. The entire network of caves was honeycombed with countless openings. He realized that he was hopelessly lost in the underground labyrinth. He wondered if he would ever have to face the problem of finding a way out.

They came to a series of caverns off to the sides that were shut off, some with rough planks that looked to serve as doors, or barriers. Other openings, though, were closed off with sheets of the wavering greenish underworld luminescence.

When Richard saw a figure standing beyond one of those curtains of green, he stopped to look. He could tell that it wasn't one of the spirits that could be seen back in the world of the dead. This figure didn't move the same, didn't writhe and wail. It moved then stood still, like a man would. He knew that it was a person trapped on the other side of the green wall. It occurred to him that the veil of the underworld might be serving as a kind of prison door.

The Mord-Sith jabbed him lightly in the back of the shoulder with her Agiel to keep him moving. He put a hand over his shoulder as he stumbled ahead, comforting the unexpected stab of pain. From ample experience he knew that the pain could have been far worse, had she intended it. This time she had only intended to prod him along.

Not much farther along, Hannis Arc stopped and turned, watching Richard, Vika, and the mass of silent, whitewashed half people coming up around and behind Richard. When Richard came to a halt, Hannis Arc silently gestured to the Mord-Sith.

She understood what he wanted.

"Give me your sword," she said as she moved around in front of Richard. "You won't be needing it."

Handing over his sword was about the last thing in the world he wanted to do, but his options were pretty limited. He could draw the weapon and fight, but there was no way he could hold off the horde of Shun-tuk all around him. His first target, of course, would have been Hannis Arc, but the man had already demonstrated his occult powers, so such an attack would swiftly prove pointless. Lastly, trying to use the weapon against a Mord-Sith was a mistake that he had made once before in his life. He would not make that same mistake again.

Vika lifted her hands out. Richard pulled the baldric off over his head and laid the sheathed sword in her upturned palms.

She looked a bit surprised. "Very good, Lord Rahl. If I didn't know better, I would think that you had already been trained by a Mord-Sith."

Without saying anything, Hannis Arc gestured to the half people crowded in close.

One of the Shun-tuk shoved Richard, turning him down a different tunnel to the left side. Once into the opening, Hannis Arc gracefully lifted a hand and a glimmering green veil rose over the opening, trapping Richard behind it.

Richard, feeling naked without his sword, looked around in his sudden solitude, the greenish veil providing light enough to see by. He paced for a time, frustrated, angry, and feeling cornered not only by the shimmering green luminescence confining him in a chamber in the rock, but by the entire situation.

He had hoped that this would lead him to where Zedd, Nicci, Cara, and the others were being held captive. He suspected that he had to be close to them, but locked in such a spot he didn't know how he would get to them.

It was obvious that Hannis Arc had long been plotting something, and Richard had been completely unaware of the man's treacherous scheming. Richard didn't know for sure what the man had planned or what his ultimate goal was, but Richard had some ideas and none of them were good.

He hated the feeling of being too far behind the flow of events, of feeling that he had been trapped before he even realized that anything was going on. Not only had the barrier to the third kingdom, built in Naja

Moon's time back during the ancient war, finally failed, but at the same time Hannis Arc was planning something ominous. It seemed obvious enough that the two events, the barrier failing and Hannis Arc capturing Richard, were connected.

He admonished himself for concentrating so much mental effort on the problem rather than trying to think of a way out of the situation. He was in the dark about Hannis Arc's plans. He couldn't know the extent of the problem and it was useless guessing.

At least Samantha had gotten away. That meant the situation wasn't hopeless. Hannis Arc either didn't care about her, or he hadn't yet managed to catch her. Most likely he didn't consider her a serious threat and so he didn't concern himself with her. It was Richard he wanted.

Richard knew that he had to think of solutions rather than fret about the problem. He needed to tackle the obstacles one at a time. The immediate solution he needed was to see if there was a way to get out of the prison he found himself in. He had to put his mind to that, first.

Setting aside the swirl of worries and questions, he began exploring the irregular area in which he found himself confined.

There was a wooden bucket of water near a wall, but no food. He soon discovered that there were openings everywhere through the rock. Most of them were small dark holes he could fit no more than a finger or hand into. There were a few other openings barely large enough to possibly squeeze himself through, but they were dark as pitch. Richard suspected they led nowhere, so he would save them as a last resort to try. It would do him no good to try to wriggle through and get stuck. There were larger openings, like the one he had come in through, but they, too, were blocked with the glowing green walls.

Richard was careful to stay clear of that wavering greenish luminescence. He had been uncomfortably close to such boundaries to the underworld before, but he was unsure of the exact properties of the ones in this place. After all, Hannis Arc had commanded them into existence. It was impossible to know if the boundary between life and death behaved differently in the third kingdom, where life and death existed together, or if they behaved like others he had encountered in the past. More importantly, after coming through the gates into the third kingdom, those boundaries were not fixed—they moved. He didn't want to be too close and have one of these unexpectedly engulf him. All the more reason to keep his distance from the wavering greenish veil.

As he glanced around, the thought occurred to him that the boundary veils blocking him in the prison might start closing in on him in order to pull him into the underworld. That seemed unlikely, though. Hannis Arc could have simply let the Shun-tuk have him if he had wanted Richard dead.

No, Hannis Arc had wanted him alive for some purpose. Maybe the same reason he had taken the others captive rather than kill them. Richard wished he knew what that purpose could be.

Sighing in frustration, he stuffed his hands into his back pockets as he walked around, inspecting every inch of his prison. He saw nothing useful and no way out. It seemed a very secure dungeon.

He hoped that Samantha hadn't been caught by the Shun-tuk. In the back of his mind he constantly worried about her.

He considered the way he had been able to call to her beyond the greenish veil trapping him. He remembered that she could hear him, but could not see him through the greenish veil.

That thought gave him an idea.

He went to one of the passages covered over with a glimmering sheet of the green light.

"Is anyone there?" he called out.

When he called out again and still received no answer back other than the echo of his own voice, he went down the line to the next veil blocking an opening, and then another, calling out at each one.

"Can anyone hear me? Is anyone there?"

"Richard?" came the weak echo of a voice he knew.

Richard spun around to where the voice had come from across the irregular chamber. He rushed to the other side of his prison, to the green veil floating in the opening on that side.

"Zedd? Zedd is that you?"

"Dear spirits—Richard!" the voice echoed back.

It sounded distant, as if it was several chambers away, and it wasn't very loud, but it was enough to hear and it was unmistakable. Zedd's voice sounded choked with tears. That tormented sound in his grandfather's voice terrified Richard.

"Zedd, yes, it's me. Are you all right?"

The answer was a long moment in coming.

"Yes, my boy. I'm alive."

That wasn't the answer Richard had been hoping for.

"Zedd, are you all right? What are they doing to you?"

He waited a moment until the answer finally came. "They're bleeding us."

"Bleeding you? They're taking your blood?"

"Yes."

Richard pounded a fist against the stone wall beside the opening blocked by the greenish luminescence.

"Why?"

"It's a long story. I've seen a few of the others. And some people I don't know. They bleed them as well, gifted and nongifted alike."

Richard remembered how Jit had been bleeding Kahlan and drinking her blood. He had to remind himself to slow his breathing and stay calm. He had to keep his wits if he was to figure something out.

It was all he could do not to try to dive through the greenish boundary of the underworld to get to his grandfather.

"I'm sorry they have you, too, my boy. But it is heartwarming to hear your voice."

The anguish in Zedd's voice was unmistakable. Zedd rarely sounded that despairing.

"Zedd, hang on. I'll think of something."

Richard could hear a soft chuckle. "That's the Richard I've missed so much."

Richard swallowed. "Zedd, what do they want with your blood. Why are they taking your blood?"

"They are using it to try to raise the dead."

Richard blinked. "What?"

"They don't do much talking, but from what I can gather, they think that the blood of the gifted can somehow bring the dead back to life."

"That's crazy, but it's far from the craziest thing I've heard recently."

The silence dragged on for a moment before Zedd spoke again.

"So tired . . . Richard, I have to rest. So tired . . ."

Richard was nodding. "It's all right, Zedd. Rest. I'll think of something. I'll get us out of here, I swear I will. Hang on. Rest for now. Save your strength."

"Hush. They're coming for me again. I love you, my boy. . . ."

Zedd's voice trailed off.

Richard pounded the side of his fist against the wall again as he heard his grandfather cry out in the distance as he was being dragged away.

Richard had to do something.

63

Kahlan caught the handle on the side to help herself stay upright when the coach bounced over a rut. Abruptly rocking so violently hurt her abdominal muscles injured by the Agiel. It still hurt to take a deep breath.

Both the Mord-Sith and the abbot were watching her as they rode through a gloomy landscape of towering trees and craggy, inhospitable terrain. Kahlan turned her eyes to look out the window so that she wouldn't have to look at the two of them. It made her anger boil to look at them. It made her furious that they were doing this.

The New World had for years fought a gruesome war with the Old World. Emperor Jagang had caused incalculable suffering. There was no way to tell how many hundreds of thousands of people had lost their lives in that war. Families lost fathers, mothers, brothers, daughters and sons. Entire generations of people had been wiped out. More people yet would be crippled for life. Many would not be entirely healed for years, if ever.

And for what?

So that Emperor Jagang could rule the world, so that the Imperial Order could bring about their vision that everyone must live for the Imperial Order and their beliefs, live as subjects of those twisted ideas of the common good imposed by force.

Like so many other rulers who preached a common good, they had been willing to kill everyone who didn't agree with their delusion of a better life. They had been willing to wipe out entire cities, the entire New World if need be, to have their way.

The suffering they'd brought to the world had been staggering, all in the absurd notion of a better life for all.

But Richard had led the New World to victory. Freedom had prevailed. The long ordeal, the suffering and sacrifice that sometimes seemed as if it would never end, was now over.

The world was at peace.

And now these people from some forsaken dark land wanted to throw the world into chains again, just as the Imperial Order had done? And for what? So that they could rule?

It was insane.

Kahlan clenched her jaw as she glared out the window.

"What was it like?"

Kahlan frowned back at the abbot sitting on the seat across from her.

"What?"

His self-satisfied smile seemed comfortably at home on his features as he watched her. He could see how angry she was, and he was enjoying it. He was enjoying that he had taken her prisoner, that the Mother Confessor, the Lord Rahl's wife, the woman who had helped defeat the Imperial Order, was now nothing more than his chattel.

"I asked what it was like."

Kahlan glared at him without answering. She turned her gaze out the window at the endless expanse of dark woods. The leaden overcast made all the trees look a greenish gray. The forest looked ancient, as if the world of man had not touched it. It was an uncharted wilderness, a primal, inhospitable wasteland where death and decay was the way of life.

The crooked limbs arching over the small road nearly closed them in, turning the poorly made road into a somber tunnel through hostile territory. They seemed to her to be like the great arms of monsters continually reaching for victims. It was as malicious-looking a woods as she had ever seen.

A sudden, violent blow to her face sent Kahlan sprawling across the seat.

She gasped from the pain and shock of the blow from the Mord-Sith's fist. Her world seemed to tilt as it spun. For a moment, Kahlan had trouble understanding where she was or what was happening. Her arms lay limp, one across her legs, the other hanging down over the front of the black leather seat.

Kahlan groaned as the pain from the blow started to blossom. Her jaw throbbed. Her lips and nose tingled as if from a thousand needles.

Erika yanked Kahlan upright by her hair and then backhanded her across the other side of the face, finally shoving her back into her seat.

As Kahlan sat, arms dangling limp at her sides, she felt warm blood running down her chin, dripping onto her pants.

"The abbot asked you a question," the Mord-Sith growled. "You had better learn to respect your superiors. If you don't wish to do that, then I would be only too happy to ask the driver to stop the coach so that I can drag you out onto the road and teach you to show proper deference and obedience."

She leaned forward, again grabbing Kahlan by the hair, pulled her forward, and put her face close. "Would you like that?"

"No," Kahlan said before the Mord-Sith struck her again.

Erika smirked as she released Kahlan's hair, leaned back in her seat, and folded her arms.

With the back of her wrist Kahlan wiped the blood from her mouth.

Abbot Dreier watched in quiet satisfaction for a moment before finally repeating the question.

"I asked, what was it like? I expect an answer. Erika expects an answer. We are both burning with curiosity."

Kahlan shot him a black look. "What are you talking about? What was what like?"

With a fluttering hand, he indicated the long, falling descent from a high place. "You know, the drop, the fall from the cliff. You really must learn to be more careful. Being clumsy and falling like that could get you killed one day. So, what was it like?"

Kahlan could feel her lip swelling and the pain setting in earnest. She wanted more than anything at that moment to strangle the life out of the man.

"I didn't like it much."

He arched an eyebrow in amusement. "Really. And why not?"

Kahlan glanced to the Mord-Sith and then back at him. "It was frightening."

He let out a brief chuckle. "I imagine it was." He folded his arms as he leaned back, watching her. "But that was the whole point."

"It had a point?"

He shrugged. "Of course."

"I'm afraid that I'm not very good at guessing. Why don't you tell me what the point was."

"Why, to scare the life out of you, of course. You were scared nearly to death, weren't you? You know, right when you were almost at the bottom, when you were about to hit the ground going full speed from a fall from on high?"

"So the point was to scare me? All right. You succeeded. I was scared. Happy?"

He turned his smile on the Mord-Sith. "She still doesn't understand."

"She will," the Mord-Sith said, rocking back and forth as the coach went over a series of bumps. "Eventually."

"I suppose you're right," he said with a sigh.

Kahlan sat silently, not wanting to give him the satisfaction of her asking what he meant.

"Aren't you curious?" he finally asked. "Don't you wonder how I did it?"

Kahlan knew exactly what he was talking about. He was asking if she was curious as to how he had managed to use his gift to stop her fall right before she hit the ground.

Kahlan had grown up around wizards. She knew a lot about magic and what it could do. Those with the gift could lift things, even heavy things, and catch objects that were falling before they hit the ground.

But they couldn't do that with living things, especially people.

Life somehow interfered with that sort of manipulation. Something about having a soul prevented people from being lifted, except in rare circumstances and for brief periods of time. Even then, it required monumental effort. Otherwise, they would all be able to fly. They had explained the principle to her once, but at the moment it seemed unimportant.

What was important, what was relevant, was how Ludwig Dreier had managed to do it, especially with such precision that he was able to catch her that close to the ground and halt her fall. When she had stopped, her face had been inches from the dirt. He had then smoothly, gently, lowered her to the ground.

It was an appalling, frightful, horrifying experience that had left her shaking like a leaf.

"Yes," Kahlan said, "as a matter of fact, I am curious. How did you do it? You obviously have the gift, a fact that you kept from us before, at the palace. I've never known a wizard who could do such a thing. From what I learned, the gift isn't able to do something like that."

He smiled with satisfaction. "Quite right. The gift can't do such a thing. But you see, I have a different sort of power."

"The gift is the gift."

"Well, yes, that is true enough, but those of us like myself and Lord Arc have acquired the additional ability to use occult powers with our gift. The rest of the world simply doesn't understand the powers we have, or what we can do with those powers." He gestured out the window. "One of the advantages of living way out here, away from everyone else, is being able to learn such dark crafts from the cunning folk and then develop it into something altogether different, something more than they could ever imagine. But then, they don't have the gift and so they could never imagine such things."

"You should be very careful conjuring such dark arts."

His smile widened again. She was getting tired of seeing it. His gloating seemed to be an end in itself.

"I am not afraid," he said in a low, dangerous sort of voice.

Kahlan wanted to say that he should be afraid. She decided better of it.

He brightened, then. "But you were afraid. When you fell, I mean. You were afraid."

"I already told you I was," Kahlan said as they bounced over a rocky section of the road.

The jolt hurt her abdomen, taking her breath, and made her jaw throb. At least her lip had stopped bleeding.

"That was what I had intended."

Kahlan renewed the black look. "I would think that you would have long ago outgrown scaring girls."

The Mord-Sith laughed out loud. "She's funny." She looked over at Abbot Dreier. "She's funny."

He made a face but otherwise ignored the Mord-Sith. "There is a point to the fear," he said patiently to Kahlan. "I'm trying to explain my purpose, and in that context the larger purpose of my life's work."

Kahlan took a deep breath. She didn't really want to talk. Since Erika had clouted her across the jaw it hurt to try to talk. She supposed there was no avoiding it.

Besides, she realized that she needed to know what the man was up to, what his "life's work" was all about, and what he was doing at the abbey. She could tell that it wouldn't take a lot to encourage him to reveal such things about himself.

"I'm sorry, Abbot, but falling from a cliff and being caught at the last possible instant before smacking the ground is all new to me. I'm afraid that if you have some purpose in doing it, that purpose is lost on me."

He dispensed with the smile as he leaned in toward her. "Right there, at the end, right at that last instant before you knew with absolute certainty that you were about to die, did you have any revelations? Any last thoughts? Any memories of the meaning of your life? In rare near-death encounters, many people say that they experience in a single instant the entirety of their life— see it all.

"So, I was wondering what your last thoughts were in that final instant before you knew that you were about to die."

Kahlan had to look away from his eyes. She stared out the window instead, watching the endless expanse of trees and limbs flash past the coach.

"Well?" he asked. "What last thought did you have?"

"You wouldn't understand," she said in a quiet voice without looking at him.

They rode in silence for a moment.

"In that case," he finally said, "why don't you explain it to me."

She knew it was not simple curiosity. It was a request she dared not ignore.

"I experienced the total and complete feelings I have for my husband."

He held up a finger. "Ah, love."

She was about to say that he wouldn't know what love really was, but decided not to waste the effort.

"Well, you see, the thing is," he went on as he picked at one of his fingernails, "we have learned, through our abilities with occult powers, how to alter that experience."

Kahlan's eyes turned to him. "Alter the 'experience'? The 'experience' of death? What do you mean?"

"In that last instant before death—real, certain death, actual death—people experience many different things. They may experience regret, paralyzing fear, love, even the instantaneous memory of the sum of their entire life, as I hear it told. That sort of thing."

"So?"

"Well, you see, we—by we, I mean I, of course—I have learned through long experimentation and effort how to alter that experience so that those about to pass through the veil and into the world of the dead are able to do something useful for those of us remaining behind in the world of life."

Kahlan frowned, now sincerely curious.

"Useful? What could you possibly get from people right before they die that is useful to you?"

His smile returned, but this time there was no amusement in it, no gloating. It was as malevolent a look as she had ever seen.

"Prophecy."

64

Kahlan was stunned. "Prophecy?"

"Yes. We get prophecy."

"What are you talking about?"

"Well, you see," he said as he leaned back, "when altered through my abilities near the end of life, that life remaining within a person, the life that is draining away, is altered so that in that last, singular instant when they are crossing over through the veil, for that brief flicker of time when they are still holding on to life and at the same time touching death, rather than seeing their life's experiences, or feeling some sense of loss, or even feelings of love, they instead, because of the changes I've made within them, as they touch the timeless world of the dead they are able to tap into that same flow of time that prophets experience.

"In that extraordinary moment, connected to the convergence of life and death, they are able to see the sweep of time, stand in its flow, and thus give forth prophecy, the same as a genuine prophet."

Kahlan was horrified. "You think that you can

somehow use occult powers to get prophecy out of people as they are dying?"

He shot her a condescending look. "It is a process I created and developed, thoroughly understand, and control. There is no speculation involved."

"And you've done this before? You intend to do it again?"

"That is the purpose of the abbey. There I use this process to collect prophecies and then deliver them to Lord Arc. Lord Arc uses prophecy, you see, to guide him."

Kahlan stared in disbelief. "Are you saying that you take people to the abbey and murder them so that they will cry out prophecy to you as they're dying? You murder people in the hope that with their last dying breath they will give you a prophecy?"

"Murder? No, not exactly. We are harvesting prophecy from the great abyss of eternity. We are reaping what is there for those who know how to obtain it."

"Through murder."

He dismissed the charge with a gesture. "The people chosen to help us in this great work are not murder victims. To the contrary. It is an honor for them that they have been chosen to give their lives to such a noble cause. They may not be able to realize that right then, of course, but they are heroic people sacrificing their lives for the benefit of others."

"That's madness," Kahlan whispered.

"Madness? No, not at all," he said, prickling at the suggestion. "The sacrifice of these few is all done for the greater good of the many. It is brilliant both in its conception and in its execution."

"'Execution' is the right word," Kahlan said. "Execution plain and simple for your twisted cause."

He gave her a testy look. "You do the same thing."

"We do no such thing and you know it."

"You who use prophecy. Those at the People's Palace use it—those like your husband who collect and hoard the life's work of prophets who have tapped that great flow of time from beyond, as I am doing, only to keep that precious prophecy in secret libraries so as to use it to control the lives of others rather than benefit those lives. Those who give prophecy—prophets—are also giving their lives into such prophecy, no less than those at the abbey, and you suck dry that effort for selfish reasons, not for the common good as it is intended by the Creator."

Kahlan knew better than to say anything.

He leaned forward and pointed a finger at her. "You and Lord Rahl keep prophecy to yourselves in order to use it as a weapon to enslave people.

"We, on the other hand, use the prophecy we gather from those who make such a final sacrifice in order to help guide the lives of our people. We use such prophecy to guide the people of Fajin Province, we don't hide it from them as you and Lord Rahl do for selfish gain. Prophecy rightly belongs to everyone, not just the few.

"And now others in other lands have asked to join with us and benefit from the insights we gain from prophecy."

Kahlan didn't bother to try to argue with such madness. She was sick to death of trying to make people understand how prophecy worked, and how it did not work. She was disheartened with the lands that had left the D'Haran Empire to follow Hannis Arc for promises of prophecy freely given to them.

In the end, people believed what they wanted to believe. The truth had very little to do with it.

"You have been chosen to contribute to this great

work," he said at last as he finally leaned back in his seat. "You will in the end be one of those who gives prophecy to those who need it. Because of your renown, prominence, and birthright as a Confessor, we expect remarkable prophecy from you."

Kahlan glanced at the Mord-Sith and then back at the abbot. "So you're going to kill me. Big surprise. Evil men have been killing innocent people since the dawn of time.

"You are going to chop off my head, expecting me to babble prophecy first? Fine, just don't try to convince yourself that I lay my head on the block willingly. It will be a simple act of murder, nothing more, and certainly not noble."

He dismissed her words with a wave and a sour expression.

"It's not that simple," the Mord-Sith said with a knowing smile.

"Not that simple," Kahlan repeated. "And why not? You said that you kill people so that they will give prophecy right as they're dying. That may be lunacy, but it is simple lunacy."

"No, you misunderstand," she said. "I meant that the process is not that simple."

"They must be prepared, first," Abbot Dreier put in with a kind of twisted zeal.

"Prepared? How do you prepare them to be murdered?"

He lifted an eyebrow. "Torture."

Kahlan stared back. "You torture people at the abbey."

"That is the function of the facility—to process people on their path to giving their gift of prophecy. It is through torture that people are properly brought to that cusp of life and death and held there at the boundary between worlds until they are finally ready to accept into themselves what we offer them."

Kahlan was incredulous. "What you offer? What could you possibly offer them as you torture them?"

"Release," the Mord-Sith said.

"Release?" Kahlan asked, still staring at them both in disbelief.

"Release," Abbot Dreier confirmed. "Only when they willingly embrace the greater good and allow themselves to be the conduit for this gift to mankind, do we release them and allow them the privilege of crossing over into death."

Kahlan felt sick. She now understood all too well the part that the Mord-Sith played in this scheme.

Erika smiled when she saw that Kahlan finally understood.

"There is transcendent glory in profound agony," the Mord-Sith said with quiet conviction, as if to justify what they were doing.

"Glory," Kahlan said, sarcastically, repulsed by the evil of it all.

"Yes, indeed, glory." The Mord-Sith's wicked satisfaction in her work surfaced. "We intend to bring you such glory as you cannot yet imagine."

Ludwig Dreier was staring at Kahlan. "And then you, too, like all the others who have come before you, will willingly give forth prophecy in order to be allowed to cross over into death."

Richard sat on the stone floor of the cavern, his back leaned up against the wall, half dozing, weary from the inner sickness weighing him down. He looked up when he heard muffled voices. It was not Zedd's voice, but voices outside of the barrier, out beyond his main prison entrance. Someone was saying something he couldn't quite make out.

He saw movement on the other side of the undulating green veil and then several figures came to a halt. It was not the kind of movement he was used to seeing from the writhing spirits inside the world of the dead who had been taunting him for days, promising him the peace of eternal nothingness, whispering for him to step through and join them in that eternal peace.

These other figures were instead standing outside his green prison door.

It had been several days since he had seen or heard anyone even passing by beyond that rippling wall of green light. At least, he thought it had been several days. He couldn't be sure. It was hard to tell time in the timeless twilight of the imprisoning cavern.

He had slept little and paced a lot as the time slowly passed. They had brought him no food. He had found a recess worn down into the rock itself by the steady drip of water. Over time that slow, steady drip had hollowed out a bowl-shaped depression. That at least provided him a source of water, since the bucket was empty.

But without food, he was beginning to think that maybe they had simply left him there to die. With the touch of death always there in the background inside him, he wondered if that poison left by the Hedge Maid might beat them to it.

Richard had gone back a number of times to the place where he had talked to Zedd, but his grandfather never answered. As he had paced, Richard had frequently checked the other openings that were also blocked by the greenish veil to the underworld. No word came back from beyond any of them. He wondered if the guards had moved people away from the cells near his so that no one could talk to him or tell him what was happening. It would make sense for them to want to isolate him.

Richard told himself that it was either that, or Zedd had not returned because it was more likely that prisoners were stuffed into any handy hole, rather than bothering to bring them back to a specific place. After all, the rock was honeycombed with caverns. He tried very hard to convince himself of that. He refused to allow himself to consider the possibility that after Richard had last spoken with him, they had again bled his grandfather and he had finally died. Richard reminded himself that Zedd was stronger than he looked, and that he would hold on now that Richard was there.

But what hope could there be just because Richard was now also a prisoner? He was more likely to die along with the rest of them.

The greenish light abruptly dissipated, twisting as it dissolved like smoke spiraling up and vanishing.

There were a number of Shun-tuk standing outside in the maze of passageways, as well as a few of the walking dead standing farther back in dark openings, watching with glowing red eyes. The half people stared as if trying to see his soul.

The Mord-Sith stood at the entrance. It was her shape he had seen beyond the veil.

Richard stayed seated where he was.

Down in the chamber where they had put him, there was no opening to the outside world, no daylight, so it was impossible for him to tell precisely how many days it had been since he had last seen anyone, or even if it was day or night. Since he had been left in his private prison, not even the Mord-Sith had come to torment him, as Mord-Sith were wont to do.

While he felt weak from lack of food, in contrast Vika looked well rested and fresh. With Mord-Sith, that was generally a bad sign.

Richard, though, wasn't in the mood for any of their nonsense or games. His time was running out and his patience was well past wearing thin.

Vika stepped into his prison room in a commanding manner that brought back a lot of very unpleasant memories. He tried to remind himself not to impose past situations on this one. This was different. He was different. He had to think of what he faced now, not what he had faced in the past.

The Mord-Sith's single blond braid looked clean and freshly made up. Her red leather was spotless and cut to stretch tightly over her muscular form.

"It is time," she said in a silky, cool voice.

"Time?" Richard, resting his forearms over his knees, didn't make a move to get up. "Time for what?"

"Time for you to come with me," she said, with a practiced lack of emotion.

Richard sighed and stood up before she came to retrieve him. He brushed the stone grit off his hands. He mentally readied himself for the dance that was about to begin. He took a calming breath. He was not going to let her lead.

"Look, Vika, I know a lot more about Mord-Sith than you can imagine, and I think you know a lot less about the outside world than you realize. You've been kept in the Dark Lands and at the same time kept in the dark.

"You need to listen to me. Darken Rahl was an evil man. Don't mark me with his crimes or sins.

"The world beyond Fajin Province, beyond these backward Dark Lands, has changed for the better. I know how Darken Rahl collected young girls to become Mord-Sith, how they were trained. I can see why any Mord-Sith would have left him . . . but I'm not him.

"I'm not like he was. I don't allow the collection of girls to become Mord-Sith, and I don't treat those women who are already Mord-Sith the way he treated them. The Mord-Sith are my friends."

She arched an eyebrow. "Like Cara?"

"Cara. Cara is here?" Richard took a step forward. "Is she all right? Is she safe?"

"She is weak."

"From being bled?"

Vika twitched a frown. "No. She is weak from being your Mord-Sith. She is weak because you are weak and allowed her to grow weak."

"Cara is a lot stronger than you could ever be because I allowed her to grow," Richard said through gritted teeth. "She had the strength to grow into the person she wanted to be. You could never be as strong as she is."

"Please," Vika scoffed with a roll of her eyes. "Her Agiel doesn't even work. She is nothing, now." She smiled. "That is how Lord Arc knew that your gift really had failed. The Agiel of your Mord-Sith do not work because your gift, your bond, has failed them. You have failed them. They are helpless, now. You are helpless now."

Richard had been wondering exactly how Hannis Arc had known about Richard's gift not working. It had been a simpler answer than he had considered.

"Did you talk to Cara? Did you try to learn anything about how things are now with—"

"I talked. She listened."

Richard didn't like what she was implying.

"You can choose to change, Vika."

"Change? Like her? Become weak? I was at the People's Palace with Abbot Dreier. I was there right under your nose, unseen, helping him set things into motion. When I was there I heard talk, and the abbot confirmed it. He said that Cara—a Mord-Sith—had wed."

"I know," Richard said in a quiet voice. "I'm the one who married them."

Vika, looking surprised, studied his face for a long moment. "Why would she do such a thing? She is Mord-Sith."

"She is also a woman, Vika, just like you. She fell in love and wanted to share her life with the man she loved."

Her frown returned. She looked sincerely puzzled. "And you allowed this? Why would you marry them?"

"Because I care about her, about all the Mord-Sith. I wanted her to be happy. After what she has been through in her life, what all of you have been through, she deserved to have some happiness come into her life. The other Mord-Sith wept with joy at her wedding." Richard tapped his own chest. "I wept with joy for her."

As Vika studied him in silence for a time, he went on.

"She changed—by her own choice, changed to have the life she wanted. You, too, have the ability to use your head, to change, but the time for you to make that choice for your own life is shrinking. You still have the choice of setting things right and of helping me to set things right. That's the only way.

"Don't let the opportunity pass you by, Vika. Once that chance slips away from you, it will be gone forever."

She was incredulous. "Chance for what?"

"Chance not to be the property of an evil man."

"He is the Lord Arc, my master."

"You are your own master. You just don't know it."

Her patience gone, her anger exploding to the surface, Vika abruptly rammed her Agiel toward his middle.

Richard caught the weapon in his fist before she could push it into his abdomen. Vika held one end, he the other, enduring the agony the way he had been taught in terrible lessons he thought he would never need.

Now, he needed those lessons.

Now, he was thankful for those lessons.

Now, those lessons were the only thing keeping him standing.

He was inches away from Vika's face, staring into her blue eyes and she into his, sharing the same pain of the Agiel that she felt, enduring it the same as she endured it.

The Shun-tuk watched without reaction from beyond the doorway, without realizing the full extent of what was happening, what the two of them were feeling, or what they were sharing. The chalky figures with blacked-out eyes made no move to intervene as the two of them stood motionless, face-to-face, sharing the withering agony of her Agiel.

Looking into her eyes, Richard finally saw the shadow of fear.

After he saw that specter of fear in her eyes, after enough time had passed to make sure she understood that he saw it and recognized it, he shoved her back while releasing the Agiel.

As she watched him, panting to get her breath, her smooth brow drew into an emotional frown. "You are a rare person, Richard Rahl, to be able to do that."

"I am the Lord Rahl," he told her with quiet authority. "Despite what you may believe, I am in control, not you. Don't ever forget that or it will cost you your life when you least expect it."

"I expect to die in battle—"

"Not old and toothless in bed," he finished.

She frowned. "So, you know more of Mord-Sith than I had thought."

"Vika, I know more of Mord-Sith than you can imagine. I know that they can choose life again. I know it isn't too late. I have worn around my neck the Agiel of Mord-Sith who have died. Some of them died fighting me, others, fighting for me. All of them were individuals who had the ability to choose more for their own lives than to be only Mord-Sith. Some chose wisely, some did not."

Vika looked deeply into his eyes as she weighed his words. She finally lifted her Agiel, pointing it at his face as the iron returned to her expression.

"I am Mord-Sith. You will do as I say, when I say it."

Richard smiled softly. "Of course, Mistress Vika." He held his arm out. "Now, get going. You are supposed to come collect me for something. The pathetic excuse for a man who you follow will be angry with you if you delay any longer. That is the way he treats Mord-Sith—no differently, really, than Darken Rahl used to treat them.

"Your choice to go with Hannis Arc instead of Darken Rahl was no improvement. You traded one tyrant for another, that's all. But at least it should show you that you have the power to choose for yourself what you want for yourself. You made that choice. I hope that you will learn from it and come to make a better choice the next time."

She did not look pleased. "I hope Lord Arc allows me to kill you."

"That's a false hope. It just isn't ever going to happen."

Her face turned red with rage. "And what makes you think so?"

"Do you really think that Hannis Arc would go to all the trouble he went through to capture me simply in order to let you kill me? I hardly think so.

"He has much bigger plans than your amusement. He wants me for some reason. He is not going to let you kill me, and I expect that he has given you explicit orders to that effect. Isn't that right?"

"You're right," she said in a calmer voice, "you do have a higher purpose than dying by my hand." She lifted her chin. "But that doesn't mean I won't enjoy your fate."

"Fine, just knock off the empty threats. Now, let's get going."

Richard started away when she didn't. He stepped aside to let her take the lead as she cut in front of him. He had pushed her enough. If he pushed any more right then it would only harden her.

Richard knew that he could have killed the woman. He knew how to kill Mord-Sith. Most people didn't, but sadly, he did.

He needed to get away and would have been willing to kill her to do so, but what ultimately prevented him from doing anything right then was the Shun-tuk crowding the corridors outside his dungeon chamber, all watching him, along with maybe a dozen corpses standing behind them.

He knew that she was the only thing keeping him alive right then. If he'd taken her down, they would have flooded into the cell and eaten him alive.

66

Richard glared at the grim faces watching him follow Vika out of his prison. The dark areas painted in around their eyes, with the chalky white ash smeared all over their shaved heads, made them look like skulls with empty eye sockets. From that inner darkness, they stared out at him the way a predator watched passing prey. And, given the go-ahead, these predators would have ripped into him in a heartbeat.

Richard thought he could see in their empty eyes that they missed some inner spark, some connection to the Grace and therefore to humanity. They were alive, after all, but they were empty, living vessels lacking a soul.

Even so, he had seen the kind of emotion the half people could exhibit when attacking those who did have souls. Then, they could be frenzied, mad, maniacal killers obsessed with devouring human flesh.

With an escort of what looked to be hundreds of Shun-tuk following behind like hungry animals hoping for a meal, Vika led Richard through a maze of chambers and passageways honeycombed through the heavily cratered and pitted rock. Behind them, the silent, ever-present awakened dead followed, lumbering stiffly along, ready to fight on command to stop any threat.

In places the tunnels and passageways through the craggy rock led them lower, descending down into a series of natural caverns that grew in complexity and size. Passages and openings seemed to run in every direction. Some of the smoother passages looked to have been sculpted by flowing water. There seemed to be even more of the silent, ghostly white onlookers in every hole or pocket in the rock.

Passing under a low opening where they had to duck under a leaning slab of rock that had apparently fallen and lodged against the walls to either side, they at last entered a vast chamber that appeared to be their destination. The arched sides and domed roof were different colors of tan, browns, and white struck through with rusty stains. Off in the distance to the sides near networks of holes and crevices riddling the outer walls, immense tapered columns hung from the ceiling above forests of their twins pointing up from below them.

The enormous, hushed chamber was packed full with what must have been thousands of silent half people. The vast numbers of chalky white Shun-tuk stood anywhere they could find space—on rocks, shelves, and ledges—covering every inch of available space. Yet more dark eyes peered out from corridors all around the cavern, or from jagged openings and fissures in the walls. They watched from behind tapered columns of what looked like melted stone. Higher up, Richard could see them looking down from yawning holes leading to other chambers. In the light of hundreds of torches Richard could see some of the walls sparkle as if adorned with shimmering jewels.

The floor of the immense chamber sloped downward

toward the center, so that the Shun-tuk all crowded in together created what looked like a vast, white bowl.

Richard could see Hannis Arc, standing out in his dark robes, down in the center of that milky basin.

Even at a distance Richard could see the man's red eyes watching Vika in her red leather leading Richard into the cavern. The Shun-tuk shuffled back out of the Mord-Sith's way as she walked without pause, expecting them to move, as she led Richard downward toward where her master waited.

In the center of the room, behind Hannis Arc, rose a platform to the height of his hips. It looked like a stone altar that had melted into soft yellow and tan shapes, almost like drippings of candle wax that had mounded up over time.

As he got close enough, Richard could see that there was a small, withered corpse lying on the rock platform.

Torches all around, popping and hissing, giving off pungent clouds of smoke, lit the desiccated cadaver. As he got closer, Richard saw that the body was mummified and looked ancient. Dark, hardened skin stretched over the nose and face so that the bones of the skull created a clearly discernible skeletal topography beneath the leathery skin.

The carcass looked like it had ossified over millennia. It was hard to tell from the shrunken husk what the once-living person had actually looked like.

Richard could see traces of whitish residue on the leathery skin. It looked like ashes or white pigment of some sort might have been rubbed onto the body at one time, likely as it had been prepared for preservation after death. Thin lips had pulled back from the teeth, giving the skull a grin. The sunken eye sockets showed indications that dark oils had once been rubbed around the eyes, so that now the sunken sockets were even darker than they otherwise might have been.

The Shun-tuk, with their ash-rubbed bodies, dark-circled eyes, and painted-on toothy grins, looked like they were paying ghastly homage by trying to mimic the look of the shriveled corpse.

As Richard got closer, he could see that the body was partially wrapped in what looked to have once been an elaborate ceremonial costume and was now little more than darkly discolored remnants of cloth decorated with gold and silver medallions strung together with precious stones. The robes lay open from the neck to the waist, exposing a skeletal rib cage.

Taking a better look, Richard realized that the dark stains on the robes were from dried blood.

Relatively fresh blood.

When he glanced down, he saw that blood also covered the floor all around the platform in the center of the cavern. It looked like something had been butchered.

"Welcome, to the momentous ceremony," Hannis Arc said.

When Richard didn't answer, Hannis Arc lifted a tattooed hand around at the crowd watching. "These people have long awaited the arrival of *fuer grissa ost drauka,* for prophecy has promised that he will be the one to resurrect their king."

At the mention of the king, all the Shun-tuk in the enormous chamber went to their knees. The rustling sound of them all kneeling in concert echoed around the room, dying out slowly in a hushed whisper of knees against stone.

"And what are you doing here in their land?" Richard asked.

"With my help, the ancient gates that for so long held them captive in this place have at long last been broken open, finally enabling them to bring in the living, those with souls, to help in returning life to their beloved king, the king of the third kingdom who will become the king of the world of life and death united in one purpose."

"In other words," Richard said, "they are trying to use the blood of living people with souls to bring life back to a corpse, and it isn't working the way they had hoped."

Hannis Arc smiled in a way that distorted the tattooed symbols on his face. "Not a very generous way to put it, but essentially correct. In their ignorance, they believed that the blood of those with souls—strong soldiers for example—would again give strength to their king, and that the blood of the gifted would give him back his powers in the world of life. In their simplistic grasp of ancient lore, they thought that if they drenched their king in the warm blood of people with souls, then it would bring warmth and life to him."

"That's it?" Richard thought there had to be more to it. "You're saying they believed that by simply pouring blood over a corpse it would come back to life?"

"Well," Hannis Arc admitted with a gesture, "there was more to the procedure. Although they didn't fully understand the process, they weren't quite as ignorant as you make it sound.

"Along with the living blood from those with souls, they were to add in the vital component of occult conjuring their kind had been taught since ancient times before they were banished, conjuring long forgotten by the rest of the world. Such spells and incantations have long fallen into disuse and have been largely forgotten by the outside world, but not here. All they lacked was the blood of those with souls, and now they have it."

"I don't know," Richard said, "he still looks dead to me."

Only Hannis Arc's red eyes betrayed his annoyance. The smile, as insincere as it was, remained in place. But even though it was hard to tell because of the way their faces were covered in pale ash and dark circles that made their eyes look like hollow sockets, there was no mistaking the silent displeasure on the faces of all the Shun-tuk watching.

"They were closer to the truth than you might think. Unfortunately," Hannis Arc said as he gestured to the masses, "they lacked access to prophecy, or they would know better."

"Prophecy?"

"Yes. You see, they had lost the living link to those who knew the old ways and could bring them the prophetic knowledge necessary to assist in their ancient task. Those who banished them to this forsaken land stripped them of any who might possess knowledge of prophecy. They were left as children, thirsting for knowledge but it was beyond their grasp."

He lifted an arm and signaled for someone to come forward. One of the bare-chested Shun-tuk women rushed down with a small pot, a bit like a teapot, suspended on a chain decorated with what looked to be gold-covered human teeth. She poured liquid from the pot into a half-dozen flat bowls set around the corpse. Another woman followed behind with a flaming splinter, lighting the fluid. Slowly wavering blue flames sprang up, giving off a pungent, yellowish smoke. Both women bowed to the corpse of the king before rushing away.

"So," Richard said, "I take it that they have been missing your leadership for all this time." He met Hannis Arc's gaze. "And, I would bet, some other important element."

Hannis Arc smiled again, but it was not what could

be described in any way as a pleasant smile. "Oh yes. They have waited all this time for someone who understands how such occult procedures would have once been practiced."

"Such as all those spells and instructions tattooed all over you," Richard said, gesturing, "all those ancient symbols in the language of Creation."

The man smiled as he arched an eyebrow. "So you know something of these sacred writings."

"I've run into them before," Richard said without saying much. "So, without you, these 'children' have been endlessly pouring a whole lot of blood over a corpse for nothing."

"I'm afraid so."

"But you know what they might have been missing."

"Precisely what they have been missing," Hannis Arc said with a small bow of his head. "Prophecy dictates that for this to work properly, it requires something extraordinary."

"And you're here to provide that extraordinary final ingredient."

"Actually," Hannis Arc said as his small smile returned, "it is you who is here to provide the extraordinary final ingredient."

"With your guidance, of course."

Hannis Arc shrugged. "Only I, a man who lives the ancient ways, practices the occult arts, and listens to the obscure whispers of prophecy, would be able to understand the larger picture of what this is all about, what was intended when this was all set into motion, and so could provide what they need. Only I would be able to bring the element of prophecy to such a task and thus be able to complete what no one else could."

"Prophecy," Richard repeated with a frown. "I get the occult magic, in a strange, sick, ritualistic way—and even the blood. But what does prophecy have to do with any of it?"

Hannis Arc arched an eyebrow. "Prophecy reveals the extraordinary final ingredient that is needed."

Richard sighed, tired of the game. "And what would that extraordinary final ingredient be?"

"To bring their dead king back to life requires life and death mixed together. It requires *fuer grissa ost drauka*, the bringer of death, to bring life again to the emperor."

This time, Richard didn't say anything.

"Ah," Hannis Arc said, pleased by what the silence meant. "I see that you are finally beginning to understand your part in all this. These people simply don't grasp how it all works. They didn't understand that this doesn't merely require the blood of the living with a soul.

"Rather, it requires the right blood, blood from one of them, one who is of the third kingdom, one who carries death within him, and yet, has a soul.

"There is only one such person, one such bringer of death. You, Richard Rahl, are the one."

"So I've been told."

"You dismissed my belief in prophecy, but it is my study of prophecy that has once again shown me the way. You are a fool for so easily shunning prophecy, and now it is going to cost you everything, Richard Rahl."

Richard cried out as Vika, from behind him, drove her Agiel into the base of his skull.

67

When Richard began to become aware of the world around him again, there was nothing in that world but paralyzed pain, leaving him frozen in place, unable to move. He remembered that shattering, one-of-a-kind pain from having the Agiel pressed into that spot at the base of his skull, but the memory was nothing like the reality of it being done again.

He realized that he was down on his hands and knees, trembling with the shock of what Vika had done to him. His screams still echoed around the otherwise silent cavern. His tears from that all-consuming pain dripped onto the bloody floor beneath him.

As the echo of his scream died out, the Shun-tuk all let out an otherworldly howling that in some odd way felt in tune with the unbearable ringing in his head. It made the air drone and vibrate.

He felt that old, familiar, icy sense of helplessness and despair, the feeling that he had been traveling a very long road and this was all there was when he reached the end of it.

Despite all those around him, for Richard, at that moment, there was only the overpowering pain that gave him the sense of being entirely alone in the world in his own private realm where there was nothing but the wasteland of suffering. Once again he remembered that old longing for death, for that release that would make the pain finally stop.

He fought those feelings of hopelessness, fought the urge to surrender, to give in to it all, the haunting desire to accept death. It felt like that desire had always been there inside him, out of sight, waiting to come out.

Death would at last bring peace, but only for his private suffering. He held on to the lifeline that it would not do anything to help anyone else or to end their suffering.

But his death would deny these half people what they wanted . . . blood of a living man with a soul to bring back the one who had been so long dead. Richard realized that he was trying to find an excuse to give in to death. Yet in that way, his death really would protect everyone else, so he wondered if it would be right to give in.

Naja's warning, though, had told him that only he could end the madness of what Emperor Sulachan had started, but only by ending prophecy. If he gave in to death, he would not have the chance to do that, and then, eventually, there would be no hope for anyone.

He was the one.

He was the only one to end the coming terror of the awakened dead and the half people, of the boundary between life and death ripped aside to let death loose in the world of life.

At the same time, he was also the one to bring back their king and free those monsters upon the world.

He was both, he realized. He was life and death together. He was savior and destroyer together.

That, too, had been the warning that Magda Searus had left for him.

Richard watched tears of pain drip down onto the floor of the cave covered with the blood of so many people. Zedd's blood. Probably Nicci's, and Cara's, and those soldiers who had protected him so many times. Those people had come to help him. They had been willing to lay down their lives for him if they had to. In the past, many like them had.

For all those people and more, he couldn't allow himself to be weak. For them, if not for himself, he had to be strong and endure whatever they did to him so that once beyond the ordeal, he could find a way to help save everyone from what was descending on the world of life. It was up to him to protect their lives in return.

They had been the steel against steel. He now had to be the magic against magic, even if he couldn't use his gift.

As the ringing in his head subsided, he began to hear the Shun-tuk all around beginning to chant softly in some language Richard didn't recognize. The haunting sound echoed around the vast chamber, almost making the whole place hum.

In a perverse way, it reminded him of the ancient devotion to the Lord Rahl. It was probably something like that, he guessed, some chant of dedication to their long-dead king.

As the half people chanted softly, Hannis Arc worked over the body of the dead man. He spoke in the same dead language, conjuring things Richard couldn't imagine. Some of the Shun-tuk brought bowls of oily potions forward. From time to time Hannis Arc dipped a tattooed finger in them and used it to draw symbols on the dead man.

As Richard watched as he recovered, Hannis Arc next drew emblems on the forehead of the corpse. The greasy lines of the design began to glow a dull, yellowish orange, as if lit from within. Hannis Arc lifted his arms, urgently signaling the watching horde, and the Shuntuk murmured a new chant. As the sound of it built, he bent back over the body.

Richard then saw the most remarkable sight. A sight both so terrifying and spellbinding at the same time that he could not look away.

Hannis Arc's tattoos began to glow.

As he spoke the words of the dead language, the lines composing different symbols on his body brightened to the same luminous yellow-orange color as the symbol aglow on the forehead of the dead king. First one, then another tattoo brightened for a brief moment only to fade as another began to illuminate from within in a continually rolling, ever-changing series.

Hannis Arc turned to those watching and lifted a hand as he shouted a series of words Richard didn't recognize.

The coordinated shouts of sacred words in answer to each prompt from the man in the center rumbled through the chamber like thunder.

As Hannis Arc worked, laying down symbols in glowing lines on the body while symbols on his own flesh glowed in sequence as if in response to the symbols he drew, the Shun-tuk began a new chant, a steady beat repeated over and over. Each beat seemed to ignite a different symbol. As the drone of it went on, the sound gradually built until even Richard felt caught up in its power, its perverse majesty.

The symbols all over Hannis Arc glowed in rhythm

with the chanting, first one, then another, each brightening in sequence then dimming as another took its place, one at a time in rapid succession, as if different symbols meaning different things were responding in turn to the murmur of the chant.

Richard had never imagined a conjuring so complex, or one that involved so many others.

At last the tattooed man turned to the Mord-Sith with a grim look that she had been anticipating.

"Get up," Vika commanded from behind Richard.

Her voice, more than anything else, seemed less than real and more like a memory from the darkest times of his life. Richard didn't move. He wasn't sure he could.

She leaned down and growled in his ear. "I said, get up."

He could only nod weakly as he struggled to get his feet under himself. He felt her hand under his arm, helping to lift him and get him upright.

With Vika's help, he walked the rest of the distance to the corpse lying on the stone table.

Hannis Arc turned with a flourish of his black robes, like some frightening apparition from another world. His red eyes fixed on Richard with fiery intensity.

Vika pressed her Agiel to the back of Richard's head, immobilizing him in place. His vision blurred and twisted. He opened his mouth to cry out, but he couldn't make the sound.

Vika pushed his arm forward. Hannis Arc seized Richard's wrist and pulled it close, over the withered corpse. Richard was helpless to do anything about it. He watched as if from a different world.

Hannis Arc pulled out a stone knife, its blade as black as the darkest depths of the underworld.

He slashed the blade across Richard's forearm.

Richard didn't feel pain from the cut. The pain of the Agiel overrode anything else.

Anything physical, anyway.

It didn't override the sudden, ripping agony inside. It felt as if the knife had cut into that place of death within him, bleeding that along with his life's blood and his soul.

Blood gushed from the gash in Richard's arm and out over the body of the king. Rivulets of it ran down the depressions between each rib.

Hannis Arc pulled Richard's arm farther forward, holding it over the desiccated mouth of the king.

When he seemed satisfied with the amount of blood splashed across the carcass of the king, Hannis Arc shoved Richard back out of his way. Richard saw his blood soaking the robes and dried flesh of the dead man. Bright red runnels ran down the rounded sides of the platform to join the darker blood all over the floor.

After Hannis Arc had shoved him aside, Vika pulled Richard back out of the way. He was too weak to resist. There was no point in trying. They were going to do what they were going to do and there was nothing Richard could do about it right then.

Richard went to his knees, too weary to stand. Hannis Arc's attention, along with all the Shun-tuk, was on the body laid out on the platform. He was too absorbed in what he was doing to care about Richard.

Vika leaned over and put her mouth close to his ear. "Put your other hand over it."

Richard heard her talking, but didn't really know what she meant. The lingering pain from the Agiel, even though long since withdrawn, was still scrambling his thoughts.

She grasped his left hand and placed it over the bleeding gash on his right arm.

"Press," she said in a low, confidential voice. "Press your hand there and hold it tight."

Richard nodded. "Thank you . . ."

He wasn't sure what he was thanking her for. It just seemed the right thing to do.

Richard saw that the king's whole body was beginning to glow, as if the symbols had lit something from within and there were a ghost now emerging from the dead husk of his body.

Vika helped lift Richard to his feet. He felt dizzy and faint, likely from loss of blood. As the effects of the contact of the Agiel to the back of his head gradually faded, he began feeling slightly more stable on his feet. Still, she had to help balance him to make sure he wasn't going to fall over before he fully recovered.

It was the sickness inside—the pain of the poison from death's touch—more than the touch of the Agiel, that threatened to overwhelm him. He remembered Samantha telling him that he was going to get worse.

He felt himself getting worse. What Vika and especially Hannis Arc had done with that wicked-looking blade had made him suddenly worse, had weakened him and made him more susceptible to the sickness deep inside him.

The weapon Hannis Arc had used had been a sinister-looking thing unlike any knife Richard had ever seen before. It had a bone handle of some sort, no doubt a human bone, and a blade made of the blackest of glassy stone affixed to that handle with thin strips of leather that also looked suspiciously like it had been made from human skin. The flaked edge of the blade had been so razor-sharp that Richard hadn't really felt it cutting him. It had that in common with the Sword of Truth.

The painted heads of the half people bobbed up and down as they shouted in unison with grim exultation at what was happening. The entire chamber reverberated with the chanting. They were at last fulfilling their purpose. This was what they had been trying to accomplish for thousands of years.

And Richard had been the one to help them accomplish their purpose.

He glanced down at the Grace on the ring he wore and remembered again the warning from Magda Searus that he could be the one to end the world of life. He feared that he very well might have done just that.

"What was that knife?" he asked Vika in a flat, hoarse voice.

"The one he used to cut you?"

Richard nodded, not wanting to have to summon his voice again if he could help it.

Vika leaned close to his ear so that he could hear over the rumbling thunder of the chanting. She watched Hannis Arc to be sure he was busy. He wondered if she did not want to incur his wrath for disturbing him, or if there was another reason.

"It's a knife made by the Shun-tuk," Vika said. "Lord Arc has several weapons made by the Shun-tuk. The Shun-tuk say that their knives can slay the dead."

"They talk?"

"When they want to."

Richard wasn't quite sure that he understood what that meant—a knife that could slay the dead—but he judged it clear enough that he didn't feel the need to press for an explanation. He spotted a number of those dead that had been brought back from their graves and pressed into service as guardians for the Shun-tuk's underground prison. Now, they stood like stiff corpses around the perimeter of the cavern, their eyes glowing red as they watched the proceedings from the shadows. Richard knew all too well that if they wanted they could move with surprising speed.

He supposed that if they got out of control for some reason known only to the dead or the half people, having a weapon that could put them down would be handy, if not invaluable. Richard had fought the awakened dead. They were not easy to defeat. It was a difficult task, even with his sword.

He wished he still had his sword with him. He knew that in this place filled with the half people and the walking dead it wouldn't be likely to do him a lot of good in fighting his way out, but it would still be comforting to have it at his hip.

If nothing else he might be able to be quick enough with it to hack the dead king to bits.

When he looked back to the altar just beyond Hannis Arc, Richard's breath halted in his lungs when he saw the corpse take a breath.

A transparent, bluish, ghostlike form now lay in the same place as the king's body. That filmy form began to stir. When it did, the body also stirred. The two, spirit body and dead body, moved as one. It looked like the corpse was possessed by a translucent ghost.

When the Shun-tuk saw the movement on the platform down at the center of the room, some of them howled in jubilation. Others cried out in what might have been fright. They were, after all, seeing a king who had the power to return to the world of life. This was not only a master to be honored, respected, and followed, but one to be greatly feared as well. Although this was something they had all wanted, the reality of seeing it actually happen was intimidating.

This was also a new beginning for them, a new era. After several thousand years of waiting, the gates to their land were open and at long last they had a real king. A king, Richard feared, who would lead them out through those gates on a mission of conquest and domination.

Richard could tell that Vika, even though she had played a role in helping it come to pass, was disquieted by what she was seeing.

Richard hated that he was the one, though, who had played the pivotal role in bringing this evil man back to the world of life. This was a man who in an age long past had rained death and destruction down on the world. Now he was back, and Richard didn't think that his stay in the underworld had mellowed him.

Without Richard, none of it would have been possible. The Shun-tuk might have played a part, Vika might have played a part, and Hannis Arc had certainly played a part, but Richard was the one who had made it possible.

He had the potential for both in him—death as well as life. He was of this kingdom. He carried life and death in him. Good and evil mixed together. He was the one.

Richard was the leader of the D'Haran Empire. He had been named *fuer grissa ost drauka*, High D'Haran for "the bringer of death."

He had just served in his role as the bringer of death. He had just helped spawn a great evil by bringing death back into the world of life.

He knew that it was up to him to find a way to bring it to an end. There was no one else who had a chance to do anything to stop this.

All he had to do, he reminded himself, was to escape

the clutches of Hannis Arc, a Mord-Sith, and untold thousands of half people who could raise an army of the dead. After that, he only needed to end prophecy.

And, he had to keep himself alive long enough.

The glowing figure of the king sat up. The Shun-tuk gasped with excitement and wonder.

It was a terrifying sight to see a dead man awaken, even for them, but especially for Richard, and especially because of what it meant.

The king's dried flesh seemed to have grown pliable, softened no doubt by Richard's blood as well as Hannis Arc's dark conjuring that had united the spirit with its worldly form. With each passing moment, the dead man seemed to move with greater ease, even if not as fluidly as a living person. It was almost as if the transparent presence, the glowing spirit, was in part what animated the corpse.

Richard wondered if what he was really seeing was the spirit of the dead king directing events from the underworld, directing events in the world of life.

The bluish glow of the spirit actually looked more alive than the corpse. The face of the spirit existed in the same place as that of the corpse, so that the bluish glow of its features actually filled in the missing places in the shriveled remains, giving it a fuller nose, lips, and eyes.

The new eyes saw. They looked about. They reacted.

The revived lips smiled with malice at the world around him, a world to which he had once belonged.

Hannis Arc stepped back out of the way as the spirit king swung his feet down over the side of the platform. He sat for a moment as he gazed out at the adoration of the Shun-tuk, all of them in unison now thrusting fists into the air as they chanted as one.

"Sul-a-chan! Sul-a-chan! Sul-a-chan!"

As Richard had suspected, the dead king of the half people was Emperor Sulachan from the Old World, and the old war, his spirit now brought back to the world of life.

Richard wanted to die and get it over with.

The way the spirit king held his blood-soaked robes to his chest with his left arm and loosely clenched fist gave him a kingly pose. He looked around the chamber with a measured, regal grace, taking in the veneration of the masses watching his triumphant return to the world of the living. As the Shun-tuk went crazy chanting his name, the dead Sulachan finally began to smile in approval.

The fluid gaze of the king of the half people, once emperor of all the Old World, swept over the masses filling the cavern. His glowing eyes finally settled on Richard, his benefactor of blood.

Richard glared back. He would have given anything for his sword at that moment.

The awakened king dragged a finger through some of the still-wet blood, Richard's blood, running down his bony chest.

Richard wished that the poisonous touch of death that he carried in his blood would take the dead man back to the world of the dead where he belonged. He knew, though, that it was an empty wish. It was going to take a lot more than wishing to banish this man from the world of life.

Sulachan brought to his lips the finger he had run through Richard's blood, tasting it, then closed his eyes with a look of rapture. He opened his eyes again to gaze deliberately at Richard. He smiled as wicked a smile as Richard had ever seen.

All the Shun-tuk in the vast chamber stomped a foot in time to their chant of "Sul-a-chan! Sul-a-chan! Sul-a-chan!"

Still holding Richard's gaze, the dead king walked across the dried blood on the floor toward the man who had at last rescued his spirit from the underworld—Richard, the one, Richard who had brought him back.

Richard didn't allow himself to retreat as the king came to a stop before him.

The malevolent smile remained on the glowing bluish lips of the spirit. Even the tight flesh beneath stretched with the self-satisfied smile.

"I have been to the farthest, darkest reaches of the underworld," the king said in an eerie voice that made Richard's skin crawl. "I have been welcomed to travel the Keeper's realm at will."

"I hope you liked it there," Richard said with sudden venom of his own, "because I am going to send you back there for good."

The dead man's unconcerned smile widened. "When in the darkest regions of that darkest of worlds, I met your father. I rather liked him."

"I didn't," Richard said. "I'm the one who sent him to that dark eternity."

"I know. He told me."

The king and his attention began to move on. As he did, Hannis Arc, his tattoos no longer aglow, joined the glowing corpse of the resurrected king.

"Now that I have completed this part, Emperor, we have things to do."

As they strolled past Richard, the dead king nodded, no longer interested or even seeming to be aware that Richard was still standing there. "Our agreements will be honored, Lord Arc. I have given you my word. Let us begin, then." He lifted an arm, casually acknowledging the cheering, chanting masses of Shun-tuk. "I, too, am eager to begin."

Richard wondered what, exactly, they were about to begin.

As he went past, Hannis Arc flashed a dark, impatient look at Vika while gesturing at Richard. "Put him back for now. I will get to him later."

Vika, hands clasped behind her back, bowed her head. "By your command, Lord Arc."

Without a moment's hesitation, her hand came up under Richard's arm to turn him back the way they had come in. Richard saw that the dead king, in all his glowing glory, was listening to Hannis Arc's words, words Richard couldn't hear because they were being drowned out by the chanting. He could see Hannis Arc gesturing with his tattooed hands as he leaned in and spoke to the king. Over the tumult all around, the king could hear the words of that private conversation, but Richard couldn't.

Richard could, though, read in the body language of the man covered in the tattoos that he was the one in charge. Sulachan might have been an emperor who ruled the vast Old World and commanded armies of wizards as well as endless legions of soldiers, but he had been a long-dead emperor trapped in the eternal world of the dead.

Hannis Arc had been the one to use long-forgotten occult powers to help break the spells containing the third kingdom and awaken Sulachan's corpse. Those powers, along with Richard's blood, had also created a link that had pulled the emperor's spirit back from the dark eternity of the world of the dead. Hannis Arc still controlled that link between worlds and thus over the king's stay in the world of life.

Despite the dead man's imperious attitude, Hannis Arc was in charge and was not shy about exerting his authority.

Whatever the emperor's grand plans from ages long ago might be, it was clear to Richard that Hannis Arc had plans of his own and he intended the corpse of the dead Shun-tuk king to help him implement those plans. Hannis Arc would not have been foolish enough to pull a wizard of Emperor Sulachan's power back from the dead without knowing that he could control him.

As bad as the resurrected king of the half people might be, Richard was beginning to realize that Hannis Arc was even more dangerous.

Still, Richard wondered if the man had any idea of the danger in holding the leash to such beastly forces.

Vika pulled Richard onward up the bowl of the cavern, toward the passageway back out. The Shun-tuk all stared at Richard as he passed. This was the man who had brought their king back to life. They had been foolishly bleeding people to no avail, but now, Richard's blood had at last done the trick. They viewed him with a kind of respectful awe.

That, however, only put him more at risk from these half people. As far as they were concerned, Richard's blood, and likely his flesh, had just proven to be extraordinarily valuable. He was sure that they would all want to be the one to have a bite of his flesh, a swallow of his blood, in the hopes of capturing his soul.

A few reached out to drag their fingers through the

blood on his arm. They brought those fingers to their lips, tasting what their eyes lusted to have.

With Hannis Arc well out ahead of them, Vika realized the menace so close all around them and hurried Richard through the crowds. With a firm grip on his arm, she steered him through pushing throngs of half people intensely interested in her charge. Vika quickened her pace, elbowing her way through, eager to get him out of the room and the hungry gazes of the onlookers. Once through the mob of Shun-tuk and out into a passageway that tunneled back through the rock, they were able to make better time. She kept up her pace, knowing that he was a prize that Hannis Arc wanted for himself.

"My arm finally stopped bleeding," he told Vika after they had gone on in silence for a time. "Thanks."

She shot him a dark look. "I just wanted you to still have some blood left in case they needed more of it, that's all. Don't try to read anything more into it."

Richard was too upset to make a flippant remark.

When they reached his dungeon cell down in the labyrinth of passageways and chambers, Vika shoved him back inside.

Some of the Shun-tuk crowded around outside in the corridor gestured on her command and the wavering greenish wall materialized out of nothing. He had heard that some of them had occult powers, even the ability to reanimate corpses. It appeared to be true.

Richard once again found himself trapped in the cave prison with no way out, with thousands of half people who wanted to eat the flesh right off his bones and lap up his blood not far away on the other side of that greenish veil, the boundary to the underworld they were able to control at will.

If they could bring those greenish walls up, they could no doubt also bring them down.

His friends faced the same peril as Richard.

Even if he could do the impossible and somehow escape the half people, without being able to get Zedd and Nicci out, he was doomed to succumb to the poisonous touch of death within him.

Kahlan was no less doomed.

70

Hannis Arc led the king of the dead out into the dawn of a new day in the world of life. Off behind them, the half people, gathering in the tens of thousands, trailed behind at a respectful distance. More likely, he thought, it was a fearful distance.

Hannis Arc paused when the king strolled to a stop to take in the sweep of the new day. Thick clouds obscured the sky as well as the higher peaks. Veils of mist dragged low enough to blur the tops of the rock spires.

The crumbling rock pinnacles reminded Hannis Arc of tightly bundled marsh grass that had died and then turned to stone. Pieces of it flaked off the spires over time, leaving the ground covered with decomposing fragments of what looked like nothing so much as stone fingers.

Everything in this place seemed to be old and crumbling and dead. The sparse shrubs and stunted trees that clung to life in crags and sheltered areas looked only half alive. It truly was a place where life and death coexisted.

"It has been a long time since I have been in this

world," the spirit king said in a voice that seemed to come from both worlds at once. "It is good to be back. At long last, after all I have accomplished in the underworld it is time at last to bring this realm under control."

Hannis Arc watched the newly united spirit and man look out over the dreary world of life. They had accomplished all that needed accomplishing in this forsaken place. Vika had arranged for their departure and seen to it that the Shun-tuk had gathered the supplies they would need for the journey. Everything was ready.

"I want to be on our way immediately," Hannis Arc said.

"And you plan on bringing the man whose blood you used?" the king asked as he feasted on the sight of the rock wasteland as if viewing a colorful field of wildflowers.

"Richard Rahl?" Hannis Arc smiled to himself. "Of course. He needs to be made to feel the pain and anguish of losing his power and authority, suffer the humiliation of his fall from leader of an empire to a nobody."

"I see," the king said without looking over. "So, you plan to assume the burden and risk of dragging him along just to humiliate him?"

Hannis Arc frowned over at the glowing spirit. "That is the idea. I have been planning my revenge on the House of Rahl for nearly my entire life. I'm at last ready to take the rule of the D'Haran Empire. He will see it come to pass."

The glowing figure smiled in the way an elder would smile. Hannis Arc didn't particularly like the smile, but he waited for the king to have his say.

"I have had experience with such matters, and I can tell you that such men as those who come to rule empires do not feel humiliation at losing rule. They feel only a need to do whatever is necessary to get back on top, or for revenge. After all, do you feel humbled at all your family lost? I think not. I expect you to feel only a need for revenge. Am I right?"

Hannis Arc hadn't thought of it in that way. "Well yes, but I want him to suffer his fall from power."

The spirit shrugged. "You are wishing for a type of satisfaction you will never get. Powerful people who lose power do not feel anguish and heartache like a jilted lover."

Hannis Arc's brow drew tighter. "What is your point?"

The spirit king turned to face him. "You brought me in back from the world of the dead to my unfinished business in the world of life and in return I am committed to helping you to rule this world. That is what I am doing."

"By asking me to abandon my revenge against Lord Rahl?"

The spirit of Sulachan smiled again. "Do you know why I am standing here today, Lord Arc?"

Hannis Arc was pleased to hear Sulachan refer to him that way, even if he wasn't pleased to be questioned. "As you just said, because I used my talents to bring you back."

If Hannis Arc wished it, he could also send the spirit of Sulachan back to that eternal world. But for now, if his plan was to succeed, he needed what only Sulachan could provide. Besides, the arrangement was well worth it and Hannis Arc felt he was getting the best of it by far.

The spirit smiled. "Yes, but you only brought me back because you needed me, and you needed me because I long ago made myself invaluable to the right person. I could afford to wait. I had all eternity to wait.

"You were the first one to come along who was wise enough to see the potential if we joined our talents and our goals.

"Part of my value is in my vast experience. That experience in rule can help you in achieving your goal."

Hannis Arc frowned, not appreciating being treated as if he were an inexperienced, subordinate partner. As far as he was concerned, it was Sulachan who was the subordinate in their arrangement. He had, after all, returned to the world of life only as a result of Hannis Arc's power and ability. He might have all eternity to wait, but he had been stuck in the underworld for thousands of years, and would be forever, unless and until Hannis Arc brought him back out. If he was so smart, he would have been able to return to the world of life by himself.

"In what way does your experience benefit me with Richard Rahl?"

"Greatness demands the kind of dedication to purpose that I have shown, that has brought me to stand in the world of life again today. I let nothing distract me from my goal. You as well have shown great dedication to the purpose of rule.

"But for those who would be great, there is no room for distracting fixations. Such distractions drain away your energy of purpose. That is why I asked what is most important to you—dragging this man along with us, or ruling the world."

Hannis Arc's mood was getting as dark as the overcast. "There is no reason why I can't do both."

"You would be ruling one man, when you should be properly devoted to the effort of ruling all men."

"You're saying that Richard Rahl is a distraction that could keep me from succeeding?"

The spirit shrugged. "The world is full of distractions.

It is the task of a great ruler to keep them to a minimum. Distractions drain time and energy from your primary goal."

Hannis Arc glanced back at the milky half people, killers all, spread silently out across the landscape behind them. He turned back to the spirit watching him.

"Since the day my parents were killed at the orders of a Rahl, I have been planning my revenge, so that I—"

"And why do you suppose that the House of Rahl killed your parents, your father, the ruler of little, insignificant, far-off Fajin Province?"

Hannis Arc paused a moment, feeling the sparkle of mist against the tattoos on his face as he let his anger cool a bit. "To eliminate the possibility that he might rise up and challenge for rule."

The spirit smiled. "That is why the House of Rahl has ruled D'Hara for so long, and the House of Arc has ruled little Fajin Province. The House of Rahl was focused on ruling, not on humiliating your father by making him watch them rule. They simply eliminated the potential for a challenge to their power. If your aim is to rule, then you should rule."

"I believe I can do both."

"So did Richard Rahl's father. He kept the distraction of Richard Rahl around for too long, and in the end it cost him his life. A number of men like him have failed because they were stopped by someone who would never have been a problem had they been killed in the first place. Richard Rahl is the leader of the D'Haran Empire because he is strong and determined and because Darken Rahl didn't kill him when he should have.

"Richard Rahl is an incredibly dangerous man. He is, after all, *fuer grissa ost drauka*. He is not a man to be trifled with.

"If you think too much of yourself, if you think you can control him every moment, if you think that your power is strong enough to best him and keep him down, then you underestimate him. You underestimate him at your peril. You may have him captive at the moment, but every moment he is alive he will be thinking of how to kill you.

"He did not get to be Lord Rahl, the leader of the D'Haran Empire, the man who defeated Emperor Jagang and the might of the Old World, without being very good at what he does, and what he does well is to take down those who try to subjugate him. Right now, you are making yourself his target, his primary goal, and I can assure you, he will not be distracted from that goal by anything.

"If he is dead, then you don't have to worry about any of that, and you can go on to rule the world."

Hannis Arc's mouth twisted. "I hate to admit it, but you may have a point. The man has proven how determined he is."

The spirit king turned back to look Hannis Arc in the eye. "Rule is the revenge, Lord Arc. Kill your enemy now, while you have the chance, and then you can go on to rule. Ruling will be your vengeance."

"As your return to this world is yours?"

Sulachan smiled a dark, vindictive smile. "I will now be the one who in the end has triumphed over all those who would think to take my rule and banish me to the infinite recesses of the underworld while at the same time banishing all those that I created"—he lifted an arm around at the desolate landscape—"to this forsaken place. In the end, they could not contain any of us with barriers or even death itself. Now, we will each have our way and our revenge."

Being from tiny Fajin Province, Hannis Arc had no

means to raise an army to fulfill his ambitions of conquest. He commanded small numbers, really, and he would need vast might to take his objective, the People's Palace, and rule from the House of Rahl's traditional seat of power. To take that objective, he was going to need an army.

And now, through Sulachan, he had what he needed. He not only had the Shun-tuk nation of half people, he had at his disposal an endless army of the dead.

Hands clasped behind his back, he finally looked over at the wise spirit king. A spirit Hannis Arc controlled.

The tattoos covering him had been tedious, time-consuming, and painful. But they had proven to be worth it. Those symbols in the language of Creation not only helped Hannis Arc pull the spirit of Sulachan back from the underworld, they protected him from the spirit king, should he not honor his commitments. They were, in a way, Hannis Arc's armor when dealing with things dead.

"Now that the barrier is down there is no reason to remain here. I don't want to waste any time. We need to be on our way."

The spirit king bowed his head. "By your command, Lord Arc." He glanced back at the vast army of half people. "We all stand ready and march on your order."

"First I kill Richard Rahl, and then we march."

A cunning smile overcame Sulachan's spirit face. "We should allow some of the Shun-tuk to feast on the captives. Let your enemy, Richard Rahl, be among those eaten. Let him suffer the same terrifying death as the others."

Hannis Arc shook his head emphatically. "No. No, you're right that while I have the upper hand I should kill him. I've watched him over the years of war and you're right about how dangerous he is. I must not take any chances.

"But now that the decision has been made, I want to do it myself, with my own hands. I want to watch death take him. I want to see the man die before my eyes so that the threat he represents is ended once and for all. I want him to look up into my eyes and know that it is I, Hannis Arc, banishing him to the world of the dead.

"Before he dies, I want him to know that I am turning the Shun-tuk loose on all his friends to devour the living flesh off their bones.

"I will see Richard Rahl die at my feet."

The spirit lifted his chin as he drew a breath while gazing out at the desolate countryside. "My first day back in the world of life and already I am well pleased."

Hannis Arc smiled, already envisioning the terror that Richard Rahl was about to suffer as he met his sad, lonely, violent end. He motioned to Vika.

She took a single stride forward. "Yes, Lord Arc?"

He couldn't keep the smile from his face as he looked into her blue eyes. "Bring Richard Rahl to me. His time to die has come at last."

She tipped her head. "Of course, Lord Arc. I will bring him to you at once."

"Good. And there is no need to be gentle. In fact, make sure he is suffering in agony first, then bring him to me. Make sure, though, that he is still alive so I can kill him."

"I will see to it, Lord Arc," she said in that chilling tone she had when unleashed to practice her skills.

He gestured toward the distance. "We're starting out at once. Have the Shun-tuk bring all our supplies, first, then bring Richard Rahl to me."

"Of course, Lord Arc. I will catch up with you."

He glanced over at the king. "After I cut his throat

with the same knife I used to bleed him over you, we'll drag him behind as we march, and leave a trail of his blood for the Shun-tuk to lick up."

Vika looked from the spirit king's smile to Hannis Arc and then hurried away.

"What a fitting and bloody end this is going to be for the House of Rahl," Hannis Arc whispered to himself as he started south. Once through the gates out of the third kingdom, he could turn toward the heart of the D'Haran Empire.

The glowing spirit of the dead Emperor Sulachan looked thoughtfully out over the landscape they were passing through. "As long as we are on the subject of rule, do you know, Lord Arc, that I commanded great respect and utter loyalty? That I was never challenged from within?"

"Challenged from within?" Hannis Arc was beginning to see that Sulachan had come back into the world of life with a lot on his mind. "What are you getting at?"

"I mean, no one within my inner circle of command—generals, commanders, advisors—ever rose up to challenge me, ever plotted to take my place."

"Why is that?"

"Because I eliminated all of those who lusted to take my place, those who thought themselves more clever than I. Sometimes, I eliminated them because I knew they were going to have such thoughts even before they themselves knew they would eventually have such thoughts."

With a thumb, Hannis Arc rubbed a tattooed symbol

laid out along the side of his first finger. It was a symbol warning of hidden threats.

"If I might add something . . . ?" the spirit said, glancing over at Hannis Arc in his silent contemplation.

"Please, state your mind." Hannis Arc gestured between himself and Sulachan. "We are of one purpose in this, after all. We both work toward the same ends. As you have said, you acquired a lot of experience when you ruled such a vast empire. If you have something useful to say, then I would know it."

The spirit looked pleased. "You have one who serves you with prophecy."

Hannis Arc considered for a moment. A number of people served him with prophecy. He finally frowned.

"Do you mean Ludwig Dreier? My abbot?"

The spirit glanced back at the vast force of devoted Shun-tuk blanketing the rugged landscape as they followed behind, flooding around the rugged spires. "That is the one. Have you considered what trouble he might be?"

"Trouble?" Hannis Arc flicked a hand dismissively. "Ludwig Dreier is a petty abbot. A nobody. He doesn't even work at the citadel, with me. He runs a dusty old abbey off in the mountains. He performs a variety of services for me."

"In what variety of ways does this petty man serve you?"

"Well, I sometimes send him in my place on matters of state. I recently sent him to bring word to the leaders of other lands in the D'Haran Empire of the value of prophecy. As it happened, Lord Rahl had invited all the rulers of all the lands to the People's Palace, for a wedding. I had business with a Hedge Maid"—he glanced over at Sulachan—"and with you, of course.

"So I sent Ludwig Dreier to the People's Palace in

my place. He was to make overtures to other lands on the value of prophecy and begin the process of winning the loyalty of leaders to our cause, rather than the D'Haran Empire.

"But his main work is to bring me prophecy. That is his job, the work of the abbey he runs."

Hannis Arc watched the king of the dead walk in silence for a moment. He finally spoke what was on his mind.

"And has he ever told you how he collects that prophecy for you?"

Hannis Arc cast about in his memory, trying to think if Dreier had ever told him anything specific.

"It's all pretty routine work. He deals with country people, the cunning folk out in the less-populated areas of Fajin Province and the Dark Lands, looking for anyone with any modicum of talent at foretelling from whom he might be able to coax prophecy. Some such people are born with minor ability to see into prophetic visions. Ludwig Dreier tests these people for what prophecy they might be capable of giving. If there is such prophecy among the country folk and he discovers it, then it should properly come to me.

"Lord Rahl has always been secretive about prophecy, and will not share what he knows of it. People have a right to prophecy. Prophecy is not the property of the few. It belongs to all of us.

"Unlike Lord Rahl, I understand and use prophecy." He gestured at the corpse walking beside him. "After all, that is part of how you are able to be here in this world again. Had it not been for prophecy I might not have unlocked the paths necessary to bring you back from the underworld.

"Sometimes those simple country people require an incentive to get them to concentrate their minds to such a complex task as giving forth prophecy. He pressures them in various ways to focus their thoughts on what we seek so that they will be able to give prophecy, if they in fact are truly gifted in the art."

"So he tortures them to get them to focus."

Hannis Arc shrugged. "Well, yes, on occasion, when necessary, I suppose. I leave it to him to decide what is necessary. I don't need to waste my time with such petty matters. I leave it to him.

"He is very effective at his work. He has brought me some remarkable prophecy. Not the prophecy I found myself, from my own more in-depth studies that I used for all this"—he swept a hand back toward the Shun-tuk behind them—"for understanding how this fits into everything, and for calling you back. But he has proven useful over the years with prophecy that has turned out to be not only true, but quite timely and useful.

"I have books in which we record the prophecy he collects. He sends it on to the citadel, I look it all over, and then we record it."

The spirit king gazed up at a wisp of gray overcast trailing down. "Do you know that he tampers with the world of the dead in order to obtain that prophecy?"

Hannis Arc missed a step. "No. . . . In what way? And how do you know?"

"Well, since I exist in that underworld, I know what happens there. You would have been unaware of such things taking place, of course, but part of my value in this alliance is to know of events in that world. You have seen things of importance here—evidence and indications—while I have seen such things of impor-tance there, in that world."

"Yes, that has proven to be mutually beneficial, and it will be even more so in the future. But what of Ludwig Dreier? What news could you have from the underworld about him?"

"He meddles in things you don't know about. He meddles in prophecy in ways that you don't know about or suspect. I know this because he uses his talents to send tentacles into my world to draw out that prophecy."

Hannis Arc's anger rose in a hot fury. "For what purpose?"

The spirit king glanced over out of the corner of a transparent, glowing eye. "What purpose indeed? What purpose would a man have not to tell his master what he was doing, and how he was doing it . . . unless he has designs on one day taking rule for himself."

Hannis Arc felt his seething anger boil to the surface.

The glowing spirit leaned toward him. "Now that I am risen from the dead, and my spirit has joined us here, is there really any purpose for an abbot who schemes behind your back with occult conjuring of his own? For an abbot who has designs on your rule?

"What possible service could he provide you that would be worth the risk?" He gestured behind. "You have all you need to carry out any order. These half people and all the dead you can use are yours to command. You will have the world kneeling at your feet, begging to do your bidding. Why tolerate a potential threat from within?" He smiled again. "Why worry about a knife in your back?"

"Why indeed," Hannis Arc said through gritted teeth.

He had always thought of Ludwig Dreier as a loyal subject with no interest other than to assist his master. He had thought him a man without any personal designs on ruling anything more than his abbey.

Hannis Arc was furious to learn that after giving

Ludwig Dreier his position and trusting him with responsibilities such as going to the People's Palace in his place and with speaking to leaders of other lands, the man would scheme to usurp rule. Hannis Arc wondered just how much his abbot had already done to undermine him.

Dark thoughts of what he wanted to do to Ludwig Dreier drifted through his mind. He reminded himself that it was still possible that it wasn't true. Sulachan could be wrong.

But what difference did it make? Ludwig Dreier wasn't needed any longer, and Sulachan was right that it made sense to eliminate the threat, or the potential for it to become one.

The spirit king gestured back to the legions of half people blanketing the landscape, moving like a silent shadow on their march.

"For your purpose, you don't need all of these here with us. Having most of them with us is more than enough. Once we get to where we're going, we will raise all the dead we need from the catacombs, the crypts, tombs, and graves. We will have all the dead we could ever need to accomplish what you wish to accomplish. It is impossible for such a force to be disloyal. You shall have a virtually endless army that will follow your commands without question or delay. You will rule without opposition."

Hannis Arc glanced back at the half people amassed behind.

"Besides sending some behind to feast on the captives, we should send others to the abbey."

The spirit king nodded. "So be it." He turned a little and lifted a hand, using two fingers to summon a contingent of the half people to receive their orders.

Hannis Arc knew from experience that they would

be only too eager to be let off their leash to hunt the abbey, as well as feed on the captives down in the caves.

The risen spirit king was proving to be useful beyond Hannis Arc's wildest imagination. He had never before had the companionship of such an equal in determination, purpose, and ruthlessness.

Soon, they would shape the world to their will.

Richard paced the length of his cell, going back and forth in the light from the soft green luminescence of the veil over the opening where he had come in. He could do nothing other than pace in frustration.

When Vika had taken him to the cell after they had cut him and used his blood to resurrect Emperor Sulachan, Richard had asked her what they were going to do with him. She had smiled in that profoundly disturbing way that only a Mord-Sith could and told him that she would be spending time with him while the others would likely be given to the half people, who were eager to devour them for their souls.

He supposed that after that, the unholy half dead would be coming for him as well. He had imagined it a thousand times over, and then another thousand. He had tried to come up with some way he might escape once they lifted the veil and came for him. He could think of nothing that had even the remotest chance to work. He knew that they would flood in and overwhelm him.

He was beyond distressed and upset waiting for the unknown. He wanted out. If he was going to die, he at least wished he could somehow recover his sword and die fighting. Better that than the end they had planned for him.

If he could get to his sword, he might be able to at least kill the newly risen dead king. He thought that, if he could get to his sword, he might even have a chance to kill Hannis Arc. He spent a lot of time trying to decide which one he would rather kill, if he could only kill one. Without his gift working, at least with his sword he wouldn't die helpless.

But he couldn't do anything—including trying to get to his sword—unless he could find a way to get out of the prison cell. He had thought for a time that maybe Vika would choose to help him, in some little way, at least. But he had not seen her since she had left him after the ceremony.

He wondered why. As he paced hour after hour, he was left to contemplate what Hannis Arc was really up to. He must have some grand goal in mind. Richard could understand the spirit of Sulachan wanting to come back to the world of the living in order to try to implement his plans. Naja's account had been pretty emphatic about what he wanted to do.

Richard glanced down at the ring that Magda Searus had left for him. He knew what Sulachan wanted. He wanted to break the Grace.

Richard went back to pacing. He knew what Sulachan wanted, but what was Hannis Arc's role? He was not the kind to be a sycophant to a spirit king. He had to have a plan of his own, something he wanted for himself. Richard knew that people like Hannis Arc only wanted one thing: power. The symbols tattooed all over the man spoke to the lengths to which he would go in order to obtain that power. He was deeply involved in the darkest of occult conjuring.

Of course, with the war ended and the world at peace—at least until the barrier containing the half people had failed and Hannis Arc brought their king back—the only real power left was the D'Haran Empire. By getting Richard out of the way, that made it pretty obvious what Bishop Arc's intent had to be.

He wanted to be Lord Arc and rule the D'Haran Empire.

Throughout his waiting and pacing, Richard had regularly gone to every opening covered by a green veil. At each he had called out, hoping to get in contact with Zedd again, or with anyone. He wished he knew if they were still alive, still all right. He shouted until he nearly lost his voice. He never received an answer. There was no one imprisoned near him.

He tried not to take that as a bad sign.

He went back to wondering what Hannis Arc and the spirit king were doing. He wondered if they had already left. If Hannis Arc hadn't already left, he surely would have already come down to gloat, to torment Richard.

Richard wondered if maybe he was being kept around as a source of fresh blood in case Sulachan's corpse needed a bit of freshening from time to time. Maybe the emperor was waiting to see if he would need more blood. Maybe they didn't know, and were keeping Richard for the time being, just in case.

Richard wanted nothing more than to have Sulachan come down to get that blood. If he got any chance at all, he was going to take it. He needed to rip that walking corpse to pieces—with his bare hands if need be, with his teeth if he had to. He might not be able to harm the spirit, but if he could rip the worldly part of him to bits that might do something.

He knew that such a battle would cost him his life, but it would be worth it if he could put a stop to what was happening. Besides, he was likely going to be fed to the half people anyway.

He could feel the sword's magic in the distance. But even though he could feel it, it was too far away to do him any good. It was like a connection waiting to be completed, waiting for him to return. He could sense where it was, but he had no way to get to it.

If it were closer, he could summon it. He was bonded to the blade, and within a certain distance he could draw the sword to hand. He had done that before— drawn it to him. But it was too far, now. Besides, it was beyond the green boundary to the underworld. Even if it were somehow close enough, and he called it to him as he had done in the past, once it fell into the underworld it would be lost forever.

He checked his arm where he had been cut. The wound had closed and was starting to heal, but it was black under the skin. He wondered if that was from the knife, or from the poison of death inside him.

He supposed that it didn't matter. He imagined that soon enough the Shun-tuk would finally be given permission to rip him apart. They were probably only being held at bay in case Sulachan needed any more blood. The others had probably already been sacrificed. Richard's time would come soon enough.

They would likely feed him to the half people before the poison inside ever had the chance to kill him. With grim curiosity, he wondered if that poison might kill the half people who ate him. He supposed not. They were of the third kingdom.

As he sat back against the wall, tossing small stones out of boredom, he wondered if Samantha had gotten away. He had no idea what she could do now that she was alone and so far from her home, but at least she had escaped Hannis Arc's clutches. Of course, there was no guarantee that she had stayed out of the drifting greenish boundaries of death, or out of the clutches of the half people.

She had wanted so much to come with him, to help him, to try to rescue her mother. She had wanted to help fight the threat descending on the world. She had wanted to carry out the duty of the gifted who had been left in Stroyza. She had shown so much resolve.

He felt guilty for abandoning her, but of course he'd had no choice in the matter. Still, he felt bad. Having her run to keep her from being captured along with him was all he had been able do.

Richard slumped back against the wall, resting his forearms over his knees. He was exhausted from the captivity, the pain of the Agiel, and with worry. He was weak from lack of food.

Worse, he was getting weaker from the inner poison.

"Lord Rahl?"

Richard's head came up. He thought he heard a voice call his name. It was distant, and rather muffled coming through the wavering, greenish underworld wall, but he thought that it sounded like Samantha's voice.

Lord Rahl?"

It was closer the second time. He was sure that it was Samantha's voice.

Richard stood in a rush.

"Lord Rahl?"

That time the voice was right outside his prison cell door.

"Samantha? Samantha, is that you?"

"Lord Rahl! Lord Rahl! Are you all right?"

"Yes! I'm trapped in here. I can't get out. They stuck me in here behind a veil to the underworld."

"I know."

"How in the world did you find me?"

"A woman in red leather saw me hiding in the rocks just outside the caves where they took you."

"Red leather? And she didn't take you captive?"

"I thought she was going to snatch me for sure and give me to all those half people. Most of them had already passed by near where I was hiding. She was coming from the caves to catch up with the men leading the half people.

"But when she spotted me, she instead signaled for me to stay where I was, to stay out of sight, and wait. I couldn't imagine why. I was afraid and didn't know if I could trust her, but I didn't know what else to do. If I came out, then the others would snatch me for sure.

"But then, after a time, when everyone had moved on, she came back."

"And she didn't capture you?"

Samantha was quiet for a moment. "No. I don't know why not. She stared at me for a long time, thinking about something, I guess. I stood there trembling, imagining she was going to feed me to the half people I'd just seen go by. Then, the strangest thing happened. She bent down and told me where you were."

Richard was stunned. "So, she's with you, then? She helped you get down here?"

"No, she only told me where you were being held. It looked like she had a hard time of deciding to do that much. After that, she went to catch up with the others."

"Do you know where the others were going?"

"Most of them seem to be headed south, back toward the gates we came through. They had so many Shun-tuk with them that it looked like the ground was moving. I couldn't see all of them, or tell if they were all moving south. I watched for what seemed like all day as they kept coming past. But I do know that some of the half people stayed behind."

"So, there are still half people here, in the caves?"

"Yes. Lots of them. It took me a long time to work my way down here," she said, sounding frantic. "They're all over in these caves. Sometimes I had to wait hours for them to leave."

"Where are they now?"

"I don't know for sure. I know that they patrol the passageways. Lord Rahl, you have to get out of there!

The half people will come back through here soon. They haunt these caves like ghosts. I can't stay here—they'll get me. You have to get out! You have to get out now!"

Richard threw his hands up in frustration. "I can't, Samantha. The half people have the ability to banish the green veil, but I don't. I don't have a way out or I would already be out. I'm trapped in here."

"Lord Rahl, I can't stay here. The caves are full of half people. If I stay I'll be caught and—"

"Listen to me, Samantha, you need to run. You're right. You can't stay out there or you'll be caught. Get out of here. Get out now."

"I need you to come with me."

Richard raked his fingers back through his hair as he growled in anger. "Samantha—"

"I found some of the others."

"What?"

"When I was looking for you, I found some of the soldiers. I talked to them like I'm talking to you. They're trapped, too, on the other side of greenish underworld veils." There was a long pause. "Lord Rahl," she said, her voice starting to choke with tears, "I talked to my mother."

Richard froze. "Dear spirits," he whispered, not wanting her to hear him.

"Lord Rahl, please, I need you to help me get her out. I can't do it. I need you."

Richard's hands fisted as his jaw clenched. He told himself to stay calm, to think. He had to tell her the brutal truth.

"Samantha, you need to get away. I'm stuck. I can't get out. Save yourself. Your mother would want you to save yourself, to live."

"I know. That's what she told me. But I can't just give up."

Richard leaned his hands on the wall beside the wavering green light. When he came close, the spirits of the dead on the other side became more agitated and pressed against the green wall, trying to get out, trying to get at him.

Richard stared at them for a moment. He was one of them, in a way. He had death inside him. He was of the third kingdom. He was both life and death together. And yet, he was trapped by death in the world of life.

"Lord Rahl . . ."

He could hear her weeping softly.

He was her only hope.

"I'm sorry, Samantha, but I don't have a way to get out."

"But you have to. You're the one."

The one, he thought bitterly. What good was it doing him to be "the one"?

Richard straightened. He was of both worlds. He was alive, but he had death in him as well. He was already dead, but had life still attached to his spirit.

It seemed so simple. Could it be true?

Magda Searus and Merritt had left him a message. They had said *Know that you have within you what you need to survive. Use it.*

Use it.

He wondered . . .

S amantha?"

"I'm here."

He looked down at the Grace on the ring Magda and Merritt had left for him. It was meant to remind him of what mattered. The Grace was a depiction of both worlds, really, and how life blended and balanced with both—the world of life, and the world of the dead. It was also a depiction of their interconnection.

Richard looked up. "Samantha, I need you to get back. Get back away from the green wall."

"Lord Rahl, I don't have anywhere to go...."

"I mean that I need you to stand back—off to the side. In case the boundary of the underworld moves I want you back out of the way. Go back down the hall a ways."

"Why? What are you going to do?"

"Hurry, we don't know how long before more of the Shun-tuk show up. Hurry, now. Stand back out of the way."

"All right," she said from farther down the cave outside. "I'm back out of the way."

"Listen, Samantha . . . if anything goes wrong, I want

you to get away. Do you understand? Don't hesitate. If anything goes wrong, run and get out of here. Your mother would want you to live."

"Lord Rahl, you're scaring me. And I'm already scared enough. There are human bones in some of the caves down here."

That was discouraging news. "I understand, but if I can't escape from in here, then you have to get away."

"It took me a long time to get down here, sneaking past all those ghostly-looking Shun-tuk. I don't know if I can get back out."

"I know it's frightening. But if this doesn't work, you have to try. Understand?"

"I understand," she finally said.

"Now, stand back."

"I am standing back. Hurry. Lord Rahl, you've got to hurry. I can hear voices echoing. I think they're coming. Hurry."

Richard took a deep breath. It had to work. It made sense.

As Samantha had told him once, he was of that world.

He remembered the message left for him, carved in the language of Creation.

Know that you have within you what you need to survive. Use it.

That was what Magda Searus and the Wizard Merritt had told him. They knew he would come to that place and read their message. They had left their ring for him.

Still, he was loath to try such a thing. But he was dead anyway if he didn't at least try. Everyone would die. This was his only chance.

He knew that more than anything, despite how he tried to convince himself of the logic of it, it was an act of desperation.

Zedd always said that sometimes an act of desperation was magic—real magic.

He tried to slow his breathing. He couldn't afford to wait any longer. He had thought it through as best he could. There was no time to think it over any longer. He was out of options and out of time. They all were. He had to try.

He looked down at the Grace on the ring one last time. He looked at the lines coming out from the center, the lines representing the spark of the gift as it crossed the world of life and then went on into the infinite world of the dead. Each was a continuous, unbroken line crossing worlds.

Richard steeled himself, gritting his teeth. And then, he raced ahead into the glowing green luminescence that was the outer boundary of the underworld itself.

The shock of it was like walking off a cliff at midnight.

He was instantly lost in an eternity of darkness.

There were no spirits as he stepped through into their world, as there had been before when he was on life's side of the boundary. There was no more howling, no wailing, no more wavering limbs.

There was nothing.

There was no heat, no cold, no light, only a kind of darkness that was beyond darkness. In a way it reminded him of what it was like looking into a night stone, only this was more like walking into a night stone, or more accurately, being swallowed into that perfect blackness.

He felt totally and utterly lost.

Everything was dead to him.

Richard couldn't sense if he had been in that empty world for mere seconds, or for a hundred years. The void was without sight, sound, dimension, or time.

But then the darkness began to dissolve around him. The world came back in ragged patches like being able to begin to see objects when first coming awake. The sensation accelerated and as light and sound crashed in around him, he found himself standing in the cave outside his prison cell.

He looked back over his shoulder and saw that the sparkling, wavering greenish luminescence blocking the opening to where he had been held for so long was no longer there.

Samantha's big dark eyes blinked as she stared in disbelief.

"Dear spirits," she whispered. "Lord Rahl, you just stepped right out of the underworld."

Richard looked down at himself. He appeared to be in one piece. He was all there. He wasn't bleeding. He wasn't in any pain. He felt normal, other than the persistent touch of death that still festered inside him.

"How could you do such a thing?" Samantha asked.

"I have death in me, remember?"

Samantha nodded her head of bushy black hair, clearly not understanding. "But how could you step right out of the world of the dead?"

"Do you remember what you told me?" he asked as he checked ahead and behind into the darkness. "You said that I was of that world—the third kingdom. Life and death together. Because I have death in me I'm of both worlds."

"So you figured that if you are the world of life, and could exist here with death in you, at least for a while, then you could exist there, at least for a while, with life in you?"

Richard nodded. "At least for a short time."

She seemed to remember her overriding urgency, then looked around and pointed. "The other voices I heard were down that way. We have to get them out. We have to get my mother out. Hurry before any of the Shun-tuk come back this way."

Richard was nodding even as he was already moving. Samantha ran beside him.

"This way, Lord Rahl," she said as she raced out in front of him and then cut down another passageway to the right.

It was dark in the rough, crooked tunnel, with distant greenish light reflecting off the rock in places, enabling him to at least see where they were going.

Richard raced past human bones. They lay discarded, piled up against the walls and drifted into irregular depressions to the side.

Panting from the short run, he stopped when Samantha skidded to halt and thrust out her arm to point. "There."

"Your mother?" he guessed.

She nodded. "Hurry."

Richard took a deep breath and then without delay stepped into the darkness beyond the flickering green curtain. It was the same timeless, black void as the first time. It was no easier to endure the uncomfortable, lost feeling of the timeless world. In a way, it felt as if he had never left.

As the wall dissolved back into the reality of the world of life, he saw a woman with black hair standing speechless before him, staring with big, dark eyes.

Samantha raced through the now-clear opening into the room where the woman stood in silent shock. She threw herself into the woman's outstretched arms. Samantha looked like a small, frail, miniature version of her mother. Richard had expected her to look like her mother, but the striking similarity was more than he had expected.

"Sammie," the woman said with profound relief. "Dear spirits, I never thought I would see you again."

"This is Lord Rahl," Samantha said with a nod as she tugged on her mother's hand, pulling her toward the opening of the room.

"Lord Rahl . . . ?" The woman's mouth dropped open.

"Yes." As she dragged her mother, Samantha waved a hand, urging Richard to come along after her. "Hurry, Lord Rahl. We need to get the others out."

Not needing the urging, Richard was right on their heels, following them out. Samantha raced down the tunnel a short way before again skidding to a halt. She thrust out her arm, again pointing at a green curtain.

"There."

Richard didn't pause to question. Without slowing he raced through the green veil and into the coldly frightening void. As the darkness dissolved, and the inner cell came into view, he found himself standing before a number of the shocked faces of men of the First File. They were packed in, filling the room. The ones sitting, leaning against the wall, jumped to their feet.

"Lord Rahl?" one of the men said in surprise.

Suddenly, Cara raced through the men, pushing them aside to make way. She flew into his arms. "Lord Rahl! You're alive! You're alive!"

Her husband, Ben, the general in charge of the First File, was right there behind her. He looked as relieved to see Richard as Cara did, if more shocked.

Cara, as frazzled as she appeared, had never looked so good to him.

"Lord Rahl," Cara said, "you look terrible."

"Probably because a Mord-Sith has been using her Agiel on me."

"What!"

"Long story, no time," he said as he started pushing soldiers toward the now-clear opening and out into the tunnel.

Richard caught General Meiffert's arm, stopping him, and spoke in a low voice. "Ben, where are the rest of the men?"

With a haunted look, Ben glanced over his shoulder at his men racing out of their prison. "They've been coming and taking them, one at a time. Lord Rahl, I know it sounds crazy, but they've been taking them out and eating them alive. We could hear it. We could hear the screams before—"

"I know," Richard said. "I know." He let out a distraught sigh as he shared a look with the man. "I'm so sorry. I wish I could have gotten here sooner."

Ben shook his head as he looked Richard in the eye. "We are here to protect you, Lord Rahl, not the other way around."

"Richard?"

It was the muffled sound of Zedd's voice, off to the side, through another wall of greenish light.

"He's in there," Ben said, gesturing to the side. "We've been able to talk to him when we don't think anyone is around. He says that Nicci is beyond, in another cell on the far side of him. They kept the gifted separated."

Richard wasted no time in asking any questions or saying anything else. There was no time to waste on reunions or explanations of anything. There would be time enough for that if they could escape the caves and the Shun-tuk that hunted them. For now he needed to get the others and get out.

Richard raced past the men and out the now-clear opening into the craggy tunnel. He ran past Samantha and her mother to the next shimmering curtain of greenish light. Without a moment's hesitation, Richard plunged into the greenish glow.

For an eternity, he floated in a timeless place, and then, as the dark, timeless emptiness resolved into the sights and sounds of the world, Richard saw an astonished Zedd rising to his feet. The old man moved with a pained slowness, as if he had been sitting on the stone floor for far too long. His wavy white hair stuck out in disarray. His simple robes were filthy.

Richard threw his arms around his grandfather in a quick embrace, then hurriedly pushed away.

"No time to talk," he said to his grandfather before the old man had a chance to launch into a thousand questions. "We need to get out of here."

Zedd flicked a bony hand toward the wall at the side. "Nicci. Nicci is over there. Can you get her, too?"

Richard nodded as he first hurried his grandfather out into the corridor where Samantha and her mother waited. Zedd took the woman's hands, expressing wordlessly his relief at being out and seeing her out as well. Obviously, the two of them must have talked.

At the next sparkling greenish veil, the shadowed shapes of spirits beyond flailed and twisted expectantly as Richard came close. Again, without pause, he immediately plummeted into the world of the dead—his world, in a way. Beyond the first sparkling flash of greenish illumination as he made contact, there were no spirits. There was nothing. It was a frightening fall through darkness until the world of life abruptly crashed into view.

As it did, Nicci, in tears of joy at seeing him, already had her arms around his neck before he was sure that he was fully back in the world of life.

"Richard . . . how in the world—"

"Later," he said, seizing her upper arm and pulling her out of the now-clear opening. She peered around the edges of the opening as she passed through, looking amazed at seeing the deadly underworld boundary so abruptly gone.

Out in the hall, Richard paused. When everyone started to talk at once, he held up his hand as he shushed them.

"Quiet. Half people are near and could hear you. We don't want to have to fight them if we don't have to, especially not down here."

They instantly fell silent, many casting worried looks up and down the rocky tunnel.

Richard also needed quiet because he wanted to go within himself and feel the link to his sword's power. He could feel that it was closer than it had been when he had been in his prison cell. As he closed his eyes and let the world around him fade into the background, it allowed him to embrace that faint inner sense.

He at last lifted his arm to point.

"That way."

He raced down the tunnel winding its way through the pockmarked rock, at junctures of passageways taking the route where he could feel the strongest pull of the sword. He could feel himself getting closer to it all the time. He ran with a sense of urgent desperation to get his hands on it.

Along the way they encountered bones pushed to the edges of the passageway. There were so many bones in places that they looked like debris that had been washed up in a flood. There were no large sections, such as intact spines, feet, or hands. All of the bones had been completely disjointed so that the individual small bits and pieces lay in dense mounds. All the skulls had been broken open so that the Shun-tuk could get at the brains, so that only fragments remained.

Richard, leading the silent group of soldiers and gifted, at last found the place where he felt his sword the strongest, where it felt near. He knew what it felt like to sense the sword and he could tell that it was only feet away beyond another underworld barrier. He dared not call it to hand, though. He feared that if he did, he might lose it in the void of the underworld.

He looked back for a brief moment at everyone's tense expressions, and then he stepped through the boundary into the world of the dead.

Before the world even began to come back in around him, he already had his fingers around the hilt of the Sword of Truth. It was a huge relief to have the weapon back. He immediately slipped the baldric over his head and let the sword find its proper place at his left hip.

"Ben, get your men in here," he called back through

the opening where the green veil winked out of existence. He signaled with an urgent wave of his arms.

There were weapons—swords, axes, pikes, knives—stacked haphazardly in the room. The half people had thrown all the weapons they'd confiscated into the small chamber in the rock and covered it over with a wall of death.

The big men of the First File rushed in, all of them retrieving weapons as fast as they could, passing them back through the ranks to men outside in the corridor, crowded in close to the weapons cache. None of them bothered to try to find their own; they were just happy to get their hands on any weapon handed back to them. Richard understood the feeling. He felt that same sense of relief at having his own weapon back.

Out in the hall, as soon as they were once again armed, the crowd quickly gathered in close around him. Richard held up a hand before anyone could say anything.

"We have to get out of here," he said as softly as possible, but loud enough so that they could all hear him. "We can talk later. Hannis Arc could be around here somewhere, along with a resurrected spirit of—"

"No, he's not," Samantha whispered.

Richard frowned at her. "What?"

"He left. Him and masses and masses of the Shun-tuk. There's still a lot more left down here in these tunnels—hundreds and hundreds—but he and most of them have gone."

Richard nodded, remembering that she had already told him that. "All right," he said. "There are still hundreds of those flesh eaters about. For now, the important thing is that we get out of these caves before they catch us trying to escape, and then get away from here."

Nicci ignored his urgency and placed two fingers

against Richard's forehead. "It's worse," she said quietly back over her shoulder to Zedd. He nodded knowingly.

"Richard, it's important that we get you and Kahlan to the palace," Nicci said, her face set with concern and urgency. "We have to heal you both of what you have inside."

Cara looked around. "Where is the Mother Confessor?"

Richard again shushed them all with a gesture. "Kahlan was unconscious," he whispered. "I had to come alone to get you all out of here. She is undoubtedly awake by now back in Stroyza. She will be waiting for us. We'll need to go get her before we head back to the palace. But first we need to get out of these caves and out of the third kingdom."

"Come on," Samantha said. "This way."

Without delay, the entire company raced off through the dark tunnel, following after Samantha. Holding her mother's hand, she ran like her dress was on fire.

The tunnels were not really corridors, but rather a variety of natural openings through the rock. It was in part a cave system through hollow cavities, part natural channels created by floodwaters through the softer portions of the rock, and in part fissures in the more rugged stone.

In places the passageway ahead led them through long clefts where the rock had buckled and split. At other spots, they had to go through low passages under broad shelves of rock that were so low that all of them except Samantha had to bend at the waist so as not to hit their heads as they followed the steep ledge upward. In some places they had to climb up into pockmarked networks of holes.

After going under a series of flat shelves of stone, the openings found their way back into the cave system, which split into a confusing maze of jagged tunnels and rifts in the layers of what looked like melted stone. Some stone was sharp and jagged, while other openings they raced through had over great periods of time been rounded and smoothed by water. Many of the passageways had small streams running through them. In places they had to skirt pools of perfectly clear deep water. Other tunnels were crooked, cavernous passageways with many openings branching all throughout them.

The entire subterranean world was so riddled with holes, openings, and rifts that it felt to Richard like it all might lead to the underworld itself. The greenish veils of luminescence that floated sporadically through the caves only added to the illusion.

"Samantha, are you sure you know where you're going?" Richard asked in a hushed voice as he followed close behind her.

"I grew up in caves," she said. "I remember distinctive things about the rocks and openings through them."

She seemed to think that was explanation enough. Richard supposed that maybe it was. As a woods guide he did much the same kind of thing when traveling through uncharted forests. He made mental notes of particular sights along the way so he could find his way back. She was more comfortable than he was underground, so he had to trust that this was her kind of world, and she was his guide through it.

Still, he did remember certain landmarks himself, and he wasn't seeing them.

"This isn't the way we came in," he whispered urgently to her as they zigzagged among what looked like melted rock towers.

"I know," she whispered back. "I had to find a way around all the unholy half dead."

Richard was glad to hear that she had used her head to find a safe passage. The way she was taking them was a route that so far had been free of the Shun-tuk. But he knew that the half people would be patrolling the tunnels and could show up at any moment. Once they discovered that their prisoners were missing, all the Shun-tuk would be hunting them.

He didn't know how much farther they had to go, but he knew he would be relieved once they finally reached the surface. He didn't know if they would be any safer aboveground, but they certainly weren't safe underground. If they were attacked in the caves it would be difficult to fight. They could be trapped by masses of Shun-tuk blocking their way from each end of a tunnel and then picked off one at a time.

He reminded himself that they now had gifted with them, and that would certainly even the odds. But he also knew from fighting half people that they didn't fear for their lives and were unrelenting in coming after their victims.

If they had to fight off the Shun-Tuk, Richard could cut them down with his sword, but sooner or later their numbers would simply become too much. He would eventually tire and then they would have him. More troubling, though, was that he could only defend one spot, and they could come in at them from all directions.

It was much the same with the gift as with his sword, if all they faced were the half people and not the reanimated dead. The gifted, too, could kill vast numbers of an enemy, and Richard had certainly seen Zedd use wizard's fire to take down hordes of enemy troops from the Old World, but even wizard's fire had its limits. It had to be conjured and cast. Doing so was a great deal of effort and it quickly became tiring. If the enemy kept coming in vast numbers, getting closer all the time, then even a wizard could be overrun.

After all, they had been overrun and captured once, already.

And then there were the walking dead. The gift was of limited use against them. That was why, Richard imagined, the half people, like those in Sulachan's time in the old war, used the dead. They were not only very effective on the front lines, they were also expendable and there was a virtually endless supply of them, so if nothing else, they could wear down any resistance.

Richard followed after Samantha as she made one twisting turn after another, following a convoluted route that only she knew back through rock riddled with passages, clefts, and a maze of intersections. She ran through the labyrinth like a rock rat, never letting go of her mother's hand, never slowing to consider the way.

When they came to a particularly complex set of passages, Samantha stretched as she ran, looking back over the heads of some of the men to see Richard. She pointed and made a snaking gesture with her hand, indicating the turns they needed to make. Richard nodded when he saw what she meant and where they would need to go.

He grabbed Nicci's arm and pulled her forward. "Help protect her. I want to make sure everyone else makes it through this part here and doesn't get lost. I don't want to have to come back in here looking for anyone who got separated."

Nicci touched his shoulder in silent confirmation of the orders before swiftly racing forward to catch up with Samantha and her mother.

Richard slowed his pace, allowing himself to fall back as the men of the First File ran past to keep up with those ahead. They were beginning to become strung out in the series of complex turns, climbs, and descents through the snarl of passages. Richard pushed each man down the correct tunnel as they raced past, lest they miss the turn. He urged them to hurry, pointing to make sure that they saw the correct turns to take up ahead. It was difficult to see in the near darkness. Only the occasional sparkling curtain of the underworld drifting through adjoining passageways gave them any light to see by. He hoped one didn't drift across to block their way, or worse, drift in from the side and separate them.

Richard spotted Zedd, near the back of the line of men. He was managing to keep up just fine. He might have been old, but he was not only stronger than he looked, but determined to get away from the fate that had awaited them in the cave prison. Richard knew that his grandfather was staying near the rear because he wanted to watch their backs for any sign of trouble.

Cara, out ahead of her husband, followed close behind Zedd near the rear of the column of men. She saw Richard slowing to push men down the correct turn.

"Go," she growled ahead to him, motioning angrily to him over the heads of a congested knot of soldiers. "Don't wait for us. Go."

He knew that she wanted him to stay in among the protection of the men of the First File. Richard was determined, though, to make sure that in the dark cave none of them missed the turns they needed to take. He didn't want to lose any of them down in the tunnels. As men squeezed past him, he pushed them into the correct tunnel, frequently pointing the way ahead.

Cara, in back of the tail end of the men, picked up her speed. She raced past an intersection to get to Richard. She was unhappy he was slowing down and wanted to get to him so she could protect him. Finally, the last two men dashed past.

Just behind, as Cara cleared the intersection ahead of her husband, a flood of Shun-tuk spilled out of several openings to the side.

There was only one person left in line: Ben.

Sword to hand, he turned to block the tunnel.

The whitish forms of Shun-tuk crashed over him in a massive wave of bodies, taking him down.

Richard and Cara skidded to a stop.

"No!" Cara screamed as the unholy half dead ripped into her husband with their teeth.

Time seemed to stop.

It seemed like Ben had a hundred of the chalky forms diving in on him like a pack of ravenous wolves.

Richard already had his sword out as he raced back through the tunnel. He had to make it in time. He had never run so fast in his life.

Blood splashed across the savage white faces as they viciously ripped out Ben's throat. Other mouths opened to try to catch squirting blood, hoping to catch with it the escaping soul.

Richard screamed in fury as he ran toward the terrible scene.

Cara bent at her knees and threw her shoulder into Richard's chest as he flew by, knocking him against the wall, blocking him from diving into the pile of howling, growling, writhing Shun-tuk in a feeding frenzy.

"It's too late!" she shouted as she shoved him violently in the other direction. "Go! Go! Don't let his sacrifice be for nothing. Run!"

In shock at what he had just seen, Richard screamed, "Zedd!"

His grandfather was already turning back, arms thrust toward the Shun-tuk as they tore the fallen general apart with their teeth.

The last thing Richard saw before an inferno of blinding yellow flame exploded back through the tunnel was that it was far too late to save Cara's husband. He'd never even had time to scream.

Richard panted in shock and rage. It had happened too fast.

The wailing mass of liquid fire that Zedd sent back through the tunnel was deafening in the confines of the passageway. The tumbling flame exploded across the ground, splashing up along the walls as it flooded over the terrible scene, engulfing it all in a terrible, blinding conflagration.

At least the fallen general would not be eaten by the beasts. He had given his life to slow the enemy in the hopes of saving the rest of them.

Tears streamed down Cara's face as she shoved Richard. "Go! Hurry! Go!"

And then Richard was running.

Cara's hand on his back made sure she was in contact with him as she pushed him ahead of her while watching his back. Behind them, Zedd was a dark, sticklike silhouette against the brutally intense yellow blaze. In the roaring heart of that blinding light, the dark bodies of the Shun-tuk were reduced to skeletons and then ash in little more than an instant.

The lethal fire roared back through the tunnel, engulfing the leading edge of the horde coming for them. The screams of the Shun-tuk were bloodcurdling.

Those screams were not enough for Richard.

When they broke free of the caverns, racing out of the underground openings and out among the dark stone spires, they found themselves in the gloom of dusk. The day was dying in deep grays that made the craggy stone pinnacles look like shadows of spirits crowding in from all around. Yet, after the darkness of the tunnels, even this somber light seemed harsh. The silence, too, was oppressive.

The silence was short-lived.

The Shun-tuk, howling in wild fury, poured out of openings everywhere in the rock. They were aroused by the smell of blood and had their prey in sight. The lethal fire Zedd had unleashed in the tunnel had only slowed them. It couldn't reach through all the passages to reach the masses of half people after them.

They hungered for those with souls. There would be no stopping them.

They flooded out of places in the rock that Richard didn't even know were caves. They rushed out into the dying daylight, a howling, ravenous horde, pouring out from the rocks and flowing around the stone spires in unending numbers.

Once out of the confining caves and in the open, seeing the masses of the unholy half dead coming from almost every direction, Richard knew that if they tried to get away, they would be run down and overwhelmed. He skidded to a halt.

As he stopped, he seized Cara by her wrist and tossed her behind him, out of his way. The storm of magic from the sword thundered through him, demanding that he strike.

It was his turn, now, to unleash his own merciless hunger for blood.

He turned to the Shun-tuk, then, and unleashed his lethal rage, both his and his sword's, against the chalky figures charging in at him with lips drawn back and teeth bared. They came at him from every direction.

His blade met the snarling faces, shattering the skulls of those diving toward him. Each swing splintered bone or severed heads. Bone, brains, and blood smacked the rocks all around Richard as he swung the sword without pause. Blood fell in a red rain.

The Shun-tuk were being cut down by the dozens. Headless bodies, or bodies with only the lower part of their head, toppled and tumbled across the ground.

Richard lost himself in the storm of anger raging through him. He gave himself over to it without reservation or restraint. All he wanted to do was kill these soulless monsters. The blade demanded ever more blood and he was only too happy to oblige. He needed the blood of these animals more than he needed to live himself.

He abandoned himself to the need to kill, to his rage at what they had done to Ben and so many others. Each body that fell only made him want to kill more of them. There was no way that he would ever be satisfied if even one of them still stood.

As he killed men and women to one side, half people on the other side thought they had an opening to get to him and take him down. Richard let them come, then spun, cutting two men in half with one swing. Legs without bodies folded and collapsed. Torsos trailing innards and blood hit the ground with heavy thuds. The severed, ashen heads of yet more half people thunked down on the rock, cracking as they hit from their violent, tumbling fall. Empty eyes set in darkly painted rings stared up at nothing from tangles of bloody limbs.

As he screamed in rage while swinging the sword, the chalky figures toppled to the ground around him, headless, armless, lifeless.

He didn't try to run, to get away. There was no getting away. There was only the killing.

He stood his ground, slaughtering them as they came, until there were so many bodies that he needed to move out from the tangled mass of sprawling carcasses and severed body parts just in order to be able to fight. Gore from those cut in half spilled across the rocky ground. Blood covered everything. Where there had been the pale, ash-covered figures, there were now only bodies covered in a sheen of wet red.

Running recklessly, many of the Shun-tuk slipped on all the blood and gore and fell sprawling across the ground. Richard stabbed downward at forms wriggling through the blood and the dead to get at him.

Those who raced in toward him fell dead and dying around him as fast as they came, adding their numbers to those already piling up around him.

It was not skillful fighting, not a gruesomely elegant dance with death. There was no artful cut and thrust, no graceful evasion and counterstrike.

It was, instead, violent, mad, bloody butchery, nothing more, nothing less.

Not far from him, Cara, with a knife in each hand that she had gotten somewhere, fought with a wild ferocity that was frightening to witness. Richard understood her savage wrath.

He usually saw her fight with her Agiel, but her Agiel would not work because his gift did not work. His gift powered the bond, and without that bond her weapon was dead in her hand, so she had instead found knives. She was no less deadly with knives than an Agiel. If anything, at the moment it looked like she preferred them for the manifest, ripping damage they did, visible evidence of her rage.

Off to the sides behind him, the soldiers of the First File fought with the same kind of grim fury, wanting to avenge the death of their general, a leader they admired and loved. The First File were the elite of D'Haran troops, the deadliest of fighters, and they were more than proving it this day.

By the way they fought, though, Richard could see that they were not fighting to save themselves. This was purely for vengeance. The First File in want of retribution was a sight to behold.

Yet, even as hard as they fought, some of those soldiers were swamped by the flood of howling half people. He saw them go down, covered with dozens of the unholy half dead wildly tearing into them with bared teeth.

Beyond them, beyond the killing field immediately around Richard littered with hundreds of dead and dying Shun-tuk, Zedd and Nicci were unleashing their gift with deadly effectiveness.

Off in the distance, at the outer margin of the raging battle, Richard could hear the roaring wail of wizard's fire racing through the murky air, lighting the stone spires with an intense yellowish orange radiance before splashing down among the Shun-tuk as they raced out of the rocks. They were incinerated by the hundreds before even having the chance to join the battle. Despite how many of the savages died, more yet poured out to replace them.

Richard heard rock columns crash down on the chalky figures as the great spikes of spires toppled among them, no doubt brought down by Nicci, or Samantha and her mother. The falling stone crushed great numbers of them at a time. Great boulders and whole sections of fractured spires tumbled down and bounced across the ground, collecting helpless Shun-tuk before they were able to get out of the way.

The earth shook with the thunderous explosion of wizard's fire as well as the boom of rock towers hitting the ground and shattering. Massive rocks hitting the ground and splitting sounded like the crack of lightning.

Yet even the roar of wizard's fire, the booming crack of exploding rock, the shouts of the soldiers, and the screams of the dying were all only a dim drone somewhere beyond Richard's immediate attention.

He was focused on the waves of chalky white figures as they raced in to try to get his soul. These were half people who clearly wanted him above all the others. They recognized that it was his blood that had brought back their king. They wanted that blood. They wanted his soul for themselves.

That was just fine with Richard. He was pleased that they were coming for him with such passion, that they wanted at him above all else. It gave him more to kill.

Despite how weary his arms were, and how out of breath he was, Richard never for a moment paused in killing them as they came. He never slowed. If anything, his rage was only building, fed by the unleashed anger from the sword. That anger fed his, powered the blade, made him more deadly, drove his need to kill. He was lost in a world of his own, focused entirely on the task.

Yet somewhere in the back of his mind, Richard knew that he wasn't going to be able to keep it up. There were just too many continually coming for him. There seemed no way to defeat them all. Their numbers were just too great.

And then, in the failing light, in among the half people, Richard saw the hulking forms of the walking dead finally emerging out of the caves.

78

The glowing red eyes of the walking dead stood out in the murky, late day light. They were slower than the Shun-tuk—that was why so many of the Shun-tuk had emerged from underground first. Now, the dead were lumbering out of the caves, come to help reap those with souls.

Richard furiously hacked his way through the half people as he crossed the bloody ground to intercept the dark shapes of the animated dead. Their clothes hung in rotting tatters. Their dried flesh was as dark as the dirt-covered clothes they wore, so that they all looked like filth formed into men.

As slimy and grimy as they were, it didn't matter to Richard. He needed to stop them before they could get to the others. He knew how dangerous these dead driven by occult magic could be. The soldiers would have more than a difficult time handling such a threat. Even the gifted's powers were no match for the occult magic that had been invested in these monsters.

Richard vaguely perceived a figure in red—Cara—close behind him, going in for the attack with him, guarding his flank from Shun-tuk turning to come after him.

Richard redirected his attack from the Shun-tuk and instead went for the dead. With their glowing red eyes they were easy enough to spot. Even the Shun-tuk kept clear of them now that they had been set with the task of killing.

Richard gritted his teeth as he swung his sword with all his might, hacking apart the dense, dark forms. Arms and legs fell, littering the ground. Legs continued to twitch. Fingers continued to grasp. Heads and parts of heads spun through the air and cracked apart as they bounced off rock walls.

All the while, fire tumbled and rolled across the ground, swamping the severed but still-moving limbs behind Richard as he drove onward through the dead coming at him and the Shun-tuk baring their teeth, hoping for a bite of him. They tasted only steel. The air all around was filled not only with the smoke from all the fire, but the stench of burning flesh. Dust boiled up as stone spires crumbled and fell among the Shun-tuk. The night air was filled with screams of the mortally injured and those trapped under the crushing weight of toppled stone.

Everywhere the mostly naked bodies lay sprawled across the ground. Their chalky white forms only served to display the blood in stark relief. Each slash that laid them open only looked more shocking because of the way their ash-covered bodies made the terrible wounds all the more horrifyingly obvious.

Richard heard his name. It was Zedd, calling out to him.

"Richard," he called again.

In a rage of blood lust, Richard brought the sword up before him, looking for any threat. Even though it still felt like hundreds of the snarling, growling half people were rushing at him, he realized that there were none.

It was only the terrible images of them that he was still seeing flashing through his mind that made him think they might still be coming. But they weren't.

He blinked. There were no more Shun-tuk charging in at him. They were all down. There were no more of the walking dead. They, too, were all down.

In the stillness of the gathering darkness, Richard could hear the men panting from the effort of the battle. Some with wounds groaned. Some walked among the wounded Shun-tuk on the ground, stabbing any still alive.

All the axes and swords the men carried dripped blood. All of the men were covered in blood and gore. Richard was covered in more Shun-tuk blood than any of them. He was soaked in red.

Richard turned to Cara, a knife in each of her blood-soaked fists. One was a steel-bladed knife, the other stone—a Shun-tuk weapon. She had been using that weapon to put down the dead.

Cara met his gaze. The rage in her eyes was frightening to see.

It broke his heart.

With his sword still gripped in his fist and the anger of the magic still coursing through every fiber of his being, Richard put his arms around her.

Cara's arms hung at her sides as he embraced her tightly, and then she threw her head back and let out a single, long wail.

He held her close as she buried her face against his chest with a helpless sob. He held her in a comforting shelter for a long moment. He finally let her go and looked into her tear-filled blue eyes.

There were no words as they looked into each other's eyes. There could be no words.

When Richard finally turned back to Zedd and Nicci standing close, the crushing weight of the world seemed to suddenly descend on him.

He dropped to a knee, abruptly unable to stand. Cara helped hold him on the way down so that he didn't fall on his face.

Nicci and Zedd were both right there, both helping keep him upright on his knees, letting him sit back on his heels.

Through a torrent of every kind of pain imaginable, the power of the sword still in his fist sustained and supported him. He felt too tired to breathe and had to will himself to draw each breath.

Both Nicci and Zedd pressed their fingers to his forehead. Richard could feel the telltale tingle of the gift probing the poison deep within him.

Nicci looked up sharply at Zedd. "Do you feel it?"

Zedd returned her grim look and gave her a nod. "We need to get to that containment field. There's not a lot of time."

"Where's Kahlan?" Nicci asked as she looked around to see if anyone knew. "Where's Kahlan? We need to get her back there as well. She will be worse than Richard by now. We have to tend to her as soon as possible. Where is she?"

"We had to leave her in Stroyza," Samantha said from back behind Zedd. "I healed some of her injuries and she hadn't awakened yet. We had to leave her to rest and recover some of her strength. She should be awake by now and waiting for us back in Stroyza."

"South, through the gates," Richard managed.

"Then we go there first and get the Mother Confessor," Cara said with surprising power, courage, and determination as she stood over Richard's shoulder. "We can't head back to the palace until we get her."

"It's not that far," Samantha offered. "It's only a few days if we hurry."

"After we get her, then we have to get you both back to the palace so we can heal you," Nicci said to Richard in a confidential, worried tone.

Richard nodded. He forced himself to his feet. "Kahlan is in Stroyza. Like Samantha says, it's not that far. It's back near where you all were attacked and captured, after you came to rescue us from the Hedge Maid."

He looked at all the faces watching him before turning his gaze south. "Let's get going. There's still a little light. We leave now."

Sword still in his hand, not yet ready to put the power of its anger away, Richard started out across the broken ground, walking over the bodies of hundreds and hundreds of fallen Shun-tuk. Cara was half a step behind his right shoulder. The rest of them all silently fell in to follow.

79

Hannis Arc turned when he caught a glimpse of the tall woman in red leather making her way resolutely through the whitewashed bodies of the Shun-tuk spread across the forested landscape behind them. Descending the slope, the vast army of grim half people seemed to pour through and among the trees like a white avalanche.

His mood darkened when he saw that the Mord-Sith was alone.

He had been wondering where she was and what had been keeping her. Traveling across the desolate land of the third kingdom had been much easier than making their way through the uncharted forests of the Dark Lands. It would not have been so difficult with a small force, but the numbers they were dragging behind them were vast and that slowed the journey. There were so many following behind that it took most of a day for all of them to pass one spot.

The Mord-Sith did not look at all happy. Seeing that she was alone made him more than merely displeased. Vika elbowed aside a silent Shun-tuk woman who didn't move out of the Mord-Sith's way. Hannis Arc could hear the bone of her jaw crack before she fell beneath the feet of the horde.

"So where is Richard Rahl?" Hannis Arc asked when she finally caught up to walk beside him. "You had better not have let him die under torture. I want to be the one to kill him."

The muscles in her jaw flexed as she clenched her teeth for a moment. "Lord Arc, I'm afraid that it looks like he escaped."

He shared a look with Sulachan.

"What do you mean, it looks like he escaped?" the spirit of Emperor Sulachan asked as he came to a halt. Behind them the progress of the Shun-tuk nation ground to a halt as well.

Vika looked at Sulachan's ghost briefly; then her steely blue eyes turned to Hannis Arc as she answered.

"It appears that he somehow managed to escape. All the containment chambers were empty. The ground outside the caves was a sea of dead Shun-tuk. It was a slaughter. I have never seen the likes of it. The stench was unimaginable. Buzzards darken the sky. The ground seems to move as their dark bodies hop from place to place to gorge on carcasses. The dead have drawn predators of all sorts—wolves, coyotes, crows, vultures, foxes—everything you can imagine is there picking over the remains. Scavengers have come from far and wide to feast."

Hannis Arc's voice rose in a way that her eyes revealed she recognized as dangerous. "Well, what about down in the caves? What about all the prisoners we left?"

Vika swallowed. "Lord Arc, they are all gone. All of them. The soldiers, the gifted, Lord Rahl—all of them are gone."

His brow drew down in a way that caused her to

back up a step. "Richard Rahl. He is no longer Lord Rahl. That has been taken from him. I am Lord Arc, leader of the D'Haran Empire, not Richard Rahl."

She swallowed again. "My mistake, Lord Arc."

The walking corpse of the spirit king gestured. "Or, you will be, one day."

Hannis Arc looked over at the glowing form of Sulachan within his long-dead, worldly form. He did not like to be spoken to in such a manner, even by the risen Sulachan.

"Are you suggesting that I might not be? That you and your forces might fail me?"

Sulachan regarded Hannis Arc with an unreadable look before finally smiling. "Of course not, Lord Arc. Not at all. I am only saying that I warned you about Richard Rahl and leaving him alive."

Hannis Arc's hands fisted. "I didn't leave him alive! We put him in a prison sealed off by the underworld itself, with an army of half people guarding him and the rest of his people! Then I sent her to bring me Richard Rahl!"

He swung around and backhanded Vika across the mouth with his fist. "And she failed me!"

Vika stumbled back three steps from the blow. As soon as she recovered she quickly came forward again and kept her head bowed.

"I'm sorry, Lord Arc. I have failed you. I went to get him, just as you ordered, but he and the others were gone—escaped somehow. The Shun-tuk left behind must have tried to stop them as well, and they, too, failed you both."

"Why didn't you look for him?" Hannis Arc demanded. "Why didn't you go after him, find him, and bring him to me?"

She kept her head bowed. "I tried to find him, Lord

Arc, but they were gone. I checked all the caverns, just in case. They were empty except for masses of charred remains. Outside the caves there were so many tracks trampling the ground from"—she gestured behind her—"from all of the Shun-tuk nation leaving that place, that there was no way I could even begin to track Richard Rahl and the small group he has with him. For days I have been searching, but to no avail. I tried, but I have no idea where he went."

"It would appear," Sulachan said, "that Richard Rahl has managed to slip from your grasp. As I warned, he is dangerous."

Hannis Arc gave the spirit a dark look, but didn't answer.

"I have failed you, Lord Arc," Vika said. "I deserve and gratefully accept any punishment you decree. My head, if you wish it, Lord Arc."

He heaved a sigh, thinking. "He was gone when you got back there, then? You didn't see or speak with any of the Shun-tuk we left behind to feed on the soldiers? You didn't see this battle? He was already gone?"

She kept her gaze to the ground. "Yes, Lord Arc. As soon as you told me to go get him and bring him to you, I immediately started back. When I got there it was as I described. The only Shun-tuk left there were long since dead. I went down in the caves and found all the prisoners gone. I spent several days, every moment there was light, searching for any sign of where they could have gone, but I could find nothing."

He considered silently for a moment. The Shun-tuk, stone-faced, watched him. Sulachan watched him. He would like to kill the woman on the spot for failing him. But she had served him well for many years. She had never before failed him.

"Well," he said in a cooler voice, "I guess I can hardly

blame you for not bringing him if he had already escaped."

"And all of the other chambers where his companions were being held were empty as well?" Sulachan's spirit asked.

She was obviously uncomfortable looking at the spirit, so she looked instead at Hannis Arc. "Yes. I don't know how they were able to break the veils confining them, but all of the ones over the openings into where they were being kept had vanished. I suppose that it's possible the half people you left to feast on them took the prisoners out, and at that point they somehow managed to overpower the half people and get away."

"So it would appear," Hannis Arc said, glaring at Sulachan, "that it is actually your half people, the ones you left behind to handle the situation, who are the ones who failed."

"No matter," the spirit king said, sounding unconcerned. "We will have him tracked down and brought back."

Hannis Arc leaned toward the glowing spirit. "How?" he demanded. "We don't even know where they went."

The spirit smiled in that way that Hannis Arc didn't like. One cadaverous arm lifted, and the spirit king signaled to those behind them. Several Shun-tuk rushed forward and crowded in close to hear his orders.

"Bring me some of my spirit trackers."

With a whisking gesture they were sent running off into the ranks to do his bidding.

"Spirit trackers?" Hannis Arc asked.

"I created more than simply one kind of soulless weapon to serve me," Sulachan said in a patronizing tone. "Some feed. Some wield powers. Some track spirits. I will send some of the latter back to the scene of the escape to pick up the essence of their spirits. They will track down and kill those with Richard Rahl. Then they will bring him back to you so that you can do what you should have done in the first place."

"I guess it is only a temporary setback." Hannis Arc met Vika's gaze. "It looks like you will soon enough get your chance to make Richard Rahl suffer. And then I will cut his throat and bleed him out at my feet."

Vika bowed her head. "Yes, Lord Arc. I look forward to the day I might redeem myself in your eyes."

He watched her for a moment, considering, weighing her words, then turned to Sulachan.

"The sooner we get there, the sooner I take the seat of power from the House of Rahl, and the sooner I rule the D'Haran Empire."

"I agree. The trackers will go after Richard Rahl for you while we will tend to more important business." Sulachan held a long-dead arm out before them in invitation. "Shall we be on our way to the People's Palace, Lord Arc? It is a long journey."

80

Ludwig Dreier tilted his head to get a better look as he pulled a handkerchief from a pocket and held it over his nose and mouth. She had lost control of her bladder, but that wasn't the worst of the stink. The smell of blood he was used to. It was the gagging stench of feces from her ruptured bowels that made his nose wrinkle and his breath come in short, reluctant pulls. It was one of the more onerous parts of his work.

He stepped over the little river of urine running across the stone floor to get a closer look. The blood ran in every direction, so he couldn't avoid stepping in that, but he wasn't bothered by blood. He had been up to his wrists in it often enough.

It was all a necessary part of his important work.

He twisted his head to the side a little more to get a better look at her face. She stared unblinking at him with the one eye that wasn't ruined.

"Has she spoken any prophecy?" he asked the Mord-Sith standing behind one of the tightly stretched chains.

"No, not yet," Erika said. "I have been keeping her near the cusp until you had time to come and see her."

Ludwig frowned, trying to make sense of the tangled form. The chain was drawn tight, stretched from where it was pinned into the stone blocks of the wall to her bleeding wrist. He finally realized how the arm was broken and twisted back around at an unusual angle, taking all the slack out of the chain, that made her look so peculiar. He was pleased to at last unravel the puzzle and understand what at first made little sense to him.

Erika had been busy, he could see. There was no doubt about it. She was gifted at what she did. But then, so was Ludwig.

He heard small sounds.

"What was that, my dear?" he asked as he bent down. She was making small sounds he couldn't understand.

He leaned closer. "I'm afraid that I can't hear you. If you want to be released from the suffering, then you are going to have to speak up so that I can understand you."

"Please," she wheezed.

"Well now, you know what we want," Ludwig said as he straightened. "We've made it clear." He gestured at the Mord-Sith. "Erika has made it clear, I'm sure. Speak up, then."

The one eye stared at him, unable to look away. "Please . . . let me die."

"Why, of course. That is why I'm here—to give you release from your agony."

It had taken time to prepare her, to bring her to this state. It was not something that could be hurried or done with haste. Ludwig had learned over his years of study that patience yielded far better results than trying to force the issue.

Slowly building the tension, terror, and pain in the end brought far better, far more insightful prophecy.

The proper, careful building of their journey toward the climax of their existence brought the exceptional visions when they looked beyond into that other, timeless world. Those were the sort he sought. Rushing the preparations simply didn't produce quality results. Torture was a game of patience.

He knew from experience, and the work that had obviously been done on her, that what information she did give before he released her into death would be some of the better-quality prophetic perception. He was culling details from the darkest depths of the netherworld. He expected great things, this time. He could feel it. He had done this enough to know when the information was going to be special, to be important, to be meaningful.

Such especially significant tellings never went to the bishop. Ludwig kept those kind to himself. This one, he knew, would never leave the confines of the abbey.

"I'll tell you what," he said down to the agonized face watching him. "I could give you a bit of assistance. I could help you bring it forth. Would you like that?"

"Yes . . . please, help me. Please help me."

"That's why I'm here," he said with a smile. "I'm here to help. Afterwards, I will grant you what you want most."

She was close, he knew she was.

When she said nothing, he gestured to the Mord-Sith. Without delay Erika pressed her Agiel into the back of the woman's skull.

She shuddered in agony. The chains rattled. Her mouth twisted as it opened. No scream could come out, no sound.

Ludwig knew from experience that she was there, that she now hung between the world of life and the world of the dead. He knew that she was at last ready.

She was now in that realm of the third kingdom.

"You see it, don't you?" he asked intimately as he ran a hand tenderly over her hair. "You see that place beyond the veil."

The woman nodded as she trembled under his steady hand.

"You will first give me prophecy from the dark place you see. As soon as you do that, I will grant your wish and release you to cross over to eternal peace. You would like to cross over, wouldn't you?"

"Yes . . ."

He could almost taste the prophecy right there, hanging within her like fresh fruit for the picking. He would have it.

The Mother Confessor had been correct when she had once told Ludwig that if he was the one who provided the prophecy that Hannis Arc needed to rule, then Hannis Arc wasn't really the one ruling. Ludwig Dreier was.

At the time he hadn't given it much thought.

But as he had thought about it, he had come to realize that she was more correct than he had at first given her credit for. He had always known that Hannis Arc was absorbed in his own work and distracted by his own goals, so he relied on the guidance of prophecy that Ludwig provided. Since that prophecy was carefully culled, it was, in reality, Ludwig's surreptitious, carefully groomed guidance. Ludwig told Hannis Arc only what Ludwig wanted him to know from beyond the veil.

What the Mother Confessor had said that day had really cast it with crystal clarity. Ludwig was the hidden hand that moved the puppet.

Hannis Arc, as powerful as he was, as talented, as clever as he was, was too insulated, too consumed with his own narrow obsessions to know how things in the wider world worked. He could not accomplish what he did without Ludwig's guidance.

Ludwig had always planned on one day seizing that rule for himself. He was, after all, the architect behind much of the power Hannis Arc wielded, so who better to rule than he. Ludwig rightly should be the one to rule.

It would require great care, though. In spite of everything else, Hannis Arc was a profoundly dangerous man. His occult abilities were not to be taken lightly.

With a gesture from Ludwig, Erika removed her Agiel from the back of the woman's head.

She was ready. It was time.

Ludwig bent close and pressed his fingers to the sides of her temples. He let the last necessary components of his own unique conjuring, conjuring he himself had created, finally flow into the woman. It would give her the last part of what she needed in order to be able to provide what he sought.

Her mouth hung open as she shook. Her one eye stared, unblinking.

He took his fingers away. She sagged.

"Speak of what you see," he said in a voice edged with anticipation.

"They come," she said in a hoarse voice.

Ludwig Dreier straightened with a frown. This was not typically how prophecy sounded, but he knew from everything that had been properly done that it somehow was prophetic.

"They come? Who comes?"

"Those with teeth," the woman said in a hoarse, raw voice. "They come to devour you."

Ludwig frowned. It was about the strangest prophecy he had ever heard. He had seen this phenomenon before. On rare occasion, rather than a distant prophecy, those he had prepared gave more of a vision of the immediate future, a telling of what they saw elsewhere in the world at that moment, of things about to take place.

"Those with teeth?"

"The unholy half dead," she whispered. "They come."

Ludwig made a face. "I don't understand."

"He does."

"He does? Who? What are you talking about? Who understands, and what exactly does he understand? You need to be more—"

"He knows what you do, Ludwig Dreier, and he

knows that you will betray him. He is with a spirit from beyond the veil, now, a spirit from the world I can now see into, a spirit who knows of your treachery. The spirit king has told Hannis Arc what you do, what you have done, of your secret betrayals, and of what you plan to do.

"Hannis Arc knows of your deceptions and the things you keep from him, the lust you have in your heart for his rule. He knows, too, that in your vanity you have come to think of yourself as Lord Dreier. He knows it all. The spirit king has told him everything.

"Most of all, the spirit king knows of your meddling in the underworld—his world.

"He and Hannis Arc have sent the Shun-tuk—the half people—to hunt the abbey for your blood, to rip your heart out. For your treachery, he sent them to eat the flesh off your bones. They come. They come."

Ludwig felt a trickle of sweat running down between his shoulder blades. He felt goose bumps on his arms, and panic swelling in his heart.

He looked up at the Mord-Sith. She looked confused, and more than worried. Seeing fear in a Mord-Sith's eyes was something that made Ludwig's heart race even faster. She was, after all, supposed to protect him.

But she knew what the Shun-tuk were. She had reason to feel fear.

He snatched up a knife from a small table to the side and pulled it deeply across the woman's throat. She struggled to breathe through the burble of blood. Her tangled and broken arms thrashed a moment and then she sagged and began to go still as blood pumped out the opening in her throat.

Erika looked up. "What do we do now?"

He licked his lips as his mind raced. "We need more

information. Better information. We need a better-quality person to stand at the cusp between worlds, a person who is more familiar with such things and would be better able to pull more informative details from beyond for us."

"The Mother Confessor?"

Ludwig Dreier nodded. "Have you started the preparations on her?"

"Yes, Abbot. I've been letting Otto, the eunuch, begin to prepare her, put her in pain. Dora has supervised the work and made sure that her agony has been properly begun. I have personally watched her struggle."

Ludwig nodded through his distracted thoughts. "We can't afford to wait any longer. Get another Mord-Sith to assist you." He looked up into Erika's blue eyes. "Come get me just as soon as you . . ." He gestured down at the twisted form at his feet, where he stood in the blood running across the floor. "As soon as you get her to the cusp."

"You mean to try to rush her to the end, then? That's dangerous. It may go too far, too fast, and then we would lose her without any results."

"It's the only way. We must hurry it along. We must try."

"Abbot," she said, an edge of urgency in her voice, "don't you think that we should leave, instead? Shouldn't we get away from here? I mean, if Lord Arc sent half people, and they are right now on their way here, we may not have that much time."

Ludwig was having trouble ordering his thoughts. He looked around, as if searching for salvation.

"Yes, yes of course you may be right. Make preparations. Have the coach prepared and standing by at the ready. Meanwhile, have one of the others begin at once on the Mother Confessor. We need to learn more. Dora. Send Dora. Her impatient nature seems fitting. Her swift cruelty may be just what is needed. Let her have her way, for once."

Erika looked skeptical but headed toward the door. "I'll send Dora immediately—and get things ready for us to leave."

She was out in the hallway for only a moment before she ran back in, her eyes wide.

"Abbot—we have to go, now."

"What? It's impossible for them to already be—"

Erika seized his arm and spun him toward the window. She pointed. "Look! Look on the far hills, there, in the distance. Do you see them? They all look the same. It's the Shun-tuk."

Ludwig stared in disbelief for a moment, then growled in anger at Hannis Arc for doing this to him. It wasn't fair.

"Have Dora get the Mother Confessor. We'll have to take her with us."

Erika grabbed his coat sleeve as he started to turn away. "I don't think we can wait that long." She pointed out the window. Whitish figures poured down over the distant hills. "They will be here soon."

He ran his hand across his throat as he glanced out the window. "You're right." He started toward the door. "But the Mother Confessor is too valuable to leave behind. Don't take the time to explain it to Dora, just tell her to get the Mother Confessor and bring her along. Tell her to hurry."

"That will still take time. Getting her unchained and down to the stables will take time. We would have to wait."

"You're right." He licked his lips. "Tell her . . . tell

her to bring the Mother Confessor to the citadel in Saavedra. You and I will start out immediately. She can meet us there."

"What if she doesn't get out of here in time?"

He angrily waved off the question. "What choice do we have? You and I have to get out of here now, while we still can. If she makes it out then she can join us."

Erika looked relieved to hear that he wasn't going to wait on them. "We're going to Saavedra, then?"

He charged out the door, Erika right behind him. "I know what Hannis Arc wants. It has always been his ambition to overthrow the House of Rahl. He has no love for Fajin Province. He has bigger plans. Now that he has set events in motion he will be headed to the People's Palace with the Shun-tuk nation to seize power. He will not go back to Saavedra anytime soon—if ever. It's the last place he would think to look for us."

"That makes sense," she said, her voice, along with the rapid strikes of their boots, echoing through the stone hall.

"There's not a moment to lose. You tell Dora to get the Mother Confessor and meet us at the citadel in Saavedra. Don't tell her anything else. I'll get the coach. Meet me there."

Together they raced down the hall. He had to get away. Later, he would figure out how to get his revenge against Hannis Arc. For now, he had to escape the fate that Hannis Arc had planned for him.

82

Kahlan thought she heard someone coming down the hall outside the windowless room where she was chained from the ceiling. It was hard to tell between the small, helpless, guttural grunts coming from deep in her throat. It took all her effort to balance on her toes in order to keep her weight off the manacles around her wrists. The wrist restraints were drawn tight by a chain running through a pulley on the ceiling and then hooked at the wall.

If she paused to take a rest from the struggle to stay up on her toes, she couldn't put her feet on the floor, so it then put all her weight on her arms. That quickly made it difficult to breathe. As she started to panic from beginning to suffocate, she would have to get up on her toes again and stay there until her legs started to tremble from the effort, and then soon enough she would begin to slip and the manacles would take up her weight. Cuts from the manacles bled down her arms.

Her shoulder sockets burned with shooting pain. She couldn't stand it anymore. But there was no way for her to bring it to an end. She thought she would go insane.

Off to the side, the fat, barefoot Otto sat gumming a hard crust of bread. He had a projecting underbite, and only two teeth that she could see, both on the bottom just left of center. Both flat, yellow teeth tipped outward and hooked over his upper lip whenever he closed his mouth. His flattened nose looked to have been broken beyond repair ages ago, making it mostly useless for breathing. Since he usually breathed through his mouth, he rarely closed it.

It was Otto's job to torment her. He would get up from time to time and use an oak rod as fat as his thumb to beat her across the back of her ribs until she slipped and lost her balance, making her weight drop into the manacles. When she eventually succumbed to tears from the agony and the hopelessness of it, he would be satisfied and go sit against the wall and gum his food, or pick at his filthy, bare feet. He seemed to have a fixation with pulling off strips of calluses.

He never spoke, and seemed to treat his job with all the enthusiasm of beating dirty rugs. He seemed satisfied when she lost control of her balance, and would go sit for a while.

When she would finally recover and bring herself under control, stop her crying, and stabilize her balance on her toes, he would then get up again, come over, and start the whole process over. Sometimes, rather than using the oak rod on her back, he would smack it across her thighs so that the stinging blows would make her weight drop.

Kahlan thought she might lose her mind before they ever got around to killing her. She felt a sense of abject hopelessness. She had no idea where Richard and the others were, and she knew that they wouldn't know where she was. She was alone with merciless people who believed that torture would get them prophecy.

She knew that, as it got increasingly worse, she would eventually want nothing so much as to die.

Which, she knew, was exactly what Ludwig Dreier was after. He believed that on the cusp of death a person could see into the eternal, timeless underworld, and give him prophecy in return for the mercy of death.

There was only so much a person could take. She expected that at some point, she, too, would end up pleading for death.

The footsteps were coming closer. The place echoed, so it was easier than it might have otherwise been to hear people coming. Otto was busy with his crust of bread, and wasn't paying attention to the footsteps. They meant little for him, anyway. Kahlan's heart sank, knowing that it was probably the Mord-Sith Dora.

The abbey was mostly stone. The rooms were cramped and filthy. It didn't look like it had ever been swept. Dirt clung to cobwebs in all the corners.

A light scattering of straw covered the floor in her room. The straw looked to have been an attempt to soak up some of the blood. It had done a poor job, but at least most of it was long dried. She expected that there would eventually be a lot more of hers all over the floor.

Kahlan was exhausted to the point of delirium from the effort of staying up on her tiptoes and so getting almost no sleep. Otto saw to it that she was kept awake on the rare occasions they lowered her to the ground for food and water. They allowed her only brief naps.

The sickness she carried deep inside wasn't helping, either. It was always there, gnawing away at her soul, it seemed.

The footsteps grew closer. By the sound of the boots, Kahlan decided that it was a Mord-Sith. She didn't know how many Mord-Sith were at the abbey, but there were more than just Erika. The only other one she knew by name was Dora, a particularly unpleasant woman of average height and above-average bad temper.

Dora was the one who came around for routine chores, like bringing Kahlan food and water. She made Otto empty the chamber pot. She wasn't pleased to be doing any of it. She apparently thought that she deserved a higher rank in life than supervising the mute Otto and feeding prisoners. She looked impatient with the whole process of the drawn-out torture.

Kahlan knew by the looks the woman gave her sometimes what she really wanted to be doing.

Kahlan felt so sick from the poisonous touch of death inside her that most of the time she felt too ill to care. That only seemed to irritate Dora all the more. She seemed to want Kahlan to tremble at the sight of her. The Mord-Sith would sometimes spin her Agiel up into her fist as she left, pointing it, telling Kahlan that she would be back. The Agiel was an implied threat of what the woman intended to do once she returned.

On a few rare occasions, when Otto had gone off for a time, she seemed to become impatiently angry with her lot in life and took out that frustration by ramming the weapon into Kahlan's middle. It left Kahlan nearly unconscious, hanging helpless, and gasping for breath.

Too weak and exhausted after Dora finished and left to get back up on her tiptoes, Kahlan would hang by her wrists for a time, unable even to cry. She could only think of how much she missed Richard, how much she wanted to be in his arms, how much she wanted to look into his gray eyes and see his smile.

When the heavy oak door squeaked in protest, Kahlan looked over from where she hung by the manacles.

As the door was pulled open, she saw that, as expected, it was Dora in black leather.

This time, Dora looked unusually distracted and rushed. Kahlan noticed that she had a key hung on her belt by a short piece of leather thong. The key looked to be the key they had used to put the manacles on her when they had brought her in.

Kahlan wondered if she was to be taken somewhere else for the serious torture. She started trembling at the thought. She was at her wits' end and she knew that it had not even really begun in earnest.

She also knew that if the woman unlocked her from the manacles, it would be her only chance to fight and try to get away.

The way Kahlan was feeling, though, and as weak as she was, she thought that she was going to have little chance of overpowering the muscular-looking Mord-Sith. Not only that, but the woman would be expecting it and likely have her Agiel pressed against Kahlan's throat in a heartbeat once Kahlan tried anything.

Still, Kahlan's heart was already pounding because she knew that this was going to be her only chance, and she was going to have to take it. If she wanted to live, to ever see Richard again, then she was going to have to fight for her life.

Dora gestured angrily at Otto. "Let her down."

Otto jumped to do as she wished. He unhooked the chain and then used his weight to hold the chain as he lowered Kahlan to the floor. He was not gentle about it, and she landed in a heap. The chain ran to an iron bolt set into the stone of the wall, so being let down from the ceiling was not enough for her to be free. The manacles had to be unlocked.

Once Otto had let Kahlan down, Dora dismissed him

with a grunt and a gesture. He bowed and left, closing the heavy door behind himself.

"Get up," Dora growled. "I'm to take you somewhere else."

"Where?" Kahlan asked without moving. She was so weak she didn't know if her trembling legs would hold her.

"You'll find out soon enough. Now, I said get up." Dora smiled in that terrible way she had. "But don't get your hopes up. I promise you, you are not going to like where I'm taking you, or what is going to happen to you there."

CHAPTER

83

As the woman came across the room toward her, Kahlan heard footsteps running at the far end of the hall. Then, in the distance, she heard a heavy thud. Dora didn't seem to notice the footsteps, but then, before she reached Kahlan, she heard the thud.

Kahlan heard people running out in the hall.

The Mord-Sith turned just as people flung open the heavy door as they burst into the room. Kahlan was astonished to see three bare-chested men with shaved heads and smeared with whitish ash charge through the doorway. Their eyes were circled with black. It was a frightening, otherworldly sight.

Dora's Agiel spun up into her fist. The three men leaped for her without pause. The first caught the Agiel in the center of his chest. He let out a clipped cry before falling dead.

The other two crashed into the Mord-Sith, taking her off her feet and to the ground right in front of Kahlan. When Dora landed hard on her back on the stone floor, it knocked the wind from her in a loud huff.

With lightning speed, one of the two men, to Kahlan's

horror, used his teeth to rip a massive piece out of Dora's throat. Blood gushed in great gouts as the man tore at her like an animal. The second bit into her face, raking his teeth over her cheek, pulling off a mouthful of flesh, gulping it down.

Dora's feet kicked weakly as her life's blood pumped out of the gaping wound. She couldn't breathe. She stared up at the ceiling in shock.

The eyes of the first man, his whitish face smeared with blood, turned up toward Kahlan, as if suddenly noticing her for the first time there on the floor.

His head lifted as he growled like a wolf seeing prey.

While the other man feasted on the still-moving Dora, tearing at her with his teeth, the man who had ripped out Dora's throat suddenly sprang over the downed Mord-Sith toward Kahlan.

She had been expecting it. With lightning speed, as he dove in on top of her, Kahlan whipped the chain around the man's neck, spinning him around in the process.

With a grunt of effort powering her muscles, she planted her boot between his shoulder blades and gave the chain a mighty yank. The chain suddenly snapping taut crushed his windpipe. He clawed at his throat as he struggled to gasp for air.

The second man, seeing what was happening, immediately jumped over Dora to attack Kahlan.

As his full weight flew toward her, Kahlan kicked him square in the face, crushing in his nose and left cheekbone. He was stopped cold, clutching both hands over the gushing wound. The blood flooding back into his throat immediately started drowning him.

He fell blindly, rolling over on his back, writhing on the floor, struggling in vain for air. Without a moment's delay Kahlan used the heel of her boot to hammer his face as hard as she could. It broke his fingers, but it also crushed in the more fragile bones in the center of his face. She used her boot twice again in quick succession, battering his face, until he went still.

The first man, still tangled in the chain, had finally suffocated and was hardly moving any longer. Kahlan panted, catching her own breath.

She could hear people racing up and down the hall, searching the other rooms. She knew that at any moment they would find her chained to the wall. She knew that if she was to have a chance, she had to get away.

She could see the key to the manacles hanging from Dora's belt. Kahlan unwound the chain from the dead man and tried, but couldn't quite reach the key with her fingers. She switched positions, throwing her legs out instead because they would have a longer reach. She stretched the chain to its full length and was able to get her boot over Dora's middle.

With all her strength, she pressed down on her foot to keep hold of the body as she struggled to drag the woman closer. She needed the key off Dora's belt or she was going to be killed and eaten while still chained to the wall.

With grunts of effort, she made jerking pulls. She kept at it until she had dragged the Mord-Sith closer. The pool of blood helped make the floor somewhat slippery and the black leather Dora wore also helped her slide a little easier in the blood. At last she had pulled the dead weight close enough to be able to snatch the key from the belt.

As she heard people running up and down the halls, and distant screams and pleas for help, or mercy, Kahlan fumbled frantically with the key, trying to get it into the manacles.

At last the iron on one wrist sprang open. Kahlan

shoved the shackle off her wrist and went to work to open the other. With one wrist free, the second was easier and she quickly got it open. She tossed the chain aside and ran to the door.

Catching her breath, she flattened herself back against the wall behind the door just as several more of the same kind of people charged through the doorway and into the room.

Like a pack of hungry scavengers, the people dove onto the body of the Mord-Sith. Some of them tore into the exposed flesh of her face and neck while others lapped at the blood. Others, unable to get in to feed, ripped open the black leather to get at her.

Kahlan, her eyes wide at the ghastly sight, quickly slipped out of the room behind them. Once out of the room, she raced down the dark hallway, not knowing where she was going. She saw Otto, or what was left of him, down a side hall with at least a dozen of the whitewashed savages growling and tearing at him with their teeth. She realized that the thud she had heard at first was probably the attackers taking Otto down.

When she heard someone in the distance, and saw shapes coming around the corner, Kahlan quickly ducked down a stairwell. She bounded down the stairs three at a time and then raced down the dark hall at the bottom. She didn't know how many bloodthirsty monsters were after her, or how close they might be. She ran for her life without looking back.

She could hear the noise of other terrified people running. Racing past rooms, she looked through one open door and saw a number of the whitish figures piled on several servants lying dead on the floor, tearing at them with their teeth or lapping up the blood. She thought that the underworld itself must have opened up and the dead were feasting on the living.

As she raced down the hall, she heard someone coming from the other end. As they rounded a corner, she saw that they were more of the cannibals. When they saw her, they broke into a dead run toward her.

Kahlan ducked into a room to the side. She slammed shut the door but there was no bolt.

Fortunately, there was no one inside. She stood with her back against the door, panting to get her breath. There was a small fire going in the fireplace.

Bodies crashed against the other side of the door. She used all her weight and strength and managed to hold it shut each time an attacker rammed into it. As she looked around, she spotted a sword on a table.

After the next time they thudded into the door, she let go and raced for the table. Behind her, the door crashed open.

Kahlan drew the sword as she turned, flinging the scabbard aside. Without an instant's pause, she swung, nearly decapitating the first man to rush at her. She spun out of the way of the next man and as she came back around she thrust the blade through his heart from behind.

Kahlan had grown up learning how to use a sword, but it wasn't until Richard had given her lessons that she really became an expert with the weapon.

Now, with a weapon in her hands, she felt that she at least had a fighting chance. She used all her skill and knowledge to desperately slash, hack, and stab the onslaught of attackers and defend herself. It wasn't as hard as it might have been, because the men all rushing in at her were not armed, and they weren't trying to fight back. They only seemed to want to bite her, so the only weapon they used was their teeth.

Still, there were too many of them. More were rushing into the room all the time. As they raced into the room, some fell over the bodies on the floor. Kahlan stabbed them as fast as she could.

Between frantic slashes and stabs, she glanced over her shoulder at the window. The room was on the ground floor.

Right after a particularly frenzied, hacking attack to drive the men back, when she had a brief opening before they piled in at her again, she turned and raced across the room.

She dove feet-first through the window. Fortunately, the two side-hinged halves of the window flew open rather than the glass breaking and slashing her. She landed hard and rolled across the ground.

As she sprang to her feet she saw the ashen people pouring like a flood out through the window. Others prowling the grounds outside saw her come out of the building and joined in the pursuit. There was no way she could fight them all.

Kahlan turned and ran. The enemy was right on her heels.

Rounding the corner of a vine-covered stone out-building at full speed, branches of shrubs flashing past her face, slapping her arms, the savages right behind her, Kahlan ran headlong into a wall of a man.

It was Richard.

In that first fraction of an instant, that infinitesimal spark of time, her thought was that she had to be mistaken. It was impossible for it to be Richard. She thought she must be dead and this was some afterlife delusion. In that spark of time, she was heartbroken and crushed because she thought that she had to be wrong.

In the second infinitesimal spark of time, she knew that it was real. As impossible as it was, it was real.

Richard had his sword out. She could see the magic of its rage in his gray eyes.

Without pause, as Kahlan crashed into him, he smoothly circled a powerful arm around her waist, lifted her around behind him, set her down, and as he turned back, beheaded the first man to run in toward him.

The moment of seeing him, of realizing that it was really him, seemed frozen in time to her.

None of it made any sense. The whole world didn't seem to make sense. Being attacked by savage cannibals didn't make any sense. But then in that fraction of a second, that spark of time, they shared a look and she knew that nothing else mattered.

Richard was there.

The rest of the horde descended in on him before the severed head had hit the ground.

And then the killing began in earnest.

Kahlan knew enough to stay out of the way of his blade when he had it out. She turned and cut down one of the pale savages to the side—a woman. As the half-naked people with the black-painted eyes rushed in at her, she drove her sword through some of them, and as she drew it back, slashed others.

As Kahlan struck, thrusting her blade through a man, Cara threw an arm around Kahlan's waist and pulled her back out of the way of the rushing men. The Mord-Sith, with a knife in each hand, turned back to the savages and used both her blades whenever one of the ashen figures got close enough. Against their skin smeared with chalky coloring, blood looked all the more shocking.

It had seemed forever since she ran into Richard, but Kahlan knew that it actually had only been mere seconds. Suddenly, within those seconds, men of the First File flooded in all around Kahlan, shielding her, protecting her from the onslaught of the attackers smeared with white. Cara pressed in close beside her as well, protecting her from any of the strange brutes.

And then, in the next second, the ground shook with the thunderous roar of wizard's fire. She saw a fierce inferno splash down across the hillside, the liquid fire spilling out over dozens of the chalky figures, turning them to black ash amid the blinding white-orange blaze.

At the same time, a dozen men of the First File, led by Nicci, charged into the stone building, going after the cannibals still inside. The abbey was three stories tall, and from what Kahlan had seen when she was in there, the place was filled with attackers. She could hear the sounds of the battle that raged beyond the stone walls.

Those idyllic-looking walls, set in among oak trees and covered with vines, looked ancient. Had Kahlan not known what the place was, or what went on there at the hands of Ludwig Dreier and his Mord-Sith, she might have thought it a picturesque place.

As it was, it was anything but. It was a slaughter-house.

Thumps of impacts came from inside the abbey as the half-naked, painted men were hunted down, while outside, out in the open, the attackers coming for Rich-ard and other men met lethal steel, and Zedd cast a deadly inferno of wizard's fire across the hillside, incin-erating the strange figures as they continued to charge in, oblivious of the danger.

And then, almost as soon as it began, the attack seemed to be over. There were no more of the ashen figures stand-ing. Their bodies lay everywhere, bloody, with terrible, gaping wounds, and missing limbs or heads.

Richard, panting from the fierce effort, sword drip-ping in blood and gripped tightly in his right fist, swept his free arm around Kahlan, pulling her in close to him, laying his head over the top of hers in silent, wordless gratitude at having her with him and safe.

She couldn't remember ever feeling such a sense of relief. Only now that it was over, only after she was done fighting for her life, done running for her life, did she feel her hands begin to shake.

It was over. Relief washed through her. She was safe. Richard was safe.

Zedd rushed in as she started sinking toward the ground. Richard helped ease her down. Although she tried giving him a smile, Zedd wasn't interested in returning it. He instead pressed his fingers to her forehead. She knew what he was checking. She could feel the tingle of gift flowing into her.

A black-haired girl ran up and leaned in beside Zedd, looking down at her. "Mother Confessor! You're safe! We were so afraid. We raced here as fast as we could when Henrik told us who took you. We were so afraid that we wouldn't get here in time."

Kahlan, her mind humming with the tingling sensation of the magic Zedd used to infuse her with strength, found herself feeling better. She sat up and puzzled at the slender young woman. "Do I know you?"

She beamed with pride. Her mass of black hair jiggled up and down as she nodded.

"I'm Samantha. I'm the one who healed you, before, back at our village."

Kahlan, feeling stronger, with Richard's hand helping, was finally able to stand. She remembered the village where she woke, but wasn't in the mood to ask a lot of questions. She instead basked in the relief of having Richard's arm around her.

"Thank you, Samantha," Kahlan said.

"I'm sorry I couldn't take the Hedge Maid's poison out of you. I can't cure death."

Kahlan supposed not.

She saw Nicci rush out of the door to the abbey. When she saw where they were, Nicci raced up the side of the hill. With a sigh of relief the sorceress at last took up one of Kahlan's hands, clutching it in both of hers for a moment.

"Dear spirits," she said with genuine relief, "I didn't think we would make it here in time."

Kahlan glanced up at Richard. "You did. But the next time, I'd appreciate it if you didn't cut it so close."

Richard smiled. Even with the sword still in his hand, he smiled.

"I'll keep that in mind," he said.

She had forgotten how his smile touched her soul, and his voice lifted her heart.

CHAPTER

85

Kahlan gestured around at all the ashen figures of the dead sprawled across the hillside. "What is all this?"

"A long story," Richard said.

"Right now we need to get you both back to the People's Palace," Zedd told her.

Kahlan knew by the looks on all the faces around her that something was going on. "Is there a problem?"

"I'm afraid there is," Richard said. "We both have been touched with death from the Hedge Maid. We are infected with the poison of that touch."

Kahlan blinked. She remembered some of being Jit's prisoner, of being tangled helplessly in the web of thorn vines, of having those awful creatures dancing around and bleeding her. But she didn't remember all that had happened. She had lost consciousness and as she faded away, so too did her memory of those terrible events.

Apparently, she didn't recall some of the worst of it. "We were touched with death?"

"I'm afraid so," Nicci said. "Richard too. At least

before it happened, he was able to block it enough that it didn't kill you right then and there."

"You mean, you think it still might?" Kahlan asked.

"We can cure you both of it," Zedd assured her when he saw the look on her face. "But not here."

"You need to know the truth of how serious it still is," Nicci said with brutal honesty. "You both carry death within you. You need to know that if we don't get death's touch out of you, you both will die. We can do that, but only in a containment field."

"The Garden of Life," Kahlan suggested.

Zedd and Nicci both smiled as they nodded.

Kahlan was relieved that at least they had a solution. She could see why they were eager to get back to the palace. Now, she was eager as well.

"Lord Rahl," one of the men of the First File called out as he ran up to them. "There are stables here." He pointed off to a building beyond the shade of some oaks. "It looks like a few of the horses are gone, but there are still others, and there is a carriage as well."

Zedd heaved a sigh of relief. "Good. That will help get us back quicker—and save their strength. We need to leave at once."

"Did you find the abbot?" Richard asked Nicci.

She shook her head. "It looks like he's gone. I would guess that he's been gone for a while, now."

"He's probably the one who took the horses," the soldier said.

Richard's jaw clenched. "We need to go after him."

"No, we don't need to go after him," Nicci said in the kind of voice that prevented even Richard from thinking about arguing. She swept a finger around at everyone there. "And neither do any of these men. I want them all with us. I want as much protection as possible."

"I agree," Cara said. "They all stay with us."

Kahlan sensed something else was wrong. Despite their having just won a battle, there was a shadow of something over the assembled group. Kahlan didn't know what it could be. She thought Cara's voice, especially, sounded a bit somber.

Nicci nodded her agreement. "You know what happened the last time we were attacked. We had more men, then, and we were still overrun and taken captive. We can't let that happen again. Being in the hands of those half people once was one too many times."

"Half people?" Kahlan said.

Everyone ignored the question.

"It's more important to get you both back to the palace right away," Zedd said, more diplomatically. "Kahlan's life is more important than going after Abbot Dreier."

Kahlan could still read the concern in Zedd's voice. At the mention of the importance of Kahlan's well-being, she could see the tension go out of Richard's muscles as he let his anger over Ludwig Dreier go. Up until that point, he had been in a fighting mood.

"You're right," he said, his voice considerably quieter. "We'll have to deal with Abbot Dreier, Hannis Arc, and the spirit king later, after Kahlan and I are healed."

"Spirit king?" Kahlan asked.

"Long story for later," he said, not looking at her.

In his voice, she could sense the same deadly weight of the poison that she felt in herself. She knew that Zedd and Nicci weren't being extra cautious. She knew that the situation was serious, and they needed to get back to the palace right away.

"You can get this out of us, right?" she asked as she looked back and forth between Zedd and Nicci. "The truth."

"The truth?" Nicci asked. "I think so."

"But you aren't sure," Kahlan said as she tipped her head toward the sorceress.

Nicci smiled, brightening her beautiful face just a bit, although not as much as Kahlan would have liked. "I believe we can, Kahlan. That's the truth. But we need to get you to the Garden of Life if we are to have a chance. Such magic as this requires can only be done in a containment field."

Kahlan didn't like the sound of that, but she was glad that she and Richard were in the hands of the best. There was no one other than Zedd and Nicci she would rather have healing them.

Richard sighed. "I suppose the omen machine will be pleased to have me back and I'm sure it will have a lot to say about all this," he said half to himself as he finally sheathed his sword. "It did, after all, give me the key to saving Kahlan from the Hedge Maid, so it seems like it knows something about what's going on. I need to find out what it knows." He let out another sigh. "At least, before I have to end prophecy."

Zedd leaned in, his bushy white eyebrows drawing together. "End prophecy? What are you talking about, my boy?"

Richard waved dismissively. As he did, Kahlan saw a ring on his right hand that she had never seen before. "Long story for later," he told his grandfather.

The mysterious ring had a Grace on it.

"Richard," she said, reaching out and running a finger over the ancient symbol on the ring, "where did this come from?"

Richard gave her the oddest look. "From a distant ancestor of yours."

"What are you talking about?"

He waved off the question. "Part of the long story for later."

"If I survive this touch of death and live long enough. If I can even be cured of it."

Nicci laid a hand on Kahlan's arm and smiled warmly. "I didn't mean to frighten you. It's serious, and I don't want to fool you and say it's not, but I'm confident that I can take care of it. You will both be fine."

Kahlan nodded, feeling a bit better, but still sensing the odd mood.

"All right," Richard said. "We need to see to that cure." He turned to the soldiers. "Get the horses ready and let's head back to the palace."

"Won't be too soon for me," one of them said. "I've had enough of the Dark Lands to last me a lifetime."

"I'd have to agree with that," Richard said as they started for the stables.

"We'll be home before you know it," Zedd said with a reassuring smile back over his shoulder as he stepped out to lead the way for Richard and Kahlan. Kahlan thought the smile looked forced.

"Richard," Kahlan whispered as she leaned close to him, "what's wrong with Cara? She looks . . . I don't know. She doesn't look right. Something is wrong. What is it?" She glanced around at the soldiers of the First File. "And where's Ben? Shouldn't he be here?"

Richard's face paled. "We lost Ben."

Kahlan felt like the ground fell out from under her. She suddenly understood the uneasy, unspoken feeling she was picking up from everyone.

"What?"

Gaze downcast, Richard swallowed. "I tried . . . we all tried. We couldn't . . ."

A lump rising in her throat, Kahlan turned and ran to Cara, taking hold of her arms to stop the woman. "Cara . . ."

Looking into those blue eyes, Kahlan couldn't speak past that lump in her throat.

Cara nodded knowingly, her lip trembling just a little. She put her hand on the back of Kahlan's head and pulled it against her shoulder.

"He gave his life to protect us," Cara said. "It was what he would have wanted. I'm proud of him."

"Me too," Kahlan said through her tears. "Dear spirits, please protect him, now."

Richard, off by himself, leaned back against the coarse face of a small outcropping of granite ledge, watching the small campfire in the distance. He could make out the shapes of the sleeping men. The light from the fire reflected up on a short, protective wall of rock nearby and up against the bottoms of the broad limbs of pines towering all around them. The smell of the fire's smoke and the popping of the wood as it burned were comfortingly familiar—even if these woods, and this dark land, weren't.

The moon was hidden behind a thick overcast, but at least it had stopped raining. The cloud cover, though, made it the darkest of nights. Such nights were always disquieting. They always made him feel like he was being watched from the darkness.

Richard was standing watch. Everyone, of course, had objected.

He had overruled them. He wanted to be alone.

Richard was relieved to be headed back to the People's Palace at last, to say nothing of having Kahlan and most of his friends safe. He didn't know what they were going to do about the spirit king that Hannis Arc had called back from the world of the dead. He didn't know what they were going to do about the barrier to the third kingdom being down and all the half people and walking dead being loose. He didn't know what Hannis Arc was up to, either, but he knew it couldn't be anything good.

And he certainly didn't know how he was supposed to end prophecy.

Maybe the omen machine, buried for millennia under the Garden of Life, would have an answer to that question. An odd thought, that. A machine devoted to prophecy maybe being able to tell him how to end its purpose for existing.

Something told him, though, that Regula—as the omen machine was called—held the key to everything. As did his discovery of the message left for him, for *fuer grissa ost drauka*, back in the caves of Stroyza.

It was all too much to be a coincidence.

He supposed that after they got back, and Nicci and Zedd were finally able to heal him and Kahlan, he would have a chance to figure it out. He knew that in order to do that he would need to find the rest of the book *Regula*, the book about the omen machine that had long ago been hidden in the Temple of the Winds—hidden there back in the great war, in the time of Magda Searus and Wizard Merritt. Back when the barrier to the third kingdom had been built.

Magda and Merritt had left him a ring to remind him of what was at stake. In the back of his mind, he couldn't stop thinking about their message to him.

One problem at a time, he told himself with a sigh, *one problem at a time. Don't think of the problem, think of the solution,* Zedd would say.

He reminded himself to think of the positives, of all that he had gained.

They had Kahlan back and she was safe. He had managed to get Zedd and Nicci and most of the soldiers out of a prison guarded by the underworld itself. He supposed he had already gotten farther, and done more, than he would ever have thought he would be able to.

He would just have to confront the rest of the problems in due course. Now that they were back together, he would have Zedd and Nicci to help, and at the palace there would be others with vast experience, such as Nathan, the prophet.

Richard spotted Cara walking toward him in the near darkness. He stayed where he was leaning against the rock, watching her come.

She finally slowed to a stop in front of him.

"Lord Rahl, may I speak with you?"

"Of course you can, Cara. You know that."

She nodded, not wanting to meet his gaze.

"Lord Rahl, I have come to ask something of you."

He shrugged. "What would you like?"

Her head finally came up. She looked into his eyes. "I would like to have my freedom."

Richard blinked. "Your freedom?"

"That's right. I have served you honorably. Now, in return for my service, I ask that you grant me my freedom."

"Cara, I can't do that."

She lifted her chin. "May I ask why not?"

"Because I don't own you. You are already free. I've always told you that you and the rest of the Mord-Sith stay with me by your own choice. You are all free to walk away at any time. That's what we fought the war about. I have no hold over you but your desire to stay."

She nodded with a brave look. "I know. But I am still Mord-Sith. As Mord-Sith, I ask to be released. I ask you to grant my request, grant me my freedom."

Richard watched her eyes for a very long time. He had to wait until he was sure his voice would not fail him.

"Granted."

She nodded sadly and turned to leave, but stopped then and turned back. "And may I keep my Agiel? I would like to have it so that I may know when you have been healed and your gift is back. If I have the Agiel with me, then when I feel its power return, I will know that you are well again."

"Of course." He gestured vaguely, his heartache making it difficult to speak. "Cara, I'm so sorry about Ben."

She nodded her appreciation. "They may have been trying to take his soul, but they in fact stole mine."

Richard wanted to do the impossible and make it right for her. Nothing could have made him sadder than knowing that there was no way he could.

"I wish you would stay with Kahlan and me. We care about you. We love you."

She thought a moment. "I know you do. I will miss you both."

"Where are you going?"

"I need to do some killing."

Richard had thought as much. He had a thousand arguments. He showed his profound respect for her by not putting words to any of them.

"I understand."

She swallowed. "Thank you, Lord Rahl."

Again, when she turned to leave, he called her name.

"Cara, please, would you let me hold you for just a moment before I let you go?"

She at last smiled as she returned and slipped her arms around him, and he around her, as she laid her head against his chest. He tenderly put his hand to the back of her head and held her, wishing there were words, but there were none.

When she finally separated from him, Kahlan was standing there. Without saying anything, Kahlan took Cara into her arms, hugging her silently for a long moment.

"He was a dear, dear man, Cara, and he will be greatly missed," Kahlan whispered in a broken voice when they separated.

"Thank you, Mother Confessor." She took a hand of each, then. "You both have been the greatest thing in my life, other than my brass buttons . . . Ben. I love you both."

She released their hands and wiped the tears from her eyes, then wiped her palms on her hips. "It will be light soon. Get an early start. I want both of you to get back to the palace so you can be healed." She smiled. "Maybe I will see you again. You never know."

"Your home is with us," Richard said. "It will always be waiting for you."

"Thank you," she said with a nod, and turned away.

Kahlan leaned against Richard as they watched her walk away.

"I love her too much to keep her from leaving," Richard whispered, half to Kahlan and half to himself, his heart breaking as he watched her melting into the night.

There were a thousand things he wanted to say to Cara. He loved her too much to say any of them.

"I know," Kahlan said, choked with tears. "Me too. Do you think she'll be back?"

"Anything is possible," Richard said as he put his arm around Kahlan's shoulders.

"Do you think she'll be safe by herself?"

Richard had seen that Cara had a steel knife on one

hip and the Shun-tuk stone knife for putting down the dead on the other.

"Oh, I don't think Cara is the one who needs to be worried."

Richard sighed and gazed down at Kahlan.

"Well, it's going to be light soon. I think we should get all of our gear collected, the horses saddled, and be on our way. The sooner we get to the palace, the sooner Zedd and Nicci will be done meddling with us."

He saw a smile overcome her in spite of herself.

"I would have to agree with that, Lord Rahl." She hugged him then. "It will be good to get home."

"Cara will come home, too. I know she will."

Her beautiful green eyes turned to look up at him. "Promise?"

Richard could only smile in answer.

TOR

Award-winning authors
Compelling stories

Please join us at the website
below for more information
about this author and other great
Tor selections, and to sign up for
our monthly newsletter!

HOMICIDE
IN THE HOUSE

Previously published Worldwide Mystery title by
COLLEEN J. SHOGAN

STABBING IN THE SENATE

HOMICIDE
IN THE HOUSE

COLLEEN J. SHOGAN

W❂RLDWIDE.

TORONTO • NEW YORK • LONDON
AMSTERDAM • PARIS • SYDNEY • HAMBURG
STOCKHOLM • ATHENS • TOKYO • MILAN
MADRID • WARSAW • BUDAPEST • AUCKLAND

Recycling programs
for this product may
not exist in your area.

Homicide in the House

A Worldwide Mystery/August 2018

First published by Camel Press, an imprint of Epicenter Press, Inc.

ISBN-13: 978-1-335-50670-2

Printed in U.S.A.

ACKNOWLEDGMENTS

After lumbering about the deserted Madison Building at the Library of Congress for three weeks during the fall of 2013, I decided the sequel to *Stabbing in the Senate* would take place during a government shutdown. Capitol Hill assumed an unsettled eeriness during the closure. Hallways were quiet, restrooms shuttered, and all public events were canceled. A high degree of political tension layered on top of the gloomy and desolate setting provided a perfect backdrop for the second book in the Washington Whodunit series.

Thank you to my agent Dawn Dowdle and the talented publishing and editorial staff at Camel Press, Catherine Treadgold and Jennifer McCord. My social media "fans" read excerpts of this book on Facebook and provided helpful feedback, particularly when I described familiar scenes in the House of Representatives. While working on the plot, I shared several twists and turns with my colleagues at the Library of Congress, who were always willing to listen enthusiastically and patiently. Thank you to several House of Representatives employees who provided key pieces of information about congressional operations. Your input made this book possible.

Finally, without the support of my family, particularly my husband, I would have never been able to finish another mystery novel while balancing the demands of everyday life. Capitol Hill provides a great backdrop

ONE

THE DIGITAL CLOCK blinked an irritating red, glaring "11:59" in block numerals. The wait was nearly over. Every television news station had displayed the number of days, hours, minutes, and seconds remaining until the inevitable federal government shutdown. We'd peered over the cliff, and apparently, it was time to jump.

"Kit, did you approve my quote for the press release?" The high-pitched voice of my boss, Representative Maeve Dixon from the great Southern state of North Carolina, jolted me out of my brief reverie. The clock now radiated "12:01." Armageddon had officially arrived.

"Yes, Maeve. I approved your comment a few hours ago. I like the part about you standing with the people of North Carolina against the politicians who caused this mess. It's always good to run against Washington." I mustered a small smile and added, "Especially when it's shuttered."

"I can't imagine the quote will put me in good stead with my fellow colleagues in Congress, but what choice do I have?"

Representative Dixon, who insisted I call her Maeve, was right. She had been elected to the House by the narrowest of margins a little over a year ago, and it being February, she'd face reelection in nine months. Homespun constituents closely monitored her political posturing. On the other hand, the leadership of her party in Congress would also look to Maeve, who was young and energetic, to carry the day when the politics surrounding the shutdown ripened on the airwaves and Twitter-sphere. We were heading into uncharted waters. Maeve was a middle-of-the-road Democrat new to Congress and I had never dealt with such a monumental catastrophe. But as her legislative director, it was my job to know everything about the ensuing crisis.

A cacophony of telephone rings resembling a bad handbell choir served as background music. It was all hands on deck in the Dixon office. We'd been barraged with calls from constituents for several hours now, with questions ranging from Maeve's position on the shutdown to whether they could still visit the Smithsonian next week during February's Presidents' Day holiday. The negative answer to the latter question was usually met with a litany of loud expletives, routinely resulting in our interns holding the telephone receivers at least six inches from their ears.

"Kit, I asked you a question. Do I have any other options?"

I looked directly at Maeve, whose long brown hair had been drawn into a hastily assembled late-night bun. Her athletic body assumed a slumped posture, no doubt the result from tiresome workdays with no recent opportunities to relieve stress at the gym. I thought her earlier question was rhetorical, but I should have known better. Maeve was literal and straightforward. She'd completed military tours of duty in both Iraq and Afghanistan. If she asked a question, she expected a direct answer.

"Not right now, ma'am. We should move forward

with the plan we discussed. Let's not deviate until we know how long this shutdown might last."

When it became clear that Congress might not come to a resolution on the federal budget before funding ran out, Maeve and I had devised a plan for how she'd handle the crisis. She needed to walk a fine line. Our party was pushing a spending bottom line that was too high. On the other hand, the Republicans wanted to cut every social program known to mankind. Maeve couldn't stand wholeheartedly behind her party's leadership because it would kill her with the more conservative constituents in her congressional district. But if she spoke too loudly against mainstream Democrats, they would make her pay when the crisis was over.

Keeping her head down wasn't an option, either. As she'd told me many times, she'd done enough of that during her military service. For her, being labeled a backbencher for the rest of her congressional career was tantamount to a political death sentence.

Behind me, a deep voice said, "I agree with Kit. Let's stay the course." I turned around to face my immediate supervisor, Dan, the chief of staff. A few years younger than me, Dan was a nice guy who meant well. Unfortunately, the kind words ended there. He came to Washington with Maeve and knew her congressional district like the back of his hand. But he understood almost nothing about policy and Congress. It was a constant battle to educate him about how politicians operated and the distinct culture of Capitol Hill. I was a newbie to the House of Representatives, but at least I knew how a bill became a law. Dan struggled with the most basic *Schoolhouse Rock* version of events.

Dan looked as if his brain had been wiped clean. His

eyes were round with panic. He hadn't bargained for a government shutdown when he left North Carolina for Washington. He moved closer so that Maeve couldn't hear his whispered question.

"What should we do next?"

"Dan, doesn't it make sense to issue the press release?" I used my regular speaking voice. Maeve should know her top aide had no clue about handling a political crisis.

"Right. I'll make sure that gets done."

He sped down the hallway toward his small private office. I hoped he knew how to email the release to our important press contacts, but I had my doubts. Yesterday, I overheard him ask his iPhone, "Siri, what is a government shutdown?" I pretended I hadn't overheard. Ignorance is bliss, especially in Washington D.C.

All staffers in the Dixon office were working tonight, but tomorrow would be an entirely different story. A government shutdown meant no money was available to keep government programs or buildings operational. That included paying government employees. Each member of Congress had to determine how to keep his or her office functional during the shutdown. Maeve decided that Dan and I would report for work. Everyone else would remain at home unless absolutely needed. Despite the winter darkness, that meant long workdays were ahead, unless Congress resolved the dispute over government funding levels quickly. With deeply entrenched views on both sides of the aisle, it was unlikely that this fiasco would be short-lived.

My desk phone buzzed. Recognizing my live-in boyfriend's cell number, I answered it.

"You're still at work?"

"Good evening to you, Doug. Happy government shutdown."

"Sorry," he muttered. "I wanted to check because I'm headed to bed soon. Are you going to stay there all night?"

"No, I'm going to leave as soon as Maeve decides to call it a day. I'll see you soon."

"Okay, great. Bye." A click was followed by a dial tone.

The conversation with Doug was par for the course—lately, at least. I'd been at my job with Maeve for six months now. Working for a newly elected freshman member of Congress had proven more time consuming than my previous position with elder statesman Senator Lyndon Langsford. After my former boss's murder, which I helped the police solve, I interviewed for numerous jobs in Congress. My best friend Meg had accepted a job working in the House of Representatives. When the opportunity to work as a senior legislative staffer for Maeve presented itself, I eagerly applied.

I'd anticipated a steep learning curve. After all, the House and the Senate function as separate political institutions with totally disparate traditions and norms. What I had not anticipated was how much work it was to staff a member of Congress who was just starting her political career rather than approaching the end of it. As a military veteran with no track record, she had to consider every vote she made and position she took with the utmost care. Her constituents in North Carolina were watching her every move. She represented a "swing district," which meant her seat frequently changed hands between the two political parties due to the evenly divided voting electorate who resided there. Doug hadn't quite adjusted to my new 24/7 responsibilities. He was a history professor at Georgetown, and between my work and his attempt to finish yet another book, our recent time together had been limited to hastily shared late-night dinners or abbreviated, stilted phone calls.

His increasing detachment should have been causing me considerable concern, but this wasn't the time to focus on it. I glanced at my email inbox. The messages were already piling up. There were several from top staff in the Speaker's office. Maeve couldn't ignore those emails. Not only was the Speaker the leader of the entire House, he was also her party's head honcho. An almost equal number of emails came from the Minority Leader's entourage across the aisle, who knew that Maeve had tough decisions ahead, pitting her district's beliefs against her partisan loyalties. The game was on. Both parties wanted a piece of Maeve Dixon during the shutdown.

An email from Meg popped up. Ignoring the rest of my inbox, I eagerly clicked on it. Meg's new position as an investigator for a House committee focused on oversight had been time-consuming, as well. Our days of carefree happy hours had dwindled. We were lucky if we found time to share frozen yogurt in the House cafeteria.

Can you believe this is happening??? she wrote. Are you excepted? If so, let's try to meet for lunch. :) Meg

"Excepted" was slang for an "excepted federal employee." That meant that even though the government had no money to pay salaries, you still had to report for work.

My spirits lifted after reading Meg's email. At least

I wouldn't have to suffer through this mess alone. I hit reply.

I'll be here. See you at Tortilla Coast at noon. I suggested her favorite restaurant near the House office buildings. Some things never changed. Though you wouldn't know it from looking at her, Meg still had an appetite to match her ambition.

It was nearly one o'clock in the morning, and thankfully the phones had quieted. I clicked off my computer and walked toward Maeve's office. As I approached the open door, I was struck by how loudly she was speaking.

Dan was standing next to my boss, who was seated at her desk with the phone at her ear. He was sweating profusely, and when he saw me, he grabbed a tissue and blotted at his forehead and cheeks. Maeve was having an argument. Only one hour into the shutdown and the shenanigans were in full swing.

"You know the shutdown puts me in a difficult position," she yelled. "The Speaker understands that. He told me yesterday he'd rather have me in Congress next year than count on my solidarity with the party."

Who was on the other end of the line? Maybe the Majority Leader of the House, the Speaker's second-in-command? Or the Democratic party whip, who had the unenviable job of trying to make sure everyone on our side of the aisle stuck together on the problematic floor votes ahead?

I mouthed silently to Dan, "Who is it?"

He shook his head. *No idea.* Why was I surprised?

I grabbed a blank Post-it note from Maeve's desk and wrote: *Who's on the line?*

Whoever it was, his voice was getting louder. Maeve

held the receiver away from her ear to avoid being deafened. She punched the "mute" button on the phone and covered the receiver with her hand, just in case.

"Jack Drysdale."

That explained why Maeve was getting an earful. Drysdale was the Speaker's top aide and Washington politico extraordinaire. Just shy of fifty, he'd been working on the Hill for two decades and had finally ascended to the most powerful staff position in the House of Representatives. I knew him only by reputation. Even senior legislative staffers like myself were never in the same room as him. He was the Speaker's eyes and ears, and when he didn't like what he was seeing and hearing, he made your life a living hell.

Jack must have come up for air, because it was now Maeve's turn to get a word in edgewise. "I can't give you my answer now. I told the Speaker I need to take the temperature in my district. Like I said earlier, my chief of staff will be in direct contact with our North Carolina office. After he gives me a report, I'll be in a better position to tell you what's possible."

Drysdale must have said something that upset Maeve, because she frowned and then promptly gave the middle finger to the phone receiver.

"If you don't want to deal with Dan, then you can communicate with my legislative director, Kit Marshall." A brief pause as she listened to his response.

"Yes, that's Kit Marshall. She can run point for me on the policy decisions related to the shutdown. Touch base with her tomorrow and we'll go from there." She slammed the phone down with no pretense of a polite farewell.

Maeve pressed her fingertips to her forehead to forestall the inevitable headache. "That man is insufferable. I don't understand how the Speaker of the House stands him."

Dan shifted his weight from one foot to the other nervously. "Did he say something about me?"

Maeve grabbed a bottle of water on her desk and chugged several gulps. "He doesn't want to deal with you on the specifics of the shutdown."

I was embarrassed for Dan, who fiddled with his glasses and said, "Did he say why?"

Maeve looked directly at Dan before answering. Was she going to try to soften the blow? I held my breath, praying that she wouldn't make an awkward situation worse.

In her infinite wisdom, my boss must have decided to take the high road. "He knows you're going to be spending all your time on the phone with our district director and the press in North Carolina to figure out the political thinking there. That's why I told him to communicate with Kit on the details of the Speaker's proposal to end this mess."

I exhaled in relief. I doubted that Drysdale had been so diplomatic. Dan's reputation as a lightweight was well known. Maeve's ability to think on her feet and bend the truth was impressive, especially for a novice politician.

She sat down at her desk. "I can't think straight. Let's call it a night and come back fresh in the morning."

I glanced at my watch. It was 1:30. How fresh would I be after four hours of sleep? I'd have to take what I could get until Congress solved this mess.

After gathering my belongings, I took the elevator to the ground floor and walked mechanically to the south-east exit, which was closest to the Capitol South Metro station. The busy station entrance was quiet, with no one entering or leaving. Then it dawned on me that it was well after midnight and I had missed the last train. I pressed the Uber app on my iPhone, and in three minutes, my own personal taxi was on the way.

While I waited for my ride, I walked west on C Street so I could catch a glimpse of the Capitol at night between the Cannon and Longworth House Office Buildings. New Jersey Avenue provided the perfect view. The February night was cold and clear. The Capitol's iron dome stared back at me peacefully, but the tranquil silence was deceiving. Starting tomorrow, a battle would ensue within those walls. Instinct told me some unlucky politicos wouldn't survive the fight. As I climbed into my cab, I had no idea how accurate my premonition would turn out to be.

TWO

THE SNOOZE ALARM on my iPhone had already gone off twice. It was time to face the music. I silenced my favorite wake-up song, "Rainbow Connection," and threw the covers aside. According to Kermit, rainbows had nothing to hide. The same thing couldn't be said of angry politicians fighting over the federal budget.

As soon as I got out of the bed, our overweight beagle-mix rescue mutt jumped up and took my place. As a history professor, Doug usually slept later than me. Clarence might think Doug couldn't tell the difference between his two bedmates, or maybe the dog just liked curling up in a pre-warmed location. Either way, once I vacated the bed, my spot was taken.

After making myself a venti-sized latte in our complicated high-end espresso machine, I took a shower and dressed quickly. With no time to wash it, I had to wet and blow-dry my shoulder-length straight dark hair to make it behave. I was even paler than usual due to lack of sleep, and my normally plump cheeks looked almost gaunt. As someone who was always gaining and losing the same five pounds, I hoped that meant I'd lost some weight.

It was already half past seven. Not good. No doubt many congressional staff had never gone to bed, and others had already descended upon Capitol Hill. I clicked on the television in the living room to assess the damage.

While listening to the cable news reports, I began scrolling through the messages on my iPhone. Many staffers had worked through the night. Emails had arrived at all hours and were piling up. Numerous bright blue dots next to the unread messages stared at me in a long, vertical column. After determining who sent the emails, I knew there would be no swiping and deleting. These missives had come from important Capitol Hill staffers and could not be answered without careful consideration.

Doug stirred inside the bedroom. I'd had no time to walk Clarence this morning, so hopefully he was getting motivated to take him outside.

"Hey," I called out, "every channel is talking about the government shutdown. I need to head into work right now."

Doug flipped over onto his back and ran his fingers through his messy, thick brown hair. Blindly he reached for his glasses, sitting on the nightstand. He put them on and yawned loudly.

"What did you just say? I'm just waking up."

I sighed. I didn't have time for a long conversation. "The government is shuttered. I'm heading to the office because I'm running point for my boss."

"Well, good morning to you, too," Doug grumbled.

I ignored his snarky comment. "Can you take Clarence out? I'm already an hour behind schedule. There are at least a dozen emails I'll have to answer on the subway."

Doug shifted on the bed and rolled Clarence onto his side. As Doug scratched his pink belly, Clarence entered a trance-like state of ecstasy. Our dog, always passive in the morning, particularly liked being rubbed on his underside.

"That's fine, I don't have a class until this afternoon. Clarence and I know how to fend for ourselves these days, don't we, buddy?" Clarence growled softly.

This time I took the bait. "Doug, the entire federal government is closed. I work for Congress, who decided shutting down the government was preferable to agreeing on a budget. That means I need to get to work."

Doug waved his hand at me in a halfhearted attempt at dismissal. "Congress wasn't always the problem, you know. It used to function just fine."

As a historian, Doug could make comments like this and rattle off a hundred different anecdotes to back them up. Best not to argue with him when I had no time to spare. Besides, I wasn't ignorant when it came to congressional history. "I'm not dealing with Henry Clay these days. Not everyone is a great compromiser. I'll keep you posted about tonight."

Doug didn't reply, so I hustled out of the bedroom, grabbed my purse, and left the condo. He certainly hadn't won any sunshine awards for his attitude this morning. It was true I hadn't spent much time with him and Clarence lately, but this was Washington D.C., and I was trying to climb the ladder on Capitol Hill. Doug's job as a tenured Georgetown professor was far less stressful. He taught classes and wrote books. He was busy at times, like when he was trying to meet a publisher's deadline or preparing to teach a new course. But for the most part, his schedule was predictable. Mine was the opposite. Until a few months ago, our divergent lifestyles had always seemed complementary.

Lately, I wasn't so sure. I still enjoyed spending time with Doug. Since accepting this new job in the House, those carefree opportunities had almost disappeared.

I reached the eerily desolate Metro. At the height of rush hour, the long platform that lined the subway tunnel had fewer than ten people waiting for the next train from suburban Virginia into the District of Columbia. This was the reality of the shutdown. Only a miniscule portion of federal workers faced the commute into work today. Everyone else was sitting in their pajamas or robes, watching Kathie Lee and Hoda get tipsy while sipping a cup of coffee and munching on homemade waffles…or at least that's what I would be eating.

I shoved the image of leisurely furloughed life out of my mind. The shutdown was no vacation for the office of Maeve Dixon. In fact, it was precisely the opposite. It gave Maeve the opportunity to show her constituents, and maybe the whole country, that she was a rising star in American politics. My job was to make sure she was front and center when every important decision and deal transpired.

With renewed resolve, I triaged the growing list of emails requiring immediate attention. There were several messages called "Dear Colleague" letters about various legislative proposals that had been filed last night to "solve" the shutdown. After scanning those, I saved them in an email folder but did nothing further. Time would tell which bills received attention from the party leadership or the media. Those would be the solutions Maeve might want to support.

One message caught my attention. It was from Jack Drysdale, the Speaker's top staffer who had called Maeve last night. Drysdale didn't miss anything. He had obviously made note of my name when Maeve told him I would serve as her lead person on the various policy proposals to end the crisis. I'd never met Drysdale, so this email might present an opportunity to build a valuable political relationship.

Drysdale had a reputation for terseness. His message indicated the scuttlebutt was rooted in reality, Speaker wants to meet with Rep. Dixon at 2pm. Members Only meeting but come so we can talk. JD.

We had been summoned to the Speaker's lair in the Capitol. The first order of business upon arriving at work would be to make sure that Maeve had no conflict for two o'clock. I had lunch with Meg at noon, but that left plenty of time to make the afternoon appointment. I'd think about strategy for the meeting once I had time to consider how Maeve should play her cards.

The next message that caught my attention was from another VIP staffer on the Hill. The name "JUDY TALENT" stood out prominently on my list of unread iPhone emails. Judy was in the same position as Jack Drysdale, but one rung lower. She was the top aide for the Majority Leader in the House. I scanned Judy's email. She didn't request a meeting but wanted to "touch base" to make sure Maeve was "on message" for the shutdown. Who was running the show for our party, Jack or Judy? Both deserved responses, and I needed to email them pronto.

After the subway arrived at the Capitol South Metro station, I rode the long escalator to exit and was greeted by a freezing blast of arctic air. Why did wind tunnels persist in subway stations? I tightened the scarf around my neck and shoved gloved hands in my pockets. At least the shutdown hadn't taken place in a nice weather month. That would have only intensified my envy of my furloughed federal brethren.

Capitol South was more conveniently situated than my previous Senate Metro station. The House of Representatives office buildings were located less than a block away from the subway, a suburban commuter's dream. Only two minutes after leaving Capitol South, I ascended the concrete staircase to enter the Cannon House Office Building. Usually, a line snaked outside the doors, particularly during the popular tourist months. Today there was no line, and I marched right up to the heavy door. I gave it a good tug, but the door didn't budge. Cupping my hands around my eyes, I peered through the dark glass doors. The entrance was usually filled with Capitol Hill Police officers screening visitors and staff through metal detectors. Then I saw the sign proclaiming this ingress closed "due to the government shutdown." So much for convenient access to the office. I hiked down the stairs and headed up First Street toward Independence Avenue.

The Cannon Building was the oldest congressional office structure in the entire Capitol complex. On a typical working day, its entire 800,000 square feet were occupied with elected members of Congress, their staffs, tourists, lobbyists, and other visitors who came to Washington D.C. to plead their case to the nation's legislature. After I entered the building through the security checkpoint, I stared down the long hallway, flanked with numerous congressional offices on both sides. Rather than resounding with the chattering of staff and the click-clack of high heels pounding on the ornate floor, the corridor was silent. Two staffers stood outside one of the offices, their heads huddled close to-

gether in a seemingly private conversation, no doubt
trading secrets about how Congress was going to dig
itself out of the mess it had created by shutting down
the government. Other than that, the corridor was jar-
ringly empty.

A similarly uncomfortable silence greeted me inside
our office suite. No perky intern acknowledged my arrival, and the flat screen television that entertained visitors in the waiting room was turned off.

I slowly opened the door that led to our workstations
and the chief of staff's small private office. Peeking around the corner, I said tentatively, "Dan, are you
here? Representative Dixon?"

No response, but someone had to be here. I had
walked right into the office suite without using my
key. After placing my purse on my desk, I turned on
my computer. Before I started answering emails, didn't
it make sense to figure out who was inside the office?

Dan's door was closed. I knocked softly, but he didn't
reply. There was a low humming sound coming from
inside.

Ummmm. Ummmm. Ummmm. It repeated itself several times.

This was officially weird. There was no way I could
start working without identifying that noise. The last
time I barged into an office unannounced, I had discovered the body of my former boss, Lyndon Langsford,
who had been stabbed inside his Senate office. Did I
want to go down that road again? That was a ridiculous
notion. What were the chances of something like that
happening twice?

I grasped the knob, twisted it, and pushed open the
door. Dan was sitting at his desk with his shoes off and

his legs crossed, sporting bulky earphones and a blind-fold. My presence had gone completely unnoticed. His arms were outstretched and his hands were turned up-wards, as if he was summoning a higher power. Com-pletely oblivious, he continued humming, or whatever that sound was.

I decided to wait another fifteen minutes. Perhaps he'd be done by then. When I returned, I cleared my throat to get his attention. The "ummmms" grew louder.

I walked over to Dan and lifted one of the cover-ings away from his right ear. "Earth to Dan. Are you almost finished?"

Perhaps my response was foolhardy; after all, Dan was my boss. But did he realize the clock was ticking, and every minute this crisis lasted could negatively im-pact Maeve's approval rating?

My intrusion must have surprised him, because he almost levitated off his chair. He hastily removed his eye mask and earphones. "Jeez, Kit, why did you do that? I was in the middle of my meditation."

"I'm sorry I ruined your flow, or your buzz, or what-ever. But Maeve needs to make decisions, and she won't want to issue an edict without finding out how her con-stituents perceive the shutdown. Have you called our district director in North Carolina yet?"

"I was going to do that right after my morning chant." He stashed his earphones and eye shield inside a desk drawer.

I didn't have any more time for Dan. "Let me know what you find out. In the meantime, the Speaker wants to see Maeve at two o'clock this afternoon. I need to confirm the appointment and make sure she's ready."

Dan seemed surprised by this revelation, but he

didn't say anything else. I interpreted his silence as approval of my plan and marched out of his office. I almost ran into Maeve, who was taking off her coat and heading into her private sanctuary. By now I was certain Dan was out of his league. It was up to me to get Maeve through this calamity without suffering a major political setback.

THREE

My STOMACH ALWAYS seemed to know what time it was. When it rumbled, I knew it was time for lunch. The office was now under some semblance of control. Dan was scheduled for numerous phone calls with the congressional district, Maeve was reviewing a Congressional Research Service report in preparation for her meeting this afternoon with the Speaker, and I had confirmed the appointment with Jack Drysdale. Sneaking out now meant I could enjoy a quick lunch with Meg, no doubt the highlight of my day.

After exiting the Cannon Building, I retraced my steps toward the Capitol South Metro station and approached Tortilla Coast, a popular watering hole for House members, staff, and lobbyists. It was never empty, even when Congress wasn't around. Today was no exception. Faced with limited options in the cafeteria, Capitol Hill staffers forced to work during the shutdown were all congregating at the Coast. If we couldn't sit at home with a warm mug of hot chocolate, at least we could sip yummy margaritas.

As I made a beeline for the entrance, I heard a familiar voice over my shoulder.

"Howdy, stranger!"

Meg appeared out of nowhere and immediately stretched out her arms for a big hug. We'd worked together for four years in the Senate and during our tour of duty had become best friends.

"You look terrific, as always." That wasn't merely a polite comment. Meg was stylish, attractive, and smart. In Washington D.C., having all three of those qualities definitely gave her an edge.

Meg ran her fingers through her short blond bob and waved her hand to dismiss my comment. Her manicured fingernails and recent highlights indicated she hadn't let the threat of the salary hiatus during the federal government shutdown interrupt her beauty regimen.

"Are you ready to eat?" Meg headed through the doors to the restaurant and asked the hostess to seat us. Meg had a voracious appetite and good genes. The latter prevented her from gaining an ounce, no matter how much she ate.

We plopped ourselves down in a booth and the waitress delivered a basket full of warm tortilla chips, the watering hole's signature offering.

The minute the basket was on the table, Meg dove into the chips. "Can we have some Sunset queso to go with this?" The waitress looked amused at Meg's immediate request, but she nodded and scuttled off to place our appetizer order.

It was often hard to get a word in edgewise with Meg. I waited until she had stuffed her mouth with a big chip saturated in yellow cheesy dip mixed with jalapeños. Asking all my questions at once might prove the best strategy. "Why are you working during the shutdown? When is this going to end? And oh, how's Kyle?"

Kyle was Meg's clean-cut boyfriend from the other side of the political aisle. He used to work in the House of Representatives but now was a chief of staff in the

Senate. We'd met him last year while informally investigating the murder of our boss.

Meg swallowed and took a big gulp of water. "Actually, those three questions are related."

Before she could elaborate, our waitress came over to take our lunch order. Given my constant battle with the bulge, I usually stuck to a bowl of soup when I indulged in lunch at the Coast. But this was no ordinary day. Who knew how late I would have to stay tonight? "I need some shutdown comfort food. I'll have the chicken fajitas."

Meg studied the menu. "Kit, you are absolutely right. I'd like to build my own burrito with steak, guacamole, and tomatillo sauce." She handed the menu to the waitress and smiled. Her order was met with another brief stare of disbelief from our server, who undoubtedly wondered how svelte Meg could ingest a monster burrito after having inhaled a basket of chips and creamy queso.

"I'm going to have to eat lunch and run because my boss has an appointment with the Speaker in an hour. Give me the lowdown on what's happening."

"Like I was saying, your questions are tied together. I'm working during the shutdown because the committee is crashing on a big hearing involving government waste." She lowered her voice and leaned in close. "We think the White House might have tried to cover up questionable expenditures from several executive branch departments."

Meg worked for an oversight committee in the House of Representatives who kept a close eye on government spending and procedures. While our party controlled the House of Representatives, the Republicans had the White House. Divided government made the politics on her committee particularly contentious. With less than a year until the next election, Meg and her colleagues were under considerable pressure to scrutinize the current administration.

I moved in closer to the table so we could keep our conversation discreet. Washington D.C. was full of snoops who liked to listen to the private conversations taking place in adjacent restaurant booths. "When are you going to bring this scandal to light?"

Meg shrugged. "It depends how much we can dig up during the shutdown. The chairman would like to go public as soon as the government reopens, if that's possible."

We ended our conversation as our waitress approached with our lunches. My fajitas sizzled as she placed them in front of me, and Meg's burrito could have fed an army. Less than five seconds later, we had both dug into our meals. Too bad stress didn't burn calories, because if it did, calories consumed during a government shutdown wouldn't really count.

After several big bites, time was growing short. I needed to talk to Maeve before we walked over to the Speaker's office, so I had to wrap up lunch with my best pal. "You didn't answer my other two questions."

Meg smiled with her mouth full. After swallowing, she said, "Sorry. Didn't you ask how long this shutdown was going to last?"

I nodded. Meg usually had good information because of her various committee staff contacts.

"I don't think you want to know the answer to that question. My sources are telling me this isn't going to be a brief one. The sides are far apart, and neither party thinks it's to their advantage to give in."

"Do you mean several days?" How could we possibly keep the office running with just Dan and me? He didn't carry his share of the workload under normal circumstances. The intensity of a shutdown would amplify the problem.

"No, Kit. You're not getting it. I mean weeks."

I choked on the big bite of chicken I had just put in my mouth.

"Are you okay? Jeez, have some water." Meg handed me a full glass.

Sputtering, I took a gulp and then wiped my mouth quickly with a napkin. "Weeks? Are you serious?"

"Of course. It takes Congress days just to take the political temperature of the country. Then it's at least another week to start coming up with a compromise. After that, who knows how long it will take to broker the actual deal? Remember, the president and Congress don't exactly see eye to eye these days." Meg seemed unaffected by this prospect. She calmly sliced up another large bite of burrito.

"Doesn't this situation bother you?"

"It's annoying. None of us will get paid as long as this debacle continues. But we have most of our staff onsite during the shutdown, so it's business as usual. The commute's a lot better, isn't it?"

"I guess that's one way of looking at it," I muttered. I couldn't get over the reality of trying to run the office for an extended period with only Dan's help. Had Doug stocked up on some nice Virginia wine varietals? For sanity's sake, I hoped so.

I'd put a sizable dent in my fajitas, and it was time for me to head back to the office. I stood up, opened my purse, and counted out the appropriate amount of money to cover my meal. "Do you mind paying the check? I need to run."

"Sure. But didn't you have another question?"

"It was about your significant other. How is he?" Meg had dated Kyle for six months, which was a long time for her to remain attached to one guy.

"He's fine."

I raised my eyebrows at her terse response. Since we saw each other infrequently these days, Meg was usually eager to go into detail. Most of the time, she offered too many specifics. It was possible to over-share, and Meg and I had different ideas about where to draw the line.

"Just fine?"

She sighed. "It's related to everything we've been talking about. I really enjoy dating Kyle, but he's from the other political party."

"I know. But that's never been a problem before. This town is filled with political party odd couples." Mary Matalin and James Carville were the most famous, but countless others existed.

"Until this investigation started. Kyle heard about it, and he's really upset we might uncover something about the president. He thinks it's pure politics and not substantive." Divided government, perhaps not viewed negatively by our founding fathers, caused considerable political heartache in Washington these days.

Meg paused a moment, and then she blurted out in a too-loud voice, "He even asked me to delay the investigation!" She put down her fork and rubbed her temples.

"He can't ask you not to do your job. That doesn't seem fair." I sat again in the booth. Meg needed my full attention—at least for three more minutes.

She moved her fingers from massaging her temples

to rubbing her eyes. "I feel like we're at a crossroads. If I dive into this investigation, I'm not sure our relationship will survive."

I reached across the table, took hold of her hands, and gave them a reassuring squeeze. "Meg, listen to me. We've been through a lot together, and I'll be here for you if this doesn't work out. But you need to make this decision. I'd want to be sure Kyle is really issuing an ultimatum. I don't know him well, but that approach doesn't seem like his style."

She nodded and wiped away a tear. I had never seen Meg cry over a relationship. It was shocking. She usually got rid of guys at the slightest pretext—such as when they didn't order the type of wine she liked.

"Thanks. I'll keep you posted. Maybe it will work itself out."

I got up to leave again, but she caught me before I could go. "Wait. We talked about me, but what about you? Is Doug any closer to making you an honest woman?"

I gritted my teeth. Meg was just being friendly but had managed to aggravate my Achilles' heel. I raised my left hand and shook it in front of her. "Nothing to report. No diamond here." I didn't add that recent events hadn't been conducive to domestic bliss.

She shook her head in apparent disbelief. "He'd better get moving, or someone else is going to beat him to the punch."

Leave it to Meg to have the last word. With that pronouncement, I hauled my unbetrothed body back to the United States Capitol to deal with the Speaker of the House.

FOUR

By THE TIME I reached the office, I'd already decided how Maeve should handle the meeting with the Speaker. She had to listen to the man's spiel; after all, he was the most powerful member of Congress. But she shouldn't commit to supporting his proposal to end the shutdown, at least not yet. The longer she held out, the more likely the Speaker might be inclined to sweeten the pot. If pressed, she could easily claim her constituents in North Carolina didn't completely support the Speaker's plan, whatever it was.

My phone was ringing as I reached my desk. I didn't recognize the number, but given the crazy political situation, anyone might be calling to lobby Maeve Dixon. On-the-fence votes were rare in the House of Representatives, and Maeve qualified as such. I snagged the receiver after placing my handbag on my desk and removing my gloves.

"Kit Marshall speaking, can I help you?"

"Hello, Kit. This is Gary from Capitol Hill Media and Consulting. I'm calling about Clarence and the Capitol Canine contest."

Talk about a miscalculation. This wasn't exactly a call from a Beltway power player. I chuckled. "Sorry. We're in shutdown mode around here and I wasn't expecting your call. I completely forgot about Capitol Canine."

"Totally understandable, given the political circumstances these days. I hope Clarence is still ready for the competition."

I hesitated. Capitol Canine was an online contest in which members of Congress and Capitol Hill staff posted photos of their dogs with quirky bios. Internet voting determined the winners.

"Are you still going forward with the contest, despite the shutdown?"

"We thought about postponing it, but we decided that Washington needed an uplifting contest like Capitol Canine to distract itself from the shutdown. Besides, most federal employees are furloughed, so they have plenty of time to browse the web and vote."

"I'd l-like to do it," I stammered, "but it's a really busy time, and—"

Gary cut me off. "You don't have to do much. We already have the paragraph about Clarence and his photo. I just need final permission to post it so we can start the voting tonight."

"I had planned to lobby my friends to vote for Clarence. I just don't have the time to do that now. Maybe Clarence should take a pass this time around."

Gary's voice grew impatient. "According to the contest rules, if Clarence withdraws, he will not be eligible for the contest in future years. Is that what you want?"

I was caught off guard by Gary's ultimatum. Did Clarence deserve a lifetime ban from Capitol Canine? I looked at the framed photograph I kept of him on my desk. His large brown beagle mutt eyes pleaded for a chance to win the top dog title.

"Okay, you got me. I'll keep Clarence in the contest."

Gary's voice brightened. "Terrific. The voting starts this evening and lasts for forty-eight hours. Don't forget about the party two nights from now to reveal the big winner. Good luck!"

I hung up, wondering if I had a death wish. How was I going to make sure Clarence garnered a respectable number of votes in the contest and help my boss solve the shutdown crisis?

I didn't have much time to ponder my predicament before Maeve appeared. "Kit, are you ready to join me for the briefing with the Speaker?"

"Yes, ma'am."

She tapped her watch. "We only have ten minutes to get to the Capitol. We have to go now."

"Absolutely, Congresswoman." When Maeve was annoyed, it was better to call her by her title than her first name. I grabbed my notebook, iPhone, and congressional identification badge.

On the walk to the Capitol through the underground tunnel, I briefed Maeve on the proposed strategy for the meeting. She agreed it was best to play it cool for now. I reminded her this was a member-only briefing. No staff, including myself, would be in the room. To my knowledge, Maeve had never met with the Speaker one-on-one before today. I snuck a look at her. Her long hair was perfectly styled, likely the result of a professional blowout at a salon. That wasn't a bad idea for such an important day. She wore a tailored black power suit and had chosen a fitted white blouse with a crisp collar. Her only jewelry was delicate diamond-stud earrings. Like me, Maeve was an unmarried woman navigating the nation's capital, although I doubted she'd remain single for long. Ten years my senior, she was a hot commodity on the D.C. dating market. K Street power brokers, prominent lawyers, and wealthy businessmen had thrown their hats in the ring for a chance to spend a visible evening with Maeve Dixon.

We turned the corner in National Statuary Hall and approached the Speaker's lair. Other offices in Congress had gatekeepers, but they were located inside the actual suites. The Speaker stationed his gatekeeper in the hallway outside the series of rooms he and his staff occupied. Capitol Hill Police provided security at all times, ostensibly supplying actual firepower to support the staffer who worked the entrance desk.

Previously, I had only stolen a furtive glance down this corridor. The imposing "SPEAKER OF THE HOUSE" title appeared above the doorway. The only people allowed to enter were those who had business with the Speaker, and I had never been summoned before today. Crystal chandeliers hung from the ceiling, and ornate wood furniture added to the regality. The appearance of the Speaker's antechamber projected a singular message. The person who occupied this real estate was the epitome of power and authority.

The guy at the desk immediately recognized Maeve. After all, he worked for the Speaker. It was his job to recognize members of Congress, particularly those in the same party. After appropriate greetings, he asked her to take a seat while he confirmed the Speaker was ready to see her.

He peered at me from under his glasses. "Staff is not permitted to attend this meeting."

"I know. Jack Drysdale said that he wanted to speak with me while Representative Dixon meets with the Speaker." I returned his steely gaze with one of my own. He was leadership staff, a coveted position in the

House of Representatives pecking order. That didn't mean he had the right to treat me like the hired help.

He grumbled in response, but I saw him start to type something. No doubt, he was sending an instant message to Jack to confirm my story. I took a seat next to Maeve on the ornate bench. We waited in silence, shifting uncomfortably on the ceremonial furniture as the minutes droned on.

Finally, the gatekeeper told Maeve she could head to the Speaker's office for her meeting. Out of pure habit, I stood up when Maeve was summoned. He quickly motioned for me to sit until Jack graced me with his presence. This had better be worth it. I was used to waiting for members of Congress, but staff usually treated each other with a modicum of respect.

Ten minutes later, Drysdale turned the corner and strode down the hallway. I easily recognized him from all the times I had seen his photo in Capitol Hill newspapers. In his late forties, Jack was one of those politicos whose looks had improved with age. His brown hair was slicked back in a *GQ*-inspired coiffure that matched his fitted wool designer suit. I guessed Burberry, but perhaps it was Paul Smith London? Either way, Jack Drysdale was the most supremely confident man I'd ever seen in my five years of Hill experience. I couldn't stop staring.

I stood up as he approached and thankfully the gatekeeper refrained from instructing me otherwise. Jack flashed a thousand-watt smile as he extended his hand. It was like shaking hands with Bruce Wayne. "Kit, I'm pleased to meet you."

"Likewise." I shook his hand politely. I needed to play it cool. By virtue of his position and undeniable sex appeal, Drysdale was a man used to getting what he wanted. Right now, Maeve wasn't for sale.

"Why don't we chat in my office? It's on this corridor. The meeting between our bosses shouldn't take long."

Jack evidently believed that Maeve would succumb swiftly to the Speaker's proposal. No need to disabuse him. I dutifully followed him down the hallway and entered an office suite. Several people were waiting in the anteroom as we breezed past. With one dismissive glance, Jack waved them off. "Don't worry. They're just Hill reporters. We're doing a quick pen and pad session with them in a few minutes."

Jack motioned for me to take a seat in his private office, which though voluminous resembled the workspace of a typical rank-and-file House member. The formal settee was no more comfortable than the bench in the corridor. Maybe the Speaker's office believed a sore behind encouraged shorter meetings and made visitors more inclined to acquiesce. Admiring the marble fireplace and mantel behind his desk, I could picture Jack donning a smoking jacket and offering me a brandy. But his face was all business.

"I'm not going to beat around the bush here. The Speaker needs Representative Dixon's vote for his budget deal. It's imperative the party caucus stick together. If we can count on her vote, then we can figure out how to make it worth her while in the long run."

I shifted slightly in an effort to look more at ease. "Do you know the details of the Speaker's proposed deal? The level of funding for various programs will matter to her and the constituents in the district."

Drysdale chuckled. "I'm not your details person. If you want to talk policy, I can put you in touch with the people writing the legislation." He leaned across his desk and added, "But let's get real here. The details don't matter. This is a political decision, plain and simple. We need Maeve Dixon's support."

His face was less than a foot away. I suddenly had newfound respect for the politicians back in the day who were the infamous recipients of the "treatment" from Lyndon Baines Johnson. I leaned back on the settee, but that monstrosity was too heavy to budge an inch.

"Believe me, Representative Dixon wants to be helpful. Right now, she can't commit to a course of action."

Drysdale fixed me with a hard stare. The frustration on his face implied he didn't appreciate a noncommittal answer from a low-level congressional staffer. But after a few seconds, he relented. With a friendly grin, he asked, "Isn't your dog in the Capitol Canine contest?"

He'd caught me off guard with such an abrupt change in mood and topic. I narrowed my eyes in distrust. "Yes. His name is Clarence."

"I love dogs, and I'm sure you want Clarence to do well in the contest. You know, my dog won Capitol Canine a few years ago."

"I didn't know that. Congratulations." Where was this headed?

"Capitol Canine is about who you know. And I know a ton of people who would be happy to vote for Clarence. Maybe we can become better friends if we join forces?" He followed up his offer with a sexy wink.

Had I just been propositioned to sell my boss's vote for a Clarence victory in the Capitol Canine contest? A direct approach was often best. "Are you trying to trade support for the Speaker's shutdown plan for votes in a dog popularity contest?"

"Don't be so literal, Kit. We're colleagues, and I'm simply trying to help you out."

After a long moment of silence, I decided to throw him a bone—no pun intended. "Maybe I can give you an answer on the Speaker's proposal in a week? I'll have to check with my chief of staff about the conversations he's having with the voters in the district."

Apparently, Jack didn't appreciate my version of a compromise. The sexy Bruce Wayne smile disappeared instantly, and his face contorted in anger. Raising his voice, he growled, "Check with your chief of staff? This is useless. I need to make sure the Speaker seals this deal."

Jack stormed out of the office, and I followed him down the corridor until he entered the Speaker's private suite. I was gutsy, but marching uninvited into the supreme leader's office space was beyond my pay grade.

I didn't want to return to the uncomfortable wooden bench in the hallway with the gatekeeper wondering why Drysdale had dismissed me. Instead, I took a seat next to the reporters in the outside waiting room. I had a clear view of the Speaker's suite across the hallway so I'd see Maeve when she emerged from her meeting. I'd stuck to our plan. Had Maeve held firm? I'd find out soon enough.

Smartphones are great time wasters. I fiddled with various apps as I waited. The next level of "Angry Birds" was within my grasp when I heard footsteps and voices across the hallway. I got up and stood in the doorway to greet my boss.

From the look on her face, she was not pleased. She charged like a linebacker to the exit of the Speaker's lair with Jack Drysdale on her heels.

"Stop, Congresswoman Dixon. You're not listening

to reason!" From behind, Drysdale placed his hand on Maeve's left shoulder in an attempt to prevent her from leaving the suite.

Maeve had impressive reflexes. She turned her body toward him and grabbed his wrist with her right hand. "Don't touch me! Is this how the Speaker's staff treat members of the House?" Her voice was loud and filled with vitriol.

The gaggle of reporters who had been relaxing inside the anteroom trailed behind me. This was better than a boring pen and pad session. One of them murmured, "I think that's Dixon from North Carolina."

This was not a good development, but Maeve didn't know that the press had a front-row seat to her altercation.

Maeve clutched Drysdale's wrist for several seconds until she let it go. Apparently her physical assault didn't intimidate him. He ran ahead and stopped directly in front of her.

Stretching his arms out wide to slow her down, Jack made his last stand. "I apologize. I shouldn't have done that. Please come back in the office so we can sort this out. You're a valuable part of this caucus and the Speaker wants to work with you on this deal."

Maeve shook her head. "You guys in House leadership are typical politicians. You can't take no for an answer. I'm not ready to make a decision. Now get out of my way."

Unmoving, Drysdale locked eyes with Maeve. She didn't look away and squared her shoulders. I could almost feel the tension around me as the reporters anxiously waited for the outcome. What was Maeve going to do? Knee him in the groin if he didn't back down?

After a moment that seemed like an eternity, Drysdale gave in and stepped aside. I breathed a deep sigh of relief and hurried into the hallway to catch up with her. As we exited the corridor, I glanced back to the doorway where I'd been standing. Every reporter was on his or her phone, ostensibly calling in the most scandalous story of the shutdown thus far. A junior member of Congress and the Speaker's top aide had nearly come to blows in the Capitol. A high school reporter could make that story fly.

As soon as we turned the corner and left the Speaker's passageway, the interrogation began. "What happened in the meeting? Were you really going to fight Jack Drysdale?"

"I'd rather not talk about it."

"But we're going to have to talk about it. A bunch of reporters were waiting across the hallway for a briefing from the Speaker's office on the shutdown. They saw everything that happened between you and Drysdale."

Maeve stopped abruptly and turned to face me. "You mean to tell me you knew there were reporters around and didn't stop me?"

I put my hands on my hips and looked directly into my boss's eyes. She meant business, but the feeling was mutual. "I didn't have the opportunity. Even if I had signaled, you never glanced in my direction. Besides, if I had intervened, it would have made matters worse."

Maeve didn't reply immediately, hopefully reflecting on the situation. "I see your point. If you'd interrupted me, then the story becomes about both of us ganging up on Jack Drysdale, the Speaker's media darling."

I breathed a sigh of relief and gave Maeve a restrained smile. "Well, he is handsome."

Maeve seemed to consider my comment, and then

she returned the grin. "Yes, he certainly is. But that's not going to help me when this story breaks."

I didn't want to tell Maeve that in all likelihood it had already broken. "Let's get back to the office and strategize with Dan." The words "strategize" and "Dan" didn't belong in the same sentence, but at this point, he was the only ally I had.

We picked up the pace and returned to the Cannon Building ten minutes later. Upon our arrival, my suspicions were confirmed. Every Capitol Hill media outlet was already reporting the altercation between Maeve and Jack Drysdale. Phones were ringing off the hook, and after Dan had answered one call without knowing how to respond, he'd ignored the remainder of the inquiries. With our press secretary on furlough, we needed to spring into action.

Maeve and I quickly explained the situation to Dan. His pasty face, already devoid of color due to the winter doldrums, somehow paled visibly.

We needed a plan, and we needed it fast. There was no time to call in reinforcements. Even if we could, furloughed employees weren't allowed to perform government business during the shutdown under penalty of law. When the Capitol Hill Police investigated me as the lead suspect in my former boss's murder last year, visions of orange jumpsuits had flooded my consciousness. I didn't need a repeat for violating the Antideficiency Act, for sure.

Dan and Maeve both sat in silence. They needed me to help them through this maelstrom. It was time to let my political instincts take over. In situations like this, thinking too much could potentially lead to an overwrought decision and an unnecessarily complicated strategy.

I took a deep breath. "Dan, you and I are going to man the phones." I turned toward my computer and visited several key websites to assess the damage. "This isn't as bad as you think. It's the usual suspects. *Roll Call*, *Politico*, the *Hill*, the *Examiner*, and the *Daily Caller* have the story. But the *Washington Post* and the *New York Times* aren't reporting it. It's a Beltway story, and that means it'll last one day. Tops."

Maeve and Dan sat in rapt attention. I was no Bob Woodward, or even Carl Bernstein, but I had worked in Congress for almost five years now. That tenure had afforded me a modicum of media savvy. After racking my brain, I continued, "We need to decide how to respond. Maeve, we could blame Drysdale and say he bullied you, but he's a favorite amongst the Capitol Hill crowd. I don't think they'd buy it."

Maeve nodded. "Agreed."

"So we avoid that angle and simply say you and the Speaker haven't come to an agreement yet on a budget deal. We address the substance, not the petty fight. That way, you take advantage of the situation and make your position clear, and we don't muck around in the dirty details."

As a GWOT (D.C. lingo for "global war on terrorism") veteran, Maeve rarely beat around the bush. "I like it. Let's do it." With that pronouncement, she returned to her office.

I turned to Dan. "Do you think you can handle talking to the press about this? If we split up the calls, it will go a lot faster."

"I can do it." He didn't sound confident, but he was

the boss. If he said he could do it, then I wasn't going to override his decision.

We listened to the voicemail messages left by reporters on the main line, made a list of calls we needed to return, and got to work. By five o'clock, we had spoken to every reporter seeking a comment and successfully spun the story to focus on Maeve's policy position on the shutdown.

I hung up the phone for the last time and rubbed my eyes. Today's fire drill had inspired a newfound respect for press secretaries. After finishing his final call, Dan pronounced, "That wasn't too bad!"

"Really? I have a splitting headache and my ear is sore from two straight hours of badgering from Capitol Hill reporters."

"Look on the bright side. It's over, and after tomorrow, this story will be old news."

I exhaled with a mixture of exasperation and weariness. "This *story* will be old news," I said, "but we just created a new story for enterprising reporters. Maeve is now front and center on the shutdown. Every journalist out there is going to follow her position like a hawk. We'd better start preparing a more detailed policy explanation for her tomorrow."

Dan's expression was blank. Clearly he had never considered the consequences of our press strategy. It had been necessary to divert attention away from Maeve's altercation with Jack, but by venturing down that path, we'd handed the media an entirely new line of inquiry for the coming days.

I hoped that Dan's silence meant he was digesting my revelation. He finally spoke. "No sense worrying today about something we can't solve until tomorrow.

That's my motto! If you need me, I'll be in my office for my evening chant." Dan bounced toward his office and closed the door behind him.

I shook my head in disbelief. My last boss in Senator Langsford's office had been an inspiration. Matt coached us when we faced difficult choices, provided words of wisdom at opportune moments, and tried to impart lasting knowledge about Congress and the legislative process. Now my immediate supervisor depended on me for his survival. This gave new meaning to the term "managing up."

I glanced at the time—just after five o'clock. A quick scan of my inbox confirmed that nothing required my immediate attention. I'd meant what I said about the piercing headache. Luckily, I found two over-the-counter painkillers in my purse, which I swallowed with a gulp of water. Could I go home? Interrupting Dan's nighttime mantra recitation was out of the question, but Maeve's door was open. I marched toward her office.

"Congresswoman, do you mind if I call it a day? Nothing requires my immediate attention, and we finished the media calls a few minutes ago."

Maeve was ensconced in reading the local North Carolina news online. She glanced away from her computer and said, "Sure, I'd take advantage of the downtime now. When the bills providing specifics on the budget start to emerge, we'll be staying late to pore over the details."

Inwardly, I groaned. Today's press incident was going to look like child's play before this fiasco was solved and we were back to normal.

"Yes, ma'am. I will do that. Are you headed home soon?"

Maeve shook her head. "No, I just received a request to serve as the presiding officer on the House floor tonight. I thought it would be a good opportunity to gain visibility with the district. Also, after the way I manhandled Jack Drysdale, some time in the chair might help repair my standing with the Speaker, right?" She grinned wryly.

Members of the majority party in the House of Representatives took turns serving as the presiding officer of floor debate. Freshmen spent more time "in the chair" than senior legislators. It gave them prime coverage on C-SPAN and also provided them with an opportunity to learn how bills were considered and debated. It was largely a ceremonial function, but an important role since the presiding officer controlled the flow of debate on the House floor, announced the result of roll call votes, and maintained decorum at all times. The latter was achieved by banging the Speaker's gavel until the members present in the chamber hushed up or at least reduced their chatter to a dull roar.

"Absolutely, I agree. Are you sure you don't need me to stay until you're finished presiding on the floor?" A sense of duty as a staffer obligated me to ask.

She waved her hand in dismissal. "Of course not. You know the parliamentarian tells me exactly what to say as presiding officer. You earned an early departure this evening. Thanks for coming up with a strategy to minimize the press damage. I know Dan appreciates it." She gave me a knowing wink.

Two winks in one day. This was a new record for my Capitol Hill career. No reason to push my luck. I hastily said good night and headed out of the office.

The subway was busier than this morning. However, my fellow riders weren't wearing work attire. Most were in jeans or other casual clothes. Undoubtedly, they were federal employees on furlough who had decided to enjoy a night out on the town. With another day out of the office virtually guaranteed for tomorrow, why not? Luckily, the pain relievers had taken care of my earlier headache, but the pulsating sting was replaced with pangs of jealousy as plans for late-night movies and barhopping unfolded around me.

I closed my eyes until the subway arrived at my stop in the Virginia suburb of Arlington. At least Doug couldn't complain about my lateness tonight. A cold wind encouraged me to hustle the several blocks to our condo building. After exiting the elevator on the fourth floor, I braced myself before putting my key in the lock. Clarence the Wonder Mutt sensed when an opportunity for escape might present itself. He positioned himself perfectly in the entryway, waiting for the precise moment when the door opened. When it did, he pounced, showing impressive agility for a chunky canine. In three seconds flat, he could race to the end of the hallway, violating numerous condo rules in the process.

I slowly turned the knob and pulled the door toward me. Sure enough, Clarence's floppy ears and adorable snout poked out. Many evenings, Clarence caught me off guard, but tonight, I was prepared for his shenanigans. As he made a break for it, I stretched my lower leg and foot to block him. He looked up with an expression reminiscent of the famous "guilty dog" YouTube video. I nudged him back inside the condo and shut the door behind us.

Doug didn't appear immediately, which wasn't unusual. After his classes at Georgetown finished for the day, he frequently spent the remaining hours working in his office at our condo. He was currently working on yet another book about early American history. His previous two tomes had focused on the Virginia dynasty of presidents and the inaugural Supreme Court. Closer to my ken, this one aspired to be the most comprehensive historical account of the first Congress of the United States.

I wandered toward the back of our abode and Doug's scholarly lair. He was sitting in front of his iMac with at least a dozen books surrounding him. Several were open with earmarked pages. Piles of photocopied pages, which appeared to be excerpts from the *Congressional Record*, were squeezed into the spaces not occupied by books. Most scholars took advantage of note-taking software that organized sources, both documents and electronic. Despite his relative youth—particularly in comparison to other accomplished historians—Doug had never adopted modern methods of conducting research. He worked exclusively with books and paper, employing his own systematic approach to collecting information. Most of the time, I thought his professorial proclivities were endearing. However, there were times when he frustrated the hell out of me. He was so lost in this newest venture that he seemed to forget I existed.

Almost a minute passed before Doug acknowledged my presence. But when I cleared my throat, he turned around immediately. "I didn't know you were home from work. Weren't you expecting to be late tonight?"

So much for an enthusiastic greeting. "That's what I expected, but Maeve was asked to serve as the presiding officer on the House floor tonight, so I got a reprieve.

Besides, I had a difficult day." I told Doug about the encounter with Jack Drysdale.

"How long do you think this shutdown business is going to drag on?"

"I had lunch with Meg and she wasn't optimistic."

Doug frowned and adjusted his glasses, which had fallen lower on his nose. "Did you know the First Congress established the State Department, the Department of War, and the Department of the Treasury in five weeks?"

"I had no idea."

"I find it fascinating that these novice legislators, who knew almost nothing about representative democracy in practice, were able to accomplish so much of consequence in such a short period of time."

This was Doug's way of taking a shot at the current Congress. "Did you ever think that the reason they were so successful was that they didn't know any better?"

"That reasoning doesn't make much sense, Kit."

"Try working for Congress and you'll get my drift. Dealing with two hundred twenty-five years of precedent, law, and custom isn't exactly easy, either."

Doug must have failed to muster a clever retort. He turned back toward his computer and resumed typing.

I headed to the kitchen and poured myself a tall glass of diet tonic. Then I carefully measured a serving of Bombay Sapphire using my favorite sterling silver shot glass and tossed it into the drink along with a few slices of lime. Selecting one of my favorite ceramic swizzle sticks, I slowly stirred the concoction. A strong G&T was typically summer fare, but the events of the day warranted an exception. If I had known what tomorrow had in store for me, I wouldn't have stopped at just one.

FIVE

The iPhone alarm buzzed at six. I was in a deep sleep but somehow located the device to silence it. After forcing myself to get out of bed, I performed my morning ritual of walking Clarence and then taking a hasty shower. My reward for getting up on time was a few precious extra minutes to make a frothy cappuccino from our espresso machine. The coffee beans with their hint of chocolate gave off an aroma reminiscent of freshly baked brownies. I was sipping my mocha masterpiece when Doug walked into our small kitchen.

"Something smells great in here."

"If it's the morning, I'm making waffles!" I smiled. Doug usually could identify my movie quotes.

"Since there's no waffles being made, I have to assume you're quoting Donkey from *Shrek*."

"You got it. However, I could make you a cappuccino with these tasty espresso beans."

"Sure, sounds good." He gave me a gentle kiss on the forehead and then retreated to the living room with his iPad to check the morning news.

Over the grind of the beans, I asked, "Can you look at the Capitol Canine site to see how Clarence is doing in the contest?"

"What are you talking about?"

"Remember, we entered Clarence in that online contest for the top dog on Capitol Hill?"

"How could I forget?" Doug muttered under his breath.

A few moments later, Doug returned to the kitchen. "Clarence is doing quite well. He's got over a thousand votes and he's in first place."

I almost dropped the cappuccino I had made for Doug. "That doesn't make sense. With everything that happened yesterday, I didn't have any time to email friends to remind them to vote for Clarence. I meant to put it on social media but I forgot. How did he get all these votes?"

Doug shrugged and passed me the iPad. I looked at Clarence's profile. Sure, he was cute. His face was a mixture of tan, black, and white fur and he had big brown eyes with adorable floppy ears. He looked like a cross between a beagle and a rottweiler, with a Jack Russell thrown in for good measure. However, good looks only get you so far in Washington—even if you're a dog. Something else was up.

"I wonder if Jack Drysdale persuaded his contacts to vote for Clarence. Maybe to try to win me over so Maeve wouldn't hold a grudge after the altercation yesterday?"

"If that's the case, it's one of the craziest things I've heard since moving to D.C. Would he really think you could be bribed with votes on Capitol Canine?"

Doug was right. It was a little nutty, but if the former Virginia governor could be bought for a Rolex watch and a joyride in a Ferrari, maybe Drysdale thought a few votes for Capitol Canine would do the trick.

"I'll try to figure it out. Can you persuade your colleagues at Georgetown to vote for Clarence?"

Doug appeared skeptical. "I don't think academics

would understand why it's important for our dog to win a Capitol Hill popularity contest."

"Well, I don't have a lot of time during the shutdown to drum up support for him. You can't help out?"

He'd returned to reading the news on his device. Without looking up, Doug said, "He seems to be doing okay without our help, right?"

Doug's blasé attitude annoyed me. I was poised to respond with a clever retort, but my iPhone indicated I'd received a text message.

I grabbed the phone off the countertop, put in my security code, and touched the green Messages app. Come to Cannon rotunda immediately. I'm in trouble. I double-checked the sender. It was Maeve.

I typed back a reply: On my way. What's wrong?

No more time to think about dog contests or coffee. Time to bust a move and get to Capitol Hill pronto. "Doug, Maeve needs my help. Gotta run. See you tonight."

Doug didn't look up from his iPad. "Good luck."

I checked my phone as I headed downstairs. No reply yet from Maeve. It was a quarter past seven. How had she managed to involve herself in another crisis before sunrise?

After exiting our condo building, I quickly evaluated my transportation options. Should I take the subway or find a cab? Using my phone, I located the nearest Uber driver. Ten minutes away. By the time I waited for the driver to arrive, I'd be halfway to the Hill on the Metro. Maeve hadn't returned my text. What did she mean by "in trouble" exactly? Without knowing the severity of the situation, the Metro was an acceptable choice.

Absent the big commuter crowds to slow the boarding of trains, I arrived at Capitol South twenty-five minutes later. Maeve hadn't replied. Perhaps the "trouble" had already blown over. Just in case she still needed help, I headed directly to the Cannon rotunda without stopping at the office. Reporters usually camped out inside the rotunda to shoot live cable television hits from Capitol Hill. It wasn't as grandiose as the Capitol rotunda, but its Corinthian architecture with imposing columns did provide a stately backdrop for the camera.

I exited the elevator and walked past the famous Cannon Caucus Room, which hosted the House Un-American Committee hearings decades ago. Hearing Maeve's voice in the distance, I followed the narrow hallway circling the rotunda. After rounding the bend, I found my boss. She wasn't alone. Next to her was Detective O'Halloran of the Capitol Hill Police. Jack Drysdale was between them, but the Speaker's top aide wasn't looking so handsome this morning. Blood flowed from his head onto the pristine marble floor. If he'd generated Clarence's Capitol Canine votes, there wouldn't be any more favors coming my way. Jack Drysdale was dead.

SIX

MAEVE TOOK ONE look at me and almost leapt into my arms. I'd never seen her so discombobulated. "Thank God you're here. What took you so long?"

"I'm sorry. I had no idea. You didn't answer when I asked what the problem was."

She leaned close to me. "I couldn't very well text you what happened," she whispered. "I'm the lead suspect."

"You're *what*?" My voice was ten times louder than hers, but I couldn't hide my reaction.

She grabbed my arm and pulled me near. "Keep quiet. This cop just arrived, and believe me, it doesn't look good."

I lowered my voice. "Don't worry. Let me talk to him. I know Detective O'Halloran."

I couldn't tell if the look on Maeve's face expressed astonishment or utter bewilderment. It didn't matter. I raised a finger to my lips, indicating she should stay quiet while I spoke with O'Halloran.

The detective and I had become acquaintances last year when Meg and I solved the murder of our former Senate boss. O'Halloran had originally pegged me as the chief suspect for the crime, but eventually appreciated my amateur assistance after I stumbled upon several key clues.

The beefy middle-aged detective was deep in conversation with several uniformed officers who had begun to secure the perimeter. If I'd arrived any later, this area would have been sealed off. As I approached, I gave him a friendly wave. "Detective O'Halloran, remember me? It's Kit Marshall."

O'Halloran stopped talking to his colleagues. He extended his hand and I shook it politely. "Ms. Marshall, how could I forget? The better question is why you've shown up again at the scene of a murder in the United States Capitol complex."

There was no good explanation for that question, except I'd somehow managed to find trouble again. I shrugged. "I'm here because my boss, Representative Maeve Dixon, messaged me this morning to meet her in the Cannon rotunda."

O'Halloran perked up. "Dixon texted you to come here? What time?"

I opened the Messages app on my iPhone. "I got the text at seven-oh-three this morning."

O'Halloran rubbed his chin as he considered my answer. "Very interesting."

"Do you mind telling me what's so interesting besides the dead body on the floor?"

O'Halloran motioned to follow him a few steps away from the growing cadre of Capitol Hill police officers. Maeve was standing silently by herself, her head buried in her smartphone. She was likely trying to determine if news of the murder had broken yet. No reporters were on the scene, but they'd figure it out soon enough, especially when the police told them they couldn't set up for their live television shots in the rotunda today.

"Listen, I don't know how you've gotten yourself involved in another murder, but you might want to consider a different line of employment."

"I know this is a strange coincidence, but why would I do that?"

"Because I don't think you're going to have your Hill job for much longer. Your boss is our top suspect for the murder of Jack Drysdale."

I looked directly into O'Halloran's eyes. "We've been down this road before, Detective. I was your number one suspect when you investigated Lyndon Langsford's murder. Look how that turned out."

O'Halloran returned my gaze. "You're correct. But this one's different. You didn't have a motive to kill Langsford, which bothered me from the beginning. I don't have that problem with this one." He motioned toward Jack's lifeless body. "Your boss nearly came to blows yesterday with the victim, and every newspaper on Capitol Hill reported the incident." To emphasize his point, he brandished yesterday's *Roll Call* story on his smartphone.

O'Halloran worked quicker than I remembered. He'd already fingered Maeve as a suspect with a credible motive. But she wasn't the only person in D.C. who had a beef with Drysdale. "Isn't it a big leap to assume Representative Dixon killed Jack because she got into an argument with him yesterday? If I murdered every person I disagreed with on Capitol Hill, I'd have a rap sheet a mile long." There was nothing wrong with injecting a bit of humor. I gave O'Halloran a small grin.

He didn't return the smile. "It's not just motive. A police officer saw Maeve Dixon hovering over the body a few minutes before seven this morning."

The morning's events started to make more sense. I glanced in Maeve's direction. The worried expression on her face indicated she understood the gravity of the situation. "That could be purely circumstantial. Maeve might have noticed Jack's body as she walked past the Cannon Caucus Room. Any good citizen with a conscience would investigate if someone was lying on the floor."

O'Halloran shook his head. "Sorry. It doesn't add up. Your boss has an office on the first floor of this building. Why would she be on the third floor so early in the morning?"

He had me there, but there was no need to let him know it. "She's a military veteran, Detective. She doesn't believe in sleeping late. She might have been stretching her legs or looking for an available restroom. During the shutdown, they don't open them up on every floor."

O'Halloran raised his eyebrows. "Last time I checked, members of Congress had private bathrooms in their office suites. I've been on the Capitol Hill Police force for over twenty years. You're going to have to try harder to pull the wool over my eyes, Ms. Marshall."

O'Halloran was at the top of his game. He seemed more confident than when he'd investigated the murder of my former boss. Better to change the subject and get as much information as possible from him. I tried to get a peek at the body, but now a bevy of forensic investigators surrounded Drysdale. There'd been a gash on his head, indicating that some sort of physical assault had killed him.

"Do you have a murder weapon, Detective?"

"I shouldn't be sharing this information with you, but we won't be able to keep a lid on this detail for long, once the media sharks get hold of this story. It appears that Mr. Drysdale was bludgeoned with the Speaker's gavel."

I swallowed hard. It was best to watch my tongue here. O'Halloran could nail Maeve with motive and opportunity. Did he know she also had access to the weapon the night before when she presided over the House of Representatives?

"That's certainly an unusual w-weapon," I stammered.

"I agree, Ms. Marshall. Not too many people have access to the gavel used on the floor of the House. I imagine it will narrow our suspect pool considerably." He paused for a moment, deep in thought. "Tell me something. Don't members of Congress have access to the gavel when they sit in for the Speaker during debate on the House floor?"

O'Halloran knew the answer to that question. He wanted to emphasize a point. I answered him as casually as possible, "Sure. But all members of the majority party preside over the House floor from time to time."

He rubbed his chin again. "That's right. I'm sure it won't be hard to see who was in the chair yesterday evening, after your boss's fight with Jack Drysdale in the Speaker's office. Don't you agree?"

I gulped again. *Yikes.* O'Halloran had the trifecta. He'd established a plausible motive, confirmed she had the opportunity to kill Jack, and soon enough, he'd tie her to the murder weapon. My heart started to beat faster, and my mind raced with suspicious thoughts. Had Maeve slipped her trolley and killed Jack Drysdale? Sure, my boss was a handful, but I didn't peg her as a killer.

It was time to end this conversation and switch into

damage control mode. I ignored O'Halloran's question. "Thanks for your time, Detective. I'm sure we'll be in touch in the coming days."

"I'm not sure about that, but I can guarantee your boss will be hearing from me soon."

Ominous words. I trotted toward Maeve, who was chewing on her thumbnail. Before this morning, I'd never seen her so ruffled. Her air of apprehension had intensified in the past ten minutes since I arrived on the scene.

I wanted to throttle Maeve for getting herself into this predicament, but this wasn't my best pal Meg. Maeve Dixon was still my boss, and I had to treat her accordingly. In a halfhearted attempt to calm myself, I counted silently to ten before speaking.

"Congresswoman, I talked to Detective O'Halloran from the Capitol Hill Police. He said that an officer found you standing over the body around seven this morning. Can I ask what you were doing by the rotunda at that hour?"

"I woke up early this morning and planned to squeeze in a workout in the House gym. On my way there, I got a text message from Dan."

She retrieved her phone from her purse and entered her security code. Maeve turned the phone so I could read the message: Jack Drysdale wants to meet you at the Cannon rotunda at 7 this am. He wants to talk about a deal.

"Instead of heading to the gym, I decided to see what Drysdale had to offer. I got here a few minutes before seven and didn't see him anywhere. I walked past the caucus room, and then I saw him on the floor. I ran over because I thought he'd had a heart attack." She paused for a moment, clearly distraught. "I couldn't stop looking at the terrible wound on his head. There was a bloody gavel next to his body."

"Maeve, this is important. Did you touch anything?"

She shook her head vigorously. "No! I swear I didn't. It was surreal. I'm not sure how long I stared at the body. The next thing I remember is a police officer grabbed me by the arm and asked me what happened." She rubbed her temples vigorously with her fingers.

"There's something not right about this story. Why would Jack Drysdale text Dan and not me?"

Maeve frowned. "I have no idea."

"Remember, Jack said he didn't want to deal with Dan on the shutdown. He asked for another name, and you gave him mine."

"That does seem strange," Maeve said slowly.

"What it means is that Jack didn't communicate with Dan this morning. Someone else texted Dan so you'd show up at the rotunda at precisely seven this morning. Someone who wanted you to discover the body."

Maeve gasped. "You mean I was set up?"

"That appears to be the case. Your fight with Drysdale yesterday was the perfect frame for the murderer. You played right into his hands." I corrected myself quickly, "Or her hands." Last year I'd learned the hard way that with the proper motivation, both men and women could transform into killers.

"The police told me to wait while they figure out what they need from me. After I texted you, I called a lawyer in town and he said he would meet me at the police station if I'm called in for questioning."

That was a good move. It was flattering that Maeve contacted me first after she discovered the body, but I wasn't a legal eagle. If she became the prime suspect, she would need the best defense lawyer in Washington D.C.

"Let me find out what's going to happen next."

Maeve nodded. O'Halloran might take another question from me. After that, his patience would likely wear thin.

He was consulting another plainclothes police officer adjacent to the crime scene. "Detective, can I ask you one more favor?"

O'Halloran put his hand up to silence me. After he finished his conversation, he turned in my direction. "Why not? Would you like a bagel and coffee, too?"

Actually, a bagel and coffee sounded terrific. I restrained myself from asking him for toasted sesame with light cream cheese and a cup of java served light and sweet. One look told me a sarcastic retort would get my butt tossed out of the rotunda area. I was already pushing the envelope with my police comrade.

"Detective, my boss wants to know if her presence will be required at the Capitol Hill Police station today? If so, legal counsel will meet her there."

From the look of concentration on his face, I guessed that O'Halloran was carefully evaluating his answer. He might have wanted to haul Maeve to the precinct for a full-scale interrogation, but the threat of her lawyering up gave him considerable pause. He was also dealing with a member of Congress. Bringing her in officially if he wasn't absolutely certain about her status as a suspect might cause him more political trouble than she was worth at this point.

My gamble paid off. "We can have an officer conduct an interview here." Then he added, "For now. That doesn't mean we won't want to schedule a more formal Q&A at the station later on."

I breathed a sigh of relief. At least Maeve would be spared the indignity of a potential mug shot today. Her face relaxed when I told her she'd avoided an imminent trip to the pokey. However, her relief didn't stop her from barking orders. "Kit, you need to return to the office and bring Dan up to speed. I might be tied up here for a while. Get prepared for the press inquiries." She glanced about furtively. "We're not going to be able to keep a lid on my involvement. We'll need a plan."

I held my tongue, but I knew firsthand the pressure Detective O'Halloran was feeling to solve the homicide of a congressional staffer. Maeve would need more than a well-devised press plan. She'd better have Perry Mason on speed dial.

This wasn't the time or place to advise Maeve about murder investigations. I'd debrief her later in the privacy of the office and ask a few questions of my own. Number one in my mind concerned the Speaker's gavel. How in the hell did it travel from the House floor to the Cannon rotunda? The gavel was a monumental symbol of the institution. Given its unique status in the House, figuring out the path of the murder weapon would likely point to the person responsible for this horrible crime.

No amount of meditation was going to prepare Dan for this news. I hustled downstairs and found him trying to operate the fax machine. Given the morning's events, I skipped telling him that no one communicated via fax anymore.

After I told him what had happened, he buried his head in his hands and started to shake uncontrollably. His hands flew to his brown mane, and a moment later, the tugging commenced. As I watched in amazement, I realized the origin of the idiom "tearing your hair out."

I was about to suggest he needed to get a grip when the shaking and yanking suddenly stopped. His eyes were semi-crazed and intensely focused. He pointed directly at me. "You. I have the answer. You can fix this."

"Have you had a mental breakdown? Do I need to call the Employee Assistance Program for help?" EAP provided counseling to congressional staff. I hoped they made emergency office visits.

Dan ignored my question. "When I hired you, someone in House leadership told me that you solved your former boss's murder in the Senate. I couldn't believe it so I searched on the Internet and found the news stories."

"That was a completely different situation. I knew the suspects because they were associates of my boss. I was an insider. I only met Jack Drysdale yesterday, remember?"

"You have to solve this murder to clear Maeve." Dan looked at me with pleading eyes. A few tears glistened in the corners. "I left North Carolina to move to Washington D.C. for this job. No one else is going to hire me if she's accused of murder. It's not like I've exactly impressed everyone here. I haven't had a chance to prove myself yet!" Dan's tirade culminated in a high-pitched squeak.

I had to calm him down. I eased him into a chair next to my desk and put a hand on his shoulder in an attempt at a comforting gesture. "Look, I've been in a similar situation. I'm sure the police are going to solve this murder. Detective O'Halloran's not a bad cop." The last part was true. O'Halloran was an admirable public servant. His investigatory skills hadn't impressed me last year, but maybe he'd learned a few tricks since then.

Dan was a political ingénue, yet he wasn't completely clueless. "If this detective is so great, why didn't he solve the murder in the Senate?"

I sighed. "Dan, I'd like to help Maeve out. I already recovered once on Capitol Hill from being labeled a murder suspect. I'm not sure having a boss accused of murder is much better. But what I said a few minutes ago still stands. I don't know the players in Jack's world. How would I come up with a list of suspects to investigate?"

Dan stood up and towered over me. "That's not my problem. You need to figure out who killed Jack Drysdale. I don't care if you help the police or pull a Jessica Fletcher. Your job depends on it. Don't worry about the press calls. I'll take care of them. Just focus on clearing Maeve Dixon's name."

"Dan, you're being completely unreasonable—"

He cut me off. "I'm the chief of staff here. I don't assert myself too often, but I mean business. Either start sleuthing or find another job. Pronto."

As I stared into Dan's implacable gaze, I recalled the catchy 1990s Paula Cole tune. Never mind the cowboys. Where had all the chakras gone?

SEVEN

I TURNED ON my computer and consumed the headlines. Sure enough, the police hadn't been able to keep a lid on Jack Drysdale's murder. The Washington-based news outlets were reporting that a high-level staffer had become the first victim of the shutdown. One particularly sordid paper boasted the headline "Shutdown Slaughter." Despite its macabre tone, I appreciated the admirable alliteration, no pun intended.

The media hadn't yet confirmed Jack was the victim, but a treasure trove of stories about him already existed online. My ignorance of Drysdale's world was as thorough as I claimed. Luckily, Jack had never turned down an interview or press profile, especially when he was climbing the Hill ladder to his last position in the Speaker's office. Although I didn't live completely inside his world of political insider intrigue, maybe I could figure out the big players with enough Google searches.

I stretched out my arms and my fingers flew across the keyboard. This type of research wasn't as difficult as Doug's academic inquiries. At times, he spent all day searching for an obscure historical document, ledger, or letter. More often than not, he came up empty-handed. In stark contrast, when I entered "JACK DRYSDALE CONGRESS" into the search engine, over a thousand hits came up.

Would this take hours? I scanned article after article

in various Capitol Hill newspapers. Slowly, a clear profile of Jack Drysdale emerged, along with a few tanta-
lizing personal tidbits. Drysdale's congressional career
had spanned two decades, he'd worked under numerous political bosses. Slowly and methodically, Jack had
crisscrossed the Hill, working for increasingly powerful members of Congress. Finally, two years ago, he'd
picked the winning horse when his boss was elected
Speaker of the House and Jack became the most influential staffer in Congress.

Along the way he'd certainly ruffled a lot of feath-
ers. Two recent conflicts in particular had received considerable press coverage. According to newspaper and
blog accounts, Jack had developed a vicious rivalry with
Judy Talent, another top staffer who currently worked
for the House Majority Leader. Apparently Judy and
Jack had risen on the Hill on parallel career tracks.
Both were gifted, respected, and ambitious. Jack had
managed to end up with the Speaker while Judy's boss
was the second-in-command.

With Jack out of the picture permanently, wouldn't
Judy be a prime candidate to take his job in the Speaker's
office? Judy had emailed me shortly after the shutdown,
requesting we keep in touch about various solutions.
Given what I'd just read about her rocky relationship
with Jack, a chat with Judy seemed like a good place
to start. I replied to her email and asked if she had free
time tomorrow to discuss the Majority Leader's plans
for ending the shutdown.

The other promising lead involved the House Sergeant at Arms office. A series of articles described
the ongoing disagreement between the Speaker's office and the Sergeant at Arms concerning security in

the House. As the head law enforcement officer in the House, the Sergeant at Arms was responsible for maintaining safety and order. With threats issued every day to destroy the Capitol complex, both from domestic and international sources, the Sergeant at Arms had a tough job. Recently, he had issued a proposal to increase security protocols for the House of Representatives and its office buildings, which would have made it more cumbersome for visitors and tourists to traverse the hallways. Representing the Speaker's interests, Jack had strongly opposed the suggested changes. A man named Gareth Pressler, a senior aide for the Sergeant at Arms, had criticized Drysdale in several news stories. The latest story in the saga caught my eye, headlined "SPEAKER SERGEANT WAR." In the article, Pressler and Drysdale had traded barbs, each accusing the other of undermining congressional operations.

I grabbed my trusty notebook and jotted down the most relevant information about Pressler and his conflict with Jack. I'd never interacted with the House Sergeant at Arms office. Without a solid contact or a good excuse for a meeting, tracking down this lead could prove challenging.

Enough surfing the web. How else could I gather information about the complex world of Jack Drysdale? A lightbulb switched on in my brain and I immediately picked up my phone to dial one of the few House extensions I'd committed to memory.

A familiar voice chirped in my ear. "Hello, Meg Peters, House Oversight."

"It's Kit. Have you heard the news yet?"

"If you're referring to Jack Drysdale's murder, of course. Everyone is buzzing about it."

I lowered my voice. Even though Dan had commanded me to investigate, I didn't trust him. "Did you know my boss found Jack's body?"

Unfortunately, my news had the opposite auditory effect on Meg. She might as well be speaking into a megaphone. "Who did you say found Jack?" she bellowed.

"Can you please not announce it to the rest of your office? It hasn't reached the press quite yet and we're trying to keep it on the down low." Capitol Hill staff rarely had private offices. Meg was no exception.

"Sure, I'm sorry," she whispered. Now I could barely hear her.

"Dan wants me to investigate the murder so I can clear Maeve as a suspect. But I don't know anything about Jack Drysdale and his crowd."

"Did you know Drysdale recently got married?"

"No. Who's the lucky lady?"

"Wrong gender, Kit. Jack was gay. After the District of Columbia legalized same-sex marriage, he and his longtime partner Jordan Macintyre got hitched."

"It's sad that Jack died so soon after getting married."

"Maybe not. I heard a rumor that Macintyre was up to his eyeballs in debt. He owned a restaurant that went under. Now he's going to inherit a lot of money from Jack."

Not a bad motive for murder. I'd add Jordan to my growing list of suspects. I could always count on Meg for an accurate download of Capitol Hill gossip. Her knowledge of the cocktail circuit was almost as vast as Doug's scholarly expertise in American history. Both served a worthy purpose inside the Beltway.

"Thanks for the tip. You're not free for lunch today,

are you?" Meg had been a resourceful ally last summer when we tracked down Senator Langsford's killer.

"I wish. We're up to our eyeballs researching this White House investigation."

"Did you make any progress with your significant other?"

Meg sighed. "Not really. He knows we're moving forward with the hearings."

Meg was in a pickle, and I didn't envy her situation with Kyle. "Just hang in there," I said. "I bet things will resolve on their own. If not, several glasses of Prosecco might help." Meg's favorite bubbly drink usually lifted her mood.

"More like the whole bottle."

I said goodbye to Meg and thanked her again for the juicy tip about Drysdale. I'd have to figure out a way to learn more about their relationship and his husband's financial difficulties. That was going to require serious ingenuity since I'd never met Jordan Macintyre.

In the tradition of *Casablanca*'s infamous Captain Renault, who else could help me round up the usual suspects? Doug didn't know much about Hill politics, but he deserved a call. Even if he'd read about Jack's death online, he wouldn't know about my boss discovering the body. My fingers hesitated over the phone's keypad. Although my boyfriend had been relieved when the culprits were caught last summer in the Senate, he'd never wanted me to engage in novice sleuthing. Doug wasn't going to embrace a repeat performance of Kit Marshall, amateur detective extraordinaire.

I commanded my digits to dial the familiar cellphone number. Maybe Doug was busy and a long voicemail would suffice. "Doug, this is Kit. Just wanted to let you know that another murderer is loose on Capitol Hill and I'll be nosing around to solve the crime. Don't wait up!"

Just as I chuckled at my fantasy message, I heard Doug's voice on the line. "Hello. Hello? Kit, is that you?"

"Sorry. I thought it might go to voicemail."

"Should I not pick up the next time you call?"

"Never mind. Did you hear about the homicide in the House today?"

"I saw a headline in the *Washington Post* about a Speaker's aide who was found dead. Did you know him?"

"That's not an easy question to answer."

"I don't understand," Doug said, his exasperation already evident.

"I just met him yesterday. He's the guy Maeve almost got into a shoving match with outside the Speaker's office."

There was silence on the line. Now the wheels of Doug's brain were spinning. No point in turning back now, so I kept talking. "Maeve found Jack's body this morning. She had the opportunity to kill him, motive for the crime, and access to the murder weapon."

More silence.

"Doug, are you still on the line?"

His response was clipped. "I'm here. I heard what you said."

I tried to hide the annoyance in my response. "Don't you have anything to say?"

"Quite frankly, I'm speechless. How could you possibly be involved in another murder on Capitol Hill?"

"Beats me. It's not as though I'm looking for these crimes. They find me."

"I suppose you're angling for a reprisal of your Nancy Drew role?"

Since my ordeal in the Senate, Doug had taken to calling me by the names of female amateur sleuths. He preferred Trixie Belden, young Miss Marple, and Veronica Mars. Nancy Drew was a new one.

"If so, does that make you Ned Nickerson?" Two could play at this game.

"I imagine it does."

"It might be a short-lived romance. I'm not sure I have many clues to solve this one. I hardly knew Jack, and even if I can identify the main suspects, they're not people I associate with on a regular basis." To put his mind at ease, I needed to make Doug understand how remotely I was situated to solve the crime.

"You should talk to one of my former students who works in the House press gallery. She might be able to tell you about Jack's world. She frequently mentioned dealing with high-level staffers and their egos."

My eyebrows shot up. The purpose of my phone call had purely been to provide information. I never expected Doug would offer to assist my investigation. "I'm surprised you're helping me develop a lead. Did you change your mind about my sleuthing?"

"I still think it's dangerous and you should leave it to the police. But I know you're going to poke around no matter what I say. Her name is Melinda. Just tell her I sent you."

There was no sense in arguing with Doug about the perils of snooping. He had a valid point. Last time I barely escaped the killer after a scary chase along a deserted underground passage in the Senate. I ended our conversation after a quick goodbye and a promise to exercise caution.

Maeve still hadn't returned to the office, so I clicked on my email inbox. There were several messages about proposed legislation to end the shutdown and notifications about staff meetings to negotiate other proposals. Nothing about Maeve being a suspect or involved in Jack's murder.

Just as I read the last email, the door connecting the outside waiting area to the staff office space opened. Maeve looked as though she'd seen better days. In contrast to yesterday, she was a mess. Her disheveled hair and wrinkled suit matched the strained expression of defeat on her face. A few years ago, someone had approached her in North Carolina and convinced her it would be a good idea if she ran for Congress. Did Maeve regret that decision? Was the strain of another rigorous campaign, a government shutdown, and a felony murder charge worth the privilege to represent over seven hundred thousand disaffected constituents?

This wasn't a good time to wax philosophical with Congresswoman Dixon. Instead, I needed facts. "What happened with the police?"

Dan must have heard Maeve's arrival. After one glance at her uncharacteristically ruffled appearance, he furrowed his brow in concern. "Is everything okay? You look a little—"

Maeve cut him off. "I know, I know. I look terrible. It's been a tough day, all right?"

Dan fawned over Maeve as if she were a wounded puppy. After she sat down, he delivered a glass of water and her favorite nutrition bar. Despite the stress, Maeve didn't deviate from her sacrosanct low-fat, low-carb, low-sugar diet. Her willpower dwarfed mine. One bad meeting and I reached for dark chocolate and a bottle of wine with no second thoughts.

Maeve took a long drink and then launched into her own interrogation. Turning toward Dan, she asked, "Why did you send me to the rotunda this morning?"

His face twitched. "I got a call early this morning on my cellphone. It was Jack Drysdale, and he said he wanted to meet you at seven to talk about a deal on the shutdown. He apologized for everything that happened yesterday so I told him I'd get you there."

Maeve sighed. "How did you know it was Jack Drysdale?"

Dan shifted his weight from one leg to another. "I assumed it was Drysdale. Why wouldn't I?"

She continued peppering Dan with questions. "Did you recognize the number? Or his voice?"

Dan shook his head. "No, but Drysdale had never called me before."

Maeve kept her head cradled in her right hand, as if the stress of the day had made it impossible to keep herself upright. Despite her skewed posture, she fired more inquiries at Dan, who had now turned from flustered pink to a darker crimson shade of trepidation.

"Do you realize this was a setup? The person you spoke with murdered Jack Drysdale. He called you so I would appear conveniently at the scene of the crime. Do you understand the ramifications of what you did, Dan?"

The poor guy visibly flinched when Maeve screamed his name at the end of her tirade. The scene gave me a small sense of satisfaction. Dan had proven barely competent since I'd been working in the office, yet Maeve always gave him a pass. His cluelessness had finally manifested in a screwup of epic proportions. However, any selfish smugness on my part was soon put aside given the horrendous seriousness of the situation. Both of our necks were on the chopping block.

It was time for cooler heads to prevail. "Can I see your phone?" I asked.

Dan handed over his iPhone. I navigated to the "recent calls" directory and found the incoming call at 6:03 this morning. After the D.C. area code, the first three numbers were 225. That was important.

"This extension means the call was made from a phone somewhere in the House. We might be in luck." I dialed the House of Representatives operator and gave her the number from Dan's phone. After listening to her response, I thanked her and hung up.

"The number is from a phone in the Capitol Visitor Center. It's located within an information desk inside the CVC. Anyone who has Capitol complex access could have used it to make the call."

Maeve rolled her eyes. "So much for that lead."

"Not so fast. We know the call was placed around six. The only people allowed in the building that early are members, congressional staff, and journalists with all-access badges."

Maeve stood up. "Terrific. We've just narrowed down the suspect pool to ten thousand people."

As she walked toward her office, I yelled after her, "Not really. A lot of the staff has been furloughed!"

EIGHT

IF DAN HAD been a dog, he would have put his tail between his legs and run. Despite his humanity, Dan's body language mimicked the universal sign of canine defeat. With a sulking posture, he returned to his office and closed the door, likely lighting a double dose of incense to combat the negative vibes sent his way by our boss.

Several online news sources confirmed that Jack's murder was the trending story in the local media, but so far, Maeve's name hadn't appeared in connection to the crime. O'Halloran was undoubtedly responsible for the tight lips. The less they said, the more evidence the police could gather without reporters breathing down their necks. Unfortunately, in this instance, the cops were marshaling resources to build a case against my boss.

With the police focused on Maeve, who would search for the real killer? The crime wasn't going to solve itself. If I wanted to find the person responsible for Jack Drysdale's demise, I'd have to do some serious pound-the-pavement snooping. Sitting on my duff was nothing but a waste of time. Dan's directive wasn't my primary motivator. If Maeve was convicted, Dan was irrelevant. We'd both be collecting unemployment.

The phone call to Dan's cell was an important clue. That had been a clever ploy, pure and simple. Why would Jack Drysdale place a call from a phone in the

Capitol Visitor Center to Dan? He'd met me the day before and had personally requested I work on the shutdown for the congresswoman. If he needed to speak to Maeve early in the morning about a proposal, he would have called my line. Furthermore, unless his own phone was lost, he would have used his cell to call, email, or text—not some random phone in the tourist enclave of the United States Capitol.

No doubt about it. Maeve had been set up. The criminal was a crafty one. He or she had capitalized on Maeve's altercation with Drysdale, seeing her as the perfect suspect. The perp had figured out how to get Drysdale and Maeve in the same location. After he or she murdered Jack, Maeve would come across the scene and suspicion would fall on her. Using the Speaker's gavel was a nice touch, especially since Maeve had served as presiding officer the night before during the House of Representatives debate.

I glanced at my email inbox. Judy Talent hadn't replied. I had no connection whatsoever to the widower Jordan Macintyre or Gareth Pressler from the Sergeant at Arms office. That left me with one option: Doug's former student. A speedy survey of the House employee directory online turned up a Melinda Gomez. Bingo. I dialed her extension and prayed she'd pick up.

"House press gallery, Assistant Superintendent Gomez speaking."

The formality of her announcement caught me off guard. I stuttered for a second and then words flew out of my mouth in a rush. "I'm Kit Marshall and my boyfriend Doug Hollingsworth suggested I call you. He was your professor at Georgetown and thought you might be able to help."

The line was silent. "This is a House extension, right? Do you work for Congress?"

My opening gambit hadn't included that important information. If I planned to reprise my sleuthing, I'd better get a grip. "Yes, I'm sorry. Let me start over. I work for Congresswoman Maeve Dixon from North Carolina. Doug, I mean Professor Hollingsworth, suggested I call you to talk about Jack Drysdale." I always forgot to use Doug's academic title when speaking with his undergraduate minions.

There was another pause. The Drysdale request had likely thrown her for a loop. She lowered her voice to a whisper. "We're not supposed to say much to reporters about the murder."

"I understand, but I don't want to give information to the press. I need to gather information about Jack so I can figure out who killed him."

"Now I know who you are. I was interning in the press gallery last year when you solved that stabbing in the Senate. There was a rumor at Georgetown that Professor Hollingsworth was somehow connected to the investigation, but no one knew how."

Never a fan of notoriety, Doug had tried to bury that connection as deep as possible. "That's me. This time, I need a little assistance coming up with a list of suspects. You see a lot from your perch. Maybe you can help?"

She chuckled. "I do see a lot, it's true." Melinda was referring to the location of the press gallery, which overlooked the House floor.

"I bet you do. What do you say?" I glanced at my watch. Melinda hadn't been working in the House very long. Most young staffers were recent college grads motivated by the free food and drinks provided at the many receptions hosted by lobbyists and trade organizations every day on the Hill. The time for lunch had come and gone, but maybe Melinda hadn't eaten yet or would succumb to a tempting offer.

It was worth a shot. "Can I buy you a snack at the Creamery?" By far the best eating establishment in the House, the Creamery served coffee and ice cream to members and staff with cravings for caffeine, sugar, or both.

"I really shouldn't leave, given everything that's happened today and the continuing interest in the shutdown." She paused. "But I'm pretty hungry. I suppose a few minutes won't hurt."

The offer of free food had resonated. Melinda was a woman after my own heart. I'd have to thank Doug tonight for making the connection.

"Terrific. I'll see you there in ten minutes."

Should I tell Maeve or Dan where I was headed? The doors to both of their private offices were shut. I decided against it. If they needed to reach me, they could call my iPhone. The Creamery was located next to the main House cafeteria in the adjacent Longworth Building. I descended to the basement of Cannon and crossed through the underground level of the rotunda, which displayed a huge plaster model of the Capitol commissioned by the powerful Speaker Joe Cannon in 1903. Despite his autocratic rule, the extension of the Capitol envisioned by Cannon and reflected in the sculptor's model hadn't been completed until 1962.

With Congress, some things never change. It takes forever to make a difference around here.

The looming Capitol model was a constant reminder

that congressional achievements were measured not in days, months, or even years, but decades.

After sliding into a seat at the Creamery, I realized I had no way of recognizing Melinda. Steady streams of House staffers paraded through the eatery at every moment, scarfing up the coffee and ice cream treats. A few moments later, a young woman in her early twenties entered. She appeared to be Hispanic and wore stylish dark-rimmed glasses that screamed "smart, yet fashionable." She looked tentatively around the establishment. This had to be Melinda Gomez, or at least the odds were good. Given Dan's mistake earlier today, I'd better check for myself. I got up and walked toward her, extending my hand. With a questioning rise in my voice, I said, "Melinda?" At the same time, I stole a hard glance at the official House identification badge she wore around her neck. It was hard to see the entire name on the tag, but I could definitely make out a capital "M" followed by a last name starting with a "G." Pay dirt.

She returned my question with a shy smile. "Are you Professor Hollingsworth's girlfriend?"

I cringed slightly at her description of me. The feminist in me screamed, "No, I'm Kit Marshall, House staffer extraordinaire!"

I stifled my insecurity, but Melinda must have noticed me wince because she added, "I'm sorry, I just forgot your name from our phone call."

Her explanation erased my tense reaction to her initial greeting. "That's okay. Yes, I'm Kit Marshall. It's nice to meet you. Would you like some ice cream?"

Melinda laughed and responded enthusiastically. "Actually, I would *love* ice cream."

We placed our orders and sat down. I hadn't eaten lunch, so ice cream didn't constitute a terrible indulgence. Rationalizing was a dieter's bête noire, but right now a good lead on Jack's murder was a bigger priority than a trim waist. Maybe Melinda had missed lunch, too. She licked at her ice cream cone as though we were battling ninety-five-degree heat in the middle of summer.

She didn't have much time to spend with me. I set my cup of chocolate chip aside so I could begin my friendly interrogation. "Is there chatter in the press gallery about who killed Jack?"

Melinda stopped inhaling her cone for a moment to utter one word. "Sure."

Obviously, I needed to lead more with my questions. Even though Melinda was a newbie press staffer, she had apparently learned the cardinal rule of D.C. media relations: never volunteer additional information.

Flattery often worked. "The police are the formal investigators, but we know the press really drives these stories. What's the chatter on the likely suspects?"

Melinda had just stuffed the last piece of cone into her mouth. She put her finger up to indicate she had to finish chewing before answering. After a big swallow, she wiped her mouth with a napkin. She'd clearly enjoyed the ice cream. Now would she return the favor?

"It's a little early for speculating, but everyone in the press gallery is chattering about Hill Rat."

Hill Rat was an anonymous blogger who wrote scathing posts about Congress. Nothing was off limits for Hill Rat. He or she wrote about members of Congress, staffers, Capitol Hill rumors, political intrigue, internecine fighting, romantic gossip, and policy deals. Hill

Rat never had anything good to say about Congress or the people who worked there. The blog, though written by an obvious narcissist, drew heavy online traffic from the Beltway crowd. Denizens of Capitol Hill both feared and desired a mention in Hill Rat's reports. A mention from Hill Rat was almost always unfavorable, but it also meant you mattered. Only the main players appeared in Hill Rat's blog, even though the acerbic observations never portrayed our city's most prominent citizens in a flattering light. Lending to Hill Rat's fame was his or her clandestine identity. Journalists joked the identity of Hill Rat remained the best secret in D.C. since Watergate's Deep Throat.

Although I'd read Rat's most infamous entries, I wasn't a devotee. The writing was witty but the condescending tone rubbed me the wrong way. Washington had its share of snobby, self-indulgent blockheads who deserved Hill Rat's drubbings. Alongside the numbskulls, however, were hardworking bleeding-heart staffers who arrived at work each day with the goal of making the country a better place to live. Sometimes Washingtonians didn't fit neatly in either of those categories. Hill Rat either ignored or failed to appreciate the shades of gray motivating daily decision-making in our nation's capital city.

"Do you mean reporters consider Hill Rat a bona fide suspect?"

Melinda smiled. "That's a good question. Hill Rat focused on Jack Drysdale in several posts a few months back. He or she even wrote about his spouse Jordan's failed business venture." That explained how Meg knew about this tidbit. She was a dedicated Hill Rat reader.

Contemplating Melinda's response, I rubbed my

chin. "But why would Hill Rat kill Jack? It seemed like he enjoyed writing about him. I'd think bloggers would want their subjects alive and kicking so they could keep writing unseemly stories."

Melinda pushed her chair back, indicating our conversation was nearing the end. "That's true, but Jack wasn't one of Hill Rat's typical victims. After the blog about Jordan, Jack vowed to get even."

We both stood up and started walking to the Creamery's exit. "How so?"

Melinda hung her purse on her shoulder and turned toward the hallway. "Jack promised reporters that he was going to discover Hill Rat's true identity."

I raced to catch up with Melinda before she left. "You think Hill Rat might have killed Jack before he could reveal his name? Or her name?"

Melinda stopped walking and turned to face me. "Jack said he'd expose Hill Rat, even if it was the last thing he did."

NINE

AFTER PARTING WAYS with Melinda, I strolled at a leisurely pace back to the Cannon Building. The ice cream had proven a valuable investment. Hill Rat's anonymity allowed him or her to script scintillating observations about D.C. power players without repercussions. Furthermore, since Hill Rat's identity was a mystery, no one knew when to shut up. Hill Rat could be any astute observer with access to the Capitol Hill crowd. But Hill Rat's cachet would be destroyed if he or she could no longer operate as an anonymous ghost. Jack had threatened exposure, and surely Hill Rat knew that Drysdale always made good on his threats.

I returned to the office, which was as quiet as when I left. A hasty check of the relevant media outlets confirmed what I already guessed. Maeve Dixon hadn't been named as an official suspect, and her involvement in Drysdale's murder hadn't been revealed. There was little hope we could keep her name out of the press much longer. Even if Maeve could avoid an official interrogation, the police would have to eventually disclose that she'd discovered the body. It was half past four. Sighing, I hauled myself to Dan's office. I couldn't assume Dan understood our relatively peaceful office existence subsisted on borrowed time.

Dan's door was ajar. I knocked lightly and heard him say, "Kit, is that you?"

I took his question as an invitation to enter. Dan was sitting at his computer, apparently at work. At least he hadn't reverted to an emergency meditation session involving self-inflicted acupuncture.

"Where did you go? You haven't been at your desk."

I sat down in the chair opposite him. "You told me to investigate, so that's what I've been doing."

His eyes lit up. "Did you figure out who killed Jack Drysdale?" Dan leaned forward, eager for my response.

"No," I said slowly. Dan must not have read the Hardy Boys growing up. Or perhaps he watched too much *CSI* and expected murders to be solved in sixty minutes or less.

Dan's face fell. "Oh. How long do you think it's going to take?"

"I'm going to be honest with you, Dan. I have no idea. I've got a couple suspects identified but it's not going to be easy. I'm not exactly friends with the people in Jack's political and social circles."

Dan lowered his voice. "You'd better keep digging. Maeve's in there," he pointed toward her office, "with her legal counsel."

Maeve hadn't wasted any time. "Do you know the specifics of their conversation?"

"I think he's trying to outline her options."

Options? That sounded ominous. "What do you mean?"

"I wasn't invited to listen. But I did linger outside her office for a minute or two," Dan admitted sheepishly.

"You eavesdropped. It's hardly a crime in light of our current situation. What did you hear?"

"I couldn't make out everything, but I did hear the word 'resignation' several times."

I swallowed hard. "As in her resignation from Congress?"

"What else could it be? Like I said, she told me the lawyer was going to cover every alternative."

This situation was headed from bad to worse. Even if Maeve wasn't arrested, she might want to avoid a media maelstrom concerning her involvement in Drysdale's murder. Sidestepping the whole mess could include ditching her political career. Meg's wisdom about working for a freshman member of Congress rang loud and clear in my brain. She'd said something akin to "opportunity of a lifetime" since I'd help "shape her political trajectory." Unless Jack's real killer was exposed, Maeve's congressional career was headed in the notorious rather than noteworthy direction.

I glanced at my iPhone and noticed a new email message. I clicked on the mail icon. Judy Talent from the Majority Leader's office had responded to my message. Dan must have noticed my surprised reaction. "What is it? Has the news hit the press?"

"Calm down. That's not it. I requested a meeting with Judy Talent and she just replied to my email."

Dan's voice squeaked like an adolescent's. "Why did you do that? I told you solving this murder and clearing Maeve was your number one priority."

Dan's annoying persistence had pushed my patience to the limit. "I had an ulterior motive, Dan."

He looked perplexed, as if I had announced the landing of aliens on the Cannon Building's roof. Some people needed every move spelled out for them. "I used the excuse to discuss the shutdown so I could find out if she knows anything about Jack's murder."

"Wow! That's really clever of you," Dan said with enthusiasm.

Not really. "I'd better get cracking then. Is there anything else you'd like me to do before heading home tonight?"

Dan shook his head. "I'll wait to talk to Maeve, but I don't think there's anything else we can do. Let's just hope the police don't mention her involvement."

As far as that front went, the sands of the hourglass had almost run out. *No need to worry Dan. Why soil the reality of the blissfully ignorant?*

I returned to my desk and replied to Judy's email. She'd suggested the possibility of lunch. That would be ideal, since I'd likely get more out of Judy during a meal than a hurried office meeting. But Judy probably didn't have a lot of time for eating these days. An idea popped into my head and I started typing: Judy, how about lunch at We The Pizza at noon?

We The Pizza was a popular Capitol Hill restaurant situated only three blocks from the Cannon Building and the Capitol. Owned by celebrity *Top Chef* star Spike Mendelsohn, the pizzeria offered one of the best "quick" options for lunch on the Hill. With the shutdown, the typical long lunch line would be nonexistent. We could order, grab a seat, and eat within thirty minutes.

I was ready to shut down my computer for the night when another email popped up. Judy had answered, so I clicked on her reply. See you there. Get ready to talk shutdown solutions.

Sure, we could do that. But we were also going to talk a little murder, too. I clicked off my terminal and grabbed my purse. It was almost impossible to think about the case while stewing inside the office. I needed to clear my head and plan my next move.

I hustled out of the office and made my way down the empty hallway toward the only Cannon Building door that remained open for egress. As I prepared to leave, I spotted a short, mousy-haired man in a Brooks Brothers suit gathering his laptop briefcase, *Wall Street Journal*, and smartphone from the conveyor belt that scanned all personal items brought into the congressional complex. His head was turned away as he focused on retrieving his various possessions. Even though I couldn't see his face clearly, I knew who it was.

"Trevor? Is that you?"

Startled, he raised his head and peered at me from behind his horn-rimmed glasses. Yep, that was Trevor. I'd recognize that stare in my sleep.

"Kit Marshall. What a delight."

Trevor and I had been colleagues in the Senate for several years. We had never been friends, even though our cubicles had been right next to each other. Trevor wasn't the most pleasant person in the world, but when Senator Langsford was murdered, he'd supported my attempt to solve the crime. Congeniality and a basic degree of human empathy eluded Trevor. Yet his intelligence and quick thinking had proven invaluable as Meg and I sorted through the suspects last summer.

Judging by his professional appearance and expensive attire, Trevor had done well for himself. He'd accepted a position as a lobbyist for a big military contractor after the governor named Senator Langsford's successor. "Are you still working for Carter Power?"

Trevor straightened his tie and smoothed his suit

jacket. "Yes, of course. I heard you had secured employment with the newly elected Maeve Dixon?"

"That's right. I'm her LD these days." LD was Hill lingo for "legislative director."

"Another challenging position. She barely won her election, as I recall."

Leave it to Trevor to point out the shortcomings. "Right again. That's one of the reasons I took the job. I wanted to work for a House member who wasn't going to follow the party line. It makes life more interesting."

Trevor chuckled. "You could put it that way. If you consider reduced job security an acceptable work challenge."

I clenched my fist around my purse. Trevor had the uncanny ability to twist my own words against me. Two could play at this game. After all, Trevor wasn't a congressional staffer anymore. He worked off the Hill as a lobbyist. That meant he should be begging me for information and access.

"How's working on K Street? Is it everything you'd dreamed it would be?"

Trevor's face clouded over. I'd hit a nerve. "It has its perks." He sniffed defensively. "For one thing, I'm finally able to dress the way a true professional should." He gave me a brief up-and-down glance, an unspoken criticism of my unfashionable attire. Hill staff didn't make big salaries, so most of my suits came from the sales rack.

No way I was letting him off the hook. "Besides the money, what do you like about the job?"

Trevor wasn't one for small talk. A direct question often elicited a straight answer. After a brief pause, he spoke slowly. "If I can be honest with you, it's not as challenging as I would have hoped. It's more about schmoozing with the right people all over town, including the Hill. So I've been working on my relationship skills."

My eyes must have bulged out of my head. Trevor was as smart as a whip, but he wasn't Mr. Congeniality. I choked out, "How's that going?"

He straightened up. "Actually, not badly. I'm meeting the right people, going to the important social functions, and learning what I need to know, plus a lot more. I can't complain."

If Trevor could charm the pants off the Beltway crowd, there was hope for me to become a swimsuit model. "That's really impressive, Trevor. I'm proud of you."

"It's hardly worthy of commendation. But that's enough about me. How are you adjusting to life in the House of Representatives?"

Trevor really had learned some basic social skills since his time in the Senate. He'd never asked me one question about myself in the four years we shared a workspace.

"It's been harder than I thought working for a first-term House member. There's so much to do, and each vote really matters for her record. Still, I've been enjoying it…until this week, that is."

"Yes, I know the shutdown has congressional offices scrambling."

Maybe Trevor would help me again. Running into him could be a lucky break. "It's not just the shutdown. Did you hear about the murder of Jack Drysdale today?"

"I read about it in the *Washington Post*. I didn't know him well. I'd only met him a handful of times."

Good. Trevor knew him better than I did. I gave him a sideways glance. "I may need to repeat my role as a homicide detective."

Trevor did a double take. I'd captured his attention. "Kit, why on earth would you get mixed up in Drysdale's murder investigation? You don't have any close ties to the Speaker's office."

I let slide Trevor's snide comment about my lowly status in the House's pecking order. Sighing, I moved a step closer. Even though the Cannon Building was deserted, the walls had ears. I couldn't afford to let this information slip into the wrong hands.

I leaned in to whisper, "My boss might be involved."

Trevor's eyes narrowed in circumspection. He moved six inches forward to nearly close the gap between us. "Might? Either she is or she isn't."

Trevor was like many Washington type A personalities. Literal. Organized. Impatient. Demanding. For these folks, it was a strain to understand ambiguity. Beating around the bush wouldn't get me anywhere with him.

"Maeve Dixon discovered the body this morning, Trevor."

My words hung in silence. Trevor was rarely shocked by anything, but his immediate reaction indicated my revelation had thrown him for a loop.

After a long moment, Trevor said, "I assume she's a suspect?"

I reminded Trevor about her encounter the day before with Jack Drysdale. He nodded, clearly aware of the public tiff.

I leaned against the wall in the hallway, needing the

support. It had been a long day, and mental exhaustion was setting in. "You can see my predicament, right?"

Trevor smiled tightly. "The situation is a bit different than last year, but an urgency exists nonetheless. Believe me, I have great respect for Detective O'Halloran and the entire Capitol Hill Police force. If you don't solve this crime swiftly, they might end up blaming the obvious suspect." As if I needed clarification, he added, "Your boss, of course."

"The problem is I don't know the suspects as intimately as I did before." I outlined the short list I had developed today after my discreet inquiries.

After Trevor listened to my list, he rubbed his chin thoughtfully. "I know several people you've mentioned. Who do you need to meet tomorrow?"

My intuition had proven correct. Trevor wanted to assist. Probably he would leap at any opportunity to re-enter the Capitol Hill orbit. I mentally clicked through the suspects I'd identified. "I have no connection to Gareth Pressler in the Sergeant at Arms office. I also don't know Jack's husband. Now I guess he's a widower." Just pronouncing the word was depressing, even though I wasn't acquainted with him.

"I can help you with Pressler. I know a guy who works in the Sergeant's office and reports to Pressler. His name is Trent Roscoe and I can get you a few minutes with him tomorrow."

What a relief. Running into Trevor had been a godsend. "Thanks, Trevor. I appreciate it."

He pressed his lips together and gave me a curt bow. "At your service." After a moment, he added, "By the way, what is the status of your relationship with your *inamorato*? I believe his name is Doug, is it not?"

Trevor's formal way of speaking used to irk me, but now I accepted it as part of his eccentric personality. It was almost as though Trevor was a vampire, born in a different era. I pushed that thought aside. Maybe I'd read one too many fantasy e-book trilogies. Trevor had nothing in common with Edward Cullen.

"We're still living together in Arlington."

Trevor exhibited numerous personality defects, but he was no dummy. "I assume you have not formalized your relationship?" He looked pointedly at my left hand.

Reflexively, I touched my ring finger. *Damn Trevor.* He always knew how to get my goat. My annoyance obvious, I replied, "No, but we're very happy together."

"I see. Well, I think you will enjoy your meeting tomorrow with Trent. Look for an email to confirm it in the morning. Have a good evening, Kit Marshall."

Trevor didn't wear a cape, but if he did, he would have swirled it around him and disappeared in a cloud of smoke. Instead, he made a beeline down the long congressional office hallway behind us, headed for destinations unknown. I admired his long strides and swift pace, wishing I could demonstrate the same self-assurance.

What did he mean about my meeting tomorrow with Trent? That was mysterious. I dismissed his comment as typical Trevor. There was no point in trying to figure out the enigma.

On impulse, I grabbed my iPhone and shot off a text to Meg: Drink? Leaving now. I'd give her three minutes to answer. If not, I'd head home and catch up with her later.

My phone chimed to indicate an iMessage: Italian happy hour?

I wrote back immediately: See you there.

We didn't need to confirm the location. We only frequented one place with cheap drinks and food. Two blocks away from the House office buildings, Sonoma was convenient. As a bonus, it added a touch of class to our Hill outings. The dinner offerings could be pricey, but their Italian happy hour featured inexpensive wines and tasty small plates. The key for Meg was the sparkling wine, her libation of choice when stressed out. To be fair, bubbly was Meg's preferred drink even if she was just plain thirsty.

In five minutes, I was inside Sonoma and heading upstairs. The open seating and upstairs bar hosted the boisterous happy hours. This evening, only two clusters of patrons were enjoying drinks and nibbles. Pretty soon, the District's small businesses would add themselves to the growing list of victims turned upside down by the federal government's shuttering.

I sat in the corner of the lounge area. At least we could talk privately. Due to her busy work schedule, Meg's free time was limited. I wanted to make good use of the unexpected opportunity.

Meg glided into the room and saw me instantly. She signaled a "hello" with a brief waggle of her hand and bustled over to the overstuffed sofa. Meg's fashionable style was evident even in the dead of winter. She wore a fitted red peacoat accented with a dark black belt and sported a trendy crochet flower hat that sat slightly off-center on her head. All this along with tight black riding pants and leather gloves. Meg had been my best friend for years. We'd survived political campaigns together, the tribulations of being overworked and underpaid congressional staffers, and even a high-profile murder investigation. One would think that through it all, Meg's sense of style might have rubbed off on me, even via osmosis (if that was biologically possible). But it hadn't. As much as I tried, I simply couldn't adapt Meg's fashion sense to my body and coloring. Whenever I tried, it just looked wrong.

"Did you order me a glass of sparkling wine yet?"

No hello or perfunctory salutations for Meg. She meant business. "Not yet, I just got here myself." I motioned for the waiter.

Meg grabbed the happy hour menu from the coffee table next to us. I ordered the white wine on special and Meg predictably went for the Prosecco, along with Italian meatballs and prosciutto. Those riding pants hid no sins. Someone should study Meg's metabolism to figure out how it defied calories.

"I only have time for one drink, unfortunately. I need to get back to the office to finish some research for the hearings."

Meg truly was burning the midnight oil. It was rare for her to cut happy hour short. "That's okay. One drink is my limit, too. I should really get back to Doug and Clarence. I haven't been able to spend much time with them lately."

Our drinks arrived and Meg grabbed her glass and clinked it to mine. "That's right, I almost forgot. Congratulations!"

I was confused. Had Doug told Meg something in confidence she'd misinterpreted? I felt my face flush. Was Doug planning a big surprise?

"Did Doug let you in on a secret I should know about?"

"No, silly! Not Doug. Clarence! He's on track to win the top dog title, of course."

Trevor's comment about my permanently single status had muddled my thinking. Of course Doug would never tell Meg about marriage proposal plans. He barely trusted her to water our plants when we went on vacation.

"Clarence is still winning the online competition?"

"You didn't know? I thought you might have engineered his success by promising Maeve's vote to end the shutdown!" She giggled.

I pulled out my iPhone and navigated to the Capitol Canine website. Sure enough, Clarence's cute mug appeared in the number one slot. This morning's results were no fluke. Somehow he'd managed to amass five thousand votes in the past twenty-four hours. He was adorable, but this made no sense. It certainly wasn't because everyone on the Hill knew his owners, either.

"This is terrific. I'm not sure how it happened."

"You didn't orchestrate a coordinated campaign for Clarence? That's usually how you win the top dog title."

How did Meg know those details? Even though she loved Clarence, Meg didn't own a dog, or any other living thing for that matter. She once remarked betta fish were beautiful, but she wouldn't want to ruin her nails changing the water. Meg gave new meaning to the adjectives "independent" and "self-sufficient," even by Washington standards.

"No, I've been a little busy. You know, with the murder—the one where my boss is the prime suspect."

"Right. Well, it looks like someone else decided to help out Clarence with Capitol Canine. There's no dog even close in votes. What are you going to wear to the big party tomorrow evening?"

"Party?"

"Kit, I might as well accept the award on behalf of Clarence. You're clueless." She grabbed my phone out of my hand and touched the screen. She waited a moment, and then showed me the phone. "The award ceremony is tomorrow night, as soon as the voting closes."

I rolled my eyes. Not that I wasn't glad Clarence had achieved such impressive status, but I had other matters on my mind right now.

"I'm not sure how I'm going to fit that in. I really need to focus on clearing Maeve's name."

Now it was Meg's turn to roll her eyes. Her drink was almost empty. She picked up her glass and pointed it at me. "What would you do without me?" She tilted her head back and finished it off. Meg had a flair for the dramatic she occasionally used to her advantage.

"I don't know. Drink less?"

"Clarence winning this contest is the luckiest thing that could happen to you. Just look who's heading the awards committee!" She pointed to my iPhone's screen again.

"I've never met that man before in my life."

"Precisely. That's Jordan Macintyre, Jack's widower. Didn't you want to figure out a way to talk to him?"

Meg was right. Macintyre was on my short list of suspects since he likely stood to gain financially from Jack's death.

"Do you think he'll come to the ceremony tomorrow night? He might skip it because of Jack's death."

"I don't know, but you could call Capitol Canine to find out. He's deeply involved with the contest because the dog he owned with Jack is a past winner. All the proceeds go to charity so he may feel obligated to participate."

Meg had a point. Given his dedication to the contest, there was a chance Jordan might show up at the party. I didn't have any other plan to interact with him, so this opportunity could be critical.

"Thanks for letting me know. Guess who I ran into before I texted you for drinks?"

Meg was putting on her coat as if eager to return to the office for several more hours of work. Meg had progressed professionally by leaps and bounds in her new job. I buried a pang of jealousy. As a legislative director, I'd moved up in the world, too. Unlike Meg, I was fighting to keep my position. I'd managed to land on my feet once after a Hill scandal. Twice would be pushing it.

"Who? I'm sorry, but I need to run back to the office."

"Trevor. He was coming into Cannon as I was leaving."

Meg slung her sleek Kate Spade bag over her shoulder. "Tremendous. I hope he's enjoying life on the dark side as a lobbyist."

Meg and Trevor had a rocky relationship. Actually, "rocky" was an understatement. Meg detested Trevor, and the feeling was mutual.

"He's going to introduce me to someone he knows in the Sergeant at Arms office so I can find out more about the conflict between Gareth Pressler and Jack."

Meg gave a perfunctory nod, waved goodbye, and started to walk toward the staircase. Then she turned around abruptly. "Who does Trevor know in the Sergeant at Arms office?"

I racked my brain. Names were always a challenge, which disadvantaged me in the political world. "It's hard for me to remember. He's going to email us both tomorrow morning." Then it popped into my brain. "I think his first name is Trent."

Meg broke into a wide grin. "Trent Roscoe?"

"That's it."

"You're in for a treat."

"Trevor made a weird remark to that effect. Why?"

"Trent was recently named one of the fifty most beautiful Capitol Hill staffers. He's eye candy, for sure!"

Leave it to Meg to know the hotties. She'd made several appearances on the infamous Capitol Hill list of attractive people.

"I'm not there to ogle him. I need him as a contact so I can determine if Gareth killed Jack."

As Meg walked away, she yelled over her shoulder, "Be sure to remember that tomorrow when you lay eyes on him!"

When I arrived home, Doug and Clarence were watching a television documentary on the History Channel about White House pets.

"Did you know that LBJ owned two beagles named Him and Her?" asked Doug.

"No idea."

"They were on the cover of *Time* magazine with the president."

"But they never held the title of Top Dog on Capitol Hill."

Doug laughed and scratched Clarence's ears. "Good point."

A plate with crackers, veggies, and other delectable

snacks littered the coffee table, along with a half-empty bottle of pinot grigio.

"Did you and Clarence have a happy hour at home?"

"We deserved it after a hard day's work." Clarence sat up next to Doug as if to agree with this pronouncement.

I flopped down on the couch next to them and popped a carrot in my mouth.

"Stressful day?" Doug asked.

"You could say that. At least Maeve managed to escape the headlines today. That can't last forever."

Doug stayed silent, so I kept talking. "I talked to your former student Melinda today. She was helpful. Apparently Jack Drysdale had a big beef with Hill Rat. Do you read that blog?"

Doug crinkled his nose. "I try to avoid journalism written by rodents."

"I'm not a fan, either. If I want to solve this murder, I may have to figure out the Rat's identity, though."

Doug popped a sesame cracker in his mouth and answered with his mouth full. "How are you going to do that? Hasn't the entire Washington D.C. press corps been trying to expose him for months?"

"I have other leads, but there's only one way to catch a rat."

Doug looked at me expectantly. I picked up a piece of Gouda and waved it around for emphasis. "You have to set a trap with the right kind of cheese."

TEN

I woke the next morning with a renewed and determined focus. Yesterday had been a mess, but the situation wasn't disastrous, at least not yet. Maeve's involvement had remained under wraps, and other legitimate suspects with motives existed. Maybe clearing her name wouldn't prove impossible. The person who discovered the body always faced tough questions, just like I had last summer. Although it had been a rocky road, the actual perpetrators had been caught in the end. Thomas Jefferson's famous quote, "Justice cannot sleep forever," fueled my optimism.

My calendar confirmed it was going to be a busy day: lunch with Judy Talent from the Majority Leader's office, a likely meeting with Trevor's contact at the Sergeant at Arms office, and then the Capitol Canine awards ceremony in the early evening.

Clarence sat obediently next to me while I checked my phone. He was trying to behave, but I could tell from the increasing rapidity of his tail wag he was losing patience. We had already been outside for our morning jog and he wanted his breakfast. Dogs are creatures of habit, and Clarence was no exception. If I didn't comply with expectations soon, he would progress to a whimper, then a staccato bark, and finally a full-throttle beagle mutt howl. Mrs. Beauregard, our neighbor two doors down, relished documenting Clarence's lapses in canine decorum. Every unleashed escape into the hallway and each early morning howl eventually made its way back to us, usually with the threat of a condo board "pet sanction." Thus far, we'd managed to avoid an actual monetary penalty because Clarence seemed to understand subconsciously he was only allowed so many mistakes in any thirty-day period. I wondered if Clarence's triumph as top dog on Capitol Hill might buy him some slack with the powers that be on the condo board. After all, he was about to become a bona fide Washington D.C. celebrity.

After I filled the dog's bowl, Doug appeared in the kitchen. He always looked disoriented when he woke up, his bushy brown hair disheveled and his glasses slightly askew. He'd slept in the t-shirt I bought him for his birthday, which sported the slogan, "TRUST ME, I'M A HISTORY PROFESSOR." He made a bee-line for the espresso machine and began filling it up with fresh beans.

"Are you free this evening?" I asked.

Normally, I would have allowed him to ingest an initial caffeine infusion before interrogating him, but the clock was ticking.

"Um, I think so. What day is it again?"

"It's Wednesday, all day."

He grumbled as he removed the coffee mug with his espresso. He carefully tilted a small pitcher of heated milk and added it to his caffeinated masterpiece.

"I don't remember anything on my schedule tonight. I was planning on teaching my class and then heading home for a long afternoon of writing."

What else was new? That was Doug's schedule every day. When he had an evening event, like a Georgetown faculty wine and cheese reception, he complained bitterly about forfeiting precious research time.

"It looks as though Clarence is going to win the Capitol Canine contest, so can you bring him to the awards ceremony tonight?"

Doug took a long sip of his latte and wiped a frothy mustache from under his lip before responding. "He's winning? How did that happen?"

"It's another mystery to solve. I thought maybe you decided to get your students involved. I haven't had any time to marshal votes for him."

"Nope, it wasn't me. I didn't even look at the website to monitor the voting."

Clarence ran in between us and abruptly rolled over on his back. After his morning jaunt and breakfast, he typically requested a belly rub.

We both bent down to rub his pink stomach, and he gave a low growl of appreciation. Doug had to commit, since it would be almost impossible to get Clarence to the awards ceremony otherwise. "Can you meet me tonight for the event? One of the suspects in Jack Drysdale's murder might be there, and it's my best chance to talk with him."

"Now I get it. You need me to handle Clarence while you interrogate suspects."

I stood and put my hands on my hips. "No, I can handle our dog and my interrogations. But if he's going to win Capitol Canine, then Clarence needs to make an appearance!"

The exasperation in my voice had caught Doug's attention. He stopped rubbing Clarence's belly and glanced up. "All right, I get it. Clarence and I will be there with bells on. Just text me the time and the address. At least we'll spend some time together."

"That's the spirit. Thank you." After giving Clarence a pat on the head and Doug a kiss on the lips, I bolted for the door. As usual, I was already behind schedule.

With the shutdown still in full force, Metro traffic remained sparse. Absent of delays caused by overloaded cars, the subway zipped along to the Hill in record time. During the long escalator ride from the Capitol South station to the surface, I determined there was enough time for a brief stop at my favorite morning breakfast stop, Le Bon Café. The tiny French bistro next to the Library of Congress's Madison Building was reminiscent of the numerous eateries that populated Parisian neighborhoods. Usually stepping inside Le Bon Café was enough to transport me momentarily to my favorite European city, providing a nice respite from the persistent cloud of stress surrounding our nation's capital.

This morning, Le Bon Café lived up to expectations. It was filled with the aroma of rich coffee, egg strata, and freshly baked pastries. I inhaled deeply, thankful that smelling delicious food wasn't fattening.

Usually, the line stretched the length of the café. This morning, only one other person stood in front of me. If I was going to treat myself to a French breakfast, I typically went for scrambled eggs or a waffle with fresh fruit. But later today I had a pizza lunch scheduled with Judy. Sighing, I opted for a skim latte and a yogurt parfait. I had just grabbed my breakfast off the counter and was about to head for the door when Detective O'Halloran breezed through the entrance.

There was no way to avoid him in the tiny café. "Good morning, Detective!" The cheer in my voice sounded forced, but I didn't want O'Halloran to know I was worried about the status of Maeve's involvement in Jack's murder. Keeping up appearances was the better strategy.

"Ms. Marshall. Just the person I was hoping to speak with this morning."

Not a good sign. Maybe O'Halloran had some good information to share about the murder. Police weren't supposed to talk about investigations in progress, but O'Halloran had exhibited loose-lipped tendencies in the past.

"You want to talk to me?" I asked, feigning innocence. My words had fallen on deaf ears. Staring over my shoulder, O'Halloran eagerly eyed the pan of oat bran crisp, fresh out of the oven. The sweet smell of brown sugar floated past us. Since I stood between him and a delicious breakfast, he'd want to keep this conversation brief.

After a moment's pause for a deep inhale, O'Halloran returned his focus to me. "Ah, yes. Ms. Marshall. You saved me a phone call. Any reason why Jack Drysdale would place a Post-it with your name on it in the middle of his desk?"

So much for staying one step removed from this murder. "I have no idea, Detective. As you know, I met with Jack the day before he was killed. Representative Dixon had an appointment with the Speaker, and I spent fifteen minutes with Mr. Drysdale while our bosses chatted."

"Why am I not surprised to find you connected to yet another crime in Congress, Ms. Marshall?"

"I have no idea, sir. Did the note on Jack's desk say anything else other than my name?"

"Actually, it did. The name 'Clarence' was also on the Post-it."

I couldn't suppress a broad grin. At least one mystery was solved. "Clarence is my dog. Jack was trying to help him win the Capitol Canine contest. It was his attempt to persuade me to sell Dixon on the Speaker's proposal to end the shutdown. He'd help Clarence win the contest, and I'd make sure the congresswoman would support the Speaker when push came to shove."

O'Halloran shook his head. "Now I've heard everything. You're telling me Drysdale tried to bribe you by fixing a dog popularity contest?"

"Not exactly. He wasn't fixing it. But if he told his numerous contacts to vote for Clarence, they'd do it. As you know, Detective, Jack Drysdale was the most powerful staffer on the Hill."

O'Halloran sighed. "Yeah, I know. So powerful that even a member of Congress might want him out of the way." He gave me a sideways glance with a half smirk.

"What are you implying?"

"Nothing, at least yet. Your boss doesn't have a fancy congressional trip abroad planned for the near future, right?"

"Not that I'm aware of. But our scheduler is on furlough due to the shutdown."

O'Halloran huffed. "Then I'll tell you instead. She shouldn't leave Washington until we solve this murder." He saluted military style with his right hand and moved past me to place his order.

His dismissal had been abrupt and the conversation disconcerting, to say the least. Maeve was still a person of interest. Even though the police had kept her name out of the press so far, that wouldn't matter if

O'Halloran gathered enough circumstantial evidence to label her a formal suspect.

The morning had started out so promising with the speedy commute and stop at my favorite breakfast joint. As I shoved the yogurt parfait into my purse, I could feel my body tense up. No amount of tasty food or libations would give me relief. The only solution was to find Jack's killer so Maeve Dixon could resume her role as a marginal yet ambitious member of Congress.

In five minutes, I opened the front door to the office and retreated to the safety of my desk. The suite seemed quiet, but appearances could be deceiving. I had just enough time to turn on my computer and suck down half of the yogurt parfait before the door to Representative Dixon's private office opened. My boss emerged, wearing an athletic zebra tank top, gray spandex shorts, and a matching black headband.

"Early workout at the House gym?" I asked.

"Since I never made it yesterday due to the fiasco with Drysdale, I did the early morning CrossFit circuit."

Maeve was referring to a killer regimen several younger representatives followed when the House was in session. They met in the gym reserved only for members of Congress and apparently knocked out a workout fit for cage fighters. My boss was a regular, mostly for the exercise, but also because it gave her an opportunity to network with colleagues she might not interact with otherwise.

"I'm impressed. Unfortunately, I have news for you that might make you wish you stayed at the gym."

She grabbed a towel and wiped the sweat still beading on her face. "What's wrong now?"

"Nothing at the moment. But I ran into Detective

O'Halloran from the Capitol Hill Police, and he indicated you are still a person of interest in the murder."

I cringed, waiting for the explosion. Instead, Maeve
gulped down half a bottle of water, swallowed, and nodded her head.

"I expected this. That's why I consulted with an attorney yesterday."

"What are you going to do if you're named an official suspect? Won't that hurt you politically?"

"It won't help. My attorney will handle the police,
and I'll have to lie low for a while until this mess is
solved."

"What about the shutdown? I thought you wanted to
help broker the solution?"

Maeve smiled. "That's why I hired you, Kit. You're
the consummate public servant, always looking to find
the perfect public policy solution to heal our nation's
woes. I'll have to retreat from the shutdown negotiations if the murder investigation focuses on me. I would
be a distraction, and neither party would welcome my
presence."

"Did you tell Dan about this?"

In the midst of a leg stretch, she answered my question. "I have. He understands and supports my decision.
Dan may not know Washington D.C., but he has been
a loyal soldier throughout my short political career."

"Maybe I can help. You know I solved the murder
of my boss in the Senate last year."

Maeve gave a short, dry laugh. "I heard about it and
Dan reminded me last night." Her face turned serious.
"Listen to me. I don't want you investigating the murder
of Jack Drysdale. You were lucky once to find a killer

in the Capitol. Luck like that doesn't strike twice. Believe me, I know from firsthand experience in combat."

"I'm really concerned if we leave it to the police," I said. "They might settle on you as an easy target."

Maeve stepped right up to me and put her hand on my shoulder. "I appreciate the gesture, Kit. I was trained as a soldier, and that means I put my faith in the system. They might focus on me initially, but the police will figure this out. I don't want anyone getting hurt in the line of duty." Her smile returned. "And that's an order."

"I understand. You don't have to worry about me."

"I'm counting on it. Try to keep Dan focused. He's a worrywart." She gave me a playful wink, then continued, "I'm headed for a shower. After that, I'll be in my office."

Now I knew why the voters of North Carolina chose my boss to represent them in Congress. She was a class act. Despite her concern about my informal inquiries, I didn't give a second thought to my plan for the day. There was nothing wrong with asking a few innocent questions.

My email inbox indicated the push to find a solution to the shutdown had begun. Several legislative options had emerged, including one from the Majority Leader. I clicked on the file to open the document describing the proposal and groaned inwardly. A two-page summary preceded fifty pages of drafted bill language. Lunch with Judy was in three hours. At least part of that conversation hinged on an informed discussion about this deal. No time for procrastination.

Usually there was a dull roar in the background of a congressional office. Multiple televisions blared, with the House's floor activity broadcast from one set along with various cable television political talk shows on the others. Staffers were constantly on the phone, talking with colleagues, constituents, or reporters. "Controlled chaos" described it well. Ensuring consistency in all interactions executed in the congresswoman's name was no small task. Without the comforting din, my mind wandered as I stared at the computer monitor.

I was getting nowhere fast. It was time for a change of scenery. Where could I go? Smaller cafeterias throughout the congressional complex were good places to escape, but the shutdown had restricted food service to the main cafeteria in the Longworth Building. That wasn't an option because it was a lobbyist cruising ground. I'd never eaten a meal there without numerous interruptions from notorious K Street peddlers.

After a few minutes of concentration, an idea popped into the recesses of my overtaxed intellect. The problem wasn't just the lack of background noise; it was everything surrounding me. I needed to get out of this building entirely. Congress was one big tangled web of conflict and confusion these days. Before the winter chill set in, I'd accidentally happened upon an oasis of relative serenity. Adjacent to the Cannon Building was the Madison Building of the Library of Congress, where I'd attended a legislative process class on the intricacies of House committee procedure. After the class ended I was, as usual, hungry. The search for the elevators to the upstairs cafeteria led me to the La Follette Reading Room, a small resource facility at the Library reserved for members of Congress and staff. Members of Congress never used La Follette because they also had access to the ornate Congressional Reading Room in the Library's historic Jefferson Building. Since that day,

I'd made several trips to the hidden treasure when the pressures of daily Hill life became too much.

After printing the legislative proposal and grabbing my portfolio and coat, I headed to the Library. An underground tunnel connected Cannon to Madison, so going outside wasn't required. But after I was done with my work, it would be time for lunch with Judy Talent at the pizza eatery on Pennsylvania.

I exited the elevator on the second floor, hoping La Follette remained open during the shutdown. Madison was even emptier than the House office buildings. Vaguely, I remembered a librarian telling me La Follette was open as long as Congress was in session. They certainly weren't getting anything accomplished, but technically, Congress was scheduled to convene today. Grabbing the handle of the heavy door to La Follette, I saw my hunch confirmed as it swung open.

A middle-aged woman with oversized black glasses and a tight bun nodded as I entered. Sometimes clichés proved true; this was the Library of Congress, after all. Probably every librarian in the United States wanted to work here. Apparently, the need to escape Congress was not uncommon. Several other staffers sat at tables and carrels, quietly reading or working at computer terminals.

I found an empty chair and sat down. I was about to open my portfolio and begin work when I glanced over at a book on a display shelf. It was a historical monograph on the Speaker of the House, and on the cover was a photograph of Sam Rayburn holding a gavel. The image got the gears in my brain churning, but not on the subject of the legislative proposal in front of me. I shifted back to Jack's murder. How did that gavel make its way from the floor of the House of Representatives to the crime scene?

So far, this detail hadn't made it into the press, which meant the police were keeping a tight lid on it. Murder weapons were important pieces of the puzzle, but this one was such an unusual artifact, it could potentially lead investigators to the killer. Unfortunately, my boss had presided over the House floor the evening before the murder, so the weapon was pointing Detective O'Halloran squarely in the direction of Maeve Dixon.

I snuck a peek at the librarian sitting at the desk. She was flipping through the latest edition of *National Journal* magazine. Appearances suggested she wasn't overwhelmed by work. Maybe she could provide valuable research assistance.

I sauntered over and she looked up from her reading with a broad smile. This was an auspicious start.

"How can I help you?"

Returning her smile with a grin, I said, "Do you have any research materials about the Speaker's gavel?"

Her eyes narrowed. "That's an unusual request. May I ask why you want information on the gavel?"

Lying wasn't morally defensible. A college lecture on Kant's categorical imperative flashed through my mind. Could I split the baby somehow? I doubted Kant would agree, but he'd never worked in the United States Congress for a vulnerable politician accused of murder.

"It's a project for my chief of staff." That wasn't a complete fib. Dan had ordered me to figure out who killed Jack Drysdale.

Her jaw relaxed. "We're not really supposed to research issues unrelated to the shutdown." She paused.

"But no one else has asked for my help, so I guess it won't hurt."

I breathed a sigh of relief. "Thank you. I appreciate it."

She pushed her glasses up and wrinkled her nose. "No problem. Do you mind having a seat while I gather materials for you?"

"Not at all." I returned to my spot and immediately dove into the legislative proposal from the Majority Leader's office. There were several provisions in the bill my boss could support. Not surprisingly, there were also a few specific examples of language she'd oppose. As I worked through the document, I jotted down copious notes for my lunchtime discussion with Judy. I was almost at the end when the librarian walked over to my table with several sheets of paper in her hand.

"I found some information about the Speaker's gavel for you. You might also want to check with the House Historian's office."

"That's a great idea. Thanks." For good measure, I added, "My chief will be thrilled with this."

She smiled politely. "Happy to help."

I quickly rifled through the printed information. One image caught my eye. It was another photo of Speaker Sam Rayburn. He was holding an armload of gavels, handed over by the man standing next to him. According to the caption, a United States Capitol engineer was giving Rayburn a stash of gavels in anticipation of the end of the summer recess in 1943. Why multiple gavels?

After flipping through the documents, I discovered that more than one gavel existed at any given time. Many Speakers in American history had broken gavels by banging them too hard. The raucous House rarely came to order when the presiding officer asked politely;

therefore, many Speakers simply pounded the gavel harder. In 1931, John Nance Garner broke three gavels in rapid succession. This led House engineers and carpenters to supply a set of gavels to the Speaker or whoever presided over the House.

Why hadn't this possibility occurred to me earlier? There wasn't a *single* gavel. There were many gavels, and therefore, a whole array of potential murder weapons. I tapped my pen to the side of my head and allowed myself a tentative smile.

ELEVEN

THERE WAS NO TIME for self-congratulation. Multiple gavels meant the one that smashed Jack's head in wasn't necessarily the same gavel Maeve had wielded the night before the murder. Though a positive development, it didn't exonerate her.

I finished reading the document before noon with only minutes to spare. After packing up my papers and donning my coat, I waved goodbye to the helpful librarian. A few minutes later, I was hustling down Pennsylvania Avenue. We The Pizza was only one and a half blocks away, but I walked as fast as I could without breaking into a jog. Something told me Judy Talent didn't tolerate the fashionably late.

The aroma of baked cheese, garlic, and pepperoni drifted as far as the intersection of Pennsylvania and Third Street. The typical We The Pizza line usually ran the length of the restaurant's ground floor, but today there were only three patrons waiting to order at the counter. I'd never met Judy before today, but I'd seen her photograph several times in various D.C. publications listing the fifty most powerful Hill staffers. She hadn't arrived yet.

I took a deep breath and shifted my attention to the pizzas behind the display glass. The restaurant boasted an eclectic assortment. Of course, the traditional cheese and pepperoni options were available. However, the signature offerings of We The Pizza were far from conventional. Slices with unusual toppings such as pulled pork, truffles, or boneless buffalo chicken wings populated the menu du jour. I'd begun to narrow down my lunchtime options when I heard a voice behind me.

"Excuse me. Are you Kit Marshall?"

I turned around to discover my lunch companion had arrived. Judy Talent was the very model of a Washington D.C. power broker. She was in her early forties, yet her figure was as trim as that of a woman a decade younger. Her brown tresses had understated auburn highlights that fell right above her shoulders in angled layers. I was no hair snob, but I could spot an expensive cut and style, likely the work of Vidal Sassoon in Tysons Galleria or even Cristophe's. If possible, her outfit was even more impressive. She sported an unbuttoned midlength black wool coat over a chic tan designer pantsuit that screamed Saks. As she shifted her purse to shake my hand, I noticed the Burberry label on the lining of her overcoat. Hillary Clinton had nothing on Judy Talent when it came to presenting the image of a flawless female politico. Her appearance projected one unified message: *I am a professional.*

I pulled my jacket across my body to cover up my outfit, one of my standard black suits with a red blouse. Compared to Judy, I felt like a reliable Toyota next to a tricked-out Ferrari.

Judy looked at me expectantly. She'd asked me a question and was offering her hand. I took it and croaked, "Yes, that's me. I mean, I'm Kit." I followed up my awkward introduction with a nervous laugh.

Judy flashed an expensive smile. "Terrific. I didn't

know what you looked like, but they aren't exactly breaking down the doors during the shutdown, are they?"

"No crowd is certainly unusual for this place. Have you eaten here before?"

Judy made a face. "I'm embarrassed to say I haven't, even though I know it's one of the best eateries on the Hill. I'm afraid my job doesn't give me many opportunities to go out for lunch."

I nodded sympathetically. At the front of the line, I placed my order for a slice of Poblano Spicy Mexican with a side salad and a premium sour cherry soda.

Judy stared at the menu on the wall behind the counter. "I really should have the farmers market salad. But it seems like a missed opportunity not to eat the pizza."

I had just taken a big sip of my custom soda. "You should definitely treat yourself." I wiped the red fizz from my upper lip. "These homemade sodas are delicious."

Judy laughed. "Sold!" She proceeded to order the two slice special, opting for the pineapple ham combo and mushroom truffle. She topped it off with a Shirley Temple soda.

While we waited for our slices to emerge from the wood-fired oven, Judy wasted no time. "Have you seen the Majority Leader's proposal to end the shutdown?" she asked.

Before I had a chance to answer, our beepers went off, indicating our pizza was ready. Judy's eyes grew wide as an employee placed her lunch on the counter for pickup. The slices at We The Pizza were huge. As we picked up our trays and headed upstairs to find a seat, Judy shook her head in dismay. "This is the biggest lunch I've had in five years. I'll be working it off at the gym all week."

I peeked at Judy's behind as I followed her to a table. It was perfect. Even while admiring her physique, I felt sorry for her. My entire life, thinness had eluded me. But I also wasn't one to deprive myself of a pizza lunch. If I could guess, I'd wager that Judy's intensity pervaded her whole existence—her work, appearance, and personal relationships.

Judy only allowed herself one bite before cutting to the chase. After taking a sip of her soda, she opened her leather portfolio, placed the legislative proposal on the table, and slid it toward me. "Here it is. I know you've seen it already, since it made the email rounds earlier today. I don't need to tell you how important it is for the entire party caucus to stick together on this vote, and I know Representative Dixon wants to get into the action. This is her chance to make a difference, both to the people of North Carolina and the Majority Leader."

At least Judy had made a good faith attempt at persuasion. That was more than I could say for the late Jack Drysdale, with his hard sell. I gave Judy a polite smile and finished my mouthful of pizza before speaking. "I appreciate you taking the time to meet. Can we go over some details? I have a few questions."

In between bites of pizza, Judy and I went back and forth on the finer points of the bill. Not all of her answers would make my boss happy, but to her credit, Judy answered each inquiry with complete and apparently honest answers. After twenty minutes, I was satisfied, at least with the political part of the conversation.

I glanced at Judy's tray. She had plowed her way through the pineapple ham slice, but her mushroom truffle was untouched. I still had my salad to eat. Judy needed to invest a few more minutes in our lunch so I could probe her about Jack's murder. Judy glanced at her watch. Two factors were working against me, namely Judy's desire to minimize the caloric damage of our meal and the fact she'd already spent more time with me at lunch than she typically devoted to anyone.

Before she started packing up, I needed to intercede. "You haven't touched your other slice of pizza."

She laughed. "I guess my eyes are bigger than my stomach. I'll get a box for this. Someone in the office will eat it as soon as I get back." She turned to gather her purse and designer overcoat. Uh-oh.

"Wait a second," I blurted out. She turned to look at me with a curious stare.

I racked my brain for a reason to keep Judy at the table. My eyes drifted to her tray. "You don't want to take that pizza to go."

Judy narrowed her eyes. "Why not?"

"It's their specialty. You don't want to give that pizza up. Trust me."

Judy stared at me for several seconds, which felt like forever. Then she burst out laughing. "I like you, Kit. You're refreshing."

The muscles in my face relaxed, and I grinned. "Thank you. I think that was a compliment."

"Yes, it was. So this pizza is really worth it?" She pointed to the slice.

"You don't want to miss it." I was telling the truth. Their mushroom truffle was divine.

"I'll take your word for it." Judy let go of her purse and coat, picked up her knife and fork, and dived in.

This was my opportunity. Unlike Judy's pizza, my salad could wait.

"Can I ask you a question unrelated to the shutdown?"

"Sure. By the way, you're right. This pizza is fantastic. I'm glad I didn't give it to one of those scavengers in my office. It wouldn't have lasted two minutes."

"Are you upset by Jack Drysdale's death?"

I studied Judy's reaction. She didn't appear alarmed or taken aback. In fact, she didn't miss a bite. After swallowing, she offered, "Yes and no. I knew Jack for many years so it's upsetting. But we weren't friends." She raised her eyebrows before continuing. "Everyone knew that."

Playing innocent might help elicit more information. Besides, I couldn't exactly explain my interest in Jack's death. "I only met Jack the day before he died. I know what's appeared in the gossip columns, though."

Judy scoffed. "Don't believe everything you read. Especially from that menace, Hill Rat."

Just the opening I needed. "I heard Jack knew Hill Rat's real identity and wanted to expose him…or her."

Judy shrugged. "I'm not surprised. Jack despised Hill Rat. He thought scandal-driven blogging made relationships even tougher to maintain within the Capitol. No one could trust anyone with Hill Rat publishing confidential missives and secrets."

Did Judy have a motive for killing Jack? According to the rumor mill, she and Jack had routinely competed for the most prestigious Capitol Hill jobs. Emerging on top with his Speaker's job, Jack had bested Judy in the end. She might have decided the only way to eliminate the competition was murder.

I leaned in closer and softened my voice. "Do you have any idea who might have killed Jack?"

Judy's face was expressionless for several seconds, which felt like five minutes. Once again, she burst into laughter. "You're just full of surprises. Why do you care who murdered Jack Drysdale? Isn't Representative Dixon giving you enough work these days?"

Luckily, my reputation preceded me and provided the perfect alibi for my nosiness. "Last year, I helped the police solve the murder of my boss in the Senate. Jack's murder is right up my alley." I tapped two fingers to the side of my head. "It's time to put the little gray cells to work." I looked at Judy expectantly. When she didn't get my reference, I said, "Hercule Poirot. He's always calling on his little gray cells to solve the crime." I tapped my temple again for emphasis.

Judy shook her finger at me playfully. "I knew I recognized your name. You're the former Senate staffer who almost became the killer's next victim. Isn't that right?"

"It was a close call. But I wouldn't let that stop me from trying to figure out who killed Jack." Prevaricating made me feel guilty but I had limited options to keep Judy from clamming up.

"Good luck on this one. I hope your detective skills are up to the task. Because there's a long list of people who wanted to see Jack dead."

I looked Judy squarely in the eye, gauging her reaction to my next question. "Are you one of them?"

I was expecting Judy to laugh me off, but she didn't. She grimaced, showing the fine wrinkles underneath her expensive makeup. Her eyes weren't angry. Instead, they softened, and for a brief moment, I thought I noticed a trace of moisture. If there were any tears for Jack, they had dried as soon as they had appeared. Judy straightened in her chair. "Absolutely not. Why would I kill Jack?"

"Weren't you in competition with him for years over the top staffing jobs on the Hill? His boss became Speaker and he claimed the most powerful position in Congress. If something happened to Jack, wouldn't the Speaker consider you as a replacement?"

Judy scoffed. "I seriously doubt it. There are enough people in the Speaker's orbit who will be standing in line for Jack's job. He doesn't want someone with loyalties to another member of Congress. More importantly, it's well known that I'm leaving the Hill soon."

That was news to me. "You have another job lined up?"

Judy started to gather her bag and coat, indicating she'd had enough pizza and enough of me. "I'm headed to K Street as a lobbyist as soon as the shutdown is over. I said I'd never do it, but I'm not getting any younger. Are you single, Kit?"

"I live with my boyfriend but we're not married." I didn't add the word "yet" to the end of the sentence. I had a feeling if I had, Judy would have lectured me about it.

She smirked. "That means you're single. So here's some advice from one unmarried D.C. gal to another." With her coat on and her bag slung over her shoulder, she touched both of my shoulders with her hands. "Don't wait too long to cash in your chits. There's an expiration date on goodwill in this town. I need to provide for my future. That's something only you can do for yourself."

Judy gave a small salute as a goodbye, and I watched her march toward the exit, already furiously typing messages on her iPhone. Without turning around, she called out, her voice echoing from the stairwell, "Don't forget. We need Maeve Dixon's support on this bill. I'm counting on you, Kit."

The faces of Dan and Maeve flashed through my mind. I took a deep breath to ease the tension. Who wasn't counting on me these days?

TWELVE

As I WALKED back to the office, I thought about my conversation with Judy Talent, a woman who didn't suffer fools gladly. Given her success on Capitol Hill, that made perfect sense. No alibi had been offered and I hadn't prodded her for one. She'd dismissed a suggested motive by announcing her new lobbying job. Was that honesty or a clever diversion? I didn't have the luxury of eliminating anyone yet, so I'd keep my eye on Judy. The ambitious, Hill-climber side of Kit Marshall liked Judy Talent. My gumshoe alter ego still viewed her as a credible suspect.

I'd just opened my computer's email inbox when I felt someone watching me. I got a similar feeling in the early morning hours when Clarence fixated on me, hoping for a walk outside and his breakfast, in that order. This was like being ogled by a puppy dog, yet I doubted the eyes belonged to a canine.

"Dan, is that you?"

A belabored sigh broke the silence. "Yes, it's me. Do you have an update?"

I spun around in my office chair. "On the shutdown?"

He waved his hand dismissively. "I don't care about the shutdown. What about clearing Maeve's name?"

"How many times do I need to tell you it takes time to solve a murder? Especially a murder of someone I don't even know!"

"If she gets labeled a suspect, how will she ever win reelection?" Dan rubbed his forehead. "No one will hire me in D.C. after this mess. I'll be ruined."

That's nothing compared to serving thirty to life for a crime you didn't commit. Rather than issue a sarcastic retort, I held my tongue. Maeve had asked me this morning to go easy on Dan. She knew he was a fragile soul.

"Settle down. I'm making progress. But a mess like this can't be sorted out overnight."

Dan perked up, his eyes finally showing a glimmer of hope. "Progress? What have you learned?"

I didn't have the energy to explain the importance of multiple Speaker gavels. It was a nuanced clue and Dan struggled with subtleties. The gavel that killed Jack wasn't necessarily the same one Maeve had used on the House floor the night before the murder. Therefore, her prints might not turn up on the murder weapon. If that was the case, it could give Detective O'Halloran and the Capitol Hill Police pause. Reasonable doubt was all we needed.

"I can't reveal anything right now." Dan's face fell in disappointment. "Don't worry. A good detective never shows her cards." I reached out and gave Dan a pat on the shoulder.

He didn't seem comforted. "That's fine if you don't want to tell me what you've found." He paused, likely for dramatic effect. "If you've found anything. But my original instruction still stands. You need to find the real killer or look for another job."

I straightened up in my chair. "I talked to Representative Dixon this morning, and she urged me not to investigate. She thinks it's too dangerous."

Dan wavered for a moment before responding. "Of course she'd say that. She doesn't want any liability if something happens to you. She can't live with the guilt. However, I have a clear conscience."

Dan's eyes bulged and he grimaced, reminding me eerily of Bert from *Sesame Street* when he got frustrated with Ernie. Angry Bert freaked me out. Irritated Dan had the same effect.

"I'd like some clarification. You don't give a rat's ass if I become collateral damage?" I rarely cussed in a professional environment, but Dan's boorish behavior justified an exception.

"That's crude, yet accurate."

I clenched my jaw and turned to face my computer. I glanced quickly to my right. Maeve's door was open. I didn't see a coat on the rack or her briefcase on the desk. She'd likely left for lunch. No luck that she'd overheard Dan reveal his true colors. I'd pegged him for a political lightweight, not a ruthless Hill denizen who cared about little else than his political career. I'd been dead wrong.

I had nothing further to say. My brain could barely process his callous remarks, yet I forced myself to open my email inbox. Returning to work would give the impression that his crazy remarks hadn't affected me. From behind, I heard Dan return to his office and shut the door.

The list of unread email messages wasn't quite as long as yesterday's. That meant the number of credible proposals to end the shutdown had diminished. Pretty soon, there would be three or four viable alternatives. Once Maeve endorsed one of them, there would be no turning back politically.

I spotted an email from Trevor with the subject "House Sergeant at Arms." Perfect. I clicked on the message. Trent Roscoe has time to meet with you today at 3. Don't miss this opportunity.

Trevor even managed to sound bossy in an email. That required real talent. I hit reply. I'll be there. Trevor appreciated brevity.

I glanced at my watch. It was a little after two so I had some time before the meeting with Trent. I was about to focus on a long email outlining yet another solution to the shutdown when Maeve walked into the office.

I stood up to greet her and smoothed my suit jacket. "Congresswoman, if you have a moment, I'd like to tell you about a discussion I had earlier today with the lead staffer from the Majority Leader's office."

She motioned for me to follow her. Inside her office, Maeve collapsed into her high-backed chair. Her face looked drawn, and her usually energetic aura had dimmed. Her demeanor had changed drastically since this morning.

What had caused this marked deterioration? "Excuse me for asking, but is there something wrong, ma'am?"

Maeve had been staring at the wall, temporarily zoned out. She snapped to attention when she heard my question. "I'm sorry, Kit. I just met with my attorney."

She couldn't throw a loaded comment out there without an explanation. Maybe it was rude, but didn't I have the right to know what was going on?

"What did he say?"

She sighed. "The police don't have any other suspects with the big three." She ticked them off with her fingers. "Means, motive, opportunity."

"What about the other people on the Hill who hated Jack? He had plenty of enemies."

"They'll explore those leads, but I'm clearly at the nexus of the investigation. My lawyer thinks the police might name me as a formal suspect and bring me in for questioning."

I gulped. "Today?"

She shrugged. "Who knows? I'm at their beck and call."

"Look on the bright side. The media hasn't caught wind of it yet. There's a chance we can keep this quiet, even if you're questioned."

Maeve brightened. "Perhaps my attorney could negotiate those conditions."

"Absolutely. That way, once they find the real killer, no one needs to know the police suspected you were involved with the crime."

Maeve and I chatted about the Majority Leader's policy proposal and Judy's pressure to lend support to it. The situation required delicate maneuvering. Maeve didn't want to support the proposal and then get hauled downtown as a formal suspect in Jack's murder. On the other hand, jumping onboard too late would earn her little political favor with the powers that be. One more day of delay wouldn't hurt, so we'd evaluate the situation again tomorrow afternoon. As I reminded my boss, political decisions were never made quickly. In an era of contentious politics, both parties routinely procrastinated.

Unlike my congressional colleagues, I had no time to waste after wrapping up with Maeve. The House Sergeant at Arms office was appropriately located inside the Capitol itself, so I needed to boogie to make it there by three. After clearing the security checkpoint, I hustled through the underground passage connecting the Capitol to the House of Representatives office buildings.

The Cannon Tunnel was the perfect spot for a moving walkway system, but such modern amenities had not appeared yet in Congress. The tunnel always made me think of an aging airport. Those of us who walked it on a daily basis found its gray, industrial appearance uninspiring. People moved swiftly on both sides of the passage under harsh lighting, usually engaged in blatant wheeling and dealing. Staff briefed their bosses en route to an important vote, lobbyists jogged to catch up with the House member they needed to solicit, and tourists clogged the artery while gawking at politicians they recognized from cable television. Adding to the chaos was the long line of paintings covering the tunnel's walls, all winners from an annual congressional art competition featuring the best work of high school students across the country. Most visitors stopped to admire the impressive artwork or find the canvas from their congressional district. It often required the antiquated skills of an expert "Frogger" video game master to negotiate the series of obstacles in one's path.

Luckily, the shutdown had decreased the typical pandemonium of the Cannon Tunnel to a dull roar. After crossing into the Capitol, I quickly found the door labeled "House Sergeant at Arms" and pushed it open. Preoccupied with finding the correct location, I'd neglected to strategize for my meeting. Trevor's contact was the purportedly attractive Trent Roscoe, whose boss was Gareth Pressler. Jack and Gareth had gone to war in the press over the security in the Capitol complex. With little love lost between the two of them, Pressler seemed like a man with a plausible motive to kill Jack.

After providing my name to the assistant sitting at the front desk, I grabbed a seat in the small waiting room and checked my iPhone for messages. I had just clicked on a new email when I heard footsteps in the adjacent hallway.

Meg and Trevor hadn't exaggerated about Trent Roscoe. He was in his late thirties or early forties, but the years had been kind. He had a different kind of appeal than what I usually found attractive. He was ruggedly handsome, with military-style cropped brown hair, a square jaw, and the faint remainder of a tan. Although he was dressed in a nondescript black suit, I could tell he was in terrific shape. His pale yellow button-down shirt hugged his chest, showing off a chiseled upper body and trim waist. The soft, muted colors of his tie provided the perfect accent to his outfit. A guy like Trent could wear pastels and get away with it because he simply radiated testosterone.

When I stood to greet him, I might have been dreaming, but I thought he gave me a once-over. If so, it didn't last for more than a second. He immediately extended his hand. "Kit Marshall, I presume?"

Maybe I was cold—the Capitol wasn't the warmest building in the winter—but when I touched his hand, a warm sensation entered my fingers, ran up my arm, and then traveled throughout my body. I looked into his eyes briefly and he smiled. Had he felt it, too?

Then his expression turned quizzical. He'd asked me a question, after all. "That's m-me," I stammered. *Nice move, Kit*. Always the queen of suave. *Cosmo* could use me as a case study illustrating how not to behave around the opposite sex.

Trent didn't bat an eyelash at my awkwardness. "Let's head to my office so we can chat," he said.

He led me down the hallway into a very small room with only a desk and one chair. It wasn't a broom closet, but it was darn close. I squeezed past the door and slid into the available seat. He laughed at my obvious attempt to fit into the tight space. "I apologize. I realize this isn't the Oval Office."

"No worries. I've never had a private office on the Hill, so I'm insanely jealous of your real estate."

He nodded. "I'm lucky Gareth decided I could have this space. Since I frequently conduct meetings about the security of the House, he thought I should have an office with a door."

How many people could discuss the security of the House in this office at one time? A multitude of staffers might be interested, but they'd have to schedule individual meetings.

"I appreciate that you're willing to meet with me," I said. "Trevor and I worked together in the Senate before he left to become a lobbyist."

Trent nodded. "When I read Trevor's email that his friend needed my help, it was a no-brainer. Any friend of Trevor's is a friend of mine."

Times had definitely changed. Trevor hadn't exactly been the social butterfly of the Senate. He must have undergone a drastic personal makeover to succeed at his new job. The bright lights of a movie marquee flashed before my eyes: *The Wolf of K Street*. It had a nice ring to it.

"How did you meet Trevor? I wouldn't think he'd have much dealings with House security."

"There's no immediate tie. But as a lobbyist for a

big defense company, Trevor needs to know everyone on the Hill. Quite a few of our employees in the Sergeant's office are former military. That's another reason for Trevor to develop a connection with our folks."

With the killer bod and buzzed haircut, Trent looked like he'd served in the military. "Are you a veteran?"

To my surprise, Trent shook his head. "Afraid not. I was in the Secret Service for a while, but an old injury prevented me from continuing work in the field. I heard through the grapevine the Sergeant at Arms wanted to make hires with a law enforcement background. Before you know it, I'm working in the House of Representatives." Trent's smile spread from ear to ear.

Not too many people these days boasted they worked for Congress. "You must really like your job."

The grin still plastered on his face, Trent said, "I love the mission. We're here to protect the elected members, staff, and everyone who visits the Capitol complex. It's a big responsibility. Who wouldn't be excited?"

Trent's enthusiasm struck a familiar chord. "In my experience," I said, "staff work on the Hill for a variety of reasons. With all the political nonsense that goes on, sometimes we forget the bigger goal of public service."

Trent's eyes lit up. "I couldn't have said it better myself." His line of sight drifted to my left hand, which was resting on the edge of Trent's desk. He quickly averted his gaze when he realized I'd caught him checking out my ring finger.

No need for another awkward moment. It was time to get down to business. "I wanted to meet with you because my boss had mentioned there was controversy concerning the level of security in the Capitol and House buildings. We have a lot of North Carolina constituents who visit our office and she'd like to know if any changes are planned." It was a load of bunk with a grain of truth, but I needed to get Trent talking about the hullabaloo between his boss and Jack.

"Calling it a controversy is an understatement. Congress is a top terrorism target, and the Sergeant at Arms is responsible for the safety of those inside these buildings. We need to make sure we have the right protocols in place to guarantee security. Unfortunately, many of our elected members of Congress don't want to impede the flow of visitors in the chamber."

"I think I read a newspaper article about that man who was murdered, Jack Drysdale, and someone who leads your office. Didn't they disagree about this issue?" I asked innocently.

"Yes. Luckily, the papers didn't report half of it. Let's put it this way: there was no love lost between Drysdale and my boss, Gareth."

Now we were getting somewhere. "Why do you say that?"

Trent sighed. "Drysdale fought with Gareth about implementing tougher security protocols. They weren't able to arrive at a sensible compromise. Instead, their meetings usually ended up in shouting matches, with Jack storming out of Gareth's office."

"Sounds serious. How did you negotiate that land mine?"

"I didn't. Those decisions are above my pay grade. But I listened to Gareth complain after the meetings."

There was a tap at the door. Trent said loudly, "Come in."

I scooted my chair as far away from the door as I could so it could open. A middle-aged man appeared.

He seemed surprised Trent had a visitor. "Don't forget we have that meeting about identification badges in a few minutes."

Trent's demeanor changed instantly. He straightened up in his chair, all business. "I will be there. Sir, this is Kit Marshall from Representative Maeve Dixon's office. She wants to learn more about House security procedures. Ma'am, may I introduce you to the Deputy Sergeant at Arms, Mr. Gareth Pressler."

Ma'am? Wasn't I at least a "miss"?

Before I had a chance to speak, Pressler said, "What does Representative Dixon want to know about security? Is there a problem I should know about?"

"No. I mean, no, sir. She's a freshman member of Congress and we want to know about any proposed changes to tourist access or visits to the Capitol."

He stared at me intently. "I'm always available—the Sergeant at Arms is as well—to answer questions from members of Congress. We find it's better to deal with the members directly on this issue. Staff don't always act in their bosses' best interests when it comes to security."

I was about to give Gareth Pressler a piece of my mind, but Trent cut me off. "Thank you, sir. We were just finishing our conversation. I'll see you in a moment."

Pressler took the hint. He nodded curtly in my direction and closed the door behind him.

"I'm sorry about Gareth. Since his disagreement with Jack, he doesn't think highly of congressional staff."

"No problem. One more question. Is the Sergeant at Arms office involved with the Drysdale murder investigation?"

"The Sergeant himself serves on the board for the Capitol Hill Police. So he's staying informed at that level. Even though we're law enforcement within the Capitol, we're leaving the detective work to the trained investigators."

"Makes sense. Thanks again for meeting with me. My boss might have more questions down the road about this security business." He hadn't seemed to notice that my ostensible reason for visiting with him had never been satisfied. I hadn't learned anything about their security procedures. I had learned some valuable information related to my real objective, however.

Trent and I both stood up, and he came around to my side of the desk. He placed his hand lightly on the small of my back to guide me toward the door, which was completely unnecessary since only three feet separated my chair from the exit.

"I'm sure we'll stay in touch," he murmured.

I felt the heat of embarrassment traveling upwards from my neck. If my face was as red as I imagined it was, Trent paid it no mind. The last thing I saw before he shut the door behind me was a sly smile accompanied by a slow, sexy wink.

I raced out of the office suite into the first-floor hallway of the Capitol. What had just happened? Sure, I wasn't the most experienced object of male admiration, but I'd been around the block a few times. Trent Roscoe had definitely put the moves on me. I took several deep breaths to clear my head.

Almost without thinking, I rummaged through my purse to find my iPhone. After swiping it on and entering the password, I touched the "Messages" green icon in the top left corner. My last texting conversation with

Meg was never far from the top of the screen. I started typing furiously in the blank window. How did I explain what just happened in a text? Maybe Meg knew more about Trent Roscoe than she was letting on.

Trent was interesting. What's his deal?

The three dots flashed, indicating Meg was replying.

He's cute & single. No more to know :)

I'd need to talk to Meg later to get her reaction. I didn't have a moment to spare the rest of the day if I wanted to make it to the Top Dog party on time.

Then I noticed Meg was typing another message. It appeared a few seconds later.

Trent is least of your troubles. Hill Rat broke story about murder :o Damn Meg and her emoticons. I wasn't sure what that last one meant. Surprise? Shock? I picked up the pace back to the office and fired off one last question to Meg.

Is it bad?

I was hitting my stride, dodging members and staff out for a leisurely walk through the Cannon Tunnel, when my phone dinged. Meg had responded.

Fraid so :(

Not a good sign.

THIRTEEN

I BRACED MYSELF for the inevitable chaos that would assault me in Representative Dixon's congressional office suite. I imagined Dan crying, Maeve yelling, or even the reverse. Instead, complete silence. After depositing my purse on the desk, I did a 360 to see if anyone else was around. That's when I heard soft voices from the congresswoman's private office.

I knocked on the door, and Maeve instructed me to enter. She was seated behind her desk with the phone receiver to her ear. Dan was sitting across from her, so I took the chair next to his.

He leaned closer. "She's on the phone with her lawyer."

"Is this about the Hill Rat story?"

Dan nodded.

"I haven't seen it yet. I just heard about it a few minutes ago after leaving a meeting in the Capitol."

Dan pulled his iPhone from his suit jacket pocket, swiped it on, and handed it to me. I recognized the familiar icon from his blog page—a sketch of a rat with the Capitol dome behind it. The rat wasn't cute like Chuck E. Cheese or the characters from Disney's *Ratatouille*. It was menacing, with sharp teeth and red eyes. Its ugly tail was curled tightly around the top of the Capitol dome in what looked like a stranglehold.

I scrolled down to read the story. Hill Rat's blog entries were rarely long, and this one fit the form. He or she usually got right to the point. Hill Rat explained that Representative Maeve Dixon from North Carolina had discovered the bludgeoned body of Jack Drysdale yesterday morning. Due to her recent public tiff with the victim, Dixon was a prime suspect.

I closed my eyes briefly and rubbed them. It had only taken two sentences to ruin my boss's career.

Considering Dan's insensitive comments earlier today, he was the last person I wanted to consult about this nightmare. But Maeve was still on the phone so I had no other option.

"Given this mess, shouldn't we try to put our press secretary on active status?"

"I mentioned that to Maeve. She's being told by the Speaker to keep her staff at a minimum during the shutdown. He wants Americans to understand it's not business as usual. She also didn't think her lawyer would want her or the press secretary talking to the press."

"Why aren't the phones ringing off the hook?"

Dan chuckled nervously. "After I showed Maeve the story, she told me it was time to hunker down and take cover. She must have remembered her military training. That included locking the door to the office, lowering the blinds, and disconnecting all the phones."

"That's fine for now, but I'm not sure it's a strategy we can use indefinitely."

"We most certainly can."

We both turned our attention to our boss, who had just hung up the phone. "Detective O'Halloran would like to question me tomorrow afternoon at headquarters. I will comply with the request, with my lawyer present. Until this is resolved, it is counsel's recommendation that we stay absolutely silent about my involvement in this murder investigation. Do you both understand?"

We both nodded and murmured, "Yes, ma'am."

She stood up, leaned forward, and placed her hands on the desk. "That means no talking to the press, on the record or off the record. If you are asked about my actions, you will say 'no comment.' It's as simple as that."

"Congresswoman," I said, "what about the phones? They're disconnected now, but we'll have to plug them back in soon, right?"

She rubbed her chin as she thought about my question. "I suppose we can't run a congressional office without phone lines. We will plug them back in after five o'clock, which is later than most reporters' deadlines for print editions. When the phone rings, you will answer, provide the 'no comment' response, and then hang up."

Dan's face had turned ashen again. All brightness had vanished, drained by the day's unexpected stress to a zombie-like pallor. If Dan got any whiter, he'd vanish.

When Dan didn't respond, I piped up. "Don't worry. We'll take care of the calls after five."

She gave us a curt nod. "I know I can count on both of you. The press might get wind of my trip to the police station tomorrow. You might want to make yourselves scarce. I'm sure enterprising reporters will be camped outside the door to see if they can pick up a juicy tidbit."

A day away from the office meant more time for sleuthing. Maeve must have noticed the change in my expression.

"Kit, I know exactly what you're thinking. I doubt that anything I say will keep you from investigating this murder. Please keep in mind that I did not kill Jack

Drysdale. That means the person who did murder him is on the loose and might even think he or she got away with it. So be careful."

I gave her a mini-salute with two fingers. "Will do."

Maeve turned to Dan. She hesitated before giving him instructions. "Dan, try to remain inconspicuous and out of the way, if you can."

"Don't worry, boss. I'm really good at that."

For once, I completely agreed with him.

FOURTEEN

UPON RETURNING TO my desk, I took a precious moment to clear my head. We couldn't have suppressed Maeve's status as a suspect indefinitely. It was pure luck her name had been kept out of the press this long. Hill Rat's exclusive also didn't surprise me. This was the Rat's typical modus operandi, namely an exclusive yet defamatory tidbit that had the potential to ruin reputations, embarrass public officials, and even change political outcomes. The suspicion surrounding Maeve Dixon hurt her personally and the constituents she represented in North Carolina since she wouldn't be able to participate in the upcoming policy debates in Congress. But it also had the potential to weaken the entire party as it tried to negotiate favorable terms to the shutdown.

A quick time check confirmed I had twenty minutes before we'd allow the phones to ring again. Attending the Capitol Canine awards ceremony tonight was low on my priority list, but where else could I possibly meet Jordan Macintyre, Jack's grieving spouse? Even though D.C. social etiquette often eluded me, it was likely bad form to own the dog that won Capitol Canine and then not show up for the party.

I signed on to my computer and clicked on the contest website. Sure enough, Clarence was still in first place. Voting closed at five. Barring some last-minute flurry of voting, Clarence was headed to victory. But would Jordan Macintyre put his grief aside for the evening and attend the party? After locating the number for Capitol Canine's publicity contact, I grabbed my cellphone and placed the call.

A female voice answered on the second ring. "Christy from Capitol Canine. Are you a reporter looking for press photos of the dogs?"

Her question caught me off guard. "Um, no. My name is Kit Marshall, and I'm the owner of Clarence, who's participating in the contest."

She squealed, conceivably in delight. Was this my Andy Warhol moment, or more specifically, Clarence's fifteen minutes of fame? Visions of his adorable face on a package of Purina Dog Chow danced before me.

"Congratulations! The contest isn't over yet, but it's looking very good for Clarence."

Absent the pressure to solve a homicide in the House, I would have found Christy's enthusiasm infectious. Given the circumstances, faking it was the better option. "Great!"

To my ears, my response sounded forced, but the woman on the other end of the line didn't seem to notice. "What time will you arrive tonight with your little champion?"

"I'll try to be there by six thirty, but that's not why I called. Is Jordan Macintyre going to attend the party tonight?"

Christy's voice softened. "Isn't it terrible? We are so sad here at Capitol Canine. Jack was a big supporter of the contest. He and Jordan secured many of our sponsors and helped raise money for our charities. Did you know Capitol Canine benefits several rescue dog organizations in the D.C. area?"

I vaguely remembered reading about the worthy financial goals of the contest. As much as I supported the noble cause, I really needed to determine whether Jordan had decided to make an appearance at tonight's event. I tried again. "That's tremendous. Will Jordan be there tonight to present the charity checks?"

"Oh yes, he'll be there. Before we announce the winner, we'll pause for a moment of silent reflection to memorialize Jack. Did you know both of them?"

This was my opportunity. "I only met Jack once, but I'd like to pay my respects to Jordan. Can you introduce me?"

Christy responded instantly with gusto. "Of course. He'll want to meet Clarence." She quickly added, "You, too!"

I got the drift. I'd play second fiddle to Clarence tonight. That was fine with me, especially if the "little champion" could help me interrogate Jordan without drawing too much attention.

After telling Christy I'd track her down soon after my arrival, I hung up. My phone dinged a few seconds after the call ended. It was a message from Doug, asking for the address for the event. I reminded him he should arrive with Clarence by six thirty. Then I copied the address and pasted it into a new text to Meg. Besides the cute dogs, Capitol Canine's allure was primarily social. Meg loved attending soirees featured in the Capitol Hill newspapers, and this one would be front and center.

Ping. I glanced at her response.

I really should stay here and work on the investigation.

I checked the clock. Five minutes before we had to

turn the phones back on. I thought for a moment before answering. Before Meg had a boyfriend, I could usually convince her to join me at almost any event on the Hill if I promised her I'd heard attractive men were planning to attend. That argument didn't work quite as well now that she was attached.

There's free drinks and pizza.

My iPhone remained inactive for a long moment. Then the three dots appeared.

I'll meet you there.

Meg's valuable assistance in our previous murder investigation had been based largely on her remarkable ability to wrap the opposite sex around her pinky finger. Jordan wasn't interested in women, so Meg would have to devise another angle. Meg's resourcefulness continually exceeded expectations, so I had no doubt she had other tricks up her sleeve.

At five o'clock on the dot, Dan turned on the phones. The calls didn't stop for a solid hour. The fervor diminished as time went on because reporters undoubtedly let each other know that the Dixon office had offered "no comment" to every single inquiry. After Dan heard I needed to leave at six fifteen to interrogate a possible suspect, he shooed me out of the office with the warning, "Don't come back until you know whodunit." Not deigning to respond, I grabbed my purse and coat and headed outside to find a taxi.

I gave the cabbie the party's address and we sped off down Independence Avenue toward the adjacent

Penn Quarter neighborhood. Located near Chinatown, the east end of the city remained one of my favorite haunts. Home of Ford's Theater, the Newseum, the Verizon Center, the Shakespeare Theatre, the Spy Museum, and the National Portrait Gallery, this area of the District bustled. The numerous attractions supported a wide variety of restaurants, ranging from high-end contemporary Indian fare to popular chains. Penn Quarter resembled the urban core of other major American cities. Washington D.C. had its advantages, but it was a government town. With its flashing lights and busy nighttime sidewalks, the five blocks of Penn Quarter provided a glimmer of New York. Even the most devout politico needed a break from the inspiring monuments and stately federal buildings, and this part of town helped satisfy those urbane desires.

The driver turned his head sideways to glance in my direction. "You work on the Hill?"

I'd been fiddling with my phone, looking for a text from Doug indicating he and Clarence had arrived. I muttered a barely audible "yes" in response.

"That's something about the female congressman killing the staffer. Did you know the guy who got whacked?"

He had my attention. "What did you say?"

"Didn't you hear? Some woman in Congress murdered the guy who works for the Speaker. Or something like that."

"Where did you hear that?"

"It's more like where didn't I hear it. All the talk shows have the story." He motioned toward the radio in his cab, which was set on a popular station for local news.

We were almost at the destination. After swiping my

credit card and gathering my things, I piped up, "You shouldn't trust the media."

I opened the door and thrust one foot on the sidewalk. Over my shoulder, I heard his final retort. "Lady, I don't believe half the stuff I hear. All I know is if they don't end this shutdown soon, more bodies are going to pile up."

I heaved myself out of the taxi, shut the door, and watched it speed away, praying his prophecy wasn't true.

FIFTEEN

A FANCY CONSULTING FIRM had donated its office space to host Capitol Canine's festivities. After exiting the elevator, I didn't need to make sure I had the correct suite. A cacophony of excited barks traveled the length of the hallway. The entrance had been decorated with photos of the dog contestants. Clarence's cute mug was in the center of the puppy collage. Someone had pasted a crown on his head, ostensibly in anticipation of the big announcement scheduled for later this evening.

About ten dogs had already arrived with their owners. A *National Geographic* documentary I'd watched over the summer explained that domestic dogs exhibited the widest variation in size and physical characteristics of any mammal. The motley crew in attendance certainly attested to that fact. There was a Scooby-Doo look-alike Great Dane, a sizable chocolate Lab, a sturdy American bulldog, a petite Yorkie, and a slightly overweight dachshund. The remainder, I was glad to see, appeared to belong to Clarence's polyglot category, affectionately known as "mutt."

I spotted Doug and Meg in the corner of the room. Doug had put Clarence's harness on him, and he was gripping his leash tightly. I waved from across the way and walked over to join them. Their personalities being on opposite ends of the spectrum, Doug and Meg weren't best buddies. Doug was as cautious as Meg was impetuous. Doug preferred quiet evenings at home with his history books, and Meg never met a happy hour she didn't like. Doug happily ate vanilla ice cream, and Meg tried every flavor before settling on Caramel Sutra with a twist of Bohemian Raspberry. The contrasts were endless and often presented entertaining challenges when we hung out together.

If Meg and Doug had been trading barbs, Clarence looked no worse for wear. Seeing me approach, he wiggled his butt enthusiastically. I bent down to pet Clarence on the top of his head and in return, he gave me a wet kiss on the cheek.

Out of the corner of my eye, I saw Meg recoil briefly at Clarence's lick. Meg liked dogs in theory, but not in practice. Her taste for expensive couture did not mesh well with dog hair and the occasional slobber.

After giving Clarence a few more scratches behind his floppy ears, I stood up. Doug was holding the dog close. "Why do you have a death grip on his leash?"

Doug grimaced. "Clarence is acting strangely. He seems overly excited. You don't want any problems here, right?"

I looked down at Clarence. His adorable face with big brown eyes stared back at me angelically. "There's nothing wrong with him. Why are you so nervous?"

Doug tended to exaggerate risk. "He's not used to being around so many dogs at once. I'm telling you we'd better keep an eye on him."

Meg was texting on her phone, clearly bored with our argument. Without looking up, she said, "Don't be such a stick in the mud, Doug. Let Clarence live a little. After all, it's his night."

Under his breath, Doug murmured, "Thanks for your

input, Dog Whisperer." He loosened his grasp of the leash, giving Clarence more room to wander.

Meg finally put her phone away. She smiled and gave me a hug. "How are you holding up after the Hill Rat debacle?"

Before I had a chance to respond, Doug said, "That's a tough break."

I sighed. "Yes. Hill Rat, the one and only, somehow figured out Maeve discovered Jack Drysdale's body yesterday." Then I turned to Meg. "Thanks for asking. Our office is still standing. For how long, I'm not sure."

Meg lowered her voice and inched closer. She motioned for Doug to do the same. "What are our assignments for tonight?"

Doug narrowed his eyes. "Assignments?"

Meg gently punched him in the arm. Clarence growled softly, not appreciating Meg's jostling of his owner. Meg shushed him. "Clarence, be quiet. We all have to pull together to solve this mystery before Kit's boss gets tossed in the slammer." As if paying careful attention, Clarence cocked his head and sat down in the center of the tight circle the three of us had formed.

"Thanks, Meg. I need to talk to Jordan Macintyre, the grieving widower. My instincts tell me he's going to want to meet Clarence, so Doug should stick with me." I checked out Meg's attire. She sported a fitted dark purple sweater dress with gray tights and knee-length black leather boots. The small bow tucked into the side of her blonde bob perfectly matched her outfit. She looked smart, sexy, and professional. In other words, a perfect fit for this crowd. "Is your boyfriend joining us tonight?"

Her sunny visage turned gloomy. "No, Kyle isn't

coming. He has to work late due to negotiations in the Senate on the shutdown." Meg nervously fiddled with the amethyst ring on her right hand. I could tell she wasn't buying Kyle's excuse any more than I was.

"That's too bad. But it suits our purposes for solving this murder. I think you need to turn on your famous charm tonight and see what you can find out in this room."

Meg stopped staring down at her hands and perked up. "Do you think that's dishonest since I have a boyfriend?"

Doug snickered. "Are you telling me you were honestly interested in every guy you flirted with before you met Kyle?"

Meg put her hands on her hips defiantly. "I never led anyone on, Doug. Besides, you of all people should not be offering relationship advice!"

That caught Doug's attention. "What is that supposed to mean?" His body language implied his question wasn't directed only at Meg. Sensing conflict, Clarence's ears flattened.

Time to intervene. "No harm meant, Doug." I put a hand on Doug's left shoulder and Meg's right. "Let's call a truce. Can we all just get along? Let's try to pick up a few clues at tonight's party."

Meg and Doug nodded their heads slowly. I reached down to pet Clarence and he gave me his right paw, a sign that he'd accepted the plan.

"Terrific. Meg, I think many of Jack and Jordan's friends will be here tonight. See what you can find out about motives and alibis." I briefly recounted my conversations earlier today with Judy Talent, Trent Roscoe, and Gareth Pressler.

Doug listened carefully. He was always reluctant to participate in my amateur sleuthing, but his superior intellect came in handy. "It sounds like you have no shortage of suspects with solid motives. How are you going to eliminate them?"

That was the million-dollar question. I shrugged. "Right now, I don't know."

Meg patted my shoulder lightly. "Don't worry. We've been down this road before. Something will turn up."

Clarence gave a small bark, either a gentle reminder we were there to celebrate his victory or a command to get to work. Either way, we parted ways to start the interrogations.

I scanned the crowd for Christy, whom I'd chatted with earlier on the phone. I hadn't thought to ask her for a physical description. After surveying the people and the dogs in attendance, I spotted a woman bustling about and directing another volunteer about something. A nametag was stuck to the upper right-hand corner of her chest, but I couldn't make out the writing. I walked toward her for a closer look and confirmed she was my mark.

Timidity at a Washington D.C. party was verboten. I charged forward with my hand outstretched so Christy couldn't escape. "Hello, I'm Kit. We spoke earlier today about my dog, Clarence." I turned around and noticed Doug and Clarence hadn't followed, so I motioned for them to come over.

Clarence pulled enthusiastically. I followed his line of sight. Helpers were placing boxes of pizza on the table behind Christy, and the enticing smell had drifted across the room. One whiff spelled trouble. This was no ordinary cheese pizza—it was definitely pepperoni.

Doug and I often joked that Clarence would kill for pepperoni pizza. In fact, whenever we had it delivered to our condo, Clarence routinely attempted to overtake the poor soul who delivered it. To avoid a scene, we'd put Clarence behind the closed bedroom door until we secured the pizza safely on the stovetop. Then we carefully shared one piece of pepperoni per slice with him. As long as we kept it coming at a reasonable rate, Clarence waited patiently. But if we missed his share, Clarence threw the doggie equivalent of a terrible twos tantrum. It wasn't a pretty sight.

I mouthed silently to Doug, "Pepperoni." He helplessly shook his head from side to side.

After shaking my hand, Christy smiled and bent down to pet Clarence. "This must be our champion!" She quickly clapped a hand over her mouth. "Whoops. You didn't hear that from me. It's not official until Jordan makes the announcement at seven thirty."

"Our lips are sealed. By the way, this is my boyfriend Doug, who also takes care of Clarence. Can you introduce us to Jordan before we start the program?"

"Of course. I'll take you over to meet him now. Follow me."

We fell in line behind Christy. Doug tightened his grip on Clarence's leash as we passed by the tables with the pizza. Clarence's nose wrinkled and his tongue passed over his teeth and lips in anticipation. When pepperoni was involved, Clarence meant business.

Jordan Macintyre stood between the food station and the bar. He was younger than his deceased husband by a decade, but strongly resembled Jack in handsomeness and style. Jordan looked like Washington's version of Christian Grey. Tall and lean, he wore a fitted suit jacket and pants that hinted at muscular definition. His tousled, dishwater-blond hair seemed to be the product of a professional stylist, yet, like the Beltway crowd, he wore conservative clothing. The dark rectangular frames of his Prada eyeglasses made him appear both shrewd and sensual.

Christy interrupted Jordan's conversation with another contestant and owner. The cute retriever/shepherd mix was edged out of the way in favor of the three of us. "Jordan, I know you want to meet this VID." She winked at me. "That stands for Very Important Dog." Out of the corner of my eye, I saw Doug roll his eyes.

Jordan turned in our direction and smiled confidently. "This must be Clarence and his owners, Kit and Doug. Welcome to the Capitol Canine family."

I was almost mesmerized by Jordan's sparkling blue eyes and his perfect teeth. He played for the other team, but a girl could still enjoy the view, right? I eked out a response, something like, "Nice to meet you."

Immune to Jordan's charms, Doug pushed past me and extended his hand. "We're sorry about Jack and wanted to offer our condolences."

"I appreciate it. This is a difficult time. We'd only been married for a few months…" his voice trailed off, and he reached behind his glasses with a handkerchief to blot a tear.

His grief seemed genuine, but he'd have to play the part of the grieving spouse convincingly, especially if he was the killer. "Were you at home when you found out what happened to Jack?" I asked innocently.

Jordan narrowed his eyes. "Yes, I was. Jack had left early for work. He always kept strange hours, and it was worse during a political crisis."

No alibi for Jordan. Clarence wiggled and whimpered. We'd have to move quicker. Surrounded by the pungent aroma of pepperoni, Clarence was losing patience. We needed to get over to that food table and give him a slice.

"Do you have any idea who might have killed Jack?" I reached down to pet Clarence in a feeble attempt to keep him under control.

Jordan peered down at me over his designer frames. "My husband had a lot of enemies, Ms. Marshall. It came with the territory."

I took in his stoic expression. Jordan was a man of few words.

Doug piped up, perhaps sensing I had struck out thus far. "Are you planning to stay in the D.C. area?"

"As a matter of fact, once the estate is settled, I'll be putting together investors for my latest venture. I hope to open a chain of canine restaurants."

Doug looked skeptical. "Did you say restaurants for dogs?"

Jordan smoothed his suit coat. "Yes, I did. There are eighty million dogs in the United States. That's a lot of untapped consumer potential."

As if on cue, Clarence barked. Jordan laughed. "See, I think Clarence is a future customer."

Only if pepperoni is on the menu. Clarence was clearly exasperated, but I had to keep pushing with Jordan. I might not get another chance to interrogate him about Jack's murder.

"What about Hill Rat? I heard Jack knew his identity. Did he tell you?"

Jordan pursed his lips. "You certainly ask a lot of questions. Yes, Jack hated Hill Rat, and he said he'd fig-

ured out who he was. He never told me the name, but
he did start referring to Hill Rat as 'he' and mentioned
his identity was surprising."

"Did Hill Rat know Jack was going to expose him?"

"Jack hadn't confronted him in person yet. If he had,
he would have told me. As I understood it, Jack floated
the rumor he was getting ready to reveal his name to
the congressional press corps. He said something about
wanting to see if the rat took the cheese." Jordan blinked
back a tear. "That was his idea of humor."

Doug broke in, "We appreciate the opportunity to
talk with you. Once again, our sincerest condolences."

I whispered to Doug, "Let's grab pizza before Clarence explodes." We had just started to walk toward the
food table when Jordan put his hand out to prevent me
from leaving.

"Wait a second. Did I read on the Capitol Canine
website that you work for Representative Maeve Dixon?"

Uh-oh. I'd hoped Jordan hadn't noticed my place of
employment. Hill Rat's revelation earlier today fingered
Maeve as a suspect. Now I was in Jordan's crosshairs.

He shook his finger. "I remember now. Jack mentioned you the night before he died. He said something
about emailing all his contacts and telling them to vote
for your dog so he could win favor with you and therefore your boss. I told him it was a ludicrous idea—that
he shouldn't use Capitol Canine as a political pawn."

Doug offered, "Given the circumstances, would you
like us to withdraw Clarence from the contest?"

I shot daggers at Doug. Sacrifice Clarence? Was he
crazy?

"I don't really care which dog wins the contest. I do
care who killed Jack," Jordan sniffed. "I haven't heard

much from the police, but the media is reporting Maeve Dixon as the prime suspect."

Jordan glared at me. Just as Jack had transformed instantaneously in his office when annoyed, his husband stopped pouring on the charm. When I didn't respond immediately, he maintained the angry glower coupled with an uneasy silence.

Jordan wasn't going to let me end this conversation without an answer. A cardinal House of Representatives rule repeated itself in my head: when in doubt, always toe the party line. I took a deep breath and spoke in my calmest voice. "Representative Dixon sincerely hopes this murder is solved quickly. She has no further comment at this time."

Jordan's eyes bulged behind his fashionable glasses, and his cheeks flushed. "Typical Washington bullshit." He squared up and shook a defiant fist in the air. More of a lover than a fighter, Clarence immediately stood up from his reclining posture with an anxious look on his face. We'd denied him a pepperoni feast and now a random stranger had threatened violence.

Jordan turned to walk away, but not before a parting shot. "Mark my words. Whoever did this to Jack is going to pay." Again, he pumped his fist aggressively, presumably indicating he planned to deliver a mammoth knuckle sandwich to Jack's murderer. His last maneuver must have been the last straw for poor Clarence.

My dog sprang into action. With the grace of a hippo lunging at its prey in the Amazon, our normally mild-mannered puppy leapt into the air and lunged at Jordan's arm. His canine teeth weren't even visible. Maybe Clarence thought Jordan's fake punches in the air were a game. His substantial beagle snout hit Jordan in the side, which caused him to stain Clarence's white fur with the entire contents of the red wine he'd been nursing. In the midst of the confusion, Doug dropped Clarence's leash. As soon as Clarence realized he was free, he lunged toward the food table. All I saw was his chunky behind.

At the top of my lungs, I yelled, "Stop! He's going for the pepperoni!"

But it was too late. In one smooth move, Clarence put his front paws on the edge of the table, grabbed a pizza box with his teeth, and dragged it to the floor. In a matter of seconds, at least ten other dogs had joined him in the pepperoni feast.

Doug and I stared at each other, truly mortified at the mess Clarence had made. But the whole scene was so outlandish, I couldn't contain myself. The stress of the last several days must have done a number on my mental health. No one said a word, but I doubled over in unstoppable peals of laughter. Doug smiled nervously and whispered, "Kit, can you please stop? Everyone is staring at us."

I wiped the tears from my eyes, drew myself up, and gradually regained my dignity. Doug had recovered Clarence and secured his leash. Exceedingly pleased with himself, Clarence bounded over to me with his tail wagging triple time. I couldn't resist my own version of a parting shot. I reached down to pet my dog, who licked my hand appreciatively. While rubbing his ears, I remarked loudly, "We'll take that pizza to go."

SIXTEEN

"I'LL HAVE A glass of the Chardonnay."

The bartender asked dully, "Which one?"

"Cakebread, please. I need something buttery and oaky that fills up my mouth."

"You got it, sister."

Doug tossed me a disapproving glance. After the Capitol Canine debacle, we persuaded Meg to join us for a quick dinner and drink in Arlington. A District dweller, Meg rarely crossed the Potomac willingly. The three jurisdictions comprising the greater Washington D.C. metropolitan area each had their own flavor and culture. The denizens of each locale swore by their respective dominions and predictably attempted to persuade friends from the other two, usually in a futile effort, to visit them instead of venturing outside the motherland. The District/Arlington divide wasn't unbridgeable since the Orange line of the Metro connected them. Thank goodness Meg didn't live in a Maryland suburb. Due to the inconvenient lack of a subway transfer, I'd never see her outside Capitol Hill.

Within five minutes of Clarence's meltdown, the governing authority of Capitol Canine, led by Jordan Macintyre and the irrepressible Christy, decided our pepperoni-loving pooch wasn't worthy of the big prize. Citing a bylaw giving them power to override the popular vote and name the winner if a contestant "displayed behavior unworthy of the title," Jordan announced a golden retriever named Wonk as the "Top Dog" on Capitol Hill. Clarence did receive honorable mention. Given the circumstances, we concurred the consolation prize was generous.

The three of us piled into the Prius and headed for the hills. The hills of Arlington, that is. After depositing Clarence in our condo, we walked to the ever-popular Green Pig Bistro. No tables were available, which was par for the course since *Washingtonian* magazine named the French-inspired restaurant one of the top local eateries. Luckily, we claimed three open seats at the bar.

After ordering drinks and several appetizers, it was time to get down to business. With Meg on one side and Doug on the other, I summoned the gods of deduction. Turning toward my best friend, I asked, "Were you able to find out anything at the party?"

Meg stopped typing on her iPhone and shoved it into her purse. "Sorry. I had to text Kyle. I wanted to give him a heads up if my name ends up in a gossip column tomorrow related to Clarence's fiasco."

On my right flank, Doug rolled his eyes. He thought Meg's obsession with D.C. culture bordered on pathological. His assessment wasn't far off the mark, but without that influence from Meg, I'd have no idea what happened on the Hill after hours. Much to Doug's chagrin, intelligence wasn't everything on the Hill. More often than not, the political became personal, and vice versa.

After a moment of silence, she said, "Right, I almost forgot. Solving the murder. You asked me what I found out?"

Did Kay Scarpetta have to deal with such a lack of

focus amongst her band of faithful crime-solving helpers? I doubted it. Since I was no Scarpetta, I waited patiently for my comrade to elaborate.

Meg took a sip of her bubbly. I needed to get the information out of her before she had any more drinks,
particularly on an empty stomach. Meg's recollection
abilities were inversely related to the amount of the al-
cohol she consumed.

"I would have extracted additional tidbits if Clarence
hadn't imploded. That said, I was able to talk to a longtime buddy of Jack and Jordan's. He knows them from
their fundraising efforts at the Human Rights Campaign." HRC was the leading gay and lesbian national
advocacy group in Washington D.C.

Our food arrived, distracting Meg. The eatery's signature dishes looked almost too good to eat, except that
all three of us were starving. Clarence had been the only
one in our party to consume a pizza dinner. The lineup
of buffalo pork ribs, kung pao sweetbreads, and pig tos-
tadas made up for what we'd missed earlier.

After we filled our plates and enjoyed our first bites,
Meg continued, "I can't remember the guy's name, but
he was more than happy to chat with me about Jordan
and Jack's relationship."

Doug interrupted her. "Why was he so forthcoming?"

Meg smiled. "He was wearing a Gucci suit from
the winter line. The gray wool checks gave it away. As
soon as I asked him about it, he was putty in my hands."

Many times I had borne witness to the fact that
Meg's allure with the opposite sex transcended age and
race. After this interaction, I could add sexual orienta-
tion to the growing list.

"After we commiserated about the federal government shutdown for a bit, I inquired about Jack and Jordan."

"What, specifically?" I asked.

Meg finished her drink and motioned for the bartender to pour her another. Her food-to-booze ratio was too low; thus her mental focus had officially lost its edge. Ironically, "Danger Zone" from *Top Gun* played softly in the background.

Meg popped the remaining tostada in her mouth and then took a long swig from her refill. "I couldn't be too obvious. I expressed my condolences about Jack and asked how Jordan was handling it."

Doug prodded, "And? What did he say?"

"Impatient, aren't we?" Her willingness to chide Doug indicated she was getting tipsy. "He said Jordan was holding up well. Then I asked why that might be the case."

The bartender cleared our plates and asked us if we wanted anything else. I was about to ask for the check when Meg pointed to the menu. "Yes, I'd like the banana bread pudding, please."

The look of astonishment on his face said it all. I knew what he was thinking. He didn't need to say it out loud. Where the hell did this woman put all those calories?

With an amused expression, he asked, "With ice cream and caramel?"

"Of course! No need to ask," Meg stated emphatically.

I giggled. Meg was truly one of a kind.

With an incredulous look, she said, "Why are you laughing? I read online this dessert was not to be missed!"

"I'm laughing because even though you're not a dog

lover, you and Clarence have more in common than you think."

Meg tapped her chin with her finger, lost in thought. She said slowly, "You might be right. We both enjoy a delicious meal."

Doug listened without comment. He had a limited tolerance for inconsequential banter. He rarely intruded on my alone time with Meg, especially when drinks were involved.

Doug's growing impatience required an inquiring prod. "Meg, what were you going to say about Jordan holding up well under the difficult circumstances?"

"Right. The well-dressed friend said it was because he planned to use his inheritance from Jack for a new business venture."

"Do you mean the dog restaurant?" asked Doug.

As we chatted, waiting for dessert, Doug listened without comment.

Meg's banana bread pudding arrived. It smelled like a Yankee candle had just been shoved under my nose. Without a second's hesitation, Meg grabbed her spoon and dove in. After a few bites, she came up for air. I could barely make out what she was saying due to the considerable amount of caramel impeding her speech. "Delicious," she mumbled.

I cleared my throat. Meg gave me a sidelong glance and then asked sheepishly, "Would you like to try it?"

"Thank you." After stuffing a sizable helping into my mouth, I understood why Meg had been reluctant to share. The combination of banana, vanilla, walnuts, and caramel could only be described as a dessert lover's nirvana.

I pointed to the few remaining bites. "You need to try it, Doug. It's amazing."

Wrinkling his nose, Doug answered, "Smells a little too strong for my taste." Then he added, "Maybe Jordan can serve it in his new restaurant."

Meg nodded enthusiastically. "One of us should tell him!"

I licked the remnants of caramel from the corner of my mouth. "I doubt he'll be taking my calls after tonight. Meg, back to what you found out about the financing for the project...that sounds like motive to me."

Meg took the final bite and pushed the empty dish toward the edge of the bar. "You got it. That's exactly what I thought. According to my source at the party, Jordan had pitched the idea to several venture capitalists but none of them had bitten yet." She grinned. "His pun, not mine."

Doug generously placed his credit card on top of the bill. Meg tried to offer him cash, but he refused. Never mind that Doug never had to worry about finances, thanks to his old-money family and trust fund. Chivalry wasn't dead, at least at the Green Pig Bistro. After our bartender took his credit card, Doug remarked, "If Jack hadn't died, Jordan's restaurant might never have come to fruition."

We gathered our coats to prepare for the frigid weather. Meg donned her vintage floppy cloche hat, leather gloves, and matching silk blend scarf. Only Meg managed to coordinate her winter accessories in addition to her outfit. My gloves were mismatched and my scarf had a tear, mostly likely because Clarence had mistaken it for a pull toy. I'd lost my hat a few months earlier when winter first reared its ugly head. Meg and

I qualified as the contemporary female version of *The Odd Couple*.

After arranging her cute bob underneath the designer hat, Meg answered, "That's the general consensus. It would explain why Jordan isn't too broken up over Jack's death."

We walked Meg to the subway stop and said our farewells. She gave me a quick hug and motioned with her right hand to call her. When she saw my blank stare, she mouthed the name, "Trent Roscoe."

I placed a hand over my mouth so Doug wouldn't ask what was funny. In response to my reaction, Meg pointed a finger at me with a knowing look. "I want the scoop tomorrow," she whispered.

I jogged to catch up with Doug, who was speed-walking determinedly toward our condo building. The cold weather was one of his few motivations to move quickly. I knew better than to begin a conversation when he was fixed on seeking warmth so I waited until we were inside the refuge of our condo.

Due to the craziness of the afternoon, there had been no time to update Doug on the murder investigation. Before we settled on the couch, he poured us each a small glass of tawny port. A rare indulgence, a twenty-year-old dessert wine remained one of the most reliable ways to warm up on a cold winter's night. This particular selection, opaque and richly dark, had a full-bodied chocolaty velvet taste, a perfect ending to a day filled with trials and tribulations.

As Doug sipped his drink and sighed in contentment, I updated him on the case. With one notable exception, I spared no details, recounting the impromptu breakfast chat with Detective O'Halloran, my research mission at the Library of Congress, lunch with Judy Talent, the unfortunate conversation with Dan, the meeting at the Sergeant at Arms office, and then Hill Rat's breaking news.

Naturally I glossed over the meeting with Trent Roscoe, underplaying his looks and sexy vibe.

Doug mostly listened, offering brief congratulations when I mentioned what the librarian had found for me about the gavels. He rubbed his chin thoughtfully. "You're not going to like what I have to say about this."

Now it was my turn to take a generous sip of port. "Go ahead. I'd like to hear your reaction."

"I know there are clues pointing to a setup of your boss. Something tells me we're missing the obvious. Have you ever heard of Occam's razor?"

Bic and Gillette constituted the extent of my knowledge on razors. Rather than profess total ignorance, I shook my head.

"It's a principle from a fourteenth-century English philosopher. There's a lot of math behind it, but the general idea is the hypothesis with the fewest assumptions is often correct. Unnecessary complications should be shaved away because the simplest explanation is often the right one. Get it?"

Living with a professor had its ups and down. Lectures about the relationship between philosophy and razors counted as a negative. Nonetheless, I responded affably, "Keep going. What's your point?"

There was that eye roll again. This time, it was exasperation, not pure annoyance. "I was trying to break it gently to you. Maeve Dixon had the motive, means, and opportunity to kill Jack Drysdale. It's the simplest explanation of the crime."

Anger and despair welled up inside me. I didn't know if I wanted to scream or cry. Trying to keep my voice calm, I asked, "How could you say that my boss is a murderer?"

He tried to put his arm around me, but I moved toward the edge of the couch, out of reach. He seemed surprised at the rejection of his affection. "Kit, what's wrong? You asked me what I thought of the situation and I told you."

"I'm glad you weren't the head of the United States Capitol Hill Police last summer when Senator Langsford was murdered. Don't you remember? I was the prime suspect in that investigation because it was the easiest explanation."

Doug pursed his lips. "No, this situation is different. You were the obvious suspect because you discovered Langsford. You had no motive. That's not the same as what you're dealing with now."

He had a point, yet it still irked me that he thought Maeve was a murderer. "What am I supposed to do? Dan may be insane, but he's right on one account. If she's convicted, our careers are finished." I took another sip of port. "Besides that, I'll be emotionally scarred if it turns out I worked for a murderer."

"You should take the approach I've counseled all along. Don't get involved. Dan can't fire you, and if Maeve is found guilty, it won't matter because you'll be unemployed. Just stay out of it and be careful around her."

I realized I was gaping and shut my mouth. "You think Maeve could try to kill me?"

"Listen, I don't know. I'm trying to bring some logic to the table. All these other explanations seem convoluted to me. If you really don't think she did it, there is one way to prove she's innocent."

"Okay, Mr. Razor, or whatever you called it. How do I prove that she's not the murderer?"

Doug placed his drink on the coffee table and leaned toward me. "It's quite easy. Come up with an explanation with fewer assumptions than the scenario I offered. Once you're able to come up with that version of events, you've got your killer."

Another negative to living with a professor: his reasoning is always dead on. No pun intended, of course.

SEVENTEEN

REPEATED BLARES OF the Sherwood Forest trumpet interrupted my peaceful sleep. I really needed to change my text message alert, which often elicited a Pavlovian response that involved throwing my phone across the room.

This time, I resisted the conditioned response and forced open an eye to identify the early-bird texter. Our bedroom was still pitch black. The glare from the smartphone forced me to squint until I could adjust to the unwelcome intrusion of concentrated light. One minute after six a.m. The last time pre-dawn text messages started flying, my boss discovered a dead body and became a prime murder suspect. This couldn't be good. Was it Maeve, in trouble again? Or Dan, perhaps sending me a threatening message about the fragility of my job if I didn't solve Jack's murder in the next fifteen minutes?

It was neither. It was Trevor.

Breakfast at seven at Pete's?

Was he insane? Pete's Diner, a Capitol Hill favorite, was situated one block from the Metro station and two blocks from my office in Cannon. No one appreciated a calorie-laden meal more than I (well, maybe Meg) but even the tasty coziness of Pete's couldn't lure me out before daybreak in the middle of winter.

Too early. How about 8?

The three dots flashed as Trevor typed his response.

Late for me. OK.

The Pentagon crowd started their days notoriously early. Trevor must have adjusted to those hours after becoming a defense lobbyist last summer. I mentally scratched off that option as a future career move.

Both Clarence and Doug snored softly. As much as I wanted to drift back to sleep, the likelihood of that happening was the same as the government shutdown ending today. Roughly nil. Sighing, I threw off the covers and quietly closed the door behind me.

At least getting up before my alarm meant there was ample time for a custom-made coffee drink. I opened the refrigerator and scanned the contents. A bag of Italian espresso beans hid behind a box of takeout Thai. I'd bought these a week ago and never had the chance to try them. After tearing open the bag and inhaling the heady aroma, I emptied a cup of beans into our grinder and chose the appropriate setting. The aroma grew stronger as the espresso brewed. Maybe Clarence's obsession with pizza was understandable. The smell of pepperoni had the same effect on him as coffee did on me in the morning. I poured two dark shots into the steamed milk, added a spoonful of sugar, and headed to the couch to enjoy my java masterpiece.

I still had a few minutes before I had to get ready for

the day. Under normal circumstances, catching up on the news about the shutdown would make sense. My current situation was anything but normal. Although Dan, with his hostile approach to his chief of staff duties the past few days, had exhibited all the charm of Jabba the Hutt, he was correct about one thing. Coming up with a workable deal on the shutdown meant squat if the police charged Maeve with Jack's homicide. While I hated to admit it, Dan had a point. Finding the real killer, or at least identifying a plausible suspect, was the task at hand.

To that end, I grabbed an old notebook and jotted down the facts thus far. Writing down what I knew about the case helped organize my thoughts. Doug's reasoning from last night was hard to ignore. Reluctantly, I listed Maeve as a suspect, along with Judy Talent, Gareth Pressler, and Jordan Macintyre. Upon reviewing my conversations with each of them, I confirmed Doug's rational conclusions. Each person had a good motive, but the hard evidence against Maeve was more substantial than the other three. Of course, there was another person to consider, but his/her status as a suspect posed even greater complications. Hill Rat had a terrific motive for wanting Jack dead. If Jack had gone through with his plan to reveal Hill Rat's true identity, the blog would be finished. No doubt Hill Rat was a great suspect. But without knowing his (assuming Jack was right) true identity, I was just Don Quixote, tilting at windmills.

What was my next step? I had a legislative directors' meeting at ten this morning. Despite the urgency to solve Jack's murder, I couldn't completely neglect my official duties. Besides attending that convo, nothing else warranted my immediate attention. What else could I do proactively? I turned back a few pages in my notebook.

The murder weapon remained the one piece of physical evidence that warranted further investigation. Maeve's status as the prime suspect wouldn't change as long as Detective O'Halloran believed her access to the gavel placed her in the most advantageous circumstances to commit the crime. My trip to the Library of Congress had raised the possibility that multiple gavels existed, but I needed to know more. Instinct told me another trip to visit the helpful librarian would arouse unwanted suspicion about my obsession with the Speaker's gavel. I'd have to figure out another way to dig up more information on the murder weapon. Since that tidbit about the crime hadn't made its way into the press yet, hopefully my sleuthing could fly under the radar.

A cursory check of the iPhone confirmed it was time to proceed with my morning duties. I showered and dressed, escorted Clarence outside for an abbreviated walk in the cold February air, greeted Doug as he awoke from his slumber, and shuttled out the door to face the lonely commute.

Pete's Diner was an anachronism on Capitol Hill, a surviving tribute to an earlier era when trendy restaurants operated by celebrity chefs didn't dominate the culinary scene. The luncheon menu offered a few unusual Asian selections and novel vegetarian options. Otherwise, Pete's was a greasy spoon frequently patronized by old-school pols who gladly eschewed the yuppie eateries of Pennsylvania Avenue.

I pulled open the door and scanned the two rows of seating. Trevor was seated at the booth farthest from the door. Ensconced in his newspaper, he raised a hand to indicate his presence without looking up to actually acknowledge my arrival. I hurried inside, sat down opposite him, and shrugged out of my winter coat.

"What are you reading?"

Trevor raised a finger to silence me.

"Please wait a moment, Kit. I'm nearly finished with a fascinating article about the threat of asteroids traveling near Earth."

I pressed my lips together to suppress the snarky retort that almost burst from my mouth. Trevor had summoned me to breakfast, after all. I didn't haul myself here to watch him read science fiction.

Clearing my throat, I motioned to the waitress for hot coffee. She obliged immediately. Although a no-frills establishment, Pete's prided itself on prompt service. Many of its Hill patrons only had a few minutes to enjoy their meal.

"Know what you want?" she asked.

I didn't need to study the menu. "Chocolate chip pancakes, thank you."

The waitress turned her attention to Trevor, who was still reading. "What about you?"

Trevor glanced up. He must have seen the irritated expression on her face because he promptly folded up the newspaper and placed it on top of his coat. "I'll have an egg white omelet with peppers and mushrooms and two slices of rye toast. No butter or hash browns, please." He handed her the plastic-covered menu and smiled.

To my surprise, she returned the grin. "Sure, Mr. Trevor. Coming right up."

My eyes widened. "How does the waitress know you?"

Trevor arranged his paper napkin neatly on his lap.

"I often come here before spending a long day on the Hill." He adjusted his glasses, smoothed his suit jacket, and tilted his head toward the grill area. "I find it comforting."

"You never fail to surprise me, Trevor."

"No doubt. What else might be in store?"

"I'll just have to wait to find out. I like Pete's, too, but why did you ask me here for breakfast?"

Our meals arrived, along with a refill of hot coffee. I grabbed the bottle of Log Cabin syrup on the table and drenched my three pancakes.

Trevor cast a disapproving glance at my meal. "How will you enjoy the pancakes underneath that mountain of syrup?"

I deserved the comment but that still didn't make it less insulting. Leave it to Trevor to aggravate me in less than ten minutes. "If possible, I'd like to eat my pancakes without judgment. Now can you tell me why you asked me to join you this morning? I hope it wasn't to criticize my choice in breakfast foods."

"Certainly not. That's simply an added benefit. I wanted to learn the status of your informal investigation concerning the murder of Jack Drysdale."

I dipped my pancake in a pool of syrup. I would have liked a few more squirts, but I couldn't bear another smart remark from Trevor. "I wish I had more to report, like the name of the actual killer. Jack had a lot of enemies, and I can't seem to narrow down the list of suspects." I briefly recounted yesterday's interactions and the relevant details.

Trevor took a bite of his dry toast and chewed slowly. He wiped his mouth neatly before speaking. "You need more opportunities to question the suspects. You've only scratched the surface, I'm afraid."

"I agree, Trevor, but I'm running out of time. Detective O'Halloran is under pressure to solve this murder as soon as possible, and my boss fits the bill."

"What is your plan for today?"

"I thought I might try to learn more about the murder weapon."

Trevor perked up. "Which is?"

I forgot the gavel hadn't been included in the media accounts of the murder. I told him about my trip to the Library of Congress and the discovery about multiple gavels.

I could never finish an entire serving of chocolate chip pancakes at Pete's. The pancakes weren't huge but the syrupy sweetness mixed with the chocolate got me every time. At least the sugar and caffeine overload guaranteed I wouldn't fall asleep anytime soon. I pushed my plate away to indicate I couldn't ingest another bite.

Trevor listened intently. "Why not track the gavels to their point of origin? Then you can find out if they still make more than just one or two for a Speaker."

"Good idea, but for all I know, those gavels are made halfway across the country."

Trevor wrinkled his nose. "Doubtful. The Architect of the Capitol is responsible for the maintenance and construction of all congressional buildings. That includes the tradecrafts necessary for daily operations. This doesn't seem like something the Speaker of the House would outsource."

"How do you know all this stuff?"

Trevor waved his hand dismissively. "I acquire information using two different methods." He signaled with one finger, and then two fingers for emphasis as he spoke. "First, I read voraciously. Second, I ask good questions." He peered over his glasses. "If you continue to engage in these investigations, you may want to engage in both activities."

"I'll keep that in mind, Trevor. I'd still need to figure out where those gavels are made, even if it's within the Capitol complex."

The bill came, and we both threw down money for our meals plus a generous tip. Fortunately, stinginess was not one of Trevor's many off-putting personality traits. While I gathered my coat to prepare for the ten-minute walk to my office in the frigid weather, he surprised me by saying, "Don't go yet. Let me try to find an answer to your question."

He grabbed his phone, and after studying it for a few minutes, he put it to his ear. "Hey, Trent, this is Trevor. How goes it, man?"

My eyebrows arched. Did I just hear Trevor use the phrase, "How goes it, man?" He hadn't been joking when he said he'd been working on his people skills.

"Thanks for meeting with her yesterday. Hey, I have a quick question for you. I know this isn't in the Sergeant at Arms office, but is there a woodworking shop in the Capitol?"

Trevor listened to Trent's response with a fixed expression of concentration. "Got it, man. Thanks again."

How many other people did Trevor call "man"? He was almost like a different person. Kevin Spacey's infamous portrayal of Keyser Söze in *The Usual Suspects* came to mind. Which version of Trevor was real? After this performance, I wasn't quite sure. Forever his nemesis, Meg would be interested in this tidbit.

Trent must have added something before Trevor got off the phone. "Interesting. Good luck with that. See you around." He punched a button on his phone to end the call.

I placed my purse on my shoulder and edged toward the end of the booth. "Trent Roscoe, I presume?"

"You are correct."

Back to "normal" Trevor, whoever that was these days. "Does he know where the gavels are made?"

Trevor answered in a scolding tone. "You heard the conversation. I never asked him such a thing. Isn't his boss Gareth Pressler still a suspect? You don't want to reveal too much, Kit." He shook his head. "I can't watch over you like I did during the last investigation. You've got to be more careful in covering your tracks."

"You're right. I'll try to be more cautious. What did he say about a woodworking shop?"

Trevor stood up and I followed. "My instincts were correct. There is a carpentry facility in the Capitol. I'm sure you can locate it using HouseNet." Trevor was referring to the internal House of Representatives website that provided employees with directories and useful administrative information about the Capitol complex.

"I'll do that. Thanks for your help, Trevor."

I was just about to cross Second Street to head toward the Cannon Building when he caught my arm. "I almost forgot something important, Kit."

I turned around to face him. "What is it? It's almost nine, and I need to report for work."

"Trent told me he's going to ask you out for drinks tonight."

I gulped. Despite the cold, my face flushed. "As in a date?"

Trevor shrugged and responded with a question. "Isn't everything in life what you make of it?"

EIGHTEEN

I DIDN'T LINGER to discuss the details of Trent's romantic intentions. After muttering an awkward goodbye, I fled to my office and thought about Trevor's revelation. Yes, Trent had sent signals during our meeting yesterday. For a variety of reasons, I'd chosen to play them down, but now they had confronted me directly, like a car's glaring "check engine" light. Once the alert flashed on the dashboard, ignoring it was impossible. Trent's advances presented a similar call to action.

I couldn't deal with this conundrum alone. Immediately after clearing my building's security, I punched a text message to Meg.

Need to chat 911.

Our version of the Batman signal, the emergency designation was saved for crises requiring urgent consult.

Meg replied in less than thirty seconds.

Break in case?

Given the distress call, that would have made sense. This was a different type of predicament, but Meg would undoubtedly agree as to the gravity of the situation.

Not quite. Trent Roscoe.

Although Meg's office was located in another House building, I could practically hear her squeal of delight.

Lunch at Longworth?

I readily agreed to meet at the main House cafeteria. Meg would know exactly how to handle this problem. She received both wanted and unwanted male attention on a daily basis. It was foreign territory for me. Her help secured, I felt one hundred percent better about my dilemma. Although figuring out if Trent's interest fell in the "wanted" or "unwanted" category might require some soul-searching.

My high spirits plummeted the moment I rounded the corner of the main hallway leading to my office. I'd completely forgotten the journalists we'd dodged yesterday. They had returned today with a vengeance. Like a pack of hungry wolves, reporters had surrounded the area immediately outside the entrance to Maeve Dixon's congressional suite. A quick pivot reversed my course and I darted inside the nearest women's restroom to strategize and regroup.

Maeve's interview with the police was scheduled for later in the day. Given the press attention, she wouldn't be likely to venture into the office this morning. Instead she'd go directly to the station from her apartment building, hopefully with her lawyer in tow. That left only Dan.

Reluctantly, I texted him. He might not answer a phone call but hopefully he'd glance at an incoming message.

Are you inside the office now?

Standing inside a stall, I stared at my device, waiting for a response. Had it really come to this? When I first landed a job in Congress, I hadn't imagined it might necessitate hiding inside a public bathroom.

The three dots flashed. Dan had received my message and was composing a reply.

Yes. Help me. I'm stuck inside.

Before answering, I considered my options. It was almost nine thirty, and I had a legislative directors' meeting at ten in the Capitol Visitors Center. Why should I force my way past the reporters when I would have to force my way out in fifteen minutes to leave again? I fished around in my purse. I had a notebook so I could jot down any important information at the meeting. The only downside was lugging around my winter coat. I'd gladly make that tradeoff if it meant I could successfully dodge the bevy of reporters for now.

Dan needed to hunker down, and he wasn't going to appreciate it. A short, sweet reply would suffice.

Have meeting then lunch.

After sending the message, I added one more detail.

Important leads on case.

That wasn't a lie and maybe it would make him feel better about the abandonment.

I shoved my phone back in my purse and hightailed

it out of the restroom. With many competing priorities, the weekly Democratic meeting for all legislative directors often had spotty attendance. Due to the shutdown, today's gathering would be an exception. Everyone wanted to know if the party's leadership had decided on a proposal to end the standoff. If I arrived a few minutes early, maybe I could chat with Judy Talent. Yesterday's pizza lunch seemed like an eternity ago. When we last spoke, she'd wanted Maeve Dixon's support for the Majority Leader's proposal. However, that was before Hill Rat's revelation about Maeve's involvement in the murder.

The Cannon Tunnel was nearly empty this early in the morning. Congress didn't espouse the "early to bed, early to rise" culture. The only fellow travelers in the tunnel were other legislative directors en route to the Capitol Visitors Center and caffeine-dependent staffers returning to their offices with steaming cups of coffee in hand. Before this morning, I'd never noticed the pipes delivering heat on the left flank of the corridor, slithering like two monstrous concrete snakes alongside the tunnel's travelers. The huge volume of people routinely masked the bleakness of the passageway. This morning, lacking the usual hordes, its industrial décor was laid bare. Crowds made it difficult to navigate, but the disguise provided by the masses was preferable to the unvarnished, naked version.

Instead of heading into the Capitol, I took a hard right at the end of the tunnel and entered the Capitol Visitors Center. The CVC, as it was popularly called, was built to accommodate the throngs of tourists who regularly descended upon Capitol Hill. Patriotic Americans and sightseers eager to visit the nation's legislature streamed in throughout the calendar year, especially in the summer months. Before the CVC's construction, navigating within the Capitol complex during June and July was nearly impossible. Demonstrating that it can act reasonably, Congress decided to build a massive 580,000 square-foot visitor center underneath the east side of the Capitol. The new facility provided a comprehensive educational experience for those who wanted to learn about Congress and its history, complete with films and exhibits. At least that was the "official" justification for the $621 million spent on its construction. Privately, everyone who worked in the Capitol complex celebrated the intentional displacement of the summer tourist onslaught.

Congress hadn't forgotten its own needs when it shelled out the small fortune of taxpayer money to build the CVC. It had included a congressional auditorium and a sizable number of meeting rooms. Since we had such a large group of legislative directors in the party (after all, we were in the majority), today's meeting had been scheduled for the auditorium. Normally, members of Congress organized important events in this space. Due to the shutdown, all official business other than solving the current crisis had been canceled. That freed up the auditorium for our staff meeting. Attendance ebbed and flowed, depending on the perceived importance of legislative business in any given week. Given that congressional inaction had caused the government to stop functioning, I predicted a heavy turnout.

After zipping past the CVC gift shop, I rode the escalator to the lower level and strolled through Emancipation Hall, the centerpiece of the CVC. Congress

named the 20,000 square-foot central gathering space
after the slave laborers who built the Capitol.

I'd walked through the CVC countless times, but normally I kept my eyes fixed on my iPhone rather than
paying attention to the impressive feat of construction
surrounding me.

Those in charge of designing the CVC had mimicked the architecture of the original Capitol Building.
The sandstone pillars resembled the massive Capitol
columns built over 150 years ago by enslaved craftsmen, and the marble for the floors was obtained from
the same quarries that had produced the marble for the
Capitol in the 1800s.

The twenty-foot plaster model used to cast the Capitol Dome's famous bronze Statue of Freedom welcomed
visitors to Emancipation Hall. Other famous sculptures
formed a border around the massive open space. I gave
a silent salute to Montana's Jeannette Rankin, the first
woman elected to Congress. Chief Washakie, a Sho-
shone Native American warrior from Wyoming, was
unusual because portions of his statue were painted in
color. And everyone loved King Kamehameha, who had
unified the Hawaiian Islands. The gold and bronze of
his regal attire drew a regular crowd of admirers who
snapped photo after photo of the colossal figure.

I headed toward the corridor that led directly to the
auditorium, breezing past several House meeting rooms
and the appointments desk. I took a hard left and pulled
open the big double door. At three minutes to ten, plenty
of seats were already filled. This was no regular legislative director meeting. People were showing up en
masse to find out what in the hell was going on. It's a
myth that congressional staff know every detail about

ongoing negotiations. In reality, Capitol Hill forms a hierarchy in which a select few understand exactly what is transpiring at any given time. The rest of us rely on our precious contacts to try to piece together the puzzle for our bosses. This meeting would provide direction for those staffers whose bosses hadn't been approached earlier by leadership for their input on the critical legislative proposals.

No aisle seats were available. *Damn.* Everyone always wanted an aisle seat at briefings like this. Boredom or a demanding boss often required a quick exit. Much like on an overseas flight in coach, aisle seats were a valuable commodity and therefore scarce. I squeezed past several colleagues who were too busy surfing their phones to make room for my passage. I finally wedged into an open seat and shoved my bulky coat under my chair.

As I fished through my purse to find my notebook, I felt the not-so-casual stare of the woman sitting next to me. She looked vaguely familiar, but with 230 other legislative directors in the party, I didn't know everyone by name. Her blonde hair had been straightened yet didn't quite behave perfectly, sort of like my brown mane. She wore boxy black frames conveying the message that she preferred to be viewed as intelligent rather than fashionable.

I'd finally located my notebook and a pen that worked when she cleared her throat. I turned to her and introduced myself, offering my hand. "I'm Kit Marshall and I work for Representative Maeve Dixon from North Carolina. I've seen you around but I don't know your name."

Smart-Not-Sexy smiled, but not too broadly. "I

thought you worked for Dixon. Have you seen Hill Rat's latest posting?"

If she didn't realize I already knew what Hill Rat had posted yesterday, she wasn't fooling anyone with those smart glasses. But it wasn't good politics to alienate a friendly colleague. "Yes, we aren't commenting to the press about Representative Dixon's discovery of Jack's body."

I turned my attention to the front of the room. Judy Talent was milling around, smiling at familiar faces and shaking hands with others. The meeting was about to begin so this meaningless conversation needed to be wrapped up.

My next-door neighbor shook her head. "Not yesterday's post. This morning's."

I whipped my head around. Smart-Not-Sexy had captured my full attention. "This morning?"

She swiped open her smartphone and skillfully used two fingers to scroll down the litany of emails. She selected one and waited for it to bring up a web page in the phone's browser. Then she handed me her device. "I get notifications when Hill Rat posts a new blog," she explained. She kept talking as I enlarged the writing on the screen. "This one went up about ten minutes ago."

The meeting had come to order. Judy began her spiel summarizing the Majority Leader's proposal to fund the federal government. I'd focused on most of this information yesterday with her, although the bill might have changed since our lunch. Unfortunately, Hill Rat was the more pressing problem.

The title of the post was in big capital letters: HOMICIDE IN THE HOUSE. Underneath the headline, Hill Rat had kept it brief:

The murder weapon in the Jack Drysdale killing has been kept under wraps...until now. Drysdale was bludgeoned to death with nothing less than the symbol of the House of Representatives itself, the Speaker's gavel. Who had access to the gavel prior to the crime?

Underneath the three-sentence post, there was a video link. I didn't want to interrupt the meeting but I needed to see what Hill Rat had posted. Flipping the phone to "mute" would have to suffice. No words were needed. The video was a five-second clip of Maeve Dixon, banging the gavel on the House floor the night before Jack's murder. Damn those C-SPAN archives!

NINETEEN

FEELING A SUDDEN need to scream, I managed to remain silent as I handed the phone back to the staffer. She shot me a questioning glance. I mouthed the word "Thanks."

Maeve needed to know about this latest development, especially if she still planned to visit police headquarters today for questioning. Dan also needed to know, since the reporters camped outside the office were likely to increase both their numbers and volume. He'd have to handle that situation on his own. No way was I going back there. Images of rabid Capitol Hill reporters waving pitchforks and torches came to mind. It was better if we didn't provide them with someone they could try to interrogate.

Maeve replied quickly to my text informing her about Hill Rat's latest revelation. She agreed that returning to the office didn't make any sense and urged Dan to "stay put" as long as possible. Each of us was on our own.

Half-listening to Judy's information about the plan to end the shutdown, I scanned the auditorium. Most people were staring at their phones while ostensibly heeding the message from congressional leadership about the way forward. No doubt about it; Hill Rat's posting would go viral. Maeve Dixon's tenure as an influential legislator in Congress was about to be cut short. The only way to stop the inevitable progression leading to total career destruction was to find the real killer. Hill Rat had given me a shove in the rear. I had to find the killer *now*.

I was tempted to bust out of the meeting and resume my investigation. Under normal circumstances, listening to rapid-fire questions about the shutdown would have been enjoyable. More than anything, I loved figuring out the nitty-gritty policy details. Today's summit offered a veritable smorgasbord of wonkiness. But none of this mattered if Maeve couldn't prove her innocence. Despite the urge to split, I forced myself to remain seated; getting up in the middle of the meeting would draw even more attention. Besides, Judy Talent had a good motive to kill Jack Drysdale. She'd hated him, and her line about leaving the Hill didn't mean anything. She could turn down the K Street job in a second if the Speaker asked her to serve as Jack's replacement. Given how busy she was, I might not get another chance to talk with her. After the meeting concluded, I would have the perfect chance to pounce, especially if I waited patiently for the opportunity to present itself.

The questions concerning the finer points of the proposal kept coming. It was a quarter past eleven before the attendees collectively decided they'd heard enough. Judy surveyed the crowd. With her fingers counting off the numbers, she bellowed, "Going once, going twice." She paused. When no one interrupted her, she concluded, "Sold! Congratulations, team. We have an offer to end the government shutdown." Judy flashed a radiant smile and turned to chat with one of her dutiful acolytes.

Along with the masses, I filed out of the row of seats. Judy was yakking up a storm, and a receiving line had formed. Some people might have legitimate questions about the legislation, but the bulk of the posse surrounding her just wanted a moment of face time. Judy was the Capitol equivalent of a high school prom queen.

I took a seat a few rows away from the confab and buried my face in my iPhone. If Smart-Not-Sexy knew about Hill Rat, it was a safe bet most of those in the room did, too. In ten minutes, the crowd had dwindled. After Judy took care of the remaining devotees, I could ambush her without drawing too much attention. I was about to make my move when a legislative director from another House office appeared next to me.

"Kit, is that you?"

I looked up. His name was Stuart and he worked for another Southern member in the Democratic caucus. There weren't too many of us from the region so we'd become acquainted. I groaned inwardly. Stuart was a nice enough guy, a well-meaning nerd of sorts. This was not the time for small talk.

"Hello. I'm sorry, I can't talk right now. I'm reading an important email from my chief of staff." Mentally I crossed my fingers. I didn't typically resort to lying. I'd say an extra Hail Mary before bedtime. Although I wasn't a churchgoer, old habits die hard.

Stuart ignored my excuse. He placed his hand gently on my shoulder. "Don't worry. I'm sure another House member will hire you after the dust settles."

What did he say? I stood so he'd have to remove his hand. Keeping my voice even, I said slowly, "I'm not looking for another job, Stuart."

Stuart nodded. "I agree with your strategy. Loyalty is crucial around here. You shouldn't jump ship until the very last minute." He laughed nervously. "Of course on the *Titanic*, that meant getting sucked under."

The image of Leonardo DiCaprio hanging onto an iceberg jumped into my head. Before the *Titanic* theme song could form an earworm, I answered Stuart, a little louder this time. "Maeve Dixon didn't kill Jack Drysdale. So while I appreciate hearing your views on loyalty, it's not necessary."

I shoved my iPhone in my purse and stormed past Stuart, who appeared stunned at my response. As I hurried to the front of the room to catch up with Judy, he yelled after me, "Don't worry! I'll let you know if we decide to hire in our office!"

Stuart's riposte was loud enough to alert Judy. As I marched toward her, one of her twentysomething lieutenants whispered in her ear. Her eyes widened. Stuart had ruined my surprise attack.

Judy smoothed her hair and extended her hand. "Hello, Kit. What can I do for you?"

After politely accepting her gesture, I gave her some good news that would hopefully put her at ease. "I spoke with Representative Dixon and she's willing to support the Majority Leader's proposal. She may have a few minor issues she'll mention to him on the floor, but in the end, she'll vote for it." I flashed my highest-wattage smile.

Judy's reaction wasn't exactly what I'd anticipated. Her face scrunched up into something between a forced smile and a grimace. She almost looked constipated. "I appreciate your willingness to follow up after our meeting." She fixated on me for a long moment. Then she tugged at my sleeve, pulling me several feet away from where her young minions were drifting about.

Judy squared up to face me directly. "I'm going to be honest with you. A day ago, I would have been fighting for Maeve Dixon's support on this bill. I might have even gone to my boss with your requests to change a few of the funding numbers." Judy shook her iPhone with the Hill Rat blog displayed on the screen. "But today, thanks to her purported involvement with Jack's murder, her political future is dicey. For Pete's sake, she had the murder weapon in her hands a few hours before the police found her hovering over the body!"

I could feel the heat of acute embarrassment in my face. Stuart had alerted Judy to my approach, but his obtuseness didn't matter one bit. She'd already labeled Maeve Dixon a political liability. Considering the volatile politics surrounding the government shutdown, adding fuel to the fire made absolutely no strategic sense. My goose was cooked.

The lady doth protest too much. I knew my *Hamlet.* Still, I couldn't help myself. No matter what Doug, Judy Talent, Hill Rat, or the rest of the world thought, Representative Maeve Dixon did not kill Jack Drysdale.

"You've got it wrong. It's all circumstantial evidence. If you give me a few days, I'm sure the real killer will surface and Maeve will be exonerated."

She scoffed at my outburst. "Now you seem desperate. Your boss has enlisted your services as a detective?"

I realized I had said "give *me* a few days." I'd meant to say "give *it* a few days." Judy's comment stung. Sure, I wasn't Adrian Monk. That didn't mean I couldn't solve a murder. I'd done it six months ago and there was no reason I couldn't do it again. Her snide remark made me reckless.

"As a matter of fact, I *am* conducting an informal

investigation concerning the death of Jack Drysdale. Where were you the morning of his death? Do you have an alibi?" I stood with my arms akimbo in an attempt to deliver the message that I meant business. Just because Judy had seniority and rank didn't mean she had license to bully me...although in actuality, seniority and rank *did* imply the privilege to bully someone on Capitol Hill. I shoved that dismal thought aside.

Judy smiled, a less than friendly grin. She wrinkled her nose. "Why should I tell you my whereabouts the morning Jack was killed?"

Was she trying to avoid my question? Leaning in, I lowered my voice for dramatic effect. "If you don't have anything to hide, then what's the harm, Judy?"

She pursed her lips in obvious distaste. I'd cornered her. Either she'd 'fess up or give me good reason to think she'd murdered Jack.

"If you must know, I was at Results Gym that morning for Gary's famous Boot Camp class. Check with him or any of the other women who wake up before dawn to stay in shape." She gave me a once-over. "I can tell that's not your crowd, but believe me, I can come up with numerous alibis."

Ouch. Judy was revealing her true colors, and they were dark—not the kind that come shining through, as in Cyndi Lauper's song. She hadn't climbed her way to the top of the Capitol Hill hierarchy without the benefit of a sharp tongue. At least I'd found out she claimed to have a strong alibi for Jack's murder.

"I'm sure the police will check to make sure your story holds up. If you change your mind about needing my boss's support, let me know." I began to walk away.

"Wait a second." She jogged to catch up to me. "Sorry for being so rude. I'm not usually like that."

While I had my doubts, there was no reason to push the issue. "Apology accepted."

"When Maeve Dixon is cleared of all suspicion, then the Majority Leader will welcome her help to end the shutdown."

It wasn't ideal, but given the circumstances, Judy's proposition seemed fair. I nodded and presented my hand as a peace offering. She accepted it with a firm shake.

I retraced my steps back through Emancipation Hall, up the Capitol Visitor Center escalator, and toward the Cannon Tunnel. It wasn't quite time for lunch with Meg so I took my time walking in the tunnel, admiring the high school art competition entries that populated the drab corridor. My phone buzzed. It was a text from Doug. Are you OK?

Obviously, Doug had seen Hill Rat's latest dispatch and wanted to check in. I clicked the "return call" button on my phone. I didn't have the energy to exchange a chain of texts with him on the topic.

Doug picked up immediately. "How are you doing? I read the blog about your boss."

"It's getting ugly around here. The Democratic leadership is starting to distance themselves from Maeve."

Doug's voice was filled with concern. "Maybe you should follow their lead."

"I can't abandon my boss at a time like this. Besides, I know she didn't do it."

There was a brief silence on the line. "Kit, I'm concerned about your safety. Working in Congress shouldn't be life threatening."

His point was valid. "Doug, I'm always careful. I'm having lunch with Meg so I have to run. Talk to you tonight." Doug's circumspection sometimes annoyed me, but it was obvious his caution arose out of a desire to keep me out of harm's way. That realization buoyed my spirits and warmed my heart. Yes, Trent Roscoe was easy on the eyes. Was that a fair trade for Doug's genuine concern for my well-being? Doubtful.

When I reached the Cannon basement rotunda, I stopped to look for one of my favorite Capitol Hill employees who had operated the shoeshine stand for the past twenty years. As I peeked around the corridor, watching for my buddy, I heard a familiar voice behind me.

"Ms. Marshall, are you lost?"

I turned to face Detective O'Halloran. "No, sir. I thought I'd chat with Martha. She also operates the key cutter." With a sheepish grin, I explained, "I lose the key to my condo on a regular basis. I help keep her in business with all the requests for duplicates."

"Why am I not surprised to hear this? Perhaps if you spent less time trying to solve murders in the United States Capitol, you'd have better luck locating your keys."

"Thanks for the advice, Detective. But I don't think the two activities are connected."

After a chuckle or two, he turned serious. "I'm afraid we've asked your boss to speak with us today about the murder of Jack Drysdale."

"I'm aware, Detective. Is she an official suspect?"

O'Halloran sighed. "At this time, she's voluntarily answering questions, which we appreciate. She's not under arrest."

I released the breath I'd been holding. O'Halloran heard my audible exhale and added, "Yet."

"Detective, I'm sure that once you examine the facts of this case, you'll arrive at the same conclusion as I did. Clearly, my boss was set up to take the fall for Drysdale's murder."

"I'm listening. What evidence substantiates that theory?" O'Halloran had given me a shot to exculpate Maeve. I had to take it.

"First, the supposed phone call from Jack the morning of the murder to our chief of staff doesn't make sense. The call was made from a random phone in the Capitol Visitor's Center. Anyone could have made that call. If Jack had done it, why not use his cell?"

O'Halloran waved his hand dismissively. "He might have left his phone back in his office. Or maybe he didn't want anyone to know he wanted to speak with Maeve Dixon to patch things up after the fracas the day before."

"But why would Jack call Dan instead of me? Maeve had instructed Drysdale I was in charge of the shutdown negotiations. I even went with her to the Speaker's meeting the day before."

"I see your point, but that's easily explained. He might have forgotten your name so he simply defaulted to calling the chief of staff who runs the office."

I shifted my bulky coat to my other hand so I could emphasize my words to O'Halloran with an emphatic gesture. "That doesn't make sense, Detective. Remember, you found my name on Jack's desk. He certainly knew who I was. He'd recently emailed all his friends to make sure my dog Clarence would win the Capitol

Canine contest. There's no way he would forget I was Maeve's point person on the shutdown."

O'Halloran's eyes met mine for several seconds. "Your logic does call into question some of the circumstantial evidence against Representative Dixon." I grinned triumphantly. He quickly continued, "But it doesn't get her off the hook. Remember, we found her standing over the body. If that isn't enough, she had access to the murder weapon the night before. We all know she served as the presiding officer on the House floor less than ten hours earlier."

"Lots of people had access to the gavel, Detective."

He shook his head. "That's where were disagree, Ms. Marshall. It's the exact opposite. It's not an object that's left lying around."

I pursed my lips. *That damn gavel again.* "I've done some research, and there are several gavels, not just one."

"That is correct. Your boss contends she didn't touch anything after she discovered Drysdale's body. So if another gavel was used to kill him, we won't find her fingerprints on the murder weapon, correct?"

O'Halloran's reasoning seemed sound. Nonetheless, I didn't want to concede any point that could implicate Maeve's involvement in the crime, so I maintained a poker face as best I could. Time to go back on the offensive. "Speaking of the gavel, I'd appreciate it if the police didn't leak information about the case."

O'Halloran appeared surprised at my accusation. "We have an ironclad policy about speaking to the press informally. We take it seriously because so many of our cases involve sensitive subjects." He added pointedly, "And sensitive people."

"You might want to reexamine the policy and how it's working. This morning, Hill Rat published a blog in which he revealed the gavel as the murder weapon and linked it to my boss." I whipped out my iPhone and showed O'Halloran the online post.

He shook his head slowly. "I'm sorry about this, Kit. I will double-check, but I'm confident no one in the police gave this information to the press, especially Hill Rat. No one even knows who Hill Rat is."

"Precisely, Detective. So it's entirely possible that Hill Rat might have overheard one of your officers talking about the case. His anonymity gives him or her a lot of power around here."

"I can't disagree with you there, Ms. Marshall."

It was almost time to meet Meg at the cafeteria. "Thanks for the chat. I hope you'll think about the evidence you've collected against my boss. It's circumstantial and it doesn't add up."

"You may have a point. But she's our best suspect, and you know what they say."

"What do they say, Detective?"

"The simplest explanation is usually the best one."

Damn. Occam's razor strikes again.

TWENTY

DURING THE SHUTDOWN, discontented souls, or excepted staff, wandered the hallways in search of any news about a viable solution. Bathrooms were shuttered, wastebaskets overflowed, and abandoned committee rooms added an extra creep factor.

The Longworth cafeteria was an exception. The only available lunchtime eatery inside the House, it had the gravitational pull of the Death Star. Everyone, no matter who they were, migrated to Longworth from their desolate, depressing office suites to find sustenance and solace.

On a typical workday, Longworth was swamped with diners. Those who built the Capitol Visitor Center had included a cafeteria to accommodate tourists. But the fancy bill of fare at the CVC had prices to match. The cost of the visitor center food mirrored Washington's economy of scale, yet most sightseers had much more modest lifestyles. Aunt Dottie and Cousin Fred took one look at the sophisticated menu in the CVC cafeteria and immediately complained to their congressman they couldn't afford the trip. In an attempt to help out cash-strapped constituents, every House office promptly directed visitors to the Longworth employee cafeteria, where the food was cheaper. Even though the visitor center planners had meant to keep the vacationer crowd at bay by attracting them to the fancy CVC cafeteria, the unintentional result had been to increase traffic in the cramped Longworth cafeteria.

I scanned the upper section of the seating area, looking for my dining companion. Not spotting her, I moved to the main section of the cafeteria, which included tables and several food service lines. A familiar hand shot up in the corner. Meg had scored the perfect seat. Given the high volume of staff, lobbyists, and journalists who frequented Longworth, even during the shutdown, nothing was private within its confines. At least Meg had found us a table on the perimeter.

"Happy fourth day of the shutdown!"

"Thanks, but the way things are going, who's counting?"

"Every news organization and interest group in town is counting, Kit."

She was right. Meg's prediction at Tortilla Coast before the murder seemed like years ago. She'd said this would be no short-lived crisis, and apparently she was right.

"Should we get some lunch before we chat?"

"Absolutely."

I followed Meg into the food court-style cafeteria. Today's outfit was tan riding pants, a black sweater sheath, and a blazer, paired with stylish boots and a silver barrette in her blonde bob. She looked ready to go fox hunting with the Queen. I, on the other hand, awkwardly toted a cumbersome winter jacket and a monstrosity of a purse. Did we make for an endearing pair, like Alvy Singer and Annie Hall? I hoped so.

Five minutes later, we were seated and ready to dish. Meg wrinkled her nose.

"Is there something wrong?" I asked.

"It's nothing. We all have to make sacrifices during the shutdown."

"What do you mean?"

"They've had to cut back on the number of cafeteria workers, and there's no supreme pizza today. Just cheese." Meg pouted and stared at her two plain slices.

Compared to my turkey on wheat sandwich, Meg's lunch looked positively delightful. It wasn't worth an argument. Better to commiserate so we could move on to the matter at hand, namely Trent Roscoe. Chewing on a big mouthful of sandwich, I barely managed an audible reply. "Yes, it's really tough these days."

Meg nodded solemnly. Her food diatribe over with, we could proceed to meatier topics, no pun intended. "You texted me a 911 message about Trent Roscoe? It must be important. You used the distress call."

We tried not to overuse the emergency code so that when we did resort to it, we both understood the severity of the situation. Once she heard what I had to say, she would fully understand my decision to employ 911.

I took a long sip of my Coke Zero, cleared my throat, and said, "Trent Roscoe is going to ask me out on a date."

The look on Meg's face resembled my free-spirited parents' when I'd told them I had a job working in Congress. For once, Meg was speechless.

"Go ahead, say something. What should I do?"

Slack-jawed shock was swiftly replaced with a wide grin. "Kit Marshall, I'm shocked you would even consider going on a date with Trent."

"The situation isn't what it seems. How am I going to solve Jack Drysdale's murder if I don't meet with suspects? Or the people who know them?"

"You can't tell me the only reason you'd accept is to solve the mystery." She waggled her index finger. "Don't lie to me. You don't find Trent at all attractive?"

I fiddled with the crust of my sandwich. "I didn't say that. But the only reason for me to go on the date would be to extract more information about his boss, Gareth Pressler."

Meg leaned back in her seat. "Fine. I see how you want to play this. I won't argue with you. But at least remain open to the possibility Trent might be a good catch."

"Am I supposed to leave Doug in the dust and run off into the sunset with Trent?"

Meg rubbed her chin thoughtfully, as if seriously considering my question. Given Meg's oil-and-water relationship with Doug, she probably was. "Of course not. At least not yet. But keeping your options open is always a good thing, *n'est-ce pas*?" She gave me a devilish smirk.

"Unless Doug finds out. Then it would be *très mal*." Meg didn't have the market cornered on basic French.

Meg stuffed the remainder of her pizza into her mouth. "I guess so. But he hasn't proposed. It's something to consider, Kit."

Meg's words were true, but they still hurt. She must have seen the pained look on my face because she retreated with lightning speed. "I didn't mean anything by that. It was a stupid comment."

If I was honest with myself, Meg's remark had validity. After all, Doug and I had lived together for almost three years. Still, I couldn't imagine life without him. "Apology accepted. I know what you were trying to say."

Her face brightened. "Let's move on. If you're going out with Trent tonight, what's the plan?"

I grabbed my iPhone and scanned my email. A ton of messages waited for my attention. Sure enough, Trent Roscoe had contacted me an hour ago. I opened his email and read it aloud to Meg.

Want to grab drinks tonight? Swing by my office at 5?

Normally, that would have been way too early to knock off work, but considering that Maeve Dixon had no political input on the negotiations taking place, it didn't make sense to burn the midnight oil. Meg gave the matter some thought before offering her opinion. "This could be the perfect plan. He invited you to his office."

I ate the last piece of my pathetic yet healthy turkey sandwich. "So what?"

Meg narrowed her eyes in disbelief. "Of all people, I shouldn't have to spell it out for you."

"I've got a lot on my mind these days. Enlighten me."

"Kit, Gareth Pressler is a suspect. His office is near Trent's, right?"

"Yes, it's around the corner."

She rolled her eyes. "This is a perfect opportunity to snoop!"

I shook my head. "No way. Last time we distracted someone to spy, you kept him occupied while I rummaged around. And that only worked because he was already in love with you." I was referring to Meg's current boyfriend Kyle. I still felt guilty that their relationship had begun with my deception, although it didn't bother Meg one bit.

Meg tapped the side of her iPhone while she mulled over the predicament. Suddenly her face lit up. "I got it! What if you had a better reason to excuse yourself from the conversation? Like an important phone call?"

"You've got my attention. Tell me more."

"It would only work if I kept the conversation going while you were gone. Didn't you say Trent loves to talk about security in the Capitol?"

"Sure. It's his job. He's enthusiastic about it."

"Perfect. You can bring me along. Write him back and tell him one of your friends wants to ask a few questions about security. After we start chatting, your phone will ring and you'll have to take the call. You can excuse yourself from the conversation for at least ten minutes. Of course, it will only work if Gareth isn't in his office. We'll have to take that chance."

"One problem, Meg. If you're along for the ride, who is going to call me on my phone? As usual, Doug is acting weird about my investigation. I don't think it's a good idea to involve him. He doesn't want me to get hurt. You know the drill."

"Yes, Doug is about as adventurous as my eighty-five-year-old grandmother. In fact, she might have him beat."

"No need to get personal, Meg."

"Sorry." She waved her hand in an apparent attempt to dismiss her impolite remark. "It doesn't matter. I have a solution."

"I'm listening."

"Have you heard about the FAC app?"

"Come again?"

She spelled out the acronym: "F-A-C. It stands for fake a call."

"I must have missed that one. Tell me about it."

"After installing the app on your smartphone, you can program it to make pretend phone calls. Let me show you."

Meg whipped out her iPhone and opened the app. In a few seconds, she had programmed her phone to ring. A few moments later, it buzzed, complete with a fake screen showing the fictitious name of the person who had supposedly called her. She swiped her phone open and answered. To my complete amazement, I could hear a voice conversing with her!

I grabbed Meg's hand. "Give me the phone. Who are you talking to?"

I put the device next to my ear and heard a guy asking me when my report would be finished. A few seconds later, he barked, "It better be on my desk in an hour!"

I must have looked utterly perplexed because Meg burst into laughter. "This is the deluxe call. It's supposed to be from your boss. It gives you the extra cover of having a real voice on the other end of the line when you answer the phone."

"I get it. So I can program my phone to ring during our conversation with Trent. I'll answer the call and excuse myself. After that, I can sneak into Gareth's office."

Meg sat back in her chair with a satisfied look. "Precisely."

"What should I look for in Pressler's office?"

"Beats me. Anything that might give him the means or motive for the crime, right?"

I gathered up my coat, purse, and trash. "Sure. I'll keep my eyes peeled. Part of the problem is there are really two related mysteries I'm trying to solve." I raised

"Especially when you work for Representative Dixon these days, as I understand."

I frowned in frustration. Pressler had turned the tables. He was interrogating me, not the other way around. "What are you implying?"

Pressler didn't blink an eyelash. Staring me down, he said evenly, "She's the prime suspect for the murder of Jack Drysdale. At least that's the story being reported."

His matter-of-fact proclamation of my boss's probable guilt galled me. *Calm down.* He's fishing for information. A deep breath steadied my voice. "She discovered Jack's body. That's it. She didn't kill him and we're confident the police will find the person who actually committed the crime."

Pressler laughed softly. "You have a lot of faith in the police."

He appeared surprised when I took a step closer. The cafeteria was full of eavesdroppers, but Pressler needed to know I meant business. "You bet I do. Justice will be served."

Pressler maintained the impassive demeanor of an expert poker player. Several seconds of silence passed. Finally he picked up his lunch tray. "I'm glad we agree that the safety of the United States Capitol complex is critical. If your boss is cleared of any wrongdoing, I would be happy to answer additional questions about our security operations." He nodded politely and strode toward the nearby exit.

What an odd duck. He reminded me of Wilford Brimley shilling for Quaker Oats. His cool, calm, and collected demeanor might mean he had nothing to hide. On the other hand, weren't psychopaths eerily hard to read?

Instead of following Pressler out the door, I sat down

at his table to plot my next move. Unexpectedly running into him had thrown me off my game, and I needed to refocus.

I had several hours at my disposal before meeting Trent at his office. But first, I needed to accept his offer of drinks. My reply to Trent's email was short and sweet.

Free for drinks after work tonight. Can I bring a friend to your office first who wants to ask questions about Capitol security?

That settled my evening plans. Right now, I was running out of leads. Then I remembered Trevor's suggestion about the gavel. If I could figure out where it was constructed, then I might be able to determine if multiple gavels existed. That would at least pave the way for the possibility that someone else could have had access to the murder weapon.

I couldn't wander the bowels of the Capitol looking for the carpentry shop. I needed to use my desktop computer to find the location. Sighing deeply, I texted Dan.

Reporters still outside?

Dan replied: Gone. Are you coming back?
Yes I was, but not to see him.

Be there in 10.

Luckily, I didn't run into anyone else in the short walk to the Cannon Building. Dan had told the truth. No reporters were camped outside the main door. When it became clear Maeve Dixon wasn't showing up for work today, the press contingent must have decided it was a waste of time to stake out her office. I pulled the door, but it didn't budge. Locked up as tight as Fort Knox. As I scrambled to find my key, I heard a familiar voice from the other side. "Who is it?"

"What do you want, Dan? A clever knock-knock joke? It's Kit, of course. I told you I'd be here in a few minutes."

The door cracked open and one eye peered through.

I waved my hand. "See, it's me. I'm alone. No worries."

He opened the door and whispered hastily, "Get in! I don't want anyone to know there's someone in the office."

After I stepped across the threshold, he hurriedly shut the door behind me. The gravity of the situation notwithstanding, I couldn't resist an attempt at humor. "Are you running Fight Club again? You know that's not allowed on federal government property. Don't make me turn you in."

He grimaced. "I'm glad you find this whole situation amusing. Do you know what it was like to be trapped inside the office all day with bloodthirsty reporters outside?"

I approached my desk, hung up the coat I'd lugged around all day, and turned on my computer. A clever retort was on the tip of my tongue, but I resisted. Dan was clearly upset and fueling the fire would only make the situation worse, if that was at all possible. Instead, it was better to commiserate and find out if he knew anything about Maeve's status.

"That sounds like a terrible way to spend the morning. I'm glad you survived." It took every ounce of concentration to remove all semblance of sarcasm from my voice. Before he had a chance to chime in, I added, "Do you have an update on our boss and her meeting with the police?"

Dan buried his face in his hands. Not a good sign. I grabbed his arm and tugged it. "What's wrong? Dan, you have to tell me."

He took several deep breaths, as if to keep from hyperventilating. "She called a few minutes before you texted. The interrogation isn't going well."

Odd that she called Dan, not me. Then I remembered her saying that she didn't want me to investigate the murder because she thought it was too dangerous. Bad news provided an excuse to kick into high gear.

"Are the police going to arrest her?" I held my breath as I waited for his answer.

He shook his head. "Not today. Unless she blows a gasket and confesses."

Maybe Dan was losing faith in Maeve's innocence. "Wait a second. If they don't have enough to arrest her, then why is the news so terrible?"

Dan raised his right hand and wiggled his fingers. "The evidence is mounting."

"Is that a secret signal? I'm not following."

Dan sighed impatiently. "I can see it was ridiculous to put my faith in you to solve the crime. What kind of detective are you? Fingerprints, of course!"

"Whose prints? Maeve's?"

"Yes! What else would matter? If they belonged to the Queen of England?"

"Calm down. I'm not the Mentalist. Her fingerprints were found at the crime scene?"

"Now you're getting warmer." Dan's voice dripped with sarcasm.

Oh, no. This *was* bad news. I almost whispered the question, "The murder weapon?"

"Bingo! Give this woman a prize! Guess what you've just won? A one-way ticket to the unemployment line." In a fit of uncontrolled anger, Dan picked up the first object in his path and threw it against the wall. Unfortunately, it was Maeve's North Carolina Woman of the Year Award. It shattered into several pieces.

Dan stared at me for a long moment. Finally, I broke the silence. It was unfortunate information, but all was not lost. "Her fingerprints were on the gavel that killed Jack. Is that correct?"

Dan nodded.

"It looks grim, but I think there's more than one gavel. If that's the case, Maeve might have been set up."

"Or she pocketed the gavel after presiding, replaced it with a new one, and then killed Jack with it."

"That doesn't sound like Maeve Dixon. The woman who survived Iraq and Afghanistan uses a world-famous symbol to kill a well-known political adversary? Then she leaves the weapon alongside the body with her fingerprints on it? Come on, Dan. It doesn't smell right."

"I'm not sure what I should think anymore. But I'm certain about one thing: if she's arrested and I'm still her chief of staff, I'll never work in politics again."

Dan's reasoning was accurate, yet his obsession with self-preservation bugged the heck out of me. Didn't he care that an innocent woman could go to prison for a crime she didn't commit?

It was time to bring this conversation to an end. "If

you'll excuse me, I have work to finish." I turned toward my computer, which was booting up.

Before returning to his office, he issued a final jab: "Do yourself a favor. Add polishing your resume to the to-do list for today."

Oh, ye of little faith. There were hundreds of emails to read, but that work could be avoided until Maeve Dixon had been cleared. The government shutdown would have to wait. Unless I figured out what happened to Jack Drysdale, the country would lose a dedicated public servant—permanently. In that light, wouldn't Uncle Sam agree I was faithfully discharging my duties, as I'd promised when taking the federal oath of office on my first day as a congressional staffer?

This morning's breakfast conversation with Trevor rattled around in my brain. He'd called Trent about the carpentry shop in the Capitol. If I could locate it, then perhaps someone who worked there might be able to tell me more about the supply of gavels for the House floor. How many were made? Would one missing gavel attract attention? If Maeve's fingerprints were on the gavel and she didn't kill Jack, then a switch had somehow occurred between the time she presided over the House of Representatives and the next morning when Jack had been killed. Any details about the plausibility of such a switch would help Maeve Dixon establish reasonable doubt.

It took a little digging online, but I finally found the location of the Capitol carpentry shop. A quick check of the clock indicated there was plenty of time to squeeze in a call to Doug before heading out on my latest quest.

My so-called "date" later on made me uneasy. Meg clearly thought I should play the field and see what developed with Trent. There was no denying he was eye-catching, yet his appeal was the complete opposite of Doug's. The man of action versus the man of intellect. How could I find total opposites sexy? I shoved thoughts of Trent aside. No matter what Meg thought, my motivation for having a drink with Trent tonight was purely the desire to find out more about Jack Drysdale's dispute with the House Sergeant at Arms office.

I punched in Doug's cell number and waited for him to pick up. After a few rings, I heard a sleepy "Hello?"

"It's me. Did I wake you up?"

"No, but you got up early this morning and it interrupted my sleep."

"Sorry. There's a lot going on here. You know, such as a federal government shutdown and my boss being accused of murder. That kind of stuff."

"Are there new developments in the case?"

I caught him up concerning Dan's information about the unfortunate placement of Maeve's fingerprints on the murder weapon.

After a few minutes of silence, Doug said, "Kit, this doesn't look good for your boss. Like I said earlier today, it might make sense for you to disengage."

"If she's guilty, there's nothing I can do about it. But what about the possibility she's innocent? I might be her only hope."

"Even if you're right, the real killer thinks he or she got away with it since so much suspicion has been focused on your boss. If you keep asking questions, you'll become a liability to him or her."

"I'm always careful. The reason I'm calling is that tonight I need to have drinks with a guy who knows one of the suspects."

"Who's that?"

"His name is Trent Roscoe. Trevor knows him and put me in touch." The less said, the better. Doug didn't need to know the gory details.

"Are you going by yourself?"

Doug never asked questions about my social obligations on the Hill. He realized evening happy hours and receptions were part of working for Congress. Did he really know me so well that he guessed something was amiss?

"I think so, but Meg is coming with me to his office to help with the interrogation."

He hesitated before replying, "Perhaps she can join you for drinks. Meg never turns down cocktails."

"That's true, but she's got this investigation she's working on for her committee. She took off early last night to join us for Capitol Canine, remember?"

"How could I forget? Clarence's pizza escapade will be seared in my memory forever."

I giggled at the image of Clarence devouring the pepperoni. At least he'd enjoyed himself.

"I'll text you when I'm headed home. Talk to you later."

He said goodbye, and I hung up, thinking that I wished I could spend more time with Doug. When all of this nonsense was over, I'd have to focus on him. There was only so long a relationship could survive on autopilot.

I gathered my belongings and headed to Dan's office to tell him I was leaving. Then I reversed course and bolted. What was the point of informing Dan? I'd always considered him a lightweight, but he'd shown his true colors the past several days. Even if the police cleared Maeve of any wrongdoing, I knew one thing for certain: there was no way in hell I could continue to work for Dan. Any ounce of respect I'd had for him disappeared when he threw our boss under the bus.

In less than five minutes, I was chugging through the Cannon Tunnel once again. This time, instead of veering to the right to enter the Capitol Visitors Center, I tacked left. This was the hinterland of the Capitol Building, known as the basement or "terrace" level. The ever-popular flag office was located around the corner, where members could obtain United States flags flown on the Capitol grounds for worthy constituents. Dan had asked me once to retrieve a flag on short notice so Maeve could provide it to a fellow veteran visiting Washington D.C.

The dimly lit corridor resembled the abandoned basement of a dilapidated high school. There were no offices down here, just uninviting steel doors with room numbers etched above them. I was definitely in the right place for the various craftsman shops. The only other people occupying this part of the building were workmen sporting blue jumpsuits with the Architect of the Capitol insignia emblazoned on them.

After traversing the corridor several times to no avail, I concluded the room number for the carpentry shop I'd unearthed on the Internet had ceased to exist. It was time for Plan B. Several Architect employees had come and gone through a particular double-door entryway. With any luck, it was the main point of access for one of the trade shops.

I stood next to the door and waited. Sure enough, a man in a blue jumpsuit rounded the corner and reached for the handle. Before he could enter, I blocked the entrance.

"Excuse me, sir. Can you help me with something?" I flashed the toothiest smile I could muster.

My innocent victim was caught off guard. Not too many congressional staffers ambushed AOC craftsmen. Once he saw the staff identification badge around my neck, he relaxed. "What's wrong, honey? Are you lost? The flag office is closed during the shutdown."

"Actually, I'm looking for the carpentry shop. Can you tell me where it is?"

"Did something break in your office? If that's the case, there's a form you need to fill out online."

"No, that's not it. I'm looking for the place where they make the Speaker's gavels."

My friend narrowed his eyes suspiciously. "That's a new one. Why do you need to know that?"

Somehow I didn't think telling him the unvarnished truth would get me far. "My boss has this guy she owes a favor. His kid is writing a research paper on the Speaker of the House and he wants to know more about the gavels. Since there's nothing going on these days, she sent me down here to find the place where they're made so I can take a photo for the little scholar." I waved my iPhone at him.

"Huh. Now congressmen are writing research papers for voters. They do everything but passing the bills to pay our salaries."

"You're not telling me anything I don't already know."

He shrugged. "Tell you what. Wait outside here and I'll see if my supervisor can come talk to you about the carpentry shop."

"Thank you so much."

I blew out a long breath. Lying had never been my strong suit, but lately, the deceptions rolled off my tongue smooth as butter.

A few minutes later, the door opened and a heavy-set, middle-aged guy in a blue uniform emerged. GENO was written in big block letters on the upper right corner of his shirt. He had bushy hair that stuck out from all sides, scrunched under a well-worn Architect of the Capitol baseball hat.

He gave me a quick once-over. "Are you the lady who wants to know about the gavels?"

"That's me. My name is Kit and I appreciate your time."

"You're in luck. We're not supposed to be doing any work around here except what's absolutely necessary to keep the Capitol operating. Due to the shutdown and all that political business."

"Thanks, Geno. Can you show me where you folks make the gavels?"

Geno removed a stick of gum from his pocket, carefully unwrapped it, placed it in his mouth, and started chewing. "This is my replacement for cigarettes. Somehow, it's not the same."

Like a true D.C. politico, Geno had avoided my question by changing the topic. But there was no way I'd give up that easily.

"I bet it's not nearly as satisfying. Are the gavels made inside this workshop?" I pointed toward the double door behind us.

"Nah. It's not here. But it doesn't matter. I can't show you inside our workshops for a million reasons. A nice lady like you might get hurt in a dangerous place. One misstep and bam!" He smacked his hands together. "You've lost a finger."

His ominous tone vaguely reminded me of my high school shop teacher and my subsequent fear of band saws. Maybe I didn't need to see where the gavels were actually constructed.

"I understand, Geno. But do your colleagues make the gavels somewhere in this building?"

He blew a small bubble. "Sure, we do. Done it since the 1930s. At least we have photographs going back that far showing Architect craftsmen with the Speaker's gavel."

Now I was getting somewhere. "I just have a few more questions. How many gavels do you make each year?"

"No idea."

"Is it more than one at a time?"

He laughed. "Of course. The Speaker needs more than one gavel. After all, sometimes they break, even though they're made from lacquered maple these days."

Bingo. "Where do they go once you've completed your work?"

"We hand them over to the parliamentarian's office. They take possession so they can be used on the House floor. Where they get stored after that, I have no idea."

"Geno, you've been a real lifesaver." I stuck my hand out for a friendly shake.

He plopped another piece of gum in his mouth and chomped away. "No problem. All this interest in the Speaker's gavel is pretty strange, though."

I whipped my head around. "What do you mean?"

He leaned up against the dingy wall next to the door leading to the shop. "I've worked here for a little over twenty years and no one has ever asked me about the

Speaker's gavel. Today, you're the second person with questions about it."

"Someone else asked about the gavel today?"

"Yeah, that's the funny thing. This morning, I had almost the same conversation with some guy."

"Do you remember his name?"

"I don't think he offered it. Said he was doing research on the Speaker's gavel and wanted to know where it was made and where it was stored. That type of stuff."

Who could have been asking about the gavel? Was the murderer trying to cover his tracks? Gareth Pressler came to mind. "Geno, would you recognize the guy if you saw him again?"

He rubbed his chin thoughtfully. "I think so. Today hasn't been too busy, so his face is pretty clear in my mind."

"Give me a second." I grabbed my iPhone from my purse and searched for a photo of Gareth Pressler online. Google Images didn't fail me. There was a recent photograph of him on LinkedIn. I pulled it up on the screen and enlarged it for Geno.

"Is this the guy you spoke with?"

Geno took my phone and held it close to his eyes. He quickly replied, "Nope" and handed it back to me.

Darn. Nothing was ever easy. "Are you sure? His name is Gareth and he works in the Capitol."

"I've seen this guy around. He's some high yuckety-muck with the Sergeant's office. He wasn't asking about the gavel."

Geno seemed sure of himself. No point in pressing. "It's been a pleasure talking with you. If you ever need anything, I'd be happy to help."

"Sure, you can do something for me."

"What's that?"

"Get those politicians to agree on a budget so me and my guys can get paid."

Not an unreasonable request. I waved goodbye to Geno and retraced my steps back through the long, bleak underground Capitol corridor.

TWENTY-TWO

I HAD TIME to kill before meeting Meg at Trent's office for our evening escapade. Under normal conditions, returning to the office would have been an option. But I didn't need another dose of Dan and his meltdown mentality. Instead, I found a seat in the basement of Cannon near the array of vending machines. Luckily, the machines were still fully operational. Junk food was typically verboten, but I'd had a rough day. After finding a few stray dollar bills in my purse, I settled in with a bottle of Diet Coke, a Hershey's bar, and my iPhone. Sleuthing required sustenance, after all.

Cyberspace engulfed me with a myriad of emails, e-alerts, and notices. A breakthrough wouldn't happen tomorrow, yet the early signs of a favorable deal were emerging. If Maeve was going to have a chance to play a notable role in solving this crisis, her name would have to be cleared soon. Trains were starting to leave the station, and they wouldn't return for wayward passengers. Time flew by and five o'clock quickly approached.

I grabbed my iPhone and searched for a message from Trent. He'd confirmed our drinks and said it was fine to bring a friend to "talk shop first." Now I had to program the Fake A Call app so it would ring during our conversation. Fifteen minutes would give us enough time to begin the chatter about security. At 5:20, my iPhone would buzz, I'd excuse myself, and commence my mission. A fast text to Meg confirmed she was still on board.

After gathering my belongings, I navigated the Cannon Tunnel once again to reach the Capitol Building. The *Mission Impossible* theme might have been playing in the background—or at least I imagined it was.

I pushed open the door at the Sergeant at Arms office and was greeted by no one. Not totally shocking, given the shutdown situation and the evening hour. The silence didn't last long. Before I could whip out my phone to message Meg, Trent Roscoe appeared with a wide grin.

"Kit, I'm so glad to see you again!"

Trent rushed toward me with his arms outstretched. A handshake seemed perfectly acceptable, but Trent was not going to settle for a professional gesture. Instead, he gave me a quick hug and let his hand linger on the small of my back. He wore a dark gray suit with a deep violet buttoned shirt that hugged his broad chest. Light crinkles emerged when he smiled, yet the fine lines of age only enhanced his physical attractiveness. There was no denying it. Trent had classic good looks with a buff body to match. Pretending otherwise would be the equivalent of denying Meg's fashion acumen or Clarence's craving for pepperoni. Some things in life resembled mathematical certainties, and Trent Roscoe's hotness qualified as such.

Before I had a chance to reply, the door swung open and Meg entered the fray. Her arrival allowed me to move several steps away from Trent so I could escape the touch of his hand on my back. It wasn't exactly unwanted. If I tolerated his touchy-feely gestures, where would the night lead us? The objective was to solve the murder, not cheat on Doug.

Meg flashed a killer smile and offered her hand. "Trent Roscoe, I presume? I've heard a lot about you."

He shook her hand politely. "Hope all of it's good, ma'am."

"Of course! Don't be silly. My name is Meg, and Kit told me about your security conversation the other day. You don't mind if we can spend a few minutes chatting in your office about it?"

Trent led us through the hallway. "We can chat all you'd like, if both of you can fit into my office."

We wedged ourselves into the tiny space across from Trent's desk. I shoved Meg in first so an easy, graceful escape would be possible when my pretend phone call came in.

Meg turned on her famous charm as we talked. She giggled at Trevor's witticisms, touched his arm lightly, complimented him on his attire, and batted her long eyelashes. This was classic Meg flirtation behavior. Usually it didn't bother me one bit. Even though I intended to avoid an awkward situation with Trent, her amorous overtures irked me. She knew he'd asked *me* out. Didn't she respect any boundaries, even if my ulterior motive for accepting his invitation was investigatory rather than romantic?

Amazingly enough, Trent reacted in an unusual fashion. More precisely, he didn't react. I couldn't remember the last time a man had been so impervious to Meg's wiles. Instead, he glanced at me several times during nversation, sending cute smiles my way.

zed by his attentions, I bounced several
t when my iPhone rang. Sure

enough, the screen displayed "Dan" as my supposed caller.

"Sorry, I need to answer this." I held the phone slightly away from my ear so Trent and Meg could hear the conversation.

"Where are you?" barked the voice on the line.

"Um, visiting a friend."

"You didn't even tell me you left the office."

Strange. How did Fake A Call know I'd left the office several hours ago?

I kept up appearances and excused myself from the office. The voice on the line kept talking. "Are you abandoning me?"

Something was wrong. I looked at my phone. The number looked familiar. Shoot. This wasn't the fake phone call. It was actually my chief of staff.

"Sorry, Dan. I didn't realize it was you. I'm sort of busy right now."

"Busy? I find that hard to believe. I got off the phone with our boss. She wasn't arrested today, but her lawyer thinks they could issue a warrant tomorrow or the next day."

I was standing at the entrance of Gareth's office. It was now or never if I wanted to inspect it. That required getting rid of Dan. "Hmm. Bad news. Listen, I have to run. I'm on the case. Don't worry!"

As I swiped the phone to end the call, I heard Dan's voice. "Wait! Don't hang up. I need to tell you something!"

Too late. Right now, I needed to focus on snooping. I had five minutes max if I wanted to avoid getting caught.

Pressler's office was immacul

clip was out of place. His desk was completely un-adorned, except for a huge three-ring binder. Carefully, I cracked it open. The table of contents indicated the three-hundred-page document was nothing less than a sweeping plan to revamp security for the House of Representatives. A quick glance indicated that Pressler's overhaul included changes to entrance and exit pro-tocol, tourist access, computer security, surveillance, Capitol Hill police presence, and identification. There was no time to digest the details of the plan, but I saw enough to know that if these procedures were imple-mented, public access to Congress would drastically diminish. To add fuel to the fire, member and congres-sional staff's freedom to roam the Capitol complex was headed for the chopping block. Access to certain loca-tions would be determined on an "as needed" basis, whatever that meant.

I'd seen enough. I closed the book and scanned the rest of his office. A computer rested on his desk, pre-dictably locked. There was no way a guy like Gareth Pressler would leave his office with his email or files exposed. But in the far corner of the office, another monitor emitted flashes of light. I hustled over to it. It took me several seconds before I could figure out what I was looking at. It was a wide screen divided into four quadrants. People walked through the shots, ostensi-bly in real time. One video displayed the Cannon Tun-nel. Others showed the rotunda and the cafeteria in Longworth. After several seconds, the screen changed. Entirely different segments of the House of Represen-tatives buildings presented themselves. Gareth Pressler had a security monitor in his office that gave him a bird's-eye view of at least three Capitol Hill buildings.

Mesmerized by the changing visual display, I heard a faint rustle from the direction of the open door. Just as I turned to make my grand escape, a loud "ruff" came from my purse. I fumbled to reach inside to locate my phone. *Damn*. I'd forgotten about the fake call I'd arranged to ring at 5:20. I'd set the ringer to mimic a dog's bark so Trent would remember I'd taken a call and excused myself. After finally retrieving the device, I swiped it to answer the call and then quickly hung up. My fingers were nowhere near fast enough to avert disaster. The sound of footsteps grew louder from the hallway as I braced myself to meet my unfortunate fate.

TWENTY-THREE

THE PATRON SAINT of sleuths must have been looking down from heaven with sympathy. To my surprise, Meg rounded the corner and grabbed my arm.

"Ouch! What are you doing?" I whispered.

"What am I doing?" she hissed. She pulled me closer before continuing her verbal assault. "What are you doing? You've been gone for fifteen minutes already. I can't keep Trent occupied forever."

I reclaimed my appendage. "That's never been a problem before. You couldn't hold Trent's interest for a little extra time?"

Meg's face contorted with frustration. "He's not biting. I don't know why. Maybe he really is in love with you."

My best friend's glare bored into me like a phaser set to stun on the Starship Enterprise. "Never mind. Let's get back to it. I can make up some story about Dan calling me. Actually, Dan did call me. That wasn't a fake."

"I heard your phone all the way down the hall. That's why I excused myself to come find you. If someone else had heard it, you would have been toast."

I motioned for Meg to lean in closer so I could whisper softly, "It was worth it. I found an extensive plan to overhaul House security on Pressler's desk. Plus, he has a monitor in his office tracking the cameras in the office buildings. He would have known Jack's location, even early in the morning."

Meg's eyes widened. "Do you think he's your guy?"

We walked toward Trent's office. "I think so. I might have to check a few things out tomorrow to confirm it."

"Are you keeping your date with Trent tonight?" Meg made air quotes around the word "date."

"I don't think it will hurt. Maybe I can find out more valuable information about his boss." I elbowed Meg. "Especially if I'm really charming."

Meg gave me a suspicious look. "I wouldn't overplay your hand, Kit. Leave the art of seductive interrogation to the professionals. If you're not interested in Trent romantically, just have a drink and go home."

I resented Meg's remark. Yes, she was pretty and men adored her. But occasionally, a good-looking guy might be interested in yours truly. Doug wasn't the beefy, bulging muscles type, but he was tall, fit, and attractive in a refined sort of way.

"I'll try to control myself."

We walked back inside Trent's tiny office and returned to our seats. Trent seemed to buy my explanation about Dan's phone call and my apology. After politely thanking him for his time, Meg excused herself. Outside the doorway, she mouthed "Call me tonight" and waved goodbye.

I returned my attention to Trent. His grin was the type I'd have plastered on my face if I heard my boss had given everyone the afternoon off. Best to keep it casual. "Ready to go?" I suggested.

"Absolutely. I know she's your friend, but I thought she'd never leave." He grabbed his coat and escorted me out of the office suite. As we left the Capitol Building, I realized we hadn't discussed where we were going. We were headed in the direction of Pennsylvania Avenue, home to a number of bars and dining establishments.

"Trent, where are we having drinks tonight?" I tried to keep my voice steady. I was shooting for friendly yet not overly encouraging.

"I thought we'd go to my favorite place on the Hill." He winked playfully.

He wasn't making this easy. "Which is?"

"I don't go out after work too often, but when I do, I go to this place called the Tune Inn. Do you know it?"

My heart sank. "Sure," I said. "Isn't it on Pennsylvania and Fourth?"

"Yep. It's right on the corner. It's not the fanciest establishment in the world, but I like the homey feel."

"Not the fanciest" was an understatement. Most thought of the Tune Inn as Capitol Hill's neighborhood dive bar. I hid my disappointment, even though there was no need to take offense. After all, it wasn't a real date, right? If Trent thought we were on a date, he must not have cared about spending a lot to impress me.

In ten minutes, we'd reached the entrance. Trent politely opened the door, and I walked inside. Dark and dingy, the décor wasn't conducive to romance. Stuffed deer, bears, boar, and swordfish adorned the wood-paneled walls. Obviously, the Tune Inn single-handedly kept several taxidermists in business. In the spaces without mounted animals, a variety of guns and swords enhanced the atmosphere.

This wasn't a place with a hostess so we sailed past the bar underneath the antler chandelier and wood rafters lined with Christmas lights to find an empty booth.

Trent was almost giddy with delight. "Isn't this place great?"

"It's certainly unique. It's the only place in D.C. where I can eat dinner across from a stuffed deer's butt." I pointed at the specimen on the opposite wall.

Trent nodded approvingly. "Don't forget the big bear with a beer in his hand at the entrance."

He handed me a menu. I took it politely. "I'll probably just have a drink. I'm not terribly hungry."

He frowned. "That's not possible. The food here is legendary. Guy Fieri even said so!" Trent offered the last comment as legitimate proof.

I stifled a sarcastic retort. If I sounded too snide with Trent, he'd wonder why I agreed to go out with him in the first place. It was in my best interest to keep him motivated...and talking.

Instead I asked in all seriousnes~~~ ~~~~at was his recommendation?"

Trent grinned. "He loved the beer-batt~~~~

How many calories would that have, I thousand? I'd have to work out from now u~~~ day. "Is that what it sounds like?"

"Yep. A beef burger dipped in batter and ~~~ to perfection."

"Did the Food Network have any other sugge~~~ It was a shot in the dark. Guy rarely sampled ~~~ burgers or salads.

"He also liked Joe's West Virginia roast beef ~~~ wich with the special sauce."

That didn't give me too much to work with. "~~~ are you having?"

"I always want to try something new, but I us~~~ get the fried burger."

Despite my earlier pronouncement, my stomach rumbled with hunger. If I was going to drink, I could use a little something. I scanned the menu, searching for a snack that wouldn't bust my calorie count for the next week. Trent looked at me expectantly. Sometimes it was just easier to play along. "I'll go with Joe's West Virginia special."

Trent's face lit up. "Excellent choice, Kit! Is Pabst Blue Ribbon on tap okay for you?"

"Sure." At least the PBR would cut the richness of the beef, cheese, and special sauce.

We made small talk while we waited for the waitress to take our order. It seemed like an eternity, but Trent appeared to be at ease. When I remarked that the service seemed a little slow, he called it "part of the ambiance" and kept chattering.

Finally we placed our orders. It was time to get down to business. If I was going to binge on fried food, my sacrifice had better pay off.

"So," I said, "tell me more about your job. What's it like working in the Sergeant at Arms office?" The pitcher of beer arrived, and Trent poured us frothy glasses.

"It's a great job. The best part is keeping everyone safe who visits the House of Representatives. It's rewarding, and I take it very seriously."

"So does your boss. His name is Gareth, right?"

"Yep. We're in lockstep on our priorities."

I took a long sip of the PBR. Its hipster cool status aside, it was remarkably refreshing. Maybe Trent had a point about the Tune Inn.

I needed Trent to divulge details about Pressler that might help finger him for Jack's murder. Commiseration often pushed the right buttons. "These days, my chief of staff is acting paranoid." I paused for a moment to increase the dramatic effect. "Now that I think of it, he's a pretty weird guy. What's it like working for Gareth?"

Trent took a swig of his beer and wiped his mouth. "He's intense. Definitely wants to make his mark at the Sergeant's office. Former military. You know the type." He gave me a knowing glance.

"What branch of the service?" I asked casually.

"Special Forces. Army Green Beret."

Something stuck in my head from one of the meetings I'd conducted with military officers from Fort Bragg. "Aren't Green Berets proficient at direct combat?"

Trent appeared surprised at my grasp of military knowledge. "That's right. They're organized into elite commando units and often engage in ambushes or other stealthy operations." He took a sip of PBR. "Or so Gareth tells me."

If the details Trent told me were true, Gareth would have had no trouble overpowering Jack Drysdale and killing him with the gavel. Time to try another line of attack, figuratively speaking.

"Given your jobs, do you have to arrive at work early in the morning?"

Trent shrugged. "We're largely concerned with the time of day when House members, staff, and the public are inside the buildings. But we have all-access identification badges, so that means we can be at work at any time, if necessary."

Gareth had the physical ability to commit the crime and access to the building during the early hours. That made him a promising suspect, but what about motive?

Just as I was about to ask, our food arrived. The waitress plunked down my specialty sandwich. The roast beef and cheese oozed out the sides of the buttered rye bread. Alongside this delectable delight sat a formidable mound of crispy french fries. I popped one in my mouth. Absolute heaven.

"Why are these fries so good?" I hoovered in a few more before Trent had a chance to answer.

"I forgot to tell you. The fries are battered, too. So they're particularly scrumptious." He grinned mischievously.

I grabbed Joe's West Virginia special and took a bite. Fattening food tasted fantastic. No wonder Meg was so darn happy all the time.

Trent refilled my glass as I polished off the first half of my sandwich. After a long swig of brew, I resumed my interrogation. "When we met, you told me your boss wanted to tighten security, but Jack Drysdale from the Speaker's office didn't agree. Now that he's dead, do you think Gareth's plans will move forward?" The huge binder in Pressler's office proved that he meant business. That plan hadn't been put together overnight.

Trent raised an eyebrow. "You seem really interested in this topic. Do you feel unsafe at work?"

His question seemed innocent enough. "No, I have faith in your office and the Capitol Hill Police. I wondered if Jack's murder changed the situation." I gave Trent my most angelic smile. Then, I added, "I'm just trying to ask polite questions about your job. It's really impressive."

Stroking egos wasn't my forte. But this time, I seemed to be doing an okay job. "It's too early to tell, but I think there will be increased security in the House.

As the Speaker's top aide, Jack threw up roadblocks to maintain open access for everyone and his brother to traipse through Congress."

Trent's altered tone caught me off guard. I couldn't resist a quick comeback. "Isn't it the people's House?"

Trent snorted. "The people have their say when they go to the voting booth. That's my opinion."

To keep our meal congenial, I bit my tongue. Trent had a lot to learn about Congress. Politicians cared about what their constituents thought, and they wanted to meet with them on a regular basis—both in Washington D.C. and in the home district. To prevent myself from spouting off, I took a big bite of the second half of my sandwich.

Trent eyeballed me. "What about you? How did you get a job with Maeve Dixon?"

I'd wanted to keep the conversation as much about him as possible, but I had to play along a bit or he might get suspicious. "I accepted a position with Dixon after the senator I worked for passed away."

"Was that the guy who was murdered last summer in his office?"

With my mouth full of roast beef and french fries, I could only nod. Trent kept talking. "I knew you looked familiar. Weren't you involved in solving that case?"

I sipped my beer. "You could say that," I answered vaguely.

"Is that why you're so interested in Jack Drysdale's murder? Trying to reprise your role as Sherlock Holmes?" Trent laughed.

"I'm no Sherlock, for sure. I don't look for crimes to solve in my spare time. I'm concerned because Representative Dixon is a prime suspect. But she didn't do it." Time to change the subject. I glanced at his plate, which was nearly clean. "Did you like your burger?"

Trent didn't seem focused on his food anymore. He was an intensely attractive guy so it was doubly uncomfortable to feel his crystal-blue eyes fixed on me. He ignored my question. "Why do you think she's innocent?"

"She claims that she didn't do it, and I know my boss fairly well. I'd prefer to give her the benefit of the doubt unless evidence proves otherwise."

Trent seemed to accept my explanation. "Makes sense, I guess. Otherwise, you'll have to find a new job."

I smiled wryly. "Yes, exactly. I'd rather not have to go through that again."

Our food and drink almost entirely consumed, it was time to wrap up this pseudo-date. I fished around in my purse for my wallet. Trent saw what I was doing. "This is my treat, Kit. Remember, I asked you out."

Despite his comment, I kept rummaging until I found cash. I threw down a twenty. "I insist. I'm glad you introduced me to the Tune Inn."

Trent grabbed the money and tossed it back to me. "You're my guest for dinner." Reluctantly, I put the money back inside my purse. Splitting the bill would have kept it platonic, but since I wanted to keep this so-called date under the radar, avoiding a scene made sense.

After putting on my coat, I stood to leave. Trent asked, "Can I walk you to the Metro?"

I'd been trying to avoid it. I wanted to call Meg and give her a report on the evening. "Don't worry about it. I'll be fine. Thanks for dinner. I enjoyed it." I gave him a little wave. Trent sat back down in his seat with an odd expression on his face. I couldn't tell if he was hurt, disappointed, annoyed, angry—or all of the above. None of the possibilities were positive, so sticking around to find out wasn't a good idea. I turned on my heels and weaved through the mob scene at the bar. Once outside, I took a deep breath of the cold evening air. Thank goodness it was over.

Walking toward the Metro, I pulled out my phone and called Meg. She didn't even bother to say hello. "How was it? Where did you go? Are you going out with him again?"

She would have kept going if I didn't interrupt. "If you'd shut up for a second, I could tell you what happened."

With a pouty voice, she said, "Fine. Go ahead."

I gave her a quick recap of the evening's events. Meg listened without interrupting until I finished. I could sense her disappointment through the phone. "I guess there's no love connection, then." She sighed.

"That wasn't the point of the evening, Meg. I'm trying to solve Jack's murder, remember?"

"You don't need to remind me. I just thought Trent might be your perfect match."

I was halfway to the Metro. Debating the current status of my love life with my best friend would have to wait. "I'm still glad I agreed to go out with him. He gave me a lot of good tidbits that might help solve the murder."

"Like what?" Meg asked.

"Gareth Pressler had access to all House buildings early in the morning. Those security monitors in his office would have made it easy to track Jack's whereabouts. Furthermore, he's former Special Forces, so killing Jack wouldn't have been difficult for him." I paused to take a breath before continuing, "And if that's not enough, he had a motive to want Jack dead."

"It sounds plausible, but your boss had access to the murder weapon only hours before she found Jack's body."

I was at the top of the escalator leading to the Capitol South subway station. "That's the last missing piece of the puzzle."

"It's not inconsequential. What are you going to do about it?"

"I'm not sure. I'll deal with it tomorrow."

"I don't want to put more pressure on you, but I heard through the grapevine today at work that the police might arrest Dixon soon. Your window of opportunity for finding the killer is closing quickly."

At this time of the evening, the long, descending moving staircase appeared to have no end, disappearing into a dark abyss, not unlike the trajectory of Maeve Dixon's political future and my Capitol Hill career unless someone exposed the real killer soon.

TWENTY-FOUR

THAT NIGHT, I tossed and turned as fleeting, bizarre images of a bloody gavel, the menacing Hill Rat logo, Gareth's face, the stuffed deer's butt at the Tune Inn, and Clarence wolfing down an entire pizza invaded my dreams. The craziness and stress of the past several days had caught up with me. At six, I gave up and threw back the bedcovers. The fried food and beer hadn't helped, not to mention my guilt: I'd gone on a pretend date with a hot guy and neglected to tell my live-in boyfriend.

But there was no time for wallowing. Clarence's internal alarm was more precise than an atomic clock, and six o'clock was too early for him to give up his cozy position in bed for a romp outside. That meant I had uninterrupted time to think about the murder. After pouring myself a frothy latte, I settled into an overstuffed chair to ruminate. The caffeine slowly energized my gray cells, and they led me to one answer: Gareth Pressler.

Other than Maeve Dixon, he was the only suspect who could have done it. He'd monitored Jack's whereabouts that morning, stalked him, and committed the crime. But there was one big problem. How did he get his hands on the Speaker's gavel? My investigation wasn't over yet. If I hurried, I could get to work early and corroborate my theory. With a little luck and some sympathy from Detective O'Halloran, maybe I could prevent Maeve's supposedly imminent arrest.

After a quick shower, I threw on my last clean pantsuit and poked my head inside the bedroom. Doug and Clarence were waking up.

Rubbing his eyes, Doug asked, "What time is it? Are you leaving for work early?"

"I don't have time to explain. I might have an idea who really killed Jack Drysdale. If I'm right, there's a chance I can convince Detective O'Halloran to hold off charging my boss for the murder."

After sitting up in bed, Clarence ambled over to Doug and plopped himself down on his lap. He licked Doug's hand, indicating that he was ready for his morning massage. Then he yawned loudly. Clarence was apparently less than impressed by my pronouncement.

Rubbing Clarence's ears, Doug put on his glasses and focused on me. "Who do you think did it?"

"Gareth Pressler. He works in the Sergeant at Arms office in the House. That's why I went out for drinks last night with that guy, Trent. I wanted to pump him for information about his boss."

Doug wrinkled his nose. Was he reading something into my words? I hadn't said the word "date." Doug didn't know I'd allowed Trent to think it was more than a casual happy hour affair. "Are you sure about this, Kit? It sounds circumstantial."

I didn't have the time to convince Doug. "I know Maeve Dixon didn't kill Jack Drysdale. That means someone else is responsible for his death. Pressler is the best alternative. I need to leave now so I can wrap this up."

Doug looked disappointed. "Clarence has a grooming appointment today. I thought we'd drive in together." Clarence's groomer was located in the Capitol Hill neighborhood. If the appointment was early enough, I usually dropped him off and then brought him to the office for part of the day. Dogs were welcome in Capitol Hill buildings during working hours. Members of Congress believed they brought happy relief to the partisan battles of Congress. At least Democrats and Republicans could agree on something.

As for Clarence, he appeared to relish spending the occasional working day on the Hill. The constant attention, pats on the head, and belly rubs were appropriate compensation. He seemed to know when he looked his best. He liked to show off, particularly if the groomer gave him a doggie scarf to wear. Unfortunately, this wasn't a good time for a Clarence visit to the Maeve Dixon office.

"I forgot about that. Thanks for taking him. It's been absolutely crazy the past several days. Between the shutdown and trying to solve this murder, I can't remember if I'm coming or going."

"I noticed," Doug murmured.

"What did you say?"

"Nothing. Don't worry about it. I'll make sure Clarence gets to the groomer."

I gave Doug a quick peck on the cheek and bent down to pet Clarence. He responded with a wet puppy kiss.

"By tonight, life should start to return to normal, especially if Detective O'Halloran listens to reason."

Doug looked skeptical. "Be careful. If you're right, this guy isn't going to appreciate being fingered for the murder. He probably thinks he got away with it."

While heading out of the condo, I called over my

shoulder, "Don't worry! Once I get what's needed, I'm turning everything over to the police. I'm not going to confront Pressler."

Less than thirty minutes later, I walked with purpose toward the entrance of the Cannon Building. The first-floor corridor was completely empty. After several days into the crisis, most "essential" congressional employees had given up on early bird arrivals in the hopes of discovering a miraculous solution. Meg had been right all along. We were in for a long haul.

I headed to my office and then reversed course. Stopping there would be an enormous waste of time. Dan had called last night when I was in the process of snooping around Gareth's office and I'd never called him back. Most likely he wanted to engage in another rant about the futility of our situation and the dismal, downward direction of Maeve Dixon's political career. He'd only delay the last part of my investigation, and it made little sense to explain my theory to him. After the police realized Pressler was a viable suspect and eased off Maeve, I could circle back to Dan, walk him through the details, and make him eat crow. After all, even though he'd asked me to investigate Jack's murder, he'd never actually thought I'd solve it.

Instead, I headed downstairs, breezed through the Capitol Hill Police metal detectors, and marched toward the dismal Cannon Tunnel. Over the course of the past week, I'd traveled the connector between my office building and the Capitol more times than I could count. The collage of paintings decorating the walls was becoming increasingly familiar. All in all, the collective talent of the high school artists was impressive. Their colorful canvases were the only sign of life in the monotone hallway. After weaving through the basement corridors and boarding the elevators tucked away in an inauspicious corner, I entered the House press gallery on the Capitol's third floor.

It would have been prudent to email Melinda on the walk over to the gallery. It seemed like ages since I'd met her to learn more about Jack Drysdale and potential suspects. With any luck, she'd remember me as her professor's generous girlfriend who liked ice cream breaks.

I provided my name at the front desk and asked for Melinda Gomez. Thus far, there hadn't been many lucky breaks in this case. This morning I was looking for the final nail to pound into Gareth Pressler's coffin.

To my relief, Melinda appeared in under a minute. Shaking her hand vigorously, I bellowed, "Thanks for seeing me on absolutely zero notice."

She adjusted her glasses with a shy smile. "No problem. You're Professor Hollingsworth's girlfriend. We met for ice cream."

I groaned inwardly. No time to educate Melinda about identifying women by their male romantic partners. "Yes, that's me. It's Kit. I'm glad you didn't forget."

Melinda shifted her weight nervously. "Oh, I'd never forget Professor Hollingsworth."

Her affinity was definitely with Doug, not me. But her willingness to talk worked in my favor. There was no point beating around the bush.

"I think you might be able to help me with my murder investigation."

Her eyes widened. "That's right. You're trying to figure out who killed Jack Drysdale. Isn't your boss the prime suspect?"

I gritted my teeth. "Yes, but she didn't do it. There's a credible suspect out there the police haven't focused on. But I need your help with the final clue."

Her face brightened, then she looked nervously at her watch. "This sounds exciting but we need to be quick about it. The House floor opens in thirty minutes. When we're live, I have to make myself available for questions from reporters, especially due to the shutdown."

I nodded. "This won't take long. Here's a question for you. Who is allowed on the dais when the House is debating a bill?" In the front of the House chamber, a tiered platform served as the stage for legislative action. Only certain people who were involved in House floor operations were allowed on it. The presiding officer— the substitute for the Speaker of the House—stands or sits at the very top of the raised platform. Maeve Dixon had served in this role on the night in question.

After giving the matter some thought, Melinda said, "Several House staffers work on the dais. The enrolling clerk, the bill clerk, the journal clerk, the tally clerk..." her voice trailed off.

I shook my head. "Not on the lower levels of the platform. What about the top level? Where the Speaker or whoever is presiding over the House of Representatives at the time sits or stands."

She adjusted her glasses again. "That's a smaller number. You have the presiding House member in the Speaker's chair, the parliamentarian, the timekeeper, and the Sergeant at Arms. Sometimes the Clerk of the House is also on the top tier. I think that's everyone who's supposed to be up there."

Bingo. "So the Sergeant at Arms always has a place on the top level?" From my many hours of watching endless debate in the House, I'd thought that was the case. But I needed to make sure.

"I'm not certain there's always a staffer from the Sergeant's office at that table, but there's definitely a space reserved for the Sergeant or his deputy."

Now we were getting warmer. "Have you ever seen Gareth Pressler sitting on the top level of the dais?"

Melinda wrinkled her nose. "I haven't worked here too long. I'm not sure what he looks like."

That was easy to remedy. I whipped out my iPhone and searched for an image of Pressler. I found his official congressional employee photograph and showed it to Melinda.

She nodded. "Yep. I've seen that guy around. He's definitely sat on the platform before. The Sergeant at Arms is in charge of the mace, so that's why a representative is entitled to a spot on the top tier."

The mace is the symbol of legislative authority for the House of Representatives. It resembles an ancient fighting weapon, consisting of a long stick with an ornate eagle at the tip. It remains on the House platform during debate, and depending on its position, it indicates the type of legislative session the House is engaged in. Since it looks rather menacing, the Sergeant at Arms supposedly uses it as a way to regain order if a member of Congress becomes unruly. Personally, I didn't think the Sergeant at Arms capitalized on the intimidation afforded by the mace nearly enough during heated debates. If the Sergeant waved the mace more regularly at House members who caused problems, then maybe we wouldn't find ourselves in the current political mess.

"Thanks, Melinda. You've been very helpful. I have one more question for you. I know there are extra gavels in case one breaks during House proceedings. Do you know where the extra gavels are kept and who has access to them?"

She shook her head. "Sorry. You got me there. I have no idea."

This was literally the last kernel of information I needed before contacting Detective O'Halloran. Hopefully Maeve hadn't been arrested yet.

Grasping at straws, I asked, "Maybe your boss would know?"

"I doubt it. We never actually go on the dais during debate. And I don't think a reporter would ask about a detail like that."

We were both lost in thought for several minutes. Then Melinda snapped her fingers. "I've got it. If we hurry, we might be able to catch my friend who works as one of the reading clerks. He might know. Follow me!" She took off and headed down the stairs toward the entrance to the House gallery.

A minute later, we were hurrying down a side aisle in the House chamber. We approached the Speaker's rostrum and Melinda scoured the room. Finally, she flagged down a guy scurrying around to ensure all the necessary papers were in place for the day's legislative proceedings.

She cleared her throat. "Excuse me. Is Charlie working today?"

The staffer ignored her question. "Who wants to know?"

She drew herself up, apparently not intimated by the snotty tone. "I work in the press gallery. Can you tell him that Melinda Gomez needs to speak with him?"

The guy sighed. "The floor opens in fifteen minutes." He motioned with his hand. "Members are already arriving for their opportunity to stick it to the other side about the shutdown."

Melinda didn't cede an inch. "Please. I need to speak with him." She lowered her voice. "It's a matter of life or death."

I wouldn't have been quite as dramatic as Melinda, but her approach caught Mr. Snotty's attention. "What isn't a matter of life or death these days?" he asked rhetorically. But then he said, "I'll see if I can find him. Just wait here."

Facing Melinda, I exclaimed, "You were terrific! Don't take no for an answer."

Melinda pushed up her glasses, which tended to fall down her nose. "Thanks. I'm learning to act more assertively on the job. I can't let reporters and staffers push me around."

"I doubt anyone ever pushed you around, Melinda."

A moment later, a tall, thin middle-aged man wearing a gray suit emerged from one of the side anterooms. Melinda waved so he'd see us.

"I'm sorry we asked to see you on such short notice, Charlie. This is Kit Marshall, and she has a question to ask you. We can't tell you right now why it matters, but trust me, it might be very important."

Charlie seemed to have a better attitude than his colleague. He laughed. "I'd rather not know the reason. I have too many secrets up here." He pointed to his head. "I can't keep them straight."

At Melinda's nod, I asked my question. Charlie answered immediately. "It's not a state secret about the extra gavel." He raised his eyebrows. "As long as you promise you're not going to steal it."

I crossed my heart.

"You came to the right person," he said. "The extra gavel is kept in the drawer of the reading clerk's desk. If the Speaker or presiding officer breaks a gavel, we replace it immediately with our spare."

"Charlie, does everyone have access to that drawer?"

"Certainly not! The desk belongs to the Clerk of the House and her employees."

"Is the drawer locked? You know, the one with the gavel," I added.

Charlie hesitated. "I can't say that it's always locked. We keep other items in that drawer and sometimes people forget to secure it."

"Do members of Congress know where you keep the extra gavel?"

"No, because otherwise they might try to pocket an extra one. As a souvenir for some lucky constituent or donor."

"I have a few more quick questions for you. Were you working the evening when Representative Maeve Dixon was in the chair? It was a few nights ago. She's my boss."

His face softened. "I heard she's a suspect in the Drysdale murder. I don't believe it for a second. Maeve Dixon always goes out of her way to act friendly when she's presiding over the House floor. It doesn't seem consistent with her personality. And yes, I worked that night. She liked my tie, as a matter of fact."

Charlie was a snappy dresser. He'd likely not forget it if a member of Congress complimented him. "Do you remember if you had to go to your drawer for the spare gavel that night?"

"It's such a rare occurrence, I would remember that. No, we haven't had to replace a gavel in a while."

Melinda broke in, "So that means the spare gavel should be in the drawer now, right?"

"Absolutely. There would be no reason for it not to be."

Unless Gareth Pressler had nabbed the gavel Maeve used and then replaced it with the spare gavel. If he did it swiftly enough after she exited the dais, no one would have noticed. He could have pocketed the gavel with her prints on it and then used it a few hours later to kill Jack Drysdale.

"Charlie, do you mind checking on the extra gavel?"

He glanced at his watch. "Okay, but then I have to skedaddle. If my boss thinks I'm not ready for the opening of the House, she's going to kill me."

Little did Charlie know that in our little world, bosses did kill. Only not mine. He hustled to the dais and sat down at the reading clerk's desk. The look of surprise on his face told us the result. The spare gavel was missing.

He opened a few more drawers, but came up empty-handed. He walked back over to where we were standing. "I don't know how you knew the spare gavel was missing, but it is. I'll have to tell my boss about it."

There was no time to waste. Every last detail had fallen into place. It was definitely enough to persuade Detective O'Halloran he needed to take a hard look at Pressler. Hopefully that meant he'd hold off charging Maeve later today.

"Charlie, you've been a lifesaver. You too, Melinda. If I'm going to prevent a disaster, I need to run now."

As I turned to leave, I said over my shoulder, "Drinks are on me once the shutdown is over!"

Melinda yelled after me. "Wait a second!"

I turned around. "What's wrong? I don't have a lot of time before my boss is arrested for a crime she didn't commit." Normally, I tried to avoid acting like a drama queen, but extraordinary circumstances called for desperate measures.

With a tentative look, Melinda offered, "Come upstairs for a few minutes so we can check on a detail about the night in question."

"No can do. It's almost nine thirty and the Capitol is open for business. I need to make sure the police don't file charges against Maeve Dixon." The sands of time had almost run out. I hurried toward the chamber's exit just as the House was called to order for the day and the House chaplain began the daily prayer.

Behind me, I heard, "Dear Father, grant us the fortitude and perseverance to help us do your will today."

Well said! Perhaps the Almighty had heard the chaplain's prayer. A little divine intervention never hurt.

TWENTY-FIVE

MEMBERS FLOODED THE House floor entrance. Normally, the opening of a legislative session was sparsely attended. The shutdown attracted a bigger crowd of politicians who wanted to speak on the House floor, even for one minute, about the funding fiasco. I waded through the masses until I reached the periphery of the Capitol Rotunda.

At this time of day, throngs of schoolchildren, international tourists, and patriotic Americans typically swarmed the Rotunda. This stately room was located in the absolute center of the Capitol, immediately underneath the dome. "Majestic" was an understatement. Perhaps at no other time in my life would I find myself almost completely alone inside its walls. Other than me, a single Capitol Hill Police officer remained on patrol. I was drawn to the splendor of it all—the beautiful assortment of neoclassic friezes and statues. This was America's pantheon, plain and simple.

My favorite Rotunda artwork was the group statue of leading women's suffragists. I felt the eyes of Elizabeth Cady Stanton, Susan B. Anthony, and Lucretia Mott fixed upon me. This monument had been relegated to the basement of the Capitol after its completion decades ago, but in 1997, it was relocated to its now prominent location inside the Rotunda, where thousands of visitors could appreciate it. What would the suffragists say if they knew a female congressional staffer was trying to save the career of her boss, a woman who had served proudly in two wars before winning election to Congress? There was no question. They'd be proud. That's why they fought to give women the right to vote and participate in politics in the first place. I was quite certain the foremothers would agree it was time for action.

I grabbed my phone and fired off an email to Detective O'Halloran, asking to meet him as soon as possible due to information I had come across concerning the murder of Jack Drysdale. I could provide the details later. Before sending the message, I added, Maeve Dixon didn't do it. He needed to know my scoop would cast doubt on Maeve's status as the prime suspect.

I'd wait for O'Halloran to contact me back at the office. With my head buried in my iPhone, I took off for the homestead in Cannon. There might be a chance he'd read the message and ask to meet inside the Capitol or somewhere else on the Hill. Wherever it was, I'd arrange to rendezvous with him immediately. Since my eyes were focused on my device and certainly not on the path ahead, it was no surprise that I almost suffered a direct collision with another staffer headed in the opposite direction.

A familiar voice said, "Hey, watch where you're going!"

My head jerked up. Dan gazed at me with pursed lips, his countenance scrunched in exasperation.

At precisely the same moment, I exclaimed, "Dan!" and he bellowed, "Kit!" We both chuckled.

"You never called me back last night." Dan sounded hurt, almost like a lovelorn teenager whose crush had dissed him.

"I'm sorry. I was busy tracking down a lead in the murder investigation."

Dan waved his hand dismissively. "You shouldn't waste your time. Maeve Dixon did it. The police are convinced, and there are no other suspects. You should be using these precious hours to find another job."

I shook my head. "You're wrong, Dan. Someone else had means, motive, and opportunity. In fact, I just emailed the police detective in charge of the case so I can meet with him and explain my theory. I don't think they'll charge Maeve once he hears it."

The color drained from Dan's face. He stammered, "Are you s-sure?"

"I might not have enough for a conviction, but it will cast doubt on Maeve's status as the prime suspect."

Dan gulped for air and rubbed his forehead nervously. "I wish you'd called me back last night."

"Why? What did you do?"

"I talked to several chiefs of staff and they said I should resign immediately. It's critical to get off Dixon's payroll before the bottom falls out. So I called Maeve earlier this morning and quit."

Dan's words hit hard. "How could you do that? It's going to make her look even more suspicious if her senior staff start to jump ship."

"I know, I know. But I left everything in North Carolina to move here. I can't go crawling back. I need to figure out a way to find another job in D.C." Dan looked like a puppy that had just made a mistake on the carpet.

"You can't call her back and retract?"

"I don't think so. She accused me of abandoning her."

"She's not off the mark."

Dan frowned. "None of this would have happened

if you'd kept me in the loop about the investigation. I never thought you'd actually succeed in finding a credible suspect."

Again, Dan's words stung. "I appreciate your vote of confidence. What's your plan now?" I glanced at my phone. No reply yet.

Dan's demeanor brightened. "I'm on my way for an interview as chief of staff for another member of Congress."

Astonishing. Dan was a political and policy lightweight. He didn't know the difference between a conference committee and a concurrent resolution. How could he already have another plum job lined up? There had to be a catch. "With who?"

Dan's outlook went dark again. "Jerry Bowser."

I suppressed a snicker. Representative Bowser, although a reliable vote for the left-wing establishment, had a reputation that preceded him. Specifically, a reputation for berating staff, throwing small items in fits of anger, and demanding curb-to-curb car service. Bowser went through staff like Kleenex.

"Good luck with that." My iPhone email icon showed I had an unread message. Time for Dan had dried up. I gave him a quick salute and concentrated on my device. Sure enough, I'd piqued Detective O'Halloran's interest. He asked to meet at Representative Dixon's office in twenty minutes. That was perfect timing. After replying, I shoved the phone back inside my purse.

I descended into the bowels of the Capitol basement yet again. A few minutes later, I reached to open the door leading to the Cannon Tunnel. A muscular arm reached over my right shoulder and grabbed the handle instead. Startled, I turned around to confront Trent Roscoe's handsome grin.

"Good morning, Kit. I saw you were headed for the tunnel and ran to catch up with you."

I breathed a sigh of relief. "You scared me. It's pretty deserted around here this early."

He opened the door and ushered me through. "Sorry about that. You left so abruptly last night, I figured this was my opportunity to chat with you again. Where are you headed in such a hurry?"

"Back to my office. I'm meeting a Capitol Hill Police detective shortly."

Trent fell into stride alongside me. "About what?" he asked innocently.

"Jack Drysdale's murder." I preferred a solitary walk to my office rather than answering nosy questions from Trent. It was bad luck running into him in the tunnel. Even if Doug wasn't in the picture, I couldn't imagine dating someone who worked on the Hill. Its insularity made it worse than high school. Meg continually struggled to maintain a wall between her dating and professional life. As she plowed through more guys on the Hill, successful compartmentalization was becoming statistically less possible. Besides, I'd decided Trent wasn't really my type. Sure, he was good-looking but the macho persona had worn thin.

Conspicuously avoiding Trent's stare, I trotted along at a good clip. He asked, "Did you figure out who did it?"

We were right next to the vending machines tucked inside a corner off the main basement intersection in Cannon. My stomach rumbled. There had been no time for breakfast this morning. I needed a caloric infusion, preferably sugar, to keep my mind from wandering into a fog when I met with Detective O'Halloran. I slowed down and grabbed my wallet, ignoring Trent's question.

In a noticeably impatient voice, Trent inquired again, "Well, did you?"

This man had become exasperating. Meg's fanciful notions about him as a potential romantic interest seemed like crazy talk right now. Hotness did not make up for an annoying personality, and Trent Roscoe had gotten on my last nerve.

I hit the button for a large bag of frosted animal crackers—the sweetest and most substantial option available in the quasi-healthy vending machines the House had installed in a futile attempt to impose federal nutritional standards on lowly congressional staffers. He touched my arm, ostensibly to get my attention. I whirled around to face him directly and looked into cold, implacable eyes. Something told me to stay silent.

I reached down to retrieve my breakfast. Once again, Trent leaned closer. At this point I hoped he was trying to hit on me. The alternative was too horrible.

His hand suddenly gripped my forearm. I said, "Trent, I'm really not in the mood for your overtures." I'd aimed for neutral but heard the fear in my own voice.

"Too bad. You're not a stupid girl, so I'm guessing you've figured it out." His voice had turned to ice and his grip tightened. At that precise instant, I felt a sharp object press into my right hip. As I tried to jerk away, Trent pulled me close. I could feel his breath on my neck. "You're going to do what I say or I'll kill you right here."

My eyes darted to the pressure. I saw the glint of a box cutter sandwiched against my body. Instinctively,

I wriggled against Trent's powerful grasp. True to his promise, he pressed the weapon deeper. Razor sharp, it ripped through my suit jacket and blouse and into my flesh. With one swift move, he stifled my scream with his left hand. From his efficiency, I knew that Trent had done this before.

"No funny business, Kit. You do what I say or I won't hesitate to hurt you more." I believed him.

We were hidden in the vending machine alcove without another person remotely near us. I nodded to let him know I understood. He shoved me in the direction of a desolate hallway leading deeper into the recesses of the Cannon basement. One of these hallways led to committee staff offices and the Library of Congress. But he was forcing me down a separate, deserted corridor. After we'd taken a few steps, he opened the door to the now-closed Cannon Carryout, a small cafeteria designed for quick food service. The Carryout had been shuttered for several months. Since its closure, I doubted anyone had ventured down this hallway, except the random maintenance worker. He reached into his pocket and produced a key, which he inserted into the lock. The door opened and he shoved me inside, bolting it behind us.

Even without a knife threatening to rip me to shreds, the abandoned Carryout would have sent shivers up my spine. The small window on the door had been papered over so that no one could see in or out. The open area that formerly displayed hot soup, cookies, and fruit was completely bare. The refrigerated shelves sat empty. A long metal counter had separated hungry lunchtime staffers from the made-to-order grill and food preparation area. A stale odor of french fries, onion rings, and chicken tenders lingered in the air.

Trent prodded me to keep walking. "Get behind the counter." The gravelly voice seemed to come from a different man than the one I'd dined with the night before at the Tune Inn. The box cutter's razor-sharp point restricted my options, so I followed his instructions. My back was up against the grill in the corner of the exposed kitchen area. Since he had me cornered, Trent let go of his tight grip. He stood squarely in front of me, his weapon brandished in his right hand.

There were two explanations. Either Trent knew his boss had killed Jack and he wanted to silence me, or Trent was the murderer. Unfortunately, both scenarios were equally deadly. I couldn't physically overpower him and no one would hear my screams. The only alternative would be reasoning with him.

I raised my hands to signal surrender. "Why are you doing this, Trent? Talk to me."

He sniggered. "*Now* you want to talk. That's typical female behavior. As soon as you got the information you wanted last night, you made a beeline for the door."

I tried to ignore his sexist comment but couldn't resist a retort. "From my perspective right now, it was the worst first date in history."

"Don't get snarky." He waved the knife back and forth.

"Okay, okay. But this is crazy. Last night, we were on a date. At least, I think it was a date. And now you're poking me with that." I pointed toward the box cutter in his hand.

Trent seemed to consider my argument. His face softened. "I actually liked you. But it was trouble when you came to see me about security in the House. Something seemed familiar. I remembered the news stories about a staffer who'd figured out the identity of her boss's murderer in the Senate. A quick Google search verified my concerns. Even worse, you started poking around. It wasn't hard to discover your real motivation for asking all those questions."

Just above a whisper, I softly stated what I now knew was true, "You killed Jack Drysdale."

Immediately, Trent's face became agitated. "You don't understand. Gareth is all talk and no action. He'd complain day after day about Jack." He changed the intonation of his voice to indicate he was mimicking Gareth. "We'll never tighten up security in the Capitol because JACK is standing in the way. JACK won't let the Speaker restrict access. JACK is a thorn in our side. JACK is the most powerful staffer in Congress."

Every time he said Jack's name, the volume of Trent's voice increased by several decibels. If I could keep him talking about Jack, he might speak loudly enough to alert a random passerby in the hallway.

I stated the obvious. "You killed Jack because Gareth wouldn't do it."

He snorted. "I didn't even bring it up with Gareth. He's the worst type of boss. He complains incessantly without offering any solutions. I did what had to be done."

"So it was a personal hatred of Jack that pushed you over the edge?"

Trent shook his head. "You've got it wrong. It was never personal. This was patriotic."

I'd read somewhere it was smart to empathize with

a psychotic perpetrator. "You wanted to protect Congress. Jack was standing in the way."

Trent's eyes lit up. "Exactly. Jack didn't understand how his decisions put the lives of elected politicians and even staff at risk. He had to be—"

"Eliminated?" I offered.

"I prefer to think of it as 'set aside,' actually."

"Set aside" seemed too mild a phrase for the occasion, but I wasn't in a position to argue semantics with a menacing hulk of a guy brandishing a box cutter. My side ached and I could sense a sticky wetness in the vicinity of where he had dug the box cutter into my flesh. I didn't dare look to see the damage that had already been done. I'd lose my edge. Keeping Trent chatting was my only hope.

"Jack's murder was premeditated, wasn't it?"

"The original plan was to kill Jack and pin it on Jordan Macintyre. Your friend Trevor gave me a tip that he was in dire financial straits. A good motive, you know?" He glanced at me for approval of his pre-murder plans.

This was all about acting calm. I forced myself to muster a smile. "Makes sense."

"Then your boss got into a public fight with Jack. She was a war hero and I started thinking...." He tapped his forehead in case I wasn't appreciating his criminal mastermind. "Why not pin it on Maeve Dixon?"

"So much for honoring those who served," I muttered.

Trent appeared to consider my sarcastic comment. "I didn't like that part, but everyone knows she's a gym rat, always lifting weights and staying in shape. She'd have the strength to kill, even a guy like Drysdale."

The combination of skipping breakfast and being

stabbed and held at knifepoint was doing a number on my flip-flopping, gurgling stomach. Still, the longer I could keep Trent blabbering, the more likely Detective O'Halloran was to look into why I was missing our appointment.

"Even if Congresswoman Dixon had a motive for killing Jack, it didn't mean she had the opportunity. How did you arrange that?"

He grinned broadly. By all objective standards, Trent was a ruggedly handsome guy. But now all I saw was a cold-blooded killer. Good looks and a wicked soul made for a terrifying combination.

"That was a lucky break. I'd already planned to lure her to the scene in the morning hours. Her discovery of the body along with the public fight with Jack would give the police plenty to work with."

The rest was obvious, but I said it anyway. "But then you saw she was going to preside over the House debate that night on the floor."

"Exactly. You figured everything out already, right?"

"Almost. I'd fingered your boss Gareth as the killer. So obviously I missed something."

Trent moved closer. Backed into a tight corner with the Carryout's grill at my back, I had nowhere to go.

"That's what I surmised from our conversation last night," he said. "The gavel was the last piece of evidence. Sure enough, you ran to the press gallery this morning to track it down."

His revelation caught me off guard. But then it made sense. There was no way he'd simply run into me by chance this morning. The move had been deliberate, just like his plan to kill Jack and incriminate Maeve.

"How did you know where I was this morning? Did

you place a tracker on me at the Tune Inn?" It wasn't too far-fetched for a former Secret Service agent.

"Didn't need to go to that expense. I have access to every person's movements inside this complex. Twenty-four hours a day, seven days a week."

Did Trent have some sort of magic map charting the comings and goings of all House employees? Images of a super-sized Marauder's Map flashed through my brain. But the dark eyes staring at me were more like Voldemort's, not Harry Potter's. Trent was no benevolent wizard; he was pure evil.

Then it clicked. "The security monitors in Gareth's office."

"There are cameras everywhere in this complex. I came in early this morning and scanned the screens for you. You were easy to find since not many people had reported for work yet." Trent's voice was steady. He might have been recounting the details of his latest fishing trip instead of his plans to stalk and kidnap me.

"I bet you also know where the blind spots are."

"Also correct. That knowledge came in handy when it was time to kill Jack. There are a few alcoves and corners, especially in the ornate parts, where the cameras don't reach. We disabled the cameras in this hallway when the Carryout closed down." He flashed his teeth in a menacing leer that sent shivers throughout my body. "Very convenient for today's unfortunate events."

Instinctively, I took another step backward. Trent pulled out a large roll of duct tape from his pocket. "Sit down on the floor," he commanded.

There was no way to hide the panic in my voice. "What are you going to do?"

He wrapped the tape around my wrists in front of

my body and then my legs. He made numerous loops on each of the binds, effectively creating shackles. For good measure, he wound the tape around my hands and fingers.

"Not sure yet. I can't do anything now because too many people have already shown up for work. There's no way to move you out of here without being noticed. I'll have to wait until later tonight to figure something out."

The more I could keep him talking, the greater the chance someone would find us, slim as it was. He tore off another long piece of duct tape. I knew that section would cover my mouth.

"Wait a second. What about the gavel?"

Trent stopped before putting the tape in place. "That was my last stroke of genius. Once I knew Maeve Dixon was going to preside over the House, I had my weapon. I made sure I was on the dais when she was in the chair, presiding over the floor debate. During a vote, when the clerks were busy with recording the 'yeas' and 'nays,' I swiped the extra gavel from the desk drawer. That drawer hasn't been locked for as long as I've worked in the House. I pocketed the gavel and waited."

Trent paused, adding more drama to his storytelling. The look of excitement on his face told me he was more than pleased with himself. He'd planned an airtight murder and pinned the crime on a known enemy of the victim.

"When my boss's duty as presiding officer was over, then what did you do?"

"That was easy. She left the gavel on the desk. I switched it with the duplicate. It took me less than five seconds." Trent beamed with malevolent pride.

"Maeve's prints were on the gavel used to kill Jack. If you grabbed it from the dais and bludgeoned Drysdale, why didn't your prints turn up when the police analyzed it?"

Trent shook his finger at me. "I was one step ahead. I needed Dixon's prints to be on the weapon, but not mine. That was the whole point of switching the gavel in the first place. That, and making sure no one noticed it was missing before Dixon was gone. So I wore a clear latex glove." His expression pensive, Trent added, "I knew the cops wouldn't focus on the switch. Their murderer's boxed up with a bow on her head and her fingerprints on the weapon. That's all they care about. People in Washington D.C. are so self-absorbed, they only see what they want to see. No one pays attention to details they think don't matter."

I was about to comment on Trent's explanation, but he cut me off. "Sorry, Kit. It's time for me to go. Can't have people at the Sergeant's office missing me."

Then he spied the package of animal cracker cookies I'd bought from the vending machine sticking out of my suit pocket. He grabbed them and put them into his own pocket. "You won't be needing these."

He stood up. "Sit tight. I wish I could say this will end better for you, but I won't lie. It's not looking good."

I strained against the duct tape. My struggles were futile, with the duct tape fastened securely around my limbs and mouth. Trent opened the door and closed it behind him. The sound of the lock clicking into place seemed to seal my fate.

TWENTY-SIX

FORCING MYSELF TO remain composed, I took deep breaths through my nose and counted slowly to thirty. I shouldn't have been so dismissive of Dan's meditation ritual. I could use a calming mantra right about now.

After my count, I knew Trent wasn't coming back immediately. Time to spring into action. I had one card up my sleeve, and with any luck, it was an ace.

My plan required standing up. I pushed my butt along the floor so my back was resting against the flat surface of a concrete wall. My hands and legs were tightly bound, but if I could leverage myself and summon the collective power of my thigh muscles, I might manage standing. Slowly, I inched my way vertically up the wall. My legs were killing me, but after an excruciating minute, my knees were bent. Luckily, I was the master of wall sits due to my sadistic boot camp instructor who liked to finish our sixty-minute workout torture sessions with a long stationary pose. After pausing for a few seconds, I used my last bit of strength to catapult myself into a fully upright position.

Good job, Kit. That was the first task. Now for the hard part.

Several months ago, I'd watched a news program about an abducted woman whose hands had been bound with duct tape. She'd freed herself by raising her arms over her head and thrusting downward with as much force as possible. The television show stressed that the trick worked even if the duct tape was tight. No time like the present to perform my own test.

With my legs bound closely together, it was hard to balance. I leaned against the wall for support and lifted both my arms as far back as possible. I took a deep breath, closed my eyes, and focused. I visualized Doug, Meg, and Clarence's faces. No way was I ready to say goodbye to them. Fueled by that resolve, I slammed my arms toward my midsection with every ounce of power I could muster.

I opened my eyes and looked at my hands. To my astonishment, the duct tape had a small rip. *Progress!* If one attempt had gotten me this far, another might do the trick. I repeated the process two more times until a sizable tear appeared down the middle of the binding. With all my strength, I pulled my hands in opposite directions and the tape tore apart.

Trent couldn't have gone far. Not wasting one second, I bent down and freed my legs. Now came the hard part. This was going to hurt. Bracing myself, I grabbed an edge of the duct tape binding my mouth and slowly ripped it off. The relief of breathing air through my mouth quickly replaced the searing pain of the tape's glue separating from my lips and face. I exhaled a grateful sigh.

Time to get moving. I bolted from behind the counter and unlocked the door. Trent had said he needed to make an appearance at his office. That meant he'd head toward the Capitol. I veered right down the deserted hallway and came upon the vending machines where he'd apprehended me.

The pain on my side intensified so I rubbed it with

my hand. Immediately I felt a warm and sticky liquid. Blood oozed through my blouse. *That bastard!* He'd actually stuck me with that damn box cutter. Although it felt like a rodent had been gnawing on my side, the wound wasn't life threatening. I had to find Trent and make sure the police apprehended him.

He was likely headed to the Cannon Tunnel. The metal detectors operated by the Capitol Hill Police stood between us. By the time I stopped and tried to explain my predicament, Trent might manage to flee—but only if he knew I had escaped. Confusion in the vicinity of the metal detectors might be enough to alert him of funny business. No, it was better to catch up with him and cause a fuss once I had eyes on him.

Pursuing Trent down the tunnel meant blowing through the metal detectors. The red ooze of blood on my blouse wasn't too obvious, but it would attract attention if I tried to move through security the conventional way.

I took a second to summon my last reserves of energy. Then I did what thousands of congressional staff only dream of doing one day: I ran through the security area with abandon, sprinting down the tunnel. It took the officers behind me several seconds to react. It wasn't every day a staffer blew right through security without a hello and a flash of a badge. As I raced down the hallway as fast as my legs would take me, I heard an officer yell, "Hey, why are you running away?" I hoped the guy wasn't going to shoot me, but I guess I was counting on the police not to use deadly force on a woman staffer. However, I did want him there when I caught up with Trent.

And there he was—just ahead of me. Two-thirds

of the way down the tunnel, sauntering along like he was taking a leisurely Sunday stroll beside the Tidal Basin. To add insult to injury, the jerk looked like he was eating something. Yes, he was helping himself to the blasted cookies he'd pilfered from my pocket when he left me bound and gagged in the Carryout.

Just as Trent was about to reach the exit leading to the Capitol's underground labyrinth, the door opened. I couldn't believe my eyes. It was Doug, Meg, and Melinda. For good measure, Clarence ambled along, with Doug holding his leash. Somehow, one of them had figured out there was trouble brewing.

I slowed down to a trot. Trent was trapped. I screamed ahead to my posse. "Don't let him leave the tunnel! Trent Roscoe killed Jack!"

The Capitol Hill Police had caught up with me and tried to secure my hands. Shrugging them off, I insisted, "You don't want to arrest me. It's that guy. He's a murderer!"

Twenty feet away, Doug appeared perplexed. He didn't know what Trent looked like. But Meg, who would have recognized him from the fifty most beautiful people on Capitol Hill list even if she hadn't met and flirted with the man, pointed and yelled, "It's the hot guy!"

Trent heard the ruckus and looked up. Still grasping a cookie in his hand, he made a break for it, dashing in the direction of the door leading to the Capitol basement. If he escaped into the maze of underground tunnels, it might take a while to find him. Meg, Doug, and Melinda looked as if they'd seen a ghost. Immobilized, they seemed unlikely to prevent his escape.

Then, an unlikely hero sprung into action. Clarence

spied the animal cracker in Trent's hand. He immediately charged and leapt. Forty pounds of beagle mutt hurtled through the air in Trent's direction to claim the prize. Clarence meant no harm—he simply saw a chance to score a delectable treat—but the diversion gave Meg the opening she needed. When Trent turned to shake Clarence off, Meg administered a swift kick with her stiletto-heeled winter boots directly at Trent's crotch. Wailing, he doubled over in pain, and the cookie dropped from his hand. As if nothing out of the ordinary had happened, Clarence scarfed down the remaining snack, licked his lips, and barked for joy.

TWENTY-SEVEN

"Can you pass the chicken wings?"

One week later, we were celebrating at the popular Capitol Hill eatery, the Hawk 'n' Dove. Hearty appetizers filled the table and drinks were flowing. There was ample reason to party. Jack's killer had been apprehended and the resolution of the case had restored Representative Maeve Dixon's reputation. Furthermore, the government shutdown had ended hours earlier when Congress and the president agreed on a compromise to fund the federal government for another year. Life was good in the nation's capital.

My other partners in sleuthing had joined Doug, Meg, and me at the historic bar. The past several days had been a whirlwind of activity as the police sorted out the details of Trent's twisted plot. Concurrent with the endless law enforcement interrogations and legal inquiries surrounding the murder investigation, Congress edged toward a grand bargain with the White House. My exonerated boss emerged as a key player in the negotiations. When I wasn't answering questions about my brief yet brutal abduction, I was wheeling and dealing with Beltway kingmakers. It had been an exhilarating series of events, but now it was time to unwind with good friends, both old and new.

Rising to my feet, I cleared my throat and said, "Thank you to everyone who joined us this evening in celebration. Each one of you played a critical role in figuring out who killed Jack Drysdale. Solving the crime cleared my boss, the distinguished member of Congress from North Carolina." I paused to tip my glass in Maeve's direction. "And also brought the real killer to justice."

Detective O'Halloran, who was being an awfully good sport under the circumstances, raised his glass of sparkling water and chimed in, "Hear, hear!"

Melinda couldn't resist a tribute of her own. "Let's toast to no more murders or shutdowns on Capitol Hill."

Judy Talent added, "For at least a year."

Each of them raised a glass, clinked with a neighbor, and took a long sip. After chatter around the table had died down, I addressed the convivial crew once again. "There is one more matter I'd like to address."

Seven pairs of eyes immediately shifted to me. Taking a deep breath, I spoke, my voice shaking a bit with excitement. "Another mystery was solved last week, in addition to Jack's murder. I've discovered the identity of the infamous blogger Hill Rat."

My pronouncement was met with audible gasps. I glanced briefly in the direction of the table's corner, where the culprit sat. He nodded in assent.

"Perhaps Hill Rat would like to reveal his identity now."

After several seconds of silence, which seemed like an eternity, Trevor spoke. "Kit speaks the truth. I am Hill Rat."

Another round of surprised exclamations prevented further discussion for almost a full minute. I grabbed my knife and hit my wine glass several times to silence the boisterous crowd. "I know you're shocked by this news. But let's give Trevor a chance to speak."

A hush fell over the table. Although not as high a priority as solving Jack's murder, unmasking Hill Rat was a Capitol Hill obsession. I saw several of my guests, namely Meg and Judy, furiously tapping away at their iPhones. Trevor knew his secret wouldn't remain at the table for long, so he was fully prepared for the inevitable press tsunami awaiting him once he left our company.

Trevor stood. The expression on his face was serious yet calm. Upon confirming my hunch about Hill Rat's true identity, I'd confronted Trevor privately. He agreed it was time to end Hill Rat's tenure. We decided this evening would be a good time to share the information with colleagues and friends. Trevor had planned a farewell post for his website that would self-publish at precisely the same time he revealed himself to our table at the Hawk 'n' Dove.

"Chaucer commented that all good things must come to an end. He was right. Writing my unpredictable dispatches as Hill Rat has given me much pleasure and satisfaction. Many people will ask why I did it. Although there are many good people who work on Capitol Hill," he motioned to those seated at the table, "there is also an underbelly. It's rarely mentioned publicly. Penning an anonymous blog was a way to keep the Hill elite on their toes."

Trevor took a sip of his drink then continued, "I knew the day would come when my anonymity would be compromised. In fact, Kit was not the first person to guess my secret, although she was the only person to live long enough to do something about it."

Trevor motioned for me to join him, so I reluctantly

stood and took up the thread. "During the murder investigation, I learned that Jack had figured out Hill Rat's identity before he died. For several days, I considered it as a possible motive. Once I had a hunch Hill Rat might be Trevor, it was easier to eliminate him as a suspect."

Trevor smiled wryly. "Thank you, Kit, for that vote of confidence. Although I might be an infamous blogger spilling the secrets of Washington, I am not a murderer."

Meg piped up, "But how did you figure out Trevor was Hill Rat?"

"It was an educated guess. Trevor seemed unusually interested in my progress on the case. That didn't make sense, since he had no strong connection to the victim or the accused. But the real evidence came from Geno."

Seeing their puzzled faces, I explained, "Geno works for the Architect of the Capitol as a craftsman in the Capitol basement. I talked with him to find out if the Speaker's gavels were made within one of the congressional buildings and how many were constructed at a time. Ultimately, I needed to determine where those extra gavels were kept and who had access to them."

Judy Talent broke in, "But what does this have to do with Hill Rat's identity?"

"I was just about to answer that question," I said. "When I talked to Geno about the gavels, he mentioned that a man had asked him earlier that morning about the Speaker's gavels. He thought it was strange that two people had inquired about the gavels in the same day. I showed him a photo of Gareth Pressler on my iPhone, but he wasn't the person who had talked to Geno."

Detective O'Halloran asked, "Wasn't that a clue Gareth wasn't the killer?"

I shrugged. "Sure, it was perplexing. At the time, I didn't think much of it."

Meg took a long sip of her drink and then raised her glass. "Maybe it's the Prosecco talking, but I'm still not following."

"It wasn't until after my kidnapping and the aftermath that I had time to mull over the entire series of events. How did Hill Rat know about the gavel as the weapon? I asked Detective O'Halloran if he'd leaked that detail to the press."

He shook his head. "Absolutely not."

"I knew Representative Dixon hadn't done it since that detail emerging didn't help her case one bit. She wanted to keep information about the gavel out of the press as long as possible."

Maeve spoke up. "No way we wanted anyone to know about the murder weapon."

"That left a small number of people." I ticked each person's name off my fingers. "Doug, Meg, Dan, and Trevor."

Meg giggled. "Did you think I was Hill Rat?"

I smiled. "Not for a second. Doug was a no-brainer, as well."

Doug adjusted his glasses in apparent annoyance. "Why wasn't I considered as a possibility? Even briefly?"

Meg answered, "Doug, Hill Rat writes about contemporary politics, not about what happened two hundred years ago!"

After regaining the floor, I went on, "The only credible alternative to Trevor was Dan. When I thought about it, Dan made no sense as Hill Rat. First, he didn't know any of the people Hill Rat wrote about. Second, Dan is scared of his own shadow, and Hill Rat had guts. Lastly, Hill Rat, although nefarious, certainly understood how Capitol Hill operates. Unfortunately, Dan does not." I glanced at my boss when I said the last sentence. I hoped she wasn't offended by my dig at Dan. After all, he had served as her top aide during her first year in Congress. If she was annoyed, she didn't show it. She laughed along with everyone else.

Melinda said, "The only possibility was Trevor."

"Yes, although it was still only a strong hypothesis. I thought about the big clue Geno had provided. The person who spoke with him earlier that morning was either Hill Rat or the killer. Once I knew Trent was the murderer, I paid a visit to Geno and showed him photographs of Trent and Trevor. He easily identified Trevor as the person who'd asked about the gavels. Then I figured it out. After having breakfast with me at Pete's, Trevor immediately investigated to find out more information about the gavel, and then he wrote his blog post about the gavel as the murder weapon."

"But that post fingered me as the killer." Maeve pointed to herself. "Why would you write something accusatory like that when you were trying to help Kit find the real killer?"

Trevor rubbed his forehand nervously. "That's a fair question. I never thought you killed Jack, Representative Dixon. But my motives in helping Kit's informal investigation were more self-interested, I admit. Once Hill Rat's identity was revealed, I would be named a prime suspect—in that the police would think I killed Jack to silence him. Before my identity was compromised, it was imperative the case was solved. I figured releasing the information about the gavel would speed things up since there would be more pressure on Kit to find the guilty party."

Maeve gave Trevor a skeptical look. "That was a big gamble. It might have ruined my reputation in Washington."

"Temporarily, yes. But once the real killer was discovered, I believed you would rebound politically." Trevor smiled cautiously.

Maeve remained silent, but I could tell Trevor would not be a welcome guest in the office of Representative Maeve Dixon.

Judy took advantage of the lull in the conversation. "I read in the newspaper that Trent Roscoe was apprehended in the Cannon Tunnel and several of you helped catch him. Were you simply in the right place at the right time?"

With a considerable degree of sarcasm, Doug said, "Hardly."

Meg sat up straighter in her chair. "I can tell this part of the story!" With a dramatic gesture of my hand, I gave her the floor.

Meg smoothed her bob and smiled eagerly. "After Kit determined the spare gavel was missing, she ran off. Melinda tried to stop her but Kit was in too much of a hurry."

Melinda broke in, "I wanted her to examine the C-SPAN footage of the House floor on the night in question so we could see which staffers and members of Congress were on the dais. The camera angles might have prevented us from seeing the murderer swap the gavel, but we could have scanned the various shots to confirm who was close to the Speaker's desk around the time Representative Dixon presided over the chamber."

Meg gave a dismissive wave. "Kit didn't have time for more sleuthing. But our trusty press gallery friend had a hunch something wasn't right."

Melinda nodded. "After Kit left, I scanned the video online. It's simple to do if you know how to use the online C-SPAN search engine and there's a specific time of day you want to view. Sure enough, Gareth Pressler wasn't on the dais. But Trent Roscoe did appear in several shots."

Meg offered, "Melinda emailed Kit, but thought she'd also better reach out to someone else who could notify her."

Melinda continued the story. "The only person I knew connected to Kit was Professor Hollingsworth. Luckily, I still had his contact information in my phone. When I was a student in his class at Georgetown, I used to text him all the time with questions about assignments." She blushed, confirming the crush I already suspected.

Doug said, "When I got Melinda's message, I knew Kit was in trouble. If she accused the wrong person, it would only cast more suspicion on Representative Dixon. When my texts went unanswered, I contacted Meg. Luckily, I was already on the Hill that day due to Clarence's grooming appointment. The three of us agreed to meet in the Capitol."

Meg was so excited to tell her part of the story, she could hardly remain seated. "Once we found each other, we decided to head to Kit's office in Cannon." Meg paused briefly, allowing the suspense to build. "That's when we saw her charging down the tunnel, pointing at Trent."

Judy's eyes were wide with astonishment. Clearly

impressed by the drama of the story, she asked, "Didn't I read that your dog had something to do with apprehending Trent?"

Doug chuckled. "That detail has made for good press fodder. It was not Trent's evil nature but his general nastiness that ultimately cooked his goose. He stole Kit's snack after locking her up in the abandoned café. He was chomping on the cookies as he walked down the hallway. Clarence was already exuberant because he saw Kit running toward us. Given his healthy appetite, he lunged for the goodies. Classic Clarence, I'm afraid."

Meg pointed to herself with fingers from both hands. "And that gave me the opportunity to kick Trent right where it hurt. He folded like a house of cards!"

I laughed. "It was a lovely finishing touch. Couldn't you see the Capitol Hill Police behind me, though?"

Meg replied, "Sure, but why take chances? He deserved it."

Finishing off her wine, Judy donned her coat. "I've got to run. Now that the government shutdown is over, it's time to think about my new job on K Street. But I'm not the only one with a new job these days." Judy gave me a knowing smile.

"It's official. Can we let everyone know?" I directed my question toward my boss.

Rising, Representative Dixon said loudly, "Can I have everyone's attention?" Everyone quieted down immediately. Some people had the ability to command a room, and Maeve was one of them.

"For the rest of my political career and my life, for that matter, I will be grateful to Kit and those who helped solve Jack's murder. Because of your sleuthing, I have a future. Above all, I want to thank everyone for believing in me." She raised her glass, and the rest of the crowd followed suit.

She kept the floor. "I'm not done! The best thing to happen from this fiasco is that I'm honored to name Kit Marshall as my new chief of staff."

Cheers erupted from the crowd. Doug and Meg knew about the appointment, but I hadn't shared the news with anyone else.

Rising once again to my feet, I said, "Thank you, Representative Dixon. I'm proud to work for you. I'm going to need a great deal of help as I begin my new position. I have two announcements in that regard. First, Judy Talent has agreed to serve as my mentor. Judy had a terrific career on Capitol Hill and she's going to teach me everything I need to know. Right, Judy?"

Judy was busy texting on her phone, but then, she was the consummate multitasker. "You got it, sister."

I grinned. "The other announcement also involves a talented female Capitol Hill staffer. Since I will assume the chief of staff role next week, Representative Dixon needs a new legislative director. I'm thrilled to name Meg Peters as our new LD for the office!"

This time, the cheers were even louder. People yelled "speech, speech" to persuade Meg to say a few words.

She wiped away several tears. "The United States Congress can be a tough place to work. But toiling away with a friend you trust makes the effort worthwhile. I didn't hesitate one moment when Kit offered me the job."

Only Trevor seemed skeptical. "You're leaving a professional committee staff position for this opportunity?"

Meg, never a Trevor fan, answered in a snippy tone.

"Yes, I am. It turns out committee investigations weren't for me. And, by the way, I have an announcement, too."

"What news?" I asked.

"I broke up with Kyle last night. We got into another fight about my job. No relationship is worth that much heartache. The good news is that I'm a single woman again!"

Trevor rolled his eyes and muttered softly under his breath, "Head for the hills." I also saw Doug grimace. No doubt, he liked Meg better when she was attached. With a boyfriend in tow, she was more predictable and restrained. My favorite Capitol Hill flirt was back in business. Last time I checked, living vicariously wasn't a mortal sin.

I gave Meg a hug. "I'm sorry about Kyle."

She waved me off. "No worries. Besides, I can't be attached right now."

"Dare I ask why not?"

Meg leaned in and gave my arm a squeeze. "Because there can't be any restrictions on our next adventure!"

TWENTY-EIGHT

AFTER ANOTHER HOUR of celebration, Doug and I exited the bar and breathed in the crisp air. The wind was still and the temperature didn't require gloves or hats, a welcome change from the dreariness that typically bookended January and February in Washington.

We strolled down Pennsylvania Avenue in contented silence. When we were about to turn left toward the Capitol South Metro, he grabbed my hand. "Let's keep strolling down First Street." With no work tomorrow and the Fahrenheit cooperating, I agreed.

We walked past the ornate Jefferson Building, the crown jewel of the Library of Congress, and Neptune's Fountain, the ornate statue that greeted visitors. Modeled after the Trevi Fountain in Rome, it wasn't quite as spectacular as the Italian masterpiece, but still provided a regal touch of classicism in harmony with the awesome splendor of the Capitol situated diagonally across the street.

Doug pulled me in the direction of the dome. After looking both ways, we crossed First Street to reach the east front of the Capitol. A large expanse of grass and concrete landscape separated the actual Capitol Building from the street. Doug led me down a pathway lit by rustic streetlamps. The shutdown having just ended, no tourists shared the grand expanse with us. They'd been deterred from visiting while the monuments and other attractions had been shuttered. Tomorrow, the bustle would return to Washington D.C., but for now, we relished the serenity.

With the steps of the Capitol directly ahead of us, Doug jerked me to the right. I asked, "What are you doing? I'd like to look at the dome at night for a moment. Isn't it beautiful when it's illuminated and the sky is clear behind it?"

Doug pulled us underneath a big tree. According to the metal marker on its trunk, it was an American beech as old as the Capitol itself. He turned to face me directly before he spoke. "I'm not interested in the Capitol Dome tonight."

I laughed uneasily. This wasn't like Doug. He was either laid-back or absentminded—take your pick—but rarely melodramatic.

He ignored my awkward laugh. "Kit, I know I've acted strangely the past couple of months. You've been incredibly busy with your job, but the whole time, I was preoccupied, too."

I gulped. I didn't like the sound of this. "What do you mean?"

"I was keeping a secret."

Terrific. I'd finally sorted out Jack's murder, my job, and the federal government shutdown. Now my boyfriend was about to unload something horrible. I braced myself, both mentally and physically, for his revelation.

"Go on. Don't keep me in suspense."

"You still don't get it, do you?"

"Actually, I don't. If you're going to break up with me, then let's not beat around the bush."

He smiled. "You've been working in the doom and

gloom too long, Kit. This isn't about breaking up. This is about making our relationship permanent."

Doug knelt down on one knee and withdrew a black velvet box from his coat pocket.

I gasped. Then I covered my eyes with my hands in disbelief. "You're going to propose!"

Now it was Doug's turn to laugh. "Yes, Kit. For a detective, it took a lot of clues before you figured it out. I've been preoccupied because I've had the ring for a while, but there's never been a right time to give it to you. I decided tonight was it."

He opened up the box, and a beautiful diamond ring sparkled back at me. Instinctively, I reached for it, but Doug pulled it back.

"Not so fast. You didn't answer the question yet."

"What question?" Two could play at this game.

"Kit Marshall, congressional staffer extraordinaire and amateur sleuth, will you marry me?"

For once, I was speechless. I whispered "yes" before jumping into Doug's arms. Quite appropriately, the nighttime illumination of the Capitol caused my newly adorned ring finger to sparkle.

* * * * *

Photo by Glen Fuhrmeister, GF Photography

COLLEEN J. SHOGAN is a senior executive at the Library of Congress. She is the former deputy director of the Congressional Research Service and previously served as a staffer in the United States Senate. A political scientist by training, Colleen has taught American government at Georgetown University, Penn, and George Mason.

Colleen is a native of Pittsburgh, Pennsylvania. She received her BA from Boston College and her doctorate from Yale. A member of Sisters in Crime, she lives in Arlington, Virginia, with her husband Rob Raffety and their rescue mutt, Conan.

For more information, please go to: www.colleenshogan.com.

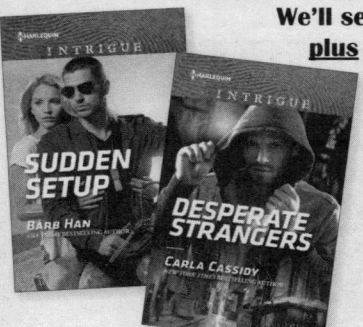

Get 4 FREE REWARDS!

We'll send you 2 FREE Books plus 2 FREE Mystery Gifts.

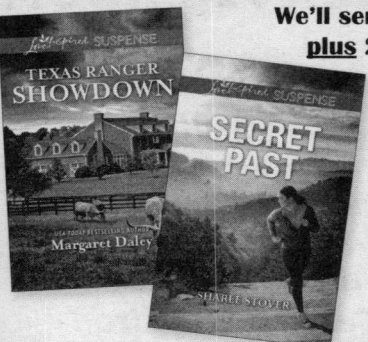

Love Inspired® Suspense books feature Christian characters facing challenges to their faith... and lives.

FREE Value Over $20